The Edith Wharton
Omnibus

THE

Edith Wharton
OMNIBUS

Introduction by
GORE VIDAL

CHARLES SCRIBNER'S SONS
New York

Introduction Copyright © 1978 Gore Vidal
The Age of Innocence, copyright 1920 D. Appleton and Company;
renewal copyright 1948 William R. Tyler.
Ethan Frome, copyright 1911 Charles Scribner's Sons;
renewal copyright 1939 William R. Tyler.
Old New York, copyright 1924 William R. Tyler;
renewal copyright 1952.

Library of Congress Cataloging in Publication Data
Wharton, Edith Newbold Jones, 1862-1937.
    The Edith Wharton omnibus.
    Contents: The age of innocence. — Ethan Frome. — Old
New York.
    I. Title.
[PZ3.W555Eam 1978b] [PS3545.H16] 813'.5'2   78-12686
ISBN 0-684-15973-2

1 3 5 7 9 11 13 15 17 19   H/C   20 18 16 14 12 10 8 6 4 2

Printed in the United States of America

CONTENTS

Introduction

by GORE VIDAL

A FEW YEARS AGO I was asked by the publisher of a biography of Edith Wharton to provide him with what is known, elegantly, in the trade as a "blurb." Now the writing of blurbs is an art form as difficult as that of the haiku; and far less appreciated. I sometimes think that a good blurb may be harder to write than a good book. Too often perfectly reputable writers will come up with the "not since General Eisenhower's *Crusade in Europe* have I laughed so much" sort of thing. Dutifully, I read the biography of Mrs. Wharton. There was new material about her private life (after twenty-three years of marriage, she had her first sexual experience at forty-six). There was a good account of the ups and downs of the reputation of a writer who . . . well, herewith, the blurb that eventually decorated the dust jacket of R. W. B. Lewis's *Edith Wharton.* "At best, there are only three or four American novelists who can be thought of as 'major' and Edith Wharton is one. Due to her sex, class (in every sense), and place of residence, she has been denied her proper place in the near-empty pantheon of American literature. Happily, Mr. Lewis's biography ought to convince the solemn of her seriousness; with much new material, he has illuminated a marvelous figure and her age." When, eventually, I collect in a single slender volume the various blurbs that I have produced over the years, I shall give, I hope not too immodestly, pride of place to this small but subtly cut zircon of the blurb-maker's tiny art (flawed only, I notice now, by the repetition of the word "place" in the second sentence).

Edith Wharton's publishers have had the good sense to make available in one volume some of her best writing. I can only say that I envy anyone reading for the first time *The Age of Innocence* or *New Year's Day.* Why? Well, let us examine the points I raised in that blurb.

"At best, there are only three or four American novelists who can be thought of as 'major' and Edith Wharton is one." Who are the other two or three? I don't think I will go into that beyond noting that, to my mind, Henry James and Edith Wharton are the two great American masters of the novel. Most of our celebrated writers have not been, properly speaking, novelists at all. Hawthorne and Melville wrote romances. Hemingway and Crane and Fitzgerald were essentially short story writers (a literary form that Americans have always excelled at). Mark Twain was a memoirist. William Dean Howells was indeed a true novelist but as Edith Wharton remarked (they were friendly acquaintances), Howells's "incurable moral timidity . . . again and again checked him on the verge of a masterpiece." She herself was never timid. Somehow in recent years a notion has got about that she was a stuffy grand old lady who wrote primly decorous novels about upper-class people of a sort that are no longer supposed to exist. She was indeed a grand lady, but she was not at all stuffy. Quite the contrary. She was witty. She was tough as nails. As for those upper-class people, they are still very much with us. But as their age ceased to be gilded and became discreetly chrome, they have decided wisely to stay out of sight. Nevertheless, they run the United States just as they did when Edith Wharton and her friend Henry James wrote about them.

"Due to her sex . . . she has been denied her proper place" as a great American writer. This seems to me to be altogether true, and sad. For a very long time it was an article of faith among American schoolteachers and writers of book-chat for newspapers that no woman could be a major writer. Predictably, it was Norman Mailer who put the conservative case: "I have nothing to say about any of the talented women who write today. . . . Indeed I doubt if there will be a really exciting woman writer until the first whore becomes a call girl and tells her tale." If anyone can figure out what that last sentence means, drop me a line. For Mailer, women writers are "fey, old-hat, Quaintsy Goysy, tiny, too dykily psychotic, crippled, creepish, fashionable, frigid, outer-Baroque, *maquillé* mannequin's whimsy, or else bright and stillborn." He then adds a nervous footnote to the effect that, well, there are *three* contemporary women writers who are not too bad. But the point that he has made not only reflects the positively Old Testament hatred that so many American men have for women (particularly notable in the fifties when the gabble that I've just quoted was written) but also the looney conviction that only men can do anything of major importance in literature, quite forgetting that the best novelist in the English language was a lady who was forced (partly by the Mailers of her day) to take the name George Eliot. Edith Wharton was quite aware that her sex was held against her. There are hundreds of Mailers in every literary generation and they write most of the book reviews. But I suspect that she was far more disturbed by the attitudes toward women of the class she was born into where a woman . . . no, that word was not used . . . where a lady was expected to be supremely ornamental, and nothing else. From the beginning, Edith Jones (later Wharton) was far too clever. Or as she ruefully noted, Boston thought her too fashionable to be clever while New York thought her too clever to be fashionable.

"Due to her . . . class" Edith Wharton was denied her proper place. Class is a delicate subject in the United States. We are not supposed to know anything about class because everyone is exactly like everyone else except, naturally, for those who are rich—and for those who are poor—and of course for the rest of us. Edith Newbold Jones was born in 1862. The Joneses were a large proud New York family (it is said that the expression "keeping up with the Joneses" referred to them). Edith was related to almost everyone. And kinship is what society with a capital "S" is all about. For that matter, society with a small "s" (at least in small communities) tends to be pretty much the same thing. One of the reasons that the American South produced so many good writers was that until recently each small town included a number of families who had become so involved with one another over the centuries that the often quite lurid stories of kin that were passed on from generation to generation on slow, hot afternoons were the very stuff of literature for any attentive child with a liking for stories, writing. One needs a well-defined society to make good novels. On the other hand, although the New York of Edith Jones's day was a splendid subject for a novelist, it was an article of faith that no one *in* Society could ever be a writer. Writers were "not like us." Of course they were brainy. But then so were chemists, and you did not have a chemist to dinner . . . or a writer.

Edith Jones's New York was still that of *The Age of Innocence.* There were dinner parties, appearances at the opera, Assembly balls; there was Newport in the summer, with the afternoon *passegiatta* along Ocean Drive; there was, best of all for her, Europe where she spent much of her childhood because her father was suddenly obliged to economize and it was cheaper to live in Paris than New York. When, finally, nervously, tentatively, she began to publish, her friends and family were deeply puzzled, and only one relative (a bedridden lady) ever admitted to having read her books. The making of literature in that world was like some wasting, sad disease which, luckily, was not thought to be contagious. Otherwise, she would have been locked up; kept permanently in quarantine.

In Edith Wharton's memoir A Backward Glance, she contemplated her long life (she died in 1937). Of her education: "I used to say that I had been taught only two things in my childhood: the modern languages and good manners. Now that I have lived to see both those branches of culture dispensed with, I perceive that there are worse systems of education." She also regarded with a sharp eye the New York gentry of her youth. They had bored her a good deal at the time. A girl who liked to read and think did not have many people to talk to in Old New York. But, later, looking back, she was surprised at her own nostalgia. "Social life with us as in the rest of the world, went on with hardly perceptible changes till the war (1917) abruptly tore down the old frame-work, and what had seemed unalterable rules of conduct became of a sudden observances as quaintly arbitrary as the domestic rites of the Pharaohs." Finally, "the compact world of my youth has receded into a past from which it can only be dug up in bits by the assiduous relic-hunter. . . ."

By and large, American writers belong to the middle class. In Edith Wharton's day they were the sons and daughters of small-town lawyers, doctors, realtors. The ruling class (which does not exist of course) is supposed to rule not write. There was—and is—a good deal of resentment on the part of the middle-middlers that a bona fide aristocrat (American style) should be not only a best-selling novelist but also a genius. The sales of her books could not be falsified. But her genius could be denied, as it so often was, and for years she has been categorized, in Mailer's phrase, as "Quaintsy Goysy."

Although Edith Wharton professed a certain nostalgia for the customs of a class that after 1917 changed its style (but kept its money), she saw to it that she herself was delivered, as soon as possible, into a happier world where she was not only admired as a writer but where she could move among intellectual equals. Needless to say, such a world was not to be found in the United States of that day but in Europe. In Paris a woman could be taken seriously as an intellectual, and it was in Paris that she finally settled.

Due to her place of residence, she was much criticized by those America Firsters who never seemed to mind the fact that writers like Ernest Hemingway seldom lived in the United States. Some sort of double standard is obviously at work.

"With much new material, [Mr. Lewis] has illuminated a marvelous figure and her age." What was the new material? Well, some of it was fairly shocking even in these candid days. In 1885 Edith Jones married the charming but dim Edward Wharton. As was the custom in that far-off time, Edith went to the bridal bed a virgin. Whether or not she was still a virgin the next day is moot. We do know that whatever happened so traumatized her that that was that: no more sex. The marriage itself was not too bad (they both liked animals). Eventually Teddy Wharton found friends elsewhere while Edith wrote, gardened, lived a full if not fulfilled life. Then, at forty-six, she had her first love affair with a clever, not entirely trustworthy bisexualist. But the lover's shortcomings made no real difference. After all, it is not who or what one loves but the emotion itself that matters. In middle life, she was rejuvenated. More to the point, the honesty with which she had always treated intimate relations between her characters now possessed a new authority. Despite her reputation as being a stuffy *grande dame*, she had always been the most direct and masculine (old sense of the word, naturally) of writers; far more so than her somewhat fussy and hesitant friend Henry James. Spades got called spades in Edith Wharton's novels. As a result, she was always at war with "editorial timidity." Early on, she was told by one of the few good editors of the day that no American magazine would publish anything that might offend "a non-existent clergyman in the Mississippi valley; . . . [I] made up my mind from the first that I would never sacrifice my literary conscience to this ghostly censor." But she lived long enough to find disquieting the explicitness of writers like D. H. Lawrence and James Joyce. With a certain dryness, she speaks of the difficulties that writers of her epoch had, turning "the wooden dolls of that literary generation into struggling suffering human beings; but we have been avenged, and more than avenged, not only by life but by the novelists, and I hope the latter will see before long that it is as hard to get dramatic interest out of a mob of irresponsible criminals as out of the Puritan marionettes who formed our stock in trade. Authentic human nature lies somewhere between the two. . . ." When the drunk Scott Fitzgerald tried to shock her by saying that he had just come from a bordello, old Mrs. Wharton silkily asked, "But what, Mr. Fitzgerald, did you *do* there?" Later, she complained of Fitzgerald's "insufficient data."

The four stories that made up the volume *Old New York* together with *The Age of Innocence* can be read as a history of New York Society from the 1840s to the 1870s, all told from the vantage point of a brilliant middle-aged woman, looking back on a world that had already become as strange to her as that of the Pharaohs. *The Age of Innocence* was published in 1920 when Wharton was fifty-eight. *False Dawn, The Old Maid, The Spark* and *New Year's Day* were published four years later.

Ethan Frome (a long short story first published in 1911) stands somewhat outside the canon of her work. For one thing, she herself is plainly outside the world that she is describing. Yet she is able to describe in a most convincing way a New England village filled with people of a sort that she could never have known well. The story is both readable and oddly remote. It could have been written by Daudet but not by her master Flaubert. Although she was very much under the influence of the French realists at the time, she does pay sly homage to Nathaniel Hawthorne, who had worked the same New England territory: a principal character in *Ethan Frome* is called Zenobia after the heroine of Hawthorne's *The Blithedale Romance*.

With the four New York stories and *The Age of Innocence* we are back in a world that she knew as intimately as Proust knew the Paris of much the same era. The stories begin. . . . But I am not going to say anything about them other than to note that they are precise and lucid, witty and passionate (there is no woman in American literature as fascinating as the doomed Madame Olenska). Not only does one live again in that lost world through Edith Wharton's art (and rather better to live in a far-off time through the medium of a great artist than to experience the real and probably awful age itself), but one is struck by the marvelous golden light that illuminates the world she reveals to us. How is this done? Through a total mastery of English. Now that our language is in trouble (reread that quotation from Mailer, read the New York *Times*), one can if not mourn the narrow world that she grew up in, at least respond with some sympathy when she observes that: "My parents' ears were wounded by an unsuitable word as those of the musical are hurt by a false note." But then "This feeling for good English was more than reverence, and nearer: it was love."

In *The Age of Innocence* the language is unusually beautiful. That is to say, the prose is simple, straightforward, loved. When it comes to rounding off her great scene where Madame Olenska is decorously destroyed by the Old New Yorkers at a dinner, Edith Wharton writes with the graceful directness of the Recording Angel: "It was the old New York way of taking life 'without effusion of blood': the way of people who dreaded scandal more than disease, who placed decency above courage, and who considered that nothing was more ill-bred than 'scenes,' except the behavior of those who gave rise to them."

Great writers are seldom great in everyday life. Edith Wharton seems to have been an exception. In the First World War she remained in Paris. She worked hard for the refugees; visited the Front; was decorated by the French government. She was a loyal if tiring friend, as Henry James noted with awe: "Her powers of devastation are ineffable, her repudiation of repose absolutely tragic and she was never more brilliant and able and interesting." Traditionally, Henry James has always been placed slightly higher up the slope of Parnassus than Edith Wharton. But now that the prejudice against the female writer is on the wane, they look to be exactly what they are: giants, equals, the tutelary and benign gods of our American literature.

*The Edith Wharton
Omnibus*

The Age of Innocence

BOOK ONE

1

On a January evening of the early seventies, Christine Nilsson was singing in *Faust* at the Academy of Music in New York.

Though there was already talk of the erection, in remote metropolitan distances "above the Forties," of a new Opera House which should compete in costliness and splendor with those of the great European capitals, the world of fashion was still content to reassemble every winter in the shabby red and gold boxes of the sociable old Academy. Conservatives cherished it for being small and inconvenient, and thus keeping out the "new people" whom New York was beginning to dread and yet be drawn to; and the sentimental clung to it for its historic associations, and the musical for its excellent acoustics, always so problematic a quality in halls built for the hearing of music.

It was Madame Nilsson's first appearance that winter, and what the daily press had already learned to describe as "an exceptionally brilliant audience" had gathered to hear her, transported through the slippery, snowy streets in private broughams, in the spacious family landau, or in the humbler but more convenient "Brown *coupé*." To come to the Opera in a Brown *coupé* was almost as honorable a way of arriving as in one's own carriage; and departure by the same means had the immense advantage of enabling one (with a playful allusion to democratic principles) to scramble into the first Brown conveyance in the line, instead of waiting till the cold-and-gin congested nose of one's own coachman gleamed under the portico of the Academy. It was one of the great livery-stableman's most masterly intuitions to have discovered that Americans want to get away from amusement even more quickly than they want to get to it.

When Newland Archer opened the door at the back of the club

box the curtain had just gone up on the garden scene. There was no reason why the young man should not have come earlier, for he had dined at seven, alone with his mother and sister, and had lingered afterward over a cigar in the Gothic library with glazed black-walnut bookcases and finial-topped chairs which was the only room in the house where Mrs. Archer allowed smoking. But, in the first place, New York was a metropolis, and perfectly aware that in metropolises it was "not the thing" to arrive early at the Opera; and what was or was not "the thing" played a part as important in Newland Archer's New York as the inscrutable totem terrors that had ruled the destinies of his forefathers thousands of years ago.

The second reason for his delay was a personal one. He had dawdled over his cigar because he was at heart a dilettante, and thinking over a pleasure to come often gave him a subtler satisfaction than its realization. This was especially the case when the pleasure was a delicate one, as his pleasures mostly were; and on this occasion the moment he looked forward to was so rare and exquisite in quality that—well, if he had timed his arrival in accord with the prima donna's stage-manager he could not have entered the Academy at a more significant moment than just as she was singing: "He loves me—he loves me not—*he loves me!*" and sprinkling the falling daisy petals with notes as clear as dew.

She sang, of course, "*M'ama!*" and not "He loves me," since an unalterable and unquestioned law of the musical world required that the German text of French operas sung by Swedish artists should be translated into Italian for the clearer understanding of English-speaking audiences. This seemed as natural to Newland Archer as all the other conventions on which his life was moulded: such as the duty of using two silver-backed brushes with his monogram in blue enamel to part his hair, and of never appearing in society without a flower (preferably a gardenia) in his buttonhole.

"*M'ama . . . non m'ama . . .*," the prima donna sang, and "*M'ama!*," with a final burst of love triumphant, as she pressed the dishevelled daisy to her lips and lifted her large eyes to the sophisticated countenance of the little brown Faust-Capoul, who was vainly trying, in a tight purple velvet doublet and plumed cap, to look as pure and true as his artless victim.

Newland Archer, leaning against the wall at the back of the club box, turned his eyes from the stage and scanned the opposite side of the house. Directly facing him was the box of old Mrs. Manson Mingott, whose monstrous obesity had long since made it impossible for her to attend the Opera, but who was always represented on fashionable nights by some of the younger members of the family. On this occasion, the front of the box was filled by her daughter-in-law, Mrs. Lovell Mingott, and her daughter, Mrs. Welland; and slightly withdrawn behind these brocaded matrons sat a young girl in white with eyes ecstatically fixed on the stage-lovers. As Madame Nilsson's *"M'ama!"* thrilled out above the silent house (the boxes always stopped talking during the Daisy Song) a warm pink mounted to the girl's cheek, mantled her brow to the roots of her fair braids, and suffused the young slope of her breast to the line where it met a modest tulle tucker fastened with a single gardenia. She dropped her eyes to the immense bouquet of lilies-of-the-valley on her knee, and Newland Archer saw her white-gloved finger tips touch the flowers softly. He drew a breath of satisfied vanity and his eyes returned to the stage.

No expense had been spared on the setting, which was acknowledged to be very beautiful even by people who shared his acquaintance with the Opera houses of Paris and Vienna. The foreground, to the footlights, was covered with emerald green cloth. In the middle distance symmetrical mounds of woolly green moss bounded by croquet hoops formed the base of shrubs shaped like orange-trees but studded with large pink and red roses. Gigantic pansies, considerably larger than the roses, and closely resembling the floral penwipers made by female parishioners for fashionable clergymen, sprang from the moss beneath the rose-trees; and here and there a daisy grafted on a rose-branch flowered with a luxuriance prophetic of Mr. Luther Burbank's far-off prodigies.

In the center of this enchanted garden Madame Nilsson, in white cashmere slashed with pale blue satin, a reticule dangling from a blue girdle, and large yellow braids carefully disposed on each side of her muslin chemisette, listened with downcast eyes to M. Capoul's impassioned wooing, and affected a guileless incomprehension of his designs whenever, by word or glance, he persuasively indicated the ground floor window of the neat brick villa projecting obliquely from the right wing.

"The darling!" thought Newland Archer, his glance flitting back to the young girl with the lilies-of-the-valley. "She doesn't even guess what it's all about." And he contemplated her absorbed young face with a thrill of possessorship in which pride in his own masculine initiation was mingled with a tender reverence for her abysmal purity. "We'll read *Faust* together . . . by the Italian lakes . . ." he thought, somewhat hazily confusing the scene of his projected honeymoon with the masterpieces of literature which it would be his manly privilege to reveal to his bride. It was only that afternoon that May Welland had let him guess that she "cared" (New York's consecrated phrase of maiden avowal), and already his imagination, leaping ahead of the engagement ring, the betrothal kiss and the march from *Lohengrin*, pictured her at his side in some scene of old European witchery.

He did not in the least wish the future Mrs. Newland Archer to be a simpleton. He meant her (thanks to his enlightening companionship) to develop a social tact and readiness of wit enabling her to hold her own with the most popular married women of the "younger set," in which it was the recognized custom to attract masculine homage while playfully discouraging it. If he had probed to the bottom of his vanity (as he sometimes nearly did) he would have found there the wish that his wife should be as worldly-wise and as eager to please as the married lady whose charms had held his fancy through two mildly agitated years; without, of course, any hint of the frailty which had so nearly marred that unhappy being's life, and had disarranged his own plans for a whole winter.

How this miracle of fire and ice was to be created, and to sustain itself in a harsh world, he had never taken the time to think out; but he was content to hold his view without analyzing it, since he knew it was that of all the carefully-brushed, white-waistcoated, buttonhole-flowered gentlemen who succeeded each other in the club box, exchanged friendly greetings with him, and turned their opera glasses critically on the circle of ladies who were the product of the system. In matters intellectual and artistic Newland Archer felt himself distinctly the superior of these chosen specimens of old New York gentility; he had probably read more, thought more, and even seen a good deal more of the world, than any other man of the number. Singly they betrayed their inferiority; but grouped together they represented "New York," and the habit of masculine solidarity made him accept their doctrine on all the issues called moral. He instinctively felt that in this respect it would be troublesome—and also rather bad form—to strike out for himself.

"Well—upon my soul!" exclaimed Lawrence Lefferts, turning his opera glass abruptly away from the stage. Lawrence Lefferts was, on the whole, the foremost authority on "form" in New York. He had probably devoted more time than anyone else to the study of this intricate and fascinating question; but study alone could not account for his complete and easy competence. One had only to look at him, from the slant of his bald forehead and the curve of his beautiful fair moustache to the long patent-leather feet at the other end of his lean and elegant person, to feel that the knowledge of "form" must be congenital in anyone who knew how to wear such good clothes so carelessly and carry such height with so much lounging grace. As a young admirer had once said of him: "If anybody can tell a fellow just when to wear a black tie with evening clothes and when not to, it's Larry Lefferts." And on the question of pumps versus patent-leather "Oxfords" his authority had never been disputed.

"My God!" he said; and silently handed his glass to old Sillerton Jackson.

Newland Archer, following Lefferts's glance, saw with surprise that his exclamation had been occasioned by the entry of a new figure into old Mrs. Mingott's box. It was that of a slim young woman, a little less tall than May Welland, with brown hair growing in close curls about her temples and held in place by a narrow band of diamonds. The suggestion of this headdress, which gave her what was then called a "Josephine look," was carried out in the cut of the dark blue velvet gown rather theatrically caught up under her bosom by a girdle with a large old-fashioned clasp. The wearer of this unusual dress, who seemed quite unconscious of the attention it was attracting, stood a moment in the center of the box, discussing with Mrs. Welland the propriety of taking the latter's place in the front right-hand corner; then she yielded with a slight smile, and seated herself in line with Mrs. Welland's sister-in-law, Mrs. Lovell Mingott, who was installed in the opposite corner.

Mr. Sillerton Jackson had returned the opera glass to Lawrence Lefferts. The whole of the club turned instinctively, waiting to hear what the old man had to say; for old Mr. Jackson was as great an authority on "family" as Lawrence Lefferts was on "form." He knew all the ramifications of New York's cousinships; and could not only elucidate such complicated questions as that of the connection between the Mingotts (through the Thorleys) with the Dallases of South Carolina, and that of the relationship of the elder branch of Philadelphia Thorleys to the Albany Chiverses (on no account to be confused with the Manson Chiverses of University Place), but could also enumerate the leading characteristics of each family: as, for instance, the fabulous stinginess of the younger lines of Leffertses (the Long Island ones); or the fatal tendency of the Rushworths to make foolish matches; or the insanity recurring in every second generation of the Albany Chiverses, with whom their New York cousins had always refused to intermarry—with the disastrous exception of poor Medora Manson, who, as everybody knew . . . but then her mother was a Rushworth.

In addition to this forest of family trees, Mr. Sillerton Jackson carried between his narrow hollow temples, and under his soft thatch of silver hair, a register of most of the scandals and mysteries that had smouldered under the unruffled surface of New York society within the last fifty years. So far indeed did his information extend, and so acutely retentive was his memory, that he was supposed to be the only man who could have told you who Julius Beaufort, the banker, really was, and what had become of handsome Bob Spicer, old Mrs. Manson Mingott's father, who had disappeared so mysteriously (with a large sum of trust money) less than a year after his marriage, on the very day that a beautiful Spanish dancer who had been delighting thronged audiences in the old Opera-house on the Battery had taken ship for Cuba. But these mysteries, and many others, were closely locked in Mr. Jackson's breast; for not only did his keen sense of honor forbid his repeating anything privately imparted, but he was fully aware that his reputation for discretion increased his opportunities of finding out what he wanted to know.

The club box, therefore, waited in visible suspense while Mr. Sillerton Jackson handed back Lawrence Lefferts's opera glass. For a moment he silently scrutinized the attentive group out of his filmy blue eyes overhung by old veined lids; then he gave his moustache a thoughtful twist, and said simply: "I didn't think the Mingotts would have tried it on."

2

NEWLAND ARCHER, during this brief episode, had been thrown into a strange state of embarrassment.

It was annoying that the box which was thus attracting the undivided attention of masculine New York should be that in which his betrothed was seated between her mother and aunt; and for a moment he could not identify the lady in the Empire dress, nor imagine why her presence created such excitement among the initiated. Then light dawned on him, and with it came a momentary rush of indignation. No, indeed; no one would have thought the Mingotts would have tried it on!

But they had; they undoubtedly had; for the low-toned comments behind him left no doubt in Archer's mind that the young woman was May Welland's cousin, the cousin always referred to in the family as "poor Ellen Olenska." Archer knew that she had suddenly arrived from Europe a day or two previously; he had even heard from Miss Welland (not disapprovingly) that she had been to see poor Ellen, who was staying with old Mrs. Mingott. Archer entirely approved of family solidarity, and one of the qualities he most admired in the Mingotts was their resolute championship of the few black sheep that their blameless stock had produced. There was nothing mean or ungenerous in the young man's heart, and he was glad that his future wife should not be restrained by false prudery from being kind (in private) to her unhappy cousin; but to receive Countess Olenska in the family circle was a different thing from producing her in public, at the Opera of all places, and in the very box with the young girl whose engagement to him, Newland Archer, was to be announced within a few weeks. No, he felt as old Sillerton Jackson felt; he did not think the Mingotts would have tried it on!

He knew, of course, that whatever man dared (within Fifth Avenue's limits) that old Mrs. Manson Mingott, the Matriarch of the line, would dare. He had always admired the high and mighty old lady, who, in spite of having been only Catherine Spicer of Staten Island, with a father mysteriously discredited, and neither money nor position enough to make people forget it, had allied herself with the head of the wealthy Mingott line, married two of her daughters to "foreigners" (an Italian Marquis and an English banker), and put the crowning touch to her audacities by building a large house of pale cream-colored stone (when brown sandstone seemed as much the only wear as a frockcoat in the afternoon) in an inaccessible wilderness near the Central Park.

Old Mrs. Mingott's foreign daughters had become a legend. They never came back to see their mother, and the latter being, like many persons of active mind and dominating will, sedentary and corpulent in her habit, had philosophically remained at home. But the cream-colored house (supposed to be modelled on the private hotels of the Parisian aristocracy) was there as a visible proof of her moral courage; and she throned in it, among pre-Revolutionary furniture and souvenirs of the Tuileries of Louis Napoleon (where she had shone in her middle age), as placidly as if there were nothing peculiar in living above Thirty-fourth Street, or in having French windows that opened like doors instead of sashes that pushed up.

Everyone (including Mr. Sillerton Jackson) was agreed that old Catherine had never had beauty—a gift which, in the eyes of New York, justified every success, and excused a certain number of failings. Unkind people said that, like her Imperial namesake, she had won her way to success by strength of will and hardness of heart, and a kind of haughty effrontery that was somehow justified by the extreme decency and dignity of her private life. Mr. Manson Mingott had died when she was only twenty-eight, and had "tied up" the money with an additional caution born of the general distrust of the Spicers; but his bold young widow went her way fearlessly, mingled freely in foreign society, married her daughters in heaven knew what corrupt and fashionable circles, hobnobbed with Dukes and Ambassadors, associated familiarly with Papists, entertained Opera singers, and was the intimate friend of Mme. Taglioni; and all the while (as Sillerton Jackson was the first to proclaim) there had never been a breath on her reputation; the only respect, he always added, in which she differed from the earlier Catherine.

Mrs. Manson Mingott had long since succeeded in untying her husband's fortune, and had lived in affluence for half a century; but memories of her early straits had made her excessively thrifty, and though, when she bought a dress or a piece of furniture, she took care that it should be of the best, she could not bring herself to spend much on the transient pleasures of the table. Therefore, for totally different reasons, her food was as poor as Mrs. Archer's, and her wines did nothing to redeem it. Her relatives considered that the penury of her table discredited the Mingott name, which had always been associated with good living; but people continued to come to her in spite of the "made dishes" and flat champagne, and in reply to the remonstrances of her son Lovell (who tried to retrieve the family credit by having the best *chef* in New York) she used to say laughingly: "What's the use of two good cooks in one family, now that I've married the girls and can't eat sauces?"

Newland Archer, as he mused on these things, had once more turned his eyes toward the Mingott box. He saw that Mrs. Welland and her sister-in-law were facing their semicircle of critics with the Mingottian *aplomb* which old Catherine had inculcated in all her tribe, and that only May Welland betrayed, by a heightened color (perhaps due to the knowledge that he was watching her), a sense of the gravity of the situation. As for the cause of the commotion, she sat gracefully in her corner of the box, her eyes fixed on the stage, and revealing, as she leaned forward, a little more shoulder and bosom than New York was accustomed to seeing, at least in ladies who had reasons for wishing to pass unnoticed.

Few things seemed to Newland Archer more awful than an offense against "Taste," that far-off divinity of whom "Form" was the mere visible representative and viceregent. Madame Olenska's pale and serious face appealed to his fancy as suited to the occasion and to her unhappy situation; but the way her dress (which had no tucker) sloped away from her thin shoulders shocked and troubled him. He hated to think of May Welland's being exposed to the influence of a young woman so careless of the dictates of Taste.

"After all," he heard one of the younger men begin behind him (everybody talked through the Mephistopheles-and-Martha scenes), "after all, just *what* happened?"

"Well—she left him; nobody attempts to deny that."

"He's an awful brute, isn't he?" continued the young enquirer, a candid Thorley, who was evidently preparing to enter the lists as the lady's champion.

"The very worst; I knew him at Nice," said Lawrence Lefferts with authority. "A half-paralyzed white sneering fellow—rather handsome head, but eyes with a lot of lashes. Well, I'll tell you the sort: when he wasn't with women he was collecting china. Paying any price for both, I understand."

There was a general laugh, and the young champion said: "Well, then——?"

"Well, then; she bolted with his secretary."

"Oh, I see." The champion's face fell.

"It didn't last long, though: I heard of her a few months later living alone in Venice. I believe Lovell Mingott went out to get her. He said she was desperately unhappy. That's all right—but this parading her at the Opera's another thing."

"Perhaps," young Thorley hazarded, "she's too unhappy to be left at home."

This was greeted with an irreverent laugh, and the youth blushed deeply, and tried to look as if he had meant to insinuate what knowing people called a "*double entendre*."

"Well—it's queer to have brought Miss Welland, anyhow," someone said in a low tone, with a side glance at Archer.

"Oh, that's part of the campaign: Granny's orders, no doubt," Lefferts laughed. "When the old lady does a thing she does it thoroughly."

The act was ending, and there was a general stir in the box. Suddenly Newland Archer felt himself impelled to decisive action. The desire to be the first man to enter Mrs. Mingott's box, to proclaim to the waiting world his engagement to May Welland, and to see her through whatever difficulties her cousin's anomalous situation might involve her in; this impulse had abruptly overruled all scruples and hesitations, and sent him hurrying through the red corridors to the farther side of the house.

As he entered the box his eyes met Miss Welland's, and he saw that she had instantly understood his motive, though the family dignity which both considered so high a virtue would not permit her to tell him so. The persons of their world lived in an atmosphere of faint implications and pale delicacies, and the fact that he and she understood each other without a word seemed to the young man to bring them nearer than any explanation would have done. Her eyes said: "You see why Mamma brought me," and his answered: "I would not for the world have had you stay away."

"You know my niece Countess Olenska?" Mrs. Welland enquired as she shook hands with her future son-in-law. Archer bowed without extending his hand, as was the custom on being introduced to a lady; and Ellen Olenska bent her head slightly, keeping her own pale-gloved hands clasped on her huge fan of eagle feathers. Having greeted Mrs. Lovell Mingott, a large blonde lady in creaking satin, he sat down beside his betrothed, and said in a low tone: "I hope you've told Madame Olenska that we're engaged? I want everybody to know—I want you to let me announce it this evening at the ball."

Miss Welland's face grew rosy as the dawn, and she looked at him with radiant eyes. "If you can persuade Mamma," she said; "but why should we change what is already settled?" He made no answer but that which his eyes returned, and she added, still more confidently smiling: "Tell my cousin yourself: I give you leave. She says she used to play with you when you were children."

She made way for him by pushing back her chair, and promptly, and a little ostentatiously, with the desire that the whole house should see what he was doing, Archer seated himself at the Countess Olenska's side.

"We *did* use to play together, didn't we?" she asked, turning her grave eyes to his. "You were a horrid boy, and kissed me once behind a door; but it was your cousin Vandie Newland, who never looked at me, that I was in love with." Her glance swept the horseshoe curve of boxes. "Ah, how this brings it all back to me—I see everybody here in knickerbockers and pantalettes," she said, with her trailing slightly foreign accent, her eyes returning to his face.

Agreeable as their expression was, the young man was shocked that they should reflect so unseemly a picture of the august tribunal before which, at that very moment, her case was being tried. Nothing could be in worse taste than misplaced flippancy; and he answered somewhat stiffly: "Yes, you have been away a very long time."

"Oh, centuries and centuries; so long," she said, "that I'm sure I'm dead and buried, and this dear old place is heaven," which, for reasons he could not define, struck Newland Archer as an even more disrespectful way of describing New York society.

3

Iᴛ invariably happened in the same way.

Mrs. Julius Beaufort, on the night of her annual ball, never failed to appear at the Opera; indeed, she always gave her ball on an Opera night in order to emphasize her complete superiority to household cares, and her possession of a staff of servants competent to organize every detail of the entertainment in her absence.

The Beauforts' house was one of the few in New York that possessed a ballroom (it antedated even Mrs. Manson Mingott's and the Headly Chiverses); and at a time when it was beginning to be thought "provincial" to put a "crash" over the drawing-room floor and move the furniture upstairs, the possession of a ballroom that was used for no other purpose, and left for three-hundred-and-sixty-four days of the year to shuttered darkness, with its gilt chairs stacked in a corner and its chandelier in a bag; this undoubted superiority was felt to compensate for whatever was regrettable in the Beaufort past.

Mrs. Archer, who was fond of coining her social philosophy into axioms, had once said: "We all have our pet common people—" and though the phrase was a daring one, its truth was secretly admitted in many an exclusive bosom. But the Beauforts were not exactly common; some people said they were even worse. Mrs. Beaufort belonged indeed to one of America's most honored families; she had been the lovely Regina Dallas (of the South Carolina branch), a penniless beauty introduced to New York society by her cousin, the imprudent Medora Manson, who was always doing the wrong thing from the right motive. When one was related to the Mansons and the Rushworths one had a *"Droit de cité"* (as Mr. Sillerton Jackson, who had frequented the Tuileries, called it) in New York society; but did one not forfeit it in marrying Julius Beaufort?

The question was: who *was* Beaufort? He passed for an English-man, was agreeable, handsome, ill-tempered, hospitable and witty. He had come to America with letters of recommendation from old Mrs. Manson Mingott's English son-in-law, the banker, and had speedily made himself an important position in the world of affairs; but his habits were dissipated, his tongue was bitter, his antecedents were mysterious; and when Medora Manson announced her cousin's engagement to him it was felt to be one more act of folly in poor Medora's long record of imprudences.

But folly is as often justified of her children as wisdom, and two years after young Mrs. Beaufort's marriage it was admitted that she had the most distinguished house in New York. No one knew exactly how the miracle was accomplished. She was indolent, passive, the caustic even called her dull; but dressed like an idol, hung with pearls, growing younger and blonder and more beautiful each year, she throned in Mr. Beaufort's heavy brownstone palace, and drew all the world there without lifting her jewelled little finger. The know-ing people said it was Beaufort himself who trained the servants, taught the *chef* new dishes, told the gardeners what hot-house flowers to grow for the dinner-table and the drawing rooms, selected the guests, brewed the after-dinner punch and dictated the little notes his wife wrote to her friends. If he did, these domestic activi-ties were privately performed, and he presented to the world the ap-pearance of a careless and hospitable millionaire strolling into his own drawing room with the detachment of an invited guest, and say-ing: "My wife's gloxinias are a marvel, aren't they? I believe she gets them out from Kew."

Mr. Beaufort's secret, people were agreed, was the way he carried things off. It was all very well to whisper that he had been "helped" to leave England by the international banking-house in which he had been employed; he carried off that rumor as easily as the rest—though New York's business conscience was no less sensitive than its moral standard—he carried everything before him, and all New York into his drawing rooms, and for over twenty years now people had said they were "going to the Beauforts'" with the same tone of secu-rity as if they had said they were going to Mrs. Manson Mingott's, and with the added satisfaction of knowing they would get hot canvasback ducks and vintage wines, instead of tepid Veuve Cliquot without a year and warmed-up croquettes from Philadelphia.

Mrs. Beaufort, then, had as usual appeared in her box just before the Jewel Song; and when, again as usual, she rose at the end of the third act, drew her opera cloak about her lovely shoulders, and disappeared, New York knew that meant that half an hour later the ball would begin.

The Beaufort house was one that New Yorkers were proud to show to foreigners, especially on the night of the annual ball. The Beauforts had been among the first people in New York to own their own red velvet carpet and have it rolled down the steps by their own footmen, under their own awning, instead of hiring it with the supper and the ballroom chairs. They had also inaugurated the custom of letting the ladies take their cloaks off in the hall, instead of shuffling up to the hostess's bedroom and recurling their hair with the aid of the gas-burner; Beaufort was understood to have said that he supposed all his wife's friends had maids who saw to it that they were properly *coiffées* when they left home.

Then the house had been boldly planned with a ballroom, so that, instead of squeezing through a narrow passage to get to it (as at the Chiverses'), one marched solemnly down a vista of enfiladed drawing rooms (the sea-green, the crimson and the *bouton d'or*), seeing from afar the many-candled lusters reflected in the polished parquetry, and beyond that the depths of a conservatory where camellias and tree ferns arched their costly foliage over seats of black and gold bamboo.

Newland Archer, as became a young man of his position, strolled in somewhat late. He had left his overcoat with the silk-stockinged footmen (the stockings were one of Beaufort's few fatuities), had dawdled awhile in the library hung with Spanish leather and furnished with buhl and malachite, where a few men were chatting and putting on their dancing-gloves, and had finally joined the line of guests whom Mrs. Beaufort was receiving on the threshold of the crimson drawing room.

Archer was distinctly nervous. He had not gone back to his club after the Opera (as the young bloods usually did), but, the night being fine, had walked for some distance up Fifth Avenue before turning back in the direction of the Beauforts' house. He was definitely afraid that the Mingotts might be going too far; that, in fact, they might have Granny Mingott's orders to bring the Countess Olenska to the ball.

From the tone of the club box he had perceived how grave a mistake that would be; and, though he was more than ever determined to "see the thing through," he felt less chivalrously eager to champion his betrothed's cousin than before their brief talk at the Opera.

Wandering on to the *bouton d'or* drawing room (where Beaufort had had the audacity to hang "Love Victorious," the much-discussed nude of Bouguereau) Archer found Mrs. Welland and her daughter standing near the ballroom door. Couples were already gliding over the floor beyond: the light of the wax candles fell on revolving tulle skirts, on girlish heads wreathed with modest blossoms, on the dashing aigrettes and ornaments of the young married women's coiffures, and on the glitter of highly glazed shirtfronts and fresh glacé gloves.

Miss Welland, evidently about to join the dancers, hung on the threshold, her lilies-of-the-valley in her hand (she carried no other bouquet), her face a little pale, her eyes burning with a candid excitement. A group of young men and girls were gathered about her, and there was much hand-clasping, laughing and pleasantry on which Mrs. Welland, standing slightly apart, shed the beam of a qualified approval. It was evident that Miss Welland was in the act of announcing her engagement, while her mother affected the air of parental reluctance considered suitable to the occasion.

Archer paused a moment. It was at his express wish that the announcement had been made, and yet it was not thus that he would have wished to have his happiness known. To proclaim it in the heat and noise of a crowded ballroom was to rob it of the fine bloom of privacy which should belong to things nearest the heart. His joy was so deep that this blurring of the surface left its essence untouched; but he would have liked to keep the surface pure too. It was something of a satisfaction to find that May Welland shared this feeling. Her eyes fled to his beseechingly, and their look said: "Remember, we're doing this because it's right."

No appeal could have found a more immediate response in Archer's breast; but he wished that the necessity of their action had been represented by some ideal reason, and not simply by poor Ellen Olenska. The group about Miss Welland made way for him with significant smiles, and after taking his share of the felicitations he drew his betrothed into the middle of the ballroom floor and put his arm about her waist.

"Now we shan't have to talk," he said, smiling into her candid eyes, as they floated away on the soft waves of the "Blue Danube."

She made no answer. Her lips trembled into a smile, but the eyes remained distant and serious, as if bent on some ineffable vision. "Dear," Archer whispered, pressing her to him: it was borne in on him that the first hours of being engaged, even if spent in a ballroom, had in them something grave and sacramental. What a new life it was going to be, with this whiteness, radiance, goodness at one's side!

The dance over, the two, as became an affianced couple, wandered into the conservatory; and sitting behind a tall screen of tree ferns and camellias Newland pressed her gloved hand to his lips.

"You see I did as you asked me to," she said.

"Yes: I couldn't wait," he answered smiling. After a moment he added: "Only I wish it hadn't had to be at a ball."

"Yes, I know." She met his glance comprehendingly. "But after all —even here we're alone together, aren't we?"

"Oh, dearest—always!" Archer cried.

Evidently she was always going to understand; she was always going to say the right thing. The discovery made the cup of his bliss overflow, and he went on gaily: "The worst of it is that I want to kiss you and I can't." As he spoke he took a swift glance about the conservatory, assured himself of their momentary privacy, and catching her to him laid a fugitive pressure on her lips. To counteract the audacity of this proceeding he led her to a bamboo sofa in a less secluded part of the conservatory, and sitting down beside her broke a lily-of-the-valley from her bouquet. She sat silent, and the world lay like a sunlit valley at their feet.

"Did you tell my cousin Ellen?" she asked presently, as if she spoke through a dream.

He roused himself, and remembered that he had not done so. Some invincible repugnance to speak of such things to the strange foreign woman had checked the words on his lips.

"No—I hadn't the chance after all," he said, fibbing hastily.

"Ah." She looked disappointed, but gently resolved on gaining her point. "You must, then, for I didn't either; and I shouldn't like her to think—"

"Of course not. But aren't you, after all, the person to do it?"

She pondered on this. "If I'd done it at the right time, yes: but now that there's been a delay I think you must explain that I'd asked you to tell her at the Opera, before our speaking about it to everybody here. Otherwise she might think I had forgotten her. You see, she's one of the family, and she's been away so long that she's rather —sensitive."

Archer looked at her glowingly. "Dear and great angel! Of course

I'll tell her." He glanced a trifle apprehensively toward the crowded ballroom. "But I haven't seen her yet. Has she come?"

"No; at the last minute she decided not to."

"At the last minute?" he echoed, betraying his surprise that she should ever have considered the alternative possible.

"Yes. She's awfully fond of dancing," the young girl answered simply. "But suddenly she made up her mind that her dress wasn't smart enough for a ball, though we thought it so lovely; and so my aunt had to take her home."

"Oh, well—" said Archer with happy indifference. Nothing about his betrothed pleased him more than her resolute determination to carry to its utmost limit that ritual of ignoring the "unpleasant" in which they had both been brought up.

"She knows as well as I do," he reflected, "the real reason of her cousin's staying away; but I shall never let her see by the least sign that I am conscious of there being a shadow of a shade on poor Ellen Olenska's reputation."

4

In the course of the next day the first of the usual betrothal visits were exchanged. The New York ritual was precise and inflexible in such matters; and in conformity with it Newland Archer first went with his mother and sister to call on Mrs. Welland, after which he and Mrs. Welland and May drove out to old Mrs. Manson Mingott's to receive the venerable ancestress' blessing.

A visit to Mrs. Manson Mingott was always an amusing episode to the young man. The house in itself was already an historic document, though not, of course, as venerable as certain other old family houses in University Place and lower Fifth Avenue. Those were of the purest 1830, with a grim harmony of cabbage-rose-garlanded carpets, rosewood consoles, round-arched fireplaces with black marble mantels, and immense glazed bookcases of mahogany; whereas old Mrs. Mingott, who had built her house later, had bodily cast out the massive furniture of her prime, and mingled with the Mingott heirlooms the frivolous upholstery of the Second Empire. It was her habit to sit in a window of her sitting room on the ground floor, as if watching calmly for life and fashion to flow northward to her solitary doors. She seemed in no hurry to have them come, for her patience was equalled by her confidence. She was sure that presently the hoardings, the quarries, the one-story saloons, the wooden greenhouses in ragged gardens, and the rocks from which goats surveyed the scene, would vanish before the advance of residences as stately as her own—perhaps (for she was an impartial woman) even statelier; and that the cobblestones over which the old clattering omnibuses bumped would be replaced by smooth asphalt, such as people reported having seen in Paris. Meanwhile, as everyone she cared to see came to *her* (and she could fill her rooms as easily as the Beauforts, and without adding a single item to the *menu* of her suppers), she did not suffer from her geographic isolation.

The immense accretion of flesh which had descended on her in middle life like a flood of lava on a doomed city had changed her from a plump active little woman with a neatly-turned foot and ankle into something as vast and august as a natural phenomenon. She had accepted this submergence as philosophically as all her other trials, and now, in extreme old age, was rewarded by presenting to her mirror an almost unwrinkled expanse of firm pink and white flesh, in the center of which the traces of a small face survived as if awaiting excavation. A flight of smooth double chins led down to the dizzy depths of a still-snowy bosom veiled in snowy muslins that were held in place by a miniature portrait of the late Mr. Mingott; and around and below, wave after wave of black silk surged away over the edges of a capacious armchair, with two tiny white hands poised like gulls on the surface of the billows.

The burden of Mrs. Manson Mingott's flesh had long since made it impossible for her to go up and down stairs, and with characteristic independence she had made her reception rooms upstairs and established herself (in flagrant violation of all the New York proprieties) on the ground floor of her house; so that, as you sat in her sitting room window with her, you caught (through a door that was always open, and a looped-back yellow damask portière) the unexpected vista of a bedroom with a huge low bed upholstered like a sofa, and a toilet-table with frivolous lace flounces and a gilt-framed mirror.

Her visitors were startled and fascinated by the foreignness of this arrangement, which recalled scenes in French fiction, and architectural incentives to immorality such as the simple American had never dreamed of. That was how women with lovers lived in the wicked old societies, in apartments with all the rooms on one floor, and all the indecent propinquities that their novels described. It amused Newland Archer (who had secretly situated the love-scenes of *Monsieur de Camors* in Mrs. Mingott's bedroom) to picture her blameless life led in the stage-setting of adultery; but he said to himself, with considerable admiration, that if a lover had been what she wanted, the intrepid woman would have had him too.

To the general relief the Countess Olenska was not present in her grandmother's drawing room during the visit of the betrothed couple. Mrs. Mingott said she had gone out; which, on a day of such

glaring sunlight, and at the "shopping hour," seemed in itself an indelicate thing for a compromised woman to do. But at any rate it
spared them the embarrassment of her presence, and the faint
shadow that her unhappy past might seem to shed on their radiant
future. The visit went off successfully, as was to have been expected.
Old Mrs. Mingott was delighted with the engagement, which, being
long foreseen by watchful relatives, had been carefully passed upon
in family council; and the engagement ring, a large thick sapphire set
in invisible claws, met with her unqualified admiration.

"It's the new setting: of course it shows the stone beautifully, but
it looks a little bare to old-fashioned eyes," Mrs. Welland had explained, with a conciliatory side glance at her future son-in-law.

"Old-fashioned eyes? I hope you don't mean mine, my dear? I like
all the novelties," said the ancestress, lifting the stone to her small
bright orbs, which no glasses had ever disfigured. "Very handsome,"
she added, returning the jewel, "very liberal. In my time a cameo set
in pearls was thought sufficient. But it's the hand that sets off the
ring, isn't it, my dear Mr. Archer?" and she waved one of her tiny
hands, with small pointed nails and rolls of aged fat encircling the
wrist like ivory bracelets. "Mine was modeled in Rome by the great
Ferrigiani. You should have May's done: no doubt he'll have it done,
my child. Her hand is large—it's these modern sports that spread the
joints—but the skin is white.—And when's the wedding to be?" she
broke off, fixing her eyes on Archer's face.

"Oh—" Mrs. Welland murmured, while the young man, smiling
at his betrothed, replied: "As soon as ever it can, if only you'll back
me up, Mrs. Mingott."

"We must give them time to get to know each other a little better, mamma," Mrs. Welland interposed, with the proper affectation
of reluctance; to which the ancestress rejoined: "Know each other?
Fiddlesticks! Everybody in New York has always known everybody.
Let the young man have his way, my dear; don't wait till the bub-
ble's off the wine. Marry them before Lent; I may catch pneumonia
any winter now, and I want to give the wedding breakfast."

These successive statements were received with the proper expressions of amusement, incredulity and gratitude; and the visit was
breaking up in a vein of mild pleasantry when the door opened to
admit the Countess Olenska, who entered in bonnet and mantle followed by the unexpected figure of Julius Beaufort.

There was a cousinly murmur of pleasure between the ladies, and

Mrs. Mingott held out Ferrigiani's model to the banker. "Ha! Beaufort, this is a rare favor!" (She had an odd foreign way of addressing men by their surnames.)

"Thanks. I wish it might happen oftener," said the visitor in his easy arrogant way. "I'm generally so tied down; but I met the Countess Ellen in Madison Square, and she was good enough to let me walk home with her."

"Ah—I hope the house will be gayer, now that Ellen's here!" cried Mrs. Mingott with a glorious effrontery. "Sit down—sit down, Beaufort: push up the yellow armchair; now I've got you I want a good gossip. I hear your ball was magnificent; and I understand you invited Mrs. Lemuel Struthers? Well—I've a curiosity to see the woman myself."

She had forgotten her relatives, who were drifting out into the hall under Ellen Olenska's guidance. Old Mrs. Mingott had always professed a great admiration for Julius Beaufort, and there was a kind of kinship in their cool domineering way and their short-cuts through the conventions. Now she was eagerly curious to know what had decided the Beauforts to invite (for the first time) Mrs. Lemuel Struthers, the widow of Struthers' Shoe-polish, who had returned the previous year from a long initiatory sojourn in Europe to lay siege to the tight little citadel of New York. "Of course if you and Regina invite her the thing is settled. Well, we need new blood and new money —and I hear she's still very good-looking," the carnivorous old lady declared.

In the hall, while Mrs. Welland and May drew on their furs, Archer saw that the Countess Olenska was looking at him with a faintly questioning smile.

"Of course you know already—about May and me," he said, answering her look with a shy laugh. "She scolded me for not giving you the news last night at the Opera: I had her orders to tell you that we were engaged—but I couldn't, in that crowd."

The smile passed from Countess Olenska's eyes to her lips: she looked younger, more like the bold, brown Ellen Mingott of his boyhood. "Of course I know; yes. And I'm so glad. But one doesn't tell such things first in a crowd." The ladies were on the threshold and she held out her hand.

"Good-bye; come and see me some day," she said, still looking at Archer.

In the carriage, on the way down Fifth Avenue, they talked pointedly of Mrs. Mingott, of her age, her spirit, and all her wonderful attributes. No one alluded to Ellen Olenska; but Archer knew that Mrs. Welland was thinking: "It's a mistake for Ellen to be seen, the very day after her arrival, parading up Fifth Avenue at the crowded hour with Julius Beaufort—" and the young man himself mentally added: "And she ought to know that a man who's just engaged doesn't spend his time calling on married women. But I daresay in the set she's lived in they do—they never do anything else." And, in spite of the cosmopolitan views on which he prided himself, he thanked heaven that he was a New Yorker, and about to ally himself with one of his own kind.

5

THE next evening old Mr. Sillerton Jackson came to dine with the Archers.

Mrs. Archer was a shy woman and shrank from society; but she liked to be well informed as to its doings. Her old friend Mr. Sillerton Jackson applied to the investigation of his friends' affairs the patience of a collector and the science of a naturalist; and his sister, Miss Sophy Jackson, who lived with him, and was entertained by all the people who could not secure her much-sought-after brother, brought home bits of minor gossip that filled out usefully the gaps in his picture.

Therefore, whenever anything happened that Mrs. Archer wanted to know about, she asked Mr. Jackson to dine; and as she honored few people with her invitations, and as she and her daughter Janey were an excellent audience, Mr. Jackson usually came himself instead of sending his sister. If he could have dictated all the conditions, he would have chosen the evenings when Newland was out; not because the young man was uncongenial to him (the two got on capitally at their club) but because the old anecdotist sometimes felt, on Newland's part, a tendency to weigh his evidence that the ladies of the family never showed.

Mr. Jackson, if perfection had been attainable on earth, would also have asked that Mrs. Archer's food should be a little better. But then New York, as far back as the mind of man could travel, had been divided into the two great fundamental groups of the Mingotts and Mansons and all their clan, who cared about eating and clothes and money, and the Archer-Newland-van-der-Luyden tribe, who were devoted to travel, horticulture and the best fiction, and looked down on the grosser forms of pleasure.

You couldn't have everything, after all. If you dined with the Lovell Mingotts you got canvasback and terrapin and vintage wines; at Adeline Archer's you could talk about Alpine scenery and "The Marble Faun"; and luckily the Archer Madeira had gone round the Cape. Therefore when a friendly summons came from Mrs. Archer, Mr. Jackson, who was a true eclectic, would usually say to his sister: "I've been a little gouty since my last dinner at the Lovell Mingotts' —it will do me good to diet at Adeline's."

Mrs. Archer, who had long been a widow, lived with her son and daughter in West Twenty-eighth Street. An upper floor was dedicated to Newland, and the two women squeezed themselves into narrower quarters below. In an unclouded harmony of tastes and interests they cultivated ferns in Wardian cases, made macramé lace and wool embroidery on linen, collected American Revolutionary glazed ware, subscribed to "Good Words," and read Ouida's novels for the sake of the Italian atmosphere. (They preferred those about peasant life, because of the descriptions of scenery and the pleasanter sentiments, though in general they liked novels about people in society, whose motives and habits were more comprehensible, spoke severely of Dickens, who "had never drawn a gentleman," and considered Thackeray less at home in the great world than Bulwer—who, however, was beginning to be thought old-fashioned.)

Mrs. and Miss Archer were both great lovers of scenery. It was what they principally sought and admired on their occasional travels abroad; considering architecture and painting as subjects for men, and chiefly for learned persons who read Ruskin. Mrs. Archer had been born a Newland, and mother and daughter, who were as like as sisters, were both, as people said, "true Newlands"; tall, pale, and slightly round-shouldered, with long noses, sweet smiles and a kind of drooping distinction like that in certain faded Reynolds portraits. Their physical resemblance would have been complete if an elderly *embonpoint* had not stretched Mrs. Archer's black brocade, while Miss Archer's brown and purple poplins hung, as the years went on, more and more slackly on her virgin frame.

Mentally, the likeness between them, as Newland was aware, was less complete than their identical mannerisms often made it appear. The long habit of living together in mutually dependent intimacy had given them the same vocabulary, and the same habit of beginning their phrases "Mother thinks" or "Janey thinks," according as one or the other wished to advance an opinion of her own; but in reality, while Mrs. Archer's serene unimaginativeness rested easily in the accepted and familiar, Janey was subject to starts and aberrations of fancy welling up from springs of suppressed romance.

Mother and daughter adored each other and revered their son and brother; and Archer loved them with a tenderness made compunctious and uncritical by the sense of their exaggerated admiration, and by his secret satisfaction in it. After all, he thought it a good thing for a man to have his authority respected in his own house, even if his sense of humor sometimes made him question the force of his mandate.

On this occasion the young man was very sure that Mr. Jackson would rather have had him dine out; but he had his own reasons for not doing so.

Of course old Jackson wanted to talk about Ellen Olenska, and of course Mrs. Archer and Janey wanted to hear what he had to tell. All three would be slightly embarrassed by Newland's presence, now that his prospective relation to the Mingott clan had been made known; and the young man waited with an amused curiosity to see how they would turn the difficulty.

They began, obliquely, by talking about Mrs. Lemuel Struthers.

"It's a pity the Beauforts asked her," Mrs. Archer said gently. "But then Regina always does what he tells her; and *Beaufort*—"

"Certain *nuances* escape Beaufort," said Mr. Jackson, cautiously inspecting the broiled shad, and wondering for the thousandth time why Mrs. Archer's cook always burnt the roe to a cinder. (Newland, who had long shared his wonder, could always detect it in the older man's expression of melancholy disapproval.)

"Oh, necessarily; Beaufort is a vulgar man," said Mrs. Archer. "My grandfather Newland always used to say to my mother: 'Whatever you do, don't let that fellow Beaufort be introduced to the girls.' But at least he's had the advantage of associating with gentlemen; in England too, they say. It's all very mysterious—" She glanced at Janey and paused. She and Janey knew every fold of the Beaufort mystery, but in public Mrs. Archer continued to assume that the subject was not one for the unmarried.

"But this Mrs. Struthers," Mrs. Archer continued; "what did you say *she* was, Sillerton?"

"Out of a mine: or rather out of the saloon at the head of the pit. Then with Living Wax-Works, touring New England. After the police broke *that* up, they say she lived—" Mr. Jackson in his turn

glanced at Janey, whose eyes began to bulge from under her prominent lids. There were still hiatuses for her in Mrs. Struthers's past.

"Then," Mr. Jackson continued (and Archer saw he was wondering why no one had told the butler never to slice cucumbers with a
steel knife), "then Lemuel Struthers came along. They say his advertiser used the girl's head for the shoe-polish posters; her hair's intensely black, you know—the Egyptian style. Anyhow, he—eventually—married her." There were volumes of innuendo in the way
the "eventually" was spaced, and each syllable given its due stress.

"Oh, well—at the pass we've come to nowadays, it doesn't matter," said Mrs. Archer indifferently. The ladies were not really interested in Mrs. Struthers just then; the subject of Ellen Olenska was
too fresh and too absorbing to them. Indeed, Mrs. Struthers's name
had been introduced by Mrs. Archer only that she might presently
be able to say: "And Newland's new cousin—Countess Olenska?
Was *she* at the ball too?"

There was a faint touch of sarcasm in the reference to her son, and
Archer knew it and had expected it. Even Mrs. Archer, who was seldom unduly pleased with human events, had been altogether glad of
her son's engagement. ("Especially after that silly business with Mrs.
Rushworth," as she had remarked to Janey, alluding to what had
once seemed to Newland a tragedy of which his soul would always
bear the scar.) There was no better match in New York than May
Welland, look at the question from whatever point you chose. Of
course such a marriage was only what Newland was entitled to; but
young men are so foolish and incalculable—and some women so en-
snaring and unscrupulous—that it was nothing short of a miracle to
see one's only son safe past the Siren Isle and in the haven of a
blameless domesticity.

All this Mrs. Archer felt, and her son knew she felt; but he knew
also that she had been perturbed by the premature announcement of
his engagement, or rather by its cause; and it was for that reason—
because on the whole he was a tender and indulgent master—that he
had stayed at home that evening. "It's not that I don't approve of
the Mingotts' *esprit de corps*; but why Newland's engagement
should be mixed up with that Olenska woman's comings and goings
I don't see," Mrs. Archer grumbled to Janey, the only witness of her
slight lapses from perfect sweetness.

She had behaved beautifully—and in beautiful behavior she was
unsurpassed—during the call on Mrs. Welland; but Newland knew

(and his betrothed doubtless guessed) that all through the visit she and Janey were nervously on the watch for Madame Olenska's possible intrusion; and when they left the house together she had permitted herself to say to her son: "I'm thankful that Augusta Welland received us alone."

These indications of inward disturbance moved Archer the more that he too felt that the Mingotts had gone a little too far. But, as it was against all the rules of their code that the mother and son should ever allude to what was uppermost in their thoughts, he simply replied: "Oh, well, there's always a phase of family parties to be gone through when one gets engaged, and the sooner it's over the better." At which his mother merely pursed her lips under the lace veil that hung down from her gray velvet bonnet trimmed with frosted grapes.

Her revenge, he felt—her lawful revenge—would be to "draw" Mr. Jackson that evening on the Countess Olenska; and, having publicly done his duty as a future member of the Mingott clan, the young man had no objection to hearing the lady discussed in private—except that the subject was already beginning to bore him.

Mr. Jackson had helped himself to a slice of the tepid *filet* which the mournful butler had handed him with a look as skeptical as his own, and had rejected the mushroom sauce after a scarcely perceptible sniff. He looked baffled and hungry, and Archer reflected that he would probably finish his meal on Ellen Olenska.

Mr. Jackson leaned back in his chair, and glanced up at the candlelit Archers, Newlands and van der Luydens hanging in dark frames on the dark walls.

"Ah, how your grandfather Archer loved a good dinner, my dear Newland!" he said, his eyes on the portrait of a plump full-chested young man in a stock and a blue coat, with a view of a white-columned country house behind him. "Well—well—well . . . I wonder what he would have said to all these foreign marriages!"

Mrs. Archer ignored the allusion to the ancestral *cuisine* and Mr. Jackson continued with deliberation: "No, she was *not* at the ball."

"Ah—" Mrs. Archer murmured, in a tone that implied: "She had that decency."

"Perhaps the Beauforts don't know her," Janey suggested, with her artless malice.

Mr. Jackson gave a faint sip, as if he had been tasting invisible Madeira. "Mrs. Beaufort may not—but Beaufort certainly does, for she was seen walking up Fifth Avenue this afternoon with him by the whole of New York."

"Mercy—" moaned Mrs. Archer, evidently perceiving the uselessness of trying to ascribe the actions of foreigners to a sense of delicacy.

"I wonder if she wears a round hat or a bonnet in the afternoon," Janey speculated. "At the Opera I know she had on dark blue velvet, perfectly plain and flat—like a nightgown."

"Janey!" said her mother; and Miss Archer blushed and tried to look audacious.

"It was, at any rate, in better taste not to go to the ball," Mrs. Archer continued.

A spirit of perversity moved her son to rejoin: "I don't think it was a question of taste with her. May said she meant to go, and then decided that the dress in question wasn't smart enough."

Mrs. Archer smiled at this confirmation of her inference. "Poor Ellen," she simply remarked; adding compassionately: "We must always bear in mind what an eccentric bringing-up Medora Manson gave her. What can you expect of a girl who was allowed to wear black satin at her coming-out ball?"

"Ah—don't I remember her in it!" said Mr. Jackson; adding: "Poor girl!" in the tone of one who, while enjoying the memory, had fully understood at the time what the sight portended.

"It's odd," Janey remarked, "that she should have kept such an ugly name as Ellen. I should have changed it to Elaine." She glanced about the table to see the effect of this.

Her brother laughed. "Why Elaine?"

"I don't know; it sounds more—more Polish," said Janey, blushing.

"It sounds more conspicuous; and that can hardly be what she wishes," said Mrs. Archer distantly.

"Why not?" broke in her son, growing suddenly argumentative. "Why shouldn't she be conspicuous if she chooses? Why should she slink about as if it were she who had disgraced herself? She's 'poor Ellen' certainly, because she had the bad luck to make a wretched marriage; but I don't see that that's a reason for hiding her head as if she were the culprit."

"That, I suppose," said Mr. Jackson, speculatively, "is the line the Mingotts mean to take."

The young man reddened. "I didn't have to wait for their cue, if that's what you mean, sir. Madame Olenska has had an unhappy life: that doesn't make her an outcast."

"There are rumors," began Mr. Jackson, glancing at Janey.

"Oh, I know: the secretary," the young man took him up. "Nonsense, mother; Janey's grown-up. They say, don't they," he went on, "that the secretary helped her to get away from her brute of a husband, who kept her practically a prisoner? Well, what if he did? I hope there isn't a man among us who wouldn't have done the same in such a case."

Mr. Jackson glanced over his shoulder to say to the sad butler: "Perhaps . . . that sauce . . . just a little, after all—"; then, having helped himself, he remarked: "I'm told she's looking for a house. She means to live here."

"I hear she means to get a divorce," said Janey boldly.

"I hope she will!" Archer exclaimed.

The word had fallen like a bombshell in the pure and tranquil atmosphere of the Archer dining room. Mrs. Archer raised her delicate eyebrows in the particular curve that signified: "The butler—" and the young man, himself mindful of the bad taste of discussing such intimate matters in public, hastily branched off into an account of his visit to old Mrs. Mingott.

After dinner, according to immemorial custom, Mrs. Archer and Janey trailed their long silk draperies up to the drawing room, where, while the gentlemen smoked below stairs, they sat beside a Carcel lamp with an engraved globe, facing each other across a rosewood work-table with a green silk bag under it, and stitched at the two ends of a tapestry band of field flowers destined to adorn an "occasional" chair in the drawing room of young Mrs. Newland Archer.

While this rite was in progress in the drawing room, Archer settled Mr. Jackson in an armchair near the fire in the Gothic library and handed him a cigar. Mr. Jackson sank into the armchair with satisfaction, lit his cigar with perfect confidence (it was Newland who bought them), and stretching his thin old ankles to the coals, said: "You say the secretary merely helped her to get away, my dear fellow? Well, he was still helping her a year later, then; for somebody met 'em living at Lausanne together."

Newland reddened. "Living together? Well, why not? Who had the right to make her life over if she hadn't? I'm sick of the hypocrisy that would bury alive a woman of her age if her husband prefers to live with harlots."

He stopped and turned away angrily to light his cigar. "Women ought to be free—as free as we are," he declared, making a discovery of which he was too irritated to measure the terrific consequences.

Mr. Sillerton Jackson stretched his ankles nearer the coals and emitted a sardonic whistle.

"Well," he said after a pause, "apparently Count Olenski takes your view; for I never heard of his having lifted a finger to get his wife back."

6

THAT evening, after Mr. Jackson had taken himself away, and the ladies had retired to their chintz-curtained bedroom, Newland Archer mounted thoughtfully to his own study. A vigilant hand had, as usual, kept the fire alive and the lamp trimmed; and the room, with its rows and rows of books, its bronze and steel statuettes of "The Fencers" on the mantelpiece and its many photographs of famous pictures, looked singularly homelike and welcoming.

As he dropped into his armchair near the fire his eyes rested on a large photograph of May Welland, which the young girl had given him in the first days of their romance, and which had now displaced all the other portraits on the table. With a new sense of awe he looked at the frank forehead, serious eyes and gay innocent mouth of the young creature whose soul's custodian he was to be. That terrifying product of the social system he belonged to and believed in, the young girl who knew nothing and expected everything, looked back at him like a stranger through May Welland's familiar features; and once more it was borne in on him that marriage was not the safe anchorage he had been taught to think, but a voyage on uncharted seas.

The case of the Countess Olenska had stirred up old settled convictions and set them drifting dangerously through his mind. His own exclamation: "Women should be free—as free as we are," struck to the root of a problem that it was agreed in his world to regard as non-existent. "Nice" women, however wronged, would never claim the kind of freedom he meant, and generous-minded men like himself were therefore—in the heat of argument—the more chivalrously ready to concede it to them. Such verbal generosities were in fact only a humbugging disguise of the inexorable conventions that tied things together and bound people down to the old pattern. But here he was pledged to defend, on the part of his betrothed's cousin, conduct that, on his own wife's part, would justify him in calling down on her all the thunders of Church and State. Of course the dilemma was purely hypothetical; since he wasn't a blackguard Polish nobleman, it was absurd to speculate what his wife's rights would be if he *were*. But Newland Archer was too imaginative not to feel that, in his case and May's, the tie might gall for reasons far less gross and palpable. What could he and she really know of each other, since it was his duty, as a "decent" fellow, to conceal his past from her, and hers, as a marriageable girl, to have no past to conceal? What if, for some one of the subtler reasons that would tell with both of them, they should tire of each other, misunderstand or irritate each other? He reviewed his friends' marriages—the supposedly happy ones—and saw none that answered, even remotely, to the passionate and tender comradeship which he pictured as his permanent relation with May Welland. He perceived that such a picture presupposed, on her part, the experience, the versatility, the freedom of judgment, which she had been carefully trained not to possess; and with a shiver of foreboding he saw his marriage becoming what most of the other marriages about him were: a dull association of material and social interests held together by ignorance on the one side and hypocrisy on the other. Lawrence Lefferts occurred to him as the husband who had most completely realized this enviable ideal. As became the high priest of form, he had formed a wife so completely to his own convenience that, in the most conspicuous moments of his frequent love affairs with other men's wives, she went about in smiling unconsciousness, saying that "Lawrence was so frightfully strict"; and had been known to blush indignantly, and avert her gaze, when someone alluded in her presence to the fact that Julius Beaufort (as became a "foreigner" of doubtful origin) had what was known in New York as "another establishment."

Archer tried to console himself with the thought that he was not quite such an ass as Larry Lefferts, nor May such a simpleton as poor Gertrude; but the difference was after all one of intelligence and not of standards. In reality they all lived in a kind of hieroglyphic world, where the real thing was never said or done or even thought, but only represented by a set of arbitrary signs; as when Mrs. Welland, who knew exactly why Archer had pressed her to announce her daughter's engagement at the Beaufort ball (and had indeed expected him to do no less), yet felt obliged to simulate reluctance, and the air of having had her hand forced, quite as, in the books on Primitive Man that people of advanced culture were beginning to read, the savage bride is dragged with shrieks from her parents' tent.

The result, of course, was that the young girl who was the center of this elaborate system of mystification remained the more inscrutable for her very frankness and assurance. She was frank, poor darling, because she had nothing to conceal, assured because she knew of nothing to be on her guard against; and with no better preparation than this, she was to be plunged overnight into what people evasively called "the facts of life."

The young man was sincerely but placidly in love. He delighted in the radiant good looks of his betrothed, in her health, her horsemanship, her grace and quickness at games, and the shy interest in books and ideas that she was beginning to develop under his guidance. (She had advanced far enough to join him in ridiculing the "Idyls of the King," but not to feel the beauty of "Ulysses" and the "Lotus Eaters.") She was straightforward, loyal and brave; she had a sense of humor (chiefly proved by her laughing at *his* jokes); and he suspected, in the depths of her innocently-gazing soul, a glow of feeling that it would be a joy to waken. But when he had gone the brief round of her he returned discouraged by the thought that all this frankness and innocence were only an artificial product. Untrained human nature was not frank and innocent; it was full of the twists and defenses of an instinctive guile. And he felt himself oppressed by this creation of factitious purity, so cunningly manufactured by a conspiracy of mothers and aunts and grandmothers and long-dead ancestresses, because it was supposed to be what he wanted, what he had a right to, in order that he might exercise his lordly pleasure in smashing it like an image made of snow.

There was a certain triteness in these reflections: they were those habitual to young men on the approach of their wedding day. But they were generally accompanied by a sense of compunction and self-abasement of which Newland Archer felt no trace. He could not deplore (as Thackeray's heroes so often exasperated him by doing) that he had not a blank page to offer his bride in exchange for the unblemished one she was to give to him. He could not get away from the fact that if he had been brought up as she had they would have been no more fit to find their way about than the Babes in the Wood; nor could he, for all his anxious cogitations, see any honest reason (any, that is, unconnected with his own momentary pleasure, and the passion of masculine vanity) why his bride should not have been allowed the same freedom of experience as himself.

Such questions, at such an hour, were bound to drift through his mind; but he was conscious that their uncomfortable persistence and precision were due to the inopportune arrival of the Countess Olenska. Here he was, at the very moment of his betrothal—a moment for pure thoughts and cloudless hopes—pitchforked into a coil of scandal which raised all the special problems he would have preferred to let lie. "Hang Ellen Olenska!" he grumbled, as he covered his fire and began to undress. He could not really see why her fate should have the least bearing on his; yet he dimly felt that he had only just begun to measure the risks of the championship which his engagement had forced upon him.

A few days later the bolt fell.

The Lovell Mingotts had sent out cards for what was known as "a formal dinner" (that is, three extra footmen, two dishes for each course, and a Roman punch in the middle), and had headed their invitations with the words "To meet the Countess Olenska," in accordance with the hospitable American fashion, which treats strangers as if they were royalties, or at least as their ambassadors.

The guests had been selected with a boldness and discrimination in which the initiated recognized the firm hand of Catherine the Great. Associated with such immemorial standbys as the Selfridge Merrys, who were asked everywhere because they always had been, the Beauforts, on whom there was a claim of relationship, and Mr. Sillerton Jackson and his sister Sophy (who went wherever her brother told her to), were some of the most fashionable and yet most irreproachable of the dominant "young married" set; the Lawrence Leffertses, Mrs. Lefferts Rushworth (the lovely widow), the Harry Thorleys, the Reggie Chiverses and young Morris Dagonet and his wife (who was a van der Luyden). The company indeed was perfectly assorted, since all the members belonged to the little inner group of people who, during the long New York season, disported themselves together daily and nightly with apparently undiminished zest.

Forty-eight hours later the unbelievable had happened; everyone had refused the Mingotts' invitation except the Beauforts and old Mr. Jackson and his sister. The intended slight was emphasized by the fact that even the Reggie Chiverses, who were of the Mingott clan, were among those inflicting it; and by the uniform wording of the notes, in all of which the writers "regretted that they were unable to accept," without the mitigating plea of a "previous engagement" that ordinary courtesy prescribed.

New York society was, in those days, far too small, and too scant in its resources, for everyone in it (including livery-stablekeepers, butlers and cooks) not to know exactly on which evenings people were free; and it was thus possible for the recipients of Mrs. Lovell Mingott's invitations to make cruelly clear their determination not to meet the Countess Olenska.

The blow was unexpected; but the Mingotts, as their way was, met it gallantly. Mrs. Lovell Mingott confided the case to Mrs. Welland, who confided it to Newland Archer; who, aflame at the outrage, appealed passionately and authoritatively to his mother; who, after a painful period of inward resistance and outward temporizing, succumbed to his instances (as she always did), and immediately embracing his cause with an energy redoubled by her previous hesitations, put on her gray velvet bonnet and said: "I'll go and see Louisa van der Luyden."

The New York of Newland Archer's day was a small and slippery pyramid, in which, as yet, hardly a fissure had been made or a foothold gained. At its base was a firm foundation of what Mrs. Archer called "plain people"; an honorable but obscure majority of respectable families who (as in the case of the Spicers or the Leffertses or the Jacksons) had been raised above their level by marriage with one of the ruling clans. People, Mrs. Archer always said, were not as particular as they used to be; and with old Catherine Spicer ruling one end of Fifth Avenue, and Julius Beaufort the other, you couldn't expect the old traditions to last much longer.

Firmly narrowing upward from this wealthy but inconspicuous substratum was the compact and dominant group which the Mingotts, Newlands, Chiverses and Mansons so actively represented. Most people imagined them to be the very apex of the pyramid; but they themselves (at least those of Mrs. Archer's generation) were aware that, in the eyes of the professional genealogist, only a still smaller number of families could lay claim to that eminence.

"Don't tell me," Mrs. Archer would say to her children, "all this modern newspaper rubbish about a New York aristocracy. If there is one, neither the Mingotts nor the Mansons belong to it; no, nor the

Newlands or the Chiverses either. Our grandfathers and great-grandfathers were just respectable English or Dutch merchants, who came
to the colonies to make their fortune, and stayed here because they
did so well. One of your great-grandfathers signed the Declaration,
and another was a general on Washington's staff, and received General Burgoyne's sword after the battle of Saratoga. These are things
to be proud of, but they have nothing to do with rank or class. New
York has always been a commercial community, and there are not
more than three families in it who can claim an aristocratic origin in
the real sense of the word."

Mrs. Archer and her son and daughter, like everyone else in New
York, knew who these privileged beings were: the Dagonets of
Washington Square, who came of an old English county family allied with the Pitts and Foxes; the Lannings, who had intermarried
with the descendants of Count de Grasse; and the van der Luydens,
direct descendants of the first Dutch governor of Manhattan, and related by pre-Revolutionary marriages to several members of the
French and British aristocracy.

The Lannings survived only in the person of two very old but
lively Miss Lannings, who lived cheerfully and reminiscently among
family portraits and Chippendale; the Dagonets were a considerable
clan, allied to the best names in Baltimore and Philadelphia; but the
van der Luydens, who stood above all of them, had faded into a kind
of super-terrestrial twilight, from which only two figures impressively
emerged; those of Mr. and Mrs. Henry van der Luyden.

Mrs. Henry van der Luyden had been Louisa Dagonet, and her
mother had been the granddaughter of Colonel du Lac, of an old
Channel Island family, who had fought under Cornwallis and had
settled in Maryland, after the war, with his bride, Lady Angelica
Trevenna, fifth daughter of the Earl of St. Austrey. The tie between
the Dagonets, the du Lacs of Maryland, and their aristocratic
Cornish kinfolk, the Trevennas, had always remained close and cordial. Mr. and Mrs. van der Luyden had more than once paid long
visits to the present head of the house of Trevenna, the Duke of St.
Austrey, at his country-seat in Cornwall and at St. Austrey in
Gloucestershire; and His Grace had frequently announced his intention of some day returning their visit (without the Duchess, who
feared the Atlantic).

Mr. and Mrs. van der Luyden divided their time between Trevenna, their place in Maryland, and Skuytercliff, the great estate on

the Hudson which had been one of the colonial grants of the Dutch government to the famous first governor, and of which Mr. van der Luyden was still "Patroon." Their large solemn house in Madison Avenue was seldom opened, and when they came to town they received in it only their most intimate friends.

"I wish you would go with me, Newland," his mother said, suddenly pausing at the door of the Brown *coupé*. "Louisa is fond of you; and of course it's on account of dear May that I'm taking this step—and also because, if we don't all stand together, there'll be no such thing as Society left."

7

Mrs. Henry van der Luyden listened in silence to her cousin Mrs. Archer's narrative.

It was all very well to tell yourself in advance that Mrs. van der Luyden was always silent, and that, though noncommittal by nature and training, she was very kind to the people she really liked. Even personal experience of these facts was not always a protection from the chill that descended on one in the high-ceilinged white-walled Madison Avenue drawing room, with the pale brocaded armchairs so obviously uncovered for the occasion, and the gauze still veiling the ormolu mantel ornaments and the beautiful old carved frame of Gainsborough's "Lady Angelica du Lac."

Mrs. van der Luyden's portrait by Huntington (in black velvet and Venetian point) faced that of her lovely ancestress. It was generally considered "as fine as a Cabanel," and, though twenty years had elapsed since its execution, was still "a perfect likeness." Indeed the Mrs. van der Luyden who sat beneath it listening to Mrs. Archer might have been the twin-sister of the fair and still youngish woman drooping against a gilt armchair before a green rep curtain. Mrs. van der Luyden still wore black velvet and Venetian point when she went into society—or rather (since she never dined out) when she threw open her own doors to receive it. Her fair hair, which had faded without turning gray, was still parted in flat overlapping points on her forehead, and the straight nose that divided her pale blue eyes was only a little more pinched about the nostrils than when the portrait had been painted. She always, indeed, struck Newland Archer as having been rather gruesomely preserved in the airless atmosphere of a perfectly irreproachable existence, as bodies caught in glaciers keep for years a rosy life-in-death.

Like all his family, he esteemed and admired Mrs. van der Luyden; but he found her gentle bending sweetness less approachable than the grimness of some of his mother's old aunts, fierce spinsters who said "No" on principle before they knew what they were going to be asked.

Mrs. van der Luyden's attitude said neither yes nor no, but always appeared to incline to clemency till her thin lips, wavering into the shadow of a smile, made the almost invariable reply: "I shall first have to talk this over with my husband."

She and Mr. van der Luyden were so exactly alike that Archer often wondered how, after forty years of the closest conjugality, two such merged identities ever separated themselves enough for anything as controversial as a talking-over. But as neither had ever reached a decision without prefacing it by this mysterious conclave, Mrs. Archer and her son, having set forth their case, waited resignedly for the familiar phrase.

Mrs. van der Luyden, however, who had seldom surprised anyone, now surprised them by reaching her long hand toward the bell-rope.

"I think," she said, "I should like Henry to hear what you have told me."

A footman appeared, to whom she gravely added: "If Mr. van der Luyden has finished reading the newspaper, please ask him to be kind enough to come."

She said "reading the newspaper" in the tone in which a Minister's wife might have said: "Presiding at a Cabinet meeting"—not from any arrogance of mind, but because the habit of a lifetime, and the attitude of her friends and relations, had led her to consider Mr. van der Luyden's least gesture as having an almost sacerdotal importance.

Her promptness of action showed that she considered the case as pressing as Mrs. Archer; but, lest she should be thought to have committed herself in advance, she added, with the sweetest look: "Henry always enjoys seeing you, dear Adeline; and he will wish to congratulate Newland."

The double doors had solemnly reopened and between them appeared Mr. Henry van der Luyden, tall, spare and frock-coated, with faded fair hair, a straight nose like his wife's and the same look of frozen gentleness in eyes that were merely pale gray instead of pale blue.

Mr. van der Luyden greeted Mrs. Archer with cousinly affability, proffered to Newland low-voiced congratulations couched in the same language as his wife's, and seated himself in one of the brocade armchairs with the simplicity of a reigning sovereign.

"I had just finished reading *The Times*," he said, laying his long fingertips together. "In town my mornings are so much occupied that I find it more convenient to read the newspapers after luncheon."

"Ah, there's a great deal to be said for that plan—indeed I think my Uncle Egmont used to say he found it less agitating not to read the morning papers till after dinner," said Mrs. Archer responsively.

"Yes: my good father abhorred hurry. But now we live in a constant rush," said Mr. van der Luyden in measured tones, looking with pleasant deliberation about the large shrouded room which to Archer was so complete an image of its owners.

"But I hope you *had* finished your reading, Henry?" his wife interposed.

"Quite—quite," he reassured her.

"Then I should like Adeline to tell you—"

"Oh, it's really Newland's story," said his mother smiling; and proceeded to rehearse once more the monstrous tale of the affront inflicted on Mrs. Lovell Mingott.

"Of course," she ended, "Augusta Welland and Mary Mingott both felt that, especially in view of Newland's engagement, you and Henry *ought to know*."

"Ah—" said Mr. van der Luyden, drawing a deep breath.

There was a silence during which the tick of the monumental ormolu clock on the white marble mantelpiece grew as loud as the boom of a minute-gun. Archer contemplated with awe the two slender faded figures, seated side by side in a kind of viceregal rigidity, mouthpieces of some remote ancestral authority which fate compelled them to wield, when they would so much rather have lived in simplicity and seclusion, digging invisible weeds out of the perfect lawns of Skuytercliff, and playing Patience together in the evenings.

Mr. van der Luyden was the first to speak.

"You really think this is due to some—some intentional interference of Lawrence Lefferts's?" he enquired, turning to Archer.

"I'm certain of it, sir. Larry has been going it rather harder than usual lately—if Cousin Louisa won't mind my mentioning it—having rather a stiff affair with the postmaster's wife in their village, or someone of that sort; and whenever poor Gertrude Lefferts begins to suspect anything, and he's afraid of trouble, he gets up a fuss of this

kind, to show how awfully moral he is, and talks at the top of his
voice about the impertinence of inviting his wife to meet people he
doesn't wish her to know. He's simply using Madame Olenska as a
lightning-rod; I've seen him try the same thing often before."

"The *Leffertses!*—" said Mrs. van der Luyden.

"The *Leffertses!*—" echoed Mrs. Archer. "What would Uncle Egmont have said of Lawrence Lefferts's pronouncing on anybody's social position? It shows what Society has come to."

"We'll hope it has not quite come to that," said Mr. van der
Luyden firmly.

"Ah, if only you and Louisa went out more!" sighed Mrs. Archer.

But instantly she became aware of her mistake. The van der Luydens were morbidly sensitive to any criticism of their secluded existence. They were the arbiters of fashion, the Court of Last Appeal,
and they knew it, and bowed to their fate. But being shy and retiring
persons, with no natural inclination for their part, they lived as
much as possible in the sylvan solitude of Skuytercliff, and when
they came to town, declined all invitations on the plea of Mrs. van
der Luyden's health.

Newland Archer came to his mother's rescue. "Everybody in New
York knows what you and Cousin Louisa represent. That's why Mrs.
Mingott felt she ought not to allow this slight on Countess Olenska
to pass without consulting you."

Mrs. van der Luyden glanced at her husband, who glanced back at
her.

"It is the principle that I dislike," said Mr. van der Luyden. "As
long as a member of a well-known family is backed up by that family
it should be considered—final."

"It seems so to me," said his wife, as if she were producing a new
thought.

"I had no idea," Mr. van der Luyden continued, "that things had
come to such a pass." He paused, and looked at his wife again. "It
occurs to me, my dear, that the Countess Olenska is already a sort of
relation—through Medora Manson's first husband. At any rate, she
will be when Newland marries." He turned toward the young man.
"Have you read this morning's *Times*, Newland?"

"Why, yes, sir," said Archer, who usually tossed off half a dozen
papers with his morning coffee.

Husband and wife looked at each other again. Their pale eyes

clung together in prolonged and serious consultation; then a faint
smile fluttered over Mrs. van der Luyden's face. She had evidently
guessed and approved.

Mr. van der Luyden turned to Mrs. Archer. "If Louisa's health allowed her to dine out—I wish you would say to Mrs. Lovell Mingott
—she and I would have been happy to—er—fill the places of the
Lawrence Leffertses at her dinner." He paused to let the irony of this
sink in. "As you know, this is impossible." Mrs. Archer sounded a
sympathetic assent. "But Newland tells me he has read this morning's *Times*; therefore he has probably seen that Louisa's relative, the
Duke of St. Austrey, arrives next week on the 'Russia.' He is coming
to enter his new sloop, the 'Guinevere,' in next summer's International Cup Race; and also to have a little canvasback shooting at
Trevenna." Mr. van der Luyden paused again, and continued with
increasing benevolence: "Before taking him down to Maryland we
are inviting a few friends to meet him here—only a little dinner—
with a reception afterward. I am sure Louisa will be as glad as I am
if Countess Olenska will let us include her among our guests." He
got up, bent his long body with a stiff friendliness toward his cousin,
and added: "I think I have Louisa's authority for saying that she will
herself leave the invitation to dine when she drives out presently:
with our cards—of course with our cards."

Mrs. Archer, who knew this to be a hint that the seventeen-hand
chestnuts which were never kept waiting were at the door, rose with
a hurried murmur of thanks. Mrs. van der Luyden beamed on her
with the smile of Esther interceding with Ahasuerus; but her husband raised a protesting hand.

"There is nothing to thank me for, dear Adeline; nothing whatever. This kind of thing must not happen in New York; it shall not,
as long as I can help it," he pronounced with sovereign gentleness as
he steered his cousins to the door.

Two hours later, everyone knew that the great C-spring barouche
in which Mrs. van der Luyden took the air at all seasons had been
seen at old Mrs. Mingott's door, where a large square envelope was
handed in; and that evening at the Opera Mr. Sillerton Jackson was
able to state that the envelope contained a card inviting the Countess Olenska to the dinner which the van der Luydens were giving the
following week for their cousin, the Duke of St. Austrey.

Some of the younger men in the club box exchanged a smile at this announcement, and glanced sideways at Lawrence Lefferts, who sat carelessly in the front of the box, pulling his long fair moustache, and who remarked with authority, as the soprano paused: "No one but Patti ought to attempt the *Sonnambula.*"

8

It was generally agreed in New York that the Countess Olenska had "lost her looks."

She had appeared there first, in Newland Archer's boyhood, as a brilliantly pretty little girl of nine or ten, of whom people said that she "ought to be painted." Her parents had been continental wanderers, and after a roaming babyhood she had lost them both, and been taken in charge by her aunt, Medora Manson, also a wanderer, who was herself returning to New York to "settle down."

Poor Medora, repeatedly widowed, was always coming home to settle down (each time in a less expensive house), and bringing with her a new husband or an adopted child; but after a few months she invariably parted from her husband or quarrelled with her ward, and, having got rid of her house at a loss, set out again on her wanderings. As her mother had been a Rushworth, and her last unhappy marriage had linked her to one of the crazy Chiverses, New York looked indulgently on her eccentricities; but when she returned with her little orphaned niece, whose parents had been popular in spite of their regrettable taste for travel, people thought it a pity that the pretty child should be in such hands.

Everyone was disposed to be kind to little Ellen Mingott, though her dusky red cheeks and tight curls gave her an air of gaiety that seemed unsuitable in a child who should still have been in black for her parents. It was one of the misguided Medora's many peculiarities to flout the unalterable rules that regulated American mourning, and when she stepped from the steamer her family were scandalized to see that the crepe veil she wore for her own brother was seven inches shorter than those of her sisters-in-law, while little Ellen was in crimson merino and amber beads, like a gipsy foundling.

But New York had so long resigned itself to Medora that only a few old ladies shook their heads over Ellen's gaudy clothes, while her other relations fell under the charm of her high color and high spirits. She was a fearless and familiar little thing, who asked disconcerting questions, made precocious comments, and possessed outlandish arts, such as dancing a Spanish shawl dance and singing Neapolitan love-songs to a guitar. Under the direction of her aunt (whose real name was Mrs. Thorley Chivers, but who, having received a Papal title, had resumed her first husband's patronymic, and called herself the Marchioness Manson, because in Italy she could turn it into Manzoni) the little girl received an expensive but incoherent education, which included "drawing from the model," a thing never dreamed of before, and playing the piano in quintets with professional musicians.

Of course no good could come of this; and when, a few years later, poor Chivers finally died in a madhouse, his widow (draped in strange weeds) again pulled up stakes and departed with Ellen, who had grown into a tall bony girl with conspicuous eyes. For some time no more was heard of them; then news came of Ellen's marriage to an immensely rich Polish nobleman of legendary fame, whom she had met at a ball at the Tuileries, and who was said to have princely establishments in Paris, Nice and Florence, a yacht at Cowes, and many square miles of shooting in Transylvania. She disappeared in a kind of sulphurous apotheosis, and when a few years later Medora again came back to New York, subdued, impoverished, mourning a third husband, and in quest of a still smaller house, people wondered that her rich niece had not been able to do something for her. Then came the news that Ellen's own marriage had ended in disaster, and that she was herself returning home to seek rest and oblivion among her kinsfolk.

These things passed through Newland Archer's mind a week later as he watched the Countess Olenska enter the van der Luyden drawing room on the evening of the momentous dinner. The occasion was a solemn one, and he wondered a little nervously how she would carry it off. She came rather late, one hand still ungloved, and fastening a bracelet about her wrist; yet she entered without any appearance of haste or embarrassment the drawing room in which New York's most chosen company was somewhat awfully assembled.

In the middle of the room she paused, looking about her with a grave mouth and smiling eyes; and in that instant Newland Archer

rejected the general verdict on her looks. It was true that her early radiance was gone. The red cheeks had paled; she was thin, worn, a little older-looking than her age, which must have been nearly thirty.
But there was about her the mysterious authority of beauty, a
sureness in the carriage of the head, the movement of the eyes,
which, without being in the least theatrical, struck him as highly
trained and full of a conscious power. At the same time she was
simpler in manner than most of the ladies present, and many people
(as he heard afterward from Janey) were disappointed that her appearance was not more "stylish"—for stylishness was what New York
most valued. It was, perhaps, Archer reflected, because her early vi-
vacity had disappeared; because she was so quiet—quiet in her movements, her voice, and the tones of her low-pitched voice. New York
had expected something a good deal more resonant in a young
woman with such a history.

The dinner was a somewhat formidable business. Dining with the
van der Luydens was at best no light matter, and dining there with a
Duke who was their cousin was almost a religious solemnity. It
pleased Archer to think that only an old New Yorker could perceive
the shade of difference (to New York) between being merely a Duke
and being the van der Luydens' Duke. New York took stray noble-
men calmly, and even (except in the Struthers set) with a certain
distrustful *hauteur*; but when they presented such credentials as
these they were received with an old-fashioned cordiality that they
would have been greatly mistaken in ascribing solely to their standing in Debrett. It was for just such distinctions that the young man
cherished his old New York even while he smiled at it.

The van der Luydens had done their best to emphasize the importance of the occasion. The du Lac Sèvres and the Trevenna George
II plate were out; so was the van der Luyden "Lowestoft" (East
India Company) and the Dagonet Crown Derby. Mrs. van der Luyden looked more than ever like a Cabanel, and Mrs. Archer, in her
grandmother's seed-pearls and emeralds, reminded her son of an Isabey miniature. All the ladies had on their handsomest jewels, but it
was characteristic of the house and the occasion that these were
mostly in rather heavy old-fashioned settings; and old Miss Lanning,
who had been persuaded to come, actually wore her mother's cameos
and a Spanish blonde shawl.

The Countess Olenska was the only young woman at the dinner;
yet, as Archer scanned the smooth plump elderly faces between their

diamond necklaces and towering ostrich feathers, they struck him as curiously immature compared with hers. It frightened him to think what must have gone to the making of her eyes.

The Duke of St. Austrey, who sat at his hostess' right, was naturally the chief figure of the evening. But if the Countess Olenska was less conspicuous than had been hoped, the Duke was almost invisible. Being a well-bred man he had not (like another recent ducal visitor) come to the dinner in a shooting-jacket; but his evening clothes were so shabby and baggy, and he wore them with such an air of their being homespun, that (with his stooping way of sitting, and the vast beard spreading over his shirt-front) he hardly gave the appearance of being in dinner attire. He was short, round-shouldered, sunburnt, with a thick nose, small eyes and a sociable smile; but he seldom spoke, and when he did it was in such low tones that, despite the frequent silences of expectation about the table, his remarks were lost to all but his neighbors.

When the men joined the ladies after dinner the Duke went straight up to the Countess Olenska, and they sat down in a corner and plunged into animated talk. Neither seemed aware that the Duke should first have paid his respects to Mrs. Lovell Mingott and Mrs. Headly Chivers, and the Countess have conversed with that amiable hypochondriac, Mr. Urban Dagonet of Washington Square, who, in order to have the pleasure of meeting her, had broken through his fixed rule of not dining out between January and April. The two chatted together for nearly twenty minutes; then the Countess rose and, walking alone across the wide drawing room, sat down at Newland Archer's side.

It was not the custom in New York drawing rooms for a lady to get up and walk away from one gentleman in order to seek the company of another. Etiquette required that she should wait, immovable as an idol, while the men who wished to converse with her succeeded each other at her side. But the Countess was apparently unaware of having broken any rule; she sat at perfect ease in a corner of the sofa beside Archer, and looked at him with the kindest eyes.

"I want you to talk to me about May," she said.

Instead of answering her he asked: "You knew the Duke before?"

"Oh, yes—we used to see him every winter at Nice. He's very fond of gambling—he used to come to the house a great deal." She said it in the simplest manner, as if she had said: "He's fond of wildflowers";

and after a moment she added candidly: "I think he's the dullest man I ever met."

This pleased her companion so much that he forgot the slight shock her previous remark had caused him. It was undeniably exciting to meet a lady who found the van der Luydens' Duke dull, and dared to utter the opinion. He longed to question her, to hear more about the life of which her careless words had given him so illuminating a glimpse; but he feared to touch on distressing memories, and before he could think of anything to say she had strayed back to her original subject.

"May is a darling; I've seen no young girl in New York so handsome and so intelligent. Are you very much in love with her?"

Newland Archer reddened and laughed. "As much as a man can be."

She continued to consider him thoughtfully, as if not to miss any shade of meaning in what he said, "Do you think, then, there is a limit?"

"To being in love? If there is, I haven't found it!"

She glowed with sympathy. "Ah—it's really and truly a romance?"

"The most romantic of romances!"

"How delightful! And you found it all out for yourselves—it was not in the least arranged for you?"

Archer looked at her incredulously. "Have you forgotten," he asked with a smile, "that in our country we don't allow our marriages to be arranged for us?"

A dusky blush rose to her cheek, and he instantly regretted his words.

"Yes," she answered, "I'd forgotten. You must forgive me if I sometimes make these mistakes. I don't always remember that everything here is good that was—that was bad where I've come from." She looked down at her Viennese fan of eagle feathers, and he saw that her lips trembled.

"I'm so sorry," he said impulsively; "but you *are* among friends here, you know."

"Yes—I know. Wherever I go I have that feeling. That's why I came home. I want to forget everything else, to become a complete American again, like the Mingotts and Wellands, and you and your delightful mother, and all the other good people here tonight. Ah, here's May arriving, and you will want to hurry away to her," she added, but without moving; and her eyes turned back from the door to rest on the young man's face.

The drawing rooms were beginning to fill up with after-dinner guests, and following Madame Olenska's glance Archer saw May Welland entering with her mother. In her dress of white and silver, with a wreath of silver blossoms in her hair, the tall girl looked like a Diana just alight from the chase.

"Oh," said Archer, "I have so many rivals: you see she's already surrounded. There's the Duke being introduced."

"Then stay with me a little longer," Madame Olenska said in a low tone, just touching his knee with her plumed fan. It was the lightest touch, but it thrilled him like a caress.

"Yes, let me stay," he answered in the same tone, hardly knowing what he said; but just then Mr. van der Luyden came up, followed by old Mr. Urban Dagonet. The Countess greeted them with her grave smile, and Archer, feeling his host's admonitory glance on him, rose and surrendered his seat.

Madame Olenska held out her hand as if to bid him good-bye.

"Tomorrow, then, after five—I shall expect you," she said; and then turned back to make room for Mr. Dagonet.

"Tomorrow—" Archer heard himself repeating, though there had been no engagement, and during their talk she had given him no hint that she wished to see him again.

As he moved away he saw Lawrence Lefferts, tall and resplendent, leading his wife up to be introduced; and heard Gertrude Lefferts say, as she beamed on the Countess with her large unperceiving smile: "But I think we used to go to dancing-school together when we were children—." Behind her, waiting their turn to name themselves to the Countess, Archer noticed a number of the recalcitrant couples who had declined to meet her at Mrs. Lovell Mingott's. As Mrs. Archer remarked: when the van der Luydens chose, they knew how to give a lesson. The wonder was that they chose so seldom.

The young man felt a touch on his arm and saw Mrs. van der Luyden looking down on him from the pure eminence of black velvet and the family diamonds. "It was good of you, dear Newland, to devote yourself so unselfishly to Madame Olenska. I told your Cousin Henry he must really come to the rescue."

He was aware of smiling at her vaguely, and she added, as if condescending to his natural shyness: "I've never seen May looking lovelier. The Duke thinks her the handsomest girl in the room."

9

THE Countess Olenska had said "after five"; and at half after the hour Newland Archer rang the bell of the peeling stucco house with a giant wisteria throttling its feeble cast-iron balcony, which she had hired, far down West Twenty-third Street, from the vagabond Medora.

It was certainly a strange quarter to have settled in. Small dressmakers, bird-stuffers and "people who wrote" were her nearest neighbors; and further down the disheveled street Archer recognized a dilapidated wooden house, at the end of a paved path, in which a writer and journalist called Winsett, whom he used to come across now and then, had mentioned that he lived. Winsett did not invite people to his house; but he had once pointed it out to Archer in the course of a nocturnal stroll, and the latter had asked himself, with a little shiver, if the humanities were so meanly housed in other capitals.

Madame Olenska's own dwelling was redeemed from the same appearance only by a little more paint about the window frames; and as Archer mustered its modest front he said to himself that the Polish Count must have robbed her of her fortune as well as of her illusions.

The young man had spent an unsatisfactory day. He had lunched with the Wellands, hoping afterward to carry off May for a walk in the Park. He wanted to have her to himself, to tell her how enchanting she had looked the night before, and how proud he was of her, and to press her to hasten their marriage. But Mrs. Welland had firmly reminded him that the round of family visits was not half over, and, when he hinted at advancing the date of the wedding, had raised reproachful eyebrows and sighed out: "Twelve dozen of everything—hand-embroidered—"

Packed in the family landau they rolled from one tribal doorstep to another, and Archer, when the afternoon's round was over, parted from his betrothed with the feeling that he had been shown off like a wild animal cunningly trapped. He supposed that his readings in anthropology caused him to take such a coarse view of what was after all a simple and natural demonstration of family feeling; but when he remembered that the Wellands did not expect the wedding to take place till the following autumn, and pictured what his life would be till then, a dampness fell upon his spirit.

"Tomorrow," Mrs. Welland called after him, "we'll do the Chiverses and the Dallases"; and he perceived that she was going through their two families alphabetically, and that they were only in the first quarter of the alphabet.

He had meant to tell May of the Countess Olenska's request—her command, rather—that he should call on her that afternoon; but in the brief moments when they were alone he had had more pressing things to say. Besides, it struck him as a little absurd to allude to the matter. He knew that May most particularly wanted him to be kind to her cousin; was it not that wish which had hastened the announcement of their engagement? It gave him an odd sensation to reflect that, but for the Countess's arrival, he might have been, if not still a free man, at least a man less irrevocably pledged. But May had willed it so, and he felt himself somehow relieved of further responsibility—and therefore at liberty, if he chose, to call on her cousin without telling her.

As he stood on Madame Olenska's threshold curiosity was his uppermost feeling. He was puzzled by the tone in which she had summoned him; he concluded that she was less simple than she seemed.

The door was opened by a swarthy foreign-looking maid, with a prominent bosom under a gay neckerchief, whom he vaguely fancied to be Sicilian. She welcomed him with all her white teeth, and answering his enquiries by a head-shake of incomprehension led him through the narrow hall into a low firelit drawing room. The room was empty, and she left him, for an appreciable time, to wonder whether she had gone to find her mistress, or whether she had not understood what he was there for, and thought it might be to wind the clocks—of which he perceived that the only visible specimen had stopped. He knew that the southern races communicated with each other in the language of pantomime, and was mortified to find her shrugs and smiles so unintelligible. At length she returned with a lamp; and Archer, having meanwhile put together a phrase out of Dante and Petrarch, evoked the answer: "*La signora è fuori; ma verrà subito*"; which he took to mean: "She's out—but you'll soon see."

What he saw, meanwhile, with the help of the lamp, was the faded shadowy charm of a room unlike any room he had known. He knew that the Countess Olenska had brought some of her possessions with her—bits of wreckage, she called them—and these, he supposed, were represented by some small slender tables of dark wood, a delicate little Greek bronze on the chimney-piece, and a stretch of red damask nailed on the discolored wallpaper behind a couple of Italian-looking pictures in old frames.

Newland Archer prided himself on his knowledge of Italian art. His boyhood had been saturated with Ruskin, and he had read all the latest books: John Addington Symonds, Vernon Lee's "Euphorion," the essays of P. G. Hamerton and a wonderful new volume called *The Renaissance* by Walter Pater. He talked easily of Botticelli, and spoke of Fra Angelico with a faint condescension. But these pictures bewildered him, for they were like nothing that he was accustomed to look at (and therefore able to see) when he travelled in Italy; and perhaps, also, his powers of observation were impaired by the oddness of finding himself in this strange empty house, where apparently no one expected him. He was sorry that he had not told May Welland of Countess Olenska's request, and a little disturbed by the thought that his betrothed might come in to see her cousin. What would she think if she found him sitting there with the air of intimacy implied by waiting alone in the dusk at a lady's fireside?

But since he had come he meant to wait; and he sank into a chair and stretched his feet to the logs.

It was odd to have summoned him in that way, and then forgotten him; but Archer felt more curious than mortified. The atmosphere of the room was so different from any he had ever breathed that self-consciousness vanished in the sense of adventure. He had been before in drawing rooms hung with red damask, with pictures "of the Italian school"; what struck him was the way in which Medora Manson's shabby hired house, with its blighted background of pampas grass and Rogers statuettes, had, by a turn of the hand, and the skilful use of a few properties, been transformed into something intimate, "foreign," subtly suggestive of old romantic scenes and sentiments. He tried to analyze the trick, to find a clue to it in the way

the chairs and tables were grouped, in the fact that only two Jacqueminot roses (of which nobody ever bought less than a dozen) had
been placed in the slender vase at his elbow, and in the vague pervading perfume that was not what one put on handkerchiefs, but
rather like the scent of some far-off bazaar, a smell made up of Turkish
coffee and ambergris and dried roses.

His mind wandered away to the question of what May's drawing
room would look like. He knew that Mr. Welland, who was behaving "very handsomely," already had his eye on a newly built house in
East Thirty-ninth Street. The neighborhood was thought remote,
and the house was built in a ghastly greenish-yellow stone that the
younger architects were beginning to employ as a protest against the
brownstone of which the uniform hue coated New York like a cold
chocolate sauce; but the plumbing was perfect. Archer would have
liked to travel, to put off the housing question; but, though the
Wellands approved of an extended European honeymoon (perhaps
even a winter in Egypt), they were firm as to the need of a house for
the returning couple. The young man felt that his fate was sealed:
for the rest of his life he would go up every evening between the
cast-iron railings of that greenish-yellow doorstep, and pass through a
Pompeian vestibule into a hall with a wainscoting of varnished yellow wood. But beyond that his imagination could not travel. He
knew the drawing room above had a bay window, but he could not
fancy how May would deal with it. She submitted cheerfully to the
purple satin and yellow tuftings of the Welland drawing room, to its
sham buhl tables and gilt vitrines full of modern Saxe. He saw no
reason to suppose that she would want anything different in her own
house; and his only comfort was to reflect that she would probably
let him arrange his library as he pleased—which would be, of course,
with "sincere" Eastlake furniture, and the plain new bookcases without glass doors.

The round-bosomed maid came in, drew the curtains, pushed back
a log, and said consolingly: "*Verrà—verrà.*" When she had gone
Archer stood up and began to wander about. Should he wait any
longer? His position was becoming rather foolish. Perhaps he had
misunderstood Madame Olenska—perhaps she had not invited him
after all.

Down the cobblestones of the quiet street came the ring of a
stepper's hoofs; they stopped before the house, and he caught the
opening of a carriage door. Parting the curtains he looked out into

the early dusk. A street lamp faced him, and in its light he saw Julius Beaufort's compact English brougham, drawn by a big roan, and the banker descending from it, and helping out Madame Olenska.

Beaufort stood, hat in hand, saying something which his companion seemed to negative; then they shook hands, and he jumped into his carriage while she mounted the steps.

When she entered the room she showed no surprise at seeing Archer there; surprise seemed the emotion that she was least addicted to.

"How do you like my funny house?" she asked. "To me it's like heaven."

As she spoke she untied her little velvet bonnet and tossing it away with her long cloak stood looking at him with meditative eyes.

"You've arranged it delightfully," he rejoined, alive to the flatness of the words, but imprisoned in the conventional by his consuming desire to be simple and striking.

"Oh, it's a poor little place. My relations despise it. But at any rate it's less gloomy than the van der Luydens'."

The words gave him an electric shock, for few were the rebellious spirits who would have dared to call the stately home of the van der Luydens gloomy. Those privileged to enter it shivered there, and spoke of it as "handsome." But suddenly he was glad that she had given voice to the general shiver.

"It's delicious—what you've done here," he repeated.

"I like the little house," she admitted; "but I suppose what I like is the blessedness of its being here, in my own country and my own town; and then, of being alone in it." She spoke so low that he hardly heard the last phrase; but in his awkwardness he took it up.

"You like so much to be alone?"

"Yes; as long as my friends keep me from feeling lonely." She sat down near the fire, said: "Nastasia will bring the tea presently," and signed to him to return to his armchair, adding: "I see you've already chosen your corner."

Leaning back, she folded her arms behind her head, and looked at the fire under drooping lids.

"This is the hour I like best—don't you?"

A proper sense of his dignity caused him to answer: "I was afraid you'd forgotten the hour. Beaufort must have been very engrossing."

She looked amused. "Why—have you waited long? Mr. Beaufort took me to see a number of houses—since it seems I'm not to be allowed to stay in this one." She appeared to dismiss both Beaufort and himself from her mind, and went on: "I've never been in a city where there seems to be such a feeling against living in *des quartiers excentriques*. What does it matter where one lives? I'm told this street is respectable."

"It's not fashionable."

"Fashionable! Do you all think so much of that? Why not make one's own fashions? But I suppose I've lived too independently; at any rate, I want to do what you all do—I want to feel cared for and safe."

He was touched, as he had been the evening before when she spoke of her need of guidance.

"That's what your friends want you to feel. New York's an awfully safe place," he added with a flash of sarcasm.

"Yes, isn't it? One feels that," she cried, missing the mockery. "Being here is like—like—being taken on a holiday when one has been a good little girl and done all one's lessons."

The analogy was well meant, but did not altogether please him. He did not mind being flippant about New York, but disliked to hear anyone else take the same tone. He wondered if she did not begin to see what a powerful engine it was, and how nearly it had crushed her. The Lovell Mingotts' dinner, patched up *in extremis* out of all sorts of social odds and ends, ought to have taught her the narrowness of her escape; but either she had been all along unaware of having skirted disaster, or else she had lost sight of it in the triumph of the van der Luyden evening. Archer inclined to the former theory; he fancied that her New York was still completely undifferentiated, and the conjecture nettled him.

"Last night," he said, "New York laid itself out for you. The van der Luydens do nothing by halves."

"No: how kind they are! It was such a nice party. Everyone seems to have such an esteem for them."

The terms were hardly adequate; she might have spoken in that way of a tea-party at the dear old Miss Lannings'.

"The van der Luydens," said Archer, feeling himself pompous as he spoke, "are the most powerful influence in New York society. Unfortunately—owing to her health—they receive very seldom."

She unclasped her hands from behind her head, and looked at him meditatively.

"Isn't that perhaps the reason?"

"The reason—?"

"For their great influence; that they make themselves so rare."

He colored a little, stared at her—and suddenly felt the penetration of the remark. At a stroke she had pricked the van der Luydens and they collapsed. He laughed, and sacrificed them.

Nastasia brought the tea, with handleless Japanese cups and little covered dishes, placing the tray on a low table.

"But you'll explain these things to me—you'll tell me all I ought to know," Madame Olenska continued, leaning forward to hand him his cup.

"It's you who are telling me; opening my eyes to things I'd looked at so long that I'd ceased to see them."

She detached a small gold cigarette-case from one of her bracelets, held it out to him, and took a cigarette herself. On the chimney were long spills for lighting them.

"Ah, then we can both help each other. But I want help so much more. You must tell me just what to do."

It was on the tip of his tongue to reply: "Don't be seen driving about the streets with Beaufort—" but he was being too deeply drawn into the atmosphere of the room, which was her atmosphere, and to give advice of that sort would have been like telling someone who was bargaining for attar-of-roses in Samarkand that one should always be provided with arctics for a New York winter. New York seemed much farther off than Samarkand, and if they were indeed to help each other she was rendering what might prove the first of their mutual services by making him look at his native city objectively. Viewed thus, as through the wrong end of a telescope, it looked disconcertingly small and distant; but then from Samarkand it would.

A flame darted from the logs and she bent over the fire, stretching her thin hands so close to it that a faint halo shone above the oval nails. The light touched to russet the rings of dark hair escaping from her braids, and made her pale face paler.

"There are plenty of people to tell you what to do," Archer rejoined, obscurely envious of them.

"Oh—all my aunts? And my dear old Granny?" She considered the idea impartially. "They're all a little vexed with me for setting up for myself—poor Granny especially. She wanted to keep me with her; but I had to be free—" He was impressed by this light way of speaking of the formidable Catherine, and moved by the thought of what must have given Madame Olenska this thirst for even the loneliest kind of freedom. But the idea of Beaufort gnawed him.

"I think I understand how you feel," he said. "Still, your family can advise you; explain differences; show you the way."

She lifted her thin black eyebrows. "Is New York such a labyrinth? I thought it so straight up and down—like Fifth Avenue. And with all the cross streets numbered!" She seemed to guess his faint disapproval of this, and added, with the rare smile that enchanted her whole face: "If you know how I like it for just *that*—the straight-up-and-downness, and the big honest labels on everything!"

He saw his chance. "Everything may be labeled—but everybody is not."

"Perhaps. I may simplify too much—but you'll warn me if I do." She turned from the fire to look at him. "There are only two people here who make me feel as if they understood what I mean and could explain things to me: you and Mr. Beaufort."

Archer winced at the joining of the names, and then, with a quick readjustment, understood, sympathized and pitied. So close to the powers of evil she must have lived that she still breathed more freely in their air. But since she felt that he understood her also, his business would be to make her see Beaufort as he really was, with all he represented—and abhor it.

He answered gently: "I understand. But just at first don't let go of your old friends' hands: I mean the older women, your Granny Mingott, Mrs. Welland, Mrs. van der Luyden. They like and admire you —they want to help you."

She shook her head and sighed. "Oh, I know—I know! But on condition that they don't hear anything unpleasant. Aunt Welland put it in those very words when I tried. . . . Does no one want to know the truth here, Mr. Archer? The real loneliness is living among all these kind people who only ask one to pretend!" She lifted her hands to her face, and he saw her thin shoulders shaken by a sob.

"Madame Olenska!—Oh, don't, Ellen," he cried, starting up and bending over her. He drew down one of her hands, clasping and chafing it like a child's while he murmured reassuring words; but in a moment she freed herself, and looked up at him with wet lashes.

"Does no one cry here, either? I suppose there's no need to, in heaven," she said, straightening her loosened braids with a laugh, and bending over the tea-kettle. It was burnt into his consciousness that he had called her "Ellen"—called her so twice; and that she had not noticed it. Far down the inverted telescope he saw the faint white figure of May Welland—in New York.

Suddenly Nastasia put her head in to say something in her rich Italian.

Madame Olenska, again with a hand at her hair, uttered an exclamation of assent—a flashing "*Già—già*"—and the Duke of St. Austrey entered, piloting a tremendous black-wigged and red-plumed lady in overflowing furs.

"My dear Countess, I've brought an old friend of mine to see you—Mrs. Struthers. She wasn't asked to the party last night, and she wants to know you."

The Duke beamed on the group, and Madame Olenska advanced with a murmur of welcome toward the queer couple. She seemed to have no idea how oddly matched they were, nor what a liberty the Duke had taken in bringing his companion—and to do him justice, as Archer perceived, the Duke seemed as unaware of it himself.

"Of course I want to know you, my dear," cried Mrs. Struthers in a round rolling voice that matched her bold feathers and her brazen wig. "I want to know everybody who's young and interesting and charming. And the Duke tells me you like music—didn't you, Duke? You're a pianist yourself, I believe? Well, do you want to hear Sarasate play tomorrow evening at my house? You know I've something going on every Sunday evening—it's the day when New York doesn't know what to do with itself, and so I say to it: 'Come and be amused.' And the Duke thought you'd be tempted by Sarasate. You'll find a number of your friends."

Madame Olenska's face grew brilliant with pleasure. "How kind! How good of the Duke to think of me!" She pushed a chair up to the tea-table and Mrs. Struthers sank into it delectably. "Of course I shall be too happy to come."

"That's all right, my dear. And bring your young gentleman with you." Mrs. Struthers extended a hail-fellow hand to Archer. "I can't put a name to you—but I'm sure I've met you—I've met everybody, here, or in Paris or London. Aren't you in diplomacy? All the diplomatists come to me. You like music too? Duke, you must be sure to bring him."

The Duke said "Rather" from the depths of his beard, and Archer withdrew with a stiffly circular bow that made him feel as full of spine as a self-conscious schoolboy among careless and unnoticing elders.

He was not sorry for the *dénouement* of his visit: he only wished it had come sooner, and spared him a certain waste of emotion. As he went out into the wintry night, New York again became vast and imminent, and May Welland the loveliest woman in it. He turned into his florist's to send her the daily box of lilies-of-the-valley which, to his confusion, he found he had forgotten that morning.

As he wrote a word on his card and waited for an envelope he glanced about the embowered shop, and his eye lit on a cluster of yellow roses. He had never seen any as sun-golden before, and his first impulse was to send them to May instead of the lilies. But they did not look like her—there was something too rich, too strong, in their fiery beauty. In a sudden revulsion of mood, and almost without knowing what he did, he signed to the florist to lay the roses in another long box, and slipped his card into a second envelope, on which he wrote the name of the Countess Olenska; then, just as he was turning away, he drew the card out again, and left the empty envelope on the box.

"They'll go at once?" he enquired, pointing to the roses.

The florist assured him that they would.

10

THE next day he persuaded May to escape for a walk in the Park after luncheon. As was the custom in old-fashioned Episcopalian New York, she usually accompanied her parents to church on Sunday afternoons; but Mrs. Welland condoned her truancy, having that very morning won her over to the necessity of a long engagement, with time to prepare a hand-embroidered trousseau containing the proper number of dozens.

The day was delectable. The bare vaulting of trees along the Mall was ceiled with lapis lazuli, and arched above snow that shone like splintered crystals. It was the weather to call out May's radiance, and she burned like a young maple in the frost. Archer was proud of the glances turned on her, and the simple joy of possessorship cleared away his underlying perplexities.

"It's so delicious—waking every morning to smell lilies-of-the-valley in one's room!" she said.

"Yesterday they came late. I hadn't time in the morning—"

"But your remembering each day to send them makes me love them so much more than if you'd given a standing order, and they came every morning on the minute, like one's music-teacher—as I know Gertrude Lefferts's did, for instance, when she and Lawrence were engaged."

"Ah—they would!" laughed Archer, amused at her keenness. He looked sideways at her fruit-like cheek and felt rich and secure enough to add: "When I sent your lilies yesterday afternoon I saw some rather gorgeous yellow roses and packed them off to Madame Olenska. Was that right?"

"How dear of you! Anything of that kind delights her. It's odd she didn't mention it: she lunched with us today, and spoke of Mr.

Beaufort's having sent her wonderful orchids, and Cousin Henry van der Luyden a whole hamper of carnations from Skuytercliff. She seems so surprised to receive flowers. Don't people send them in Europe? She thinks it such a pretty custom."

"Oh, well, no wonder mine were overshadowed by Beaufort's," said Archer irritably. Then he remembered that he had not put a card with the roses, and was vexed at having spoken of them. He wanted to say: "I called on your cousin yesterday," but hesitated. If Madame Olenska had not spoken of his visit it might seem awkward that he should. Yet not to do so gave the affair an air of mystery that he disliked. To shake off the question he began to talk of their own plans, their future, and Mrs. Welland's insistence on a long engagement.

"If you call it long! Isabel Chivers and Reggie were engaged for two years: Grace and Thorley for nearly a year and a half. Why aren't we very well off as we are?"

It was the traditional maidenly interrogation, and he felt ashamed of himself for finding it singularly childish. No doubt she simply echoed what was said for her; but she was nearing her twenty-second birthday, and he wondered at what age "nice" women began to speak for themselves.

"Never, if we won't let them, I suppose," he mused, and recalled his mad outburst to Mr. Sillerton Jackson: "Women ought to be as free as we are—"

It would presently be his task to take the bandage from this young woman's eyes, and bid her look forth on the world. But how many generations of the women who had gone to her making had descended bandaged to the family vault? He shivered a little, remembering some of the new ideas in his scientific books, and the much-cited instance of the Kentucky cave-fish, which had ceased to develop eyes because they had no use for them. What if, when he had bidden May Welland to open hers, they could only look out blankly at blankness?

"We might be much better off. We might be altogether together —we might travel."

Her face lit up. "That would be lovely," she owned: she would love to travel. But her mother would not understand their wanting to do things so differently.

"As if the mere 'differently' didn't account for it!" the wooer insisted.

"Newland! You're so original!" she exulted.

His heart sank, for he saw that he was saying all the things that young men in the same situation were expected to say, and that she was making the answers that instinct and tradition taught her to make—even to the point of calling him original.

"Original! We're all as like each other as those dolls cut out of the same folded paper. We're like patterns stencilled on a wall. Can't you and I strike out for ourselves, May?"

He had stopped and faced her in the excitement of their discussion, and her eyes rested on him with a bright unclouded admiration.

"Mercy—shall we elope?" she laughed.

"If you would—"

"You *do* love me, Newland! I'm so happy."

"But then—why not be happier?"

"We can't behave like people in novels, though, can we?"

"Why not—why not—why not?"

She looked a little bored by his insistence. She knew very well that they couldn't, but it was troublesome to have to produce a reason. "I'm not clever enough to argue with you. But that kind of thing is rather—vulgar, isn't it?" she suggested, relieved to have hit on a word that would assuredly extinguish the whole subject.

"Are you so much afraid, then, of being vulgar?"

She was evidently staggered by this. "Of course I should hate it—so would you," she rejoined, a trifle irritably.

He stood silent, beating his stick nervously against his boot-top; and feeling that she had indeed found the right way of closing the discussion, she went on lightheartedly: "Oh, did I tell you that I showed Ellen my ring? She thinks it the most beautiful setting she ever saw. There's nothing like it in the rue de la Paix, she said. I do love you, Newland, for being so artistic!"

The next afternoon, as Archer, before dinner, sat smoking sullenly in his study, Janey wandered in on him. He had failed to stop at his club on the way up from the office where he exercised the profession of the law in the leisurely manner common to well-to-do New Yorkers of his class. He was out of spirits and slightly out of temper, and a haunting horror of doing the same thing every day at the same hour besieged his brain.

"Sameness—sameness!" he muttered, the word running through

his head like a persecuting tune as he saw the familiar tall-hatted figures lounging behind the plate glass; and because he usually dropped in at the club at that hour he had gone home instead. He knew not only what they were likely to be talking about, but the part each one would take in the discussion. The Duke of course would be their principal theme; though the appearance in Fifth Avenue of a golden-haired lady in a small canary-colored brougham with a pair of black cobs (for which Beaufort was generally thought responsible) would also doubtless be thoroughly gone into. Such "women" (as they were called) were few in New York, those driving their own carriages still fewer, and the appearance of Miss Fanny Ring in Fifth Avenue at the fashionable hour had profoundly agitated society. Only the day before, her carriage had passed Mrs. Lovell Mingott's, and the latter had instantly rung the little bell at her elbow and ordered the coachman to drive her home. "What if it had happened to Mrs. van der Luyden?" people asked each other with a shudder. Archer could hear Lawrence Lefferts, at that very hour, holding forth on the disintegration of society.

He raised his head irritably when his sister Janey entered, and then quickly bent over his book (Swinburne's *Chastelard*—just out) as if he had not seen her. She glanced at the writing-table heaped with books, opened a volume of the *Contes Drôlatiques*, made a wry face over the archaic French, and sighed: "What learned things you read!"

"Well—?" he asked, as she hovered Cassandra-like before him.

"Mother's very angry."

"Angry? With whom? About what?"

"Miss Sophy Jackson has just been here. She brought word that her brother would come in after dinner: she couldn't say very much, because he forbade her to: he wishes to give all the details himself. He's with Cousin Louisa van der Luyden now."

"For heaven's sake, my dear girl, try a fresh start. It would take an omniscient Deity to know what you're talking about."

"It's not a time to be profane, Newland. . . . Mother feels badly enough about your not going to church. . . ."

With a groan he plunged back into his book.

"*Newland!* Do listen. Your friend Madame Olenska was at Mrs. Lemuel Struthers's party last night: she went there with the Duke and Mr. Beaufort."

At the last clause of this announcement a senseless anger swelled the young man's breast. To smother it he laughed. "Well, what of it? I knew she meant to."

Janey paled and her eyes began to project. "You knew she meant to—and you didn't try to stop her? To warn her?"

"Stop her? Warn her?" He laughed again. "I'm not engaged to be married to the Countess Olenska!" The words had a fantastic sound in his own ears.

"You're marrying into her family."

"Oh, family—family!" he jeered.

"Newland—don't you care about Family?"

"Not a brass farthing."

"Nor about what Cousin Louisa van der Luyden will think?"

"Not the half of one—if she thinks such old maid's rubbish."

"Mother is not an old maid," said his virgin sister with pinched lips.

He felt like shouting back: "Yes, she is, and so are the van der Luydens, and so we all are, when it comes to being so much as brushed by the wing-tip of Reality." But he saw her long gentle face puckering into tears, and felt ashamed of the useless pain he was inflicting.

"Hang Countess Olenska! Don't be a goose, Janey—I'm not her keeper."

"No; but you *did* ask the Wellands to announce your engagement sooner so that we might all back her up; and if it hadn't been for that Cousin Louisa would never have invited her to the dinner for the Duke."

"Well—what harm was there in inviting her? She was the best-looking woman in the room; she made the dinner a little less funereal than the usual van der Luyden banquet."

"You know Cousin Henry asked her to please you: he persuaded Cousin Louisa. And now they're so upset that they're going back to Skuytercliff tomorrow. I think, Newland, you'd better come down. You don't seem to understand how Mother feels."

In the drawing room Newland found his mother. She raised a troubled brow from her needlework to ask: "Has Janey told you?"

"Yes." He tried to keep his tone as measured as her own. "But I can't take it very seriously."

"Not the fact of having offended Cousin Louisa and Cousin Henry?"

"The fact that they can be offended by such a trifle as Countess Olenska's going to the house of a woman they consider common."

"*Consider—!*"

"Well, who is; but who has good music, and amuses people on Sunday evenings, when the whole of New York is dying of inanition."

"Good music? All I know is, there was a woman who got up on a table and sang the things they sing at the places you go to in Paris. There was smoking and champagne."

"Well—that kind of thing happens in other places, and the world still goes on."

"I don't suppose, dear, you're really defending the French Sunday?"

"I've heard you often enough, Mother, grumble at the English Sunday when we've been in London."

"New York is neither Paris nor London."

"Oh, no, it's not!" her son groaned.

"You mean, I suppose, that society here is not as brilliant? You're right, I daresay; but we belong here, and people should respect our ways when they come among us. Ellen Olenska especially: she came back to get away from the kind of life people lead in brilliant societies."

Newland made no answer, and after a moment his mother ventured: "I was going to put on my bonnet and ask you to take me to see Cousin Louisa for a moment before dinner." He frowned, and she continued: "I thought you might explain to her what you've just said: that society abroad is different . . . that people are not as particular, and that Madame Olenska may not have realized how we feel about such things. It would be, you know, dear," she added with an innocent adroitness, "in Madame Olenska's interests if you did."

"Dearest Mother, I really don't see how we're concerned in the matter. The Duke took Madame Olenska to Mrs. Struthers's—in fact he brought Mrs. Struthers to call on her. I was there when they came. If the van der Luydens want to quarrel with anybody, the real culprit is under their own roof."

"Quarrel? Newland, did you ever know of Cousin Henry's quarrelling? Besides, the Duke's his guest; and a stranger too. Strangers don't discriminate: how should they? Countess Olenska is a New Yorker, and should have respected the feelings of New York."

"Well, then, if they must have a victim, you have my leave to throw Madame Olenska to them," cried her son, exasperated. "I don't see myself—or you either—offering ourselves up to expiate her crimes."

"Oh, of course you see only the Mingott side," his mother answered, in the sensitive tone that was her nearest approach to anger.

The sad butler drew back the drawing-room portières and announced: "Mr. Henry van der Luyden."

Mrs. Archer dropped her needle and pushed her chair back with an agitated hand.

"Another lamp," she cried to the retreating servant, while Janey bent over to straighten her mother's cap.

Mr. van der Luyden's figure loomed on the threshold, and Newland Archer went forward to greet his cousin.

"We were just talking about you, sir," he said.

Mr. van der Luyden seemed overwhelmed by the announcement. He drew off his glove to shake hands with the ladies, and smoothed his tall hat shyly, while Janey pushed an armchair forward, and Archer continued: "And the Countess Olenska."

Mrs. Archer paled.

"Ah—a charming woman. I have just been to see her," said Mr. van der Luyden, complacency restored to his brow. He sank into the chair, laid his hat and gloves on the floor beside him in the old-fashioned way, and went on: "She has a real gift for arranging flowers. I had sent her a few carnations from Skuytercliff, and I was astonished. Instead of massing them in big bunches as our head-gardener does, she had scattered them about loosely, here and there . . . I can't say how. The Duke had told me: he said: 'Go and see how cleverly she's arranged her drawing room.' And she has. I should really like to take Louisa to see her, if the neighborhood were not so—unpleasant."

A dead silence greeted this unusual flow of words from Mr. van der Luyden. Mrs. Archer drew her embroidery out of the basket into which she had nervously tumbled it, and Newland, leaning against the chimney-place and twisting a hummingbird-feather screen in his hand, saw Janey's gaping countenance lit up by the coming of the second lamp.

"The fact is," Mr. van der Luyden continued, stroking his long gray leg with a bloodless hand weighed down by the Patroon's great signet ring, "the fact is, I dropped in to thank her for the very pretty note she wrote me about my flowers; and also—but this is between ourselves, of course—to give her a friendly warning about allowing the Duke to carry her off to parties with him. I don't know if you've heard—"

Mrs. Archer produced an indulgent smile. "Has the Duke been carrying her off to parties?"

"You know what these English grandees are. They're all alike. Louisa and I are very fond of our cousin—but it's hopeless to expect people who are accustomed to the European courts to trouble themselves about our little republican distinctions. The Duke goes where he's amused." Mr. van der Luyden paused, but no one spoke. "Yes— it seems he took her with him last night to Mrs. Lemuel Struthers's. Sillerton Jackson has just been to us with the foolish story, and Louisa was rather troubled. So I thought the shortest way was to go straight to Countess Olenska and explain—by the merest hint, you know—how we feel in New York about certain things. I felt I might, without indelicacy, because the evening she dined with us she rather suggested . . . rather let me see that she would be grateful for guidance. And she *was*."

Mr. van der Luyden looked about the room with what would have been self-satisfaction on features less purged of the vulgar passions. On his face it became a mild benevolence which Mrs. Archer's countenance dutifully reflected.

"How kind you both are, dear Henry—always! Newland will particularly appreciate what you have done because of dear May and his new relations."

She shot an admonitory glance at her son, who said: "Immensely, sir. But I was sure you'd like Madame Olenska."

Mr. van der Luyden looked at him with extreme gentleness. "I never ask to my house, my dear Newland," he said, "anyone whom I do not like. And so I have just told Sillerton Jackson." With a glance at the clock he rose and added: "But Louisa will be waiting. We are dining early, to take the Duke to the Opera."

After the portières had solemnly closed behind their visitor a silence fell upon the Archer family.

"Gracious—how romantic!" at last broke explosively from Janey. No one knew exactly what inspired her elliptic comments, and her relations had long since given up trying to interpret them.

Mrs. Archer shook her head with a sigh. "Provided it all turns out for the best," she said, in the tone of one who knows how surely it will not. "Newland, you must stay and see Sillerton Jackson when he comes this evening: I really shan't know what to say to him."

"Poor mother! But he won't come—" her son laughed, stooping to kiss away her frown.

11

Some two weeks later, Newland Archer, sitting in abstracted idleness in his private compartment of the office of Letterblair, Lamson and Low, attorneys at law, was summoned by the head of the firm.

Old Mr. Letterblair, the accredited legal adviser of three generations of New York gentility, throned behind his mahogany desk in evident perplexity. As he stroked his close-clipped white whiskers and ran his hand through the rumpled gray locks above his jutting brows, his disrespectful junior partner thought how much he looked like the Family Physician annoyed with a patient whose symptoms refuse to be classified.

"My dear sir—" he always addressed Archer as "sir"—"I have sent for you to go into a little matter; a matter which, for the moment, I prefer not to mention either to Mr. Skipworth or Mr. Redwood." The gentlemen he spoke of were the other senior partners of the firm; for, as was always the case with legal associations of old standing in New York, all the partners named on the office letter-head were long since dead; and Mr. Letterblair, for example, was, professionally speaking, his own grandson.

He leaned back in his chair with a furrowed brow. "For family reasons—" he continued.

Archer looked up.

"The Mingott family," said Mr. Letterblair with an explanatory smile and bow. "Mrs. Manson Mingott sent for me yesterday. Her grand-daughter the Countess Olenska wishes to sue her husband for divorce. Certain papers have been placed in my hands." He paused and drummed on his desk. "In view of your prospective alliance with the family I should like to consult you—to consider the case with you—before taking any further steps."

Archer felt the blood in his temples. He had seen the Countess Olenska only once since his visit to her, and then at the Opera, in the Mingott box. During this interval she had become a less vivid and importunate image, receding from his foreground as May Welland resumed her rightful place in it. He had not heard her divorce spoken of since Janey's first random allusion to it, and had dismissed the tale as unfounded gossip. Theoretically, the idea of divorce was almost as distasteful to him as to his mother; and he was annoyed that Mr. Letterblair (no doubt prompted by old Catherine Mingott) should be so evidently planning to draw him into the affair. After all, there were plenty of Mingott men for such jobs, and as yet he was not even a Mingott by marriage.

He waited for the senior partner to continue. Mr. Letterblair unlocked a drawer and drew out a packet. "If you will run your eye over these papers—"

Archer frowned. "I beg your pardon, sir; but just because of the prospective relationship, I should prefer your consulting Mr. Skipworth or Mr. Redwood."

Mr. Letterblair looked surprised and slightly offended. It was unusual for a junior to reject such an opening.

He bowed. "I respect your scruple, sir; but in this case I believe true delicacy requires you to do as I ask. Indeed, the suggestion is not mine but Mrs. Manson Mingott's and her son's. I have seen Lovell Mingott; and also Mr. Welland. They all named you."

Archer felt his temper rising. He had been somewhat languidly drifting with events for the last fortnight, and letting May's fair looks and radiant nature obliterate the rather importunate pressure of the Mingott claims. But this behest of old Mrs. Mingott's roused him to a sense of what the clan thought they had the right to exact from a prospective son-in-law; and he chafed at the rôle.

"Her uncles ought to deal with this," he said.

"They have. The matter has been gone into by the family. They are opposed to the Countess's idea; but she is firm, and insists on a legal opinion."

The young man was silent: he had not opened the packet in his hand.

"Does she want to marry again?"

"I believe it is suggested; but she denies it."

"Then—"

"Will you oblige me, Mr. Archer, by first looking through these papers? Afterward, when we have talked the case over, I will give you my opinion."

Archer withdrew reluctantly with the unwelcome documents. Since their last meeting he had half-unconsciously collaborated with events in ridding himself of the burden of Madame Olenska. His hour alone with her by the firelight had drawn them into a momentary intimacy on which the Duke of St. Austrey's intrusion with Mrs. Lemuel Struthers, and the Countess's joyous greeting of them, had rather providentially broken. Two days later Archer had assisted at the comedy of her reinstatement in the van der Luydens' favor, and had said to himself, with a touch of tartness, that a lady who knew how to thank all-powerful elderly gentlemen to such good purpose for a bunch of flowers did not need either the private consolations or the public championship of a young man of his small compass. To look at the matter in this light simplified his own case and surprisingly furbished up all the dim domestic virtues. He could not picture May Welland, in whatever conceivable emergency, hawking about her private difficulties and lavishing her confidences on strange men; and she had never seemed to him finer or fairer than in the week that followed. He had even yielded to her wish for a long engagement, since she had found the one disarming answer to his plea for haste.

"You know, when it comes to the point, your parents have always let you have your way ever since you were a little girl," he argued; and she had answered, with her clearest look: "Yes; and that's what makes it so hard to refuse the very last thing they'll ever ask of me as a little girl."

That was the old New York note; that was the kind of answer he would like always to be sure of his wife's making. If one had habitually breathed the New York air there were times when anything less crystalline seemed stifling.

The papers he had retired to read did not tell him much in fact; but they plunged him into an atmosphere in which he choked and spluttered. They consisted mainly of an exchange of letters between Count Olenski's solicitors and a French legal firm to whom the Countess had applied for the settlement of her financial situation. There was also a short letter from the Count to his wife: after reading it, Newland Archer rose, jammed the papers back into their envelope, and reentered Mr. Letterblair's office.

"Here are the letters, sir. If you wish I'll see Madame Olenska," he said in a constrained voice.

"Thank you—thank you, Mr. Archer. Come and dine with me tonight if you're free, and we'll go into the matter afterward: in case you wish to call on our client tomorrow."

Newland Archer walked straight home again that afternoon. It was a winter evening of transparent clearness, with an innocent young moon above the housetops; and he wanted to fill his soul's lungs with the pure radiance, and not exchange a word with anyone till he and Mr. Letterblair were closeted together after dinner. It was impossible to decide otherwise than he had done: he must see Madame Olenska himself rather than let her secrets be bared to other eyes. A great wave of compassion had swept away his indifference and impatience: she stood before him as an exposed and pitiful figure, to be saved at all costs from farther wounding herself in her mad plunges against fate.

He remembered what she had told him of Mrs. Welland's request to be spared whatever was "unpleasant" in her history, and winced at the thought that it was perhaps this attitude of mind which kept the New York air so pure. "Are we only Pharisees after all?" he wondered, puzzled by the effort to reconcile his instinctive disgust at human vileness with his equally instinctive pity for human frailty.

For the first time he perceived how elementary his own principles had always been. He passed for a young man who had not been afraid of risks, and he knew that his secret love-affair with poor silly Mrs. Thorley Rushworth had not been too secret to invest him with a becoming air of adventure. But Mrs. Rushworth was "that kind of woman"; foolish, vain, clandestine by nature, and far more attracted by the secrecy and peril of the affair than by such charms and qualities as he possessed. When the fact dawned on him it nearly broke his heart, but now it seemed the redeeming feature of the case. The affair, in short, had been of the kind that most of the young men of his age had been through, and emerged from with calm consciences and an undisturbed belief in the abysmal distinction between the women one loved and respected and those one enjoyed—and pitied. In this view they were sedulously abetted by their mothers, aunts and other elderly female relatives, who all shared Mrs. Archer's belief that when "such things happened" it was undoubtedly foolish of the man, but somehow always criminal of the woman. All the elderly ladies whom Archer knew regarded any woman who loved imprudently as necessarily unscrupulous and designing, and mere simple-minded man as powerless in her clutches. The only thing to do was to persuade him, as early as possible, to marry a nice girl, and then trust to her to look after him.

In the complicated old European communities, Archer began to guess, love-problems might be less simple and less easily classified. Rich and idle and ornamental societies must produce many more such situations; and there might even be one in which a woman naturally sensitive and aloof would yet, from the force of circumstances, from sheer defenselessness and loneliness, be drawn into a tie inexcusable by conventional standards.

On reaching home he wrote a line to the Countess Olenska, asking at what hour of the next day she could receive him, and despatched it by a messenger-boy, who returned presently with a word to the effect that she was going to Skuytercliff the next morning to stay over Sunday with the van der Luydens, but that he would find her alone that evening after dinner. The note was written on a rather untidy half-sheet, without date or address, but her hand was firm and free. He was amused at the idea of her week-ending in the stately solitude of Skuytercliff, but immediately afterward felt that there, of all places, she would most feel the chill of minds rigorously averted from the "unpleasant."

He was at Mr. Letterblair's punctually at seven, glad of the pretext for excusing himself soon after dinner. He had formed his own opinion from the papers entrusted to him, and did not especially want to go into the matter with his senior partner. Mr. Letterblair was a widower, and they dined alone, copiously and slowly, in a dark shabby room hung with yellowing prints of "The Death of Chatham" and "The Coronation of Napoleon." On the sideboard, between fluted Sheraton knife-cases, stood a decanter of Haut Brion, and another of the old Lanning port (the gift of a client), which the wastrel Tom Lanning had sold off a year or two before his mysterious and discreditable death in San Francisco—an incident less publicly humiliating to the family than the sale of the cellar.

After a velvety oyster soup came shad and cucumbers, then a young broiled turkey with corn fritters, followed by a canvasback with currant jelly and a celery mayonnaise. Mr. Letterblair, who lunched on a sandwich and tea, dined deliberately and deeply, and insisted on his guest's doing the same. Finally, when the closing rites had been accomplished, the cloth was removed, cigars were lit, and Mr. Letterblair, leaning back in his chair and pushing the port westward, said, spreading his back agreeably to the coal fire behind him: "The whole family are against a divorce. And I think rightly."

Archer instantly felt himself on the other side of the argument. "But why, sir? If there ever was a case—"

"Well—what's the use? *She's* here—he's there; the Atlantic's between them. She'll never get back a dollar more of her money than what he's voluntarily returned to her: their damned heathen marriage settlements take precious good care of that. As things go over there, Olenski's acted generously: he might have turned her out without a penny."

The young man knew this and was silent.

"I understand, though," Mr. Letterblair continued, "that she attaches no importance to the money. Therefore, as the family say, why not let well enough alone?"

Archer had gone to the house an hour earlier in full agreement with Mr. Letterblair's view; but put into words by this selfish, wellfed and supremely indifferent old man it suddenly became the Pharisaic voice of a society wholly absorbed in barricading itself against the unpleasant.

"I think that's for her to decide."

"H'm—have you considered the consequences if she decides for divorce?"

"You mean the threat in her husband's letter? What weight would that carry? It's no more than the vague charge of an angry blackguard."

"Yes; but it might make some unpleasant talk if he really defends the suit."

"Unpleasant—!" said Archer explosively.

Mr. Letterblair looked at him from under enquiring eyebrows, and the young man, aware of the uselessness of trying to explain what was in his mind, bowed acquiescently while his senior continued: "Divorce is always unpleasant."

"You agree with me?" Mr. Letterblair resumed, after a waiting silence.

"Naturally," said Archer.

"Well, then, I may count on you; the Mingotts may count on you; to use your influence against the idea?"

Archer hesitated. "I can't pledge myself till I've seen the Countess Olenska," he said at length.

"Mr. Archer, I don't understand you. Do you want to marry into a family with a scandalous divorce-suit hanging over it?"

"I don't think that has anything to do with the case."

Mr. Letterblair put down his glass of port and fixed on his young partner a cautious and apprehensive gaze.

Archer understood that he ran the risk of having his mandate withdrawn, and for some obscure reason he disliked the prospect. Now that the job had been thrust on him he did not propose to relinquish it; and, to guard against the possibility, he saw that he must reassure the unimaginative old man who was the legal conscience of the Mingotts.

"You may be sure, sir, that I shan't commit myself till I've reported to you; what I meant was that I'd rather not give an opinion till I've heard what Madame Olenska has to say."

Mr. Letterblair nodded approvingly at an excess of caution worthy of the best New York tradition, and the young man, glancing at his watch, pleaded an engagement and took leave.

12

OLD-FASHIONED New York dined at seven, and the habit of after-dinner calls, though derided in Archer's set, still generally prevailed. As the young man strolled up Fifth Avenue from Waverley Place, the long thoroughfare was deserted but for a group of carriages standing before the Reggie Chiverses' (where there was a dinner for the Duke), and the occasional figure of an elderly gentleman in heavy overcoat and muffler ascending a brownstone doorstep and disappearing into a gas-lit hall. Thus, as Archer crossed Washington Square, he remarked that old Mr. du Lac was calling on his cousins the Dagonets, and turning down the corner of West Tenth Street he saw Mr. Skipworth, of his own firm, obviously bound on a visit to the Miss Lannings. A little farther up Fifth Avenue, Beaufort appeared on his doorstep, darkly projected against a blaze of light, descended to his private brougham, and rolled away to a mysterious and probably unmentionable destination. It was not an Opera night, and no one was giving a party, so that Beaufort's outing was undoubtedly of a clandestine nature. Archer connected it in his mind with a little house beyond Lexington Avenue in which beribboned window curtains and flower-boxes had recently appeared, and before whose newly painted door the canary-colored brougham of Miss Fanny Ring was frequently seen to wait.

Beyond the small and slippery pyramid which composed Mrs. Archer's world lay the almost unmapped quarter inhabited by artists, musicians and "people who wrote." These scattered fragments of humanity had never shown any desire to be amalgamated with the social structure. In spite of odd ways they were said to be, for the most part, quite respectable; but they preferred to keep to themselves. Medora Manson, in her prosperous days, had inaugurated a "literary salon"; but it had soon died out owing to the reluctance of the literary to frequent it.

Others had made the same attempt, and there was a household of Blenkers—an intense and voluble mother, and three blowsy daughters who imitated her—where one met Edwin Booth and Patti and William Winter, and the new Shakespearian actor George Rignold, and some of the magazine editors and musical and literary critics.

Mrs. Archer and her group felt a certain timidity concerning these persons. They were odd, they were uncertain, they had things one didn't know about in the background of their lives and minds. Literature and art were deeply respected in the Archer set, and Mrs. Archer was always at pains to tell her children how much more agreeable and cultivated society had been when it included such figures as Washington Irving, Fitz-Greene Halleck and the poet of "The Culprit Fay." The most celebrated authors of that generation had been "gentlemen"; perhaps the unknown persons who succeeded them had gentlemanly sentiments, but their origin, their appearance, their hair, their intimacy with the stage and the Opera, made any old New York criterion inapplicable to them.

"When I was a girl," Mrs. Archer used to say, "we knew everybody between the Battery and Canal Street; and only the people one knew had carriages. It was perfectly easy to place anyone then; now one can't tell, and I prefer not to try."

Only old Catherine Mingott, with her absence of moral prejudices and almost *parvenu* indifference to the subtler distinctions, might have bridged the abyss; but she had never opened a book or looked at a picture, and cared for music only because it reminded her of gala nights at the *Italiens*, in the days of her triumph at the Tuileries. Possibly Beaufort, who was her match in daring, would have succeeded in bringing about a fusion; but his grand house and silk-stockinged footmen were an obstacle to informal sociability. Moreover, he was as illiterate as old Mrs. Mingott, and considered "fellows who wrote" as the mere paid purveyors of rich men's pleasures; and no one rich enough to influence his opinion had ever questioned it.

Newland Archer had been aware of these things ever since he could remember, and had accepted them as part of the structure of his universe. He knew that there were societies where painters and poets and novelists and men of science, and even great actors, were as sought after as Dukes; he had often pictured to himself what it would have been to live in the intimacy of drawing rooms dominated

by the talk of Mérimée (whose *Lettres à une Inconnue* was one of
his inseparables), of Thackeray, Browning or William Morris. But
such things were inconceivable in New York, and unsettling to think
of. Archer knew most of the "fellows who wrote," the musicians and
the painters: he met them at the Century, or at the little musical
and theatrical clubs that were beginning to come into existence. He
enjoyed them there, and was bored with them at the Blenkers',
where they were mingled with fervid and dowdy women who passed
them about like captured curiosities; and even after his most exciting
talks with Ned Winsett he always came away with the feeling that if
his world was small, so was theirs, and that the only way to enlarge
either was to reach a stage of manners where they would naturally
merge.

He was reminded of this by trying to picture the society in which
the Countess Olenska had lived and suffered, and also—perhaps—
tasted mysterious joys. He remembered with what amusement she
had told him that her grandmother Mingott and the Wellands objected to her living in a "Bohemian" quarter given over to "people
who wrote." It was not the peril but the poverty that her family
disliked; but that shade escaped her, and she supposed they considered literature compromising.

She herself had no fears of it, and the books scattered about her
drawing room (a part of the house in which books were usually supposed to be "out of place"), though chiefly works of fiction, had
whetted Archer's interest with such new names as those of Paul
Bourget, Huysmans, and the Goncourt brothers. Ruminating on
these things as he approached her door, he was once more conscious
of the curious way in which she reversed his values, and of the need
of thinking himself into conditions incredibly different from any that
he knew if he were to be of use in her present difficulty.

Nastasia opened the door, smiling mysteriously. On the bench in
the hall lay a sable-lined overcoat, a folded opera hat of dull silk with
a gold J. B. on the lining, and a white silk muffler: there was no mistaking the fact that these costly articles were the property of Julius
Beaufort.

Archer was angry: so angry that he came near scribbling a word on
his card and going away; then he remembered that in writing to
Madame Olenska he had been kept by excess of discretion from saying that he wished to see her privately. He had therefore no one but

himself to blame if she had opened her doors to other visitors; and he entered the drawing room with the dogged determination to make Beaufort feel himself in the way, and to outstay him.

The banker stood leaning against the mantelshelf, which was draped with an old embroidery held in place by brass candelabra containing church candles of yellowish wax. He had thrust his chest out, supporting his shoulders against the mantel and resting his weight on one large patent-leather foot. As Archer entered he was smiling and looking down on his hostess, who sat on a sofa placed at right angles to the chimney. A table banked with flowers formed a screen behind it, and against the orchids and azaleas which the young man recognized as tributes from the Beaufort hot-houses, Madame Olenska sat half-reclined, her head propped on a hand and her wide sleeve leaving the arm bare to the elbow.

It was usual for ladies who received in the evening to wear what were called "simple dinner dresses": a close-fitting armor of whale-boned silk, slightly open in the neck, with lace ruffles filling in the crack, and tight sleeves with a flounce uncovering just enough wrist to show an Etruscan gold bracelet or a velvet band. But Madame Olenska, heedless of tradition, was attired in a long robe of red velvet bordered about the chin and down the front with glossy black fur. Archer remembered, on his last visit to Paris, seeing a portrait by the new painter, Carolus Duran, whose pictures were the sensation of the Salon, in which the lady wore one of these bold sheath-like robes with her chin nestling in fur. There was something perverse and provocative in the notion of fur worn in the evening in a heated drawing room, and in the combination of a muffled throat and bare arms; but the effect was undeniably pleasing.

"Lord love us—three whole days at Skuytercliff!" Beaufort was saying in his loud sneering voice as Archer entered. "You'd better take all your furs, and a hot water-bottle."

"Why? Is the house so cold?" she asked, holding out her left hand to Archer in a way mysteriously suggesting that she expected him to kiss it.

"No; but the missus is," said Beaufort, nodding carelessly to the young man.

"But I thought her so kind. She came herself to invite me. Granny says I must certainly go."

"Granny would, of course. And I say it's a shame you're going to miss the little oyster supper I'd planned for you at Delmonico's next Sunday, with Campanini and Scalchi and a lot of jolly people."

She looked doubtfully from the banker to Archer.

"Ah—that does tempt me! Except the other evening at Mrs. Struthers's, I've not met a single artist since I've been here."

"What kind of artists? I know one or two painters, very good fellows, that I could bring to see you if you'd allow me," said Archer boldly.

"Painters? Are there painters in New York?" asked Beaufort, in a tone implying that there could be none since he did not buy their pictures; and Madame Olenska said to Archer, with her grave smile: "That would be charming. But I was really thinking of dramatic artists, singers, actors, musicians. My husband's house was always full of them."

She said the words "my husband" as if no sinister associations were connected with them, and in a tone that seemed almost to sigh over the lost delights of her married life. Archer looked at her perplexedly, wondering if it were lightness or dissimulation that enabled her to touch so easily on the past at the very moment when she was risking her reputation in order to break with it.

"I do think," she went on, addressing both men, "that the *imprévu* adds to one's enjoyment. It's perhaps a mistake to see the same people every day."

"It's confoundedly dull, anyhow; New York is dying of dullness," Beaufort grumbled. "And when I try to liven it up for you, you go back on me. Come—think better of it! Sunday is your last chance, for Campanini leaves next week for Baltimore and Philadelphia; and I've a private room, and a Steinway, and they'll sing all night for me."

"How delicious! May I think it over, and write to you tomorrow morning?"

She spoke amiably, yet with the least hint of dismissal in her voice. Beaufort evidently felt it, and being unused to dismissals, stood staring at her with an obstinate line between his eyes.

"Why not now?"

"It's too serious a question to decide at this late hour."

"Do you call it late?"

She returned his glance coolly. "Yes; because I have still to talk business with Mr. Archer for a little while."

"Ah," Beaufort snapped. There was no appeal from her tone, and with a slight shrug he recovered his composure, took her hand, which he kissed with a practiced air, and calling out from the threshold: "I say, Newland, if you can persuade the Countess to stop in town of course you're included in the supper," left the room with his heavy important step.

For a moment Archer fancied that Mr. Letterblair must have told her of his coming; but the irrelevance of her next remark made him change his mind.

"You know painters, then? You live in their *milieu?*" she asked, her eyes full of interest.

"Oh, not exactly. I don't know that the arts have a *milieu* here, any of them; they're more like a very thinly settled outskirt."

"But you care for such things?"

"Immensely. When I'm in Paris or London I never miss an exhibition. I try to keep up."

She looked down at the tip of the little satin boot that peeped from her long draperies.

"I used to care immensely too: my life was full of such things. But now I want to try not to."

"You want to try not to?"

"Yes: I want to cast off all my old life, to become just like everybody else here."

Archer reddened. "You'll never be like everybody else," he said.

She raised her straight eyebrows a little. "Ah, don't say that. If you knew how I hate to be different!"

Her face had grown as somber as a tragic mask. She leaned forward, clasping her knee in her thin hands, and looking away from him into remote dark distances.

"I want to get away from it all," she insisted.

He waited a moment and cleared his throat. "I know. Mr. Letterblair has told me."

"Ah?"

"That's the reason I've come. He asked me to—you see I'm in the firm."

She looked slightly surprised, and then her eyes brightened. "You mean you can manage it for me? I can talk to you instead of Mr. Letterblair? Oh, that will be so much easier!"

Her tone touched him, and his confidence grew with his self-satisfaction. He perceived that she had spoken of business to Beaufort simply to get rid of him; and to have routed Beaufort was something of a triumph.

"I am here to talk about it," he repeated.

She sat silent, her head still propped by the arm that rested on the back of the sofa. Her face looked pale and extinguished, as if dimmed by the rich red of her dress. She struck Archer, of a sudden, as a pathetic and even pitiful figure.

"Now we're coming to hard facts," he thought, conscious in himself of the same instinctive recoil that he had so often criticized in his mother and her contemporaries. How little practice he had had in dealing with unusual situations! Their very vocabulary was unfamiliar to him, and seemed to belong to fiction and the stage. In face of what was coming he felt as awkward and embarrassed as a boy.

After a pause Madame Olenska broke out with unexpected vehemence: "I want to be free; I want to wipe out all the past."

"I understand that."

Her face warmed. "Then you'll help me?"

"First—" he hesitated—"perhaps I ought to know a little more."

She seemed surprised. "You know about my husband—my life with him?"

He made a sign of assent.

"Well—then—what more is there? In this country are such things tolerated? I'm a Protestant—our church does not forbid divorce in such cases."

"Certainly not."

They were both silent again, and Archer felt the specter of Count Olenski's letter grimacing hideously between them. The letter filled only half a page, and was just what he had described it to be in speaking of it to Mr. Letterblair: the vague charge of an angry blackguard. But how much truth was behind it? Only Count Olenski's wife could tell.

"I've looked through the papers you gave to Mr. Letterblair," he said at length.

"Well—can there be anything more abominable?"

"No."

She changed her position slightly, screening her eyes with her lifted hand.

"Of course you know," Archer continued, "that if your husband chooses to fight the case—as he threatens to—"

"Yes—?"

"He can say things—things that might be unpl—might be disagreeable to you: say them publicly, so that they would get about, and harm you even if—"

"If—?"

"I mean: no matter how unfounded they were."

She paused for a long interval; so long that, not wishing to keep his eyes on her shaded face, he had time to imprint on his mind the exact shape of her other hand, the one on her knee, and every detail of the three rings on her fourth and fifth fingers; among which, he noticed, a wedding ring did not appear.

"What harm could such accusations, even if he made them publicly, do me here?"

It was on his lips to exclaim: "My poor child—far more harm than anywhere else!" Instead, he answered, in a voice that sounded in his ears like Mr. Letterblair's: "New York society is a very small world compared with the one you've lived in. And it's ruled, in spite of appearances, by a few people with—well, rather old-fashioned ideas."

She said nothing, and he continued: "Our ideas about marriage and divorce are particularly old-fashioned. Our legislation favors divorce—our social customs don't."

"Never?"

"Well—not if the woman, however injured, however irreproachable, has appearances in the least degree against her, has exposed herself by any unconventional action to—to offensive insinuations—"

She drooped her head a little lower, and he waited again, intensely hoping for a flash of indignation, or at least a brief cry of denial. None came.

A little traveling clock ticked purringly at her elbow, and a log broke in two and sent up a shower of sparks. The whole hushed and brooding room seemed to be waiting silently with Archer.

"Yes," she murmured at length, "that's what my family tell me."

He winced a little. "It's not unnatural—"

"*Our* family," she corrected herself; and Archer colored. "For you'll be my cousin soon," she continued gently.

"I hope so."

"And you take their view?"

He stood up at this, wandered across the room, stared with void eyes at one of the pictures against the old red damask, and came back irresolutely to her side. How could he say: "Yes, if what your husband hints is true, or if you've no way of disproving it?"

"Sincerely—" she interjected, as he was about to speak.

He looked down into the fire. "Sincerely, then—what should you gain that would compensate for the possibility—the certainty—of a lot of beastly talk?"

"But my freedom—is that nothing?"

It flashed across him at that instant that the charge in the letter was true, and that she hoped to marry the partner of her guilt. How was he to tell her that, if she really cherished such a plan, the laws of the State were inexorably opposed to it? The mere suspicion that the thought was in her mind made him feel harshly and impatiently toward her. "But aren't you as free as air as it is?" he returned. "Who can touch you? Mr. Letterblair tells me the financial question has been settled—"

"Oh, yes," she said indifferently.

"Well, then: is it worth while to risk what may be infinitely disagreeable and painful? Think of the newspapers—their vileness! It's all stupid and narrow and unjust—but one can't make over society."

"No," she acquiesced; and her tone was so faint and desolate that he felt a sudden remorse for his own hard thoughts.

"The individual, in such cases, is nearly always sacrificed to what is supposed to be the collective interest: people cling to any convention that keeps the family together—protects the children, if there are any," he rambled on, pouring out all the stock phrases that rose to his lips in his intense desire to cover over the ugly reality which her silence seemed to have laid bare. Since she would not or could not say the one word that would have cleared the air, his wish was not to let her feel that he was trying to probe into her secret. Better keep on the surface, in the prudent old New York way, than risk uncovering a wound he could not heal.

"It's my business, you know," he went on, "to help you to see these things as the people who are fondest of you see them. The Mingotts, the Wellands, the van der Luydens, all your friends and relations: if I didn't show you honestly how they judge such questions, it wouldn't be fair of me, would it?" He spoke insistently, almost pleading with her in his eagerness to cover up that yawning silence.

She said slowly: "No; it wouldn't be fair."

The fire had crumbled down to grayness, and one of the lamps made a gurgling appeal for attention. Madame Olenska rose, wound it up and returned to the fire, but without resuming her seat.

Her remaining on her feet seemed to signify that there was nothing more for either of them to say, and Archer stood up also.

"Very well; I will do what you wish," she said abruptly. The blood rushed to his forehead; and, taken aback by the suddenness of her surrender, he caught her two hands awkwardly in his.

"I—I do want to help you," he said.

"You do help me. Goodnight, my cousin."

He bent and laid his lips on her hands, which were cold and lifeless. She drew them away, and he turned to the door, found his coat and hat under the faint gaslight of the hall, and plunged out into the winter night bursting with the belated eloquence of the inarticulate.

13

It was a crowded night at Wallack's Theater.

The play was *The Shaughraun*, with Dion Boucicault in the title rôle and Harry Montague and Ada Dyas as the lovers. The popularity of the admirable English company was at its height, and *The Shaughraun* always packed the house. In the galleries the enthusiasm was unreserved; in the stalls and boxes, people smiled a little at the hackneyed sentiments and claptrap situations, and enjoyed the play as much as the galleries did.

There was one episode, in particular, that held the house from floor to ceiling. It was that in which Harry Montague, after a sad, almost monosyllabic scene of parting with Miss Dyas, bade her good-bye, and turned to go. The actress, who was standing near the mantelpiece and looking down into the fire, wore a gray cashmere dress without fashionable loopings or trimmings, moulded to her tall figure and flowing in long lines about her feet. Around her neck was a narrow black velvet ribbon with the ends falling down her back.

When her wooer turned from her she rested her arms against the mantel-shelf and bowed her face in her hands. On the threshold he paused to look at her; then he stole back, lifted one of the ends of velvet ribbon, kissed it, and left the room without her hearing him or changing her attitude. And on this silent parting the curtain fell.

It was always for the sake of that particular scene that Newland Archer went to see *The Shaughraun*. He thought the adieux of Montague and Ada Dyas as fine as anything he had ever seen Croisette and Bressant do in Paris, or Madge Robertson and Kendal in London; in its reticence, its dumb sorrow, it moved him more than the most famous histrionic outpourings.

On the evening in question the little scene acquired an added poignancy by reminding him—he could not have said why—of his leave-taking from Madame Olenska after their confidential talk a week or ten days earlier.

It would have been as difficult to discover any resemblance between the two situations as between the appearance of the persons concerned. Newland Archer could not pretend to anything approaching the young English actor's romantic good looks, and Miss Dyas was a tall red-haired woman of monumental build whose pale and pleasantly ugly face was utterly unlike Ellen Olenska's vivid countenance. Nor were Archer and Madame Olenska two lovers parting in heartbroken silence; they were client and lawyer separating after a talk which had given the lawyer the worst possible impression of the client's case. Wherein, then, lay the resemblance that made the young man's heart beat with a kind of retrospective excitement? It seemed to be in Madame Olenska's mysterious faculty of suggesting tragic and moving possibilities outside the daily run of experience. She had hardly ever said a word to him to produce this impression, but it was a part of her, either a projection of her mysterious and outlandish background or of something inherently dramatic, passionate and unusual in herself. Archer had always been inclined to think that chance and circumstance played a small part in shaping people's lots compared with their innate tendency to have things happen to them. This tendency he had felt from the first in Madame Olenska. The quiet, almost passive young woman struck him as exactly the kind of person to whom things were bound to happen, no matter how much she shrank from them and went out of her way to avoid them. The exciting fact was her having lived in an atmosphere so thick with drama that her own tendency to provoke it had apparently passed unperceived. It was precisely the odd absence of surprise in her that gave him the sense of her having been plucked out of a very maelstrom: the things she took for granted gave the measure of those she had rebelled against.

Archer had left her with the conviction that Count Olenski's accusation was not unfounded. The mysterious person who figured in his wife's past as "the secretary" had probably not been unrewarded for his share in her escape. The conditions from which she had fled were intolerable, past speaking of, past believing: she was young, she was frightened, she was desperate—what more natural than that she should be grateful to her rescuer? The pity was that her gratitude put her, in the law's eyes and the world's, on a par with her abominable husband. Archer had made her understand this, as he was bound to do; he had also made her understand that simple-hearted kindly New York, on whose larger charity she had apparently counted, was precisely the place where she could least hope for indulgence.

To have to make this fact plain to her—and to witness her resigned acceptance of it—had been intolerably painful to him. He felt himself drawn to her by obscure feelings of jealousy and pity, as if her dumbly-confessed error had put her at his mercy, humbling yet endearing her. He was glad it was to him she had revealed her secret, rather than to the cold scrutiny of Mr. Letterblair, or the embarrassed gaze of her family. He immediately took it upon himself to assure them both that she had given up her idea of seeking a divorce, basing her decision on the fact that she had understood the uselessness of the proceeding; and with infinite relief they had all turned their eyes from the "unpleasantness" she had spared them.

"I was sure Newland would manage it," Mrs. Welland had said proudly of her future son-in-law; and old Mrs. Mingott, who had summoned him for a confidential interview, had congratulated him on his cleverness, and added impatiently: "Silly goose! I told her myself what nonsense it was. Wanting to pass herself off as Ellen Mingott and an old maid, when she has the luck to be a married woman and a Countess!"

These incidents had made the memory of his last talk with Madame Olenska so vivid to the young man that as the curtain fell on the parting of the two actors his eyes filled with tears, and he stood up to leave the theater.

In doing so, he turned to the side of the house behind him, and saw the lady of whom he was thinking seated in a box with the Beauforts, Lawrence Lefferts and one or two other men. He had not spoken with her alone since their evening together, and had tried to avoid being with her in company; but now their eyes met, and as Mrs. Beaufort recognized him at the same time, and made her languid little gesture of invitation, it was impossible not to go into the box.

Beaufort and Lefferts made way for him, and after a few words with Mrs. Beaufort, who always preferred to look beautiful and not have to talk, Archer seated himself behind Madame Olenska. There was no one else in the box but Mr. Sillerton Jackson, who was telling Mrs. Beaufort in a confidential undertone about Mrs. Lemuel Struthers's last Sunday reception (where some people reported that there had been dancing). Under cover of this circumstantial narrative, to which Mrs. Beaufort listened with her perfect smile, and her head at just the right angle to be seen in profile from the stalls, Madame Olenska turned and spoke in a low voice.

"Do you think," she asked, glancing toward the stage, "he will send her a bunch of yellow roses tomorrow morning?"

Archer reddened, and his heart gave a leap of surprise. He had called only twice on Madame Olenska, and each time he had sent her a box of yellow roses, and each time without a card. She had never before made any allusion to the flowers, and he supposed she had never thought of him as the sender. Now her sudden recognition of the gift, and her associating it with the tender leave-taking on the stage, filled him with an agitated pleasure.

"I was thinking of that too—I was going to leave the theater in order to take the picture away with me," he said.

To his surprise her color rose, reluctantly and duskily. She looked down at the mother-of-pearl opera glass in her smoothly gloved hands, and said, after a pause: "What do you do while May is away?"

"I stick to my work," he answered, faintly annoyed by the question.

In obedience to a long-established habit, the Wellands had left the previous week for St. Augustine, where, out of regard for the supposed susceptibility of Mr. Welland's bronchial tubes, they always spent the latter part of the winter. Mr. Welland was a mild and silent man, with no opinions but with many habits. With these habits none might interfere; and one of them demanded that his wife and daughter should always go with him on his annual journey to the south. To preserve an unbroken domesticity was essential to his peace of mind; he would not have known where his hair-brushes were, or how to provide stamps for his letters, if Mrs. Welland had not been there to tell him.

As all the members of the family adored each other, and as Mr. Welland was the central object of their idolatry, it never occurred to his wife and May to let him go to St. Augustine alone; and his sons, who were both in the law, and could not leave New York during the winter, always joined him for Easter and traveled back with him.

It was impossible for Archer to discuss the necessity of May's accompanying her father. The reputation of the Mingotts' family physician was largely based on the attack of pneumonia which Mr. Welland had never had; and his insistence on St. Augustine was therefore inflexible. Originally, it had been intended that May's engagement should not be announced till her return from Florida, and the fact that it had been made known sooner could not be expected to alter Mr. Welland's plans. Archer would have liked to join the travelers and have a few weeks of sunshine and boating with his betrothed; but he too was bound by custom and conventions. Little arduous as his professional duties were, he would have been convicted of frivolity by the whole Mingott clan if he had suggested asking for a holiday in mid-winter; and he accepted May's departure with the resignation which he perceived would have to be one of the principal constituents of married life.

He was conscious that Madame Olenska was looking at him under lowered lids. "I have done what you wished—what you advised," she said abruptly.

"Ah—I'm glad," he returned, embarrassed by her broaching the subject at such a moment.

"I understand—that you were right," she went on a little breathlessly; "but sometimes life is difficult . . . perplexing. . . ."

"I know."

"And I wanted to tell you that I *do* feel you were right; and that I'm grateful to you," she ended, lifting her opera glass quickly to her eyes as the door of the box opened and Beaufort's resonant voice broke in on them.

Archer stood up, and left the box and the theater.

Only the day before he had received a letter from May Welland in which, with characteristic candor, she had asked him to "be kind to Ellen" in their absence. "She likes you and admires you so much—and you know, though she doesn't show it, she's still very lonely and unhappy. I don't think Granny understands her, or Uncle Lovell Mingott either; they really think she's much worldlier and fonder of society than she is. And I can quite see that New York must seem dull to her, though the family won't admit it. I think she's been used to lots of things we haven't got; wonderful music, and picture shows, and celebrities—artists and authors and all the clever people you admire. Granny can't understand her wanting anything but lots of dinners and clothes—but I can see that you're almost the only person in New York who can talk to her about what she really cares for."

His wise May—how he had loved her for that letter! But he had not meant to act on it; he was too busy, to begin with, and he did not care, as an engaged man, to play too conspicuously the part of

Madame Olenska's champion. He had an idea that she knew how to take care of herself a good deal better than the ingenuous May imagined. She had Beaufort at her feet, Mr. van der Luyden hovering above her like a protecting deity, and any number of candidates (Lawrence Lefferts among them) waiting their opportunity in the middle distance. Yet he never saw her, or exchanged a word with her, without feeling that, after all, May's ingenuousness almost amounted to a gift of divination. Ellen Olenska was lonely and she was unhappy.

14

As he came out into the lobby Archer ran across his friend Ned Winsett, the only one among what Janey called his "clever people" with whom he cared to probe into things a little deeper than the average level of club and chop-house banter.

He had caught sight, across the house, of Winsett's shabby round-shouldered back, and had once noticed his eyes turned toward the Beaufort box. The two men shook hands, and Winsett proposed a bock at a little German restaurant around the corner. Archer, who was not in the mood for the kind of talk they were likely to get there, declined on the plea that he had work to do at home; and Winsett said: "Oh, well, so have I for that matter, and I'll be the Industrious Apprentice too."

They strolled along together, and presently Winsett said: "Look here, what I'm really after is the name of the dark lady in that swell box of yours—with the Beauforts, wasn't she? The one your friend Lefferts seems so smitten by."

Archer, he could not have said why, was slightly annoyed. What the devil did Ned Winsett want with Ellen Olenska's name? And above all, why did he couple it with Lefferts's? It was unlike Winsett to manifest such curiosity; but after all, Archer remembered, he was a journalist.

"It's not for an interview, I hope?" he laughed.

"Well—not for the press; just for myself," Winsett rejoined. "The fact is she's a neighbor of mine—queer quarter for such a beauty to settle in—and she's been awfully kind to my little boy, who fell down her area chasing his kitten, and gave himself a nasty cut. She rushed in bareheaded, carrying him in her arms, with his knee all beautifully bandaged, and was so sympathetic and beautiful that my wife was too dazzled to ask her name."

A pleasant glow dilated Archer's heart. There was nothing extraordinary in the tale: any woman would have done as much for a neighbor's child. But it was just like Ellen, he felt, to have rushed in bareheaded, carrying the boy in her arms, and to have dazzled poor Mrs. Winsett into forgetting to ask who she was.

"That is the Countess Olenska—a granddaughter of old Mrs. Mingott's."

"Whew—a Countess!" whistled Ned Winsett. "Well, I didn't know Countesses were so neighborly. Mingotts ain't."

"They would be, if you'd let them."

"Ah, well—" It was their old interminable argument as to the obstinate unwillingness of the "clever people" to frequent the fashionable, and both men knew that there was no use in prolonging it.

"I wonder," Winsett broke off, "how a Countess happens to live in our slum?"

"Because she doesn't care a hang about where she lives—or about any of our little social sign-posts," said Archer, with a secret pride in his own picture of her.

"H'm—been in bigger places, I suppose," the other commented. "Well, here's my corner."

He slouched off across Broadway, and Archer stood looking after him and musing on his last words.

Ned Winsett had those flashes of penetration; they were the most interesting thing about him, and always made Archer wonder why they had allowed him to accept failure so stolidly at an age when most men are still struggling.

Archer had known that Winsett had a wife and child, but he had never seen them. The two men always met at the Century, or at some haunt of journalists and theatrical people, such as the restaurant where Winsett had proposed to go for a bock. He had given Archer to understand that his wife was an invalid; which might be true of the poor lady, or might merely mean that she was lacking in social gifts or in evening clothes, or in both. Winsett himself had a savage abhorrence of social observances: Archer, who dressed in the evening because he thought it cleaner and more comfortable to do so, and who had never stopped to consider that cleanliness and comfort are two of the costliest items in a modest budget, regarded Winsett's attitude as part of the boring "Bohemian" pose that always made fashionable people who changed their clothes without talking about it, and were not forever harping on the number of servants one kept, seem so much simpler and less self-conscious than the others. Nevertheless, he was always stimulated by Winsett, and whenever he caught sight of the journalist's lean bearded face and melancholy eyes he would rout him out of his corner and carry him off for a long talk.

Winsett was not a journalist by choice. He was a pure man of letters, untimely born in a world that had no need of letters; but after publishing one volume of brief and exquisite literary appreciations, of which one hundred and twenty copies were sold, thirty given away, and the balance eventually destroyed by the publishers (as per contract) to make room for more marketable material, he had abandoned his real calling, and taken a sub-editorial job on a women's weekly, where fashion-plates and paper patterns alternated with New England love-stories and advertisements of temperance drinks.

On the subject of "Hearth-fires" (as the paper was called) he was inexhaustibly entertaining; but beneath his fun lurked the sterile bitterness of the still young man who has tried and given up. His conversation always made Archer take the measure of his own life, and feel how little it contained; but Winsett's, after all, contained still less, and though their common fund of intellectual interests and curiosities made their talks exhilarating, their exchange of views usually remained within the limits of a pensive dilettantism.

"The fact is, life isn't much a fit for either of us," Winsett had once said. "I'm down and out; nothing to be done about it. I've got only one ware to produce, and there's no market for it here, and won't be in my time. But you're free and you're well-off. Why don't *you* get into touch? There's only one way to do it: to go into politics."

Archer threw his head back and laughed. There one saw at a flash the unbridgeable difference between men like Winsett and the others—Archer's kind. Everyone in polite circles knew that, in America, "a gentleman couldn't go into politics." But, since he could hardly put it in that way to Winsett, he answered evasively: "Look at the career of the honest man in American politics! They don't want us."

"Who's 'they'? Why don't you all get together and be 'they' yourselves?"

Archer's laugh lingered on his lips in a slightly condescending smile. It was useless to prolong the discussion: everybody knew the melancholy fate of the few gentlemen who had risked their clean

linen in municipal or state politics in New York. The day was past
when that sort of thing was possible: the country was in possession
of the bosses and the emigrant, and decent people had to fall back
on sport or culture.

"Culture! Yes—if we had it! But there are just a few little local
patches, dying out here and there for lack of—well, hoeing and cross-
fertilizing: the last remnants of the old European tradition that your
forebears brought with them. But you're in a pitiful little minority:
you've got no center, no competition, no audience. You're like the
pictures on the walls of a deserted house: 'The Portrait of a Gentleman.' You'll never amount to anything, any of you, till you roll up
your sleeves and get right down into the muck. That, or emigrate
. . . God! If I could emigrate. . . ."

Archer mentally shrugged his shoulders and turned the conversation back to books, where Winsett, if uncertain, was always interesting. Emigrate! As if a gentleman could abandon his own country! One could no more do that than one could roll up one's sleeves
and go down into the muck. A gentleman simply stayed at home and
abstained. But you couldn't make a man like Winsett see that; and
that was why the New York of literary clubs and exotic restaurants,
though a first shake made it seem more of a kaleidoscope, turned
out, in the end, to be a smaller box, with a more monotonous pattern, than the assembled atoms of Fifth Avenue.

The next morning Archer scoured the town in vain for more yellow roses. In consequence of this search he arrived late at the office,
perceived that his doing so made no difference whatever to anyone,
and was filled with sudden exasperation at the elaborate futility of
his life. Why should he not be, at that moment, on the sands of St.
Augustine with May Welland? No one was deceived by his pretense
of professional activity. In old-fashioned legal firms like that of
which Mr. Letterblair was the head, and which were mainly engaged
in the management of large estates and "conservative" investments,
there were always two or three young men, fairly well-off, and without professional ambition, who, for a certain number of hours of
each day, sat at their desks accomplishing trivial tasks, or simply
reading the newspapers. Though it was supposed to be proper for
them to have an occupation, the crude fact of moneymaking was still
regarded as derogatory, and the law, being a profession, was accounted a more gentlemanly pursuit than business. But none of

these young men had much hope of really advancing in his profession, or any earnest desire to do so; and over many of them the green mould of the perfunctory was already perceptibly spreading.

It made Archer shiver to think that it might be spreading over him too. He had, to be sure, other tastes and interests; he spent his vacations in European travel, cultivated the "clever people" May spoke of, and generally tried to "keep up," as he had somewhat wistfully put it to Madame Olenska. But once he was married, what would become of this narrow margin of life in which his real experiences were lived? He had seen enough of other young men who had dreamed his dream, though perhaps less ardently, and who had gradually sunk into the placid and luxurious routine of their elders.

From the office he sent a note by messenger to Madame Olenska, asking if he might call that afternoon, and begging her to let him find a reply at his club; but at the club he found nothing, nor did he receive any letter the following day. This unexpected silence mortified him beyond reason, and though the next morning he saw a glorious cluster of yellow roses behind a florist's window-pane, he left it there. It was only on the third morning that he received a line by post from the Countess Olenska. To his surprise it was dated from Skuytercliff, whither the van der Luydens had promptly retreated after putting the Duke on board his steamer.

"I ran away," the writer began abruptly (without the usual preliminaries), "the day after I saw you at the play, and these kind friends have taken me in. I wanted to be quiet, and think things over. You were right in telling me how kind they were; I feel myself so safe here. I wish that you were with us." She ended with a conventional "Yours sincerely," and without any allusion to the date of her return.

The tone of the note surprised the young man. What was Madame Olenska running away from, and why did she feel the need to be safe? His first thought was of some dark menace from abroad; then he reflected that he did not know her epistolary style, and that it might run to picturesque exaggeration. Women always exaggerated; and moreover she was not wholly at her ease in English, which she often spoke as if she were translating from the French. "Je me suis évadée—" put in that way, the opening sentence immediately suggested that she might merely have wanted to escape from a boring round of engagements; which was very likely true, for he judged her to be capricious, and easily wearied of the pleasure of the moment.

It amused him to think of the van der Luydens' having carried her off to Skuytercliff on a second visit, and this time for an indefinite period. The doors of Skuytercliff were rarely and grudgingly opened to visitors, and a chilly weekend was the most ever offered to the few thus privileged. But Archer had seen, on his last visit to Paris, the delicious play of Labiche, *Le Voyage de M. Perrichon*, and he remembered M. Perrichon's dogged and undiscouraged attachment to the young man whom he had pulled out of the glacier. The van der Luydens had rescued Madame Olenska from a doom almost as icy; and though there were many other reasons for being attracted to her, Archer knew that beneath them all lay the gentle and obstinate determination to go on rescuing her.

He felt a distinct disappointment on learning that she was away; and almost immediately remembered that, only the day before, he had refused an invitation to spend the following Sunday with the Reggie Chiverses at their house on the Hudson, a few miles below Skuytercliff.

He had had his fill long ago of the noisy friendly parties at Highbank, with coasting, ice-boating, sleighing, long tramps in the snow, and a general flavor of mild flirting and milder practical jokes. He had just received a box of new books from his London bookseller, and had preferred the prospect of a quiet Sunday at home with his spoils. But he now went into the club writing-room, wrote a hurried telegram, and told the servant to send it immediately. He knew that Mrs. Reggie didn't object to her visitors' suddenly changing their minds, and that there was always a room to spare in her elastic house.

15

NEWLAND ARCHER arrived at the Chiverses' on Friday evening, and on Saturday went conscientiously through all the rites appertaining to a weekend at Highbank.

In the morning he had a spin in the ice-boat with his hostess and a few of the hardier guests; in the afternoon he "went over the farm" with Reggie, and listened, in the elaborately appointed stables, to long and impressive disquisitions on the horse; after tea he talked in a corner of the firelit hall with a young lady who had professed herself broken-hearted when his engagement was announced, but was now eager to tell him of her own matrimonial hopes; and finally, about midnight, he assisted in putting a goldfish in one visitor's bed, dressed up a burglar in the bathroom of a nervous aunt, and saw in the small hours by joining in a pillow-fight that ranged from the nurseries to the basement. But on Sunday after luncheon he borrowed a cutter, and drove over to Skuytercliff.

People had always been told that the house at Skuytercliff was an Italian villa. Those who had never been to Italy believed it; so did some who had. The house had been built by Mr. van der Luyden in his youth, on his return from the "grand tour," and in anticipation of his approaching marriage with Miss Louisa Dagonet. It was a large square wooden structure, with tongued and grooved walls painted pale green and white, a Corinthian portico, and fluted pilasters between the windows. From the high ground on which it stood a series of terraces bordered by balustrades and urns descended in the steel-engraving style to a small irregular lake with an asphalt edge overhung by rare weeping conifers. To the right and left, the famous weedless lawns studded with "specimen" trees (each of a different variety) rolled away to long ranges of grass crested with elaborate cast-iron ornaments; and below, in a hollow, lay the four-roomed stone house which the first Patroon had built on the land granted him in 1612.

Against the uniform sheet of snow and the grayish winter sky the Italian villa loomed up rather grimly; even in summer it kept its distance, and the boldest coleus bed had never ventured nearer than thirty feet from its awful front. Now, as Archer rang the bell, the long tinkle seemed to echo through a mausoleum; and the surprise of the butler who at length responded to the call was as great as though he had been summoned from his final sleep.

Happily Archer was of the family, and therefore, irregular though his arrival was, entitled to be informed that the Countess Olenska was out, having driven to afternoon service with Mrs. van der Luyden exactly three quarters of an hour earlier.

"Mr. van der Luyden," the butler continued, "is in, sir; but my impression is that he is either finishing his nap or else reading yesterday's *Evening Post*. I heard him say, sir, on his return from church this morning, that he intended to look through the *Evening Post* after luncheon; if you like, sir, I might go to the library door and listen—"

But Archer, thanking him, said that he would go and meet the ladies; and the butler, obviously relieved, closed the door on him majestically.

A groom took the cutter to the stables, and Archer struck through the park to the high-road. The village of Skuytercliff was only a mile and a half away, but he knew that Mrs. van der Luyden never walked, and that he must keep to the road to meet the carriage. Presently, however, coming down a footpath that crossed the highway, he caught sight of a slight figure in a red cloak, with a big dog running ahead. He hurried forward, and Madame Olenska stopped short with a smile of welcome.

"Ah, you've come!" she said, and drew her hand from her muff.

The red cloak made her look gay and vivid, like the Ellen Mingott of old days; and he laughed as he took her hand, and answered: "I came to see what you were running away from."

Her face clouded over, but she answered: "Ah, well—you will see, presently."

The answer puzzled him. "Why—do you mean that you've been overtaken?"

She shrugged her shoulders, with a little movement like Nastasia's, and rejoined in a lighter tone: "Shall we walk on? I'm so cold after the sermon. And what does it matter, now you're here to protect me?"

The blood rose to his temples and he caught a fold of her cloak. "Ellen—what is it? You must tell me."

"Oh, presently—let's run a race first: my feet are freezing to the ground," she cried; and gathering up the cloak she fled away across the snow, the dog leaping about her with challenging barks. For a moment Archer stood watching, his gaze delighted by the flash of the red meteor against the snow; then he started after her, and they met, panting and laughing, at a wicket that led into the park.

She looked up at him and smiled. "I knew you'd come!"

"That shows you wanted me to," he returned, with a disproportionate joy in their nonsense. The white glitter of the trees filled the air with its own mysterious brightness, and as they walked on over the snow the ground seemed to sing under their feet.

"Where did you come from?" Madame Olenska asked.

He told her, and added: "It was because I got your note."

After a pause she said, with a just perceptible chill in her voice: "May asked you to take care of me."

"I didn't need any asking."

"You mean—I'm so evidently helpless and defenseless? What a poor thing you must all think me! But women here seem not—seem never to feel the need: any more than the blessed in heaven."

He lowered his voice to ask: "What sort of a need?"

"Ah, don't ask me! I don't speak your language," she retorted petulantly.

The answer smote him like a blow, and he stood still in the path, looking down at her.

"What did I come for, if I don't speak yours?"

"Oh, my friend—!" She laid her hand lightly on his arm, and he pleaded earnestly: "Ellen—why won't you tell me what's happened?"

She shrugged again. "Does anything ever happen in heaven?"

He was silent, and they walked on a few yards without exchanging a word. Finally she said: "I will tell you—but where, where, where? One can't be alone for a minute in that great seminary of a house, with all the doors wide open, and always a servant bringing tea, or a log for the fire, or the newspaper! Is there nowhere in an American house where one may be by one's self? You're so shy, and yet you're so public. I always feel as if I were in the convent again—or on the stage, before a dreadfully polite audience that never applauds."

"Ah, you don't like us!" Archer exclaimed.

They were walking past the house of the old Patroon, with its squat walls and small square windows compactly grouped about a central chimney. The shutters stood wide, and through one of the newly-washed windows Archer caught the light of a fire.

"Why—the house is open!" he said.

She stood still. "No; only for today, at least. I wanted to see it, and Mr. van der Luyden had the fire lit and the windows opened, so that we might stop there on the way back from church this morning." She ran up the steps and tried the door. "It's still unlocked—what luck! Come in and we can have a quiet talk. Mrs. van der Luyden has driven over to see her old aunts at Rhinebeck and we shan't be missed at the house for another hour."

He followed her into the narrow passage. His spirits, which had dropped at her last words, rose with an irrational leap. The homely little house stood there, its panels and brasses shining in the firelight, as if magically created to receive them. A big bed of embers still gleamed in the kitchen chimney, under an iron pot hung from an ancient crane. Rush-bottomed armchairs faced each other across the tiled hearth, and rows of Delft plates stood on shelves against the walls. Archer stooped over and threw a log upon the embers.

Madame Olenska, dropping her cloak, sat down in one of the chairs. Archer leaned against the chimney and looked at her.

"You're laughing now; but when you wrote me you were unhappy," he said.

"Yes." She paused. "But I can't feel unhappy when you're here."

"I shan't be here long," he rejoined, his lips stiffening with the effort to say just so much and no more.

"No; I know. But I'm improvident: I live in the moment when I'm happy."

The words stole through him like a temptation, and to close his senses to it he moved away from the hearth and stood gazing out at the black tree-boles against the snow. But it was as if she too had shifted her place, and he still saw her, between himself and the trees, drooping over the fire with her indolent smile. Archer's heart was beating insubordinately. What if it were from him that she had been running away, and if she had waited to tell him so till they were here alone together in this secret room?

"Ellen, if I'm really a help to you—if you really wanted me to come—tell me what's wrong, tell me what it is you're running away from," he insisted.

He spoke without shifting his position, without even turning to look at her: if the thing was to happen, it was to happen in this way, with the whole width of the room between them, and his eyes still fixed on the outer snow.

For a long moment she was silent; and in that moment Archer imagined her, almost heard her, stealing up behind him to throw her light arms about his neck. While he waited, soul and body throbbing with the miracle to come, his eyes mechanically received the image of a heavily-coated man with his fur collar turned up who was advancing along the path to the house. The man was Julius Beaufort.

"Ah—!" Archer cried, bursting into a laugh.

Madame Olenska had sprung up and moved to his side, slipping her hand into his; but after a glance through the window her face paled and she shrank back.

"So that was it?" Archer said derisively.

"I didn't know he was here," Madame Olenska murmured. Her hand still clung to Archer's; but he drew away from her, and walking out into the passage threw open the door of the house.

"Hallo, Beaufort—this way! Madame Olenska was expecting you," he said.

During his journey back to New York the next morning, Archer relived with a fatiguing vividness his last moments at Skuytercliff.

Beaufort, though clearly annoyed at finding him with Madame Olenska, had, as usual, carried off the situation high-handedly. His way of ignoring people whose presence inconvenienced him actually gave them, if they were sensitive to it, a feeling of invisibility, of nonexistence. Archer, as the three strolled back through the park, was aware of this odd sense of disembodiment; and humbling as it was to his vanity it gave him the ghostly advantage of observing unobserved.

Beaufort had entered the little house with his usual easy assurance; but he could not smile away the vertical line between his eyes. It was fairly clear that Madame Olenska had not known that he was coming, though her words to Archer had hinted at the possibility; at any rate, she had evidently not told him where she was going when she left New York, and her unexplained departure had exasperated him. The ostensible reason of his appearance was the discovery, the very night before, of a "perfect little house," not in the market, which was really just the thing for her, but would be snapped up instantly if she didn't take it; and he was loud in mock-reproaches for the dance she had led him in running away just as he had found it.

"If only this new dodge for talking along a wire had been a little bit nearer perfection I might have told you all this from town, and been toasting my toes before the club fire at this minute, instead of tramping after you through the snow," he grumbled, disguising a real irritation under the pretense of it; and at this opening Madame Olenska twisted the talk away to the fantastic possibility that they might one day actually converse with each other from street to street, or even—incredible dream!—from one town to another. This struck from all three allusions to Edgar Poe and Jules Verne, and such platitudes as naturally rise to the lips of the most intelligent when they are talking against time, and dealing with a new invention in which it would seem ingenuous to believe too soon; and the question of the telephone carried them safely back to the big house.

Mrs. van der Luyden had not yet returned; and Archer took his leave and walked off to fetch the cutter, while Beaufort followed the Countess Olenska indoors. It was probable that, little as the van der Luydens encouraged unannounced visits, he could count on being asked to dine, and sent back to the station to catch the nine o'clock train; but more than that he would certainly not get, for it would be inconceivable to his hosts that a gentleman traveling without luggage should wish to spend the night, and distasteful to them to propose it to a person with whom they were on terms of such limited cordiality as Beaufort.

Beaufort knew all this, and must have foreseen it; and his taking the long journey for so small a reward gave the measure of his impatience. He was undeniably in pursuit of the Countess Olenska; and Beaufort had only one object in view in his pursuit of pretty women. His dull and childless home had long since palled on him; and in addition to more permanent consolations he was always in quest of amorous adventures in his own set. This was the man from whom Madame Olenska was avowedly flying: the question was whether she had fled because his importunities displeased her, or because she did not wholly trust herself to resist them; unless, indeed, all her talk of flight had been a blind, and her departure no more than a maneuver.

Archer did not really believe this. Little as he had actually seen of Madame Olenska, he was beginning to think that he could read her face, and if not her face, her voice; and both had betrayed annoyance, and even dismay, at Beaufort's sudden appearance. But, after all, if this were the case, was it not worse than if she had left New York for the express purpose of meeting him? If she had done that, she ceased to be an object of interest, she threw in her lot with the vulgarest of dissemblers: a woman engaged in a love affair with Beaufort "classed" herself irretrievably.

No, it was worse a thousand times if, judging Beaufort, and probably despising him, she was yet drawn to him by all that gave him an advantage over the other men about her: his habit of two continents and two societies, his familiar association with artists and actors and people generally in the world's eye, and his careless contempt for local prejudices. Beaufort was vulgar, he was uneducated, he was purse-proud; but the circumstances of his life, and a certain native shrewdness, made him better worth talking to than many men, morally and socially his betters, whose horizon was bounded by the Battery and the Central Park. How should anyone coming from a wider world not feel the difference and be attracted by it?

Madame Olenska, in a burst of irritation, had said to Archer that he and she did not talk the same language; and the young man knew that in some respects this was true. But Beaufort understood every turn of her dialect, and spoke it fluently: his view of life, his tone, his attitude, were merely a coarser reflection of those revealed in Count Olenski's letter. This might seem to be to his disadvantage with Count Olenski's wife; but Archer was too intelligent to think that a young woman like Ellen Olenska would necessarily recoil from everything that reminded her of her past. She might believe herself wholly in revolt against it; but what had charmed her in it would still charm her, even though it were against her will.

Thus, with a painful impartiality, did the young man make out the case for Beaufort, and for Beaufort's victim. A longing to enlighten her was strong in him; and there were moments when he imagined that all she asked was to be enlightened.

That evening he unpacked his books from London. The box was full of things he had been waiting for impatiently; a new volume of Herbert Spencer, another collection of the prolific Alphonse Daudet's brilliant tales, and a novel called *Middlemarch*, as to which there had lately been interesting things said in the reviews. He had declined three dinner invitations in favor of this feast; but though he turned the pages with the sensuous joy of the book-lover, he did not know what he was reading, and one book after another dropped from his hand. Suddenly, among them, he lit on a small volume of verse which he had ordered because the name had attracted him: *The House of Life.* He took it up, and found himself plunged in an atmosphere unlike any he had ever breathed in books; so warm, so rich, and yet so ineffably tender, that it gave a new and haunting beauty to the most elementary of human passions. All through the night he pursued through those enchanted pages the vision of a woman who had the face of Ellen Olenska; but when he woke the next morning, and looked out at the brownstone houses across the street, and thought of his desk in Mr. Letterblair's office, and the family pew in Grace Church, his hour in the park of Skuytercliff became as far outside the pale of probability as the visions of the night.

"Mercy, how pale you look, Newland!" Janey commented over the coffee cups at breakfast; and his mother added: "Newland, dear, I've noticed lately that you've been coughing; I do hope you're not letting yourself be overworked?" For it was the conviction of both ladies that, under the iron despotism of his senior partners, the young man's life was spent in the most exhausting professional labors—and he had never thought it necessary to undeceive them.

The next two or three days dragged by heavily. The taste of the usual was like cinders in his mouth, and there were moments when he felt as if he were being buried alive under his future. He heard nothing of the Countess Olenska, or of the perfect little house, and though he met Beaufort at the club they merely nodded at each other across the whist-tables. It was not till the fourth evening that he found a note awaiting him on his return home. "Come late tomorrow: I must explain to you. Ellen." These were the only words it contained.

The young man, who was dining out, thrust the note into his pocket, smiling a little at the Frenchness of the "to you." After dinner he went to a play; and it was not until his return home, after midnight, that he drew Madame Olenska's missive out again and reread it slowly a number of times. There were several ways of answering it, and he gave considerable thought to each one during the watches of an agitated night. That on which, when morning came, he finally decided was to pitch some clothes into a portmanteau and jump on board a boat that was leaving that very afternoon for St. Augustine.

16

WHEN Archer walked down the sandy main street of St. Augustine to the house which had been pointed out to him as Mr. Welland's, and saw May Welland standing under a magnolia with the sun in her hair, he wondered why he had waited so long to come.

Here was truth, here was reality, here was the life that belonged to him; and he, who fancied himself so scornful of arbitrary restraints, had been afraid to break away from his desk because of what people might think of his stealing a holiday!

Her first exclamation was: "Newland—has anything happened?" and it occurred to him that it would have been more "feminine" if she had instantly read in his eyes why he had come. But when he answered: "Yes—I found I had to see you," her happy blushes took the chill from her surprise, and he saw how easily he would be forgiven, and how soon even Mr. Letterblair's mild disapproval would be smiled away by a tolerant family.

Early as it was, the main street was no place for any but formal greetings, and Archer longed to be alone with May, and to pour out all his tenderness and his impatience. It still lacked an hour to the late Welland breakfast-time, and instead of asking him to come in she proposed that they should walk out to an old orange-garden beyond the town. She had just been for a row on the river, and the sun that netted the little waves with gold seemed to have caught her in its meshes. Across the warm brown of her cheek her blown hair glittered like silver wire; and her eyes too looked lighter, almost pale in their youthful limpidity. As she walked beside Archer with her long swinging gait her face wore the vacant serenity of a young marble athlete.

To Archer's strained nerves the vision was as soothing as the sight of the blue sky and the lazy river. They sat down on a bench under the orange-trees and he put his arm about her and kissed her. It was like drinking at a cold spring with the sun on it; but his pressure may have been more vehement than he had intended, for the blood rose to her face and she drew back as if he had startled her.

"What is it?" he asked, smiling; and she looked at him with surprise, and answered: "Nothing."

A slight embarrassment fell on them, and her hand slipped out of his. It was the only time that he had kissed her on the lips except for their fugitive embrace in the Beaufort conservatory, and he saw that she was disturbed, and shaken out of her cool boyish composure.

"Tell me what you do all day," he said, crossing his arms under his tilted-back head, and pushing his hat forward to screen the sun-dazzle. To let her talk about familiar and simple things was the easiest way of carrying on his own independent train of thought; and he sat listening to her simple chronicle of swimming, sailing and riding, varied by an occasional dance at the primitive inn when a man-of-war came in. A few pleasant people from Philadelphia and Baltimore were picnicking at the inn, and the Selfridge Merrys had come down for three weeks because Kate Merry had had bronchitis. They were planning to lay out a lawn tennis court on the sands; but no one but Kate and May had racquets, and most of the people had not even heard of the game.

All this kept her very busy, and she had not had time to do more than look at the little vellum book that Archer had sent her the week before (the *Sonnets from the Portuguese*); but she was learning by heart "How They Brought the Good News from Ghent to Aix," because it was one of the first things he had ever read to her; and it amused her to be able to tell him that Kate Merry had never even heard of a poet called Robert Browning.

Presently she started up, exclaiming that they would be late for breakfast; and they hurried back to the tumble-down house with its paintless porch and unpruned hedge of plumbago and pink geraniums where the Wellands were installed for the winter. Mr. Welland's sensitive domesticity shrank from the discomforts of the slovenly southern hotel, and at immense expense, and in face of almost insuperable difficulties, Mrs. Welland was obliged, year after year, to improvise an establishment partly made up of discontented New York servants and partly drawn from the local African supply.

"The doctors want my husband to feel that he is in his own home;

otherwise he would be so wretched that the climate would not do him any good," she explained, winter after winter, to the sympathizing Philadelphians and Baltimoreans; and Mr. Welland, beaming across a breakfast table miraculously supplied with the most varied delicacies, was presently saying to Archer: "You see, my dear fellow, we camp—we literally camp. I tell my wife and May that I want to teach them how to rough it."

Mr. and Mrs. Welland had been as much surprised as their daughter by the young man's sudden arrival; but it had occurred to him to explain that he had felt himself on the verge of a nasty cold, and this seemed to Mr. Welland an all-sufficient reason for abandoning any duty.

"You can't be too careful, especially toward spring," he said, heaping his plate with straw-colored griddle-cakes and drowning them in golden syrup. "If I'd only been as prudent at your age May would have been dancing at the Assemblies now, instead of spending her winters in a wilderness with an old invalid."

"Oh, but I love it here, Papa; you know I do. If only Newland could stay I should like it a thousand times better than New York."

"Newland must stay till he has quite thrown off his cold," said Mrs. Welland indulgently; and the young man laughed, and said he supposed there was such a thing as one's profession.

He managed, however, after an exchange of telegrams with the firm, to make his cold last a week; and it shed an ironic light on the situation to know that Mr. Letterblair's indulgence was partly due to the satisfactory way in which his brilliant young junior partner had settled the troublesome matter of the Olenski divorce. Mr. Letterblair had let Mrs. Welland know that Mr. Archer had "rendered an invaluable service" to the whole family, and that old Mrs. Manson Mingott had been particularly pleased; and one day when May had gone for a drive with her father in the only vehicle the place produced Mrs. Welland took occasion to touch on a topic which she always avoided in her daughter's presence.

"I'm afraid Ellen's ideas are not at all like ours. She was barely eighteen when Medora Manson took her back to Europe—you remember the excitement when she appeared in black at her coming-out ball? Another of Medora's fads—really this time it was almost prophetic! That must have been at least twelve years ago; and since then Ellen has never been to America. No wonder she is completely Europeanized."

"But European society is not given to divorce: Countess Olenska thought she would be conforming to American ideas in asking for her freedom." It was the first time that the young man had pronounced her name since he had left Skuytercliff, and he felt the color rise to his cheek.

Mrs. Welland smiled compassionately. "That is just like the extraordinary things that foreigners invent about us. They think we dine at two o'clock and countenance divorce! That is why it seems to me so foolish to entertain them when they come to New York. They accept our hospitality, and then they go home and repeat the same stupid stories."

Archer made no comment on this, and Mrs. Welland continued: "But we do most thoroughly appreciate your persuading Ellen to give up the idea. Her grandmother and her Uncle Lovell could do nothing with her; both of them have written that her changing her mind was entirely due to your influence—in fact she said so to her grandmother. She has an unbounded admiration for you. Poor Ellen —she was always a wayward child. I wonder what her fate will be?"

"What we've all contrived to make it," he felt like answering. "If you'd all of you rather she should be Beaufort's mistress than some decent fellow's wife you've certainly gone the right way about it."

He wondered what Mrs. Welland would have said if he had uttered the words instead of merely thinking them. He could picture the sudden decomposure of her firm placid features, to which a life-long mastery over trifles had given an air of factitious authority. Traces still lingered on them of a fresh beauty like her daughter's; and he asked himself if May's face was doomed to thicken into the same middle-aged image of invincible innocence.

Ah, no, he did not want May to have that kind of innocence, the innocence that seals the mind against imagination and the heart against experience!

"I verily believe," Mrs. Welland continued, "that if the horrible business had come out in the newspapers it would have been my husband's death-blow. I don't know any of the details; I only ask not to, as I told poor Ellen when she tried to talk to me about it. Having an invalid to care for, I have to keep my mind bright and happy. But Mr. Welland was terribly upset; he had a slight temperature every morning while we were waiting to hear what had been decided. It was the horror of his girl's learning that such things were possible—

but of course, dear Newland, you felt that too. We all knew that you were thinking of May."

"I'm always thinking of May," the young man rejoined, rising to cut short the conversation.

He had meant to seize the opportunity of his private talk with Mrs. Welland to urge her to advance the date of his marriage. But he could think of no arguments that would move her, and with a sense of relief he saw Mr. Welland and May driving up to the door.

His only hope was to plead again with May, and on the day before his departure he walked with her to the ruinous garden of the Spanish Mission. The background lent itself to allusions to European scenes; and May, who was looking her loveliest under a wide-brimmed hat that cast a shadow of mystery over her too-clear eyes, kindled into eagerness as he spoke of Granada and the Alhambra.

"We might be seeing it all this spring—even the Easter ceremonies at Seville," he urged, exaggerating his demands in the hope of a larger concession.

"Easter in Seville? And it will be Lent next week!" she laughed.

"Why shouldn't we be married in Lent?" he rejoined; but she looked so shocked that he saw his mistake.

"Of course I didn't mean that, dearest; but soon after Easter—so that we could sail at the end of April. I know I could arrange it at the office."

She smiled dreamily upon the possibility; but he perceived that to dream of it sufficed her. It was like hearing him read aloud out of his poetry books the beautiful things that could not possibly happen in real life.

"Oh, do go on, Newland; I do love your descriptions."

"But why should they be only descriptions? Why shouldn't we make them real?"

"We shall, dearest, of course; next year." Her voice lingered over it.

"Don't you want them to be real sooner? Can't I persuade you to break away now?"

She bowed her head, vanishing from him under her conniving hat-brim.

"Why should we dream away another year? Look at me, dear! Don't you understand how I want you for my wife?"

For a moment she remained motionless; then she raised on him eyes of such despairing clearness that he half-released her waist from his hold. But suddenly her look changed and deepened inscrutably. "I'm not sure if I *do* understand," she said. "Is it—is it because you're not certain of continuing to care for me?"

Archer sprang up from his seat. "My God—perhaps—I don't know," he broke out angrily.

May Welland rose also; as they faced each other she seemed to grow in womanly stature and dignity. Both were silent for a moment, as if dismayed by the unforeseen trend of their words: then she said in a low voice: "If that is it—is there someone else?"

"Someone else—between you and me?" He echoed her words slowly, as though they were only half-intelligible and he wanted time to repeat the question to himself. She seemed to catch the uncertainty of his voice, for she went on in a deepening tone: "Let us talk frankly, Newland. Sometimes I've felt a difference in you; especially since our engagement has been announced."

"Dear—what madness!" he recovered himself to exclaim.

She met his protest with a faint smile. "If it is, it won't hurt us to talk about it." She paused, and added, lifting her head with one of her noble movements: "Or even if it's true: why shouldn't we speak of it? You might so easily have made a mistake."

He lowered his head, staring at the black leaf-pattern on the sunny path at their feet. "Mistakes are always easy to make; but if I had made one of the kind you suggest, is it likely that I should be imploring you to hasten our marriage?"

She looked downward too, disturbing the pattern with the point of her sunshade while she struggled for expression. "Yes," she said at length. "You might want—once for all—to settle the question: it's one way."

Her quiet lucidity startled him, but did not mislead him into thinking her insensible. Under her hat-brim he saw the pallor of her profile, and a slight tremor of the nostril above her resolutely steadied lips.

"Well—?" he questioned, sitting down on the bench, and looking up at her with a frown that he tried to make playful.

She dropped back into her seat and went on: "You mustn't think that a girl knows as little as her parents imagine. One hears and one notices—one has one's feelings and ideas. And of course, long before you told me that you cared for me, I'd known that there was someone else you were interested in; everyone was talking about it two years ago at Newport. And once I saw you sitting together on the verandah at a dance—and when she came back into the house her face was sad, and I felt sorry for her; I remembered it afterward, when we were engaged."

Her voice had sunk almost to a whisper, and she sat clasping and unclasping her hands about the handle of her sunshade. The young man laid his upon them with a gentle pressure; his heart dilated with an inexpressible relief.

"My dear child—was *that* it? If you only knew the truth!"

She raised her head quickly. "Then there is a truth I don't know?"

He kept his hand over hers. "I meant, the truth about the old story you speak of."

"But that's what I want to know, Newland—what I ought to know. I couldn't have my happiness made out of a wrong—an unfairness—to somebody else. And I want to believe that it would be the same with you. What sort of a life could we build on such foundations?"

Her face had taken on a look of such tragic courage that he felt like bowing himself down at her feet. "I've wanted to say this for a long time," she went on. "I've wanted to tell you that, when two people really love each other, I understand that there may be situations which make it right that they should—should go against public opinion. And if you feel yourself in any way pledged . . . pledged to the person we've spoken of . . . and if there is any way . . . any way in which you can fulfill your pledge . . . even by her getting a divorce . . . Newland, don't give her up because of me!"

His surprise at discovering that her fears had fastened upon an episode so remote and so completely of the past as his love affair with Mrs. Thorley Rushworth gave way to wonder at the generosity of her view. There was something superhuman in an attitude so recklessly unorthodox, and if other problems had not pressed on him he would have been lost in wonder at the prodigy of the Wellands' daughter urging him to marry his former mistress. But he was still dizzy with the glimpse of the precipice they had skirted, and full of a new awe at the mystery of young-girlhood.

For a moment he could not speak; then he said: "There is no pledge—no obligation whatever—of the kind you think. Such cases don't always—present themselves quite as simply as . . . But that's no matter . . . I love your generosity, because I feel as you do about those things . . . I feel that each case must be judged individually, on its own merits . . . irrespective of stupid conventionalities . . . I mean, each woman's right to her liberty—" He pulled himself up, startled by the turn his thoughts had taken, and went on, looking at her with a smile: "Since you understand so many things, dearest, can't you go a little farther, and understand the uselessness of our submitting to another form of the same foolish conventionalities? If there's no one and nothing between us, isn't that an argument for marrying quickly, rather than for more delay?"

She flushed with joy and lifted her face to his; as he bent to it he saw that her eyes were full of happy tears. But in another moment she seemed to have descended from her womanly eminence to help-less and timorous girlhood; and he understood that her courage and initiative were all for others, and that she had none for herself. It was evident that the effort of speaking had been much greater than her studied composure betrayed, and that at his first word of reassur-ance she had dropped back into the usual, as a too adventurous child takes refuge in its mother's arms.

Archer had no heart to go on pleading with her; he was too much disappointed at the vanishing of the new being who had cast that one deep look at him from her transparent eyes. May seemed to be aware of his disappointment, but without knowing how to alleviate it; and they stood up and walked silently home.

17

"Your cousin the Countess called on Mother while you were away," Janey Archer announced to her brother on the evening of his return.

The young man, who was dining alone with his mother and sister, glanced up in surprise and saw Mrs. Archer's gaze demurely bent on her plate. Mrs. Archer did not regard her seclusion from the world as a reason for being forgotten by it; and Newland guessed that she was slightly annoyed that he should be surprised by Madame Olenska's visit.

"She had on a black velvet polonaise with jet buttons, and a tiny green monkey muff; I never saw her so stylishly dressed," Janey continued. "She came alone, early on Sunday afternoon; luckily the fire was lit in the drawing room. She had one of those new card-cases. She said she wanted to know us because you'd been so good to her."

Newland laughed. "Madame Olenska always takes that tone about her friends. She's very happy at being among her own people again."

"Yes, so she told us," said Mrs. Archer. "I must say she seems thankful to be here."

"I hope you liked her, mother."

Mrs. Archer drew her lips together. "She certainly lays herself out to please, even when she is calling on an old lady."

"Mother doesn't think her simple," Janey interjected, her eyes screwed upon her brother's face.

"It's just my old-fashioned feeling; dear May is my ideal," said Mrs. Archer.

"Ah," said her son, "they're not alike."

Archer had left St. Augustine charged with many messages for old

Mrs. Mingott; and a day or two after his return to town he called on her.

The old lady received him with unusual warmth; she was grateful to him for persuading the Countess Olenska to give up the idea of a divorce; and when he told her that he had deserted the office without leave, and rushed down to St. Augustine simply because he wanted to see May, she gave an adipose chuckle and patted his knee with her puff-ball hand.

"Ah, ah—so you kicked over the traces, did you? And I suppose Augusta and Welland pulled long faces, and behaved as if the end of the world had come? But little May—she knew better, I'll be bound?"

"I hoped she did; but after all she wouldn't agree to what I'd gone down to ask for."

"Wouldn't she indeed? And what was that?"

"I wanted to get her to promise that we should be married in April. What's the use of our wasting another year?"

Mrs. Manson Mingott screwed up her little mouth into a grimace of mimic prudery and twinkled at him through malicious lids. "'Ask Mamma,' I suppose—the usual story. Ah, these Mingotts—all alike! Born in a rut, and you can't root 'em out of it. When I built this house you'd have thought I was moving to California! Nobody ever *had* built above Fortieth Street—no, says I, nor above the Battery either, before Christopher Columbus discovered America. No, no; not one of them wants to be different; they're as scared of it as the small-pox. Ah, my dear Mr. Archer, I thank my stars I'm nothing but a vulgar Spicer; but there's not one of my own children that takes after me but my little Ellen." She broke off, still twinkling at him, and asked, with the casual irrelevance of old age: "Now, why in the world didn't you marry my little Ellen?"

Archer laughed. "For one thing, she wasn't there to be married."

"No—to be sure; more's the pity. And now it's too late; her life is finished." She spoke with the cold-blooded complacency of the aged throwing earth into the grave of young hopes. The young man's heart grew chill, and he said hurriedly: "Can't I persuade you to use your influence with the Wellands, Mrs. Mingott? I wasn't made for long engagements."

Old Catherine beamed on him approvingly. "No; I can see that. You've got a quick eye. When you were a little boy I've no doubt you liked to be helped first." She threw back her head with a laugh that made her chins ripple like little waves. "Ah, here's my Ellen now!" she exclaimed, as the portières parted behind her.

Madame Olenska came forward with a smile. Her face looked vivid and happy, and she held out her hand gaily to Archer while she stooped to her grandmother's kiss.

"I was just saying to him, my dear: 'Now, why didn't you marry my little Ellen?' "

Madame Olenska looked at Archer, still smiling. "And what did he answer?"

"Oh, my darling, I leave you to find that out! He's been down to Florida to see his sweetheart."

"Yes, I know." She still looked at him. "I went to see your mother, to ask where you'd gone. I sent a note that you never answered, and I was afraid you were ill."

He muttered something about leaving unexpectedly, in a great hurry, and having intended to write to her from St. Augustine.

"And of course once you were there you never thought of me again!" She continued to beam on him with a gaiety that might have been a studied assumption of indifference.

"If she still needs me, she's determined not to let me see it," he thought, stung by her manner. He wanted to thank her for having been to see his mother, but under the ancestress's malicious eye he felt himself tongue-tied and constrained.

"Look at him—in such hot haste to get married that he took French leave and rushed down to implore the silly girl on his knees! That's something like a lover—that's the way handsome Bob Spicer carried off my poor mother; and then got tired of her before I was weaned—though they only had to wait eight months for me! But there—you're not a Spicer, young man; luckily for you and for May. It's only my poor Ellen that has kept any of their wicked blood; the rest of them are all model Mingotts," cried the old lady scornfully.

Archer was aware that Madame Olenska, who had seated herself at her grandmother's side, was still thoughtfully scrutinizing him. The gaiety had faded from her eyes, and she said with great gentleness: "Surely, Granny, we can persuade them between us to do as he wishes."

Archer rose to go, and as his hand met Madame Olenska's he felt that she was waiting for him to make some allusion to her unanswered letter.

"When can I see you?" he asked, as she walked with him to the door of the room.

"Whenever you like; but it must be soon if you want to see the little house again. I am moving next week."

A pang shot through him at the memory of his lamplit hours in the low-studded drawing room. Few as they had been, they were thick with memories.

"Tomorrow evening?"

She nodded. "Tomorrow; yes; but early. I'm going out."

The next day was a Sunday, and if she were "going out" on a Sunday evening it could, of course, be only to Mrs. Lemuel Struthers's. He felt a slight movement of annoyance, not so much at her going there (for he rather liked her going where she pleased in spite of the van der Luydens), but because it was the kind of house at which she was sure to meet Beaufort, where she must have known beforehand that she would meet him—and where she was probably going for that purpose.

"Very well; tomorrow evening," he repeated, inwardly resolved that he would not go early, and that by reaching her door late he would either prevent her from going to Mrs. Struthers's, or else arrive after she had started—which, all things considered, would no doubt be the simplest solution.

It was only half-past eight, after all, when he rang the bell under the wisteria; not as late as he had intended by half an hour—but a singular restlessness had driven him to her door. He reflected, however, that Mrs. Struthers's Sunday evenings were not like a ball, and that her guests, as if to minimize their delinquency, usually went early.

The one thing he had not counted on, in entering Madame Olenska's hall, was to find hats and overcoats there. Why had she bidden him to come early if she was having people to dine? On a closer inspection of the garments besides which Nastasia was laying his own, his resentment gave way to curiosity. The overcoats were in fact the very strangest he had ever seen under a polite roof; and it took but a glance to assure himself that neither of them belonged to Julius Beaufort. One was a shaggy yellow ulster of "reach-me-down" cut, the other a very old and rusty cloak with a cape—something like what the French called a "Macfarlane." This garment, which appeared to be made for a person of prodigious size, had evidently seen long and hard wear, and its greenish-black folds gave out a moist saw-dusty smell suggestive of prolonged sessions against barroom walls. On it lay a ragged gray scarf and an odd felt hat of semi-clerical shape.

Archer raised his eyebrows enquiringly at Nastasia, who raised hers in return with a fatalistic "Già!" as she threw open the drawing-room door.

The young man saw at once that his hostess was not in the room; then, with surprise, he discovered another lady standing by the fire. This lady, who was long, lean and loosely put together, was clad in raiment intricately looped and fringed, with plaids and stripes and bands of plain color disposed in a design to which the clue seemed missing. Her hair, which had tried to turn white and only succeeded in fading, was surmounted by a Spanish comb and black lace scarf, and silk mittens, visibly darned, covered her rheumatic hands.

Beside her, in a cloud of cigar-smoke, stood the owners of the two overcoats, both in morning clothes that they had evidently not taken off since morning. In one of the two, Archer, to his surprise, recognized Ned Winsett; the other and older, who was unknown to him, and whose gigantic frame declared him to be the wearer of the "Macfarlane," had a feebly leonine head with crumpled gray hair, and moved his arms with large pawing gestures, as though he were distributing lay blessings to a kneeling multitude.

These three persons stood together on the hearth-rug, their eyes fixed on an extraordinarily large bouquet of crimson roses, with a knot of purple pansies at their base, that lay on the sofa where Madame Olenska usually sat.

"What they must have cost at this season—though of course it's the sentiment one cares about!" The lady was saying in a sighing staccato as Archer came in.

The three turned with surprise at his appearance, and the lady, advancing, held out her hand.

"Dear Mr. Archer—almost my nephew Newland!" she said. "I am the Marchioness Manson."

Archer bowed, and she continued: "My Ellen has taken me in for a few days. I came from Cuba, where I have been spending the winter with Spanish friends—such delightful distinguished people: the highest nobility of old Castile—how I wish you could know them! But I was called away by our dear great friend here, Dr. Carver. You don't know Dr. Agathon Carver, founder of the Valley of Love Community?"

Dr. Carver inclined his leonine head, and the Marchioness continued: "Ah, New York—New York—how little the life of the spirit has reached it! But I see you do know Mr. Winsett."

"Oh, yes—I reached him some time ago; but not by that route," Winsett said with his dry smile.

The Marchioness shook her head reprovingly. "How do you know, Mr. Winsett? The spirit bloweth where it listeth."

"List—oh, list!" interjected Dr. Carver in a stentorian murmur.

"But do sit down, Mr. Archer. We four have been having a delightful little dinner together, and my child has gone up to dress. She expects you; she will be down in a moment. We were just admiring these marvelous flowers, which will surprise her when she reappears."

Winsett remained on his feet. "I'm afraid I must be off. Please tell Madame Olenska that we shall all feel lost when she abandons our street. This house has been an oasis."

"Ah, but she won't abandon *you*. Poetry and art are the breath of life to her. It *is* poetry you write, Mr. Winsett?"

"Well, no; but I sometimes read it," said Winsett, including the group in a general nod and slipping out of the room.

"A caustic spirit—*un peu sauvage*. But so witty; Dr. Carver, you *do* think him witty?"

"I never think of wit," said Dr. Carver severely.

"Ah—ah—you never think of wit! How merciless he is to us weak mortals, Mr. Archer! But he lives only in the life of the spirit; and tonight he is mentally preparing the lecture he is to deliver presently at Mrs. Blenker's. Dr. Carver, would there be time, before you start for the Blenkers' to explain to Mr. Archer your illuminating discovery of the Direct Contact? But no; I see it is nearly nine o'clock, and we have no right to detain you while so many are waiting for your message."

Dr. Carver looked slightly disappointed at this conclusion, but, having compared his ponderous gold timepiece with Madame Olenska's little traveling-clock, he reluctantly gathered up his mighty limbs for departure.

"I shall see you later, dear friend?" he suggested to the Marchioness, who replied with a smile: "As soon as Ellen's carriage comes I will join you; I do hope the lecture won't have begun."

Dr. Carver looked thoughtfully at Archer. "Perhaps, if this young gentleman is interested in my experiences, Mrs. Blenker might allow you to bring him with you?"

"Oh, dear friend, if it were possible—I am sure she would be too happy. But I fear my Ellen counts on Mr. Archer herself."

"That," said Dr. Carver, "is unfortunate—but here is my card." He handed it to Archer, who read on it, in Gothic characters:

Agathon Carver
The Valley of Love
Kittasquattamy, N. Y.

Dr. Carver bowed himself out, and Mrs. Manson, with a sigh that might have been either of regret or relief, again waved Archer to a seat.

"Ellen will be down in a moment; and before she comes, I am so glad of this quiet moment with you."

Archer murmured his pleasure at their meeting, and the Marchioness continued, in her low sighing accents: "I know everything, dear Mr. Archer—my child has told me all you have done for her. Your wise advice: your courageous firmness—thank heaven it was not too late!"

The young man listened with considerable embarrassment. Was there anyone, he wondered, to whom Madame Olenska had not proclaimed his intervention in her private affairs?

"Madame Olenska exaggerates; I simply gave her a legal opinion, as she asked me to."

"Ah, but in doing it—in doing it you were the unconscious instrument of—of—what word have we moderns for Providence, Mr. Archer?" cried the lady, tilting her head on one side and drooping her lids mysteriously. "Little did you know that at that very moment I was being appealed to: being approached, in fact—from the other side of the Atlantic!"

She glanced over her shoulder, as though fearful of being overheard, and then, drawing her chair nearer, and raising a tiny ivory fan to her lips, breathed behind it: "By the Count himself—my poor, mad, foolish Olenski; who asks only to take her back on her own terms."

"Good God!" Archer exclaimed, springing up.

"You are horrified? Yes, of course; I understand. I don't defend poor Stanislas, though he has always called me his best friend. He does not defend himself—he casts himself at her feet: in my person." She tapped her emaciated bosom. "I have his letter here."

"A letter?—Has Madame Olenska seen it?" Archer stammered, his brain whirling with the shock of the announcement.

The Marchioness Manson shook her head softly. "Time—time; I must have time. I know my Ellen—haughty, intractable; shall I say, just a shade unforgiving?"

"But, good heavens, to forgive is one thing; to go back into that hell—"

"Ah, yes," the Marchioness acquiesced. "So she describes it—my sensitive child! But on the material side, Mr. Archer, if one may stoop to consider such things; do you know what she is giving up? Those roses there on the sofa—acres like them, under glass and in the open, in his matchless terraced gardens at Nice! Jewels—historic pearls: the Sobieski emeralds—sables—but she cares nothing for all these! Art and beauty, those she does care for, she lives for, as I always have; and those also surrounded her. Pictures, priceless furniture, music, brilliant conversation—ah, that, my dear young man, if you'll excuse me, is what you've no conception of here! And she had it all; and the homage of the greatest. She tells me she is not thought handsome in New York—good heavens! Her portrait has been painted nine times; the greatest artists in Europe have begged for the privilege. Are these things nothing? And the remorse of an adoring husband?"

As the Marchioness Manson rose to her climax her face assumed an expression of ecstatic retrospection which would have moved Archer's mirth had he not been numb with amazement.

He would have laughed if anyone had foretold to him that his first sight of poor Medora Manson would have been in the guise of a messenger of Satan; but he was in no mood for laughing now, and she seemed to him to come straight out of the hell from which Ellen Olenska had just escaped.

"She knows nothing yet—of all this?" he asked abruptly.

Mrs. Manson laid a purple finger on her lips. "Nothing directly—but does she suspect? Who can tell? The truth is, Mr. Archer, I have been waiting to see you. From the moment I heard of the firm stand you had taken, and of your influence over her, I hoped it might be possible to count on your support—to convince you. . . ."

"That she ought to go back? I would rather see her dead!" cried the young man violently.

"Ah," the Marchioness murmured, without visible resentment. For a while she sat in her armchair, opening and shutting the absurd ivory fan between her mittened fingers; but suddenly she lifted her head and listened.

"Here she comes," she said in a rapid whisper; and then, pointing to the bouquet on the sofa: "Am I to understand that you prefer *that*, Mr. Archer? After all, marriage is marriage . . . and my niece is still a wife. . . ."

18

"What are you two plotting together, Aunt Medora?" Madame Olenska cried as she came into the room.

She was dressed as if for a ball. Everything about her shimmered and glimmered softly, as if her dress had been woven out of candle beams; and she carried her head high, like a pretty woman challenging a roomful of rivals.

"We were saying, my dear, that here was something beautiful to surprise you with," Mrs. Manson rejoined, rising to her feet and pointing archly to the flowers.

Madame Olenska stopped short and looked at the bouquet. Her color did not change, but a sort of white radiance of anger ran over her like summer lightning. "Ah," she exclaimed, in a shrill voice that the young man had never heard, "who is ridiculous enough to send me a bouquet? Why a bouquet? And why tonight of all nights? I am not going to a ball; I am not a girl engaged to be married. But some people are always ridiculous."

She turned back to the door, opened it, and called out: "Nastasia!"

The ubiquitous handmaiden promptly appeared, and Archer heard Madame Olenska say, in an Italian that she seemed to pronounce with intentional deliberateness in order that he might follow it: "Here —throw this into the dustbin!" and then, as Nastasia stared protestingly: "But no—it's not the fault of the poor flowers. Tell the boy to carry them to the house three doors away, the house of Mr. Winsett, the dark gentleman who dined here. His wife is ill—they may give her pleasure. . . . The boy is out, you say? Then, my dear one, run yourself; here, put my cloak over you and fly. I want the thing out of the house immediately! And, as you live, don't say they come from me!"

She flung her velvet opera cloak over the maid's shoulders and turned back into the drawing room, shutting the door sharply. Her bosom was rising high under its lace, and for a moment Archer thought she was about to cry; but she burst into a laugh instead, and looking from the Marchioness to Archer, asked abruptly: "And you two—have you made friends!"

"It's for Mr. Archer to say, darling; he has waited patiently while you were dressing."

"Yes—I gave you time enough: my hair wouldn't go," Madame Olenska said, raising her hand to the heaped-up curls of her *chignon*. "But that reminds me: I see Dr. Carver is gone, and you'll be late at the Blenkers'. Mr. Archer, will you put my aunt in the carriage?"

She followed the Marchioness into the hall, saw her fitted into a miscellaneous heap of overshoes, shawls and tippets, and called from the doorstep: "Mind, the carriage is to be back for me at ten!" Then she returned to the drawing room, where Archer, on re-entering it, found her standing by the mantelpiece, examining herself in the mirror. It was not usual, in New York society, for a lady to address her parlor-maid as "my dear one," and send her out on an errand wrapped in her own opera cloak; and Archer, through all his deeper feelings, tasted the pleasurable excitement of being in a world where action followed on emotion with such Olympian speed.

Madame Olenska did not move when he came up behind her, and for a second their eyes met in the mirror; then she turned, threw herself into her sofa-corner, and sighed out: "There's time for a cigarette."

He handed her the box and lit a spill for her; and as the flame flashed up into her face she glanced at him with laughing eyes and said: "What do you think of me in a temper?"

Archer paused a moment; then he answered with sudden resolution: "It makes me understand what your aunt has been saying about you."

"I knew she'd been talking about me. Well?"

"She said you were used to all kinds of things—splendors and amusements and excitements—that we could never hope to give you here."

Madame Olenska smiled faintly into the circle of smoke about her lips.

"Medora is incorrigibly romantic. It has made up to her for so many things!"

Archer hesitated again, and again took his risk. "Is your aunt's romanticism always consistent with accuracy?"

"You mean: does she speak the truth?" Her niece considered. "Well, I'll tell you: in almost everything she says, there's something true and something untrue. But why do you ask? What has she been telling you?"

He looked away into the fire, and then back at her shining presence. His heart tightened with the thought that this was their last evening by that fireside, and that in a moment the carriage would come to carry her away.

"She says—she pretends that Count Olenski has asked her to persuade you to go back to him."

Madame Olenska made no answer. She sat motionless, holding her cigarette in her half-lifted hand. The expression of her face had not changed; and Archer remembered that he had before noticed her apparent incapacity for surprise.

"You knew, then?" he broke out.

She was silent for so long that the ash dropped from her cigarette. She brushed it to the floor. "She has hinted about a letter: poor darling! Medora's hints—"

"Is it at your husband's request that she has arrived here suddenly?"

Madame Olenska seemed to consider this question also. "There again: one can't tell. She told me she had had a 'spiritual summons,' whatever that is, from Dr. Carver. I'm afraid she's going to marry Dr. Carver . . . poor Medora, there's always someone she wants to marry. But perhaps the people in Cuba just got tired of her! I think she was with them as a sort of paid companion. Really, I don't know why she came."

"But you do believe she has a letter from your husband?"

Again Madame Olenska brooded silently; then she said: "After all, it was to be expected."

The young man rose and went to lean against the fireplace. A sudden restlessness possessed him, and he was tongue-tied by the sense that their minutes were numbered, and that at any moment he might hear the wheels of the returning carriage.

"You know that your aunt believes you will go back?"

Madame Olenska raised her head quickly. A deep blush rose to her face and spread over her neck and shoulders. She blushed seldom and painfully, as if it hurt her like a burn.

"Many cruel things have been believed of me," she said.

"Oh, Ellen—forgive me; I'm a fool and a brute!"

She smiled a little. "You are horribly nervous; you have your own troubles. I know you think the Wellands are unreasonable about your marriage, and of course I agree with you. In Europe people don't understand our long American engagements; I suppose they are not as calm as we are." She pronounced the "we" with a faint emphasis that gave it an ironic sound.

Archer felt the irony but did not dare to take it up. After all, she had perhaps purposely deflected the conversation from her own affairs, and after the pain his last words had evidently caused her he felt that all he could do was to follow her lead. But the sense of the waning hour made him desperate: he could not bear the thought that a barrier of words should drop between them again.

"Yes," he said abruptly; "I went south to ask May to marry me after Easter. There's no reason why we shouldn't be married then."

"And May adores you—and yet you couldn't convince her? I thought her too intelligent to be the slave of such absurd superstitions."

"She *is* too intelligent—she's not their slave."

Madame Olenska looked at him. "Well, then—I don't understand."

Archer reddened, and hurried on with a rush. "We had a frank talk—almost the first. She thinks my impatience is a bad sign."

"Merciful heavens—a bad sign?"

"She thinks it means that I can't trust myself to go on caring for her. She thinks, in short, I want to marry her at once to get away from someone that I—care for more."

Madame Olenska examined this curiously. "But if she thinks that —why isn't she in a hurry too?"

"Because she's not like that: she's so much nobler. She insists all the more on the long engagement, to give me time—"

"Time to give her up for the other woman?"

"If I want to."

Madame Olenska leaned toward the fire and gazed into it with fixed eyes. Down the quiet street Archer heard the approaching trot of her horses.

"That *is* noble," she said, with a slight break in her voice.

"Yes. But it's ridiculous."

"Ridiculous? Because you don't care for anyone else?"

"Because I don't mean to marry anyone else."

"Ah." There was another long interval. At length she looked up at him and asked: "This other woman—does she love you?"

"Oh, there's no other woman; I mean, the person that May was thinking of is—was never—"

"Then, why, after all, are you in such haste?"

"There's your carriage," said Archer.

She half-rose and looked about her with absent eyes. Her fan and gloves lay on the sofa beside her and she picked them up mechanically.

"Yes; I suppose I must be going."

"You're going to Mrs. Struthers's?"

"Yes." She smiled and added: "I must go where I am invited, or I should be too lonely. Why not come with me?"

Archer felt that at any cost he must keep her beside him, must make her give him the rest of her evening. Ignoring her question, he continued to lean against the chimney-piece, his eyes fixed on the hand in which she held her gloves and fan, as if watching to see if he had the power to make her drop them.

"May guessed the truth," he said. "There is another woman—but not the one she thinks."

Ellen Olenska made no answer, and did not move. After a moment he sat down beside her, and, taking her hand, softly unclasped it, so that the gloves and fan fell on the sofa between them.

She started up, and freeing herself from him moved away to the other side of the hearth. "Ah, don't make love to me! Too many people have done that," she said, frowning.

Archer, changing color, stood up also: it was the bitterest rebuke she could have given him. "I have never made love to you," he said, "and I never shall. But you are the woman I would have married if it had been possible for either of us."

"Possible for either of us?" She looked at him with unfeigned astonishment. "And you say that—when it's you who've made it impossible?"

He stared at her, groping in a blackness through which a single arrow of light tore its blinding way.

"*I've* made it impossible—?"

"You, you, *you!*" she cried, her lip trembling like a child's on the verge of tears. "Isn't it you who made me give up divorcing—give it up because you showed me how selfish and wicked it was, how one must sacrifice one's self to preserve the dignity of marriage . . . and to spare one's family the publicity, the scandal? And because my family was going to be your family—for May's sake and for yours—I did what you told me, what you proved to me that I ought to do. Ah," she broke out with a sudden laugh, "I've made no secret of having done it for you!"

She sank down on the sofa again, crouching among the festive ripples of her dress like a stricken masquerader; and the young man stood by the fireplace and continued to gaze at her without moving.

"Good God," he groaned. "When I thought—"

"You thought?"

"Ah, don't ask me what I thought!"

Still looking at her, he saw the same burning flush creep up her neck to her face. She sat upright, facing him with a rigid dignity.

"I do ask you."

"Well, then: there were things in that letter you asked me to read—"

"My husband's letter?"

"Yes."

"I had nothing to fear from that letter: absolutely nothing! All I feared was to bring notoriety, scandal, on the family—on you and May."

"Good God," he groaned again, bowing his face in his hands.

The silence that followed lay on them with the weight of things final and irrevocable. It seemed to Archer to be crushing him down like his own grave-stone; in all the wide future he saw nothing that would ever lift that load from his heart. He did not move from his place, or raise his head from his hands; his hidden eyeballs went on staring into utter darkness.

"At least I loved you—" he brought out.

On the other side of the hearth, from the sofa-corner where he supposed that she still crouched, he heard a faint stifled crying like a child's. He started up and came to her side.

"Ellen! What madness! Why are you crying? Nothing's done that can't be undone. I'm still free, and you're going to be." He had her in his arms, her face like a wet flower at his lips, and all their vain terrors shrivelling up like ghosts at sunrise. The one thing that astonished him now was that he should have stood for five minutes arguing with her across the width of the room, when just touching her made everything so simple.

She gave him back all his kiss, but after a moment he felt her stiffening in his arms, and she put him aside and stood up.

"Ah, my poor Newland—I suppose this had to be. But it doesn't in the least alter things," she said, looking down at him in her turn from the hearth.

"It alters the whole of life for me."

"No, no—it mustn't, it can't. You're engaged to May Welland; and I'm married."

He stood up too, flushed and resolute. "Nonsense! It's too late for that sort of thing. We've no right to lie to other people or to ourselves. We won't talk of your marriage; but do you see me marrying May after this?"

She stood silent, resting her thin elbows on the mantelpiece, her profile reflected in the glass behind her. One of the locks of her *chignon* had become loosened and hung on her neck; she looked haggard and almost old.

"I don't see you," she said at length, "putting that question to May. Do you?"

He gave a reckless shrug. "It's too late to do anything else."

"You say that because it's the easiest thing to say at this moment —not because it's true. In reality it's too late to do anything but what we'd both decided on."

"Ah, I don't understand you!"

She forced a pitiful smile that pinched her face instead of smoothing it. "You don't understand because you haven't yet guessed how you've changed things for me: oh, from the first—long before I knew all you'd done."

"All I'd done?"

"Yes. I was perfectly unconscious at first that people here were shy of me—that they thought I was a dreadful sort of person. It seems they had even refused to meet me at dinner. I found that out afterward; and how you'd made your mother go with you to the van der Luydens'; and how you'd insisted on announcing your engagement at the Beaufort ball, so that I might have two families to stand by me instead of one—"

At that he broke into a laugh.

"Just imagine," she said, "how stupid and unobservant I was! I knew nothing of all this till Granny blurted it out one day. New York simply meant peace and freedom to me: it was coming home. And I was so happy at being among my own people that everyone I met seemed kind and good, and glad to see me. But from the very beginning," she continued, "I felt there was no one as kind as you; no one who gave me reasons that I understood for doing what at first seemed so hard and—unnecessary. The very good people didn't convince me; I felt they'd never been tempted. But you knew; you understood; you had felt the world outside tugging at one with all its golden hands—and yet you hated the things it asks of one; you hated happiness bought by disloyalty and cruelty and indifference. That was what I'd never known before—and it's better than anything I've known."

She spoke in a low even voice, without tears or visible agitation; and each word, as it dropped from her, fell into his breast like burning lead. He sat bowed over, his head between his hands, staring at the hearth-rug, and at the tip of the satin shoe that showed under her dress. Suddenly he knelt down and kissed the shoe.

She bent over him, laying her hands on his shoulders, and looking at him with eyes so deep that he remained motionless under her gaze.

"Ah, don't let us undo what you've done!" she cried. "I can't go back now to that other way of thinking. I can't love you unless I give you up."

His arms were yearning up to her; but she drew away, and they remained facing each other, divided by the distance that her words had created. Then, abruptly, his anger overflowed.

"And Beaufort? Is he to replace me?"

As the words sprang out he was prepared for an answering flare of anger; and he would have welcomed it as fuel for his own. But Madame Olenska only grew a shade paler, and stood with her arms hanging down before her, and her head slightly bent, as her way was when she pondered a question.

"He's waiting for you now at Mrs. Struthers's; why don't you go to him?" Archer sneered.

She turned to ring the bell. "I shall not go out this evening; tell the carriage to go and fetch the Signora Marchesa," she said when the maid came.

After the door had closed again Archer continued to look at her with bitter eyes. "Why this sacrifice? Since you tell me that you're lonely I've no right to keep you from your friends."

She smiled a little under her wet lashes. "I shan't be lonely now. I *was* lonely; I *was* afraid. But the emptiness and the darkness are gone; when I turn back into myself now I'm like a child going at night into a room where there's always a light."

Her tone and her look still enveloped her in a soft inaccessibility, and Archer groaned out again: "I don't understand you!"

"Yet you understand May!"

He reddened under the retort, but kept his eyes on her. "May is ready to give me up."

"What! Three days after you've entreated her on your knees to hasten your marriage?"

"She's refused; that gives me the right—"

"Ah, you've taught me what an ugly word that is," she said.

He turned away with a sense of utter weariness. He felt as though he had been struggling for hours up the face of a steep precipice, and now, just as he had fought his way to the top, his hold had given way and he was pitching down headlong into darkness.

If he could have got her in his arms again he might have swept away her arguments; but she still held him at a distance by something inscrutably aloof in her look and attitude, and by his own awed sense of her sincerity. At length he began to plead again.

"If we do this now it will be worse afterward—worse for every-one—"

"No—no—no!" she almost screamed, as if he frightened her.

At that moment the bell sent a long tinkle through the house. They had heard no carriage stopping at the door, and they stood motionless, looking at each other with startled eyes.

Outside, Nastasia's step crossed the hall, the outer door opened, and a moment later she came in carrying a telegram which she handed to the Countess Olenska.

"The lady was very happy at the flowers," Nastasia said, smoothing her apron. "She thought it was her *signor marito* who had sent them, and she cried a little and said it was a folly."

Her mistress smiled and took the yellow envelope. She tore it open and carried it to the lamp; then, when the door had closed again, she handed the telegram to Archer.

It was dated from St. Augustine, and addressed to the Countess Olenska. In it he read: "Granny's telegram successful. Papa and Mamma agree marriage after Easter. Am telegraphing Newland. Am too happy for words and love you dearly. Your grateful May."

Half an hour later, when Archer unlocked his own front-door, he found a similar envelope on the hall-table on top of his pile of notes and letters. The message inside the envelope was also from May Welland, and ran as follows: "Parents consent wedding Tuesday after Easter at twelve Grace Church eight bridesmaids please see Rector so happy love May."

Archer crumpled up the yellow sheet as if the gesture could annihilate the news it contained. Then he pulled out a small pocket-diary and turned over the pages with trembling fingers; but he did not find what he wanted, and cramming the telegram into his pocket he mounted the stairs.

A light was shining through the door of the little hall room which served Janey as a dressing room and boudoir, and her brother rapped impatiently on the panel. The door opened, and his sister stood before him in her immemorial purple flannel dressing-gown, with her hair "on pins." Her face looked pale and apprehensive.

"Newland! I hope there's no bad news in that telegram? I waited on purpose, in case—" (No item of his correspondence was safe from Janey.)

He took no notice of her question. "Look here—what day is Easter this year?"

She looked shocked at such unchristian ignorance. "Easter? Newland! Why, of course, the first week in April. Why?"

"The first week?" He turned again to the pages of his diary, calculating rapidly under his breath. "The first week, did you say?" He threw back his head with a long laugh.

"For mercy's sake what's the matter?"

"Nothing's the matter, except that I'm going to be married in a month."

Janey fell upon his neck and pressed him to her purple flannel breast. "Oh Newland, how wonderful! I'm so glad! But, dearest, why do you keep on laughing? Do hush, or you'll wake Mamma."

BOOK TWO

19

Tʜᴇ day was fresh, with a lively spring wind full of dust. All the old ladies in both families had got out their faded sables and yellowing ermines, and the smell of camphor from the front pews almost smothered the faint spring scent of the lilies banking the altar.

Newland Archer, at a signal from the sexton, had come out of the vestry and placed himself with his best man on the chancel step of Grace Church.

The signal meant that the brougham bearing the bride and her father was in sight; but there was sure to be a considerable interval of adjustment and consultation in the lobby, where the bridesmaids were already hovering like a cluster of Easter blossoms. During this unavoidable lapse of time the bridegroom, in proof of his eagerness, was expected to expose himself alone to the gaze of the assembled company; and Archer had gone through this formality as resignedly as through all the others which made of a nineteenth-century New York wedding a rite that seemed to belong to the dawn of history. Everything was equally easy—or equally painful, as one chose to put it—in the path he was committed to tread, and he had obeyed the flurried injunctions of his best man as piously as other bridegrooms had obeyed his own, in the days when he had guided them through the same labyrinth.

So far he was reasonably sure of having fulfilled all his obligations. The bridesmaids' eight bouquets of white lilac and lilies-of-the-valley had been sent in due time, as well as the gold and sapphire sleeve-links of the eight ushers and the best man's cat's-eye scarf-pin; Archer had sat up half the night trying to vary the wording of his thanks for the last batch of presents from men friends and ex-lady-loves; the fees for the Bishop and the Rector were safely in the pocket of his best man; his own luggage was already at Mrs. Manson Mingott's, where the wedding-breakfast was to take place, and so were the traveling clothes into which he was to change; and a private compartment had been engaged in the train that was to carry the young couple to their unknown destination—concealment of the spot in which the bridal night was to be spent being one of the most sacred taboos of the prehistoric ritual.

"Got the ring all right?" whispered young van der Luyden Newland, who was inexperienced in the duties of a best man, and awed by the weight of his responsibility.

Archer made the gesture which he had seen so many bridegrooms make: with his ungloved right hand he felt in the pocket of his dark gray waistcoat, and assured himself that the little gold circlet (engraved inside: *Newland to May, April* ——, 187—) was in its place; then, resuming his former attitude, his tall hat and pearl-gray gloves with black stitchings grasped in his left hand, he stood looking at the door of the church.

Overhead, Handel's March swelled pompously through the imitation stone vaulting, carrying on its waves the faded drift of the many weddings at which, with cheerful indifference, he had stood on the same chancel step watching other brides float up the nave toward other bridegrooms.

"How like a first night at the Opera!" he thought, recognizing all the same faces in the same boxes (no, pews), and wondering if, when the Last Trump sounded, Mrs. Selfridge Merry would be there with the same towering ostrich feathers in her bonnet, and Mrs. Beaufort with the same diamond earrings and the same smile—and whether suitable proscenium seats were already prepared for them in another world.

After that there was still time to review, one by one, the familiar countenances in the first rows; the women's sharp with curiosity and excitement, the men's sulky with the obligation of having to put on their frock-coats before luncheon, and fight for food at the wedding-breakfast.

"Too bad the breakfast is at old Catherine's," the bridegroom could fancy Reggie Chivers saying. "But I'm told that Lovell Mingott insisted on its being cooked by his own *chef,* so it ought to be good if one can only get at it." And he could imagine Sillerton Jackson adding with authority: "My dear fellow, haven't you heard? It's to be served at small tables, in the new English fashion."

Archer's eyes lingered a moment on the left-hand pew, where his mother, who had entered the church on Mr. Henry van der Luyden's arm, sat weeping softly under her Chantilly veil, her hands in her grandmother's ermine muff.

"Poor Janey!" he thought, looking at his sister, "even by screwing her head around she can see only the people in the few front pews; and they're mostly dowdy Newlands and Dagonets."

On the hither side of the white ribbon dividing off the seats reserved for the families he saw Beaufort, tall and red-faced, scrutinizing the women with his arrogant stare. Beside him sat his wife, all silvery chinchilla and violets; and on the far side of the ribbon, Lawrence Lefferts's sleekly brushed head seemed to mount guard over the invisible deity of "Good Form" who presided at the ceremony.

Archer wondered how many flaws Lefferts's keen eyes would discover in the ritual of his divinity; then he suddenly recalled that he too had once thought such questions important. The things that had filled his days seemed now like a nursery parody of life, or like the wrangles of medieval schoolmen over metaphysical terms that nobody had ever understood. A stormy discussion as to whether the wedding presents should be "shown" had darkened the last hours before the wedding; and it seemed inconceivable to Archer that grown-up people should work themselves into a state of agitation over such trifles, and that the matter should have been decided (in the negative) by Mrs. Welland's saying, with indignant tears: "I should as soon turn the reporters loose in my house." Yet there was a time when Archer had had definite and rather aggressive opinions on all such problems, and when everything concerning the manners and customs of his little tribe had seemed to him fraught with world-wide significance.

"And all the while, I suppose," he thought, "real people were living somewhere, and real things happening to them . . ."

"*There they come!*" breathed the best man excitedly; but the bridegroom knew better.

The cautious opening of the door of the church meant only that Mr. Brown the livery-stable keeper (gowned in black in his intermittent character of sexton) was taking a preliminary survey of the scene before marshaling his forces. The door was softly shut again; then after another interval it swung majestically open, and a murmur ran through the church: "The family!"

Mrs. Welland came first, on the arm of her eldest son. Her large pink face was appropriately solemn, and her plum-colored satin with pale blue side-panels, and blue ostrich plumes in a small satin bonnet, met with general approval; but before she had settled herself with a stately rustle in the pew opposite Mrs. Archer's the spectators were craning their necks to see who was coming after her. Wild rumors had been abroad the day before to the effect that Mrs. Manson Mingott, in spite of her physical disabilities, had resolved on being present at the ceremony; and the idea was so much in keeping with her sporting character that bets ran high at the clubs as to her being able to walk up the nave and squeeze into a seat. It was known that she had insisted on sending her own carpenter to look into the possibility of taking down the end panel of the front pew, and to measure the space between the seat and the front; but the result had been discouraging, and for one anxious day her family had watched her dallying with the plan of being wheeled up the nave in her enormous Bath chair and sitting enthroned in it at the foot of the chancel.

The idea of this monstrous exposure of her person was so painful to her relations that they could have covered with gold the ingenious person who suddenly discovered that the chair was too wide to pass between the iron uprights of the awning which extended from the church door to the curbstone. The idea of doing away with this awning, and revealing the bride to the mob of dressmakers and newspaper reporters who stood outside fighting to get near the joints of the canvas, exceeded even old Catherine's courage, though for a moment she had weighed the possibility. "Why, they might take a photograph of my child *and put it in the papers!*" Mrs. Welland exclaimed when her mother's last plan was hinted to her; and from this unthinkable indecency the clan recoiled with a collective shudder. The ancestress had had to give in; but her concession was bought only by the promise that the wedding-breakfast should take place under her roof, though (as the Washington Square connection said) with the Wellands' house in easy reach it was hard to have to make a special price with Brown to drive one to the other end of nowhere.

Though all these transactions had been widely reported by the Jacksons a sporting minority still clung to the belief that old Catherine would appear in church, and there was a distinct lowering of the temperature when she was found to have been replaced by her daughter-in-law. Mrs. Lovell Mingott had the high color and glassy stare induced in ladies of her age and habit by the effort of getting into a new dress; but once the disappointment occasioned by her mother-in-law's non-appearance had subsided, it was agreed that her black Chantilly over lilac satin, with a bonnet of Parma violets, formed the happiest contrast to Mrs. Welland's blue and plum-color. Far different was the impression produced by the gaunt and mincing lady who followed on Mr. Mingott's arm, in a wild dishevelment of stripes and fringes and floating scarves; and as this last apparition glided into view Archer's heart contracted and stopped beating.

He had taken it for granted that the Marchioness Manson was still in Washington, where she had gone some four weeks previously with her niece, Madame Olenska. It was generally understood that their abrupt departure was due to Madame Olenska's desire to remove her aunt from the baleful eloquence of Dr. Agathon Carver, who had nearly succeeded in enlisting her as a recruit for the Valley of Love; and in the circumstances no one had expected either of the ladies to return for the wedding. For a moment Archer stood with his eyes fixed on Medora's fantastic figure, straining to see who came behind her; but the little procession was at an end, for all the lesser members of the family had taken their seats, and the eight tall ushers, gathering themselves together like birds or insects preparing for some migratory maneuver, were already slipping through the side doors into the lobby.

"Newland—I say: *she's here!*" the best man whispered.

Archer roused himself with a start.

A long time had apparently passed since his heart had stopped beating, for the white and rosy procession was in fact half-way up the nave, the Bishop, the Rector and two white-winged assistants were hovering about the flower-banked altar, and the first chords of the Spohr symphony were strewing their flower-like notes before the bride.

Archer opened his eyes (but could they really have been shut, as he imagined?), and felt his heart beginning to resume its usual task. The music, the scent of the lilies on the altar, the vision of the cloud of tulle and orange-blossoms floating nearer and nearer, the sight of Mrs. Archer's face suddenly convulsed with happy sobs, the low benedictory murmur of the Rector's voice, the ordered evolutions of the eight pink bridesmaids and the eight black ushers: all these sights, sounds and sensations, so familiar in themselves, so unutterably strange and meaningless in his new relation to them, were confusedly mingled in his brain.

"My God," he thought, "*have* I got the ring?"—and once more he went through the bridegroom's convulsive gesture.

Then, in a moment, May was beside him, such radiance streaming from her that it sent a faint warmth through his numbness, and he straightened himself and smiled into her eyes.

"Dearly beloved, we are gathered together here," the Rector began . . .

The ring was on her hand, the Bishop's benediction had been given, the bridesmaids were apoise to resume their place in the procession, and the organ was showing preliminary symptoms of breaking out into the Mendelssohn March, without which no newly-wedded couple had ever emerged upon New York.

"Your arm—*I say, give her your arm!*" young Newland nervously hissed; and once more Archer became aware of having been adrift far off in the unknown. What was it that had sent him there, he wondered? Perhaps the glimpse, among the anonymous spectators in the transept, of a dark coil of hair under a hat which, a moment later, revealed itself as belonging to an unknown lady with a long nose, so laughably unlike the person whose image she had evoked that he asked himself if he were becoming subject to hallucinations.

And now he and his wife were pacing slowly down the nave, carried forward on the light Mendelssohn ripples, the spring day beckoning to them through widely opened doors, and Mrs. Welland's chestnuts, with big white favors on their frontlets, curvetting and showing off at the far end of the canvas tunnel.

The footman, who had a still bigger white favor on his lapel, wrapped May's white cloak about her, and Archer jumped into the brougham at her side. She turned to him with a triumphant smile and their hands clasped under her veil.

"Darling!" Archer said—and suddenly the same black abyss yawned before him and he felt himself sinking into it, deeper and deeper, while his voice rambled on smoothly and cheerfully: "Yes, of course I thought I'd lost the ring; no wedding would be complete if the poor devil of a bridegroom didn't go through that. But you *did* keep me waiting, you know! I had time to think of every horror that might possibly happen."

She surprised him by turning, in full Fifth Avenue, and flinging her arms about his neck. "But none ever *can* happen now, can it, Newland, as long as we two are together?"

Every detail of the day had been so carefully thought out that the young couple, after the wedding-breakfast, had ample time to put on their traveling clothes, descend the wide Mingott stairs between laughing bridesmaids and weeping parents, and get into the brougham under the traditional shower of rice and satin slippers; and there was still half an hour left in which to drive to the station, buy the last weeklies at the bookstall with the air of seasoned travellers, and settle themselves in the reserved compartment in which May's maid had already placed her dove-colored traveling cloak and glaringly new dressing-bag from London.

The old du Lac aunts at Rhinebeck had put their house at the disposal of the bridal couple, with a readiness inspired by the prospect of spending a week in New York with Mrs. Archer; and Archer, glad to escape the usual "bridal suite" in a Philadelphia or Baltimore hotel, had accepted with an equal alacrity.

May was enchanted at the idea of going to the country, and childishly amused at the vain efforts of the eight bridesmaids to discover where their mysterious retreat was situated. It was thought "very English" to have a country-house lent to one, and the fact gave a last touch of distinction to what was generally conceded to be the most brilliant wedding of the year; but where the house was no one was permitted to know, except the parents of bride and groom, who, when taxed with the knowledge, pursed their lips and said mysteriously: "Ah, they didn't tell us—" which was manifestly true, since there was no need to.

Once they were settled in their compartment, and the train, shaking off the endless wooden suburbs, had pushed out into the pale landscape of spring, talk became easier than Archer had expected. May was still, in look and tone, the simple girl of yesterday, eager to compare notes with him as to the incidents of the wedding, and discussing them as impartially as a bridesmaid talking it all over with an usher. At first Archer had fancied that this detachment was the disguise of an inward tremor; but her clear eyes revealed only the most tranquil unawareness. She was alone for the first time with her husband; but her husband was only the charming comrade of yesterday. There was no one whom she liked as much, no one whom she trusted as completely, and the culminating "lark" of the whole delightful adventure of engagement and marriage was to be off with him alone on a journey, like a grown-up person, like a "married woman," in fact.

It was wonderful that—as he had learned in the Mission garden at St. Augustine—such depths of feeling could coexist with such absence of imagination. But he remembered how, even then, she had surprised him by dropping back to inexpressive girlishness as soon as her conscience had been eased of its burden; and he saw that she would probably go through life dealing to the best of her ability with each experience as it came, but never anticipating any by so much as a stolen glance.

Perhaps that faculty of unawareness was what gave her eyes their transparency, and her face the look of representing a type rather than a person; as if she might have been chosen to pose for a Civic Virtue or a Greek goddess. The blood that ran so close to her fair skin might have been a preserving fluid rather than a ravaging element; yet her look of indestructible youthfulness made her seem neither hard nor dull, but only primitive and pure. In the thick of this meditation Archer suddenly felt himself looking at her with the startled gaze of a stranger, and plunged into a reminiscence of the wedding-breakfast and of Granny Mingott's immense and triumphant pervasion of it.

May settled down to frank enjoyment of the subject. "I was surprised, though—weren't you?—that Aunt Medora came after all. Ellen wrote that they were neither of them well enough to take the journey; I do wish it had been she who had recovered! Did you see the exquisite old lace she sent me?"

He had known that the moment must come sooner or later, but he had somewhat imagined that by force of willing he might hold it at bay.

"Yes—I—no: yes, it was beautiful," he said, looking at her blindly, and wondering if, whenever he heard those two syllables, all his carefully built-up world would tumble about him like a house of cards.

"Aren't you tired? It will be good to have some tea when we arrive —I'm sure the aunts have got everything beautifully ready," he rattled on, taking her hand in his; and her mind rushed away instantly to the magnificent tea and coffee service of Baltimore silver which the Beauforts had sent, and which "went" so perfectly with Uncle Lovell Mingott's trays and side-dishes.

In the spring twilight the train stopped at the Rhinebeck station, and they walked along the platform to the waiting carriage.

"Ah, how awfully kind of the van der Luydens—they've sent their man over from Skuytercliff to meet us," Archer exclaimed, as a sedate person out of livery approached them and relieved the maid of her bags.

"I'm extremely sorry, sir," said this emissary, "that a little accident has occurred at the Miss du Lacs': a leak in the water-tank. It happened yesterday, and Mr. van der Luyden, who heard of it this morning, sent a housemaid up by the early train to get the Patroon's house ready. It will be quite comfortable, I think you'll find, sir; and the Miss du Lacs have sent their cook over, so that it will be exactly the same as if you'd been at Rhinebeck."

Archer stared at the speaker so blankly that he repeated in still more apologetic accents: "It'll be exactly the same, sir, I do assure you—" and May's eager voice broke out, covering the embarrassed silence: "The same as Rhinebeck? The Patroon's house? But it will be a hundred thousand times better—won't it, Newland? It's too dear and kind of Mr. van der Luyden to have thought of it."

And as they drove off, with the maid beside the coachman, and their shining bridal bags on the seat before them, she went on excitedly: "Only fancy, I've never been inside it—have you? The van der Luydens show it to so few people. But they opened it for Ellen, it seems, and she told me what a darling little place it was: she says it's the only house she's seen in America that she could imagine being perfectly happy in."

"Well—that's what we're going to be, isn't it?" cried her husband gaily; and she answered with her boyish smile: "Ah, it's just our luck beginning—the wonderful luck we're always going to have together!"

20

"Of course we must dine with Mrs. Carfry, dearest," Archer said; and his wife looked at him with an anxious frown across the monumental Britannia ware of their lodging house breakfast-table.

In all the rainy desert of autumnal London there were only two people whom the Newland Archers knew; and these two they had sedulously avoided, in conformity with the old New York tradition that it was not "dignified" to force one's self on the notice of one's acquaintances in foreign countries.

Mrs. Archer and Janey, in the course of their visits to Europe, had so unflinchingly lived up to this principle, and met the friendly advances of their fellow-travelers with an air of such impenetrable reserve, that they had almost achieved the record of never having exchanged a word with a "foreigner" other than those employed in hotels and railway-stations. Their own compatriots—save those previously known or properly accredited—they treated with an even more pronounced disdain; so that, unless they ran across a Chivers, a Dagonet or a Mingott, their months abroad were spent in an unbroken *tête-à-tête*. But the utmost precautions are sometimes unavailing; and one night at Botzen one of the two English ladies in the room across the passage (whose names, dress and social situation were already intimately known to Janey) had knocked on the door and asked if Mrs. Archer had a bottle of liniment. The other lady—the intruder's sister, Mrs. Carfry—had been seized with a sudden attack of bronchitis; and Mrs. Archer, who never traveled without a complete family pharmacy, was fortunately able to produce the required remedy.

Mrs. Carfry was very ill, and as she and her sister Miss Harle were traveling alone they were profoundly grateful to the Archer ladies, who supplied them with ingenious comforts and whose efficient maid helped to nurse the invalid back to health.

When the Archers left Botzen they had no idea of ever seeing Mrs. Carfry and Miss Harle again. Nothing, to Mrs. Archer's mind, would have been more "undignified" than to force one's self on the notice of a "foreigner" to whom one had happened to render an accidental service. But Mrs. Carfry and her sister, to whom this point of view was unknown, and who would have found it utterly incomprehensible, felt themselves linked by an eternal gratitude to the "delightful Americans" who had been so kind at Botzen. With touching fidelity they seized every chance of meeting Mrs. Archer and Janey in the course of their continental travels, and displayed a supernatural acuteness in finding out when they were to pass through London on their way to or from the States. The intimacy became indissoluble, and Mrs. Archer and Janey, whenever they alighted at Brown's Hotel, found themselves awaited by two affectionate friends who, like themselves, cultivated ferns in Wardian cases, made macramé lace, read the memoirs of the Baroness Bunsen and had views about the occupants of the leading London pulpits. As Mrs. Archer said, it made "another thing of London" to know Mrs. Carfry and Miss Harle; and by the time that Newland became engaged the tie between the families was so firmly established that it was thought "only right" to send a wedding invitation to the two English ladies, who sent, in return, a pretty bouquet of pressed Alpine flowers under glass. And on the dock, when Newland and his wife sailed for England, Mrs. Archer's last word had been: "You must take May to see Mrs. Carfry."

Newland and his wife had had no idea of obeying this injunction; but Mrs. Carfry, with her usual acuteness, had run them down and sent them an invitation to dine; and it was over this invitation that May Archer was wrinkling her brows across the tea and muffins.

"It's all very well for you, Newland; you *know* them. But I shall feel so shy among a lot of people I've never met. And what shall I wear?"

Newland leaned back in his chair and smiled at her. She looked handsomer and more Diana-like than ever. The moist English air seemed to have deepened the bloom of her cheeks and softened the slight hardness of her virginal features; or else it was simply the inner glow of happiness, shining through like a light under ice.

"Wear, dearest? I thought a trunkful of things had come from Paris last week."

"Yes, of course. I meant to say that I shan't know *which* to wear." She pouted a little. "I've never dined out in London; and I don't want to be ridiculous."

He tried to enter into her perplexity. "But don't Englishwomen dress just like everybody else in the evening?"

"Newland! How can you ask such funny questions? When they go to the theater in old ball-dresses and bare heads."

"Well, perhaps they wear new ball-dresses at home; but at any rate Mrs. Carfry and Miss Harle won't. They'll wear caps like my mother's—and shawls; very soft shawls."

"Yes; but how will the other women be dressed?"

"Not as well as you, dear," he rejoined, wondering what had suddenly developed in her Janey's morbid interest in clothes.

She pushed back her chair with a sigh. "That's dear of you, Newland; but it doesn't help me much."

He had an inspiration. "Why not wear your wedding-dress? That can't be wrong, can it?"

"Oh, dearest! If I only had it here! But it's gone to Paris to be made over for next winter, and Worth hasn't sent it back."

"Oh, well—" said Archer, getting up. "Look here—the fog's lifting. If we made a dash for the National Gallery we might manage to catch a glimpse of the pictures."

The Newland Archers were on their way home, after a three months' wedding-tour which May, in writing to her girl friends, vaguely summarized as "blissful."

They had not gone to the Italian Lakes: on reflection, Archer had not been able to picture his wife in that particular setting. Her own inclination (after a month with the Paris dressmakers) was for mountaineering in July and swimming in August. This plan they punctually fulfilled, spending July at Interlaken and Grindelwald, and August at a little place called Etretat, on the Normandy coast, which someone had recommended as quaint and quiet. Once or twice, in the mountains, Archer had pointed southward and said: "There's Italy"; and May, her feet in a gentian-bed, had smiled cheerfully, and replied: "It would be lovely to go there next winter, if only you didn't have to be in New York."

But in reality traveling interested her even less than he had expected. She regarded it (once her clothes were ordered) as merely an enlarged opportunity for walking, riding, swimming, and trying her hand at the fascinating new game of lawn tennis; and when they finally got back to London (where they were to spend a fortnight while he ordered *his* clothes) she no longer concealed the eagerness with which she looked forward to sailing.

In London nothing interested her but the theaters and the shops; and she found the theaters less exciting than the Paris *cafés chantants* where, under the blossoming horse-chestnuts of the Champs Élysées, she had had the novel experience of looking down from the restaurant terrace on an audience of "cocottes," and having her husband interpret to her as much of the songs as he thought suitable for bridal ears.

Archer had reverted to all his old inherited ideas about marriage. It was less trouble to conform with the tradition and treat May exactly as all his friends treated their wives than to try to put into practice the theories with which his untrammeled bachelorhood had dallied. There was no use in trying to emancipate a wife who had not the dimmest notion that she was not free; and he had long since discovered that May's only use of the liberty she supposed herself to possess would be to lay it on the altar of her wifely adoration. Her innate dignity would always keep her from making the gift abjectly; and a day might even come (as it once had) when she would find strength to take it altogether back if she thought she were doing it for his own good. But with a conception of marriage so uncomplicated and incurious as hers such a crisis could be brought about only by something visibly outrageous in his own conduct; and the fineness of her feeling for him made that unthinkable. Whatever happened, he knew, she would always be loyal, gallant and unresentful; and that pledged him to the practice of the same virtues.

All this tended to draw him back into his old habits of mind. If her simplicity had been the simplicity of pettiness he would have chafed and rebelled; but since the lines of her character, though so few, were on the same fine mould as her face, she became the tutelary divinity of all his old traditions and reverences.

Such qualities were scarcely of the kind to enliven foreign travel, though they made her so easy and pleasant a companion; but he saw at once how they would fall into place in their proper setting. He had no fear of being oppressed by them, for his artistic and intellectual life would go on, as it always had, outside the domestic circle; and within it there would be nothing small and stifling—coming back to his wife would never be like entering a stuffy room after a tramp in the open. And when they had children the vacant corners in both their lives would be filled.

All these things went through his mind during their long slow drive from Mayfair to South Kensington, where Mrs. Carfry and her sister lived. Archer too would have preferred to escape their friends' hospitality: in conformity with the family tradition he had always traveled as a sight-seer and looker-on, affecting a haughty unconsciousness of the presence of his fellow-beings. Once only, just after Harvard, he had spent a few gay weeks at Florence with a band of queer Europeanized Americans, dancing all night with titled ladies in palaces, and gambling half the day with the rakes and dandies of the fashionable club; but it had all seemed to him, though the greatest fun in the world, as unreal as a carnival. These queer cosmopolitan women, deep in complicated love affairs which they appeared to feel the need of retailing to everyone they met, and the magnificent young officers and elderly dyed wits who were the subjects or the recipients of their confidences, were too different from the people Archer had grown up among, too much like expensive and rather malodorous hot-house exotics, to detain his imagination long. To introduce his wife into such a society was out of the question; and in the course of his travels no other had shown any marked eagerness for his company.

Not long after their arrival in London he had run across the Duke of St. Austrey, and the Duke, instantly and cordially recognizing him, had said: "Look me up, won't you?"—but no proper-spirited American would have considered that a suggestion to be acted on, and the meeting was without a sequel. They had even managed to avoid May's English aunt, the banker's wife, who was still in Yorkshire; in fact, they had purposely postponed going to London till the autumn in order that their arrival during the season might not appear pushing and snobbish to these unknown relatives.

"Probably there'll be nobody at Mrs. Carfry's—London's a desert at this season, and you've made yourself much too beautiful," Archer said to May, who sat at his side in the hansom so spotlessly splendid in her sky-blue cloak edged with swansdown that it seemed wicked to expose her to the London grime.

"I don't want them to think that we dress like savages," she replied, with a scorn that Pocahontas might have resented; and he was struck again by the religious reverence of even the most unworldly American women for the social advantages of dress.

"It's their armor," he thought, "their defense against the unknown, and their defiance of it." And he understood for the first time the earnestness with which May, who was incapable of tying a ribbon in her hair to charm him, had gone through the solemn rite of selecting and ordering her extensive wardrobe.

He had been right in expecting the party at Mrs. Carfry's to be a small one. Besides their hostess and her sister, they found, in the long chilly drawing room, only another shawled lady, a genial Vicar who was her husband, a silent lad whom Mrs. Carfry named as her nephew, and a small dark gentleman with lively eyes whom she introduced as his tutor, pronouncing a French name as she did so.

Into this dimly-lit and dim-featured group May Archer floated like a swan with the sunset on her: she seemed larger, fairer, more voluminously rustling than her husband had ever seen her; and he perceived that the rosiness and rustlingness were the tokens of an extreme and infantile shyness.

"What on earth will they expect me to talk about?" her helpless eyes implored him, at the very moment that her dazzling apparition was calling forth the same anxiety in their own bosoms. But beauty, even when distrustful of itself, awakens confidence in the manly heart; and the Vicar and the French-named tutor were soon manifesting to May their desire to put her at her ease.

In spite of their best efforts, however, the dinner was a languishing affair. Archer noticed that his wife's way of showing herself at her ease with foreigners was to become more uncompromisingly local in her references, so that, though her loveliness was an encouragement to admiration, her conversation was a chill to repartee. The Vicar soon abandoned the struggle; but the tutor, who spoke the most fluent and accomplished English, gallantly continued to pour it out to her until the ladies, to the manifest relief of all concerned, went up to the drawing room.

The Vicar, after a glass of port, was obliged to hurry away to a meeting, and the shy nephew, who appeared to be an invalid, was packed off to bed. But Archer and the tutor continued to sit over their wine, and suddenly Archer found himself talking as he had not done since his last symposium with Ned Winsett. The Carfry nephew, it turned out, had been threatened with consumption, and had had to leave Harrow for Switzerland, where he had spent two

years in the milder air of Lake Léman. Being a bookish youth, he
had been entrusted to M. Rivière, who had brought him back to
England, and was to remain with him till he went up to Oxford the
following spring; and M. Rivière added with simplicity that he
should then have to look out for another job.

It seemed impossible, Archer thought, that he should be long
without one, so varied were his interests and so many his gifts. He
was a man of about thirty, with a thin ugly face (May would certainly have called him common-looking) to which the play of his
ideas gave an intense expressiveness; but there was nothing frivolous
or cheap in his animation.

His father, who had died young, had filled a small diplomatic post,
and it had been intended that the son should follow the same career;
but an insatiable taste for letters had thrown the young man into
journalism, then into authorship (apparently unsuccessful), and at
length—after other experiments and vicissitudes which he spared his
listener—into tutoring English youths in Switzerland. Before that,
however, he had lived much in Paris, frequented the Goncourt *gre-
nier*, been advised by Maupassant not to attempt to write (even that
seemed to Archer a dazzling honor!), and had often talked with
Mérimée in his mother's house. He had obviously always been desperately poor and anxious (having a mother and an unmarried sister
to provide for), and it was apparent that his literary ambitions had
failed. His situation, in fact, seemed, materially speaking, no more
brilliant than Ned Winsett's; but he had lived in a world in which,
as he said, no one who loved ideas need hunger mentally. As it was
precisely of that love that poor Winsett was starving to death,
Archer looked with a sort of vicarious envy at this eager impecunious
young man who had fared so richly in his poverty.

"You see, Monsieur, it's worth everything, isn't it, to keep one's intellectual liberty, not to enslave one's powers of appreciation, one's
critical independence? It was because of that that I abandoned journalism, and took to so much duller work: tutoring and private secretaryship. There is a good deal of drudgery, of course; but one preserves one's moral freedom, what we call in French one's *quant à soi*.
And when one hears good talk one can join in it without compromising any opinions but one's own; or one can listen, and answer it inwardly. Ah, good conversation—there's nothing like it, is there? The
air of ideas is the only air worth breathing. And so I have never regretted giving up either diplomacy or journalism—two different

forms of the same self-abdication." He fixed his vivid eyes on Archer as he lit another cigarette. "Voyez-vous, Monsieur, to be able to look life in the face: that's worth living in a garret for, isn't it? But, after all, one must earn enough to pay for the garret; and I confess that to grow old as a private tutor—or a 'private' anything—is almost as chilling to the imagination as a second secretaryship at Bucharest. Sometimes I feel I must make a plunge: an immense plunge. Do you suppose, for instance, there would be any opening for me in America —in New York?"

Archer looked at him with startled eyes. New York, for a young man who had frequented the Goncourts and Flaubert, and who thought the life of ideas the only one worth living! He continued to stare at M. Rivière perplexedly, wondering how to tell him that his very superiorities and advantages would be the surest hindrance to success.

"New York—New York—but must it be especially New York?" he stammered, utterly unable to imagine what lucrative opening his native city could offer to a young man to whom good conversation appeared to be the only necessity.

A sudden flush rose under M. Rivière's sallow skin. "I—I thought it your metropolis: is not the intellectual life more active there?" he rejoined; then, as if fearing to give his hearer the impression of having asked a favor, he went on hastily: "One throws out random suggestions—more to one's self than to others. In reality, I see no immediate prospect—" and rising from his seat he added, without a trace of constraint: "But Mrs. Carfry will think that I ought to be taking you upstairs."

During the homeward drive Archer pondered deeply on this episode. His hour with M. Rivière had put new air into his lungs, and his first impulse had been to invite him to dine the next day; but he was beginning to understand why married men did not always immediately yield to their first impulses.

"That young tutor is an interesting fellow: we had some awfully good talk after dinner about books and things," he threw out tentatively in the hansom.

May roused herself from one of the dreamy silences into which he had read so many meanings before six months of marriage had given him the key to them.

"The little Frenchman? Wasn't he dreadfully common?" she

questioned coldly; and he guessed that she nursed a secret disappointment at having been invited out in London to meet a clergyman and a French tutor. The disappointment was not occasioned by the sentiment ordinarily defined as snobbishness, but by old New York's sense of what was due to it when it risked its dignity in foreign lands. If May's parents had entertained the Carfrys in Fifth Avenue they would have offered them something more substantial than a parson and a schoolmaster.

But Archer was on edge, and took her up.

"Common—common *where?*" he queried; and she returned with unusual readiness: "Why, I should say anywhere but in his schoolroom. Those people are always awkward in society. But then," she added disarmingly, "I suppose I shouldn't have known if he was clever."

Archer disliked her use of the word "clever" almost as much as her use of the word "common"; but he was beginning to fear his tendency to dwell on the things he disliked in her. After all, her point of view had always been the same. It was that of all the people he had grown up among, and he had always regarded it as necessary but negligible. Until a few months ago he had never known a "nice" woman who looked at life differently; and if a man married it must necessarily be among the nice.

"Ah—then I won't ask him to dine!" he concluded with a laugh; and May echoed, bewildered: "Goodness—ask the Carfrys' tutor?"

"Well, not on the same day with the Carfrys, if you prefer I shouldn't. But I did rather want another talk with him. He's looking for a job in New York."

Her surprise increased with her indifference: he almost fancied that she suspected him of being tainted with "foreignness."

"A job in New York? What sort of a job? People don't have French tutors: what does he want to do?"

"Chiefly to enjoy good conversation, I understand," her husband retorted perversely; and she broke into an appreciative laugh. "Oh, Newland, how funny! Isn't that *French?*"

On the whole, he was glad to have the matter settled for him by her refusing to take seriously his wish to invite M. Rivière. Another after-dinner talk would have made it difficult to avoid the question of New York; and the more Archer considered it the less he was able to fit M. Rivière into any conceivable picture of New York as he knew it.

He perceived with a flash of chilling insight that in future many problems would be thus negatively solved for him; but as he paid the hansom and followed his wife's long train into the house he took refuge in the comforting platitude that the first six months were always the most difficult in marriage. "After that I suppose we shall have pretty nearly finished rubbing off each other's angles," he reflected; but the worst of it was that May's pressure was already bearing on the very angles whose sharpness he most wanted to keep.

21

Tʜᴇ small bright lawn stretched away smoothly to the big bright sea.

The turf was hemmed with an edge of scarlet geranium and coleus, and cast-iron vases painted in chocolate color, standing at intervals along the winding path that led to the sea, looped their garlands of petunia and ivy geranium above the neatly raked gravel.

Halfway between the edge of the cliff and the square wooden house (which was also chocolate-colored, but with the tin roof of the verandah striped in yellow and brown to represent an awning) two large targets had been placed against a background of shrubbery. On the other side of the lawn, facing the targets, was pitched a real tent, with benches and garden-seats about it. A number of ladies in summer dresses and gentlemen in gray frock-coats and tall hats stood on the lawn or sat upon the benches; and every now and then a slender girl in starched muslin would step from the tent, bow in hand, and speed her shaft at one of the targets, while the spectators interrupted their talk to watch the result.

Newland Archer, standing on the verandah of the house, looked curiously down upon this scene. On each side of the shiny painted steps was a large blue china flower-pot on a bright yellow china stand. A spiky green plant filled each pot, and below the verandah ran a wide border of blue hydrangeas edged with more red geraniums. Behind him, the French windows of the drawing rooms through which he had passed gave glimpses, between swaying lace curtains, of glassy parquet floors islanded with chintz *poufs*, dwarf armchairs, and velvet tables covered with trifles in silver.

The Newport Archery Club always held its August meeting at the Beauforts'. The sport, which had hitherto known no rival but croquet, was beginning to be discarded in favor of lawn tennis; but the latter game was still considered too rough and inelegant for social occasions, and as an opportunity to show off pretty dresses and graceful attitudes the bow and arrow held their own.

Archer looked down with wonder at the familiar spectacle. It surprised him that life should be going on in the old way when his own reactions to it had so completely changed. It was Newport that had first brought home to him the extent of the change. In New York, during the previous winter, after he and May had settled down in the new greenish-yellow house with the bow-window and the Pompeian vestibule, he had dropped back with relief into the old routine of the office, and the renewal of this daily activity had served as a link with his former self. Then there had been the pleasurable excitement of choosing a showy gray stepper for May's brougham (the Wellands had given the carriage), and the abiding occupation and interest of arranging his new library, which, in spite of family doubts and disapprovals, had been carried out as he had dreamed, with a dark embossed paper, Eastlake bookcases and "sincere" armchairs and tables. At the Century he had found Winsett again, and at the Knickerbocker the fashionable young men of his own set; and what with the hours dedicated to the law and those given to dining out or entertaining friends at home, with an occasional evening at the Opera or the play, the life he was living had still seemed a fairly real and inevitable sort of business.

But Newport represented the escape from duty into an atmosphere of unmitigated holiday-making. Archer had tried to persuade May to spend the summer on a remote island off the coast of Maine (called, appropriately enough, Mount Desert), where a few hardy Bostonians and Philadelphians were camping in "native" cottages, and whence came reports of enchanting scenery and a wild, almost trapper-like existence amid woods and waters.

But the Wellands always went to Newport, where they owned one of the square boxes on the cliffs, and their son-in-law could adduce no good reason why he and May should not join them there. As Mrs. Welland rather tartly pointed out, it was hardly worth while for May to have worn herself out trying on summer clothes in Paris if she was not to be allowed to wear them; and this argument was of a kind to which Archer had as yet found no answer.

May herself could not understand his obscure reluctance to fall in with so reasonable and pleasant a way of spending the summer. She reminded him that he had always liked Newport in his bachelor days, and as this was indisputable he could only profess that he was sure he was going to like it better than ever now that they were to be there together. But as he stood on the Beaufort verandah and looked out on the brightly peopled lawn it came home to him with a shiver that he was not going to like it at all.

It was not May's fault, poor dear. If, now and then, during their travels, they had fallen slightly out of step, harmony had been restored by their return to the conditions she was used to. He had always foreseen that she would not disappoint him; and he had been right. He had married (as most young men did) because he had met a perfectly charming girl at the moment when a series of rather aimless sentimental adventures were ending in premature disgust; and she had represented peace, stability, comradeship, and the steadying sense of an unescapable duty.

He could not say that he had been mistaken in his choice, for she had fulfilled all that he had expected. It was undoubtedly gratifying to be the husband of one of the handsomest and most popular young married women in New York, especially when she was also one of the sweetest-tempered and most reasonable of wives; and Archer had never been insensible to such advantages. As for the momentary madness which had fallen upon him on the eve of his marriage, he had trained himself to regard it as the last of his discarded experiments. The idea that he could ever, in his senses, have dreamed of marrying the Countess Olenska had become almost unthinkable, and she remained in his memory simply as the most plaintive and poignant of a line of ghosts.

But all these abstractions and eliminations made of his mind a rather empty and echoing place, and he supposed that was one of the reasons why the busy animated people on the Beaufort lawn shocked him as if they had been children playing in a graveyard.

He heard a murmur of skirts beside him, and the Marchioness Manson fluttered out of the drawing-room window. As usual, she was extraordinarily festooned and bedizened, with a limp Leghorn hat anchored to her head by many windings of faded gauze, and a little black velvet parasol on a carved ivory handle absurdly balanced over her much larger hat-brim.

"My dear Newland, I had no idea that you and May had arrived! You yourself came only yesterday, you say? Ah, business—business—professional duties . . . I understand. Many husbands, I know, find it impossible to join their wives here except for the weekend."

She cocked her head on one side and languished at him through screwed-up eyes. "But marriage is one long sacrifice, as I used often to remind my Ellen—"

Archer's heart stopped with a queer jerk which it had given once before, and which seemed suddenly to slam a door between himself and the outer world; but this break of continuity must have been of the briefest, for he presently heard Medora answering a question he had apparently found voice to put.

"No, I am not staying here, but with the Blenkers, in their delicious solitude at Portsmouth. Beaufort was kind enough to send his famous trotters for me this morning, so that I might have at least a glimpse of one of Regina's garden-parties; but this evening I go back to rural life. The Blenkers, dear original beings, have hired a primitive old farm-house at Portsmouth where they gather about them representative people. . . ." She drooped slightly beneath her protecting brim, and added with a faint blush: "This week Dr. Agathon Carver is holding a series of Inner Thought meetings there. A contrast indeed to this gay scene of worldly pleasure—but then I have always lived on contrasts! To me the only death is monotony. I always say to Ellen: Beware of monotony; it's the mother of all the deadly sins. But my poor child is going through a phase of exaltation, of abhorrence of the world. You know, I suppose, that she has declined all invitations to stay at Newport, even with her grandmother Mingott? I could hardly persuade her to come with me to the Blenkers', if you believe it! The life she leads is morbid, unnatural. Ah, if she had only listened to me when it was still possible . . . When the door was still open. . . . But shall we go down and watch this absorbing match? I hear your May is one of the competitors."

Strolling toward them from the tent Beaufort advanced over the lawn, tall, heavy, too tightly buttoned into a London frock-coat, with one of his own orchids in its buttonhole. Archer, who had not seen him for two or three months, was struck by the change in his appearance. In the hot summer light his floridness seemed heavy and bloated, and but for his erect square-shouldered walk he would have looked like an over-fed and over-dressed old man.

There were all sorts of rumors afloat about Beaufort. In the spring he had gone off on a long cruise to the West Indies in his new steam-yacht, and it was reported that, at various points where he had touched, a lady resembling Miss Fanny Ring had been seen in his company. The steam-yacht, built in the Clyde, and fitted with tiled bathrooms and other unheard-of luxuries, was said to have cost him half a million; and the pearl necklace which he had presented to his wife on his return was as magnificent as such expiatory offerings are apt to be. Beaufort's fortune was substantial enough to stand the strain; and yet the disquieting rumors persisted, not only in Fifth Avenue but in Wall Street. Some people said he had speculated unfortunately in railways, others that he was being bled by one of the most insatiable members of her profession; and to every report of threatened insolvency Beaufort replied by a fresh extravagance: the building of a new row of orchid-houses, the purchase of a new string of race-horses, or the addition of a new Meissonnier or Cabanel to his picture gallery.

He advanced toward the Marchioness and Newland with his usual half-sneering smile. "Hullo, Medora! Did the trotters do their business? Forty minutes, eh? . . . Well, that's not so bad, considering your nerves had to be spared." He shook hands with Archer, and then, turning back with them, placed himself on Mrs. Manson's other side, and said, in a low voice, a few words which their companion did not catch.

The Marchioness replied by one of her queer foreign jerks, and a "Que voulez-vous?" which deepened Beaufort's frown; but he produced a good semblance of a congratulatory smile as he glanced at Archer to say: "You know May's going to carry off the first prize."

"Ah, then it remains in the family," Medora rippled; and at that moment they reached the tent and Mrs. Beaufort met them in a girlish cloud of mauve muslin and floating veils.

May Welland was just coming out of the tent. In her white dress, with a pale green ribbon about the waist and a wreath of ivy on her hat, she had the same Diana-like aloofness as when she had entered the Beaufort ballroom on the night of her engagement. In the interval not a thought seemed to have passed behind her eyes or a feeling through her heart; and though her husband knew that she had the capacity for both he marveled afresh at the way in which experience dropped away from her.

She had her bow and arrow in her hand, and placing herself on the chalk-mark traced on the turf she lifted the bow to her shoulder and took aim. The attitude was so full of a classic grace that a murmur of appreciation followed her appearance, and Archer felt the glow of proprietorship that so often cheated him into momentary well-being. Her rivals—Mrs. Reggie Chivers, the Merry girls, and divers rosy

Thorleys, Dagonets and Mingotts, stood behind her in a lovely anxious group, brown heads and golden bent above the scores, and pale muslins and flower-wreathed hats mingled in a tender rainbow. All were young and pretty, and bathed in summer bloom; but not one had the nymph-like ease of his wife, when, with tense muscles and happy frown, she bent her soul upon some feat of strength.

"Gad," Archer heard Lawrence Lefferts say, "not one of the lot holds the bow as she does"; and Beaufort retorted: "Yes; but that's the only kind of target she'll ever hit."

Archer felt irrationally angry. His host's contemptuous tribute to May's "niceness" was just what a husband should have wished to hear said of his wife. The fact that a coarse-minded man found her lacking in attraction was simply another proof of her quality; yet the words sent a faint shiver through his heart. What if "niceness" carried to that supreme degree were only a negation, the curtain dropped before an emptiness? As he looked at May, returning flushed and calm from her final bull's-eye, he had the feeling that he had never yet lifted that curtain.

She took the congratulations of her rivals and of the rest of the company with the simplicity that was her crowning grace. No one could ever be jealous of her triumphs because she managed to give the feeling that she would have been just as serene if she had missed them. But when her eyes met her husband's her face glowed with the pleasure she saw in his.

Mrs. Welland's basket-work pony-carriage was waiting for them, and they drove off among the dispersing carriages, May handling the reins and Archer sitting at her side.

The afternoon sunlight still lingered upon the bright lawns and shrubberies, and up and down Bellevue Avenue rolled a double line of victorias, dog-carts, landaus and "vis-à-vis," carrying well-dressed ladies and gentlemen away from the Beaufort garden-party, or homeward from their daily afternoon turn along the Ocean Drive.

"Shall we go to see Granny?" May suddenly proposed. "I should like to tell her myself that I've won the prize. There's lots of time before dinner."

Archer acquiesced, and she turned the ponies down Narragansett Avenue, crossed Spring Street and drove out toward the rocky moorland beyond. In this unfashionable region Catherine the Great, always indifferent to precedent and thrifty of purse, had built herself in her youth a many-peaked and cross-beamed *cottage orné* on a bit of cheap land overlooking the bay. Here, in a thicket of stunted oaks, her verandahs spread themselves above the island-dotted waters. A winding drive led up between iron stags and blue glass balls embedded in mounds of geraniums to a front door of highly-varnished walnut under a striped verandah-roof; and behind it ran a narrow hall with a black and yellow star-patterned parquet floor, upon which opened four small square rooms with heavy flock-papers under ceilings on which an Italian house-painter had lavished all the divinities of Olympus. One of these rooms had been turned into a bedroom by Mrs. Mingott when the burden of flesh descended on her, and in the adjoining one she spent her days, enthroned in a large armchair between the open door and window, and perpetually waving a palm-leaf fan which the prodigious projection of her bosom kept so far from the rest of her person that the air it set in motion stirred only the fringe of the antimacassars on the chair-arms.

Since she had been the means of hastening his marriage old Catherine had shown to Archer the cordiality which a service rendered excites toward the person served. She was persuaded that irrepressible passion was the cause of his impatience; and being an ardent admirer of impulsiveness (when it did not lead to the spending of money) she always received him with a genial twinkle of complicity and a play of allusion to which May seemed fortunately impervious.

She examined and appraised with much interest the diamond-tipped arrow which had been pinned on May's bosom at the conclusion of the match, remarking that in her day a filigree brooch would have been thought enough, but that there was no denying that Beaufort did things handsomely.

"Quite an heirloom, in fact, my dear," the old lady chuckled. "You must leave it in fee to your eldest girl." She pinched May's white arm and watched the color flood her face. "Well, well, what have I said to make you shake out the red flag? Ain't there going to be any daughters—only boys, eh? Good gracious, look at her blushing again all over her blushes! What—can't I say that either? Mercy me —when my children beg me to have all those gods and goddesses painted out overhead I always say I'm too thankful to have somebody about me that *nothing* can shock!"

Archer burst into a laugh, and May echoed it, crimson to the eyes.

"Well, now tell me all about the party, please, my dears, for I shall never get a straight word about it out of that silly Medora," the ancestress continued; and, as May exclaimed: "Aunt Medora? But I thought she was going back to Portsmouth?" she answered placidly: "So she is—but she's got to come here first to pick up Ellen. Ah— you didn't know Ellen had come to spend the day with me? Such fol-de-rol, her not coming for the summer; but I gave up arguing with young people about fifty years ago. Ellen—*Ellen!*" she cried in her shrill old voice, trying to bend forward far enough to catch a glimpse of the lawn beyond the verandah.

There was no answer, and Mrs. Mingott rapped impatiently with her stick on the shiny floor. A mulatto maidservant in a bright tur- ban, replying to the summons, informed her mistress that she had seen "Miss Ellen" going down the path to the shore; and Mrs. Min- gott turned to Archer.

"Run down and fetch her, like a good grandson; this pretty lady will describe the party to me," she said; and Archer stood up as if in a dream.

He had heard the Countess Olenska's name pronounced often enough during the year and a half since they had last met, and was even familiar with the main incidents of her life in the interval. He knew that she had spent the previous summer at Newport, where she appeared to have gone a great deal into society, but that in the au- tumn she had suddenly sub-let the "perfect house" which Beaufort had been at such pains to find for her, and decided to establish her- self in Washington. There, during the winter, he had heard of her (as one always heard of pretty women in Washington) as shining in the "brilliant diplomatic society" that was supposed to make up for the social shortcomings of the Administration. He had listened to these accounts, and to various contradictory reports on her appear- ance, her conversation, her point of view and her choice of friends, with the detachment with which one listens to reminiscences of someone long since dead; not till Medora suddenly spoke her name at the archery match had Ellen Olenska become a living presence to him again. The Marchioness's foolish lisp had called up a vision of the little fire-lit drawing room and the sound of the carriage-wheels returning down the deserted street. He thought of a story he had read, of some peasant children in Tuscany lighting a bunch of straw in a wayside cavern, and revealing old silent images in their painted tomb. . . .

The way to the shore descended from the bank on which the house was perched to a walk above the water planted with weeping

willows. Through their veil Archer caught the glint of the Lime
Rock, with its white-washed turret and the tiny house in which the
heroic lighthouse keeper, Ida Lewis, was living her last venerable
years. Beyond it lay the flat reaches and ugly government chimneys
of Goat Island, the bay spreading northward in a shimmer of gold to
Prudence Island with its low growth of oaks, and the shores of
Conanicut faint in the sunset haze.

From the willow walk projected a slight wooden pier ending in a
sort of pagoda-like summer-house; and in the pagoda a lady stood,
leaning against the rail, her back to the shore. Archer stopped at the
sight as if he had waked from sleep. That vision of the past was a
dream, and the reality was what awaited him in the house on the
bank overhead: was Mrs. Welland's pony-carriage circling around
and around the oval at the door, was May sitting under the shame-
less Olympians and glowing with secret hopes, was the Welland villa
at the far end of Bellevue Avenue, and Mr. Welland, already dressed
for dinner, and pacing the drawing-room floor, watch in hand, with
dyspeptic impatience—for it was one of the houses in which one always knew exactly what is happening at a given hour.

"What am I? A son-in-law—" Archer thought.

The figure at the end of the pier had not moved. For a long moment the young man stood halfway down the bank, gazing at the
bay furrowed with the coming and going of sailboats, yacht-launches,
fishing-craft and the trailing black coal-barges hauled by noisy tugs.
The lady in the summer-house seemed to be held by the same sight.
Beyond the gray bastions of Fort Adams a long-drawn sunset was
splintering up into a thousand fires, and the radiance caught the sail
of a catboat as it beat out through the channel between the Lime
Rock and the shore. Archer, as he watched, remembered the scene in
The Shaughraun, and Montague lifting Ada Dyas's ribbon to his lips
without her knowing that he was in the room.

"She doesn't know—she hasn't guessed. Shouldn't I know if she
came up behind me; I wonder?" he mused; and suddenly he said to
himself: "If she doesn't turn before that sail crosses the Lime Rock
light I'll go back."

The boat was gliding out on the receding tide. It slid before the
Lime Rock, blotted out Ida Lewis's little house, and passed across
the turret in which the light was hung. Archer waited till a wide
space of water sparkled between the last reef of the island and the

stern of the boat; but still the figure in the summer-house did not move.

He turned and walked up the hill.

"I'm sorry you didn't find Ellen—I should have liked to see her again," May said as they drove home through the dusk. "But perhaps she wouldn't have cared—she seems so changed."

"Changed?" echoed her husband in a colorless voice, his eyes fixed on the ponies' twitching ears.

"So indifferent to her friends, I mean; giving up New York and her house, and spending her time with such queer people. Fancy how hideously uncomfortable she must be at the Blenkers'! She says she does it to keep Aunt Medora out of mischief: to prevent her marrying dreadful people. But I sometimes think we've always bored her."

Archer made no answer, and she continued, with a tinge of hardness that he had never before noticed in her frank fresh voice: "After all, I wonder if she wouldn't be happier with her husband."

He burst into a laugh. "*Sancta simplicitas!*" he exclaimed; and as she turned a puzzled frown on him he added: "I don't think I ever heard you say a cruel thing before."

"Cruel?"

"Well—watching the contortions of the damned is supposed to be a favorite sport of the angels; but I believe even they don't think people happier in hell."

"It's a pity she ever married abroad then," said May, in the placid tone with which her mother met Mr. Welland's vagaries; and Archer felt himself gently relegated to the category of unreasonable husbands.

They drove down Bellevue Avenue and turned in between the chamfered wooden gate-posts surmounted by cast-iron lamps which marked the approach to the Welland villa. Lights were already shining through its windows, and Archer, as the carriage stopped, caught a glimpse of his father-in-law, exactly as he had pictured him, pacing the drawing room, watch in hand and wearing the pained expression that he had long since found to be much more efficacious than anger.

The young man, as he followed his wife into the hall, was conscious of a curious reversal of mood. There was something about the luxury of the Welland house and the density of the Welland atmosphere, so charged with minute observances and exactions, that always stole into his system like a narcotic. The heavy carpets, the watchful servants, the perpetually reminding tick of disciplined clocks, the perpetually renewed stack of cards and invitations on the hall table, the whole chain of tyrannical trifles binding one hour to the next, and each member of the household to all the others, made any less systematized and affluent existence seem unreal and precarious. But now it was the Welland house, and the life he was expected to lead in it, that had become unreal and irrelevant, and the brief scene on the shore, when he had stood irresolute, halfway down the bank, was as close to him as the blood in his veins.

All night he lay awake in the big chintz bedroom at May's side, watching the moonlight slant along the carpet, and thinking of Ellen Olenska driving home across the gleaming beaches behind Beaufort's trotters.

22

"A party for the Blenkers—the Blenkers?"

Mr. Welland laid down his knife and fork and looked anxiously and incredulously across the luncheon table at his wife, who, adjusting her gold eye-glasses, read aloud, in the tone of high comedy: "Professor and Mrs. Emerson Sillerton request the pleasure of Mr. and Mrs. Welland's company at the meeting of the Wednesday Afternoon Club on August 25th at 3 o'clock punctually. To meet Mrs. and the Misses Blenker.

Red Gables, Catherine Street.   R. S. V. P."

"Good gracious—" Mr. Welland gasped, as if a second reading had been necessary to bring the monstrous absurdity of the thing home to him.

"Poor Amy Sillerton—you never can tell what her husband will do next," Mrs. Welland sighed. "I suppose he's just discovered the Blenkers."

Professor Emerson Sillerton was a thorn in the side of Newport society; and a thorn that could not be plucked out, for it grew on a venerable and venerated family tree. He was, as people said, a man who had had "every advantage." His father was Sillerton Jackson's uncle, his mother a Pennilow of Boston; on each side there was wealth and position, and mutual suitability. Nothing—as Mrs. Welland had often remarked—nothing on earth obliged Emerson Sillerton to be an archeologist, or indeed a Professor of any sort, or to live in Newport in winter, or do any of the other revolutionary things that he did. But at least, if he was going to break with tradition and flout society in the face, he need not have married poor Amy Dagonet, who had a right to expect "something different," and money enough to keep her own carriage.

No one in the Mingott set could understand why Amy Sillerton had submitted so tamely to the eccentricities of a husband who filled the house with long-haired men and short-haired women, and, when he traveled, took her to explore tombs in Yucatan instead of going to Paris or Italy. But there they were, set in their ways, and apparently unaware that they were different from other people; and when they gave one of their dreary annual garden-parties every family on the Cliffs, because of the Sillerton-Pennilow-Dagonet connection, had to draw lots and send an unwilling representative.

"It's a wonder," Mrs. Welland remarked, "that they didn't choose the Cup Race day! Do you remember, two years ago, their giving a party for a black man on the day of Julia Mingott's *thé dansant?* Luckily this time there's nothing else going on that I know of—for of course some of us will have to go."

Mr. Welland sighed nervously. " 'Some of us,' my dear—more than one? Three o'clock is such a very awkward hour. I have to be here at half-past three to take my drops: it's really no use trying to follow Bencomb's new treatment if I don't do it systematically; and if I join you later, of course I shall miss my drive." At the thought he laid down his knife and fork again, and a flush of anxiety rose to his finely-wrinkled cheek.

"There's no reason why you should go at all, my dear," his wife answered with a cheerfulness that had become automatic. "I have some cards to leave at the other end of Bellevue Avenue, and I'll drop in at about half-past three and stay long enough to make poor Amy feel that she hasn't been slighted." She glanced hesitatingly at her daughter. "And if Newland's afternoon is provided for perhaps May can drive you out with the ponies, and try their new russet harness."

It was a principle in the Welland family that people's days and hours should be what Mrs. Welland called "provided for." The melancholy possibility of having to "kill time" (especially for those who did not care for whist or solitaire) was a vision that haunted her as the specter of the unemployed haunts the philanthropist. Another of her principles was that parents should never (at least visibly) interfere with the plans of their married children; and the difficulty of adjusting this respect for May's independence with the exigency of Mr. Welland's claims could be overcome only by the exercise of an ingenuity which left not a second of Mrs. Welland's own time unprovided for.

"Of course I'll drive with Papa—I'm sure Newland will find something to do," May said, in a tone that gently reminded her husband of his lack of response. It was a cause of constant distress to Mrs. Welland that her son-in-law showed so little foresight in planning his days. Often already, during the fortnight that he had passed under her roof, when she enquired how he meant to spend his afternoon, he had answered paradoxically: "Oh, I think for a change I'll just save it instead of spending it—" and once, when she and May had had to go on a long-postponed round of afternoon calls, he had confessed to having lain all the afternoon under a rock on the beach below the house.

"Newland never seems to look ahead," Mrs. Welland once ventured to complain to her daughter; and May answered serenely: "No; but you see it doesn't matter, because when there's nothing particular to do he reads a book."

"Ah, yes—like his father!" Mrs. Welland agreed, as if allowing for an inherited oddity; and after that the question of Newland's unemployment was tacitly dropped.

Nevertheless, as the day for the Sillerton reception approached, May began to show a natural solicitude for his welfare, and to suggest a tennis match at the Chiverses', or a sail on Julius Beaufort's cutter, as a means of atoning for her temporary desertion. "I shall be back by six, you know, dear: Papa never drives later than that—" and she was not reassured till Archer said that he thought of hiring a run-about and driving up the island to a stud-farm to look at a second horse for her brougham. They had been looking for this horse for some time, and the suggestion was so acceptable that May glanced at her mother as if to say: "You see he knows how to plan out his time as well as any of us."

The idea of the stud-farm and the brougham horse had germinated in Archer's mind on the very day when the Emerson Sillerton invitation had first been mentioned; but he had kept it to himself as if there were something clandestine in the plan, and discovery might prevent its execution. He had, however, taken the precaution to engage in advance a run-about with a pair of old livery-stable trotters that could still do their eighteen miles on level roads; and at two o'clock, hastily deserting the luncheon-table, he sprang into the light carriage and drove off.

The day was perfect. A breeze from the north drove little puffs of white cloud across an ultramarine sky, with a bright sea running under it. Bellevue Avenue was empty at that hour, and after dropping the stable-lad at the corner of Mill Street Archer turned down the Old Beach Road and drove across Eastman's Beach.

He had the feeling of unexplained excitement with which, on half-holidays at school, he used to start off into the unknown. Taking his pair at an easy gait, he counted on reaching the stud-farm, which was not far beyond Paradise Rocks, before three o'clock; so that, after looking over the horse (and trying him if he seemed promising) he would still have four golden hours to dispose of.

As soon as he heard of the Sillertons' party he had said to himself that the Marchioness Manson would certainly come to Newport with the Blenkers, and that Madame Olenska might again take the opportunity of spending the day with her grandmother. At any rate, the Blenker habitation would probably be deserted, and he would be able, without indiscretion, to satisfy a vague curiosity concerning it. He was not sure that he wanted to see the Countess Olenska again; but ever since he had looked at her from the path above the bay he had wanted, irrationally and indescribably, to see the place she was living in, and to follow the movements of her imagined figure as he had watched the real one in the summer-house. The longing was with him day and night, an incessant undefinable craving, like the sudden whim of a sick man for food or drink once tasted and long since forgotten. He could not see beyond the craving, or picture what it might lead to, for he was not conscious of any wish to speak to Madame Olenska or to hear her voice. He simply felt that if he could carry away the vision of the spot of earth she walked on, and the way the sky and sea enclosed it, the rest of the world might seem less empty.

When he reached the stud-farm a glance showed him that the horse was not what he wanted; nevertheless he took a turn behind it in order to prove to himself that he was not in a hurry. But at three o'clock he shook out the reins over the trotters and turned into the by-roads leading to Portsmouth. The wind had dropped and a faint haze on the horizon showed that a fog was waiting to steal up the Saconnet on the turn of the tide; but all about him fields and woods were steeped in golden light.

He drove past gray-shingled farm-houses in orchards, past hay-fields and groves of oak, past villages with white steeples rising sharply into the fading sky; and at last, after stopping to ask the way of some men at work in a field, he turned down a lane between high banks of goldenrod and brambles. At the end of the lane was the blue glimmer of the river; to the left, standing in front of a clump of oaks and maples, he saw a long tumbledown house with white paint peeling from its clapboards.

On the road-side facing the gateway stood one of the open sheds in which the New Englander shelters his farming implements and visitors "hitch" their "teams." Archer, jumping down, led his pair into the shed, and after tying them to a post turned toward the house. The patch of lawn before it had relapsed into a hay-field; but to the left an overgrown box-garden full of dahlias and rusty rose-bushes encircled a ghostly summer-house of trellis-work that had once been white, surmounted by a wooden Cupid who had lost his bow and arrow but continued to take ineffectual aim.

Archer leaned for a while against the gate. No one was in sight, and not a sound came from the open windows of the house: a grizzled Newfoundland dozing before the door seemed as ineffectual a guardian as the arrowless Cupid. It was strange to think that this place of silence and decay was the home of the turbulent Blenkers; yet Archer was sure that he was not mistaken.

For a long time he stood there, content to take in the scene, and gradually falling under its drowsy spell; but at length he roused himself to the sense of the passing time. Should he look his fill and then drive away? He stood irresolute, wishing suddenly to see the inside of the house, so that he might picture the room that Madame Olenska sat in. There was nothing to prevent his walking up to the door and ringing the bell; if, as he supposed, she was away with the rest of the party, he could easily give his name, and ask permission to go into the sitting room to write a message.

But instead, he crossed the lawn and turned toward the box-garden. As he entered it he caught sight of something bright-colored in the summer-house, and presently made it out to be a pink parasol. The parasol drew him like a magnet: he was sure it was hers. He went into the summer-house, and sitting down on the rickety seat picked up the silken thing and looked at its carved handle, which was made of some rare wood that gave out an aromatic scent. Archer lifted the handle to his lips.

He heard a rustle of skirts against the box, and sat motionless, leaning on the parasol handle with clasped hands, and letting the rustle come nearer without lifting his eyes. He had always known that this must happen. . . .

"Oh, Mr. Archer!" exclaimed a loud young voice; and looking up he saw before him the youngest and largest of the Blenker girls, blonde and blowsy, in bedraggled muslin. A red blotch on one of her cheeks seemed to show that it had recently been pressed against a pillow, and her half-awakened eyes stared at him hospitably but confusedly.

"Gracious—where did you drop from? I must have been sound asleep in the hammock. Everybody else has gone to Newport. Did you ring?" she incoherently enquired.

Archer's confusion was greater than hers. "I—no—that is, I was just going to. I had to come up the island to see about a horse, and I drove over on a chance of finding Mrs. Blenker and your visitors. But the house seemed empty—so I sat down to wait."

Miss Blenker, shaking off the fumes of sleep, looked at him with increasing interest. "The house *is* empty. Mother's not here, or the Marchioness—or anybody but me." Her glance became faintly reproachful. "Didn't you know that Professor and Mrs. Sillerton are giving a garden-party for mother and all of us this afternoon? It was too unlucky that I couldn't go; but I've had a sore throat, and mother was afraid of the drive home this evening. Did you ever know anything so disappointing? Of course," she added gaily, "I shouldn't have minded half as much if I'd known you were coming."

Symptoms of a lumbering coquetry became visible in her, and Archer found the strength to break in: "But Madame Olenska—has she gone to Newport too?"

Miss Blenker looked at him with surprise. "Madame Olenska—didn't you know she'd been called away?"

"Called away?—"

"Oh, my best parasol! I lent it to that goose of a Katie, because it matched her ribbons, and the careless thing must have dropped it here. We Blenkers are all like that . . . real Bohemians!" Recovering the sunshade with a powerful hand she unfurled it and suspended its rosy dome above her head. "Yes, Ellen was called away yesterday: she lets us call her Ellen, you know. A telegram came from Boston: she said she might be gone for two days. I do *love* the way she does her hair, don't you?" Miss Blenker rambled on.

Archer continued to stare through her as though she had been transparent. All he saw was the trumpery parasol that arched its pinkness above her giggling head.

After a moment he ventured: "You don't happen to know why

Madame Olenska went to Boston? I hope it was not on account of bad news?"

Miss Blenker took this with a cheerful incredulity. "Oh, I don't believe so. She didn't tell us what was in the telegram. I think she didn't want the Marchioness to know. She's so romantic-looking, isn't she? Doesn't she remind you of Mrs. Scott-Siddons when she reads *Lady Geraldine's Courtship?* Did you never hear her?"

Archer was dealing hurriedly with crowding thoughts. His whole future seemed suddenly to be unrolled before him; and passing down its endless emptiness he saw the dwindling figure of a man to whom nothing was ever to happen. He glanced about him at the unpruned garden, the tumbledown house, and the oak-grove under which the dusk was gathering. It had seemed so exactly the place in which he ought to have found Madame Olenska; and she was far away, and even the pink sunshade was not hers. . . .

He frowned and hesitated. "You don't know, I suppose—I shall be in Boston tomorrow. If I could manage to see her—"

He felt that Miss Blenker was losing interest in him, though her smile persisted. "Oh, of course; how lovely of you! She's staying at the Parker House; it must be horrible there in this weather."

After that Archer was but intermittently aware of the remarks they exchanged. He could only remember stoutly resisting her entreaty that he should await the returning family and have high tea with them before he drove home. At length, with his hostess still at his side, he passed out of range of the wooden Cupid, unfastened his horses and drove off. At the turn of the lane he saw Miss Blenker standing at the gate and waving the pink parasol.

23

THE next morning, when Archer got out of the Fall River train, he emerged upon a steaming mid-summer Boston. The streets near the station were full of the smell of beer and coffee and decaying fruit, and a shirt-sleeved populace moved through them with the intimate abandon of boarders going down the passage to the bathroom.

Archer found a cab and drove to the Somerset Club for breakfast. Even the fashionable quarters had the air of untidy domesticity to which no excess of heat ever degrades the European cities. Caretakers in calico lounged on the doorsteps of the wealthy, and the Common looked like a pleasure-ground on the morrow of a Masonic picnic. If Archer had tried to imagine Ellen Olenska in improbable scenes he could not have called up any into which it was more difficult to fit her than this heat-prostrated and deserted Boston.

He breakfasted with appetite and method, beginning with a slice of melon, and studying a morning paper while he waited for his toast and scrambled eggs. A new sense of energy and activity had possessed him ever since he had announced to May the night before that he had business in Boston, and should take the Fall River boat that night and go on to New York the following evening. It had always been understood that he would return to town early in the week, and when he got back from his expedition to Portsmouth a letter from the office, which fate had conspicuously placed on a corner of the hall table, sufficed to justify his sudden change of plan. He was even ashamed of the ease with which the whole thing had been done: it reminded him, for an uncomfortable moment, of Lawrence Lefferts's masterly contrivances for securing his freedom. But this did not long trouble him, for he was not in an analytic mood.

After breakfast he smoked a cigarette and glanced over the *Com-*

mercial Advertiser. While he was thus engaged two or three men he knew came in, and the usual greetings were exchanged: it was the same world after all, though he had such a queer sense of having slipped through the meshes of time and space.

He looked at his watch, and finding that it was half-past nine got up and went into the writing room. There he wrote a few lines, and ordered a messenger to take a cab to the Parker House and wait for the answer. He then sat down behind another newspaper and tried to calculate how long it would take a cab to get to the Parker House.

"The lady was out, sir," he suddenly heard a waiter's voice at his elbow; and he stammered: "Out?—" as if it were a word in a strange language.

He got up and went into the hall. It must be a mistake: she could not be out at that hour. He flushed with anger at his own stupidity: why had he not sent the note as soon as he arrived?

He found his hat and stick and went forth into the street. The city had suddenly become as strange and vast and empty as if he were a traveler from distant lands. For a moment he stood on the doorstep hesitating; then he decided to go to the Parker House. What if the messenger had been misinformed, and she were still there?

He started to walk across the Common; and on the first bench, under a tree, he saw her sitting. She had a gray silk sunshade over her head—how could he ever have imagined her with a pink one? As he approached he was struck by her listless attitude: she sat there as if she had nothing else to do. He saw her drooping profile, and the knot of hair fastened low in the neck under her dark hat, and the long wrinkled glove on the hand that held the sunshade. He came a step or two nearer, and she turned and looked at him.

"Oh"—she said; and for the first time he noticed a startled look on her face; but in another moment it gave way to a slow smile of wonder and contentment.

"Oh"—she murmured again, on a different note, as he stood looking down at her; and without rising she made a place for him on the bench.

"I'm here on business—just got here," Archer explained; and, without knowing why, he suddenly began to feign astonishment at seeing her. "But what on earth are *you* doing in this wilderness?" He had really no idea what he was saying: he felt as if he were shouting at her across endless distances, and she might vanish again before he could overtake her.

"I? Oh, I'm here on business too," she answered, turning her head toward him so that they were face to face. The words hardly reached him: he was aware only of her voice, and of the startling fact that not an echo of it had remained in his memory. He had not even remembered that it was low-pitched, with a faint roughness on the consonants.

"You do your hair differently," he said, his heart beating as if he had uttered something irrevocable.

"Differently? No—it's only that I do it as best I can when I'm without Nastasia."

"Nastasia; but isn't she with you?"

"No; I'm alone. For two days it was not worthwhile to bring her."

"You're alone—at the Parker House?"

She looked at him with a flash of her old malice. "Does it strike you as dangerous?"

"No; not dangerous—"

"But unconventional? I see; I suppose it is." She considered a moment. "I hadn't thought of it, because I've just done something so much more unconventional." The faint tinge of irony lingered in her eyes. "I've just refused to take back a sum of money—that belonged to me."

Archer sprang up and moved a step or two away. She had furled her parasol and sat absently drawing patterns on the gravel. Presently he came back and stood before her.

"Someone—has come here to meet you?"

"Yes."

"With this offer?"

She nodded.

"And you refused—because of the conditions?"

"I refused," she said after a moment.

He sat down by her again. "What were the conditions?"

"Oh, they were not onerous: just to sit at the head of his table now and then."

There was another interval of silence. Archer's heart had slammed itself shut in the queer way it had, and he sat vainly groping for a word.

"He wants you back—at any price?"

"Well—a considerable price. At least the sum is considerable for me."

He paused again, beating about the question he felt he must put.

"It was to meet him here that you came?"

She stared, and then burst into a laugh. "Meet him—my husband? *Here?* At this season he's always at Cowes or Baden."

"He sent someone?"

"Yes."

"With a letter?"

She shook her head. "No; just a message. He never writes. I don't think I've had more than one letter from him." The allusion brought the color to her cheek, and it reflected itself in Archer's vivid blush.

"Why does he never write?"

"Why should he? What does one have secretaries for?"

The young man's blush deepened. She had pronounced the word as if it had no more significance than any other in her vocabulary. For a moment it was on the tip of his tongue to ask: "Did he send his secretary, then?" But the remembrance of Count Olenski's only letter to his wife was too present to him. He paused again, and then took another plunge.

"And the person?"—

"The emissary? The emissary," Madame Olenska rejoined, still smiling, "might, for all I care, have left already; but he has insisted on waiting till this evening . . . in case . . . on the chance. . . ."

"And you came out here to think the chance over?"

"I came out to get a breath of air. The hotel's too stifling. I'm taking the afternoon train back to Portsmouth."

They sat silent, not looking at each other, but straight ahead at the people passing along the path. Finally she turned her eyes again to his face and said: "You're not changed."

He felt like answering: "I was, till I saw you again"; but instead he stood up abruptly and glanced about him at the untidy sweltering park.

"This is horrible. Why shouldn't we go out a little on the bay? There's a breeze, and it will be cooler. We might take the steamboat down to Point Arley." She glanced up at him hesitatingly and he went on: "On a Monday morning there won't be anybody on the boat. My train doesn't leave till evening: I'm going back to New York. Why shouldn't we?" he insisted, looking down at her: and suddenly he broke out: "Haven't we done all we could?"

"Oh"—she murmured again. She stood up and reopened her sunshade, glancing about her as if to take counsel of the scene, and assure herself of the impossibility of remaining in it. Then her eyes returned to his face. "You mustn't say things like that to me," she said.

"I'll say anything you like; or nothing. I won't open my mouth unless you tell me to. What harm can it do to anybody? All I want is to listen to you," he stammered.

She drew out a little gold-faced watch on an enameled chain. "Oh, don't calculate," he broke out; "give me the day! I want to get you away from that man. At what time was he coming?"

Her color rose again. "At eleven."

"Then you must come at once."

"You needn't be afraid—if I don't come."

"Nor you either—if you do. I swear I only want to hear about you, to know what you've been doing. It's a hundred years since we've met—it may be another hundred before we meet again."

She still wavered, her anxious eyes on his face. "Why didn't you come down to the beach to fetch me, the day I was at Granny's?" she asked.

"Because you didn't look round—because you didn't know I was there. I swore I wouldn't unless you looked round." He laughed as the childishness of the confession struck him.

"But I didn't look round on purpose."

"On purpose?"

"I knew you were there; when you drove in I recognized the ponies. So I went down to the beach."

"To get away from me as far as you could?"

She repeated in a low voice: "To get away from you as far as I could."

He laughed out again, this time in boyish satisfaction. "Well, you see it's no use. I may as well tell you," he added, "that the business I came here for was just to find you. But, look here, we must start or we shall miss our boat."

"Our boat?" She frowned perplexedly, and then smiled. "Oh, but I must go back to the hotel first: I must leave a note—"

"As many notes as you please. You can write here." He drew out a note-case and one of the new stylographic pens. "I've even got an envelope—you see how everything's predestined! There—steady the thing on your knee, and I'll get the pen going in a second. They have to be humored; wait—" He banged the hand that held the pen against the back of the bench. "It's like jerking down the mercury in a thermometer: just a trick. Now try—"

She laughed, and bending over the sheet of paper which he had laid on his note-case, began to write. Archer walked away a few steps, staring with radiant unseeing eyes at the passers-by, who, in their turn, paused to stare at the unwonted sight of a fashionably-dressed lady writing a note on her knee on a bench in the Common.

Madame Olenska slipped the sheet into the envelope, wrote a name on it, and put it into her pocket. Then she too stood up.

They walked back toward Beacon Street, and near the club Archer caught sight of the plush-lined "herdic" which had carried his note to the Parker House, and whose driver was reposing from this effort by bathing his brow at the corner hydrant.

"I told you everything was predestined! Here's a cab for us. You see!" They laughed, astonished at the miracle of picking up a public conveyance at that hour, and in that unlikely spot, in a city where cab-stands were still a "foreign" novelty.

Archer, looking at his watch, saw that there was time to drive to the Parker House before going to the steamboat landing. They rattled through the hot streets and drew up at the door of the hotel.

Archer held out his hand for the letter. "Shall I take it in?" he asked; but Madame Olenska, shaking her head, sprang out and disappeared through the glazed doors. It was barely half-past ten; but what if the emissary, impatient for her reply, and not knowing how else to employ his time, were already seated among the travelers with cooling drinks at their elbows of whom Archer had caught a glimpse as she went in?

He waited, pacing up and down before the herdic. A Sicilian youth with eyes like Nastasia's offered to shine his boots, and an Irish matron to sell him peaches; and every few moments the doors opened to let out hot men with straw hats tilted far back, who glanced at him as they went by. He marveled that the door should open so often, and that all the people it let out should look so like each other, and so like all the other hot men who, at that hour, through the length and breadth of the land, were passing continuously in and out of the swinging doors of hotels.

And then, suddenly, came a face that he could not relate to the other faces. He caught but a flash of it, for his pacings had carried him to the farthest point of his beat, and it was in turning back to the hotel that he saw, in a group of typical countenances—the lank and weary, the round and surprised, the lantern-jawed and mild—this other face that was so many more things at once, and things so different. It was that of a young man, pale too, and half-extinguished by the heat, or worry, or both, but somehow, quicker, vivider, more conscious; or perhaps seeming so because he was so different. Archer hung a moment on a thin thread of memory, but it snapped and floated off with the disappearing face—apparently that of some foreign business man, looking doubly foreign in such a setting. He vanished in the stream of passers-by, and Archer resumed his patrol.

He did not care to be seen watch in hand within view of the hotel, and his unaided reckoning of the lapse of time led him to conclude that, if Madame Olenska was so long in reappearing, it could only be because she had met the emissary and been waylaid by him. At the thought Archer's apprehension rose to anguish.

"If she doesn't come soon I'll go in and find her," he said.

The doors swung open again and she was at his side. They got into the herdic, and as it drove off he took out his watch and saw that she had been absent just three minutes. In the clatter of loose windows that made talk impossible they bumped over the disjointed cobblestones to the wharf.

Seated side by side on a bench of the half-empty boat they found that they had hardly anything to say to each other, or rather that what they had to say communicated itself best in the blessed silence of their release and their isolation.

As the paddle-wheels began to turn, and wharves and shipping to recede through the veil of heat, it seemed to Archer that everything in the old familiar world of habit was receding also. He longed to ask Madame Olenska if she did not have the same feeling: the feeling that they were starting on some long voyage from which they might never return. But he was afraid to say it, or anything else that might disturb the delicate balance of her trust in him. In reality he had no wish to betray that trust. There had been days and nights when the memory of their kiss had burned and burned on his lips; the day before even, on the drive to Portsmouth, the thought of her had run through him like fire; but now that she was beside him, and they were drifting forth into this unknown world, they seemed to have reached the kind of deeper nearness that a touch may sunder.

As the boat left the harbor and turned seaward a breeze stirred about them and the bay broke up into long oily undulations, then into ripples tipped with spray. The fog of sultriness still hung over the city, but ahead lay a fresh world of ruffled waters, and distant promontories with lighthouses in the sun. Madame Olenska, leaning back against the boat-rail, drank in the coolness between parted lips. She had wound a long veil about her hat, but it left her face uncovered, and Archer was struck by the tranquil gaiety of her expression. She seemed to take their adventure as a matter of course, and to be neither in fear of unexpected encounters, nor (what was worse) unduly elated by their possibility.

In the bare dining room of the inn, which he had hoped they would have to themselves, they found a strident party of innocent-looking young men and women—school-teachers on a holiday, the landlord told them—and Archer's heart sank at the idea of having to talk through their noise.

"This is hopeless—I'll ask for a private room," he said; and Madame Olenska, without offering any objection, waited while he went in search of it. The room opened on a long wooden verandah, with the sea coming in at the windows. It was bare and cool, with a table covered with a coarse checkered cloth and adorned by a bottle of pickles and a blueberry pie under a cage. No more guileless-looking *cabinet particulier* ever offered its shelter to a clandestine couple: Archer fancied he saw the sense of its reassurance in the faintly amused smile with which Madame Olenska sat down opposite to him. A woman who had run away from her husband—and reputedly with another man—was likely to have mastered the art of taking things for granted; but something in the quality of her composure took the edge from his irony. By being so quiet, so unsurprised, and so simple she had managed to brush away the conventions and make him feel that to seek to be alone was the natural thing for two old friends who had so much to say to each other. . . .

24

THEY lunched slowly and meditatively, with mute intervals between rushes of talk; for, the spell once broken, they had much to say, and yet moments when saying became the mere accompaniment to long duologues of silence. Archer kept the talk from his own affairs, not with conscious intention but because he did not want to miss a word of her history; and leaning on the table, her chin resting on her clasped hands, she talked to him of the year and a half since they had met.

She had grown tired of what people called "society"; New York was kind, it was almost oppressively hospitable; she should never forget the way in which it had welcomed her back; but after the first flush of novelty she had found herself, as she phrased it, too "different" to care for the things it cared about—and so she had decided to try Washington, where one was supposed to meet more varieties of people and of opinion. And on the whole she should probably settle down in Washington, and make a home there for poor Medora, who had worn out the patience of all her other relations just at the time when she most needed looking after and protecting from matrimonial perils.

"But Dr. Carver—aren't you afraid of Dr. Carver? I hear he's been staying with you at the Blenkers'."

She smiled. "Oh, the Carver danger is over. Dr. Carver is a very clever man. He wants a rich wife to finance his plans, and Medora is simply a good advertisement as a convert."

"A convert to what?"

"To all sorts of new and crazy social schemes. But, do you know, they interest me more than the blind conformity to tradition—somebody else's tradition—that I see among our own friends. It seems stupid to have discovered America only to make it into a copy of another country." She smiled across the table. "Do you suppose Christopher Columbus would have taken all that trouble just to go to the Opera with the Selfridge Merrys?"

Archer changed color. "And Beaufort—do you say these things to Beaufort?" he asked abruptly.

"I haven't seen him for a long time. But I used to; and he understands."

"Ah, it's what I've always told you; you don't like us. And you like Beaufort because he's so unlike us." He looked about the bare room and out at the bare beach and the row of stark white village houses strung along the shore. "We're damnably dull. We've no character, no color, no variety—I wonder," he broke out, "why you don't go back?"

Her eyes darkened, and he expected an indignant rejoinder. But she sat silent, as if thinking over what he had said, and he grew frightened lest she should answer that she wondered too.

At length she said: "I believe it's because of you."

It was impossible to make the confession more dispassionately, or in a tone less encouraging to the vanity of the person addressed. Archer reddened to the temples, but dared not move or speak: it was as if her words had been some rare butterfly that the least motion might drive off on startled wings, but that might gather a flock about it if it were left undisturbed.

"At least," she continued, "it was you who made me understand that under the dullness there are things so fine and sensitive and delicate that even those I most cared for in my other life look cheap in comparison. I don't know how to explain myself"—she drew together her troubled brows—"but it seems as if I'd never before understood with how much that is hard and shabby and base the most exquisite pleasures may be paid."

"Exquisite pleasures—it's something to have had them!" he felt like retorting; but the appeal in her eyes kept him silent.

"I want," she went on, "to be perfectly honest with you—and with myself. For a long time I've hoped this chance would come: that I might tell you how you've helped me, what you've made of me—"

Archer sat staring beneath frowning brows. He interrupted her with a laugh. "And what do you make out that you've made of me?"

She paled a little. "Of you?"

"Yes: for I'm of your making much more than you ever were of mine. I'm the man who married one woman because another one told him to."

Her paleness turned to a fugitive flush. "I thought—you promised —you were not to say such things today."

"Ah—how like a woman! None of you will ever see a bad business through!"

She lowered her voice. "*Is* it a bad business—for May?"

He stood in the window, drumming against the raised sash, and feeling in every fiber the wistful tenderness with which she had spoken her cousin's name.

"For that's the thing we've always got to think of—haven't we—by your own showing?" she insisted.

"My own showing?" he echoed, his blank eyes still on the sea.

"Or if not," she continued, pursuing her own thought with a painful application, "if it's not worthwhile to have given up, to have missed things, so that others may be saved from disillusionment and misery—then everything I came home for, everything that made my other life seem by contrast so bare and so poor because no one there took account of them—all these things are a sham or a dream—"

He turned around without moving from his place. "And in that case there's no reason on earth why you shouldn't go back?" he concluded for her.

Her eyes were clinging to him desperately. "Oh, *is* there no reason?"

"Not if you staked your all on the success of my marriage. My marriage," he said savagely, "isn't going to be a sight to keep you here." She made no answer, and he went on: "What's the use? You gave me my first glimpse of a real life, and at the same moment you asked me to go on with a sham one. It's beyond human enduring—that's all."

"Oh, don't say that; when I'm enduring it!" she burst out, her eyes filling.

Her arms had dropped along the table, and she sat with her face abandoned to his gaze as if in the recklessness of a desperate peril. The face exposed her as much as if it had been her whole person, with the soul behind it: Archer stood dumb, overwhelmed by what it suddenly told him.

"You too—oh, all this time, you too?"

For answer, she let the tears on her lids overflow and run slowly downward.

Half the width of the room was still between them, and neither made any show of moving. Archer was conscious of a curious indifference to her bodily presence: he would hardly have been aware of it if one of the hands she had flung out on the table had not drawn his gaze as on the occasion when, in the little Twenty-third Street house, he had kept his eye on it in order not to look at her face. Now his imagination spun about the hand as about the edge of a vortex; but still he made no effort to draw nearer. He had known the love that is fed on caresses and feeds them; but this passion that was closer than his bones was not to be superficially satisfied. His one terror was to do anything which might efface the sound and impression of her words; his one thought, that he should never again feel quite alone.

But after a moment the sense of waste and ruin overcame him. There they were, close together and safe and shut in; yet so chained to their separate destinies that they might as well have been half the world apart.

"What's the use—when you will go back?" he broke out, a great hopeless *How on earth can I keep you?* crying out to her beneath his words.

She sat motionless, with lowered lids. "Oh—I shan't go yet!"

"Not yet? Some time, then? Some time that you already foresee?"

At that she raised her clearest eyes. "I promise you: not as long as you hold out. Not as long as we can look straight at each other like this."

He dropped into his chair. What her answer really said was: "If you lift a finger you'll drive me back: back to all the abominations you know of, and all the temptations you half guess." He understood it as clearly as if she had uttered the words, and the thought kept him anchored to his side of the table in a kind of moved and sacred submission.

"What a life for you!—" he groaned.

"Oh—as long as it's a part of yours."

"And mine a part of yours?"

She nodded.

"And that's to be all—for either of us?"

"Well; it *is* all, isn't it?"

At that he sprang up, forgetting everything but the sweetness of her face. She rose too, not as if to meet him or to flee from him, but quietly, as though the worst of the task were done and she had only to wait; so quietly that, as he came close, her outstretched hands acted not as a check but as a guide to him. They fell into his, while her arms, extended but not rigid, kept him far enough off to let her surrendered face say the rest.

They may have stood in that way for a long time, or only for a few moments; but it was long enough for her silence to communicate all she had to say, and for him to feel that only one thing mattered. He must do nothing to make this meeting their last; he must leave their future in her care, asking only that she should keep fast hold of it.

"Don't—don't be unhappy," she said, with a break in her voice, as she drew her hands away; and he answered: "You won't go back— you won't go back?" as if it were the one possibility he could not bear.

"I won't go back," she said; and turning away she opened the door and led the way into the public dining room.

The strident school-teachers were gathering up their possessions preparatory to a straggling flight to the wharf; across the beach lay the white steam-boat at the pier; and over the sunlit waters Boston loomed in a line of haze.

25

ONCE more on the boat, and in the presence of others, Archer felt a tranquillity of spirit that surprised as much as it sustained him.

The day, according to any current valuation, had been a rather ridiculous failure; he had not so much as touched Madame Olenska's hand with his lips, or extracted one word from her that gave promise of further opportunities. Nevertheless, for a man sick with unsatisfied love, and parting for an indefinite period from the object of his passion, he felt himself almost humiliatingly calm and comforted. It was the perfect balance she had held between their loyalty to others and their honesty to themselves that had so stirred and yet tranquillized him; a balance not artfully calculated, as her tears and her falterings showed, but resulting naturally from her unabashed sincerity. It filled him with a tender awe, now the danger was over, and made him thank the fates that no personal vanity, no sense of playing a part before sophisticated witnesses, had tempted him to tempt her. Even after they had clasped hands for good-bye at the Fall River station, and he had turned away alone, the conviction remained with him of having saved out of their meeting much more than he had sacrificed.

He wandered back to the club, and went and sat alone in the deserted library, turning and turning over in his thoughts every separate second of their hours together. It was clear to him, and it grew more clear under closer scrutiny, that if she should finally decide on returning to Europe—returning to her husband—it would not be because her old life tempted her, even on the new terms offered. No: she would go only if she felt herself becoming a temptation to Archer, a temptation to fall away from the standard they had both set up. Her choice would be to stay near him as long as he did not ask her to come nearer; and it depended on himself to keep her just there, safe but secluded.

In the train these thoughts were still with him. They enclosed him in a kind of golden haze, through which the faces about him looked remote and indistinct: he had a feeling that if he spoke to his fellow-travelers they would not understand what he was saying. In this state of abstraction he found himself, the following morning, waking to the reality of a stifling September day in New York. The heat-withered faces in the long train streamed past him, and he continued to stare at them through the same golden blur; but suddenly, as he left the station, one of the faces detached itself, came closer and forced itself upon his consciousness. It was, as he instantly recalled, the face of the young man he had seen, the day before, passing out of the Parker House, and had noted as not conforming to type, as not having an American hotel face.

The same thing struck him now; and again he became aware of a dim stir of former associations. The young man stood looking about him with the dazed air of the foreigner flung upon the harsh mercies of American travel; then he advanced toward Archer, lifted his hat, and said in English: "Surely, Monsieur, we met in London?"

"Ah, to be sure: in London!" Archer grasped his hand with curiosity and sympathy. "So you *did* get here, after all?" he exclaimed, casting a wondering eye on the astute and haggard little countenance of young Carfry's French tutor.

"Oh, I got here—yes," M. Rivière smiled with drawn lips. "But not for long; I return the day after tomorrow." He stood grasping his light valise in one neatly gloved hand, and gazing anxiously, perplexedly, almost appealingly, into Archer's face.

"I wonder, Monsieur, since I've had the good luck to run across you, if I might—"

"I was just going to suggest it: come to luncheon, won't you? Down town, I mean: if you'll look me up in my office I'll take you to a very decent restaurant in that quarter."

M. Rivière was visibly touched and surprised. "You're too kind. But I was only going to ask if you would tell me how to reach some sort of conveyance. There are no porters, and no one here seems to listen—"

"I know: our American stations must surprise you. When you ask for a porter they give you chewing-gum. But if you'll come along I'll extricate you; and you must really lunch with me, you know."

The young man, after a just perceptible hesitation, replied, with profuse thanks, and in a tone that did not carry complete conviction, that he was already engaged; but when they had reached the comparative reassurance of the street he asked if he might call that afternoon.

Archer, at ease in the midsummer leisure of the office, fixed an hour and scribbled his address, which the Frenchman pocketed with reiterated thanks and a wide flourish of his hat. A horse-car received him, and Archer walked away.

Punctually at the hour M. Rivière appeared, shaved, smoothed-out, but still unmistakably drawn and serious. Archer was alone in his office, and the young man, before accepting the seat he proffered, began abruptly: "I believe I saw you, sir, yesterday in Boston."

The statement was insignificant enough, and Archer was about to frame an assent when his words were checked by something mysterious yet illuminating in his visitor's insistent gaze.

"It is extraordinary, very extraordinary," M. Rivière continued, "that we should have met in the circumstances in which I find myself."

"What circumstances?" Archer asked, wondering a little crudely if he needed money.

M. Rivière continued to study him with tentative eyes. "I have come, not to look for employment, as I spoke of doing when we last met, but on a special mission—"

"Ah—!" Archer exclaimed. In a flash the two meetings had connected themselves in his mind. He paused to take in the situation thus suddenly lighted up for him, and M. Rivière also remained silent, as if aware that what he had said was enough.

"A special mission," Archer at length repeated.

The young Frenchman, opening his palms, raised them slightly, and the two men continued to look at each other across the office-desk till Archer roused himself to say: "Do sit down"; whereupon M. Rivière bowed, took a distant chair, and again waited.

"It was about this mission that you wanted to consult me?" Archer finally asked.

M. Rivière bent his head. "Not in my own behalf: on that score I—I have fully dealt with myself. I should like—if I may—to speak to you about the Countess Olenska."

Archer had known for the last few minutes that the words were coming; but when they came they sent the blood rushing to his temples as if he had been caught by a bent-back branch in a thicket.

"And on whose behalf," he said, "do you wish to do this?"

M. Rivière met the question sturdily. "Well—I might say *hers,* if it did not sound like a liberty. Shall I say instead: on behalf of abstract justice?"

Archer considered him ironically. "In other words: you are Count Olenski's messenger?"

He saw his blush more darkly reflected in M. Rivière's sallow countenance. "Not to *you,* Monsieur. If I come to you, it is on quite other grounds."

"What right have you, in the circumstances, to *be* on any other ground?" Archer retorted. "If you're an emissary, you're an emissary."

The young man considered. "My mission is over: as far as the Countess Olenska goes, it has failed."

"I can't help that," Archer rejoined on the same note of irony.

"No: but you can help—" M. Rivière paused, turned his hat about in his still carefully gloved hands, looked into its lining and then back at Archer's face. "You can help, Monsieur, I am convinced, to make it equally a failure with her family."

Archer pushed back his chair and stood up. "Well—and by God I will!" he exclaimed. He stood with his hands in his pockets, staring down wrathfully at the little Frenchman, whose face, though he too had risen, was still an inch or two below the line of Archer's eyes.

M. Rivière paled to his normal hue: paler than that his complexion could hardly turn.

"Why the devil," Archer explosively continued, "should you have thought—since I suppose you're appealing to me on the ground of my relationship to Madame Olenska—that I should take a view contrary to the rest of her family?"

The change of expression in M. Rivière's face was for a time his only answer. His look passed from timidity to absolute distress: for a young man of his usually resourceful mien it would have been difficult to appear more disarmed and defenseless. "Oh, Monsieur—"

"I can't imagine," Archer continued, "why you should have come to me when there are others so much nearer to the Countess; still less why you thought I should be more accessible to the arguments I suppose you were sent over with."

M. Rivière took this onslaught with a disconcerting humility.

"The arguments I want to present to you, Monsieur, are my own and not those I was sent over with."

"Then I see still less reason for listening to them."

M. Rivière again looked into his hat, as if considering whether these last words were not a sufficiently broad hint to put it on and be gone. Then he spoke with sudden decision. "Monsieur—will you tell me one thing? Is it my right to be here that you question? Or do you perhaps believe the whole matter to be already closed?"

His quiet insistence made Archer feel the clumsiness of his own bluster. M. Rivière had succeeded in imposing himself: Archer, reddening slightly, dropped into his chair again, and signed to the young man to be seated.

"I beg your pardon: but why isn't the matter closed?"

M. Rivière gazed back at him with anguish. "You do, then, agree with the rest of the family that, in face of the new proposals I have brought, it is hardly possible for Madame Olenska not to return to her husband?"

"Good God!" Archer exclaimed; and his visitor gave out a low murmur of confirmation.

"Before seeing her, I saw—at Count Olenski's request—Mr. Lovell Mingott, with whom I had several talks before going to Boston. I understand that he represents his mother's view; and that Mrs. Manson Mingott's influence is great throughout her family."

Archer sat silent, with the sense of clinging to the edge of a sliding precipice. The discovery that he had been excluded from a share in these negotiations, and even from the knowledge that they were on foot, caused him a surprise hardly dulled by the acuter wonder of what he was learning. He saw in a flash that if the family had ceased to consult him it was because some deep tribal instinct warned them that he was no longer on their side; and he recalled, with a start of comprehension, a remark of May's during their drive home from Mrs. Manson Mingott's on the day of the Archery Meeting: "Perhaps, after all, Ellen would be happier with her husband."

Even in the tumult of new discoveries Archer remembered his indignant exclamation, and the fact that since then his wife had never named Madame Olenska to him. Her careless allusion had no doubt been the straw held up to see which way the wind blew; the result had been reported to the family, and thereafter Archer had been tacitly omitted from their counsels. He admired the tribal discipline which made May bow to this decision. She would not have done so, he knew, had her conscience protested; but she probably shared the family view that Madame Olenska would be better off as an unhappy wife than as a separated one, and that there was no use in discussing the case with Newland, who had an awkward way of suddenly not seeming to take the most fundamental things for granted.

Archer looked up and met his visitor's anxious gaze. "Don't you know, Monsieur—is it possible you don't know—that the family begin to doubt if they have the right to advise the Countess to refuse her husband's last proposals?"

"The proposals you brought?"

"The proposals I brought."

It was on Archer's lips to exclaim that whatever he knew or did not know was no concern of M. Rivière's; but something in the humble and yet courageous tenacity of M. Rivière's gaze made him reject this conclusion, and he met the young man's question with another. "What is your object in speaking to me of this?"

He had not to wait a moment for the answer. "To beg you, Monsieur—to beg you with all the force I'm capable of—not to let her go back.—Oh, don't let her!" M. Rivière exclaimed.

Archer looked at him with increasing astonishment. There was no mistaking the sincerity of his distress or the strength of his determination: he had evidently resolved to let everything go by the board but the supreme need of thus putting himself on record. Archer considered.

"May I ask," he said at length, "if this is the line you took with the Countess Olenska?"

M. Rivière reddened, but his eyes did not falter. "No, Monsieur: I accepted my mission in good faith. I really believed—for reasons I need not trouble you with—that it would be better for Madame Olenska to recover her situation, her fortune, the social consideration that her husband's standing gives her."

"So I supposed: you could hardly have accepted such a mission otherwise."

"I should not have accepted it."

"Well, then—?" Archer paused again, and their eyes met in another protracted scrutiny.

"Ah, Monsieur, after I had seen her, after I had listened to her, I knew she was better off here."

"You knew—?"

"Monsieur, I discharged my mission faithfully: I put the Count's arguments, I stated his offers, without adding any comment of my own. The Countess was good enough to listen patiently; she carried her goodness so far as to see me twice; she considered impartially all I had come to say. And it was in the course of these two talks that I changed my mind, that I came to see things differently."

"May I ask what led to this change?"

"Simply seeing the change in *her*," M. Rivière replied.

"The change in her? Then you knew her before?"

The young man's color again rose. "I used to see her in her husband's house. I have known Count Olenski for many years. You can imagine that he would not have sent a stranger on such a mission."

Archer's gaze, wandering away to the blank walls of the office, rested on a hanging calendar surmounted by the rugged features of the President of the United States. That such a conversation should be going on anywhere within the millions of square miles subject to his rule seemed as strange as anything that the imagination could invent.

"The change—what sort of a change?"

"Ah, Monsieur, if I could tell you!" M. Rivière paused. "*Tenez*—the discovery, I suppose, of what I'd never thought of before: that she's an American. And that if you're an American of *her* kind—of your kind—things that are accepted in certain other societies, or at least put up with as part of a general convenient give-and-take—become unthinkable, simply unthinkable. If Madame Olenska's relations understood what these things were, their opposition to her returning would no doubt be as unconditional as her own; but they seem to regard her husband's wish to have her back as proof of an irresistible longing for domestic life." M. Rivière paused, and then added: "Whereas it's far from being as simple as that."

Archer looked back to the President of the United States, and then down at his desk and at the papers scattered on it. For a second or two he could not trust himself to speak. During this interval he heard M. Rivière's chair pushed back, and was aware that the young man had risen. When he glanced up again he saw that his visitor was as moved as himself.

"Thank you," Archer said simply.

"There's nothing to thank me for, Monsieur: it is I, rather—" M. Rivière broke off, as if speech for him too were difficult. "I should like, though," he continued in a firmer voice, "to add one thing. You asked me if I was in Count Olenski's employ. I am at this moment:

I returned to him, a few months ago, for reasons of private necessity such as may happen to anyone who has persons, ill and older persons, dependent on him. But from the moment that I have taken the step of coming here to say these things to you I consider myself discharged, and I shall tell him so on my return, and give him the reasons. That's all, Monsieur."

M. Rivière bowed and drew back a step.

"Thank you," Archer said again, as their hands met.

26

EVERY year on the fifteenth of October Fifth Avenue opened its shutters, unrolled its carpets and hung up its triple layer of window-curtains.

By the first of November this household ritual was over, and society had begun to look about and take stock of itself. By the fifteenth the season was in full blast, Opera and theaters were putting forth their new attractions, dinner-engagements were accumulating, and dates for dances being fixed. And punctually at about this time Mrs. Archer always said that New York was very much changed.

Observing it from the lofty standpoint of a non-participant, she was able, with the help of Mr. Sillerton Jackson and Miss Sophy, to trace each new crack in its surface, and all the strange weeds pushing up between the ordered rows of social vegetables. It had been one of the amusements of Archer's youth to wait for this annual pronouncement of his mother's, and to hear her enumerate the minute signs of disintegration that his careless gaze had overlooked. For New York, to Mrs. Archer's mind, never changed without changing for the worse; and in this view Miss Sophy Jackson heartily concurred.

Mr. Sillerton Jackson, as became a man of the world, suspended his judgment and listened with an amused impartiality to the lamentations of the ladies. But even he never denied that New York had changed; and Newland Archer, in the winter of the second year of his marriage, was himself obliged to admit that if it had not actually changed it was certainly changing.

These points had been raised, as usual, at Mrs. Archer's Thanksgiving dinner. At the date when she was officially enjoined to give thanks for the blessings of the year it was her habit to take a mournful though not embittered stock of her world, and wonder what there was to be thankful for. At any rate, not the state of society; society, if it could be said to exist, was rather a spectacle on which to call down Biblical imprecations—and in fact, everyone knew what the Reverend Dr. Ashmore meant when he chose a text from Jeremiah (chap. ii., verse 25) for his Thanksgiving sermon. Dr. Ashmore, the new Rector of St. Matthew's, had been chosen because he was very "advanced": his sermons were considered bold in thought and novel in language. When he fulminated against fashionable society he always spoke of its "trend"; and to Mrs. Archer it was terrifying and yet fascinating to feel herself part of a community that was trending.

"There's no doubt that Dr. Ashmore is right: there *is* a marked trend," she said, as if it were something visible and measurable, like a crack in a house.

"It was odd, though, to preach about it on Thanksgiving," Miss Jackson opined; and her hostess drily rejoined: "Oh, he means us to give thanks for what's left."

Archer had been wont to smile at these annual vaticinations of his mother's; but this year even he was obliged to acknowledge, as he listened to an enumeration of the changes, that the "trend" was visible.

"The extravagance in dress—" Miss Jackson began. "Sillerton took me to the first night of the Opera, and I can only tell you that Jane Merry's dress was the only one I recognized from last year; and even that had had the front panel changed. Yet I know she got it out from Worth only two years ago, because my seamstress always goes in to make over her Paris dresses before she wears them."

"Ah, Jane Merry is one of *us*," said Mrs. Archer sighing, as if it were not such an enviable thing to be in an age when ladies were beginning to flaunt abroad their Paris dresses as soon as they were out of the Custom House, instead of letting them mellow under lock and key, in the manner of Mrs. Archer's contemporaries.

"Yes; she's one of the few. In my youth," Miss Jackson rejoined, "it was considered vulgar to dress in the newest fashions; and Amy Sillerton has always told me that in Boston the rule was to put away one's Paris dresses for two years. Old Mrs. Baxter Pennilow, who did everything handsomely, used to import twelve a year, two velvet, two satin, two silk, and the other six of poplin and the finest cashmere. It was a standing order, and as she was ill for two years before she died they found forty-eight Worth dresses that had never been taken out of tissue paper; and when the girls left off their mourning they were able to wear the first lot at the Symphony concerts without looking in advance of the fashion."

"Ah, well, Boston is more conservative than New York; but I always think it's a safe rule for a lady to lay aside her French dresses for one season," Mrs. Archer conceded.

"It was Beaufort who started the new fashion by making his wife clap her new clothes on her back as soon as they arrived: I must say at times it takes all Regina's distinction not to look like . . . like . . ." Miss Jackson glanced around the table, caught Janey's bulging gaze, and took refuge in an unintelligible murmur.

"Like her rivals," said Mr. Sillerton Jackson, with the air of producing an epigram.

"Oh,—" the ladies murmured; and Mrs. Archer added, partly to distract her daughter's attention from forbidden topics: "Poor Regina! Her Thanksgiving hasn't been a very cheerful one, I'm afraid. Have you heard the rumors about Beaufort's speculations, Sillerton?"

Mr. Jackson nodded carelessly. Everyone had heard the rumors in question, and he scorned to confirm a tale that was already common property.

A gloomy silence fell upon the party. No one really liked Beaufort, and it was not wholly unpleasant to think the worst of his private life; but the idea of his having brought financial dishonor on his wife's family was too shocking to be enjoyed even by his enemies. Archer's New York tolerated hypocrisy in private relations; but in business matters it exacted a limpid and impeccable honesty. It was a long time since any well-known banker had failed discreditably; but everyone remembered the social extinction visited on the heads of the firm when the last event of the kind had happened. It would be the same with the Beauforts, in spite of his power and her popularity; not all the leagued strength of the Dallas connection would save poor Regina if there were any truth in the reports of her husband's unlawful speculations.

The talk took refuge in less ominous topics; but everything they touched on seemed to confirm Mrs. Archer's sense of an accelerated trend.

"Of course, Newland, I know you let dear May go to Mrs. Struthers's Sunday evenings—" she began; and May interposed gaily: "Oh, you know, everybody goes to Mrs. Struthers's now; and she was invited to Granny's last reception."

It was thus, Archer reflected, that New York managed its transitions: conspiring to ignore them till they were well over, and then, in all good faith, imagining that they had taken place in a preceding age. There was always a traitor in the citadel; and after he (or generally she) had surrendered the keys, what was the use of pretending that it was impregnable? Once people had tasted of Mrs. Struthers's easy Sunday hospitality they were not likely to sit at home remembering that her champagne was transmuted Shoe-Polish.

"I know, dear, I know," Mrs. Archer sighed. "Such things have to be, I suppose, as long as *amusement* is what people go out for; but I've never quite forgiven your cousin Madame Olenska for being the first person to countenance Mrs. Struthers."

A sudden blush rose to young Mrs. Archer's face; it surprised her husband as much as the other guests about the table. "Oh, *Ellen*—" she murmured, much in the same accusing and yet deprecating tone in which her parents might have said: "Oh, *the Blenkers*—."

It was the note which the family had taken to sounding on the mention of the Countess Olenska's name, since she had surprised and inconvenienced them by remaining obdurate to her husband's advances; but on May's lips it gave food for thought, and Archer looked at her with the sense of strangeness that sometimes came over him when she was most in the tone of her environment.

His mother, with less than her usual sensitiveness to atmosphere, still insisted: "I've always thought that people like the Countess Olenska, who have lived in aristocratic societies, ought to help us to keep up our social distinctions, instead of ignoring them."

May's blush remained permanently vivid: it seemed to have a significance beyond that implied by the recognition of Madame Olenska's social bad faith.

"I've no doubt we all seem alike to foreigners," said Miss Jackson tartly.

"I don't think Ellen cares for society; but nobody knows exactly what she does care for," May continued, as if she had been groping for something noncommittal.

"Ah, well—" Mrs. Archer sighed again.

Everybody knew that the Countess Olenska was no longer in the good graces of her family. Even her devoted champion, old Mrs. Manson Mingott, had been unable to defend her refusal to return to her husband. The Mingotts had not proclaimed their disapproval aloud: their sense of solidarity was too strong. They had simply, as

Mrs. Welland said, "let poor Ellen find her own level"—and that, mortifyingly and incomprehensibly, was in the dim depths where the Blenkers prevailed, and "people who wrote" celebrated their untidy rites. It was incredible, but it was a fact, that Ellen, in spite of all her opportunities and her privileges, had become simply "Bohemian." The fact enforced the contention that she had made a fatal mistake in not returning to Count Olenski. After all, a young woman's place was under her husband's roof, especially when she had left it in circumstances that . . . well . . . if one had cared to look into them. . . .

"Madame Olenska is a great favorite with the gentlemen," said Miss Sophy, with her air of wishing to put forth something conciliatory when she knew that she was planting a dart.

"Ah, that's the danger that a young woman like Madame Olenska is always exposed to," Mrs. Archer mournfully agreed; and the ladies, on this conclusion, gathered up their trains to seek the carcel globes of the drawing room, while Archer and Mr. Sillerton Jackson withdrew to the Gothic library.

Once established before the grate, and consoling himself for the inadequacy of the dinner by the perfection of his cigar, Mr. Jackson became portentous and communicable.

"If the Beaufort smash comes," he announced, "there are going to be disclosures."

Archer raised his head quickly: he could never hear the name without the sharp vision of Beaufort's heavy figure, opulently furred and shod, advancing through the snow at Skuytercliff.

"There's bound to be," Mr. Jackson continued, "the nastiest kind of a cleaning up. He hasn't spent all his money on Regina."

"Oh, well—that's discounted, isn't it? My belief is he'll pull out yet," said the young man, wanting to change the subject.

"Perhaps—perhaps. I know he was to see some of the influential people today. Of course," Mr. Jackson reluctantly conceded, "it's to be hoped they can tide him over—this time anyhow. I shouldn't like to think of poor Regina's spending the rest of her life in some shabby foreign watering-place for bankrupts."

Archer said nothing. It seemed to him so natural—however tragic —that money ill-gotten should be cruelly expiated, that his mind, hardly lingering over Mrs. Beaufort's doom, wandered back to closer questions. What was the meaning of May's blush when the Countess Olenska had been mentioned?

Four months had passed since the midsummer day that he and Madame Olenska had spent together; and since then he had not seen her. He knew that she had returned to Washington, to the little house which she and Medora Manson had taken there: he had written to her once—a few words, asking when they were to meet again—and she had even more briefly replied: "Not yet."

Since then there had been no farther communication between them, and he had built up within himself a kind of sanctuary in which she throned among his secret thoughts and longings. Little by little it became the scene of his real life, of his only rational activities; thither he brought the books he read, the ideas and feelings which nourished him, his judgments and his visions. Outside it, in the scene of his actual life, he moved with a growing sense of unreality and insufficiency, blundering against familiar prejudices and traditional points of view as an absent-minded man goes on bumping into the furniture of his own room. Absent—that was what he was: so absent from everything most densely real and near to those about him that it sometimes startled him to find they still imagined he was there.

He became aware that Mr. Jackson was clearing his throat preparatory to farther revelations.

"I don't know, of course, how far your wife's family are aware of what people say about—well, about Madame Olenska's refusal to accept her husband's latest offer."

Archer was silent, and Mr. Jackson obliquely continued: "It's a pity—it's certainly a pity—that she refused it."

"A pity? In God's name, why?"

Mr. Jackson looked down his leg to the unwrinkled sock that joined it to a glossy pump.

"Well—to put it on the lowest ground—what's she going to live on now?"

"Now—?"

"If Beaufort—"

Archer sprang up, his fist banging down on the black walnut-edge of the writing-table. The wells of the brass double inkstand danced in their sockets.

"What the devil do you mean, sir?"

Mr. Jackson, shifting himself slightly in his chair, turned a tranquil gaze on the young man's burning face.

"Well—I have it on pretty good authority—in fact, on old Catherine's herself—that the family reduced Countess Olenska's allowance considerably when she definitely refused to go back to her husband; and as, by this refusal, she also forfeits the money settled on her when she married—which Olenski was ready to make over to her if she returned—why, what the devil do *you* mean, my dear boy, by asking me what *I* mean?" Mr. Jackson good-humoredly retorted.

Archer moved toward the mantelpiece and bent over to knock his ashes into the grate.

"I don't know anything of Madame Olenska's private affairs; but I don't need to, to be certain that what you insinuate—"

"Oh, *I* don't: it's Lefferts, for one," Mr. Jackson interposed.

"Lefferts—who made love to her and got snubbed for it!" Archer broke out contemptuously.

"Ah—*did* he?" snapped the other, as if this were exactly the fact he had been laying a trap for. He still sat sideways from the fire, so that his hard old gaze held Archer's face as if in a spring of steel.

"Well, well: it's a pity she didn't go back before Beaufort's cropper," he repeated. "If she goes *now*, and if he fails, it will only confirm the general impression: which isn't by any means peculiar to Lefferts, by the way."

"Oh, she won't go back now: less than ever!" Archer had no sooner said it than he had once more the feeling that it was exactly what Mr. Jackson had been waiting for.

The old gentleman considered him attentively. "That's your opinion, eh? Well, no doubt you know. But everybody will tell you that the few pennies Medora Manson has left are all in Beaufort's hands; and how the two women are to keep their heads above water unless he does, I can't imagine. Of course, Madame Olenska may still soften old Catherine, who's been the most inexorably opposed to her staying; and old Catherine could make her any allowance she chooses. But we all know that she hates parting with good money; and the rest of the family have no particular interest in keeping Madame Olenska here."

Archer was burning with unavailing wrath: he was exactly in the state when a man is sure to do something stupid, knowing all the while that he is doing it.

He saw that Mr. Jackson had been instantly struck by the fact that Madame Olenska's differences with her grandmother and her other relations were not known to him, and that the old gentleman had drawn his own conclusions as to the reasons for Archer's exclusion from the family councils. This fact warned Archer to go warily; but the insinuations about Beaufort made him reckless. He was mindful, however, if not of his own danger, at least of the fact that Mr. Jackson was under his mother's roof, and consequently his guest. Old New York scrupulously observed the etiquette of hospitality, and no discussion with a guest was ever allowed to degenerate into a disagreement.

"Shall we go up and join my mother?" he suggested curtly, as Mr. Jackson's last cone of ashes dropped into the brass ash-tray at his elbow.

On the drive homeward May remained oddly silent; through the darkness, he still felt her enveloped in her menacing blush. What its menace meant he could not guess: but he was sufficiently warned by the fact that Madame Olenska's name had evoked it.

They went upstairs, and he turned into the library. She usually followed him; but he heard her passing down the passage to her bedroom.

"May!" he called out impatiently; and she came back, with a slight glance of surprise at his tone.

"This lamp is smoking again; I should think the servants might see that it's kept properly trimmed," he grumbled nervously.

"I'm so sorry: it shan't happen again," she answered, in the firm bright tone she had learned from her mother; and it exasperated Archer to feel that she was already beginning to humor him like a younger Mr. Welland. She bent over to lower the wick, and as the light struck up on her white shoulders and the clear curves of her face he thought: "How young she is! For what endless years this life will have to go on!"

He felt, with a kind of horror, his own strong youth and the bounding blood in his veins. "Look here," he said suddenly, "I may have to go to Washington for a few days—soon; next week perhaps."

Her hand remained on the key of the lamp as she turned to him slowly. The heat from its flame had brought back a glow to her face, but it paled as she looked up.

"On business?" she asked, in a tone which implied that there could be no other conceivable reason, and that she had put the question automatically, as if merely to finish his own sentence.

"On business, naturally. There's a patent case coming up before the Supreme Court—" He gave the name of the inventor, and went on furnishing details with all Lawrence Lefferts's practiced glibness, while she listened attentively, saying at intervals: "Yes, I see."

"The change will do you good," she said simply, when he had finished; "and you must be sure to go and see Ellen," she added, looking him straight in the eyes with her cloudless smile, and speaking in the tone she might have employed in urging him not to neglect some irksome family duty.

It was the only word that passed between them on the subject; but in the code in which they had both been trained it meant: "Of course you understand that I know all that people have been saying about Ellen, and heartily sympathize with my family in their effort to get her to return to her husband. I also know that, for some reason you have not chosen to tell me, you have advised her against this course, which all the older men of the family, as well as our grandmother, agree in approving; and that it is owing to your encouragement that Ellen defies us all, and exposes herself to the kind of criticism of which Mr. Sillerton Jackson probably gave you, this evening, the hint that has made you so irritable. . . . Hints have indeed not been wanting; but since you appear unwilling to take them from others, I offer you this one myself, in the only form in which well-bred people of our kind can communicate unpleasant things to each other: by letting you understand that I know you mean to see Ellen when you are in Washington, and are perhaps going there expressly for that purpose; and that, since you are sure to see her, I wish you to do so with my full and explicit approval—and to take the opportunity of letting her know what the course of conduct you have encouraged her in is likely to lead to."

Her hand was still on the key of the lamp when the last word of this mute message reached him. She turned the wick down, lifted off the globe, and breathed on the sulky flame.

"They smell less if one blows them out," she explained, with her bright housekeeping air. On the threshold she turned and paused for his kiss.

27

WALL Street, the next day, had more reassuring reports of Beaufort's situation. They were not definite, but they were hopeful. It was generally understood that he could call on powerful influences in case of emergency, and that he had done so with success; and that evening, when Mrs. Beaufort appeared at the Opera wearing her old smile and a new emerald necklace, society drew a breath of relief.

New York was inexorable in its condemnation of business irregularities. So far there had been no exception to its tacit rule that those who broke the law of probity must pay; and everyone was aware that even Beaufort and Beaufort's wife would be offered up unflinchingly to this principle. But to be obliged to offer them up would be not only painful but inconvenient. The disappearance of the Beauforts would leave a considerable void in their compact little circle; and those who were too ignorant or too careless to shudder at the moral catastrophe bewailed in advance the loss of the best ballroom in New York.

Archer had definitely made up his mind to go to Washington. He was waiting only for the opening of the law-suit of which he had spoken to May, so that its date might coincide with that of his visit; but on the following Tuesday he learned from Mr. Letterblair that the case might be postponed for several weeks. Nevertheless, he went home that afternoon determined in any event to leave the next evening. The chances were that May, who knew nothing of his professional life, and had never shown any interest in it, would not learn of the postponement, should it take place, nor remember the names of the litigants if they were mentioned before her; and at any rate he could no longer put off seeing Madame Olenska. There were too many things that he must say to her.

On the Wednesday morning, when he reached his office, Mr. Letterblair met him with a troubled face. Beaufort, after all, had not managed to "tide over"; but by setting afloat the rumor that he had done so he had reassured his depositors, and heavy payments had poured into the bank till the previous evening, when disturbing reports again began to predominate. In consequence, a run on the bank had begun, and its doors were likely to close before the day was over. The ugliest things were being said of Beaufort's dastardly maneuver, and his failure promised to be one of the most discreditable in the history of Wall Street.

The extent of the calamity left Mr. Letterblair white and incapacitated. "I've seen bad things in my time; but nothing as bad as this. Everybody we know will be hit, one way or another. And what will be done about Mrs. Beaufort? What *can* be done about her? I pity Mrs. Manson Mingott as much as anybody: coming at her age, there's no knowing what effect this affair may have on her. She always believed in Beaufort—she made a friend of him! And there's the whole Dallas connection: poor Mrs. Beaufort is related to every one of you. Her only chance would be to leave her husband—yet how can anyone tell her so? Her duty is at his side; and luckily she seems always to have been blind to his private weaknesses."

There was a knock, and Mr. Letterblair turned his head sharply. "What is it? I can't be disturbed."

A clerk brought in a letter for Archer and withdrew. Recognizing his wife's hand, the young man opened the envelope and read: "Won't you please come up town as early as you can? Granny had a slight stroke last night. In some mysterious way she found out before anyone else this awful news about the bank. Uncle Lovell is away shooting, and the idea of the disgrace has made poor Papa so nervous that he has a temperature and can't leave his room. Mamma needs you dreadfully, and I do hope you can get away at once and go straight to Granny's."

Archer handed the note to his senior partner, and a few minutes later was crawling northward in a crowded horse-car, which he exchanged at Fourteenth Street for one of the high staggering omnibuses of the Fifth Avenue line. It was after twelve o'clock when this laborious vehicle dropped him at old Catherine's. The sitting-room window on the ground floor, where she usually throned, was tenanted by the inadequate figure of her daughter, Mrs. Welland, who signed a haggard welcome as she caught sight of Archer; and at

the door he was met by May. The hall wore the unnatural appearance peculiar to well-kept houses suddenly invaded by illness: wraps
and furs lay in heaps on the chairs, a doctor's bag and overcoat were
on the table, and beside them letters and cards had already piled up
unheeded.

May looked pale but smiling: Dr. Bencomb, who had just come
for the second time, took a more hopeful view, and Mrs. Mingott's
dauntless determination to live and get well was already having an
effect on her family. May led Archer into the old lady's sitting room,
where the sliding doors opening into the bedroom had been drawn
shut, and the heavy yellow damask portières dropped over them; and
here Mrs. Welland communicated to him in horrified undertones
the details of the catastrophe. It appeared that the evening before
something dreadful and mysterious had happened. At about eight
o'clock, just after Mrs. Mingott had finished the game of solitaire
that she always played after dinner, the door-bell had rung, and a
lady so thickly veiled that the servants did not immediately recognize
her had asked to be received.

The butler, hearing a familiar voice, had thrown open the sitting-
room door, announcing: "Mrs. Julius Beaufort"—and had then
closed it again on the two ladies. They must have been together, he
thought, about an hour. When Mrs. Mingott's bell rang Mrs. Beaufort had already slipped away unseen, and the old lady, white and
vast and terrible, sat alone in her great chair, and signed to the butler
to help her into her room. She seemed, at that time, though obviously distressed, in complete control of her body and brain. The mulatto maid put her to bed, brought her a cup of tea as usual, laid everything straight in the room, and went away; but at three in the
morning the bell rang again, and the two servants, hastening in at
this unwonted summons (for old Catherine usually slept like a
baby), had found their mistress sitting up against her pillows with a
crooked smile on her face and one little hand hanging limp from its
huge arm.

The stroke had clearly been a slight one, for she was able to articu-
late and to make her wishes known; and soon after the doctor's first
visit she had begun to regain control of her facial muscles. But the
alarm had been great; and proportionately great was the indignation
when it was gathered from Mrs. Mingott's fragmentary phrases that
Regina Beaufort had come to ask her—incredible effrontery!—to
back up her husband, see them through—not to "desert" them, as

she called it—in fact to induce the whole family to cover and con-
done their monstrous dishonor.

"I said to her: 'Honor's always been honor, and honesty honesty,
in Manson Mingott's house, and will be till I'm carried out of it feet
first,' " the old woman had stammered into her daughter's ear, in the
thick voice of the partly paralyzed. "And when she said: 'But my
name, Auntie—my name's Regina Dallas,' I said: 'It was Beaufort
when he covered you with jewels, and it's got to stay Beaufort now
that he's covered you with shame.' "

So much, with tears and gasps of horror, Mrs. Welland imparted,
blanched and demolished by the unwonted obligation of having at
last to fix her eyes on the unpleasant and the discreditable. "If only I
could keep it from your father-in-law: he always says: 'Augusta, for
pity's sake, don't destroy my last illusions'—and how am I to prevent
his knowing these horrors?" the poor lady wailed.

"After all, Mamma, he won't have *seen* them," her daughter
suggested; and Mrs. Welland sighed: "Ah, no; thank heaven he's
safe in bed. And Dr. Bencomb has promised to keep him there till
poor Mamma is better, and Regina has been got away somewhere."

Archer had seated himself near the window and was gazing out
blankly at the deserted thoroughfare. It was evident that he had
been summoned rather for the moral support of the stricken ladies
than because of any specific aid that he could render. Mr. Lovell
Mingott had been telegraphed for, and messages were being despatched by hand to the members of the family living in New York;
and meanwhile there was nothing to do but to discuss in hushed
tones the consequences of Beaufort's dishonor and of his wife's
unjustifiable action.

Mrs. Lovell Mingott, who had been in another room writing
notes, presently reappeared, and added her voice to the discussion. In
their day, the elder ladies agreed, the wife of a man who had done
anything disgraceful in business had only one idea: to efface herself,
to disappear with him. "There was the case of poor Grandmamma
Spicer; your great-grandmother, May. Of course," Mrs. Welland hastened to add, "your great-grandfather's money difficulties were private—losses at cards, or signing a note for somebody—I never quite
knew, because Mamma would never speak of it. But she was brought
up in the country because her mother had to leave New York after
the disgrace, whatever it was: they lived up the Hudson alone, winter
and summer, till Mamma was sixteen. It would never have occurred

to Grandmamma Spicer to ask the family to 'countenance' her, as I understand Regina calls it; though a private disgrace is nothing compared to the scandal of ruining hundreds of innocent people."

"Yes, it would be more becoming in Regina to hide her own countenance than to talk about other people's," Mrs. Lovell Mingott agreed. "I understand that the emerald necklace she wore at the Opera last Friday had been sent on approval from Ball and Black's in the afternoon. I wonder if they'll ever get it back?"

Archer listened unmoved to the relentless chorus. The idea of absolute financial probity as the first law of a gentleman's code was too deeply ingrained in him for sentimental considerations to weaken it. An adventurer like Lemuel Struthers might build up the millions of his Shoe Polish on any number of shady dealings; but unblemished honesty was the *noblesse oblige* of old financial New York. Nor did Mrs. Beaufort's fate greatly move Archer. He felt, no doubt, more sorry for her than her indignant relatives; but it seemed to him that the tie between husband and wife, even if breakable in prosperity, should be indissoluble in misfortune. As Mr. Letterblair had said, a wife's place was at her husband's side when he was in trouble; but society's place was not at his side, and Mrs. Beaufort's cool assumption that it was seemed almost to make her his accomplice. The mere idea of a woman's appealing to her family to screen her husband's business dishonor was inadmissible, since it was the one thing that the Family, as an institution, could not do.

The mulatto maid called Mrs. Lovell Mingott into the hall, and the latter came back in a moment with a frowning brow.

"She wants me to telegraph for Ellen Olenska. I had written to Ellen, of course, and to Medora; but now it seems that's not enough. I'm to telegraph to her immediately, and to tell her that she's to come alone."

The announcement was received in silence. Mrs. Welland sighed resignedly, and May rose from her seat and went to gather up some newspapers that had been scattered on the floor.

"I suppose it must be done," Mrs. Lovell Mingott continued, as if hoping to be contradicted; and May turned back toward the middle of the room.

"Of course it must be done," she said. "Granny knows what she wants, and we must carry out all her wishes. Shall I write the telegram for you, Auntie? If it goes at once Ellen can probably catch tomorrow morning's train." She pronounced the syllables of the name with a peculiar clearness, as if she had tapped on two silver bells.

"Well, it can't go at once. Jasper and the pantry-boy are both out with notes and telegrams."

May turned to her husband with a smile. "But here's Newland, ready to do anything. Will you take the telegram, Newland? There'll be just time before luncheon."

Archer rose with a murmur of readiness, and she seated herself at old Catherine's rosewood bonheur du jour, and wrote out the message in her large immature hand. When it was written she blotted it neatly and handed it to Archer.

"What a pity," she said, "that you and Ellen will cross each other on the way!—Newland," she added, turning to her mother and aunt, "is obliged to go to Washington about a patent law-suit that is coming up before the Supreme Court. I suppose Uncle Lovell will be back by tomorrow night, and with Granny improving so much it doesn't seem right to ask Newland to give up an important engagement for the firm—does it?"

She paused, as if for an answer, and Mrs. Welland hastily declared: "Oh, of course not, darling. Your Granny would be the last person to wish it." As Archer left the room with the telegram, he heard his mother-in-law add, presumably to Mrs. Lovell Mingott: "But why on earth she should make you telegraph for Ellen Olenska—" and May's clear voice rejoin: "Perhaps it's to urge on her again that after all her duty is with her husband."

The outer door closed on Archer and he walked hastily away toward the telegraph office.

28

"Ol—ol—howjer spell it, anyhow?" asked the tart young lady to whom Archer had pushed his wife's telegram across the brass ledge of the Western Union office.

"Olenska—O-len-ska," he repeated, drawing back the message in order to print out the foreign syllables above May's rambling script.

"It's an unlikely name for a New York telegraph office; at least in this quarter," an unexpected voice observed; and turning around Archer saw Lawrence Lefferts at his elbow, pulling an imperturbable moustache and affecting not to glance at the message.

"Hallo, Newland: thought I'd catch you here. I've just heard of old Mrs. Mingott's stroke; and as I was on my way to the house I saw you turning down this street and nipped after you. I suppose you've come from there?"

Archer nodded, and pushed his telegram under the lattice.

"Very bad, eh?" Lefferts continued. "Wiring to the family, I suppose. I gather it *is* bad, if you're including Countess Olenska."

Archer's lips stiffened; he felt a savage impulse to dash his fist into the long, vain, handsome face at his side.

"Why?" he questioned.

Lefferts, who was known to shrink from discussion, raised his eyebrows with an ironic grimace that warned the other of the watching damsel behind the lattice. Nothing could be worse "form" the look reminded Archer, than any display of temper in a public place.

Archer had never been more indifferent to the requirements of form; but his impulse to do Lawrence Lefferts a physical injury was only momentary. The idea of bandying Ellen Olenska's name with him at such a time, and on whatsoever provocation, was unthinkable. He paid for his telegram, and the two young men went out together into the street. There Archer, having regained his self-control, went on: "Mrs. Mingott is much better: the doctor feels no anxiety whatever"; and Lefferts, with profuse expressions of relief, asked him if he had heard that there were beastly bad rumors again about Beaufort. . . .

That afternoon the announcement of the Beaufort failure was in all the papers. It overshadowed the report of Mrs. Manson Mingott's stroke, and only the few who had heard of the mysterious connection between the two events thought of ascribing old Catherine's illness to anything but the accumulation of flesh and years.

The whole of New York was darkened by the tale of Beaufort's dishonor. There had never, as Mr. Letterblair said, been a worse case in his memory, nor, for that matter, in the memory of the far-off Letterblair who had given his name to the firm. The bank had continued to take in money for a whole day after its failure was inevitable; and as many of its clients belonged to one or another of the ruling clans, Beaufort's duplicity seemed doubly cynical. If Mrs. Beaufort had not taken the tone that such misfortunes (the word was her own) were "the test of friendship," compassion for her might have tempered the general indignation against her husband. As it was—and especially after the object of her nocturnal visit to Mrs. Manson Mingott had become known—her cynicism was held to exceed his; and she had not the excuse—nor her detractors the satisfaction—of pleading that she was "a foreigner." It was some comfort (to those whose securities were not in jeopardy) to be able to remind themselves that Beaufort *was*; but, after all, if a Dallas of South Carolina took his view of the case, and glibly talked of his soon being "on his feet again," the argument lost its edge, and there was nothing to do but to accept this awful evidence of the indissolubility of marriage. Society must manage to get on without the Beauforts, and there was an end of it—except indeed for such hapless victims of the disaster as Medora Manson, the poor old Miss Lannings, and certain other misguided ladies of good family who, if only they had listened to Mr. Henry van der Luyden. . . .

"The best thing the Beauforts can do," said Mrs. Archer, summing it up as if she were pronouncing a diagnosis and prescribing a course of treatment, "is to go and live at Regina's little place in North Carolina. Beaufort has always kept a racing stable, and he had better breed trotting horses. I should say he had all the qualities of a successful horse-dealer." Everyone agreed with her, but no one condescended to enquire what the Beauforts really meant to do.

The next day Mrs. Manson Mingott was much better: she recovered her voice sufficiently to give orders that no one should mention the Beauforts to her again, and asked—when Dr. Bencomb appeared—what in the world her family meant by making such a fuss about her health.

"If people of my age *will* eat chicken salad in the evening what are they to expect?" she enquired; and, the doctor having opportunely modified her dietary, the stroke was transformed into an attack of indigestion. But in spite of her firm tone old Catherine did not wholly recover her former attitude toward life. The growing remoteness of old age, though it had not diminished her curiosity about her neighbors, had blunted her never very lively compassion for their troubles; and she seemed to have no difficulty in putting the Beaufort disaster out of her mind. But for the first time she became absorbed in her own symptoms, and began to take a sentimental interest in certain members of her family to whom she had hitherto been contemptuously indifferent.

Mr. Welland, in particular, had the privilege of attracting her notice. Of her sons-in-law he was the one she had most consistently ignored; and all his wife's efforts to represent him as a man of forceful character and marked intellectual ability (if he had only "chosen") had been met with a derisive chuckle. But his eminence as a valetudinarian now made him an object of engrossing interest, and Mrs. Mingott issued an imperial summons to him to come and compare diets as soon as his temperature permitted; for old Catherine was now the first to recognize that one could not be too careful about temperatures.

Twenty-four hours after Madame Olenska's summons a telegram announced that she would arrive from Washington on the evening of the following day. At the Wellands', where the Newland Archers chanced to be lunching, the question as to who should meet her at Jersey City was immediately raised; and the material difficulties amid which the Welland household struggled as if it had been a frontier outpost, lent animation to the debate. It was agreed that Mrs. Welland could not possibly go to Jersey City because she was to accompany her husband to old Catherine's that afternoon, and the brougham could not be spared, since, if Mr. Welland were "upset" by seeing his mother-in-law for the first time after her attack, he might have to be taken home at a moment's notice. The Welland sons would of course be "down town," Mr. Lovell Mingott would be just hurrying back from his shooting, and the Mingott carriage engaged in meeting him; and one could not ask May, at the close of a winter afternoon, to go alone across the ferry to Jersey City, even in her own carriage. Nevertheless, it might appear inhospitable—and contrary to old Catherine's express wishes—if Madame Olenska were allowed to arrive without any of the family being at the station to receive her. It was just like Ellen, Mrs. Welland's tired voice implied, to place the family in such a dilemma. "It's always one thing after another," the poor lady grieved, in one of her rare revolts against fate; "the only thing that makes me think Mamma must be less well than Dr. Bencomb will admit is this morbid desire to have Ellen come at once, however inconvenient it is to meet her."

The words had been thoughtless, as the utterances of impatience often are; and Mr. Welland was upon them with a pounce.

"Augusta," he said, turning pale and laying down his fork, "have you any other reason for thinking that Bencomb is less to be relied on than he was? Have you noticed that he has been less conscientious than usual in following up my case or your mother's?"

It was Mrs. Welland's turn to grow pale as the endless consequences of her blunder unrolled themselves before her; but she managed to laugh, and take a second helping of scalloped oysters, before she said, struggling back into her old armor of cheerfulness: "My dear, how could you imagine such a thing? I only meant that, after the decided stand Mamma took about its being Ellen's duty to go back to her husband, it seems strange that she should be seized with this sudden whim to see her, when there are half a dozen other grandchildren that she might have asked for. But we must never forget that Mamma, in spite of her wonderful vitality, is a very old woman."

Mr. Welland's brow remained clouded, and it was evident that his perturbed imagination had fastened at once on this last remark. "Yes: your mother's a very old woman; and for all we know Bencomb may not be as successful with very old people. As you say, my dear, it's always one thing after another; and in another ten or fifteen years I suppose I shall have the pleasing duty of looking about for a new doctor. It's always better to make such a change before it's absolutely necessary." And having arrived at this Spartan decision Mr. Welland firmly took up his fork.

"But all the while," Mrs. Welland began again, as she rose from the luncheon table, and led the way into the wilderness of purple satin and malachite known as the back drawing room, "I don't see how Ellen's to be got here tomorrow evening; and I do like to have things settled for at least twenty-four hours ahead."

Archer turned from the fascinated contemplation of a small painting representing two Cardinals carousing, in an octagonal ebony frame set with medallions of onyx.

"Shall I fetch her?" he proposed. "I can easily get away from the office in time to meet the brougham at the ferry, if May will send it there." His heart was beating excitedly as he spoke.

Mrs. Welland heaved a sigh of gratitude, and May, who had moved away to the window, turned to shed on him a beam of approval. "So you see, Mamma, everything *will* be settled twenty-four hours in advance," she said, stooping over to kiss her mother's troubled forehead.

May's brougham awaited her at the door, and she was to drive Archer to Union Square, where he could pick up a Broadway car to carry him to the office. As she settled herself in her corner she said: "I didn't want to worry Mamma by raising fresh obstacles; but how can you meet Ellen tomorrow, and bring her back to New York, when you're going to Washington?"

"Oh, I'm not going," Archer answered.

"Not going? Why, what's happened?" Her voice was as clear as a bell, and full of wifely solicitude.

"The case is off—postponed."

"Postponed? How odd! I saw a note this morning from Mr. Letterblair to Mamma saying that he was going to Washington tomorrow for the big patent case that he was to argue before the Supreme Court. You said it was a patent case, didn't you?"

"Well—that's it: the whole office can't go. Letterblair decided to go this morning."

"Then it's *not* postponed?" she continued, with an insistence so unlike her that he felt the blood rising to his face, as if he were blushing for her unwonted lapse from all the traditional delicacies.

"No: but my going is," he answered, cursing the unnecessary explanations that he had given when he had announced his intention of going to Washington, and wondering where he had read that clever liars give details, but that the cleverest do not. It did not hurt him half as much to tell May an untruth as to see her trying to pretend that she had not detected him.

"I'm not going till later on: luckily for the convenience of your family," he continued, taking base refuge in sarcasm. As he spoke he felt that she was looking at him, and he turned his eyes to hers in order not to appear to be avoiding them. Their glances met for a second, and perhaps let them into each other's meanings more deeply than either cared to go.

"Yes; it *is* awfully convenient," May brightly agreed, "that you should be able to meet Ellen after all; you saw how much Mamma appreciated your offering to do it."

"Oh, I'm delighted to do it." The carriage stopped, and as he jumped out she leaned to him and laid her hand on his. "Good-bye, dearest," she said, her eyes so blue that he wondered afterward if they had shone on him through tears.

He turned away and hurried across Union Square, repeating to himself, in a sort of inward chant: "It's all of two hours from Jersey City to old Catherine's. It's all of two hours—and it may be more."

29

His wife's dark blue brougham (with the wedding varnish still on it) met Archer at the ferry, and conveyed him luxuriously to the Pennsylvania terminus in Jersey City.

It was a somber snowy afternoon, and the gas-lamps were lit in the big reverberating station. As he paced the platform, waiting for the Washington express, he remembered that there were people who thought there would one day be a tunnel under the Hudson through which the trains of the Pennsylvania railway would run straight into New York. They were of the brotherhood of visionaries who likewise predicted the building of ships that would cross the Atlantic in five days, the invention of a flying machine, lighting by electricity, telephonic communication without wires, and other Arabian Night marvels.

"I don't care which of their visions comes true," Archer mused, "as long as the tunnel isn't built yet." In his senseless schoolboy happiness he pictured Madame Olenska's descent from the train, his discovery of her a long way off, among the throngs of meaningless faces, her clinging to his arm as he guided her to the carriage, their slow approach to the wharf among slipping horses, laden carts, vociferating teamsters, and then the startling quiet of the ferry-boat, where they would sit side by side under the snow, in the motionless carriage, while the earth seemed to glide away under them, rolling to the other side of the sun. It was incredible, the number of things he had to say to her, and in what eloquent order they were forming themselves on his lips. . . .

The clanging and groaning of the train came nearer, and it staggered slowly into the station like a prey-laden monster into its lair. Archer pushed forward, elbowing through the crowd, and staring blindly into window after window of the high-hung carriages. And then, suddenly, he saw Madame Olenska's pale and surprised face close at hand, and had again the mortified sensation of having forgotten what she looked like.

They reached each other, their hands met, and he drew her arm through his. "This way—I have the carriage," he said.

After that it all happened as he had dreamed. He helped her into the brougham with her bags, and had afterward the vague recollection of having properly reassured her about her grandmother and given her a summary of the Beaufort situation (he was struck by the softness of her: "Poor Regina!"). Meanwhile the carriage had worked its way out of the coil about the station, and they were crawling down the slippery incline to the wharf, menaced by swaying coal-carts, bewildered horses, dishevelled express-wagons, and an empty hearse—ah, that hearse! She shut her eyes as it passed, and clutched at Archer's hand.

"If only it doesn't mean—poor Granny!"

"Oh, no, no—she's much better—she's all right, really. There—we've passed it!" he exclaimed, as if that made all the difference. Her hand remained in his, and as the carriage lurched across the gangplank onto the ferry he bent over, unbuttoned her tight brown glove, and kissed her palm as if he had kissed a relic. She disengaged herself with a faint smile, and he said: "You didn't expect me today?"

"Oh, no."

"I meant to go to Washington to see you. I'd made all my arrangements—I very nearly crossed you in the train."

"Oh—" she exclaimed, as if terrified by the narrowness of their escape.

"Do you know—I hardly remembered you?"

"Hardly remembered me?"

"I mean: how shall I explain? I—it's always so. *Each time you happen to me all over again.*"

"Oh, yes: I know! I know!"

"Does it—do I too: to you?" he insisted.

She nodded, looking out of the window.

"Ellen—Ellen—Ellen!"

She made no answer, and he sat in silence, watching her profile grow indistinct against the snow-streaked dusk beyond the window. What had she been doing in all those four long months, he wondered? How little they knew of each other, after all! The precious moments were slipping away, but he had forgotten everything that he had meant to say to her and could only helplessly brood on the mystery of their remoteness and their proximity, which seemed to be symbolized by the fact of their sitting so close to each other, and yet being unable to see each other's faces.

"What a pretty carriage! Is it May's?" she asked, suddenly turning her face from the window.

"Yes."

"It was May who sent you to fetch me, then? How kind of her!"

He made no answer for a moment; then he said explosively: "Your husband's secretary came to see me the day after we met in Boston."

In his brief letter to her he had made no allusion to M. Rivière's visit, and his intention had been to bury the incident in his bosom. But her reminder that they were in his wife's carriage provoked him to an impulse of retaliation. He would see if she liked his reference to Rivière any better than he liked hers to May! As on certain other occasions when he had expected to shake her out of her usual composure, she betrayed no sign of surprise: and at once he concluded: "He writes to her, then."

"M. Rivière went to see you?"

"Yes: didn't you know?"

"No," she answered simply.

"And you're not surprised?"

She hesitated. "Why should I be? He told me in Boston that he knew you; that he'd met you in England I think."

"Ellen—I must ask you one thing."

"Yes."

"I wanted to ask it after I saw him, but I couldn't put it in a letter. It was Rivière who helped you to get away—when you left your husband?"

His heart was beating suffocatingly. Would she meet this question with the same composure?

"Yes: I owe him a great debt," she answered, without the least tremor in her quiet voice.

Her tone was so natural, so almost indifferent, that Archer's turmoil subsided. Once more she had managed, by her sheer simplicity, to make him feel stupidly conventional just when he thought he was flinging convention to the winds.

"I think you're the most honest woman I ever met!" he exclaimed.

"Oh, no—but probably one of the least fussy," she answered, a smile in her voice.

"Call it what you like: you look at things as they are."

"Ah—I've had to. I've had to look at the Gorgon."

"Well—it hasn't blinded you! You've seen that she's just an old bogey like all the others."

"She doesn't blind one; but she dries up one's tears."

The answer checked the pleading on Archer's lips: it seemed to come from depths of experience beyond his reach. The slow advance of the ferry-boat had ceased, and her bows bumped against the piles of the slip with a violence that made the brougham stagger, and flung Archer and Madame Olenska against each other. The young man, trembling, felt the pressure of her shoulder, and passed his arm about her.

"If you're not blind, then, you must see that this can't last."

"What can't?"

"Our being together—and not together."

"No. You ought not to have come today," she said in an altered voice; and suddenly she turned, flung her arms about him and pressed her lips to his. At the same moment the carriage began to move, and a gas-lamp at the head of the slip flashed its light into the window. She drew away, and they sat silent and motionless while the brougham struggled through the congestion of carriages about the ferry-landing. As they gained the street Archer began to speak hurriedly.

"Don't be afraid of me: you needn't squeeze yourself back into your corner like that. A stolen kiss isn't what I want. Look: I'm not even trying to touch the sleeve of your jacket. Don't suppose that I don't understand your reasons for not wanting to let this feeling between us dwindle into an ordinary hole-and-corner love affair. I couldn't have spoken like this yesterday, because when we've been apart, and I'm looking forward to seeing you, every thought is burnt up in a great flame. But then you come; and you're so much more than I remembered, and what I want of you is so much more than an hour or two every now and then, with wastes of thirsty waiting between, that I can sit perfectly still beside you, like this, with that other vision in my mind, just quietly trusting to it to come true."

For a moment she made no reply; then she asked, hardly above a whisper: "What do you mean by trusting to it to come true?"

"Why—you know it will, don't you?"

"Your vision of you and me together?" She burst into a sudden hard laugh. "You choose your place well to put it to me!"

"Do you mean because we're in my wife's brougham? Shall we get out and walk, then? I don't suppose you mind a little snow?"

She laughed again, more gently. "No; I shan't get out and walk, because my business is to get to Granny's as quickly as I can. And you'll sit beside me, and we'll look, not at visions, but at realities."

"I don't know what you mean by realities. The only reality to me is this."

She met the words with a long silence, during which the carriage rolled down an obscure side-street and then turned into the searching illumination of Fifth Avenue.

"Is it your idea, then, that I should live with you as your mistress —since I can't be your wife?" she asked.

The crudeness of the question startled him: the word was one that women of his class fought shy of, even when their talk flitted closest about the topic. He noticed that Madame Olenska pronounced it as if it had a recognized place in her vocabulary, and he wondered if it had been used familiarly in her presence in the horrible life she had fled from. Her question pulled him up with a jerk, and he floundered.

"I want—I want somehow to get away with you into a world where words like that—categories like that—won't exist. Where we shall be simply two human beings who love each other, who are the whole of life to each other; and nothing else on earth will matter."

She drew a deep sigh that ended in another laugh. "Oh, my dear— where is that country? Have you ever been there?" she asked; and as he remained sullenly dumb she went on: "I know so many who've tried to find it; and, believe me, they all got out by mistake at wayside stations: at places like Boulogne, or Pisa, or Monte Carlo —and it wasn't at all different from the old world they'd left, but only rather smaller and dingier and more promiscuous."

He had never heard her speak in such a tone, and he remembered the phrase she had used a little while before.

"Yes, the Gorgon *has* dried your tears," he said.

"Well, she opened my eyes too; it's a delusion to say that she blinds people. What she does is just the contrary—she fastens their eyelids open, so that they're never again in the blessed darkness. Isn't there a Chinese torture like that? There ought to be. Ah, believe me, it's a miserable little country!"

The carriage had crossed Forty-second Street: May's sturdy brougham-horse was carrying them northward as if he had been a Kentucky trotter. Archer choked with the sense of wasted minutes and vain words.

"Then what, exactly, is your plan for us?" he asked.

"For *us?* But there's no *us* in that sense! We're near each other only if we stay far from each other. Then we can be ourselves. Otherwise we're only Newland Archer, the husband of Ellen Olenska's cousin, and Ellen Olenska, the cousin of Newland Archer's wife, trying to be happy behind the backs of the people who trust them."

"Ah, I'm beyond that," he groaned.

"No, you're not! You've never been beyond. And *I* have," she said, in a strange voice, "and I know what it looks like there."

He sat silent, dazed with inarticulate pain. Then he groped in the darkness of the carriage for the little bell that signaled orders to the coachman. He remembered that May rang twice when she wished to stop. He pressed the bell, and the carriage drew up beside the curbstone.

"Why are we stopping? This is not Granny's," Madame Olenska exclaimed.

"No: I shall get out here," he stammered, opening the door and jumping to the pavement. By the light of a street-lamp he saw her startled face, and the instinctive motion she made to detain him. He closed the door, and leaned for a moment in the window.

"You're right: I ought not to have come today," he said, lowering his voice so that the coachman should not hear. She bent forward, and seemed about to speak; but he had already called out the order to drive on, and the carriage rolled away while he stood on the corner. The snow was over, and a tingling wind had sprung up, that lashed his face as he stood gazing. Suddenly he felt something stiff and cold on his lashes, and perceived that he had been crying, and that the wind had frozen his tears.

He thrust his hands in his pockets, and walked at a sharp pace down Fifth Avenue to his own house.

30

THAT evening when Archer came down before dinner he found the drawing room empty.

He and May were dining alone, all the family engagements having been postponed since Mrs. Manson Mingott's illness; and as May was the more punctual of the two he was surprised that she had not preceded him. He knew that she was at home, for while he dressed he had heard her moving about in her room; and he wondered what had delayed her.

He had fallen into the way of dwelling on such conjectures as a means of tying his thoughts fast to reality. Sometimes he felt as if he had found the clue to his father-in-law's absorption in trifles; perhaps even Mr. Welland, long ago, had had escapes and visions, and had conjured up all the hosts of domesticity to defend himself against them.

When May appeared he thought she looked tired. She had put on the low-necked and tightly-laced dinner-dress which the Mingott ceremonial exacted on the most informal occasions, and had built her fair hair into its usual accumulated coils; and her face, in contrast, was wan and almost faded. But she shone on him with her usual tenderness, and her eyes had kept the blue dazzle of the day before.

"What became of you, dear?" she asked. "I was waiting at Granny's, and Ellen came alone, and said she had dropped you on the way because you had to rush off on business. There's nothing wrong?"

"Only some letters I'd forgotten, and wanted to get off before dinner."

"Ah—" she said; and a moment afterward: "I'm sorry you didn't come to Granny's—unless the letters were urgent."

"They were," he rejoined, surprised at her insistence. "Besides, I don't see why I should have gone to your grandmother's. I didn't know you were there."

She turned and moved to the looking-glass above the mantelpiece. As she stood there, lifting her long arm to fasten a puff that had slipped from its place in her intricate hair, Archer was struck by something languid and inelastic in her attitude, and wondered if the deadly monotony of their lives had laid its weight on her also. Then he remembered that, as he had left the house that morning, she had called over the stairs that she would meet him at her grandmother's so that they might drive home together. He had called back a cheery "Yes!" and then, absorbed in other visions, had forgotten his promise. Now he was smitten with compunction, yet irritated that so trifling an omission should be stored up against him after nearly two years of marriage. He was weary of living in a perpetual tepid honeymoon, without the temperature of passion yet with all its exactions. If May had spoken out her grievances (he suspected her of many) he might have laughed them away; but she was trained to conceal imaginary wounds under a Spartan smile.

To disguise his own annoyance he asked how her grandmother was, and she answered that Mrs. Mingott was still improving, but had been rather disturbed by the last news about the Beauforts.

"What news?"

"It seems they're going to stay in New York. I believe he's going into an insurance business, or something. They're looking about for a small house."

The preposterousness of the case was beyond discussion, and they went in to dinner. During dinner their talk moved in its usual limited circle; but Archer noticed that his wife made no allusion to Madame Olenska, nor to old Catherine's reception of her. He was thankful for the fact, yet felt it to be vaguely ominous.

They went up to the library for coffee, and Archer lit a cigar and took down a volume of Michelet. He had taken to history in the evenings since May had shown a tendency to ask him to read aloud whenever she saw him with a volume of poetry: not that he disliked the sound of his own voice, but because he could always foresee her comments on what he read. In the days of their engagement she had simply (as he now perceived) echoed what he told her; but since he had ceased to provide her with opinions she had begun to hazard her own, with results destructive to his enjoyment of the works commented on.

Seeing that he had chosen history she fetched her work-basket, drew up an armchair to the green-shaded student lamp, and uncovered a cushion she was embroidering for his sofa. She was not a clever needlewoman; her large capable hands were made for riding, rowing and open-air activities; but since other wives embroidered cushions for their husbands she did not wish to omit this last link in her devotion.

She was so placed that Archer, by merely raising his eyes, could see her bent above her work-frame, her ruffled elbow-sleeves slipping back from her firm round arms, the betrothal sapphire shining on her left hand above her broad gold wedding-ring, and the right hand slowly and laboriously stabbing the canvas. As she sat thus, the lamplight full on her clear brow, he said to himself with a secret dismay that he would always know the thoughts behind it, that never, in all the years to come, would she surprise him by an unexpected mood, by a new idea, a weakness, a cruelty or an emotion. She had spent her poetry and romance on their short courting: the function was exhausted because the need was past. Now she was simply ripening into a copy of her mother, and mysteriously, by the very process, trying to turn him into a Mr. Welland. He laid down his book and stood up impatiently; and at once she raised her head.

"What's the matter?"

"The room is stifling: I want a little air."

He had insisted that the library curtains should draw backward and forward on a rod, so that they might be closed in the evening, instead of remaining nailed to a gilt cornice, and immovably looped up over layers of lace, as in the drawing room; and he pulled them back and pushed up the sash, leaning out into the icy night. The mere fact of not looking at May, seated beside his table, under his lamp, the fact of seeing other houses, roofs, chimneys, of getting the sense of other lives outside his own, other cities beyond New York, and a whole world beyond his world, cleared his brain and made it easier to breathe.

After he had leaned out into the darkness for a few minutes he heard her say: "Newland! Do shut the window. You'll catch your death."

He pulled the sash down and turned back. "Catch my death!" he echoed; and he felt like adding: "But I've caught it already. I *am* dead—I've been dead for months and months."

And suddenly the play of the word flashed up a wild suggestion. What if it were *she* who was dead! If she were going to die—to die soon—and leave him free! The sensation of standing there, in that warm familiar room, and looking at her, and wishing her dead, was so strange, so fascinating and overmastering, that its enormity did not immediately strike him. He simply felt that chance had given him a new possibility to which his sick soul might cling. Yes, May might die—people did: young people, healthy people like herself: she might die, and set him suddenly free.

She glanced up, and he saw by her widening eyes that there must be something strange in his own.

"Newland! Are you ill?"

He shook his head and turned toward his armchair. She bent over her work-frame, and as he passed he laid his hand on her hair. "Poor May!" he said.

"Poor? Why poor?" she echoed with a strained laugh.

"Because I shall never be able to open a window without worrying you," he rejoined, laughing also.

For a moment she was silent; then she said very low, her head bowed over her work: "I shall never worry if you're happy."

"Ah, my dear; and I shall never be happy unless I can open the windows!"

"In *this* weather?" she remonstrated; and with a sigh he buried his head in his book.

Six or seven days passed. Archer heard nothing from Madame Olenska, and became aware that her name would not be mentioned in his presence by any member of the family. He did not try to see her; to do so while she was at old Catherine's guarded bedside would have been almost impossible. In the uncertainty of the situation he let himself drift, conscious, somewhere below the surface of his thoughts, of a resolve which had come to him when he had leaned out from his library window into the icy night. The strength of that resolve made it easy to wait and make no sign.

Then one day May told him that Mrs. Manson Mingott had asked to see him. There was nothing surprising in the request, for the old lady was steadily recovering, and she had always openly declared that she preferred Archer to any of her other grandsons-in-law. May gave the message with evident pleasure: she was proud of old Catherine's appreciation of her husband.

There was a moment's pause, and then Archer felt it incumbent on him to say: "All right. Shall we go together this afternoon?"

His wife's face brightened, but she instantly answered: "Oh, you'd much better go alone. It bores Granny to see the same people too often."

Archer's heart was beating violently when he rang old Mrs. Mingott's bell. He had wanted above all things to go alone, for he felt sure the visit would give him the chance of saying a word in private to the Countess Olenska. He had determined to wait till the chance presented itself naturally; and here it was, and here he was on the doorstep. Behind the door, behind the curtains of the yellow damask room next to the hall, she was surely awaiting him; in another moment he should see her, and be able to speak to her before she led him to the sickroom.

He wanted only to put one question: after that his course would be clear. What he wished to ask was simply the date of her return to Washington; and that question she could hardly refuse to answer.

But in the yellow sitting room it was the mulatto maid who waited. Her white teeth shining like a keyboard, she pushed back the sliding doors and ushered him into old Catherine's presence.

The old woman sat in a vast throne-like armchair near her bed. Beside her was a mahogany stand bearing a cast bronze lamp with an engraved globe, over which a green paper shade had been balanced. There was not a book or a newspaper in reach, nor any evidence of feminine employment: conversation had always been Mrs. Mingott's sole pursuit, and she would have scorned to feign an interest in fancywork.

Archer saw no trace of the slight distortion left by her stroke. She merely looked paler, with darker shadows in the folds and recesses of her obesity; and, in the fluted mobcap tied by a starched bow between her first two chins, and the muslin kerchief crossed over her billowing purple dressing-gown, she seemed like some shrewd and kindly ancestress of her own who might have yielded too freely to the pleasures of the table.

She held out one of the little hands that nestled in a hollow of her huge lap like pet animals, and called to the maid: "Don't let in anyone else. If my daughters call, say I'm asleep."

The maid disappeared, and the old lady turned to her grandson.

"My dear, am I perfectly hideous?" she asked gaily, launching out one hand in search of the folds of muslin on her inaccessible bosom. "My daughters tell me it doesn't matter at my age—as if hideousness didn't matter all the more the harder it gets to conceal!"

"My dear, you're handsomer than ever!" Archer rejoined in the same tone; and she threw back her head and laughed.

"Ah, but not as handsome as Ellen!" she jerked out, twinkling at him maliciously; and before he could answer she added: "Was she so awfully handsome the day you drove her up from the ferry?"

He laughed, and she continued: "Was it because you told her so that she had to put you out on the way? In my youth young men didn't desert pretty women unless they were made to!" She gave another chuckle, and interrupted it to say almost querulously: "It's a pity she didn't marry you; I always told her so. It would have spared me all this worry. But who ever thought of sparing their grandmother worry?"

Archer wondered if her illness had blurred her faculties; but suddenly she broke out: "Well, it's settled, anyhow: she's going to stay with me, whatever the rest of the family say! She hadn't been here five minutes before I'd have gone down on my knees to keep her—if only, for the last twenty years, I'd been able to see where the floor was!"

Archer listened in silence, and she went on: "They'd talked me over, as no doubt you know: persuaded me, Lovell, and Letterblair, and Augusta Welland, and all the rest of them, that I must hold out and cut off her allowance, till she was made to see that it was her duty to go back to Olenski. They thought they'd convinced me when the secretary, or whatever he was, came out with the last proposals: handsome proposals I confess they were. After all, marriage is marriage, and money's money—both useful things in their way . . . and I didn't know what to answer—" She broke off and drew a long breath, as if speaking had become an effort. "But the minute I laid eyes on her, I said: 'You sweet bird, you! Shut you up in that cage again? Never!' And now it's settled that she's to stay here and nurse her Granny as long as there's a Granny to nurse. It's not a gay prospect, but she doesn't mind; and of course I've told Letterblair that she's to be given her proper allowance."

The young man heard her with veins aglow; but in his confusion of mind he hardly knew whether her news brought joy or pain. He had so definitely decided on the course he meant to pursue that for the moment he could not readjust his thoughts. But gradually there stole over him the delicious sense of difficulties deferred and opportunities miraculously provided. If Ellen had consented to come and live with her grandmother it must surely be because she had recognized the impossibility of giving him up. This was her answer to his final appeal of the other day: if she would not take the extreme step he had urged, she had at last yielded to half-measures. He sank back into the thought with the involuntary relief of a man who has been ready to risk everything, and suddenly tastes the dangerous sweetness of security.

"She couldn't have gone back—it was impossible!" he exclaimed.

"Ah, my dear, I always knew you were on her side; and that's why I sent for you today, and why I said to your pretty wife, when she proposed to come with you: 'No, my dear, I'm pining to see Newland, and I don't want anybody to share our transports.' For you see, my dear—" she drew her head back as far as its tethering chins permitted, and looked him full in the eyes—"you see, we shall have a fight yet. The family don't want her here, and they'll say it's because I've been ill, because I'm a weak old woman, that she's persuaded me. I'm not well enough yet to fight them one by one, and you've got to do it for me."

"I?" he stammered.

"You. Why not?" she jerked back at him, her round eyes suddenly as sharp as pen-knives. Her hand fluttered from its chair-arm and lit on his with a clutch of little pale nails like bird-claws. "Why not?" she searchingly repeated.

Archer, under the exposure of her gaze, had recovered his self-possession.

"Oh, I don't count—I'm too insignificant."

"Well, you're Letterblair's partner, ain't you? You've got to get at them through Letterblair. Unless you've got a reason," she insisted.

"Oh, my dear, I back you to hold your own against them all without my help; but you shall have it if you need it," he reassured her.

"Then we're safe!" she sighed; and smiling on him with all her ancient cunning she added, as she settled her head among the cushions: "I always knew you'd back us up, because they never quote you when they talk about its being her duty to go home."

He winced a little at her terrifying perspicacity, and longed to ask: "And May—do they quote her?" But he judged it safer to turn the question.

"And Madame Olenska? When am I to see her?" he said.

The old lady chuckled, crumpled her lids, and went through the pantomime of archness. "Not today. One at a time, please. Madame Olenska's gone out."

He flushed with disappointment, and she went on: "She's gone out, my child: gone in my carriage to see Regina Beaufort."

She paused for this announcement to produce its effect. "That's what she's reduced me to already. The day after she got here she put on her best bonnet, and told me, as cool as a cucumber, that she was going to call on Regina Beaufort. 'I don't know her; who is she?' says I. 'She's your grand-niece, and a most unhappy woman,' she says. 'She's the wife of a scoundrel,' I answered. 'Well,' she says, 'and so am I, and yet all my family want me to go back to him.' Well, that floored me, and I let her go; and finally one day she said it was raining too hard to go out on foot, and she wanted me to lend her my carriage. 'What for?' I asked her; and she said: 'To go and see Cousin Regina'—*cousin!* Now, my dear, I looked out of the window, and saw it wasn't raining a drop; but I understood her, and I let her have the carriage. . . . After all, Regina's a brave woman, and so is she; and I've always liked courage above everything."

Archer bent down and pressed his lips on the little hand that still lay on his.

"Eh—eh—eh! Whose hand did you think you were kissing, young man—your wife's, I hope?" the old lady snapped out with her mocking cackle; and as he rose to go she called out after him: "Give her her Granny's love; but you'd better not say anything about our talk."

31

ARCHER had been stunned by old Catherine's news. It was only natural that Madame Olenska should have hastened from Washington in response to her grandmother's summons; but that she should have decided to remain under her roof—especially now that Mrs. Mingott had almost regained her health—was less easy to explain.

Archer was sure that Madame Olenska's decision had not been influenced by the change in her financial situation. He knew the exact figure of the small income which her husband had allowed her at their separation. Without the addition of her grandmother's allowance it was hardly enough to live on, in any sense known to the Mingott vocabulary; and now that Medora Manson, who shared her life, had been ruined, such a pittance would barely keep the two women clothed and fed. Yet Archer was convinced that Madame Olenska had not accepted her grandmother's offer from interested motives.

She had the heedless generosity and the spasmodic extravagance of persons used to large fortunes, and indifferent to money; but she could go without many things which her relations considered indispensable, and Mrs. Lovell Mingott and Mrs. Welland had often been heard to deplore that anyone who had enjoyed the cosmopolitan luxuries of Count Olenski's establishments should care so little about "how things were done." Moreover, as Archer knew, several months had passed since her allowance had been cut off; yet in the interval she had made no effort to regain her grandmother's favor. Therefore if she had changed her course it must be for a different reason.

He did not have far to seek for that reason. On the way from the ferry she had told him that he and she must remain apart; but she had said it with her head on his breast. He knew that there was no calculated coquetry in her words; she was fighting her fate as he had fought his, and clinging desperately to her resolve that they should not break faith with the people who trusted them. But during the ten days which had elapsed since her return to New York she had perhaps guessed from his silence, and from the fact of his making no attempt to see her, that he was meditating a decisive step, a step from which there was no turning back. At the thought, a sudden fear of her own weakness might have seized her, and she might have felt that, after all, it was better to accept the compromise usual in such cases, and follow the line of least resistance.

An hour earlier, when he had rung Mrs. Mingott's bell, Archer had fancied that his path was clear before him. He had meant to have a word alone with Madame Olenska, and failing that, to learn from her grandmother on what day, and by which train, she was returning to Washington. In that train he intended to join her, and travel with her to Washington, or as much farther as she was willing to go. His own fancy inclined to Japan. At any rate she would understand at once that, wherever she went, he was going. He meant to leave a note for May that should cut off any other alternative.

He had fancied himself not only nerved for this plunge but eager to take it; yet his first feeling on hearing that the course of events was changed had been one of relief. Now, however, as he walked home from Mrs. Mingott's, he was conscious of a growing distaste for what lay before him. There was nothing unknown or unfamiliar in the path he was presumably to tread; but when he had trodden it before it was as a free man, who was accountable to no one for his actions, and could lend himself with an amused detachment to the game of precautions and prevarications, concealments and compliances, that the part required. This procedure was called "protecting a woman's honor"; and the best fiction, combined with the after-dinner talk of his elders, had long since initiated him into every detail of its code.

Now he saw the matter in a new light, and his part in it seemed singularly diminished. It was, in fact, that which, with a secret fatuity, he had watched Mrs. Thorley Rushworth play toward a fond and unperceiving husband: a smiling, bantering, humoring, watchful, and incessant lie. A lie by day, a lie by night, a lie in every touch and every look; a lie in every caress and every quarrel; a lie in every word and in every silence.

It was easier, and less dastardly on the whole, for a wife to play such a part toward her husband. A woman's standard of truthfulness was tacitly held to be lower: she was the subject creature, and versed in the arts of the enslaved. Then she could always plead moods and nerves, and the right not to be held too strictly to account; and even in the most straight-laced societies the laugh was always against the husband.

But in Archer's little world no one laughed at a wife deceived, and a certain measure of contempt was attached to men who continued their philandering after marriage. In the rotation of crops there was a recognized season for wild oats; but they were not to be sown more than once.

Archer had always shared this view: in his heart he thought Lefferts despicable. But to love Ellen Olenska was not to become a man like Lefferts: for the first time Archer found himself face to face with the dread argument of the individual case. Ellen Olenska was like no other woman, he was like no other man: their situation, therefore, resembled no one else's, and they were answerable to no tribunal but that of their own judgment.

Yes, but in ten minutes more he would be mounting his own doorstep; and there were May, and habit, and honor, and all the old decencies that he and his people had always believed in. . . .

At his corner he hesitated, and then walked on down Fifth Avenue.

Ahead of him, in the winter night, loomed a big unlit house. As he drew near he thought how often he had seen it blazing with lights, its steps awninged and carpeted, and carriages waiting in double line to draw up at the curbstone. It was in the conservatory that stretched its dead-black bulk down the side street that he had taken his first kiss from May; it was under the myriad candles of the ballroom that he had seen her appear, tall and silver-shining as a young Diana.

Now the house was as dark as the grave, except for a faint flare of gas in the basement, and a light in one upstairs room where the blind had not been lowered. As Archer reached the corner he saw that the carriage standing at the door was Mrs. Manson Mingott's. What an opportunity for Sillerton Jackson, if he should chance to pass! Archer had been greatly moved by old Catherine's account of Madame Olenska's attitude toward Mrs. Beaufort; it made the righteous reprobation of New York seem like a passing-by on the other side. But he knew well enough what construction the clubs and drawing rooms would put on Ellen Olenska's visits to her cousin.

He paused and looked up at the lighted window. No doubt the two women were sitting together in that room: Beaufort had probably sought consolation elsewhere. There were even rumors that he had left New York with Fanny Ring; but Mrs. Beaufort's attitude made the report seem improbable.

Archer had the nocturnal perspective of Fifth Avenue almost to himself. At that hour most people were indoors, dressing for dinner; and he was secretly glad that Ellen's exit was likely to be unobserved. As the thought passed through his mind the door opened, and she came out. Behind her was a faint light, such as might have been carried down the stairs to show her the way. She turned to say a word to someone; then the door closed, and she came down the steps.

"Ellen," he said in a low voice, as she reached the pavement.

She stopped with a slight start, and just then he saw two young men of fashionable cut approaching. There was a familiar air about their overcoats and the way their smart silk mufflers were folded over their white ties; and he wondered how youths of their quality happened to be dining out so early. Then he remembered that the Reggie Chiverses, whose house was a few doors above, were taking a large party that evening to see Adelaide Neilson in *Romeo and Juliet*, and guessed that the two were of the number. They passed under a lamp, and he recognized Lawrence Lefferts and a young Chivers.

A mean desire not to have Madame Olenska seen at the Beauforts' door vanished as he felt the penetrating warmth of her hand.

"I shall see you now—we shall be together," he broke out, hardly knowing what he said.

"Ah," she answered, "Granny has told you?"

While he watched her he was aware that Lefferts and Chivers, on reaching the farther side of the street corner, had discreetly struck away across Fifth Avenue. It was the kind of masculine solidarity that he himself often practiced; now he sickened at their connivance. Did she really imagine that he and she could live like this? And if not, what else did she imagine?

"Tomorrow I must see you—somewhere where we can be alone," he said, in a voice that sounded almost angry to his own ears.

She wavered, and moved toward the carriage.

"But I shall be at Granny's—for the present that is," she added, as if conscious that her change of plans required some explanation.

"Somewhere where we can be alone," he insisted.

She gave a faint laugh that grated on him.

"In New York? But there are no churches . . . no monuments."

"There's the Art Museum—in the Park," he explained, as she looked puzzled. "At half-past two. I shall be at the door. . . ."

She turned away without answering and got quickly into the carriage. As it drove off she leaned forward, and he thought she waved her hand in the obscurity. He stared after her in a turmoil of contradictory feelings. It seemed to him that he had been speaking not to the woman he loved but to another, a woman he was indebted to for pleasures already wearied of: it was hateful to find himself the prisoner of this hackneyed vocabulary.

"She'll come!" he said to himself, almost contemptuously.

Avoiding the popular "Wolfe collection," whose anecdotic canvases filled one of the main galleries of the queer wilderness of cast-iron and encaustic tiles known as the Metropolitan Museum, they had wandered down a passage to the room where the "Cesnola antiquities" mouldered in unvisited loneliness.

They had this melancholy retreat to themselves, and seated on the divan enclosing the central steam-radiator, they were staring silently at the glass cabinets mounted in ebonized wood which contained the recovered fragments of Ilium.

"It's odd," Madame Olenska said, "I never came here before."

"Ah, well—. Some day, I suppose, it will be a great Museum."

"Yes," she assented absently.

She stood up and wandered across the room. Archer, remaining seated, watched the light movements of her figure, so girlish even under its heavy furs, the cleverly planted heron wing in her fur cap, and the way a dark curl lay like a flattened vine spiral on each cheek above the ear. His mind, as always when they first met, was wholly absorbed in the delicious details that made her herself and no other. Presently he rose and approached the case before which she stood. Its glass shelves were crowded with small broken objects—hardly recognizable domestic utensils, ornaments and personal trifles—made of glass, of clay, of discolored bronze and other time-blurred substances.

"It seems cruel," she said, "that after a while nothing matters . . . any more than these little things, that used to be necessary and important to forgotten people, and now have to be guessed at under a magnifying glass and labeled: 'Use unknown.'"

"Yes; but meanwhile—"

"Ah, meanwhile—"

As she stood there, in her long sealskin coat, her hands thrust in a small round muff, her veil drawn down like a transparent mask to the tip of her nose, and the bunch of violets he had brought her stirring with her quickly-taken breath, it seemed incredible that this pure harmony of line and color should ever suffer the stupid law of change.

"Meanwhile everything matters—that concerns you," he said.

She looked at him thoughtfully, and turned back to the divan. He sat down beside her and waited; but suddenly he heard a step echoing far off down the empty rooms, and felt the pressure of the minutes.

"What is it you wanted to tell me?" she asked, as if she had received the same warning.

"What I wanted to tell you?" he rejoined. "Why, that I believe you came to New York because you were afraid."

"Afraid?"

"Of my coming to Washington."

She looked down at her muff, and he saw her hands stir in it uneasily.

"Well—?"

"Well—yes," she said.

"You *were* afraid? You knew—?"

"Yes: I knew. . . ."

"Well, then?" he insisted.

"Well, then: this is better, isn't it?" she returned with a long questioning sigh.

"Better—?"

"We shall hurt others less. Isn't it, after all, what you always wanted?"

"To have you here, you mean—in reach and yet out of reach? To meet you in this way, on the sly? It's the very reverse of what I want. I told you the other day what I wanted."

She hesitated. "And you still think this—worse?"

"A thousand times!" He paused. "It would be easy to lie to you; but the truth is I think it detestable."

"Oh, so do I!" she cried with a deep breath of relief.

He sprang up impatiently. "Well, then—it's my turn to ask: what is it, in God's name, that you think better?"

She hung her head and continued to clasp and unclasp her hands in her muff. The step drew nearer, and a guardian in a braided cap walked listlessly through the room like a ghost stalking through a necropolis. They fixed their eyes simultaneously on the case opposite them, and when the official figure had vanished down a vista of mummies and sarcophagi Archer spoke again.

"What do you think better?"

Instead of answering she murmured: "I promised Granny to stay with her because it seemed to me that here I should be safer."

"From me?"

She bent her head slightly, without looking at him.

"Safer from loving me?"

Her profile did not stir, but he saw a tear overflow on her lashes and hang in a mesh of her veil.

"Safer from doing irreparable harm. Don't let us be like all the others!" she protested.

"What others? I don't profess to be different from my kind. I'm consumed by the same wants and the same longings."

She glanced at him with a kind of terror, and he saw a faint color steal into her cheeks.

"Shall I—once come to you; and then go home?" she suddenly hazarded in a low clear voice.

The blood rushed to the young man's forehead. "Dearest!" he said, without moving. It seemed as if he held his heart in his hands, like a full cup that the least motion might overbrim.

Then her last phrase struck his ear and his face clouded. "Go home? What do you mean by going home?"

"Home to my husband."

"And you expect me to say yes to that?"

She raised her troubled eyes to his. "What else is there? I can't stay here and lie to the people who've been good to me."

"But that's the very reason why I ask you to come away!"

"And destroy their lives, when they've helped me to remake mine?"

Archer sprang to his feet and stood looking down on her in inarticulate despair. It would have been easy to say: "Yes, come; come once." He knew the power she would put in his hands if she consented; there would be no difficulty then in persuading her not to go back to her husband.

But something silenced the word on his lips. A sort of passionate honesty in her made it inconceivable that he should try to draw her into that familiar trap. "If I were to let her come," he said to himself, "I should have to let her go again." And that was not to be imagined.

But he saw the shadow of the lashes on her wet cheek, and wavered.

"After all," he began again, "we have lives of our own. . . . There's no use attempting the impossible. You're so unprejudiced about some things, so used, as you say, to looking at the Gorgon, that I don't know why you're afraid to face our case, and see it as it really is—unless you think the sacrifice is not worth making."

She stood up also, her lips tightening under a rapid frown.

"Call it that, then—I must go," she said, drawing her little watch from her bosom.

She turned away, and he followed and caught her by the wrist. "Well, then: come to me once," he said, his head turning suddenly at the thought of losing her; and for a second or two they looked at each other almost like enemies.

"When?" he insisted. "Tomorrow?"

She hesitated. "The day after."

"Dearest—!" he said again.

She had disengaged her wrist; but for a moment they continued to hold each other's eyes, and he saw that her face, which had grown very pale, was flooded with a deep inner radiance. His heart beat with awe: he felt that he had never before beheld love visible.

"Oh, I shall be late—good-bye. No, don't come any farther than this," she cried, walking hurriedly away down the long room, as if the reflected radiance in his eyes had frightened her. When she reached the door she turned for a moment to wave a quick farewell.

Archer walked home alone. Darkness was falling when he let himself into his house, and he looked about at the familiar objects in the hall as if he viewed them from the other side of the grave.

The parlormaid, hearing his step, ran up the stairs to light the gas on the upper landing.

"Is Mrs. Archer in?"

"No, sir; Mrs. Archer went out in the carriage after luncheon, and hasn't come back."

With a sense of relief he entered the library and flung himself down in his armchair. The parlormaid followed, bringing the student lamp and shaking some coals onto the dying fire. When she left he continued to sit motionless, his elbows on his knees, his chin on his clasped hands, his eyes fixed on the red grate.

He sat there without conscious thoughts, without sense of the lapse of time, in a deep and grave amazement that seemed to suspend life rather than quicken it. "This was what had to be, then . . . this was what had to be," he kept repeating to himself, as if he hung in the clutch of doom. What he had dreamed of had been so different that there was a mortal chill in his rapture.

The door opened and May came in.

"I'm dreadfully late—you weren't worried, were you?" she asked, laying her hand on his shoulder with one of her rare caresses.

He looked up astonished. "Is it late?"

"After seven. I believe you've been asleep!" She laughed, and drawing out her hatpins tossed her velvet hat on the sofa. She looked paler than usual, but sparkling with an unwonted animation.

"I went to see Granny, and just as I was going away Ellen came in from a walk; so I stayed and had a long talk with her. It was ages since we'd had a real talk. . . ." She had dropped into her usual armchair, facing his, and was running her fingers through her rumpled hair. He fancied she expected him to speak.

"A really good talk," she went on, smiling with what seemed to Archer an unnatural vividness. "She was so dear—just like the old Ellen. I'm afraid I haven't been fair to her lately. I've sometimes thought—"

Archer stood up and leaned against the mantelpiece, out of the radius of the lamp.

"Yes, you've thought—?" he echoed as she paused.

"Well, perhaps I haven't judged her fairly. She's so different—at least on the surface. She takes up such odd people—she seems to like to make herself conspicuous. I suppose it's the life she's led in that fast European society; no doubt we seem dreadfully dull to her. But I don't want to judge her unfairly."

She paused again, a little breathless with the unwonted length of her speech, and sat with her lips slightly parted and a deep blush on her cheeks.

Archer, as he looked at her, was reminded of the glow which had suffused her face in the Mission Garden at St. Augustine. He became aware of the same obscure effort in her, the same reaching out toward something beyond the usual range of her vision.

"She hates Ellen," he thought, "and she's trying to overcome the feeling, and to get me to help her to overcome it."

The thought moved him, and for a moment he was on the point of breaking the silence between them, and throwing himself on her mercy.

"You understand, don't you," she went on, "why the family have sometimes been annoyed? We all did what we could for her at first; but she never seemed to understand. And now this idea of going to see Mrs. Beaufort, of going there in Granny's carriage! I'm afraid she's quite alienated the van der Luydens. . . ."

"Ah," said Archer with an impatient laugh. The open door had closed between them again.

"It's time to dress; we're dining out, aren't we?" he asked, moving from the fire.

She rose also, but lingered near the hearth. As he walked past her she moved forward impulsively, as though to detain him: their eyes met, and he saw that hers were of the same swimming blue as when he had left her to drive to Jersey City.

She flung her arms about his neck and pressed her cheek to his.

"You haven't kissed me today," she said in a whisper; and he felt her tremble in his arms.

32

"At the Court of the Tuileries," said Mr. Sillerton Jackson with his reminiscent smile, "such things were pretty openly tolerated."

The scene was the van der Luydens' black walnut dining room in Madison Avenue, and the time the evening after Newland Archer's visit to the Museum of Art. Mr. and Mrs. van der Luyden had come to town for a few days from Skuytercliff, whither they had precipitately fled at the announcement of Beaufort's failure. It had been represented to them that the disarray into which society had been thrown by this deplorable affair made their presence in town more necessary than ever. It was one of the occasions when, as Mrs. Archer put it, they "owed it to society" to show themselves at the Opera, and even to open their own doors.

"It will never do, my dear Louisa, to let people like Mrs. Lemuel Struthers think they can step into Regina's shoes. It is just at such times that new people push in and get a footing. It was owing to the epidemic of chicken-pox in New York the winter Mrs. Struthers first appeared that the married men slipped away to her house while their wives were in the nursery. You and dear Henry, Louisa, must stand in the breach as you always have."

Mr. and Mrs. van der Luyden could not remain deaf to such a call, and reluctantly but heroically they had come to town, unmuffled the house, and sent out invitations for two dinners and an evening reception.

On this particular evening they had invited Sillerton Jackson, Mrs. Archer and Newland and his wife to go with them to the Opera, where *Faust* was being sung for the first time that winter. Nothing was done without ceremony under the van der Luyden roof, and though there were but four guests the repast had begun at seven punctually, so that the proper sequence of courses might be served without haste before the gentlemen settled down to their cigars.

Archer had not seen his wife since the evening before. He had left early for the office, where he had plunged into an accumulation of unimportant business. In the afternoon one of the senior partners had made an unexpected call on his time; and he had reached home so late that May had preceded him to the van der Luydens', and sent back the carriage.

Now, across the Skuytercliff carnations and the massive plate, she struck him as pale and languid; but her eyes shone, and she talked with exaggerated animation.

The subject which had called forth Mr. Sillerton Jackson's favorite allusion had been brought up (Archer fancied not without intention) by their hostess. The Beaufort failure, or rather the Beaufort attitude since the failure, was still a fruitful theme for the drawing-room moralist; and after it had been thoroughly examined and condemned Mrs. van der Luyden had turned her scrupulous eyes on May Archer.

"Is it possible, dear, that what I hear is true? I was told your Grandmother Mingott's carriage was seen standing at Mrs. Beaufort's door." It was noticeable that she no longer called the offending lady by her Christian name.

May's color rose, and Mrs. Archer put in hastily: "If it was, I'm convinced it was there without Mrs. Mingott's knowledge."

"Ah, you think—?" Mrs. van der Luyden paused, sighed, and glanced at her husband.

"I'm afraid," Mr. van der Luyden said, "that Madame Olenska's kind heart may have led her into the imprudence of calling on Mrs. Beaufort."

"Or her taste for peculiar people," put in Mrs. Archer in a dry tone, while her eyes dwelt innocently on her son's.

"I'm sorry to think it of Madame Olenska," said Mrs. van der Luyden; and Mrs. Archer murmured: "Ah, my dear—and after you'd had her twice at Skuytercliff!"

It was at this point that Mr. Jackson seized the chance to place his favorite allusion.

"At the Tuileries," he repeated, seeing the eyes of the company expectantly turned on him, "the standard was excessively lax in some respects; and if you'd asked where Morny's money came from—! Or who paid the debts of some of the Court beauties. . . ."

"I hope, dear Sillerton," said Mrs. Archer, "you are not suggesting that we should adopt such standards?"

"I never suggest," returned Mr. Jackson imperturbably. "But Madame Olenska's foreign bringing-up may make her less particular—"

"Ah," the two elder ladies sighed.

"Still, to have kept her grandmother's carriage at a defaulter's door!" Mr. van der Luyden protested; and Archer guessed that he was remembering, and resenting, the hampers of carnations he had sent to the little house in Twenty-third Street.

"Of course I've always said that she looks at things quite differently," Mrs. Archer summed up.

A flush rose to May's forehead. She looked across the table at her husband, and said precipitately: "I'm sure Ellen meant it kindly."

"Imprudent people are often kind," said Mrs. Archer, as if the fact were scarcely an extenuation; and Mrs. van der Luyden murmured: "If only she had consulted someone—"

"Ah, that she never did!" Mrs. Archer rejoined.

At this point Mr. van der Luyden glanced at his wife, who bent her head slightly in the direction of Mrs. Archer; and the glimmering trains of the three ladies swept out of the door while the gentlemen settled down to their cigars. Mr. van der Luyden supplied short ones on Opera nights; but they were so good that they made his guests deplore his inexorable punctuality.

Archer, after the first act, had detached himself from the party and made his way to the back of the club box. From there he watched, over various Chivers, Mingott and Rushworth shoulders, the same scene that he had looked at, two years previously, on the night of his first meeting with Ellen Olenska. He had half-expected her to appear again in old Mrs. Mingott's box, but it remained empty; and he sat motionless, his eyes fastened on it, till suddenly Madame Nilsson's pure soprano broke out into "M'ama, non m'ama. . . ."

Archer turned to the stage, where, in the familiar setting of giant roses and pen-wiper pansies, the same large blonde victim was succumbing to the same small brown seducer.

From the stage his eyes wandered to the point of the horseshoe where May sat between two older ladies, just as, on that former evening, she had sat between Mrs. Lovell Mingott and her newly-arrived "foreign" cousin. As on that evening, she was all in white; and Archer, who had not noticed what she wore, recognized the blue-white satin and old lace of her wedding-dress.

It was the custom, in old New York, for brides to appear in this costly garment during the first year or two of marriage: his mother, he knew, kept hers in tissue paper in the hope that Janey might some day wear it, though poor Janey was reaching the age when pearl gray poplin and no bridesmaids would be thought more "appropriate."

It struck Archer that May, since their return from Europe, had seldom worn her bridal satin, and the surprise of seeing her in it made him compare her appearance with that of the young girl he had watched with such blissful anticipations two years earlier.

Though May's outline was slightly heavier, as her goddess-like build had foretold, her athletic erectness of carriage, and the girlish transparency of her expression, remained unchanged: but for the slight languor that Archer had lately noticed in her she would have been the exact image of the girl playing with the bouquet of lilies-of-the-valley on her betrothal evening. The fact seemed an additional appeal to his pity: such innocence was as moving as the trustful clasp of a child. Then he remembered the passionate generosity latent under that incurious calm. He recalled her glance of understanding when he had urged that their engagement should be announced at the Beaufort ball; he heard the voice in which she had said, in the Mission garden: "I couldn't have my happiness made out of a wrong —a wrong to someone else"; and an uncontrollable longing seized him to tell her the truth, to throw himself on her generosity, and ask for the freedom he had once refused.

Newland Archer was a quiet and self-controlled young man. Conformity to the discipline of a small society had become almost his second nature. It was deeply distasteful to him to do anything melodramatic and conspicuous, anything Mr. van der Luyden would have deprecated and the club box condemned as bad form. But he had become suddenly unconscious of the club box, of Mr. van der Luyden, of all that had so long enclosed him in the warm shelter of habit. He walked along the semi-circular passage at the back of the house, and opened the door of Mrs. van der Luyden's box as if it had been a gate into the unknown.

"M'ama!" thrilled out the triumphant Marguerite; and the occupants of the box looked up in surprise at Archer's entrance. He had already broken one of the rules of his world, which forbade the entering of a box during a solo.

Slipping between Mr. van der Luyden and Sillerton Jackson, he leaned over his wife.

"I've got a beastly headache; don't tell anyone, but come home, won't you?" he whispered.

May gave him a glance of comprehension, and he saw her whisper to his mother, who nodded sympathetically; then she murmured an excuse to Mrs. van der Luyden, and rose from her seat just as Marguerite fell into Faust's arms. Archer, while he helped her on with her opera cloak, noticed the exchange of a significant smile between the older ladies.

As they drove away May laid her hand shyly on his. "I'm so sorry you don't feel well. I'm afraid they've been over-working you again at the office."

"No—it's not that: do you mind if I open the window?" he returned confusedly, letting down the pane on his side. He sat staring out into the street, feeling his wife beside him as a silent watchful interrogation, and keeping his eyes steadily fixed on the passing houses. At their door she caught her skirt in the step of the carriage, and fell against him.

"Did you hurt yourself?" he asked, steadying her with his arm.

"No; but my poor dress—see how I've torn it!" she exclaimed. She bent to gather up a mud-stained breadth, and followed him up the steps into the hall. The servants had not expected them so early, and there was only a glimmer of gas on the upper landing.

Archer mounted the stairs, turned up the light, and put a match to the brackets on each side of the library mantelpiece. The curtains were drawn, and the warm friendly aspect of the room smote him like that of a familiar face met during an unavowable errand.

He noticed that his wife was very pale, and asked if he should get her some brandy.

"Oh, no," she exclaimed with a momentary flush, as she took off her cloak. "But hadn't you better go to bed at once?" she added, as he opened a silver box on the table and took out a cigarette.

Archer threw down the cigarette and walked to his usual place by the fire.

"No; my head is not as bad as that." He paused. "And there's something I want to say; something important—that I must tell you at once."

She had dropped into an armchair, and raised her head as he spoke. "Yes, dear?" she rejoined, so gently that he wondered at the lack of wonder with which she received this preamble.

"May—" he began, standing a few feet from her chair, and looking over at her as if the slight distance between them were an unbridgeable abyss. The sound of his voice echoed uncannily through the homelike hush, and he repeated: "There is something I've got to tell you . . . about myself. . . ."

She sat silent, without a movement or a tremor of her lashes. She was still extremely pale, but her face had a curious tranquillity of expression that seemed drawn from some secret inner source.

Archer checked the conventional phrases of self-accusal that were crowding to his lips. He was determined to put the case baldly, without vain recrimination or excuse.

"Madame Olenska—" he said; but at the name his wife raised her hand as if to silence him. As she did so the gaslight struck on the gold of her wedding-ring.

"Oh, why should we talk about Ellen tonight?" she asked, with a slight pout of impatience.

"Because I ought to have spoken before."

Her face remained calm. "Is it really worthwhile, dear? I know I've been unfair to her at times—perhaps we all have. You've understood her, no doubt, better than we did: you've always been kind to her. But what does it matter, now it's all over?"

Archer looked at her blankly. Could it be possible that the sense of unreality in which he felt himself imprisoned had communicated itself to his wife?

"All over—what do you mean?" he asked in an indistinct stammer.

May still looked at him with transparent eyes. "Why—since she's going back to Europe so soon; since Granny approves and understands, and has arranged to make her independent of her husband—"

She broke off, and Archer, grasping the corner of the mantelpiece in one convulsed hand, and steadying himself against it, made a vain effort to extend the same control to his reeling thoughts.

"I supposed," he heard his wife's even voice go on, "that you had been kept at the office this evening about the business arrangements. It was settled this morning, I believe." She lowered her eyes under his unseeing stare, and another fugitive flush passed over her face.

He understood that his own eyes must be unbearable, and turning away, rested his elbows on the mantel-shelf and covered his face. Something drummed and clanged furiously in his ears; he could not tell if it were the blood in his veins, or the tick of the clock on the mantel.

May sat without moving or speaking while the clock slowly measured out five minutes. A lump of coal fell forward in the grate, and hearing her rise to push it back, Archer at length turned and faced her.

"It's impossible," he exclaimed.

"Impossible—?"

"How do you know—what you've just told me?"

"I saw Ellen yesterday—I told you I'd seen her at Granny's."

"It wasn't then that she told you?"

"No; I had a note from her this afternoon.—Do you want to see it?"

He could not find his voice, and she went out of the room, and came back almost immediately.

"I thought you knew," she said simply.

She laid a sheet of paper on the table, and Archer put out his hand and took it up. The letter contained only a few lines.

"May dear, I have at last made Granny understand that my visit to her could be no more than a visit; and she has been as kind and generous as ever. She sees now that if I return to Europe I must live by myself, or rather with poor Aunt Medora, who is coming with me. I am hurrying back to Washington to pack up, and we sail next week. You must be very good to Granny when I'm gone—as good as you've always been to me, Ellen.

"If any of my friends wish to urge me to change my mind, please tell them it would be utterly useless."

Archer read the letter over two or three times; then he flung it down and burst out laughing.

The sound of his laugh startled him. It recalled Janey's midnight fright when she had caught him rocking with incomprehensible mirth over May's telegram announcing that the date of their marriage had been advanced.

"Why did she write this?" he asked, checking his laugh with a supreme effort.

May met the question with her unshaken candor. "I suppose because we talked things over yesterday—"

"What things?"

"I told her I was afraid I hadn't been fair to her—hadn't always understood how hard it must have been for her here, alone among so many people who were relations and yet strangers; who felt the right to criticize, and yet didn't always know the circumstances." She paused. "I knew you'd been the one friend she could always count on; and I wanted her to know that you and I were the same—in all our feelings."

She hesitated, as if waiting for him to speak, and then added slowly: "She understood my wishing to tell her this. I think she understands everything."

She went up to Archer, and taking one of his cold hands pressed it quickly against her cheek.

"My head aches too; good-night, dear," she said, and turned to the door, her torn and muddy wedding-dress dragging after her across the room.

33

It was, as Mrs. Archer smilingly said to Mrs. Welland, a great event for a young couple to give their first big dinner.

The Newland Archers, since they had set up their household, had received a good deal of company in an informal way. Archer was fond of having three or four friends to dine, and May welcomed them with the beaming readiness of which her mother had set her the example in conjugal affairs. Her husband questioned whether, if left to herself, she would ever have asked anyone to the house; but he had long given up trying to disengage her real self from the shape into which tradition and training had moulded her. It was expected that well-off young couples in New York should do a good deal of informal entertaining, and a Welland married to an Archer was doubly pledged to the tradition.

But a big dinner, with a hired *chef* and two borrowed footmen, with Roman punch, roses from Henderson's, and *menus* on gilt-edged cards, was a different affair, and not to be lightly undertaken. As Mrs. Archer remarked, the Roman punch made all the difference; not in itself but by its manifold implications—since it signified either canvasbacks or terrapin, two soups, a hot and a cold sweet, full *décolletage* with short sleeves, and guests of a proportionate importance.

It was always an interesting occasion when a young pair launched their first invitations in the third person, and their summons was seldom refused even by the seasoned and sought-after. Still, it was admittedly a triumph that the van der Luydens, at May's request, should have stayed over in order to be present at her farewell dinner for the Countess Olenska.

The two mothers-in-law sat in May's drawing room on the afternoon of the great day, Mrs. Archer writing out the *menus* on Tiffany's thickest gilt-edged bristol, while Mrs. Welland superintended the placing of the palms and standard lamps.

Archer, arriving late from his office, found them still there. Mrs. Archer had turned her attention to the namecards for the table, and Mrs. Welland was considering the effect of bringing forward the large gilt sofa, so that another "corner" might be created between the piano and the window.

May, they told him, was in the dining room inspecting the mound of Jacqueminot roses and maidenhair in the center of the long table, and the placing of the Maillard bonbons in openwork silver baskets between the candelabra. On the piano stood a large basket of orchids which Mr. van der Luyden had had sent from Skuytercliff. Everything was, in short, as it should be on the approach of so considerable an event.

Mrs. Archer ran thoughtfully over the list, checking off each name with her sharp gold pen.

"Henry van der Luyden—Louisa—the Lovell Mingotts—the Reggie Chiverses—Lawrence Lefferts and Gertrude—(yes, I suppose May was right to have them)—the Selfridge Merrys, Sillerton Jackson, Van Newland and his wife. (How time passes! It seems only yesterday that he was your best man, Newland)—and Countess Olenska—yes, I think that's all. . . ."

Mrs. Welland surveyed her son-in-law affectionately. "No one can say, Newland, that you and May are not giving Ellen a handsome send-off."

"Ah, well," said Mrs. Archer, "I understand May's wanting her cousin to tell people abroad that we're not quite barbarians."

"I'm sure Ellen will appreciate it. She was to arrive this morning, I believe. It will make a most charming last impression. The evening before sailing is usually so dreary," Mrs. Welland cheerfully continued.

Archer turned toward the door, and his mother-in-law called to him: "Do go in and have a peep at the table. And don't let May tire herself too much." But he affected not to hear, and sprang up the stairs to his library. The room looked at him like an alien countenance composed into a polite grimace; and he perceived that it had been ruthlessly "tidied," and prepared, by a judicious distribution of ash-trays and cedar-wood boxes, for the gentlemen to smoke in.

"Ah, well," he thought, "it's not for long—" and he went on to his dressing room.

Ten days had passed since Madame Olenska's departure from New York. During those ten days Archer had had no sign from her but that conveyed by the return of a key wrapped in tissue paper, and sent to his office in a sealed envelope addressed in her hand. This retort to his last appeal might have been interpreted as a classic move in a familiar game; but the young man chose to give it a different meaning. She was still fighting against her fate; but she was going to Europe, and she was not returning to her husband. Nothing, therefore, was to prevent his following her; and once he had taken the irrevocable step, and had proved to her that it was irrevocable, he believed she would not send him away.

This confidence in the future had steadied him to play his part in the present. It had kept him from writing to her, or betraying, by any sign or act, his misery and mortification. It seemed to him that in the deadly silent game between them the trumps were still in his hands; and he waited.

There had been, nevertheless, moments sufficiently difficult to pass; as when Mr. Letterblair, the day after Madame Olenska's departure, had sent for him to go over the details of the trust which Mrs. Manson Mingott wished to create for her granddaughter. For a couple of hours Archer had examined the terms of the deed with his senior, all the while obscurely feeling that if he had been consulted it was for some reason other than the obvious one of his cousinship; and that the close of the conference would reveal it.

"Well, the lady can't deny that it's a handsome arrangement," Mr. Letterblair had summed up, after mumbling over a summary of the settlement. "In fact I'm bound to say she's been treated pretty handsomely all round."

"All round?" Archer echoed with a touch of derision. "Do you refer to her husband's proposal to give her back her own money?"

Mr. Letterblair's bushy eyebrows went up a fraction of an inch. "My dear sir, the law's the law; and your wife's cousin was married under the French law. It's to be presumed she knew what that meant."

"Even if she did, what happened subsequently—." But Archer paused. Mr. Letterblair had laid his pen-handle against his big corrugated nose, and was looking down it with the expression assumed by virtuous elderly gentlemen when they wish their youngers to understand that virtue is not synonymous with ignorance.

"My dear sir, I've no wish to extenuate the Count's transgressions; but—but on the other side . . . I wouldn't put my hand in the fire . . . well, that there hadn't been tit for tat . . . with the young champion. . . ." Mr. Letterblair unlocked a drawer and pushed a folded paper toward Archer. "This report, the result of discreet enquiries. . . ." And then, as Archer made no effort to glance at the paper or to repudiate the suggestion, the lawyer somewhat flatly continued: "I don't say it's conclusive, you observe; far from it. But straws show . . . and on the whole it's eminently satisfactory for all parties that this dignified solution has been reached."

"Oh, eminently," Archer assented, pushing back the paper.

A day or two later, on responding to a summons from Mrs. Manson Mingott, his soul had been more deeply tried.

He had found the old lady depressed and querulous.

"You know she's deserted me?" she began at once; and without waiting for his reply: "Oh, don't ask me why! She gave so many reasons that I've forgotten them all. My private belief is that she couldn't face the boredom. At any rate that's what Augusta and my daughters-in-law think. And I don't know that I altogether blame her. Olenski's a finished scoundrel; but life with him must have been a good deal gayer than it is in Fifth Avenue. Not that the family would admit that: they think Fifth Avenue is Heaven with the rue de la Paix thrown in. And poor Ellen, of course, has no idea of going back to her husband. She held out as firmly as ever against that. So she's to settle down in Paris with that fool Medora. . . . Well, Paris is Paris; and you can keep a carriage there on next to nothing. But she was as gay as a bird, and I shall miss her." Two tears, the parched tears of the old, rolled down her puffy cheeks and vanished in the abysses of her bosom.

"All I ask is," she concluded, "that they shouldn't bother me any more. I must really be allowed to digest my gruel. . . ." And she twinkled a little wistfully at Archer.

It was that evening, on his return home, that May announced her intention of giving a farewell dinner to her cousin. Madame Olenska's name had not been pronounced between them since the night of her flight to Washington; and Archer looked at his wife with surprise.

"A dinner—why?" he interrogated.

Her color rose. "But you like Ellen—I thought you'd be pleased."

"It's awfully nice—your putting it in that way. But I really don't see—"

"I mean to do it, Newland," she said, quietly rising and going to her desk. "Here are the invitations all written. Mother helped me— she agrees that we ought to." She paused, embarrassed and yet smiling, and Archer suddenly saw before him the embodied image of the Family.

"Oh, all right," he said, staring with unseeing eyes at the list of guests that she had put in his hand.

When he entered the drawing room before dinner May was stooping over the fire and trying to coax the logs to burn in their unaccustomed setting of immaculate tiles.

The tall lamps were all lit, and Mr. van der Luyden's orchids had been conspicuously disposed in various receptacles of modern porcelain and knobby silver. Mrs. Newland Archer's drawing room was generally thought a great success. A gilt bamboo *jardinière*, in which the primulas and cinerarias were punctually renewed, blocked the access to the bay window (where the old-fashioned would have preferred a bronze reduction of the Venus of Milo); the sofas and armchairs of pale brocade were cleverly grouped about little plush tables densely covered with silver toys, porcelain animals and efflorescent photograph frames; and tall rosy-shaded lamps shot up like tropical flowers among the palms.

"I don't think Ellen has ever seen this room lighted up," said May, rising flushed from her struggle, and sending about her a glance of pardonable pride. The brass tongs which she had propped against the side of the chimney fell with a crash that drowned her husband's answer; and before he could restore them Mr. and Mrs. van der Luyden were announced.

The other guests quickly followed, for it was known that the van der Luydens liked to dine punctually. The room was nearly full, and Archer was engaged in showing to Mrs. Selfridge Merry a small highly-varnished Verbeckhoven "Study of Sheep," which Mr. Welland had given May for Christmas, when he found Madame Olenska at his side.

She was excessively pale, and her pallor made her dark hair seem denser and heavier than ever. Perhaps that, or the fact that she had wound several rows of amber beads about her neck, reminded him suddenly of the little Ellen Mingott he had danced with at children's parties, when Medora Manson had first brought her to New York.

The amber beads were trying to her complexion, or her dress was perhaps unbecoming: her face looked lusterless and almost ugly, and he had never loved it as he did at that minute. Their hands met, and he thought he heard her say: "Yes, we're sailing tomorrow in the *Russia*—"; then there was an unmeaning noise of opening doors, and after an interval May's voice: "Newland! Dinner's been announced. Won't you please take Ellen in?"

Madame Olenska put her hand on his arm, and he noticed that the hand was ungloved, and remembered how he had kept his eyes fixed on it the evening that he had sat with her in the little Twenty-third Street drawing room. All the beauty that had forsaken her face seemed to have taken refuge in the long pale fingers and faintly dimpled knuckles on his sleeve, and he said to himself: "If it were only to see her hand again I should have to follow her—."

It was only at an entertainment ostensibly offered to a "foreign visitor" that Mrs. van der Luyden could suffer the diminution of being placed on her host's left. The fact of Madame Olenska's "foreignness" could hardly have been more adroitly emphasized than by this farewell tribute; and Mrs. van der Luyden accepted her displacement with an affability which left no doubt as to her approval. There were certain things that had to be done, and if done at all, done handsomely and thoroughly; and one of these, in the old New York code, was the tribal rally around a kinswoman about to be eliminated from the tribe. There was nothing on earth that the Wellands and Mingotts would not have done to proclaim their unalterable affection for the Countess Olenska now that her passage for Europe was engaged; and Archer, at the head of his table, sat marveling at the silent untiring activity with which her popularity had been retrieved, grievances against her silenced, her past countenanced, and her present irradiated by the family approval. Mrs. van der Luyden shone on her with the dim benevolence which was her nearest approach to cordiality, and Mr. van der Luyden, from his seat at May's right, cast down the table glances plainly intended to justify all the carnations he had sent from Skuytercliff.

Archer, who seemed to be assisting at the scene in a state of odd imponderability, as if he floated somewhere between chandelier and ceiling, wondered at nothing so much as his own share in the proceedings. As his glance traveled from one placid well-fed face to another he saw all the harmless-looking people engaged upon May's canvasbacks as a band of dumb conspirators, and himself and the pale woman on his right as the center of their conspiracy. And then it came over him, in a vast flash made up of many broken gleams, that to all of them he and Madame Olenska were lovers, lovers in the extreme sense peculiar to "foreign" vocabularies. He guessed himself to have been, for months, the center of countless silently observing eyes and patiently listening ears, he understood that, by means as yet unknown to him, the separation between himself and the partner of his guilt had been achieved, and that now the whole tribe had rallied about his wife on the tacit assumption that nobody knew anything, or had ever imagined anything, and that the occasion of the entertainment was simply May Archer's natural desire to take an affectionate leave of her friend and cousin.

It was the old New York way of taking life "without effusion of blood": the way of people who dreaded scandal more than disease, who placed decency above courage, and who considered that nothing was more ill-bred than "scenes," except the behavior of those who gave rise to them.

As these thoughts succeeded each other in his mind Archer felt like a prisoner in the center of an armed camp. He looked about the table, and guessed at the inexorableness of his captors from the tone in which, over the asparagus from Florida, they were dealing with Beaufort and his wife. "It's to show me," he thought, "what would happen to *me*—" and a deathly sense of the superiority of implication and analogy over direct action, and of silence over rash words, closed in on him like the doors of the family vault.

He laughed, and met Mrs. van der Luyden's startled eyes.

"You think it laughable?" she said with a pinched smile. "Of course poor Regina's idea of remaining in New York has its ridiculous side, I suppose"; and Archer muttered: "Of course."

At this point, he became conscious that Madame Olenska's other neighbor had been engaged for some time with the lady on his right. At the same moment he saw that May, serenely enthroned between Mr. van der Luyden and Mr. Selfridge Merry, had cast a quick glance down the table. It was evident that the host and the lady on his right could not sit through the whole meal in silence. He turned to Madame Olenska, and her pale smile met him. "Oh, do let's see it through," it seemed to say.

"Did you find the journey tiring?" he asked in a voice that surprised him by its naturalness; and she answered that, on the contrary, she had seldom traveled with fewer discomforts.

"Except, you know, the dreadful heat in the train," she added; and he remarked that she would not suffer from that particular hardship in the country she was going to.

"I never," he declared with intensity, "was more nearly frozen than once, in April, in the train between Calais and Paris."

She said she did not wonder, but remarked that, after all, one could always carry an extra rug, and that every form of travel had its hardships; to which he abruptly returned that he thought them all of no account compared with the blessedness of getting away. She changed color, and he added, his voice suddenly rising in pitch: "I mean to do a lot of traveling myself before long." A tremor crossed her face, and leaning over to Reggie Chivers, he cried out: "I say, Reggie, what do you say to a trip round the world: now, next month, I mean? I'm game if you are—" at which Mrs. Reggie piped up that she could not think of letting Reggie go till after the Martha Washington Ball she was getting up for the Blind Asylum in Easter week; and her husband placidly observed that by that time he would have to be practicing for the International Polo match.

But Mr. Selfridge Merry had caught the phrase "round the world," and having once circled the globe in his steam-yacht, he seized the opportunity to send down the table several striking items concerning the shallowness of the Mediterranean ports. Though, after all, he added, it didn't matter; for when you'd seen Athens and Smyrna and Constantinople, what else was there? And Mrs. Merry said she could never be too grateful to Dr. Bencomb for having made them promise not to go to Naples on account of the fever.

"But you must have three weeks to do India properly," her husband conceded, anxious to have it understood that he was no frivolous globe-trotter.

And at this point the ladies went up to the drawing room.

In the library, in spite of weightier presences, Lawrence Lefferts predominated.

The talk, as usual, had veered around to the Beauforts, and even Mr. van der Luyden and Mr. Selfridge Merry, installed in the honorary armchairs tacitly reserved for them, paused to listen to the younger man's philippic.

Never had Lefferts so abounded in the sentiments that adorn

Christian manhood and exalt the sanctity of the home. Indignation lent him a scathing eloquence, and it was clear that if others had followed his example, and acted as he talked, society would never have been weak enough to receive a foreign upstart like Beaufort—no, sir, not even if he'd married a van der Luyden or a Lanning instead of a Dallas. And what chance would there have been, Lefferts wrathfully questioned, of his marrying into such a family as the Dallases, if he had not already wormed his way into certain houses, as people like Mrs. Lemuel Struthers had managed to worm theirs in his wake? If society chose to open its doors to vulgar women the harm was not great, though the gain was doubtful; but once it got in the way of tolerating men of obscure origin and tainted wealth the end was total disintegration—and at no distant date.

"If things go on at this pace," Lefferts thundered, looking like a young prophet dressed by Poole, and who had not yet been stoned, "we shall see our children fighting for invitations to swindlers' houses, and marrying Beaufort's bastards."

"Oh, I say—draw it mild!" Reggie Chivers and young Newland protested, while Mr. Selfridge Merry looked genuinely alarmed, and an expression of pain and disgust settled on Mr. van der Luyden's sensitive face.

"Has he got any?" cried Mr. Sillerton Jackson, pricking up his ears; and while Lefferts tried to turn the question with a laugh, the old gentleman twittered into Archer's ear: "Queer, those fellows who are always wanting to set things right. The people who have the worst cooks are always telling you they're poisoned when they dine out. But I hear there are pressing reasons for our friend Lawrence's diatribe:—typewriter this time, I understand. . . ."

The talk swept past Archer like some senseless river running and running because it did not know enough to stop. He saw, on the faces about him, expressions of interest, amusement and even mirth. He listened to the younger men's laughter, and to the praise of the Archer Madeira, which Mr. van der Luyden and Mr. Merry were thoughtfully celebrating. Through it all he was dimly aware of a general attitude of friendliness toward himself, as if the guard of the prisoner he felt himself to be were trying to soften his captivity; and the perception increased his passionate determination to be free.

In the drawing room, where they presently joined the ladies, he met May's triumphant eyes, and read in them the conviction that everything had "gone off" beautifully. She rose from Madame Olenska's side, and immediately Mrs. van der Luyden beckoned the latter to a seat on the gilt sofa where she throned. Mrs. Selfridge Merry bore across the room to join them, and it became clear to Archer that here also a conspiracy of rehabilitation and obliteration was going on. The silent organization which held his little world together was determined to put itself on record as never for a moment having questioned the propriety of Madame Olenska's conduct, or the completeness of Archer's domestic felicity. All these amiable and inexorable persons were resolutely engaged in pretending to each other that they had never heard of, suspected, or even conceived possible, the least hint to the contrary; and from this tissue of elaborate mutual dissimulation Archer once more disengaged the fact that New York believed him to be Madame Olenska's lover. He caught the glitter of victory in his wife's eyes, and for the first time understood that she shared the belief. The discovery roused a laughter of inner devils that reverberated through all his efforts to discuss the Martha Washington Ball with Mrs. Reggie Chivers and little Mrs. Newland; and so the evening swept on, running and running like a senseless river that did not know how to stop.

At length he saw that Madame Olenska had risen and was saying good-bye. He understood that in a moment she would be gone, and tried to remember what he had said to her at dinner; but he could not recall a single word they had exchanged.

She went up to May, the rest of the company making a circle about her as she advanced. The two young women clasped hands; then May bent forward and kissed her cousin.

"Certainly our hostess is much the handsomer of the two," Archer heard Reggie Chivers say in an undertone to young Mrs. Newland; and he remembered Beaufort's coarse sneer at May's ineffectual beauty.

A moment later he was in the hall, putting Madame Olenska's cloak about her shoulders.

Through all his confusion of mind he had held fast to the resolve to say nothing that might startle or disturb her. Convinced that no power could now turn him from his purpose he had found strength to let events shape themselves as they would. But as he followed Madame Olenska into the hall he thought with a sudden hunger of being for a moment alone with her at the door of her carriage.

"Is your carriage here?" he asked; and at that moment Mrs. van der Luyden, who was being majestically inserted into her sables, said gently: "We are driving dear Ellen home."

Archer's heart gave a jerk, and Madame Olenska, clasping her cloak and fan with one hand, held out the other to him. "Good-bye," she said.

"Good-bye—but I shall see you soon in Paris," he answered aloud —it seemed to him that he had shouted it.

"Oh," she murmured, "if you and May could come—!"

Mr. van der Luyden advanced to give her his arm, and Archer turned to Mrs. van der Luyden. For a moment, in the billowy dark-ness inside the big landau, he caught the dim oval of a face, eyes shining steadily—and she was gone.

As he went up the steps he crossed Lawrence Lefferts coming down with his wife. Lefferts caught his host by the sleeve, drawing back to let Gertrude pass.

"I say, old chap: do you mind just letting it be understood that I'm dining with you at the club tomorrow night? Thanks so much, you old brick! Good-night."

"It *did* go off beautifully, didn't it?" May questioned from the threshold of the library.

Archer roused himself with a start. As soon as the last carriage had driven away, he had come up to the library and shut himself in, with the hope that his wife, who still lingered below, would go straight to her room. But there she stood, pale and drawn, yet radiating the fac-titious energy of one who has passed beyond fatigue.

"May I come and talk it over?" she asked.

"Of course, if you like. But you must be awfully sleepy—"

"No, I'm not sleepy. I should like to sit with you a little."

"Very well," he said, pushing her chair near the fire.

She sat down and he resumed his seat; but neither spoke for a long time. At length Archer began abruptly: "Since you're not tired, and want to talk, there's something I must tell you. I tried to the other night—."

She looked at him quickly. "Yes, dear. Something about yourself?"

"About myself. You say you're not tired: well, I am. Horribly tired. . . ."

In an instant she was all tender anxiety. "Oh, I've seen it coming on, Newland! You've been so wickedly overworked—"

"Perhaps it's that. Anyhow, I want to make a break—"

"A break? To give up the law?"

"To go away, at any rate—at once. On a long trip, ever so far off—away from everything—"

He paused, conscious that he had failed in his attempt to speak with the indifference of a man who longs for a change, and is yet too weary to welcome it. Do what he would, the chord of eagerness vibrated. "Away from everything—" he repeated.

"Ever so far? Where, for instance?" she asked.

"Oh, I don't know. India—or Japan."

She stood up, and as he sat with bent head, his chin propped on his hands, he felt her warmly and fragrantly hovering over him.

"As far as that? But I'm afraid you can't, dear . . ." she said in an unsteady voice. "Not unless you'll take me with you." And then, as he was silent, she went on, in tones so clear and evenly-pitched that each separate syllable tapped like a little hammer on his brain: "That is, if the doctors will let me go . . . but I'm afraid they won't. For you see, Newland, I've been sure since this morning of something I've been so longing and hoping for—"

He looked up at her with a sick stare, and she sank down, all dew and roses, and hid her face against his knee.

"Oh, my dear," he said, holding her to him while his cold hand stroked her hair.

There was a long pause, which the inner devils filled with strident laughter; then May freed herself from his arms and stood up.

"You didn't guess—?"

"Yes—I; no. That is, of course I hoped—"

They looked at each other for an instant and again fell silent; then, turning his eyes from hers, he asked abruptly: "Have you told anyone else?"

"Only Mamma and your mother." She paused, and then added hurriedly, the blood flushing up to her forehead: "That is—and Ellen. You know I told you we'd had a long talk one afternoon—and how dear she was to me."

"Ah—" said Archer, his heart stopping.

He felt that his wife was watching him intently. "Did you *mind* my telling her first, Newland?"

"Mind? Why should I?" He made a last effort to collect himself. "But that was a fortnight ago, wasn't it? I thought you said you weren't sure till today."

Her color burned deeper, but she held his gaze. "No; I wasn't sure then—but I told her I was. And you see I was right!" she exclaimed, her blue eyes wet with victory.

34

NEWLAND ARCHER sat at the writing-table in his library in East Thirty-ninth Street.

He had just got back from a big official reception for the inauguration of the new galleries at the Metropolitan Museum, and the spectacle of those great spaces crowded with the spoils of the ages, where the throng of fashion circulated through a series of scientifically catalogued treasures, had suddenly pressed on a rusted spring of memory.

"Why, this used to be one of the old Cesnola rooms," he heard someone say; and instantly everything about him vanished, and he was sitting alone on a hard leather divan against a radiator, while a slight figure in a long sealskin cloak moved away down the meagerly-fitted vistas of the old Museum.

The vision had roused a host of other associations, and he sat looking with new eyes at the library which, for over thirty years, had been the scene of his solitary musings and of all the family confabulations.

It was the room in which most of the real things of his life had happened. There his wife, nearly twenty-six years ago, had broken to him, with a blushing circumlocution that would have caused the young women of the new generation to smile, the news that she was to have a child; and there their eldest boy, Dallas, too delicate to be taken to church in midwinter, had been christened by their old friend the Bishop of New York, the ample magnificent irreplaceable Bishop, so long the pride and ornament of his diocese. There Dallas had first staggered across the floor shouting "Dad," while May and the nurse laughed behind the door; there their second child, Mary (who was so like her mother), had announced her engagement to the dullest and most reliable of Reggie Chivers's many sons; and there Archer had kissed her through her wedding veil before they went down to the motor which was to carry them to Grace Church—for in a world where all else had reeled on its foundations the "Grace Church wedding" remained an unchanged institution.

It was in the library that he and May had always discussed the future of the children: the studies of Dallas and his young brother Bill, Mary's incurable indifference to "accomplishments," and passion for sport and philanthropy, and the vague leanings toward "art" which had finally landed the restless and curious Dallas in the office of a rising New York architect.

The young men nowadays were emancipating themselves from the law and business and taking up all sorts of new things. If they were not absorbed in state politics or municipal reform, the chances were that they were going in for Central American archeology, for architecture or landscape-engineering; taking a keen and learned interest in the pre-Revolutionary buildings of their own country, studying and adapting Georgian types, and protesting at the meaningless use of the word "Colonial." Nobody nowadays had "Colonial" houses except the millionaire grocers of the suburbs.

But above all—sometimes Archer put it above all—it was in that library that the Governor of New York, coming down from Albany one evening to dine and spend the night, had turned to his host, and said, banging his clenched fist on the table and gnashing his eyeglasses: "Hang the professional politician! You're the kind of man the country wants, Archer. If the stable's ever to be cleaned out, men like you have got to lend a hand in the cleaning."

"Men like you—" how Archer had glowed at the phrase! How eagerly he had risen up at the call! It was an echo of Ned Winsett's old appeal to roll his sleeves up and get down into the muck; but spoken by a man who set the example of the gesture, and whose summons to follow him was irresistible.

Archer, as he looked back, was not sure that men like himself *were* what his country needed, at least in the active service to which Theodore Roosevelt had pointed; in fact, there was reason to think it did not, for after a year in the State Assembly he had not been re-elected, and had dropped back thankfully into obscure if useful municipal work, and from that again to the writing of occasional articles in one of the reforming weeklies that were trying to shake the country out of its apathy. It was little enough to look back on; but when he remembered to what the young men of his generation and his set had looked forward—the narrow groove of money-making, sport and society to which their vision had been limited—even his small contribution to the new state of things seemed to count, as each brick counts in a well-built wall. He had done little in public life; he would always be by nature a contemplative and a dilettante; but he had had high things to contemplate, great things to delight in; and one great man's friendship to be his strength and pride.

He had been, in short, what people were beginning to call "a good citizen." In New York, for many years past, every new movement, philanthropic, municipal or artistic, had taken account of his opinion and wanted his name. People said: "Ask Archer" when there was a question of starting the first school for crippled children, reorganizing the Museum of Art, founding the Grolier Club, inaugurating the new Library, or getting up a new society of chamber music. His days were full, and they were filled decently. He supposed it was all a man ought to ask.

Something he knew he had missed: the flower of life. But he thought of it now as a thing so unattainable and improbable that to have repined would have been like despairing because one had not drawn the first prize in a lottery. There were a hundred million tickets in *his* lottery, and there was only one prize; the chances had been too decidedly against him. When he thought of Ellen Olenska it was abstractly, serenely, as one might think of some imaginary beloved in a book or a picture: she had become the composite vision of all that he had missed. That vision, faint and tenuous as it was, had kept him from thinking of other women. He had been what was called a faithful husband; and when May had suddenly died—carried off by the infectious pneumonia through which she had nursed their youngest child—he had honestly mourned her. Their long years together had shown him that it did not so much matter if marriage was a dull duty, as long as it kept the dignity of a duty: lapsing from that, it became a mere battle of ugly appetites. Looking about him, he honored his own past, and mourned for it. After all, there was good in the old ways.

His eyes, making the round of the room—done over by Dallas with English mezzotints, Chippendale cabinets, bits of chosen blue-and-white and pleasantly shaded electric lamps—came back to the old Eastlake writing-table that he had never been willing to banish, and to his first photograph of May, which still kept its place beside his inkstand.

There she was, tall, round-bosomed and willowy, in her starched muslin and flapping Leghorn, as he had seen her under the orange-trees in the Mission garden. And as he had seen her that day, so she had remained; never quite at the same height, yet never far below it: generous, faithful, unwearied; but so lacking in imagination, so incapable of growth, that the world of her youth had fallen into pieces and rebuilt itself without her ever being conscious of the change. This hard bright blindness had kept her immediate horizon apparently unaltered. Her incapacity to recognize change made her children conceal their views from her as Archer concealed his; there had been, from the first, a joint pretense of sameness, a kind of innocent family hypocrisy, in which father and children had unconsciously collaborated. And she had died thinking the world a good place, full of loving and harmonious households like her own, and resigned to leave it because she was convinced that, whatever happened, Newland would continue to inculcate in Dallas the same principles and prejudices which had shaped his parents' lives, and that Dallas in turn (when Newland followed her) would transmit the sacred trust to little Bill. And of Mary she was sure as of her own self. So, having snatched little Bill from the grave, and given her life in the effort, she went contentedly to her place in the Archer vault in St. Mark's, where Mrs. Archer already lay safe from the terrifying "trend" which her daughter-in-law had never even become aware of.

Opposite May's portrait stood one of her daughter. Mary Chivers was as tall and fair as her mother, but large-waisted, flat-chested and slightly slouching, as the altered fashion required. Mary Chivers's mighty feats of athleticism could not have been performed with the twenty-inch waist that May Archer's azure sash so easily spanned. And the difference seemed symbolic; the mother's life had been as closely girt as her figure. Mary, who was no less conventional, and no more intelligent, yet led a larger life and held more tolerant views. There was good in the new order too.

The telephone clicked, and Archer, turning from the photographs, unhooked the transmitter at his elbow. How far they were from the days when the legs of the brass-buttoned messenger boy had been New York's only means of quick communication!

"Chicago wants you."

Ah—it must be a long-distance from Dallas, who had been sent to Chicago by his firm to talk over the plan of the Lakeside palace they were to build for a young millionaire with ideas. The firm always sent Dallas on such errands.

"Hallo, Dad—Yes: Dallas. I say—how do you feel about sailing on Wednesday? *Mauretania:* Yes, next Wednesday as ever is. Our client wants me to look at some Italian gardens before we settle anything, and has asked me to nip over on the next boat. I've got to be back on the first of June—" the voice broke into a joyful conscious laugh—"so we must look alive. I say, Dad, I want your help: do come."

Dallas seemed to be speaking in the room: the voice was as nearby and natural as if he had been lounging in his favorite armchair by the fire. The fact would not ordinarily have surprised Archer, for long-distance telephoning had become as much a matter of course as electric lighting and five-day Atlantic voyages. But the laugh did startle him; it still seemed wonderful that across all those miles and miles of country—forest, river, mountain, prairie, roaring cities and busy indifferent millions—Dallas's laugh should be able to say: "Of course, whatever happens, I must get back on the first, because Fanny Beaufort and I are to be married on the fifth."

The voice began again: "Think it over? No, sir: not a minute. You've got to say yes now. Why not, I'd like to know? If you can allege a single reason—no; I knew it. Then it's a go, eh? Because I count on you to ring up the Cunard office first thing tomorrow; and you'd better book a return on a boat from Marseilles. I say, Dad; it'll be our last time together, in this kind of way—. Oh, good! I knew you would."

Chicago rang off, and Archer rose and began to pace up and down the room.

It would be their last time together in this kind of way: the boy was right. They would have lots of other "times" after Dallas's marriage, his father was sure; for the two were born comrades, and Fanny Beaufort, whatever one might think of her, did not seem likely to interfere with their intimacy. On the contrary, from what he had seen of her, he thought she would be naturally included in it. Still, change was change, and differences were differences, and much as he felt himself drawn toward his future daughter-in-law, it was tempting to seize this last chance of being alone with his boy.

There was no reason why he should not seize it, except the profound one that he had lost the habit of travel. May had disliked to move except for valid reasons, such as taking the children to the sea or in the mountains: she could imagine no other motive for leaving the house in Thirty-ninth Street or their comfortable quarters at the Wellands' in Newport. After Dallas had taken his degree she had thought it her duty to travel for six months; and the whole family had made the old-fashioned tour through England, Switzerland and Italy. Their time being limited (no one knew why) they had omitted France. Archer remembered Dallas's wrath at being asked to contemplate Mont Blanc instead of Rheims and Chartres. But Mary and Bill wanted mountain-climbing, and had already yawned their way in Dallas's wake through the English cathedrals; and May, always fair to her children, had insisted on holding the balance evenly between their athletic and artistic proclivities. She had indeed proposed that her husband should go to Paris for a fortnight, and join them on the Italian lakes after they had "done" Switzerland; but Archer had declined. "We'll stick together," he said; and May's face had brightened at his setting such a good example to Dallas.

Since her death, nearly two years before, there had been no reason for his continuing in the same routine. His children had urged him to travel: Mary Chivers had felt sure it would do him good to go abroad and "see the galleries." The very mysteriousness of such a cure made her the more confident of its efficacy. But Archer had found himself held fast by habit, by memories, by a sudden startled shrinking from new things.

Now, as he reviewed his past, he saw into what a deep rut he had sunk. The worst of doing one's duty was that it apparently unfitted one for doing anything else. At least that was the view that the men of his generation had taken. The trenchant divisions between right and wrong, honest and dishonest, respectable and the reverse, had left so little scope for the unforeseen. There are moments when a man's imagination, so easily subdued to what it lives in, suddenly rises above its daily level, and surveys the long windings of destiny. Archer hung there and wondered. . . .

What was left of the little world he had grown up in, and whose standards had bent and bound him? He remembered a sneering prophecy of poor Lawrence Lefferts's, uttered years ago in that very room: "If things go on at this rate, our children will be marrying Beaufort's bastards."

It was just what Archer's eldest son, the pride of his life, was doing; and nobody wondered or reproved. Even the boy's Aunt Janey, who still looked so exactly as she used to in her elderly youth, had taken her mother's emeralds and seed-pearls out of their pink cotton-wool, and carried them with her own twitching hands to the future bride; and Fanny Beaufort, instead of looking disappointed at not receiving a "set" from a Paris jeweller, had exclaimed at their old-fashioned beauty, and declared that when she wore them she should feel like an Isabey miniature.

Fanny Beaufort, who had appeared in New York at eighteen, after the death of her parents, had won its heart much as Madame Olenska had won it thirty years earlier; only instead of being distrustful and afraid of her, society took her joyfully for granted. She was pretty, amusing and accomplished: what more did anyone want? Nobody was narrow-minded enough to rake up against her the half-forgotten facts of her father's past and her own origin. Only the older people remembered so obscure an incident in the business life of New York as Beaufort's failure, or the fact that after his wife's death he had been quietly married to the notorious Fanny Ring, and had left the country with his new wife, and a little girl who inherited her beauty. He was subsequently heard of in Constantinople, then in Russia; and a dozen years later American travelers were handsomely entertained by him in Buenos Aires, where he represented a large insurance agency. He and his wife died there in the odor of prosperity; and one day their orphaned daughter had appeared in New York in charge of May Archer's sister-in-law, Mrs. Jack Welland, whose husband had been appointed the girl's guardian. The fact threw her into almost cousinly relationship with Newland Archer's children, and nobody was surprised when Dallas's engagement was announced.

Nothing could more clearly give the measure of the distance that the world had traveled. People nowadays were too busy—busy with reforms and "movements," with fads and fetishes and frivolities—to bother much about their neighbors. And of what account was anybody's past, in the huge kaleidoscope where all the social atoms spun around on the same plane?

Newland Archer, looking out of his hotel window at the stately gaiety of the Paris streets, felt his heart beating with the confusion and eagerness of youth.

It was long since it had thus plunged and reared under his widening waistcoat, leaving him, the next minute, with an empty breast and hot temples. He wondered if it was thus that his son's conducted itself in the presence of Miss Fanny Beaufort—and decided that it was not. "It functions as actively, no doubt, but the rhythm is different," he reflected, recalling the cool composure with which the young man had announced his engagement, and taken for granted that his family would approve.

"The difference is that these young people take it for granted that they're going to get whatever they want, and that we almost always took it for granted that we shouldn't. Only, I wonder—the thing one's so certain of in advance: can it ever make one's heart beat as wildly?"

It was the day after their arrival in Paris, and the spring sunshine held Archer in his open window, above the wide silvery prospect of the Place Vendôme. One of the things he had stipulated—almost the only one—when he had agreed to come abroad with Dallas, was that, in Paris, he shouldn't be made to go to one of the new-fangled "palaces."

"Oh, all right—of course," Dallas goodnaturedly agreed. "I'll take you to some jolly old-fashioned place—the Bristol say—" leaving his father speechless at hearing that the century-long home of kings and emperors was now spoken of as an old-fashioned inn, where one went for its quaint inconveniences and lingering local color.

Archer had pictured often enough, in the first impatient years, the scene of his return to Paris; then the personal vision had faded, and he had simply tried to see the city as the setting of Madame Olenska's life. Sitting alone at night in his library, after the household had gone to bed, he had evoked the radiant outbreak of spring down the avenues of horse-chestnuts, the flowers and statues in the public gardens, the whiff of lilacs from the flower-carts, the majestic roll of the river under the great bridges, and the life of art and study and pleasure that filled each mighty artery to bursting. Now the spectacle was before him in its glory, and as he looked out on it he felt shy, old-fashioned, inadequate: a mere gray speck of a man compared with the ruthless magnificent fellow he had dreamed of being. . . .

Dallas's hand came down cheerily on his shoulder. "Hullo, father: this is something like, isn't it?" They stood for a while looking out in silence, and then the young man continued: "By the way, I've got a message for you: the Countess Olenska expects us both at half-past five."

He said it lightly, carelessly, as he might have imparted any casual item of information, such as the hour at which their train was to leave for Florence the next evening. Archer looked at him, and thought he saw in his gay young eyes a gleam of his great-grand-mother Mingott's malice.

"Oh, didn't I tell you?" Dallas pursued. "Fanny made me swear to do three things while I was in Paris: get her the score of the last Debussy songs, go to the Grand-Guignol and see Madame Olenska. You know she was awfully good to Fanny when Mr. Beaufort sent her over from Buenos Aires to the Assomption. Fanny hadn't any friends in Paris, and Madame Olenska used to be kind to her and trot her about on holidays. I believe she was a great friend of the first Mrs. Beaufort's. And she's our cousin, of course. So I rang her up this morning before I went out, and told her you and I were here for two days and wanted to see her."

Archer continued to stare at him. "You told her I was here?"

"Of course—why not?" Dallas's eyebrows went up whimsically. Then, getting no answer, he slipped his arm through his father's with a confidential pressure.

"I say, Father: what was she like?"

Archer felt his color rise under his son's unabashed gaze. "Come, own up: you and she were great pals, weren't you? Wasn't she most awfully lovely?"

"Lovely? I don't know. She was different."

"Ah—there you have it! That's what it always comes to, doesn't it? When she comes, *she's different*—and one doesn't know why. It's exactly what I feel about Fanny."

His father drew back a step, releasing his arm. "About Fanny? But, my dear fellow—I should hope so! Only I don't see—"

"Dash it, Dad, don't be prehistoric. Wasn't she—once—your Fanny?"

Dallas belonged body and soul to the new generation. He was the first-born of Newland and May Archer, yet it had never been possible to inculcate in him even the rudiments of reserve. "What's the use of making mysteries? It only makes people want to nose 'em out," he always objected when enjoined to discretion. But Archer, meeting his eyes, saw the filial light under their banter.

"My Fanny—?"

"Well, the woman you'd have chucked everything for: only you didn't," continued his surprising son.

"I didn't," echoed Archer with a kind of solemnity.

"No: you date, you see, dear old boy. But Mother said—"

"Your mother?"

"Yes: the day before she died. It was when she sent for me alone—
you remember? She said she knew we were safe with you, and always
would be, because once, when she asked you to, you'd given up the
thing you most wanted."

Archer received this strange communication in silence. His eyes
remained unseeingly fixed on the thronged sunlit square below the
window. At length he said in a low voice: "She never asked me."

"No. I forgot. You never did ask each other anything, did you?
And you never told each other anything. You just sat and watched
each other, and guessed at what was going on underneath. A deaf-
and-dumb asylum, in fact. Well, I back your generation for knowing
more about each other's private thoughts than we ever have time to
find out about our own.—I say, Dad," Dallas broke off, "you're not
angry with me? If you are, let's make it up and go and lunch at
Henri's. I've got to rush out to Versailles afterward."

Archer did not accompany his son to Versailles. He preferred to
spend the afternoon in solitary roamings through Paris. He had to
deal all at once with the packed regrets and stifled memories of an
inarticulate lifetime.

After a little while he did not regret Dallas's indiscretion. It
seemed to take an iron band from his heart to know that, after all,
someone had guessed and pitied. . . . And that it should have been
his wife moved him indescribably. Dallas, for all his affectionate insight, would not have understood that. To the boy, no doubt, the episode was only a pathetic instance of vain frustration, of wasted
forces. But was it really no more? For a long time Archer sat on a
bench in the Champs Elysées and wondered, while the stream of life
rolled by. . . .

A few streets away, a few hours away, Ellen Olenska waited. She
had never gone back to her husband, and when he had died, some
years before, she had made no change in her way of living. There was
nothing now to keep her and Archer apart—and that afternoon he
was to see her.

He got up and walked across the Place de la Concorde and the
Tuileries gardens to the Louvre. She had once told him that she
often went there, and he had a fancy to spend the intervening time
in a place where he could think of her as perhaps having lately been.
For an hour or more he wandered from gallery to gallery through the
dazzle of afternoon light, and one by one the pictures burst on him

in their half-forgotten splendor, filling his soul with the long echoes of beauty. After all, his life had been too starved. . . .

Suddenly, before an effulgent Titian, he found himself saying: "But I'm only fifty-seven—" and then he turned away. For such summer dreams it was too late; but surely not for a quiet harvest of friendship, of comradeship, in the blessed hush of her nearness.

He went back to the hotel, where he and Dallas were to meet; and together they walked again across the Place de la Concorde and over the bridge that leads to the Chamber of Deputies.

Dallas, unconscious of what was going on in his father's mind, was talking excitedly and abundantly of Versailles. He had had but one previous glimpse of it, during a holiday trip in which he had tried to pack all the sights he had been deprived of when he had had to go with the family to Switzerland; and tumultuous enthusiasm and cocksure criticism tripped each other up on his lips.

As Archer listened, his sense of inadequacy and inexpressiveness increased. The boy was not insensitive, he knew; but he had the facility and self-confidence that came of looking at fate not as a master but as an equal. "That's it: they feel equal to things—they know their way about," he mused, thinking of his son as the spokesman of the new generation which had swept away all the old landmarks, and with them the sign-posts and the danger-signal.

Suddenly Dallas stopped short, grasping his father's arm. "Oh, by Jove," he exclaimed.

They had come out into the great tree-planted space before the Invalides. The dome of Mansart floated ethereally above the budding trees and the long gray front of the building: drawing up into itself all the rays of afternoon light, it hung there like the visible symbol of the race's glory.

Archer knew that Madame Olenska lived in a square near one of the avenues radiating from the Invalides; and he had pictured the quarter as quiet and almost obscure, forgetting the central splendor that lit it up. Now, by some queer process of association, that golden light became for him the pervading illumination in which she lived. For nearly thirty years, her life—of which he knew so strangely little —had been spent in this rich atmosphere that he already felt to be too dense and yet too stimulating for his lungs. He thought of the theaters she must have been to, the pictures she must have looked at, the sober and splendid old houses she must have frequented, the people she must have talked with, the incessant stir of ideas, curiosities, images and associations thrown out by an intensely social race in a setting of immemorial manners; and suddenly he remembered the young Frenchman who had once said to him: "Ah, good conversation—there is nothing like it, is there?"

Archer had not seen M. Rivière, or heard of him, for nearly thirty years; and that fact gave the measure of his ignorance of Madame Olenska's existence. More than half a lifetime divided them, and she had spent the long interval among people he did not know, in a society he but faintly guessed at, in conditions he would never wholly understand. During that time he had been living with his youthful memory of her; but she had doubtless had other and more tangible companionship. Perhaps she too had kept her memory of him as something apart; but if she had, it must have been like a relic in a small dim chapel, where there was not time to pray every day. . . .

They had crossed the Place des Invalides, and were walking down one of the thoroughfares flanking the building. It was a quiet quarter, after all, in spite of its splendor and its history; and the fact gave one an idea of the riches Paris had to draw on, since such scenes as this were left to the few and the indifferent.

The day was fading into a soft sun-shot haze, pricked here and there by a yellow electric light, and passers were rare in the little square into which they had turned. Dallas stopped again, and looked up.

"It must be here," he said, slipping his arm through his father's with a movement from which Archer's shyness did not shrink; and they stood together looking up at the house.

It was a modern building, without distinctive character, but many-windowed, and pleasantly balconied up its wide cream-colored front. On one of the upper balconies, which hung well above the rounded tops of the horse-chestnuts in the square, the awnings were still lowered, as though the sun had just left it.

"I wonder which floor—?" Dallas conjectured; and moving toward the *porte-cochère* he put his head into the porter's lodge, and came back to say: "The fifth. It must be the one with the awnings."

Archer remained motionless, gazing at the upper windows as if the end of their pilgrimage had been attained.

"I say, you know, it's nearly six," his son at length reminded him.

The father glanced away at an empty bench under the trees.

"I believe I'll sit there a moment," he said.

"Why—aren't you well?" his son exclaimed.

"Oh, perfectly. But I should like you, please, to go up without me."

Dallas paused before him, visibly bewildered. "But, I say, Dad: do you mean you won't come up at all?"

"I don't know," said Archer slowly.

"If you don't she won't understand."

"Go, my boy; perhaps I shall follow you."

Dallas gave him a long look through the twilight.

"But what on earth shall I say?"

"My dear fellow, don't you always know what to say?" his father rejoined with a smile.

"Very well. I shall say you're old-fashioned, and prefer walking up the five flights because you don't like lifts."

His father smiled again. "Say I'm old-fashioned: that's enough."

Dallas looked at him again, and then, with an incredulous gesture, passed out of sight under the vaulted doorway.

Archer sat down on the bench and continued to gaze at the awninged balcony. He calculated the time it would take his son to be carried up in the lift to the fifth floor, to ring the bell, and be admitted to the hall, and then ushered into the drawing room. He pictured Dallas entering that room with his quick assured step and his delightful smile, and wondered if the people were right who said that his boy "took after him."

Then he tried to see the persons already in the room—for probably at that sociable hour there would be more than one—and among them a dark lady, pale and dark, who would look up quickly, half rise, and hold out a long thin hand with three rings on it. . . . He thought she would be sitting in a sofa-corner near the fire, with azaleas banked behind her on a table.

"It's more real to me here than if I went up," he suddenly heard himself say; and the fear lest that last shadow of reality should lose its edge kept him rooted to his seat as the minutes succeeded each other.

He sat for a long time on the bench in the thickening dusk, his eyes never turning from the balcony. At length a light shone through the windows, and a moment later a man-servant came out on the balcony, drew up the awnings, and closed the shutters.

At that, as if it had been the signal he waited for, Newland Archer got up slowly and walked back alone to his hotel.

Ethan Frome

ETHAN FROME

I HAD THE STORY, bit by bit, from various people, and, as generally happens in such cases, each time it was a different story.

If you know Starkfield, Massachusetts, you know the post-office. If you know the post-office you must have seen Ethan Frome drive up to it, drop the reins on his hollow-backed bay and drag himself across the brick pavement to the white colonnade: and you must have asked who he was.

It was there that, several years ago, I saw him for the first time; and the sight pulled me up sharp. Even then he was the most striking figure in Starkfield, though he was but the ruin of a man. It was not so much his great height that marked him, for the "natives" were easily singled out by their lank longitude from the stockier foreign breed: it was the careless powerful look he had, in spite of a lameness checking each step like the jerk of a chain. There was something bleak and unapproachable in his face, and he was so stiffened and grizzled that I took him for an old man and was surprised to hear that he was not more than fifty-two. I had this from Harmon Gow, who had driven the stage from Bettsbridge to Starkfield in pre-trolley days and knew the chronicle of all the families on his line.

"He's looked that way ever since he had his smash-up; and that's twenty-four years ago come next February," Harmon threw out between reminiscent pauses.

The "smash-up" it was—I gathered from the same informant—which, besides drawing the red gash across Ethan Frome's forehead, had so shortened and warped his right side that it cost him a visible effort to take the few steps from his buggy to the post-office window. He used to drive in from his farm every day at about noon, and as that was my own hour for fetching my mail I often passed him in the porch or stood beside him while we waited on the motions of the distributing hand behind the grating. I noticed that, though he came so punctually, he seldom received anything but a copy of the *Betts-bridge Eagle*, which he put without a glance into his sagging pocket. At intervals, however, the post-master would hand him an envelope addressed to Mrs. Zenobia—or Mrs. Zeena—Frome, and usually bearing conspicuously in the upper left-hand corner the address of some manufacturer of patent medicine and the name of his specific. These documents my neighbour would also pocket without a glance, as if too much used to them to wonder at their number and variety, and would then turn away with a silent nod to the post-master.

Every one in Starkfield knew him and gave him a greeting tempered to his own grave mien; but his taciturnity was respected and it was only on rare occasions that one of the older men of the place detained him for a word. When this happened he would listen quietly, his blue eyes on the speaker's face, and answer in so low a tone that his words never reached me; then he would climb stiffly into his buggy, gather up the reins in his left hand and drive slowly away in the direction of his farm.

"It was a pretty bad smash-up?" I questioned Harmon, looking after Frome's retreating figure, and thinking how gallantly his lean brown head, with its shock of light hair, must have sat on his strong shoulders before they were bent out of shape.

"Wust kind," my informant assented. "More'n enough to kill most men. But the Fromes are tough. Ethan'll likely touch a hundred."

"Good God!" I exclaimed. At the moment Ethan Frome, after climbing to his seat, had leaned over to assure himself of the security of a wooden box—also with a druggist's label on it—which he had placed in the back of the buggy, and I saw his face as it probably looked when he thought himself alone. "*That* man touch a hundred? He looks as if he was dead and in hell now!"

Harmon drew a slab of tobacco from his pocket, cut off a wedge and pressed it into the leather pouch of his cheek. "Guess he's been in Starkfield too many winters. Most of the smart ones get away."

"Why didn't *he?*"

"Somebody had to stay and care for the folks. There warn't ever anybody but Ethan. Fust his father—then his mother—then his wife."

"And then the smash-up?"

Harmon chuckled sardonically. "That's so. He *had* to stay then."

"I see. And since then they've had to care for him?"

Harmon thoughtfully passed his tobacco to the other cheek. "Oh, as to that: I guess it's always Ethan done the caring."

Though Harmon Gow developed the tale as far as his mental and moral reach permitted there were perceptible gaps between his facts, and I had the sense that the deeper meaning of the story was in the gaps. But one phrase stuck in my memory and served as the nucleus about which I grouped my subsequent inferences: "Guess he's been in Starkfield too many winters."

Before my own time there was up I had learned to know what that meant. Yet I had come in the degenerate day of trolley, bicycle and rural delivery, when communication was easy between the scattered mountain villages, and the bigger towns in the valleys, such as Bettsbridge and Shadd's Falls, had libraries, theatres and Y. M. C. A. halls to which the youth of the hills could descend for recreation. But when winter shut down on Starkfield, and the village lay under a sheet of snow perpetually renewed from the pale skies, I began to see what life there—or rather its negation—must have been in Ethan Frome's young manhood.

I had been sent up by my employers on a job connected with the big power-house at Corbury Junction, and a long-drawn carpenters' strike had so delayed the work that I found myself anchored at Starkfield—the nearest habitable spot—for the best part of the winter. I chafed at first, and then, under the hypnotising effect of routine, gradually began to find a grim satisfaction in the life. During the early part of my stay I had been struck by the contrast between the vitality of the climate and the deadness of the community. Day by day, after the December snows were over, a blazing blue sky poured down torrents of light and air on the white landscape, which gave them back in an intenser glitter. One would have supposed that such an atmosphere must quicken the emotions as well as the blood; but it seemed to produce no change except that of retarding still more the sluggish pulse of Starkfield. When I had been there a little longer, and had seen this phase of crystal clearness followed by long stretches of sunless cold; when the storms of February had pitched their white tents about the devoted village and the wild cavalry of March winds had charged down to their support; I began to understand why Starkfield emerged from its six months' siege like a starved garrison capitulating without quarter. Twenty years earlier the means of resistance must have been far fewer, and the enemy in command of almost all the lines of access between the beleaguered villages; and, considering these things, I felt the sinister force of Harmon's phrase: "Most of the smart ones get away." But if that were the case, how could any combination of obstacles have hindered the flight of a man like Ethan Frome?

During my stay at Starkfield I lodged with a middle-aged widow colloquially known as Mrs. Ned Hale. Mrs. Hale's father had been the village lawyer of the previous generation, and "lawyer Varnum's house," where my landlady still lived with her mother, was the most considerable mansion in the village. It stood at one end of the main street, its classic portico and small-paned windows looking down a flagged path between Norway spruces to the slim white steeple of the Congregational church. It was clear that the Varnum fortunes were at the ebb, but the two women did what they could to preserve a decent dignity; and Mrs. Hale, in particular, had a certain wan refinement not out of keeping with her pale old-fashioned house.

In the "best parlour," with its black horse-hair and mahogany weakly illuminated by a gurgling Carcel lamp, I listened every evening to another and more delicately shaded version of the Starkfield chronicle. It was not that Mrs. Ned Hale felt, or affected, any social superiority to the people about her; it was only that the accident of a finer sensibility and a little more education had put just enough distance between herself and her neighbours to enable her to judge them with detachment. She was not unwilling to exercise this faculty, and I had great hopes of getting from her the missing facts of Ethan Frome's story, or rather such a key to his character as should co-ordinate the facts I knew. Her mind was a store-house of innocuous anecdote and any question about her acquaintances brought forth a volume of detail; but on the subject of Ethan Frome I found her unexpectedly reticent. There was no hint of disapproval in her reserve; I merely felt in her an insurmountable reluctance to speak of him or his affairs, a low "Yes, I knew them both . . . it was awful . . ." seeming to be the utmost concession that her distress could make to my curiosity.

So marked was the change in her manner, such depths of sad initiation did it imply, that, with some doubts as to my delicacy, I put the case anew to my village oracle, Harmon Gow; but got for my pains only an uncomprehending grunt.

"Ruth Varnum was always as nervous as a rat; and, come to

think of it, she was the first one to see 'em after they was picked up. It happened right below lawyer Varnum's, down at the bend of the Corbury road, just round about the time that Ruth got engaged to Ned Hale. The young folks was all friends, and I guess she just can't bear to talk about it. She's had troubles enough of her own."

All the dwellers in Starkfield, as in more notable communities, had had troubles enough of their own to make them comparatively indifferent to those of their neighbours; and though all conceded that Ethan Frome's had been beyond the common measure, no one gave me an explanation of the look in his face which, as I persisted in thinking, neither poverty nor physical suffering could have put there. Nevertheless, I might have contented myself with the story pieced together from these hints had it not been for the provocation of Mrs. Hale's silence, and—a little later—for the accident of personal contact with the man.

On my arrival at Starkfield, Denis Eady, the rich Irish grocer, who was the proprietor of Starkfield's nearest approach to a livery stable, had entered into an agreement to send me over daily to Corbury Flats, where I had to pick up my train for the Junction. But about the middle of the winter Eady's horses fell ill of a local epidemic. The illness spread to the other Starkfield stables and for a day or two I was put to it to find a means of transport. Then Harmon Gow suggested that Ethan Frome's bay was still on his legs and that his owner might be glad to drive me over.

I stared at the suggestion. "Ethan Frome? But I've never even spoken to him. Why on earth should he put himself out for me?"

Harmon's answer surprised me still more. "I don't know as he would; but I know he wouldn't be sorry to earn a dollar."

I had been told that Frome was poor, and that the saw-mill and the arid acres of his farm yielded scarcely enough to keep his household through the winter; but I had not supposed him to be in such want as Harmon's words implied, and I expressed my wonder.

"Well, matters ain't gone any too well with him," Harmon said. "When a man's been setting round like a hulk for twenty years or more, seeing things that want doing, it eats inter him, and he loses his grit. That Frome farm was always 'bout as bare's a milkpan when the cat's been round; and you know what one of them old water-mills is wuth nowadays. When Ethan could sweat over 'em both from sun-up to dark he kinder choked a living out of 'em; but his folks ate up most everything, even then, and I don't see how he makes out now. Fust his father got a kick, out haying, and went soft in the brain, and gave away money like Bible texts afore he died. Then his mother got queer and dragged along for years as weak as a baby; and his wife Zeena, she's always been the greatest hand at doctoring in the county. Sickness and trouble: that's what Ethan's had his plate full up with, ever since the very first helping."

The next morning, when I looked out, I saw the hollow-backed bay between the Varnum spruces, and Ethan Frome, throwing back his worn bearskin, made room for me in the sleigh at his side. After that, for a week, he drove me over every morning to Corbury Flats, and on my return in the afternoon met me again and carried me back through the icy night to Starkfield. The distance each way was barely three miles, but the old bay's pace was slow, and even with firm snow under the runners we were nearly an hour on the way. Ethan Frome drove in silence, the reins loosely held in his left hand, his brown seamed profile, under the helmet-like peak of the cap, relieved against the banks of snow like the bronze image of a hero. He never turned his face to mine, or answered, except in monosyllables, the questions I put, or such slight pleasantries as I ventured. He seemed a part of the mute melancholy landscape, an incarnation of its frozen woe, with all that was warm and sentient in him fast bound below the surface; but there was nothing unfriendly in his silence. I simply felt that he lived in a depth of moral isolation too remote for casual access, and I had the sense that his loneliness was not merely the result of his personal plight, tragic as I guessed that to be, but had in it, as Harmon Gow had hinted, the profound accumulated cold of many Starkfield winters.

Only once or twice was the distance between us bridged for a moment; and the glimpses thus gained confirmed my desire to know more. Once I happened to speak of an engineering job I had been on the previous year in Florida, and of the contrast between the winter landscape about us and that in which I had found myself the year before; and to my surprise Frome said suddenly: "Yes: I was down there once, and for a good while afterward I could call up the sight of it in winter. But now it's all snowed under."

He said no more, and I had to guess the rest from the inflection of his voice and his sharp relapse into silence.

Another day, on getting into my train at the Flats, I missed a volume of popular science—I think it was on some recent discoveries in bio-chemistry—which I had carried with me to read on the way. I thought no more about it till I got into the sleigh again that evening, and saw the book in Frome's hand.

"I found it after you were gone," he said.

I put the volume into my pocket and we dropped back into our usual silence; but as we began to crawl up the long hill from Corbury Flats to the Starkfield ridge I became aware in the dusk that he had turned his face to mine.

"There are things in that book that I didn't know the first word about," he said.

I wondered less at his words than at the queer note of resentment in his voice. He was evidently surprised and slightly aggrieved at his own ignorance.

"Does that sort of thing interest you?" I asked.

"It used to."

"There are one or two rather new things in the book: there have been some big strides lately in that particular line of research." I waited a moment for an answer that did not come; then I said: "If you'd like to look the book through I'd be glad to leave it with you."

He hesitated, and I had the impression that he felt himself about to yield to a stealing tide of inertia; then, "Thank you—I'll take it," he answered shortly.

I hoped that this incident might set up some more direct communication between us. Frome was so simple and straightforward that I was sure his curiosity about the book was based on a genuine interest in its subject. Such tastes and acquirements in a man of his condition made the contrast more poignant between his outer situation and his inner needs, and I hoped that the chance of giving expression to the latter might at least unseal his lips. But something in his past history, or in his present way of living, had apparently driven him too deeply into himself for any casual impulse to draw him back to his kind. At our next meeting he made no allusion to the book, and our intercourse seemed fated to remain as negative and one-sided as if there had been no break in his reserve.

Frome had been driving me over to the Flats for about a week when one morning I looked out of my window into a thick snow-fall. The height of the white waves massed against the garden-fence and along the wall of the church showed that the storm must have been going on all night, and that the drifts were likely to be heavy in the open. I thought it probable that my train would be delayed; but I had to be at the power-house for an hour or two that afternoon, and

I decided, if Frome turned up, to push through to the Flats and wait there till my train came in. I don't know why I put it in the conditional, however, for I never doubted that Frome would appear. He was not the kind of man to be turned from his business by any commotion of the elements; and at the appointed hour his sleigh glided up through the snow like a stage-apparition behind thickening veils of gauze.

I was getting to know him too well to express either wonder or gratitude at his keeping his appointment; but I exclaimed in surprise as I saw him turn his horse in a direction opposite to that of the Corbury road.

"The railroad's blocked by a freight-train that got stuck in a drift below the Flats," he explained, as we jogged off into the stinging whiteness.

"But look here—where are you taking me, then?"

"Straight to the Junction, by the shortest way," he answered, pointing up School House Hill with his whip.

"To the Junction—in this storm? Why, it's a good ten miles!"

"The bay'll do it if you give him time. You said you had some business there this afternoon. I'll see you get there."

He said it so quietly that I could only answer: "You're doing me the biggest kind of a favour."

"That's all right," he rejoined.

Abreast of the schoolhouse the road forked, and we dipped down a lane to the left, between hemlock boughs bent inward to their trunks by the weight of the snow. I had often walked that way on Sundays, and knew that the solitary roof showing through bare branches near the bottom of the hill was that of Frome's saw-mill. It looked exanimate enough, with its idle wheel looming above the black stream dashed with yellow-white spume, and its cluster of sheds sagging under their white load. Frome did not even turn his head as we drove by, and still in silence we began to mount the next slope. About a mile farther, on a road I had never travelled, we came to an orchard of starved apple-trees writhing over a hillside among outcroppings of slate that nuzzled up through the snow like animals pushing out their noses to breathe. Beyond the orchard lay a field or two, their boundaries lost under drifts; and above the fields, huddled against the white immensities of land and sky, one of those lonely New England farm-houses that make the landscape lonelier.

"That's my place," said Frome, with a sideway jerk of his lame

elbow; and in the distress and oppression of the scene I did not know
what to answer. The snow had ceased, and a flash of watery sunlight
exposed the house on the slope above us in all its plaintive ugliness.
The black wraith of a deciduous creeper flapped from the porch, and
the thin wooden walls, under their worn coat of paint, seemed to
shiver in the wind that had risen with the ceasing of the snow.

"The house was bigger in my father's time: I had to take down
the 'L,' a while back," Frome continued, checking with a twitch of
the left rein the bay's evident intention of turning in through the
broken-down gate.

I saw then that the unusually forlorn and stunted look of the
house was partly due to the loss of what is known in New England
as the "L": that long deep-roofed adjunct usually built at right angles to the main house, and connecting it, by way of store-rooms and
tool-house, with the wood-shed and cow-barn. Whether because of
its symbolic sense, the image it presents of a life linked with the soil,
and enclosing in itself the chief sources of warmth and nourishment,
or whether merely because of the consolatory thought that it enables
the dwellers in that harsh climate to get to their morning's work
without facing the weather, it is certain that the "L" rather than the
house itself seems to be the centre, the actual hearth-stone of the
New England farm. Perhaps this connection of ideas, which had
often occurred to me in my rambles about Starkfield, caused me to
hear a wistful note in Frome's words, and to see in the diminished
dwelling the image of his own shrunken body.

"We're kinder side-tracked here now," he added, "but there was
considerable passing before the railroad was carried through to the
Flats." He roused the lagging bay with another twitch; then, as if the
mere sight of the house had let me too deeply into his confidence for
any farther pretence of reserve, he went on slowly: "I've always set
down the worst of mother's trouble to that. When she got the
rheumatism so bad she couldn't move around she used to sit up
there and watch the road by the hour; and one year, when they was
six months mending the Bettsbridge pike after the floods, and Harmon Gow had to bring his stage round this way, she picked up so
that she used to get down to the gate most days to see him. But after
the trains begun running nobody ever come by here to speak of, and
mother never could get it through her head what had happened, and
it preyed on her right along till she died."

As we turned into the Corbury road the snow began to fall again, cutting off our last glimpse of the house; and Frome's silence fell with it, letting down between us the old veil of reticence. This time the wind did not cease with the return of the snow. Instead, it sprang up to a gale which now and then, from a tattered sky, flung pale sweeps of sunlight over a landscape chaotically tossed. But the bay was as good as Frome's word, and we pushed on to the Junction through the wild white scene.

In the afternoon the storm held off, and the clearness in the west seemed to my inexperienced eye the pledge of a fair evening. I finished my business as quickly as possible, and we set out for Starkfield with a good chance of getting there for supper. But at sunset the clouds gathered again, bringing an earlier night, and the snow began to fall straight and steadily from a sky without wind, in a soft universal diffusion more confusing than the gusts and eddies of the morning. It seemed to be a part of the thickening darkness, to be the winter night itself descending on us layer by layer.

The small ray of Frome's lantern was soon lost in this smothering medium, in which even his sense of direction, and the bay's homing instinct, finally ceased to serve us. Two or three times some ghostly landmark sprang up to warn us that we were astray, and then was sucked back into the mist; and when we finally regained our road the old horse began to show signs of exhaustion. I felt myself to blame for having accepted Frome's offer, and after a short discussion I persuaded him to let me get out of the sleigh and walk along through the snow at the bay's side. In this way we struggled on for another mile or two, and at last reached a point where Frome, peering into what seemed to me formless night, said: "That's my gate down yonder."

The last stretch had been the hardest part of the way. The bitter cold and the heavy going had nearly knocked the wind out of me, and I could feel the horse's side ticking like a clock under my hand.

"Look here, Frome," I began, "there's no earthly use in your going any farther—" but he interrupted me: "Nor you neither. There's been about enough of this for anybody."

I understood that he was offering me a night's shelter at the farm, and without answering I turned into the gate at his side, and followed him to the barn, where I helped him to unharness and bed down the tired horse. When this was done he unhooked the lantern from the sleigh, stepped out again into the night, and called to me over his shoulder: "This way."

Far off above us a square of light trembled through the screen of snow. Staggering along in Frome's wake I floundered toward it, and in the darkness almost fell into one of the deep drifts against the front of the house. Frome scrambled up the slippery steps of the porch, digging a way through the snow with his heavily booted foot. Then he lifted his lantern, found the latch, and led the way into the house. I went after him into a low unlit passage, at the back of which a ladder-like staircase rose into obscurity. On our right a line of light marked the door of the room which had sent its ray across the night; and behind the door I heard a woman's voice droning querulously.

Frome stamped on the worn oil-cloth to shake the snow from his boots, and set down his lantern on a kitchen chair which was the only piece of furniture in the hall. Then he opened the door.

"Come in," he said; and as he spoke the droning voice grew still. . .

It was that night that I found the clue to Ethan Frome, and began to put together this vision of his story. . . .

1

THE VILLAGE lay under two feet of snow, with drifts at the windy corners. In a sky of iron the points of the Dipper hung like icicles and Orion flashed his cold fires. The moon had set, but the night was so transparent that the white house-fronts between the elms looked gray against the snow, clumps of bushes made black stains on it, and the basement windows of the church sent shafts of yellow light far across the endless undulations.

Young Ethan Frome walked at a quick pace along the deserted street, past the bank and Michael Eady's new brick store and lawyer Varnum's house with the two black Norway spruces at the gate. Opposite the Varnum gate, where the road fell away toward the Corbury valley, the church reared its slim white steeple and narrow peristyle. As the young man walked toward it the upper windows drew a black arcade along the side wall of the building, but from the lower openings, on the side where the ground sloped steeply down to the Corbury road, the light shot its long bars, illuminating many fresh furrows in the track leading to the basement door, and showing, under an adjoining shed, a line of sleighs with heavily blanketed horses.

The night was perfectly still, and the air so dry and pure that it gave little sensation of cold. The effect produced on Frome was rather of a complete absence of atmosphere, as though nothing less tenuous than ether intervened between the white earth under his feet and the metallic dome overhead. "It's like being in an exhausted receiver," he thought. Four or five years earlier he had taken a year's course at a technological college at Worcester, and dabbled in the laboratory with a friendly professor of physics; and the images supplied by that experience still cropped up, at unexpected moments, through the totally different associations of thought in which he had since been living. His father's death, and the misfortunes following it, had put a premature end to Ethan's studies; but though they had not gone far enough to be of much practical use they had fed his fancy and made him aware of huge cloudy meanings behind the daily face of things.

As he strode along through the snow the sense of such meanings glowed in his brain and mingled with the bodily flush produced by his sharp tramp. At the end of the village he paused before the darkened front of the church. He stood there a moment, breathing quickly, and looking up and down the street, in which not another figure moved. The pitch of the Corbury road, below lawyer Varnum's spruces, was the favourite coasting-ground of Starkfield, and on clear evenings the church corner rang till late with the shouts of the coasters; but to-night not a sled darkened the whiteness of the long declivity. The hush of midnight lay on the village, and all its waking life was gathered behind the church windows, from which strains of dance-music flowed with the broad bands of yellow light.

The young man, skirting the side of the building, went down the slope toward the basement door. To keep out of range of the revealing rays from within he made a circuit through the untrodden snow and gradually approached the farther angle of the basement wall. Thence, still hugging the shadow, he edged his way cautiously forward to the nearest window, holding back his straight spare body and craning his neck till he got a glimpse of the room.

Seen thus, from the pure and frosty darkness in which he stood, it seemed to be seething in a mist of heat. The metal reflectors of the gas-jets sent crude waves of light against the whitewashed walls, and the iron flanks of the stove at the end of the hall looked as though they were heaving with volcanic fires. The floor was thronged with girls and young men. Down the side wall facing the window stood a row of kitchen chairs from which the older women had just risen. By this time the music had stopped, and the musicians—a fiddler, and the young lady who played the harmonium on Sundays—were hastily refreshing themselves at one corner of the supper-table which aligned its devastated pie-dishes and ice-cream saucers on the platform at the end of the hall. The guests were preparing to leave, and the tide had already set toward the passage where coats and wraps were hung, when a young man with a sprightly foot and a shock of black hair shot into the middle of the floor and clapped his hands. The signal took instant effect. The musicians hurried to their instruments, the dancers—some already half-muffled for departure—fell into line down each side of the room, the older spectators slipped back to their chairs, and the lively young man, after diving about here and there in the throng, drew forth a girl who had already wound a cherry-coloured "fascinator" about her head, and, leading her up to the end of the floor, whirled her down its length to the bounding tune of a Virginia reel.

Frome's heart was beating fast. He had been straining for a glimpse of the dark head under the cherry-coloured scarf and it vexed him that another eye should have been quicker than his. The leader of the reel, who looked as if he had Irish blood in his veins, danced well, and his partner caught his fire. As she passed down the line, her light figure swinging from hand to hand in circles of increasing swiftness, the scarf flew off her head and stood out behind her shoulders, and Frome, at each turn, caught sight of her laughing panting lips, the cloud of dark hair about her forehead, and the dark eyes which seemed the only fixed points in a maze of flying lines.

The dancers were going faster and faster, and the musicians, to keep up with them, belaboured their instruments like jockeys lashing their mounts on the home-stretch; yet it seemed to the young man at the window that the reel would never end. Now and then he turned his eyes from the girl's face to that of her partner, which, in the exhilaration of the dance, had taken on a look of almost impudent ownership. Denis Eady was the son of Michael Eady, the ambitious Irish grocer, whose suppleness and effrontery had given Starkfield its first notion of "smart" business methods, and whose new brick store testified to the success of the attempt. His son seemed likely to follow in his steps, and was meanwhile applying the same arts to the conquest of the Starkfield maidenhood. Hitherto Ethan Frome had been content to think him a mean fellow; but now he positively invited a horse-whipping. It was strange that the girl did not seem aware of it: that she could lift her rapt face to her dancer's, and drop her hands into his, without appearing to feel the offence of his look and touch.

Frome was in the habit of walking into Starkfield to fetch home his wife's cousin, Mattie Silver, on the rare evenings when some chance of amusement drew her to the village. It was his wife who had suggested, when the girl came to live with them, that such opportunities should be put in her way. Mattie Silver came from Stamford, and when she entered the Fromes' household to act as her cousin Zeena's aid it was thought best, as she came without pay, not to let her feel too sharp a contrast between the life she had left and the isolation of a Starkfield farm. But for this—as Frome sardonically reflected—it would hardly have occurred to Zeena to take any thought for the girl's amusement.

When his wife first proposed that they should give Mattie an occasional evening out he had inwardly demurred at having to do the extra two miles to the village and back after his hard day on the farm; but not long afterward he had reached the point of wishing that Starkfield might give all its nights to revelry.

Mattie Silver had lived under his roof for a year, and from early morning till they met at supper he had frequent chances of seeing her; but no moments in her company were comparable to those when, her arm in his, and her light step flying to keep time with his long stride, they walked back through the night to the farm. He had taken to the girl from the first day, when he had driven over to the Flats to meet her, and she had smiled and waved to him from the train, crying out, "You must be Ethan!" as she jumped down with her bundles, while he reflected, looking over her slight person: "She don't look much on housework, but she ain't a fretter, anyhow." But it was not only that the coming to his house of a bit of hopeful young life was like the lighting of a fire on a cold hearth. The girl was more than the bright serviceable creature he had thought her. She had an eye to see and an ear to hear: he could show her things and tell her things, and taste the bliss of feeling that all he imparted left long reverberations and echoes he could wake at will.

It was during their night walks back to the farm that he felt most intensely the sweetness of this communion. He had always been more sensitive than the people about him to the appeal of natural beauty. His unfinished studies had given form to this sensibility and even in his unhappiest moments field and sky spoke to him with a deep and powerful persuasion. But hitherto the emotion had remained in him as a silent ache, veiling with sadness the beauty that evoked it. He did not even know whether any one else in the world felt as he did, or whether he was the sole victim of this mournful privilege. Then he learned that one other spirit had trembled with the same touch of wonder: that at his side, living under his roof and eating his bread, was a creature to whom he could say: "That's Orion down yonder; the big fellow to the right is Aldebaran, and the

bunch of little ones—like bees swarming—they're the Pleiades . . ."
or whom he could hold entranced before a ledge of granite thrusting
up through the fern while he unrolled the huge panorama of the ice
age, and the long dim stretches of succeeding time. The fact that admiration for his learning mingled with Mattie's wonder at what he
taught was not the least part of his pleasure. And there were other
sensations, less definable but more exquisite, which drew them together with a shock of silent joy: the cold red of sunset behind winter hills, the flight of cloud-flocks over slopes of golden stubble, or
the intensely blue shadows of hemlocks on sunlit snow. When she
said to him once: "It looks just as if it was painted!" it seemed to
Ethan that the art of definition could go no farther, and that words
had at last been found to utter his secret soul. . . .

As he stood in the darkness outside the church these memories
came back with the poignancy of vanished things. Watching Mattie
whirl down the floor from hand to hand he wondered how he could
ever have thought that his dull talk interested her. To him, who was
never gay but in her presence, her gaiety seemed plain proof of
indifference. The face she lifted to her dancers was the same which,
when she saw him, always looked like a window that has caught the
sunset. He even noticed two or three gestures which, in his fatuity,
he had thought she kept for him: a way of throwing her head back
when she was amused, as if to taste her laugh before she let it out,
and a trick of sinking her lids slowly when anything charmed or
moved her.

The sight made him unhappy, and his unhappiness roused his latent fears. His wife had never shown any jealousy of Mattie, but of
late she had grumbled increasingly over the house-work and found
oblique ways of attracting attention to the girl's inefficiency. Zeena
had always been what Starkfield called "sickly," and Frome had to
admit that, if she were as ailing as she believed, she needed the help
of a stronger arm than the one which lay so lightly in his during the
night walks to the farm. Mattie had no natural turn for housekeeping, and her training had done nothing to remedy the defect. She
was quick to learn, but forgetful and dreamy, and not disposed to
take the matter seriously. Ethan had an idea that if she were to
marry a man she was fond of the dormant instinct would wake, and
her pies and biscuits become the pride of the county; but domesticity
in the abstract did not interest her. At first she was so awkward that
he could not help laughing at her; but she laughed with him and

that made them better friends. He did his best to supplement her unskilled efforts, getting up earlier than usual to light the kitchen fire, carrying in the wood overnight, and neglecting the mill for the farm that he might help her about the house during the day. He even crept down on Saturday nights to scrub the kitchen floor after the women had gone to bed; and Zeena, one day, had surprised him at the churn and had turned away silently, with one of her queer looks.

Of late there had been other signs of her disfavour, as intangible but more disquieting. One cold winter morning, as he dressed in the dark, his candle flickering in the draught of the ill-fitting window, he had heard her speak from the bed behind him.

"The doctor don't want I should be left without anybody to do for me," she said in her flat whine.

He had supposed her to be asleep, and the sound of her voice had startled him, though she was given to abrupt explosions of speech after long intervals of secretive silence.

He turned and looked at her where she lay indistinctly outlined under the dark calico quilt, her high-boned face taking a grayish tinge from the whiteness of the pillow.

"Nobody to do for you?" he repeated.

"If you say you can't afford a hired girl when Mattie goes."

Frome turned away again, and taking up his razor stooped to catch the reflection of his stretched cheek in the blotched looking-glass above the wash-stand.

"Why on earth should Mattie go?"

"Well, when she gets married, I mean," his wife's drawl came from behind him.

"Oh, she'd never leave us as long as you needed her," he returned, scraping hard at his chin.

"I wouldn't ever have it said that I stood in the way of a poor girl like Mattie marrying a smart fellow like Denis Eady," Zeena answered in a tone of plaintive self-effacement.

Ethan, glaring at his face in the glass, threw his head back to draw the razor from ear to chin. His hand was steady, but the attitude was an excuse for not making an immediate reply.

"And the doctor don't want I should be left without anybody," Zeena continued. "He wanted I should speak to you about a girl he's heard about, that might come——"

Ethan laid down the razor and straightened himself with a laugh.

"Denis Eady! If that's all, I guess there's no such hurry to look round for a girl."

"Well, I'd like to talk to you about it," said Zeena obstinately.

He was getting into his clothes in fumbling haste. "All right. But I haven't got the time now; I'm late as it is," he returned, holding his old silver turnip-watch to the candle.

Zeena, apparently accepting this as final, lay watching him in silence while he pulled his suspenders over his shoulders and jerked his arms into his coat; but as he went toward the door she said, suddenly and incisively: "I guess you're always late, now you shave every morning."

That thrust had frightened him more than any vague insinuations about Denis Eady. It was a fact that since Mattie Silver's coming he had taken to shaving every day; but his wife always seemed to be asleep when he left her side in the winter darkness, and he had stupidly assumed that she would not notice any change in his appearance. Once or twice in the past he had been faintly disquieted by Zenobia's way of letting things happen without seeming to remark them, and then, weeks afterward, in a casual phrase, revealing that she had all along taken her notes and drawn her inferences. Of late, however, there had been no room in his thoughts for such vague apprehensions. Zeena herself, from an oppressive reality, had faded into an insubstantial shade. All his life was lived in the sight and sound of Mattie Silver, and he could no longer conceive of its being otherwise. But now, as he stood outside the church, and saw Mattie spinning down the floor with Denis Eady, a throng of disregarded hints and menaces wove their cloud about his brain. . . .

2

As THE DANCERS poured out of the hall Frome, drawing back behind the projecting storm-door, watched the segregation of the grotesquely muffled groups, in which a moving lantern ray now and then lit up a face flushed with food and dancing. The villagers, being afoot, were the first to climb the slope to the main street, while the country neighbours packed themselves more slowly into the sleighs under the shed.

"Ain't you riding, Mattie?" a woman's voice called back from the throng about the shed, and Ethan's heart gave a jump. From where he stood he could not see the persons coming out of the hall till they had advanced a few steps beyond the wooden sides of the storm-door; but through its cracks he heard a clear voice answer: "Mercy no! Not on such a night."

She was there, then, close to him, only a thin board between. In another moment she would step forth into the night, and his eyes, accustomed to the obscurity, would discern her as clearly as though she stood in daylight. A wave of shyness pulled him back into the dark angle of the wall, and he stood there in silence instead of making his presence known to her. It had been one of the wonders of their intercourse that from the first, she, the quicker, finer, more expressive, instead of crushing him by the contrast, had given him something of her own ease and freedom; but now he felt as heavy and loutish as in his student days, when he had tried to "jolly" the Worcester girls at a picnic.

He hung back, and she came out alone and paused within a few yards of him. She was almost the last to leave the hall, and she stood looking uncertainly about her as if wondering why he did not show himself. Then a man's figure approached, coming so close to her that under their formless wrappings they seemed merged in one dim outline.

"Gentleman friend gone back on you? Say, Matt, that's tough! No, I wouldn't be mean enough to tell the other girls. I ain't as low-down as that." (How Frome hated his cheap banter!) "But look a here, ain't it lucky I got the old man's cutter down there waiting for us?"

Frome heard the girl's voice, gaily incredulous: "What on earth's your father's cutter doin' down there?"

"Why, waiting for me to take a ride. I got the roan colt too. I kinder knew I'd want to take a ride to-night," Eady, in his triumph, tried to put a sentimental note into his bragging voice.

The girl seemed to waver, and Frome saw her twirl the end of her scarf irresolutely about her fingers. Not for the world would he have made a sign to her, though it seemed to him that his life hung on her next gesture.

"Hold on a minute while I unhitch the colt," Denis called to her, springing toward the shed.

She stood perfectly still, looking after him, in an attitude of tranquil expectancy torturing to the hidden watcher. Frome noticed that she no longer turned her head from side to side, as though peering through the night for another figure. She let Denis Eady lead out the horse, climb into the cutter and fling back the bearskin to make room for her at his side; then, with a swift motion of flight, she turned about and darted up the slope toward the front of the church.

"Good-bye! Hope you'll have a lovely ride!" she called back to him over her shoulder.

Denis laughed, and gave the horse a cut that brought him quickly abreast of her retreating figure.

"Come along! Get in quick! It's as slippery as thunder on this turn," he cried, leaning over to reach out a hand to her.

She laughed back at him: "Good-night! I'm not getting in."

By this time they had passed beyond Frome's earshot and he could only follow the shadowy pantomime of their silhouettes as they continued to move along the crest of the slope above him. He saw Eady, after a moment, jump from the cutter and go toward the girl with the reins over one arm. The other he tried to slip through hers; but she eluded him nimbly, and Frome's heart, which had swung out over a black void, trembled back to safety. A moment later he heard the jingle of departing sleigh-bells and discerned a figure advancing alone toward the empty expanse of snow before the church.

In the black shade of the Varnum spruces he caught up with her and she turned with a quick "Oh!"

"Think I'd forgotten you, Matt?" he asked with sheepish glee.

She answered seriously: "I thought maybe you couldn't come back for me."

"Couldn't? What on earth could stop me?"

"I knew Zeena wasn't feeling any too good to-day."

"Oh, she's in bed long ago." He paused, a question struggling in him. "Then you meant to walk home all alone?"

"Oh, I ain't afraid!" she laughed.

They stood together in the gloom of the spruces, an empty world glimmering about them wide and grey under the stars. He brought his question out.

"If you thought I hadn't come, why didn't you ride back with Denis Eady?"

"Why, where *were* you? How did you know? I never saw you!"

Her wonder and his laughter ran together like spring rills in a thaw. Ethan had the sense of having done something arch and ingenious. To prolong the effect he groped for a dazzling phrase, and brought out, in a growl of rapture: "Come along."

He slipped an arm through hers, as Eady had done, and fancied it was faintly pressed against her side; but neither of them moved. It was so dark under the spruces that he could barely see the shape of her head beside his shoulder. He longed to stoop his cheek and rub it against her scarf. He would have liked to stand there with her all night in the blackness. She moved forward a step or two and then paused again above the dip of the Corbury road. Its icy slope, scored by innumerable runners, looked like a mirror scratched by travellers at an inn.

"There was a whole lot of them coasting before the moon set," she said.

"Would you like to come in and coast with them some night?" he asked.

"Oh, *would* you, Ethan? It would be lovely!"

"We'll come to-morrow if there's a moon."

She lingered, pressing closer to his side. "Ned Hale and Ruth Varnum came just as *near* running into the big elm at the bottom. We were all sure they were killed." Her shiver ran down his arm. "Wouldn't it have been too awful? They're so happy!"

"Oh, Ned ain't much at steering. I guess I can take you down all right!" he said disdainfully.

He was aware that he was "talking big," like Denis Eady; but his reaction of joy had unsteadied him, and the inflection with which she had said of the engaged couple "They're so happy!" made the words sound as if she had been thinking of herself and him.

"The elm *is* dangerous, though. It ought to be cut down," she insisted.

"Would you be afraid of it, with me?"

"I told you I ain't the kind to be afraid," she tossed back, almost indifferently; and suddenly she began to walk on with a rapid step.

These alterations of mood were the despair and joy of Ethan Frome. The motions of her mind were as incalculable as the flit of a bird in the branches. The fact that he had no right to show his feelings, and thus provoke the expression of hers, made him attach a fantastic importance to every change in her look and tone. Now he thought she understood him, and feared; now he was sure she did not, and despaired. To-night the pressure of accumulated misgivings sent the scale drooping toward despair, and her indifference was the more chilling after the flush of joy into which she had plunged him by dismissing Denis Eady. He mounted School House Hill at her side and walked on in silence till they reached the lane leading to the saw-mill; then the need of some definite assurance grew too strong for him.

"You'd have found me right off if you hadn't gone back to have that last reel with Denis," he brought out awkwardly. He could not pronounce the name without a stiffening of the muscles of his throat.

"Why, Ethan, how could I tell you were there?"

"I suppose what folks say is true," he jerked out at her, instead of answering.

She stopped short, and he felt, in the darkness, that her face was lifted quickly to his. "Why, what do folks say?"

"It's natural enough you should be leaving us," he floundered on, following his thought.

"Is that what they say?" she mocked back at him; then, with a sudden drop of her sweet treble: "You mean that Zeena—ain't suited with me any more?" she faltered.

Their arms had slipped apart and they stood motionless, each seeking to distinguish the other's face.

"I know I ain't anything like as smart as I ought to be," she went on, while he vainly struggled for expression. "There's lots of things a hired girl could do that come awkward to me still—and I haven't got much strength in my arms. But if she'd only tell me I'd try. You know she hardly ever says anything, and sometimes I can see she ain't suited, and yet I don't know why." She turned on him with a sudden flash of indignation. "You'd ought to tell me, Ethan Frome —you'd ought to! Unless *you* want me to go too——"

Unless he wanted her to go too! The cry was balm to his raw wound. The iron heavens seemed to melt and rain down sweetness. Again he struggled for the all-expressive word, and again, his arm in hers, found only a deep "Come along."

They walked on in silence through the blackness of the hemlock-shaded lane, where Ethan's saw-mill gloomed through the night, and out again into the comparative clearness of the fields. On the farther side of the hemlock belt the open country rolled away before them grey and lonely under the stars. Sometimes their way led them under the shade of an overhanging bank or through the thin obscurity of a clump of leafless trees. Here and there a farm-house stood far back among the fields, mute and cold as a grave-stone. The night was so still that they heard the frozen snow crackle under their feet. The crash of a loaded branch falling far off in the woods reverberated like a musket-shot, and once a fox barked, and Mattie shrank closer to Ethan, and quickened her steps.

At length they sighted the group of larches at Ethan's gate, and as they drew near it the sense that the walk was over brought back his words.

"Then you don't want to leave us, Matt?"

He had to stoop his head to catch her stifled whisper: "Where'd I go, if I did?"

The answer sent a pang through him but the tone suffused him with joy. He forgot what else he had meant to say and pressed her against him so closely that he seemed to feel her warmth in his veins.

"You ain't crying are you, Matt?"

"No, of course I'm not," she quavered.

They turned in at the gate and passed under the shaded knoll where, enclosed in a low fence, the Frome grave-stones slanted at crazy angles through the snow. Ethan looked at them curiously. For years that quiet company had mocked his restlessness, his desire for change and freedom. "We never got away—how should you?" seemed to be written on every headstone; and whenever he went in or out of his gate he thought with a shiver: "I shall just go on living here till I join them." But now all desire for change had vanished, and the sight of the little enclosure gave him a warm sense of continuance and stability.

"I guess we'll never let you go, Matt," he whispered, as though even the dead, lovers once, must conspire with him to keep her; and brushing by the graves, he thought: "We'll always go on living here together, and some day she'll lie there beside me."

He let the vision possess him as they climbed the hill to the house. He was never so happy with her as when he abandoned himself to these dreams. Half-way up the slope Mattie stumbled against some unseen obstruction and clutched his sleeve to steady herself. The wave of warmth that went through him was like the prolongation of his vision. For the first time he stole his arm about her, and she did not resist. They walked on as if they were floating on a summer stream.

Zeena always went to bed as soon as she had had her supper, and the shutterless windows of the house were dark. A dead cucumber-vine dangled from the porch like the crape streamer tied to the door for a death, and the thought flashed through Ethan's brain: "If it was there for Zeena—" Then he had a distinct sight of his wife lying in their bedroom asleep, her mouth slightly open, her false teeth in a tumbler by the bed . . .

They walked around to the back of the house, between the rigid gooseberry bushes. It was Zeena's habit, when they came back late from the village, to leave the key of the kitchen door under the mat. Ethan stood before the door, his head heavy with dreams, his arm still about Mattie. "Matt—" he began, not knowing what he meant to say.

She slipped out of his hold without speaking, and he stooped down and felt for the key.

"It's not there!" he said, straightening himself with a start.

They strained their eyes at each other through the icy darkness. Such a thing had never happened before.

"Maybe she's forgotten it," Mattie said in a tremulous whisper; but both of them knew that it was not like Zeena to forget.

"It might have fallen off into the snow," Mattie continued, after a pause during which they had stood intently listening.

"It must have been pushed off, then," he rejoined in the same tone. Another wild thought tore through him. What if tramps had been there—what if . . .

Again he listened, fancying he heard a distant sound in the house; then he felt in his pocket for a match, and kneeling down, passed its light slowly over the rough edges of snow about the door-step.

He was still kneeling when his eyes, on a level with the lower panel of the door, caught a faint ray beneath it. Who could be stirring in that silent house? He heard a step on the stairs, and again for an instant the thought of tramps tore through him. Then the door opened and he saw his wife.

Against the dark background of the kitchen she stood up tall and angular, one hand drawing a quilted counterpane to her flat breast, while the other held a lamp. The light, on a level with her chin, drew out of the darkness her puckered throat and the projecting wrist of the hand that clutched the quilt, and deepened fantastically the hollows and prominences of her high-boned face under its ring of crimping-pins. To Ethan, still in the rosy haze of his hour with Mattie, the sight came with the intense precision of the last dream before waking. He felt as if he had never before known what his wife looked like.

She drew aside without speaking, and Mattie and Ethan passed into the kitchen, which had the deadly chill of a vault after the dry cold of the night.

"Guess you forgot about us, Zeena," Ethan joked, stamping the snow from his boots.

"No. I just felt so mean I couldn't sleep."

Mattie came forward, unwinding her wraps, the colour of the cherry scarf in her fresh lips and cheeks. "I'm so sorry, Zeena! Isn't there anything I can do?"

"No; there's nothing." Zeena turned away from her. "You might 'a' shook off that snow outside," she said to her husband.

She walked out of the kitchen ahead of them and pausing in the hall raised the lamp at arm's-length, as if to light them up the stairs.

Ethan paused also, affecting to fumble for the peg on which he hung his coat and cap. The doors of the two bedrooms faced each other across the narrow upper landing, and to-night it was peculiarly repugnant to him that Mattie should see him follow Zeena.

"I guess I won't come up yet awhile," he said, turning as if to go back to the kitchen.

Zeena stopped short and looked at him. "For the land's sake— what you going to do down here?"

"I've got the mill accounts to go over."

She continued to stare at him, the flame of the unshaded lamp bringing out with microscopic cruelty the fretful lines of her face.

"At this time o' night? You'll ketch your death. The fire's out long ago."

Without answering he moved away toward the kitchen. As he did so his glance crossed Mattie's and he fancied that a fugitive warning gleamed through her lashes. The next moment they sank to her flushed cheeks and she began to mount the stairs ahead of Zeena.

"That's so. It *is* powerful cold down here," Ethan assented; and with lowered head he went up in his wife's wake, and followed her across the threshold of their room.

3

THERE WAS some hauling to be done at the lower end of the wood-lot, and Ethan was out early the next day.

The winter morning was as clear as crystal. The sunrise burned red in a pure sky, the shadows on the rim of the wood-lot were darkly blue, and beyond the white and scintillating fields patches of far-off forest hung like smoke.

It was in the early morning stillness, when his muscles were swinging to their familiar task and his lungs expanding with long draughts of mountain air, that Ethan did his clearest thinking. He and Zeena had not exchanged a word after the door of their room had closed on them. She had measured out some drops from a medicine-bottle on a chair by the bed and, after swallowing them, and wrapping her head in a piece of yellow flannel, had lain down with her face turned away. Ethan undressed hurriedly and blew out the light so that he should not see her when he took his place at her side. As he lay there he could hear Mattie moving about in her room, and her candle, sending its small ray across the landing, drew a scarcely perceptible line of light under his door. He kept his eyes fixed on the light till it vanished. Then the room grew perfectly black, and not a sound was audible but Zeena's asthmatic breathing. Ethan felt confusedly that there were many things he ought to think about, but through his tingling veins and tired brain only one sensation throbbed: the warmth of Mattie's shoulder against his. Why had he not kissed her when he held her there? A few hours earlier he would not have asked himself the question. Even a few minutes earlier, when they had stood alone outside the house, he would not have dared to think of kissing her. But since he had seen her lips in the lamplight he felt that they were his.

Now, in the bright morning air, her face was still before him. It was part of the sun's red and of the pure glitter on the snow. How the girl had changed since she had come to Starkfield! He remembered what a colourless slip of a thing she had looked the day he had met her at the station. And all the first winter, how she had shivered with cold when the northerly gales shook the thin clapboards and the snow beat like hail against the loose-hung windows!

He had been afraid that she would hate the hard life, the cold and loneliness; but not a sign of discontent escaped her. Zeena took the view that Mattie was bound to make the best of Starkfield since she hadn't any other place to go to; but this did not strike Ethan as conclusive. Zeena, at any rate, did not apply the principle in her own case.

He felt all the more sorry for the girl because misfortune had, in a sense, indentured her to them. Mattie Silver was the daughter of a cousin of Zenobia Frome's, who had inflamed his clan with mingled sentiments of envy and admiration by descending from the hills to Connecticut, where he had married a Stamford girl and succeeded to her father's thriving "drug" business. Unhappily Orin Silver, a man of far-reaching aims, had died too soon to prove that the end justifies the means. His accounts revealed merely what the means had been; and these were such that it was fortunate for his wife and daughter that his books were examined only after his impressive funeral. His wife died of the disclosure, and Mattie, at twenty, was left alone to make her way on the fifty dollars obtained from the sale of her piano. For this purpose her equipment, though varied, was inadequate. She could trim a hat, make molasses candy, recite "Curfew shall not ring to-night," and play "The Lost Chord" and a pot-pourri from "Carmen." When she tried to extend the field of her activities in the direction of stenography and book-keeping her health broke down, and six months on her feet behind the counter of a department store did not tend to restore it. Her nearest relations had been induced to place their savings in her father's hands, and though, after his death, they ungrudgingly acquitted themselves of the Christian duty of returning good for evil by giving his daughter all the advice at their disposal, they could hardly be expected to supplement it by material aid. But when Zenobia's doctor recommended her looking about for some one to help her with the house-work the clan instantly saw the chance of exacting a compensation from Mattie. Zenobia, though doubtful of the girl's efficiency, was tempted by the freedom to find fault without much risk of losing her; and so Mattie came to Starkfield.

Zenobia's fault-finding was of the silent kind, but not the less penetrating for that. During the first months Ethan alternately burned with the desire to see Mattie defy her and trembled with fear of the result. Then the situation grew less strained. The pure air, and the long summer hours in the open, gave back life and elasticity to Mattie, and Zeena, with more leisure to devote to her complex ailments, grew less watchful of the girl's omissions; so that Ethan, struggling on under the burden of his barren farm and failing saw-mill, could at least imagine that peace reigned in his house.

There was really, even now, no tangible evidence to the contrary; but since the previous night a vague dread had hung on his sky-line. It was formed of Zeena's obstinate silence, of Mattie's sudden look of warning, of the memory of just such fleeting imperceptible signs as those which told him, on certain stainless mornings, that before night there would be rain.

His dread was so strong that, man-like, he sought to postpone certainty. The hauling was not over till mid-day, and as the lumber was to be delivered to Andrew Hale, the Starkfield builder, it was really easier for Ethan to send Jotham Powell, the hired man, back to the farm on foot, and drive the load down to the village himself. He had scrambled up on the logs, and was sitting astride of them, close over his shaggy grays, when, coming between him and their streaming necks, he had a vision of the warning look that Mattie had given him the night before.

"If there's going to be any trouble I want to be there," was his vague reflection, as he threw to Jotham the unexpected order to unhitch the team and lead them back to the barn.

It was a slow trudge home through the heavy fields, and when the two men entered the kitchen Mattie was lifting the coffee from the stove and Zeena was already at the table. Her husband stopped short at sight of her. Instead of her usual calico wrapper and knitted shawl she wore her best dress of brown merino, and above her thin strands of hair, which still preserved the tight undulations of the crimping-pins, rose a hard perpendicular bonnet, as to which Ethan's clearest notion was that he had to pay five dollars for it at the Bettsbridge Emporium. On the floor beside her stood his old valise and a band-box wrapped in newspapers.

"Why, where are you going, Zeena?" he exclaimed.

"I've got my shooting pains so bad that I'm going over to Betts-bridge to spend the night with Aunt Martha Pierce and see that new doctor," she answered in a matter-of-fact tone, as if she had said she was going into the store-room to take a look at the preserves, or up to the attic to go over the blankets.

In spite of her sedentary habits such abrupt decisions were not without precedent in Zeena's history. Twice or thrice before she had suddenly packed Ethan's valise and started off to Bettsbridge, or even Springfield, to seek the advice of some new doctor, and her husband had grown to dread these expeditions because of their cost. Zeena always came back laden with expensive remedies, and her last visit to Springfield had been commemorated by her paying twenty dollars for an electric battery of which she had never been able to learn the use. But for the moment his sense of relief was so great as to preclude all other feelings. He had now no doubt that Zeena had spoken the truth in saying, the night before, that she had sat up because she felt "too mean" to sleep: her abrupt resolve to seek medical advice showed that, as usual, she was wholly absorbed in her health.

As if expecting a protest, she continued plaintively; "If you're too busy with the hauling I presume you can let Jotham Powell drive me over with the sorrel in time to ketch the train at the Flats."

Her husband hardly heard what she was saying. During the winter months there was no stage between Starkfield and Bettsbridge, and the trains which stopped at Corbury Flats were slow and infrequent. A rapid calculation showed Ethan that Zeena could not be back at the farm before the following evening. . . .

"If I'd supposed you'd 'a' made any objection to Jotham Powell's driving me over—" she began again, as though his silence had implied refusal. On the brink of departure she was always seized with a flux of words. "All I know is," she continued, "I can't go on the way I am much longer. The pains are clear away down to my ankles now, or I'd 'a' walked in to Starkfield on my own feet, sooner'n put you out, and asked Michael Eady to let me ride over on his wagon to the Flats, when he sends to meet the train that brings his groceries. I'd 'a' had two hours to wait in the station, but I'd sooner 'a' done it, even with this cold, than to have you say——"

"Of course Jotham'll drive you over," Ethan roused himself to an-swer. He became suddenly conscious that he was looking at Mattie while Zeena talked to him, and with an effort he turned his eyes to his wife. She sat opposite the window, and the pale light reflected from the banks of snow made her face look more than usually drawn and bloodless, sharpened the three parallel creases between ear and cheek, and drew querulous lines from her thin nose to the corners of her mouth. Though she was but seven years her husband's senior, and he was only twenty-eight, she was already an old woman.

Ethan tried to say something befitting the occasion, but there was only one thought in his mind: the fact that, for the first time since Mattie had come to live with them, Zeena was to be away for a night. He wondered if the girl were thinking of it too. . . .

He knew that Zeena must be wondering why he did not offer to drive her to the Flats and let Jotham Powell take the lumber to Starkfield, and at first he could not think of a pretext for not doing so; then he said: "I'd take you over myself, only I've got to collect the cash for the lumber."

As soon as the words were spoken he regretted them, not only because they were untrue—there being no prospect of his receiving cash payment from Hale—but also because he knew from experience the imprudence of letting Zeena think he was in funds on the eve of one of her therapeutic excursions. At the moment, however, his one desire was to avoid the long drive with her behind the ancient sorrel who never went out of a walk.

Zeena made no reply: she did not seem to hear what he had said. She had already pushed her plate aside, and was measuring out a draught from a large bottle at her elbow.

"It ain't done me a speck of good, but I guess I might as well use it up," she remarked; adding, as she pushed the empty bottle toward Mattie: "If you can get the taste out it'll do for pickles."

4

As soon as his wife had driven off Ethan took his coat and cap from the peg. Mattie was washing up the dishes, humming one of the dance tunes of the night before. He said "So long, Matt," and she answered gaily "So long, Ethan"; and that was all.

It was warm and bright in the kitchen. The sun slanted through the south window on the girl's moving figure, on the cat dozing in a chair, and on the geraniums brought in from the door-way, where Ethan had planted them in the summer to "make a garden" for Mattie. He would have liked to linger on, watching her tidy up and then settle down to her sewing; but he wanted still more to get the hauling done and be back at the farm before night.

All the way down to the village he continued to think of his return to Mattie. The kitchen was a poor place, not "spruce" and shining as his mother had kept it in his boyhood; but it was surprising what a homelike look the mere fact of Zeena's absence gave it. And he pictured what it would be like that evening, when he and Mattie were there after supper. For the first time they would be alone together indoors, and they would sit there, one on each side of the stove, like a married couple, he in his stocking feet and smoking his pipe, she laughing and talking in that funny way she had, which was always as new to him as if he had never heard her before.

The sweetness of the picture, and the relief of knowing that his fears of "trouble" with Zeena were unfounded, sent up his spirits with a rush, and he, who was usually so silent, whistled and sang aloud as he drove through the snowy fields. There was in him a slumbering spark of sociability which the long Starkfield winters had not yet extinguished. By nature grave and inarticulate, he admired recklessness and gaiety in others and was warmed to the marrow by friendly human intercourse. At Worcester, though he had the name of keeping to himself and not being much of a hand at a good time, he had secretly gloried in being clapped on the back and hailed as "Old Ethe" or "Old Stiff"; and the cessation of such familiarities had increased the chill of his return to Starkfield.

There the silence had deepened about him year by year. Left alone, after his father's accident, to carry the burden of farm and mill, he had had no time for convivial loiterings in the village; and when his mother fell ill the loneliness of the house grew more oppressive than that of the fields. His mother had been a talker in her day, but after her "trouble" the sound of her voice was seldom heard, though she had not lost the power of speech. Sometimes, in the long winter evenings, when in desperation her son asked her why she didn't "say something," she would lift a finger and answer: "Because I'm listening"; and on stormy nights, when the loud wind was about the house, she would complain, if he spoke to her: "They're talking so out there that I can't hear you."

It was only when she drew toward her last illness, and his cousin Zenobia Pierce came over from the next valley to help him nurse her, that human speech was heard again in the house. After the mortal silence of his long imprisonment Zeena's volubility was music in his ears. He felt that he might have "gone like his mother" if the sound of a new voice had not come to steady him. Zeena seemed to understand his case at a glance. She laughed at him for not knowing the simplest sick-bed duties and told him to "go right along out" and leave her to see to things. The mere fact of obeying her orders, of feeling free to go about his business again and talk with other men, restored his shaken balance and magnified his sense of what he owed her. Her efficiency shamed and dazzled him. She seemed to possess by instinct all the household wisdom that his long apprenticeship had not instilled in him. When the end came it was she who had to tell him to hitch up and go for the undertaker, and she thought it "funny" that he had not settled beforehand who was to have his mother's clothes and the sewing-machine. After the funeral, when he saw her preparing to go away, he was seized with an unreasoning dread of being left alone on the farm; and before he knew what he was doing he had asked her to stay there with him. He had often thought since that it would not have happened if his mother had died in spring instead of winter . . .

When they married it was agreed that, as soon as he could

straighten out the difficulties resulting from Mrs. Frome's long illness, they would sell the farm and saw-mill and try their luck in a
large town. Ethan's love of nature did not take the form of a taste
for agriculture. He had always wanted to be an engineer, and to live
in towns, where there were lectures and big libraries and "fellows
doing things." A slight engineering job in Florida, put in his way during his period of study at Worcester, increased his faith in his ability
as well as his eagerness to see the world; and he felt sure that, with a
"smart" wife like Zeena, it would not be long before he had made
himself a place in it.

Zeena's native village was slightly larger and nearer to the railway
than Starkfield, and she had let her husband see from the first that
life on an isolated farm was not what she had expected when she
married. But purchasers were slow in coming, and while he waited
for them Ethan learned the impossibility of transplanting her. She
chose to look down on Starkfield, but she could not have lived in a
place which looked down on her. Even Bettsbridge or Shadd's Falls
would not have been sufficiently aware of her, and in the greater
cities which attracted Ethan she would have suffered a complete loss
of identity. And within a year of their marriage she developed the
"sickliness" which had since made her notable even in a community
rich in pathological instances. When she came to take care of his
mother she had seemed to Ethan like the very genius of health, but
he soon saw that her skill as a nurse had been acquired by the absorbed observation of her own symptoms.

Then she too fell silent. Perhaps it was the inevitable effect of life
on the farm, or perhaps, as she sometimes said, it was because Ethan
"never listened." The charge was not wholly unfounded. When she
spoke it was only to complain, and to complain of things not in his
power to remedy; and to check a tendency to impatient retort he had
first formed the habit of not answering her, and finally of thinking of
other things while she talked. Of late, however, since he had had
reasons for observing her more closely, her silence had begun to trouble him. He recalled his mother's growing taciturnity, and wondered
if Zeena were also turning "queer." Women did, he knew. Zeena,
who had at her fingers' ends the pathological chart of the whole region, had cited many cases of the kind while she was nursing his
mother; and he himself knew of certain lonely farm-houses in the
neighbourhood where stricken creatures pined, and of others where
sudden tragedy had come of their presence. At times, looking at

Zeena's shut face, he felt the chill of such forebodings. At other times her silence seemed deliberately assumed to conceal far-reaching intentions, mysterious conclusions drawn from suspicions and resentments impossible to guess. That supposition was even more disturbing than the other; and it was the one which had come to him the night before, when he had seen her standing in the kitchen door.

Now her departure for Bettsbridge had once more eased his mind, and all his thoughts were on the prospect of his evening with Mattie. Only one thing weighed on him, and that was his having told Zeena that he was to receive cash for the lumber. He foresaw so clearly the consequences of this imprudence that with considerable reluctance he decided to ask Andrew Hale for a small advance on his load.

When Ethan drove into Hale's yard the builder was just getting out of his sleigh.

"Hello, Ethe!" he said. "This comes handy."

Andrew Hale was a ruddy man with a big gray moustache and a stubbly double-chin unconstrained by a collar; but his scrupulously clean shirt was always fastened by a small diamond stud. This display of opulence was misleading, for though he did a fairly good business it was known that his easygoing habits and the demands of his large family frequently kept him what Starkfield called "behind." He was an old friend of Ethan's family, and his house one of the few to which Zeena occasionally went, drawn there by the fact that Mrs. Hale, in her youth, had done more "doctoring" than any other woman in Starkfield, and was still a recognised authority on symptoms and treatment.

Hale went up to the grays and patted their sweating flanks.

"Well, sir," he said, "you keep them two as if they was pets."

Ethan set about unloading the logs and when he had finished his job he pushed open the glazed door of the shed which the builder used as his office. Hale sat with his feet up on the stove, his back propped against a battered desk strewn with papers: the place, like the man, was warm, genial and untidy.

"Sit right down and thaw out," he greeted Ethan.

The latter did not know how to begin, but at length he managed to bring out his request for an advance of fifty dollars. The blood rushed to his thin skin under the sting of Hale's astonishment. It was the builder's custom to pay at the end of three months, and there was no precedent between the two men for a cash settlement.

Ethan felt that if he had pleaded an urgent need Hale might have made shift to pay him; but pride, and an instinctive prudence, kept him from resorting to this argument. After his father's death it had taken time to get his head above water, and he did not want Andrew Hale, or any one else in Starkfield, to think he was going under again. Besides, he hated lying; if he wanted the money he wanted it, and it was nobody's business to ask why. He therefore made his demand with the awkwardness of a proud man who will not admit to himself that he is stooping; and he was not much surprised at Hale's refusal.

The builder refused genially, as he did everything else: he treated the matter as something in the nature of a practical joke, and wanted to know if Ethan meditated buying a grand piano or adding a "cupolo" to his house; offering, in the latter case, to give his services free of cost.

Ethan's arts were soon exhausted, and after an embarrassed pause he wished Hale good day and opened the door of the office. As he passed out the builder suddenly called after him: "See here—you ain't in a tight place, are you?"

"Not a bit," Ethan's pride retorted before his reason had time to intervene.

"Well, that's good! Because I *am*, a shade. Fact is, I was going to ask you to give me a little extra time on that payment. Business is pretty slack, to begin with, and then I'm fixing up a little house for Ned and Ruth when they're married. I'm glad to do it for 'em, but it costs." His look appealed to Ethan for sympathy. "The young people like things nice. You know how it is yourself: it's not so long ago since you fixed up your own place for Zeena."

Ethan left the grays in Hale's stable and went about some other business in the village. As he walked away the builder's last phrase lingered in his ears, and he reflected grimly that his seven years with Zeena seemed to Starkfield "not so long."

The afternoon was drawing to an end, and here and there a lighted pane spangled the cold gray dusk and made the snow look whiter. The bitter weather had driven every one indoors and Ethan had the long rural street to himself. Suddenly he heard the brisk play of sleigh-bells and a cutter passed him, drawn by a free-going horse. Ethan recognised Michael Eady's roan colt, and young Denis Eady, in a handsome new fur cap, leaned forward and waved a greeting. "Hello, Ethe!" he shouted and spun on.

The cutter was going in the direction of the Frome farm, and Ethan's heart contracted as he listened to the dwindling bells. What more likely than that Denis Eady had heard of Zeena's departure for Bettsbridge, and was profiting by the opportunity to spend an hour with Mattie? Ethan was ashamed of the storm of jealousy in his breast. It seemed unworthy of the girl that his thoughts of her should be so violent.

He walked on to the church corner and entered the shade of the Varnum spruces, where he had stood with her the night before. As he passed into their gloom he saw an indistinct outline just ahead of him. At his approach it melted for an instant into two separate shapes and then conjoined again, and he heard a kiss, and a half-laughing "Oh!" provoked by the discovery of his presence. Again the outline hastily disunited and the Varnum gate slammed on one half while the other hurried on ahead of him. Ethan smiled at the discomfiture he had caused. What did it matter to Ned Hale and Ruth Varnum if they were caught kissing each other? Everybody in Starkfield knew they were engaged. It pleased Ethan to have surprised a pair of lovers on the spot where he and Mattie had stood with such a thirst for each other in their hearts; but he felt a pang at the thought that these two need not hide their happiness.

He fetched the grays from Hale's stable and started on his long climb back to the farm. The cold was less sharp than earlier in the day and a thick fleecy sky threatened snow for the morrow. Here and there a star pricked through, showing behind it a deep well of blue. In an hour or two the moon would push over the ridge behind the farm, burn a gold-edged rent in the clouds, and then be swallowed by them. A mournful peace hung on the fields, as though they felt the relaxing grasp of the cold and stretched themselves in their long winter sleep.

Ethan's ears were alert for the jingle of sleigh-bells, but not a sound broke the silence of the lonely road. As he drew near the farm he saw, through the thin screen of larches at the gate, a light twinkling in the house above him. "She's up in her room," he said to himself, "fixing herself up for supper"; and he remembered Zeena's sarcastic stare when Mattie, on the evening of her arrival, had come down to supper with smoothed hair and a ribbon at her neck.

He passed by the graves on the knoll and turned his head to glance at one of the older headstones, which had interested him deeply as a boy because it bore his name.

SACRED TO THE MEMORY OF

ETHAN FROME AND ENDURANCE HIS WIFE,

WHO DWELLED TOGETHER IN PEACE

FOR FIFTY YEARS.

He used to think that fifty years sounded like a long time to live together, but now it seemed to him that they might pass in a flash. Then, with a sudden dart of irony, he wondered if, when their turn came, the same epitaph would be written over him and Zeena.

He opened the barn-door and craned his head into the obscurity, half-fearing to discover Denis Eady's roan colt in the stall beside the sorrel. But the old horse was there alone, mumbling his crib with toothless jaws, and Ethan whistled cheerfully while he bedded down the grays and shook an extra measure of oats into their mangers. His was not a tuneful throat, but harsh melodies burst from it as he locked the barn and sprang up the hill to the house. He reached the kitchen-porch and turned the door-handle; but the door did not yield to his touch.

Startled at finding it locked he rattled the handle violently; then he reflected that Mattie was alone and that it was natural she should barricade herself at nightfall. He stood in the darkness expecting to hear her step. It did not come, and after vainly straining his ears he called out in a voice that shook with joy: "Hello, Matt!"

Silence answered; but in a minute or two he caught a sound on the stairs and saw a line of light about the door-frame, as he had seen it the night before. So strange was the precision with which the incidents of the previous evening were repeating themselves that he half expected, when he heard the key turn, to see his wife before him on the threshold; but the door opened, and Mattie faced him.

She stood just as Zeena had stood, a lifted lamp in her hand, against the black background of the kitchen. She held the light at the same level, and it drew out with the same distinctness her slim young throat and the brown wrist no bigger than a child's. Then, striking upward, it threw a lustrous fleck on her lips, edged her eyes with velvet shade, and laid a milky whiteness above the black curve of her brows.

She wore her usual dress of darkish stuff, and there was no bow at her neck; but through her hair she had run a streak of crimson ribbon. This tribute to the unusual transformed and glorified her. She seemed to Ethan taller, fuller, more womanly in shape and motion. She stood aside, smiling silently, while he entered, and then moved away from him with something soft and flowing in her gait. She set the lamp on the table, and he saw that it was carefully laid for supper, with fresh dough-nuts, stewed blueberries and his favourite pickles in a dish of gay red glass. A bright fire glowed in the stove and the cat lay stretched before it, watching the table with a drowsy eye.

Ethan was suffocated with the sense of well-being. He went out into the passage to hang up his coat and pull off his wet boots. When he came back Mattie had set the teapot on the table and the cat was rubbing itself persuasively against her ankles.

"Why, Puss! I nearly tripped over you," she cried, the laughter sparkling through her lashes.

Again Ethan felt a sudden twinge of jealousy. Could it be his coming that gave her such a kindled face?

"Well, Matt, any visitors?" he threw off, stooping down carelessly to examine the fastening of the stove.

She nodded and laughed, "Yes, one," and he felt a blackness settling on his brows.

"Who was that?" he questioned, raising himself up to slant a glance at her beneath his scowl.

Her eyes danced with malice. "Why, Jotham Powell. He came in after he got back, and asked for a drop of coffee before he went down home."

The blackness lifted and light flooded Ethan's brain. "That all? Well, I hope you made out to let him have it." And after a pause he felt it right to add: "I suppose he got Zeena over to the Flats all right?"

"Oh, yes; in plenty of time."

The name threw a chill between them, and they stood a moment looking sideways at each other before Mattie said with a shy laugh, "I guess it's about time for supper."

They drew their seats up to the table, and the cat, unbidden, jumped between them into Zeena's empty chair. "Oh, Puss!" said Mattie, and they laughed again.

Ethan, a moment earlier, had felt himself on the brink of eloquence; but the mention of Zeena had paralysed him. Mattie seemed to feel the contagion of his embarrassment, and sat with downcast lids, sipping her tea, while he feigned an insatiable appetite for dough-nuts and sweet pickles. At last, after casting about for an effective opening, he took a long gulp of tea, cleared his throat, and said: "Looks as if there'd be more snow."

She feigned great interest. "Is that so? Do you suppose it'll interfere with Zeena's getting back?" She flushed red as the question escaped her, and hastily set down the cup she was lifting.

Ethan reached over for another helping of pickles. "You never can tell, this time of year, it drifts so bad on the Flats." The name had benumbed him again, and once more he felt as if Zeena were in the room between them.

"Oh, Puss, you're too greedy!" Mattie cried.

The cat, unnoticed, had crept up on muffled paws from Zeena's seat to the table, and was stealthily elongating its body in the direction of the milk-jug, which stood between Ethan and Mattie. The two leaned forward at the same moment and their hands met on the handle of the jug. Mattie's hand was underneath, and Ethan kept his clasped on it a moment longer than was necessary. The cat, profiting by this unusual demonstration, tried to effect an unnoticed retreat, and in doing so backed into the pickle-dish, which fell to the floor with a crash.

Mattie, in an instant, had sprung from her chair and was down on her knees by the fragments.

"Oh, Ethan, Ethan—it's all to pieces! What will Zeena say?"

But this time his courage was up. "Well, she'll have to say it to the cat, any way!" he rejoined with a laugh, kneeling down at Mattie's side to scrape up the swimming pickles.

She lifted stricken eyes to him. "Yes, but, you see, she never meant it should be used, not even when there was company; and I had to get up on the step-ladder to reach it down from the top shelf of the china-closet, where she keeps it with all her best things, and of course she'll want to know why I did it——"

The case was so serious that it called forth all of Ethan's latent resolution.

"She needn't know anything about it if you keep quiet. I'll get another just like it to-morrow. Where did it come from? I'll go to Shadd's Falls for it if I have to!"

"Oh, you'll never get another even there! It was a wedding present —don't you remember? It came all the way from Philadelphia, from

Zeena's aunt that married the minister. That's why she wouldn't ever use it. Oh, Ethan, Ethan, what in the world shall I do?"

She began to cry, and he felt as if every one of her tears were pouring over him like burning lead. "Don't, Matt, don't—oh, *don't!*" he implored her.

She struggled to her feet, and he rose and followed her helplessly while she spread out the pieces of glass on the kitchen dresser. It seemed to him as if the shattered fragments of their evening lay there.

"Here, give them to me," he said in a voice of sudden authority.

She drew aside, instinctively obeying his tone. "Oh, Ethan, what are you going to do?"

Without replying he gathered the pieces of glass into his broad palm and walked out of the kitchen to the passage. There he lit a candle-end, opened the china-closet, and, reaching his long arm up to the highest shelf, laid the pieces together with such accuracy of touch that a close inspection convinced him of the impossibility of detecting from below that the dish was broken. If he glued it together the next morning months might elapse before his wife noticed what had happened, and meanwhile he might after all be able to match the dish at Shadd's Falls or Bettsbridge. Having satisfied himself that there was no risk of immediate discovery he went back to the kitchen with a lighter step, and found Mattie disconsolately removing the last scraps of pickle from the floor.

"It's all right, Matt. Come back and finish supper," he commanded her.

Completely reassured, she shone on him through tear-hung lashes, and his soul swelled with pride as he saw how his tone subdued her. She did not even ask what he had done. Except when he was steering a big log down the mountain to his mill he had never known such a thrilling sense of mastery.

5

THEY FINISHED supper, and while Mattie cleared the table Ethan went to look at the cows and then took a last turn about the house. The earth lay dark under a muffled sky and the air was so still that now and then he heard a lump of snow come thumping down from a tree far off on the edge of the wood-lot.

When he returned to the kitchen Mattie had pushed up his chair to the stove and seated herself near the lamp with a bit of sewing. The scene was just as he had dreamed of it that morning. He sat down, drew his pipe from his pocket and stretched his feet to the glow. His hard day's work in the keen air made him feel at once lazy and light of mood, and he had a confused sense of being in another world, where all was warmth and harmony and time could bring no change. The only drawback to his complete well-being was the fact that he could not see Mattie from where he sat; but he was too indolent to move and after a moment he said: "Come over here and sit by the stove."

Zeena's empty rocking-chair stood facing him. Mattie rose obediently, and seated herself in it. As her young brown head detached itself against the patch-work cushion that habitually framed his wife's gaunt countenance, Ethan had a momentary shock. It was almost as if the other face, the face of the superseded woman, had obliterated that of the intruder. After a moment Mattie seemed to be affected by the same sense of constraint. She changed her position, leaning forward to bend her head above her work, so that he saw only the foreshortened tip of her nose and the streak of red in her hair; then she slipped to her feet, saying "I can't see to sew," and went back to her chair by the lamp.

Ethan made a pretext of getting up to replenish the stove, and when he returned to his seat he pushed it sideways that he might get a view of her profile and of the lamplight falling on her hands. The cat, who had been a puzzled observer of these unusual movements, jumped up into Zeena's chair, rolled itself into a ball, and lay watching them with narrowed eyes.

Deep quiet sank on the room. The clock ticked above the dresser, a piece of charred wood fell now and then in the stove, and the faint sharp scent of the geraniums mingled with the odour of Ethan's smoke, which began to throw a blue haze about the lamp and to hang its greyish cobwebs in the shadowy corners of the room.

All constraint had vanished between the two, and they began to talk easily and simply. They spoke of every-day things, of the prospect of snow, of the next church sociable, of the loves and quarrels of Starkfield. The commonplace nature of what they said produced in Ethan an illusion of long-established intimacy which no outburst of emotion could have given, and he set his imagination adrift on the fiction that they had always spent their evenings thus and would always go on doing so . . .

"This is the night we were to have gone coasting, Matt," he said at length, with the rich sense, as he spoke, that they could go on any other night they chose, since they had all time before them.

She smiled back at him. "I guess you forgot!"

"No, I didn't forget; but it's as dark as Egypt outdoors. We might go to-morrow if there's a moon."

She laughed with pleasure, her head tilted back, the lamplight sparkling on her lips and teeth. "That would be lovely, Ethan!"

He kept his eyes fixed on her, marvelling at the way her face changed with each turn of their talk, like a wheat-field under a summer breeze. It was intoxicating to find such magic in his clumsy words, and he longed to try new ways of using it.

"Would you be scared to go down the Corbury road with me on a night like this?" he asked.

Her cheeks burned redder. "I ain't any more scared than you are!"

"Well, I'd be scared, then; I wouldn't do it. That's an ugly corner down by the big elm. If a fellow didn't keep his eyes open he'd go plumb into it." He luxuriated in the sense of protection and authority which his words conveyed. To prolong and intensify the feeling he added: "I guess we're well enough here."

She let her lids sink slowly, in the way he loved. "Yes, we're well enough here," she sighed.

Her tone was so sweet that he took the pipe from his mouth and drew his chair up to the table. Leaning forward, he touched the farther end of the strip of brown stuff that she was hemming. "Say, Matt," he began with a smile, "what do you think I saw under the Varnum spruces, coming along home just now? I saw a friend of yours getting kissed."

The words had been on his tongue all the evening, but now that he had spoken them they struck him as inexpressibly vulgar and out of place.

Mattie blushed to the roots of her hair and pulled her needle rapidly twice or thrice through her work, insensibly drawing the end of it away from him. "I suppose it was Ruth and Ned," she said in a low voice, as though he had suddenly touched on something grave.

Ethan had imagined that his allusion might open the way to the accepted pleasantries, and these perhaps in turn to a harmless caress, if only a mere touch on her hand. But now he felt as if her blush had set a flaming guard about her. He supposed it was his natural awkwardness that made him feel so. He knew that most young men made nothing at all of giving a pretty girl a kiss, and he remembered that the night before, when he had put his arm about Mattie, she had not resisted. But that had been out-of-doors, under the open irresponsible night. Now, in the warm lamplit room, with all its ancient implications of conformity and order, she seemed infinitely farther away from him and more unapproachable.

To ease his constraint he said: "I suppose they'll be setting a date before long."

"Yes. I shouldn't wonder if they got married some time along in the summer." She pronounced the word *married* as if her voice caressed it. It seemed a rustling covert leading to enchanted glades. A pang shot through Ethan, and he said, twisting away from her in his chair: "It'll be your turn next, I wouldn't wonder."

She laughed a little uncertainly. "Why do you keep on saying that?"

He echoed her laugh. "I guess I do it to get used to the idea."

He drew up to the table again and she sewed on in silence, with dropped lashes, while he sat in fascinated contemplation of the way in which her hands went up and down above the strip of stuff, just as he had seen a pair of birds make short perpendicular flights over a nest they were building. At length, without turning her head or lifting her lids, she said in a low tone: "It's not because you think Zeena's got anything against me, is it?"

His former dread started up full-armed at the suggestion. "Why, what do you mean?" he stammered.

She raised distressed eyes to his, her work dropping on the table between them. "I don't know. I thought last night she seemed to have."

"I'd like to know what," he growled.

"Nobody can tell with Zeena." It was the first time they had ever spoken so openly of her attitude toward Mattie, and the repetition of the name seemed to carry it to the farther corners of the room and send it back to them in long repercussions of sound. Mattie waited, as if to give the echo time to drop, and then went on: "She hasn't said anything to *you?*"

He shook his head. "No, not a word."

She tossed the hair back from her forehead with a laugh. "I guess I'm just nervous, then. I'm not going to think about it any more."

"Oh, no—don't let's think about it, Matt!"

The sudden heat of his tone made her colour mount again, not with a rush, but gradually, delicately, like the reflection of a thought stealing slowly across her heart. She sat silent, her hands clasped on her work, and it seemed to him that a warm current flowed toward him along the strip of stuff that still lay unrolled between them. Cautiously he slid his hand palm-downward along the table till his finger-tips touched the end of the stuff. A faint vibration of her lashes seemed to show that she was aware of his gesture, and that it had sent a counter-current back to her; and she let her hands lie motionless on the other end of the strip.

As they sat thus he heard a sound behind him and turned his head. The cat had jumped from Zeena's chair to dart at a mouse in the wainscot, and as a result of the sudden movement the empty chair had set up a spectral rocking.

"She'll be rocking in it herself this time to-morrow," Ethan thought. "I've been in a dream, and this is the only evening we'll ever have together." The return to reality was as painful as the return to consciousness after taking an anæsthetic. His body and brain ached with indescribable weariness, and he could think of nothing to say or to do that should arrest the mad flight of the moments.

His alteration of mood seemed to have communicated itself to Mattie. She looked up at him languidly, as though her lids were weighted with sleep and it cost her an effort to raise them. Her glance fell on his hand, which now completely covered the end of her work and grasped it as if it were a part of herself. He saw a scarcely perceptible tremor cross her face, and without knowing what he did he stooped his head and kissed the bit of stuff in his hold. As his lips rested on it he felt it glide slowly from beneath them, and saw that Mattie had risen and was silently rolling up her work. She fastened it with a pin, and then, finding her thimble and scissors, put them with the roll of stuff into the box covered with fancy paper which he had once brought to her from Bettsbridge.

He stood up also, looking vaguely about the room. The clock above the dresser struck eleven.

"Is the fire all right?" she asked in a low voice.

He opened the door of the stove and poked aimlessly at the embers. When he raised himself again he saw that she was dragging toward the stove the old soap-box lined with carpet in which the cat made its bed. Then she recrossed the floor and lifted two of the geranium pots in her arms, moving them away from the cold window. He followed her and brought the other geraniums, the hyacinth bulbs in a cracked custard bowl and the German ivy trained over an old croquet hoop.

When these nightly duties were performed there was nothing left to do but to bring in the tin candlestick from the passage, light the candle and blow out the lamp. Ethan put the candlestick in Mattie's hand and she went out of the kitchen ahead of him, the light that she carried before her making her dark hair look like a drift of mist on the moon.

"Good night, Matt," he said as she put her foot on the first step of the stairs.

She turned and looked at him a moment. "Good night, Ethan," she answered, and went up.

When the door of her room had closed on her he remembered that he had not even touched her hand.

6

THE NEXT MORNING at breakfast Jotham Powell was between them, and Ethan tried to hide his joy under an air of exaggerated indifference, lounging back in his chair to throw scraps to the cat, growling at the weather, and not so much as offering to help Mattie when she rose to clear away the dishes.

He did not know why he was so irrationally happy, for nothing was changed in his life or hers. He had not even touched the tip of her fingers or looked her full in the eyes. But their evening together had given him a vision of what life at her side might be, and he was glad now that he had done nothing to trouble the sweetness of the picture. He had a fancy that she knew what had restrained him . . .

There was a last load of lumber to be hauled to the village, and Jotham Powell—who did not work regularly for Ethan in winter—had "come round" to help with the job. But a wet snow, melting to sleet, had fallen in the night and turned the roads to glass. There was more wet in the air and it seemed likely to both men that the weather would "milden" toward afternoon and make the going safer. Ethan therefore proposed to his assistant that they should load the sledge at the wood-lot, as they had done on the previous morning, and put off the "teaming" to Starkfield till later in the day. This plan had the advantage of enabling him to send Jotham to the Flats after dinner to meet Zenobia, while he himself took the lumber down to the village.

He told Jotham to go out and harness up the greys, and for a moment he and Mattie had the kitchen to themselves. She had plunged the breakfast dishes into a tin dish-pan and was bending above it with her slim arms bared to the elbow, the steam from the hot water beading her forehead and tightening her rough hair into little brown rings like the tendrils on the traveller's joy.

Ethan stood looking at her, his heart in his throat. He wanted to say: "We shall never be alone again like this." Instead, he reached down his tobacco-pouch from a shelf of the dresser, put it into his pocket and said: "I guess I can make out to be home for dinner."

She answered "All right, Ethan," and he heard her singing over the dishes as he went.

As soon as the sledge was loaded he meant to send Jotham back to the farm and hurry on foot into the village to buy the glue for the pickle-dish. With ordinary luck he should have had time to carry out this plan; but everything went wrong from the start. On the way over to the wood-lot one of the greys slipped on a glare of ice and cut his knee; and when they got him up again Jotham had to go back to the barn for a strip of rag to bind the cut. Then, when the loading finally began, a sleety rain was coming down once more, and the tree trunks were so slippery that it took twice as long as usual to lift them and get them in place on the sledge. It was what Jotham called a sour morning for work, and the horses, shivering and stamping under their wet blankets, seemed to like it as little as the men. It was long past the dinner-hour when the job was done, and Ethan had to give up going to the village because he wanted to lead the injured horse home and wash the cut himself.

He thought that by starting out again with the lumber as soon as he had finished his dinner he might get back to the farm with the glue before Jotham and the old sorrel had had time to fetch Zenobia from the Flats; but he knew the chance was a slight one. It turned on the state of the roads and on the possible lateness of the Betts-bridge train. He remembered afterward, with a grim flash of self-derision, what importance he had attached to the weighing of these probabilities . . .

As soon as dinner was over he set out again for the wood-lot, not daring to linger till Jotham Powell left. The hired man was still dry-ing his wet feet at the stove, and Ethan could only give Mattie a quick look as he said beneath his breath: "I'll be back early."

He fancied that she nodded her comprehension; and with that scant solace he had to trudge off through the rain.

He had driven his load half-way to the village when Jotham Pow-ell overtook him, urging the reluctant sorrel toward the Flats. "I'll have to hurry up to do it," Ethan mused, as the sleigh dropped down ahead of him over the dip of the School House Hill. He worked like ten at the unloading, and when it was over hastened on to Michael

Eady's for the glue. Eady and his assistant were both "down street," and young Denis, who seldom deigned to take their place, was lounging by the stove with a knot of the golden youth of Starkfield. They hailed Ethan with ironic compliment and offers of conviviality; but no one knew where to find the glue. Ethan, consumed with the longing for a last moment alone with Mattie, hung about impatiently while Denis made an ineffectual search in the obscurer corners of the store.

"Looks as if we were all sold out. But if you'll wait around till the old man comes along maybe he can put his hand on it."

"I'm obliged to you, but I'll try if I can get it down at Mrs. Homan's," Ethan answered, burning to be gone.

Denis's commercial instinct compelled him to aver on oath that what Eady's store could not produce would never be found at the widow Homan's; but Ethan, heedless of this boast, had already climbed to the sledge and was driving on to the rival establishment. Here, after considerable search, and sympathetic questions as to what he wanted it for, and whether ordinary flour paste wouldn't do as well if she couldn't find it, the widow Homan finally hunted down her solitary bottle of glue to its hiding-place in a medley of cough-lozenges and corset-laces.

"I hope Zeena ain't broken anything she sets store by," she called after him as he turned the greys toward home.

The fitful bursts of sleet had changed into a steady rain and the horses had heavy work even without a load behind them. Once or twice, hearing sleigh-bells, Ethan turned his head, fancying that Zeena and Jotham might overtake him; but the old sorrel was not in sight, and he set his face against the rain and urged on his ponderous pair.

The barn was empty when the horses turned into it and, after giving them the most perfunctory ministrations they had ever received from him, he strode up to the house and pushed open the kitchen door.

Mattie was there alone, as he had pictured her. She was bending over a pan on the stove; but at the sound of his step she turned with a start and sprang to him.

"See here, Matt, I've got some stuff to mend the dish with! Let me get at it quick," he cried, waving the bottle in one hand while he put her lightly aside; but she did not seem to hear him.

"Oh, Ethan—Zeena's come," she said in a whisper, clutching his sleeve.

They stood and stared at each other, pale as culprits.

"But the sorrel's not in the barn!" Ethan stammered.

"Jotham Powell brought some goods over from the Flats for his wife, and he drove right on home with them," she explained.

He gazed blankly about the kitchen, which looked cold and squalid in the rainy winter twilight.

"How is she?" he asked, dropping his voice to Mattie's whisper.

She looked away from him uncertainly. "I don't know. She went right up to her room."

"She didn't say anything?"

"No."

Ethan let out his doubts in a low whistle and thrust the bottle back into his pocket. "Don't fret; I'll come down and mend it in the night," he said. He pulled on his wet coat again and went back to the barn to feed the greys.

While he was there Jotham Powell drove up with the sleigh, and when the horses had been attended to Ethan said to him: "You might as well come back up for a bite." He was not sorry to assure himself of Jotham's neutralising presence at the supper table, for Zeena was always "nervous" after a journey. But the hired man, though seldom loth to accept a meal not included in his wages, opened his stiff jaws to answer slowly: "I'm obliged to you, but I guess I'll go along back."

Ethan looked at him in surprise. "Better come up and dry off. Looks as if there'd be something hot for supper."

Jotham's facial muscles were unmoved by this appeal and, his vocabulary being limited, he merely repeated: "I guess I'll go along back."

To Ethan there was something vaguely ominous in this stolid rejection of free food and warmth, and he wondered what had happened on the drive to nerve Jotham to such stoicism. Perhaps Zeena had failed to see the new doctor or had not liked his counsels: Ethan knew that in such cases the first person she met was likely to be held responsible for her grievance.

When he re-entered the kitchen the lamp lit up the same scene of shining comfort as on the previous evening. The table had been as carefully laid, a clear fire glowed in the stove, the cat dozed in its warmth, and Mattie came forward carrying a plate of dough-nuts.

She and Ethan looked at each other in silence; then she said, as she had said the night before: "I guess it's about time for supper."

7

ETHAN WENT OUT into the passage to hang up his wet garments. He listened for Zeena's step and, not hearing it, called her name up the stairs. She did not answer, and after a moment's hesitation he went up and opened her door. The room was almost dark, but in the obscurity he saw her sitting by the window, bolt upright, and knew by the rigidity of the outline projected against the pane that she had not taken off her travelling dress.

"Well, Zeena," he ventured from the threshold.

She did not move, and he continued: "Supper's about ready. Ain't you coming?"

She replied: "I don't feel as if I could touch a morsel."

It was the consecrated formula, and he expected it to be followed, as usual, by her rising and going down to supper. But she remained seated, and he could think of nothing more felicitous than: "I presume you're tired after the long ride."

Turning her head at this, she answered solemnly: "I'm a great deal sicker than you think."

Her words fell on his ear with a strange shock of wonder. He had often heard her pronounce them before—what if at last they were true?

He advanced a step or two into the dim room. "I hope that's not so, Zeena," he said.

She continued to gaze at him through the twilight with a mien of wan authority, as of one consciously singled out for a great fate. "I've got complications," she said.

Ethan knew the word for one of exceptional import. Almost everybody in the neighbourhood had "troubles," frankly localized and specified; but only the chosen had "complications." To have them was in itself a distinction, though it was also, in most cases, a death-warrant. People struggled on for years with "troubles," but they almost always succumbed to "complications."

Ethan's heart was jerking to and fro between two extremities of feeling, but for the moment compassion prevailed. His wife looked so hard and lonely, sitting there in the darkness with such thoughts.

"Is that what the new doctor told you?" he asked, instinctively lowering his voice.

"Yes. He says any regular doctor would want me to have an operation."

Ethan was aware that, in regard to the important question of surgical intervention, the female opinion of the neighbourhood was divided, some glorying in the prestige conferred by operations while others shunned them as indelicate. Ethan, from motives of economy, had always been glad that Zeena was of the latter faction.

In the agitation caused by the gravity of her announcement he sought a consolatory short cut. "What do you know about this doctor anyway? Nobody ever told you that before."

He saw his blunder before she could take it up: she wanted sympathy, not consolation.

"I didn't need to have anybody tell me I was losing ground every day. Everybody but you could see it. And everybody in Bettsbridge knows about Dr. Buck. He has his office in Worcester, and comes over once a fortnight to Shadd's Falls and Bettsbridge for consultations. Eliza Spears was wasting away with kidney trouble before she went to him, and now she's up and around, and singing in the choir."

"Well, I'm glad of that. You must do just what he tells you," Ethan answered sympathetically.

She was still looking at him. "I mean to," she said. He was struck by a new note in her voice. It was neither whining nor reproachful, but drily resolute.

"What does he want you should do?" he asked, with a mounting vision of fresh expenses.

"He wants I should have a hired girl. He says I oughtn't to have to do a single thing around the house."

"A hired girl?" Ethan stood transfixed.

"Yes. And Aunt Martha found me one right off. Everybody said I was lucky to get a girl to come away out here, and I agreed to give her a dollar extry to make sure. She'll be over to-morrow afternoon."

Wrath and dismay contended in Ethan. He had foreseen an immediate demand for money, but not a permanent drain on his scant resources. He no longer believed what Zeena had told him of the supposed seriousness of her state: he saw in her expedition to Bettsbridge only a plot hatched between herself and her Pierce relations to foist on him the cost of a servant; and for the moment wrath predominated.

"If you meant to engage a girl you ought to have told me before you started," he said.

"How could I tell you before I started? How did I know what Dr. Buck would say?"

"Oh, Dr. Buck—" Ethan's incredulity escaped in a short laugh. "Did Dr. Buck tell you how I was to pay her wages?"

Her voice rose furiously with his. "No, he didn't. For I'd 'a' been ashamed to tell *him* that you grudged me the money to get back my health, when I lost it nursing your own mother!"

"*You* lost your health nursing mother?"

"Yes; and my folks all told me at the time you couldn't do no less than marry me after——"

"Zeena!"

Through the obscurity which hid their faces their thoughts seemed to dart at each other like serpents shooting venom. Ethan was seized with horror of the scene and shame at his own share in it. It was as senseless and savage as a physical fight between two enemies in the darkness.

He turned to the shelf above the chimney, groped for matches and lit the one candle in the room. At first its weak flame made no impression on the shadows; then Zeena's face stood grimly out against the uncurtained pane, which had turned from grey to black.

It was the first scene of open anger between the couple in their sad seven years together, and Ethan felt as if he had lost an irretrievable advantage in descending to the level of recrimination. But the practical problem was there and had to be dealt with.

"You know I haven't got the money to pay for a girl, Zeena. You'll have to send her back: I can't do it."

"The doctor says it'll be my death if I go on slaving the way I've had to. He doesn't understand how I've stood it as long as I have."

"Slaving!—" He checked himself again, "You sha'n't lift a hand, if he says so. I'll do everything round the house myself——"

She broke in: "You're neglecting the farm enough already," and this being true, he found no answer, and left her time to add ironically: "Better send me over to the almshouse and done with it . . . I guess there's been Fromes there afore now."

The taunt burned into him, but he let it pass. "I haven't got the money. That settles it."

There was a moment's pause in the struggle, as though the combatants were testing their weapons. Then Zeena said in a level voice: "I thought you were to get fifty dollars from Andrew Hale for that lumber."

"Andrew Hale never pays under three months." He had hardly spoken when he remembered the excuse he had made for not accompanying his wife to the station the day before; and the blood rose to his frowning brows.

"Why, you told me yesterday you'd fixed it up with him to pay cash down. You said that was why you couldn't drive me over to the Flats."

Ethan had no suppleness in deceiving. He had never before been convicted of a lie, and all the resources of evasion failed him. "I guess that was a misunderstanding," he stammered.

"You ain't got the money?"

"No."

"And you ain't going to get it?"

"No."

"Well, I couldn't know that when I engaged the girl, could I?"

"No." He paused to control his voice. "But you know it now. I'm sorry, but it can't be helped. You're a poor man's wife, Zeena; but I'll do the best I can for you."

For a while she sat motionless, as if reflecting, her arms stretched along the arms of her chair, her eyes fixed on vacancy. "Oh, I guess we'll make out," she said mildly.

The change in her tone reassured him. "Of course we will! There's a whole lot more I can do for you, and Mattie——"

Zeena, while he spoke, seemed to be following out some elaborate mental calculation. She emerged from it to say: "There'll be Mattie's board less, anyhow——"

Ethan, supposing the discussion to be over, had turned to go down to supper. He stopped short, not grasping what he heard. "Mattie's board less—?" he began.

Zeena laughed. It was an odd unfamiliar sound—he did not remember ever having heard her laugh before. "You didn't suppose I was going to keep two girls, did you? No wonder you were scared at the expense!"

He still had but a confused sense of what she was saying. From the beginning of the discussion he had instinctively avoided the mention of Mattie's name, fearing he hardly knew what: criticism, complaints, or vague allusions to the imminent probability of her marrying. But the thought of a definite rupture had never come to him, and even now could not lodge itself in his mind.

"I don't know what you mean," he said. "Mattie Silver's not a hired girl. She's your relation."

"She's a pauper that's hung onto us all after her father'd done his best to ruin us. I've kep' her here a whole year: it's somebody else's turn now."

As the shrill words shot out Ethan heard a tap on the door, which he had drawn shut when he turned back from the threshold.

"Ethan—Zeena!" Mattie's voice sounded gaily from the landing, "do you know what time it is? Supper's been ready half an hour."

Inside the room there was a moment's silence; then Zeena called out from her seat: "I'm not coming down to supper."

"Oh, I'm sorry! Aren't you well? Sha'n't I bring you up a bite of something?"

Ethan roused himself with an effort and opened the door. "Go along down, Matt. Zeena's just a little tired. I'm coming."

He heard her "All right!" and her quick step on the stairs; then he shut the door and turned back into the room. His wife's attitude was unchanged, her face inexorable, and he was seized with the despairing sense of his helplessness.

"You ain't going to do it, Zeena?"

"Do what?" she emitted between flattened lips.

"Send Mattie away—like this?"

"I never bargained to take her for life!"

He continued with rising vehemence: "You can't put her out of the house like a thief—a poor girl without friends or money. She's done her best for you and she's got no place to go to. You may forget she's your kin but everybody else'll remember it. If you do a thing like that what do you suppose folks'll say of you?"

Zeena waited a moment, as if giving him time to feel the full force of the contrast between his own excitement and her composure.

Then she replied in the same smooth voice: "I know well enough what they say of my having kep' her here as long as I have."

Ethan's hand dropped from the door-knob, which he had held clenched since he had drawn the door shut on Mattie. His wife's retort was like a knife-cut across the sinews and he felt suddenly weak and powerless. He had meant to humble himself, to argue that Mattie's keep didn't cost much, after all, that he could make out to buy a stove and fix up a place in the attic for the hired girl—but Zeena's words revealed the peril of such pleadings.

"You mean to tell her she's got to go—at once?" he faltered out, in terror of letting his wife complete her sentence.

As if trying to make him see reason she replied impartially: "The girl will be over from Bettsbridge to-morrow, and I presume she's got to have somewheres to sleep."

Ethan looked at her with loathing. She was no longer the listless creature who had lived at his side in a state of sullen self-absorption, but a mysterious alien presence, an evil energy secreted from the long years of silent brooding. It was the sense of his helplessness that sharpened his antipathy. There had never been anything in her that one could appeal to; but as long as he could ignore and command he had remained indifferent. Now she had mastered him and he abhorred her. Mattie was her relation, not his: there were no means by which he could compel her to keep the girl under her roof. All the long misery of his baffled past, of his youth of failure, hardship and vain effort, rose up in his soul in bitterness and seemed to take shape before him in the woman who at every turn had barred his way. She had taken everything else from him; and now she meant to take the one thing that made up for all the others. For a moment such a flame of hate rose in him that it ran down his arm and clenched his fist against her. He took a wild step forward and then stopped.

"You're—you're not coming down?" he said in a bewildered voice.

"No. I guess I'll lay down on the bed a little while," she answered mildly; and he turned and walked out of the room.

In the kitchen Mattie was sitting by the stove, the cat curled up on her knees. She sprang to her feet as Ethan entered and carried the covered dish of meat-pie to the table.

"I hope Zeena isn't sick?" she asked.

"No."

She shone at him across the table. "Well, sit right down then. You must be starving." She uncovered the pie and pushed it over to him. So they were to have one more evening together, her happy eyes seemed to say!

He helped himself mechanically and began to eat; then disgust took him by the throat and he laid down his fork.

Mattie's tender gaze was on him and she marked the gesture.

"Why, Ethan, what's the matter? Don't it taste right?"

"Yes—it's first-rate. Only I—" He pushed his plate away, rose from his chair, and walked around the table to her side. She started up with frightened eyes.

"Ethan, there's something wrong! I *knew* there was!"

She seemed to melt against him in her terror, and he caught her in his arms, held her fast there, felt her lashes beat his cheek like netted butterflies.

"What is it—what is it?" she stammered; but he had found her lips at last and was drinking unconsciousness of everything but the joy they gave him.

She lingered a moment, caught in the same strong current; then she slipped from him and drew back a step or two, pale and troubled. Her look smote him with compunction, and he cried out, as if he saw her drowning in a dream: "You can't go, Matt! I'll never let you!"

"Go—go?" she stammered. "Must I go?"

The words went on sounding between them as though a torch of warning flew from hand to hand through a black landscape.

Ethan was overcome with shame at his lack of self-control in flinging the news at her so brutally. His head reeled and he had to support himself against the table. All the while he felt as if he were still kissing her, and yet dying of thirst for her lips.

"Ethan, what has happened? Is Zeena mad with me?"

Her cry steadied him, though it deepened his wrath and pity. "No, no," he assured her, "it's not that. But this new doctor has scared her about herself. You know she believes all they say the first time she sees them. And this one's told her she won't get well unless she lays up and don't do a thing about the house—not for months——"

He paused, his eyes wandering from her miserably. She stood silent a moment, drooping before him like a broken branch. She was so small and weak-looking that it wrung his heart; but suddenly she lifted her head and looked straight at him. "And she wants somebody handier in my place? Is that it?"

"That's what she says to-night."

"If she says it to-night she'll say it to-morrow."

Both bowed to the inexorable truth: they knew that Zeena never changed her mind, and that in her case a resolve once taken was equivalent to an act performed.

There was a long silence between them; then Mattie said in a low voice: "Don't be too sorry, Ethan."

"Oh, God—oh, God," he groaned. The glow of passion he had felt for her had melted to an aching tenderness. He saw her quick lids beating back the tears, and longed to take her in his arms and soothe her.

"You're letting your supper get cold," she admonished him with a pale gleam of gaiety.

"Oh, Matt—Matt—where'll you go to?"

Her lids sank and a tremor crossed her face. He saw that for the first time the thought of the future came to her distinctly. "I might get something to do over at Stamford," she faltered, as if knowing that he knew she had no hope.

He dropped back into his seat and hid his face in his hands. Despair seized him at the thought of her setting out alone to renew the weary quest for work. In the only place where she was known she was surrounded by indifference or animosity; and what chance had she, inexperienced and untrained, among the million bread-seekers of the cities? There came back to him miserable tales he had heard at Worcester, and the faces of girls whose lives had begun as hopefully as Mattie's. . . . It was not possible to think of such things without a revolt of his whole being. He sprang up suddenly.

"You can't go, Matt! I won't let you! She's always had her way, but I mean to have mine now——"

Mattie lifted her hand with a quick gesture, and he heard his wife's step behind him.

Zeena came into the room with her dragging down-at-the-heel step, and quietly took her accustomed seat between them.

"I felt a little mite better, and Dr. Buck says I ought to eat all I can to keep my strength up, even if I ain't got any appetite," she said in her flat whine, reaching across Mattie for the teapot. Her "good" dress had been replaced by the black calico and brown knitted shawl which formed her daily wear, and with them she had put on her usual face and manner. She poured out her tea, added a great deal of milk to it, helped herself largely to pie and pickles, and made the familiar gesture of adjusting her false teeth before she began to eat.

The cat rubbed itself ingratiatingly against her, and she said "Good Pussy," stooped to stroke it and gave it a scrap of meat from her plate.

Ethan sat speechless, not pretending to eat, but Mattie nibbled valiantly at her food and asked Zeena one or two questions about her visit to Bettsbridge. Zeena answered in her every-day tone and, warming to the theme, regaled them with several vivid descriptions of intestinal disturbances among her friends and relatives. She looked straight at Mattie as she spoke, a faint smile deepening the vertical lines between her nose and chin.

When supper was over she rose from her seat and pressed her hand to the flat surface over the region of her heart. "That pie of yours always sets a mite heavy, Matt," she said, not ill-naturedly. She seldom abbreviated the girl's name, and when she did so it was always a sign of affability.

"I've a good mind to go and hunt up those stomach powders I got last year over in Springfield," she continued. "I ain't tried them for quite a while, and maybe they'll help the heartburn."

Mattie lifted her eyes. "Can't I get them for you, Zeena?" she ventured.

"No. They're in a place you don't know about," Zeena answered darkly, with one of her secret looks.

She went out of the kitchen and Mattie, rising, began to clear the dishes from the table. As she passed Ethan's chair their eyes met and clung together desolately. The warm still kitchen looked as peaceful as the night before. The cat had sprung to Zeena's rocking-chair, and the heat of the fire was beginning to draw out the faint sharp scent of the geraniums. Ethan dragged himself wearily to his feet.

"I'll go out and take a look around," he said, going toward the passage to get his lantern.

As he reached the door he met Zeena coming back into the room, her lips twitching with anger, a flush of excitement on her sallow face. The shawl had slipped from her shoulders and was dragging at her down-trodden heels, and in her hands she carried the fragments of the red glass pickle-dish.

"I'd like to know who done this," she said, looking sternly from Ethan to Mattie.

There was no answer, and she continued in a trembling voice: "I went to get those powders I'd put away in father's old spectacle-case, top of the china-closet, where I keep the things I set store by, so's folks sha'n't meddle with them—" Her voice broke, and two small tears hung on her lashless lids and ran slowly down her cheeks. "It takes the step-ladder to get at the top shelf, and I put Aunt Philura Maple's pickle-dish up there o' purpose when we was married, and it's never been down since, 'cept for the spring cleaning, and then I always lifted it with my own hands, so's 't shouldn't get broke." She laid the fragments reverently on the table. "I want to know who done this," she quavered.

At the challenge Ethan turned back into the room and faced her. "I can tell you, then. The cat done it."

"The *cat?*"

"That's what I said."

She looked at him hard, and then turned her eyes to Mattie, who was carrying the dish-pan to the table.

"I'd like to know how the cat got into my china-closet," she said.

"Chasin' mice, I guess," Ethan rejoined. "There was a mouse round the kitchen all last evening."

Zeena continued to look from one to the other; then she emitted her small strange laugh. "I knew the cat was a smart cat," she said in a high voice, "but I didn't know he was smart enough to pick up the pieces of my pickle-dish and lay 'em edge to edge on the very shelf he knocked 'em off of."

Mattie suddenly drew her arms out of the steaming water. "It wasn't Ethan's fault, Zeena! The cat *did* break the dish; but I got it down from the china-closet, and I'm the one to blame for its getting broken."

Zeena stood beside the ruin of her treasure, stiffening into a stony image of resentment, "*You* got down my pickle-dish—what for?"

A bright flush flew to Mattie's cheeks. "I wanted to make the supper-table pretty," she said.

"You wanted to make the supper-table pretty; and you waited till my back was turned, and took the thing I set most store by of anything I've got, and wouldn't never use it, not even when the minister come to dinner, or Aunt Martha Pierce come over from Betts-bridge—" Zeena paused with a gasp, as if terrified by her own evocation of the sacrilege. "You're a bad girl, Mattie Silver, and I always known it. It's the way your father begun, and I was warned of it when I took you, and I tried to keep my things where you couldn't get at 'em—and now you've took from me the one I cared for most of all—"

She broke off in a short spasm of sobs that passed and left her more than ever like a shape of stone.

"If I'd 'a' listened to folks, you'd 'a' gone before now, and this wouldn't 'a' happened," she said; and gathering up the bits of broken glass she went out of the room as if she carried a dead body . . .

8

WHEN ETHAN was called back to the farm by his father's illness his mother gave him, for his own use, a small room behind the untenanted "best parlour." Here he had nailed up shelves for his books, built himself a box-sofa out of boards and a mattress, laid out his papers on a kitchen-table, hung on the rough plaster wall an engraving of Abraham Lincoln and a calendar with "Thoughts from the Poets," and tried, with these meagre properties, to produce some likeness to the study of a "minister" who had been kind to him and lent him books when he was at Worcester. He still took refuge there in summer, but when Mattie came to live at the farm he had had to give her his stove, and consequently the room was uninhabitable for several months of the year.

To this retreat he descended as soon as the house was quiet, and Zeena's steady breathing from the bed had assured him that there was to be no sequel to the scene in the kitchen. After Zeena's departure he and Mattie had stood speechless, neither seeking to approach the other. Then the girl had returned to her task of clearing up the kitchen for the night and he had taken his lantern and gone on his usual round outside the house. The kitchen was empty when he came back to it; but his tobacco-pouch and pipe had been laid on the table, and under them was a scrap of paper torn from the back of a seedsman's catalogue, on which three words were written: "Don't trouble, Ethan."

Going into his cold dark "study" he placed the lantern on the table and, stooping to its light, read the message again and again. It was the first time that Mattie had ever written to him, and the possession of the paper gave him a strange new sense of her nearness; yet it deepened his anguish by reminding him that henceforth they

would have no other way of communicating with each other. For the
life of her smile, the warmth of her voice, only cold paper and dead
words!

Confused motions of rebellion stormed in him. He was too young,
too strong, too full of the sap of living, to submit so easily to the de-
struction of his hopes. Must he wear out all his years at the side of a
bitter querulous woman? Other possibilities had been in him, possibilities sacrificed, one by one, to Zeena's narrow-mindedness and ignorance. And what good had come of it? She was a hundred times
bitterer and more discontented than when he had married her: the
one pleasure left her was to inflict pain on him. All the healthy in-
stincts of self-defence rose up in him against such waste . . .

He bundled himself into his old coon-skin coat and lay down on
the box-sofa to think. Under his cheek he felt a hard object with
strange protuberances. It was a cushion which Zeena had made for
him when they were engaged—the only piece of needlework he had
ever seen her do. He flung it across the floor and propped his head
against the wall . . .

He knew a case of a man over the mountain—a young fellow of
about his own age—who had escaped from just such a life of misery
by going West with the girl he cared for. His wife had divorced him,
and he had married the girl and prospered. Ethan had seen the couple the summer before at Shadd's Falls, where they had come to visit
relatives. They had a little girl with fair curls, who wore a gold locket
and was dressed like a princess. The deserted wife had not done
badly either. Her husband had given her the farm and she had managed to sell it, and with that and the alimony she had started a
lunch-room at Bettsbridge and bloomed into activity and importance. Ethan was fired by the thought. Why should he not leave
with Mattie the next day, instead of letting her go alone? He would
hide his valise under the seat of the sleigh, and Zeena would suspect
nothing till she went upstairs for her afternoon nap and found a letter on the bed . . .

His impulses were still near the surface, and he sprang up, re-lit
the lantern, and sat down at the table. He rummaged in the drawer
for a sheet of paper, found one, and began to write.

"Zeena, I've done all I could for you, and I don't see as it's been
any use. I don't blame you, nor I don't blame myself. Maybe both of
us will do better separate. I'm going to try my luck West, and you
can sell the farm and mill, and keep the money——"

His pen paused on the word, which brought home to him the relentless conditions of his lot. If he gave the farm and mill to Zeena what would be left him to start his own life with? Once in the West he was sure of picking up work—he would not have feared to try his chance alone. But with Mattie depending on him the case was different. And what of Zeena's fate? Farm and mill were mortgaged to the limit of their value, and even if she found a purchaser—in itself an unlikely chance—it was doubtful if she could clear a thousand dollars on the sale. Meanwhile, how could she keep the farm going? It was only by incessant labour and personal supervision that Ethan drew a meagre living from his land, and his wife, even if she were in better health than she imagined, could never carry such a burden alone.

Well, she could go back to her people, then, and see what they would do for her. It was the fate she was forcing on Mattie—why not let her try it herself? By the time she had discovered his whereabouts, and brought suit for divorce, he would probably—wherever he was—be earning enough to pay her a sufficient alimony. And the alternative was to let Mattie go forth alone, with far less hope of ultimate provision . . .

He had scattered the contents of the table-drawer in his search for a sheet of paper, and as he took up his pen his eye fell on an old copy of the *Bettsbridge Eagle.* The advertising sheet was folded uppermost, and he read the seductive words: "Trips to the West: Reduced Rates."

He drew the lantern nearer and eagerly scanned the fares; then the paper fell from his hand and he pushed aside his unfinished letter. A moment ago he had wondered what he and Mattie were to live on when they reached the West; now he saw that he had not even the money to take her there. Borrowing was out of the question: six months before he had given his only security to raise funds for necessary repairs to the mill, and he knew that without security no one at Starkfield would lend him ten dollars. The inexorable facts closed in on him like prison-warders handcuffing a convict. There was no way out—none. He was a prisoner for life, and now his one ray of light was to be extinguished.

He crept back heavily to the sofa, stretching himself out with limbs so leaden that he felt as if they would never move again. Tears rose in his throat and slowly burned their way to his lids.

As he lay there, the window-pane that faced him, growing gradually lighter, inlaid upon the darkness a square of moon-suffused sky. A crooked tree-branch crossed it, a branch of the apple-tree under which, on summer evenings, he had sometimes found Mattie sitting when he came up from the mill. Slowly the rim of the rainy vapours caught fire and burnt away, and a pure moon swung into the blue. Ethan, rising on his elbow, watched the landscape whiten and shape itself under the sculpture of the moon. This was the night on which he was to have taken Mattie coasting, and there hung the lamp to light them! He looked out at the slopes bathed in lustre, the silver-edged darkness of the woods, the spectral purple of the hills against the sky, and it seemed as though all the beauty of the night had been poured out to mock his wretchedness . . .

He fell asleep, and when he woke the chill of the winter dawn was in the room. He felt cold and stiff and hungry, and ashamed of being hungry. He rubbed his eyes and went to the window. A red sun stood over the grey rim of the fields, behind trees that looked black and brittle. He said to himself: "This is Matt's last day," and tried to think what the place would be without her.

As he stood there he heard a step behind him and she entered.

"Oh, Ethan—were you here all night?"

She looked so small and pinched, in her poor dress, with the red scarf wound about her, and the cold light turning her paleness sallow, that Ethan stood before her without speaking.

"You must be frozen," she went on, fixing lustreless eyes on him.

He drew a step nearer. "How did you know I was here?"

"Because I heard you go down stairs again after I went to bed, and I listened all night, and you didn't come up."

All his tenderness rushed to his lips. He looked at her and said: "I'll come right along and make up the kitchen fire."

They went back to the kitchen, and he fetched the coal and kindlings and cleared out the stove for her, while she brought in the milk and the cold remains of the meat-pie. When warmth began to radiate from the stove, and the first ray of sunlight lay on the kitchen floor, Ethan's dark thoughts melted in the mellower air. The sight of Mattie going about her work as he had seen her on so many mornings made it seem impossible that she should ever cease to be a part of the scene. He said to himself that he had doubtless exaggerated the significance of Zeena's threats, and that she too, with the return of daylight, would come to a saner mood.

He went up to Mattie as she bent above the stove, and laid his hand on her arm. "I don't want you should trouble either," he said, looking down into her eyes with a smile.

She flushed up warmly and whispered back: "No, Ethan, I ain't going to trouble."

"I guess things'll straighten out," he added.

There was no answer but a quick throb of her lids, and he went on: "She ain't said anything this morning?"

"No. I haven't seen her yet."

"Don't you take any notice when you do."

With this injunction he left her and went out to the cow-barn. He saw Jotham Powell walking up the hill through the morning mist, and the familiar sight added to his growing conviction of security.

As the two men were clearing out the stalls Jotham rested on his pitch-fork to say: "Dan'l Byrne's goin' over to the Flats to-day noon, an' he c'd take Mattie's trunk along, and make it easier ridin' when I take her over in the sleigh."

Ethan looked at him blankly, and he continued: "Mis' Frome said the new girl'd be at the Flats at five, and I was to take Mattie then, so's 't she could ketch the six o'clock train for Stamford."

Ethan felt the blood drumming in his temples. He had to wait a moment before he could find voice to say: "Oh, it ain't so sure about Mattie's going——"

"That so?" said Jotham indifferently; and they went on with their work.

When they returned to the kitchen the two women were already at breakfast. Zeena had an air of unusual alertness and activity. She drank two cups of coffee and fed the cat with the scraps left in the pie-dish; then she rose from her seat and, walking over to the window, snipped two or three yellow leaves from the geraniums. "Aunt Martha's ain't got a faded leaf on 'em; but they pine away when they ain't cared for," she said reflectively. Then she turned to Jotham and asked: "What time'd you say Dan'l Byrne'd be along?"

The hired man threw a hesitating glance at Ethan. "Round about noon," he said.

Zeena turned to Mattie. "That trunk of yours is too heavy for the sleigh, and Dan'l Byrne'll be round to take it over to the Flats," she said.

"I'm much obliged to you, Zeena," said Mattie.

"I'd like to go over things with you first," Zeena continued in an unperturbed voice. "I know there's a huckabuck towel missing; and I can't take out what you done with that match-safe 't used to stand behind the stuffed owl in the parlour."

She went out, followed by Mattie, and when the men were alone Jotham said to his employer: "I guess I better let Dan'l come round, then."

Ethan finished his usual morning tasks about the house and barn; then he said to Jotham: "I'm going down to Starkfield. Tell them not to wait dinner."

The passion of rebellion had broken out in him again. That which had seemed incredible in the sober light of day had really come to pass, and he was to assist as a helpless spectator at Mattie's banishment. His manhood was humbled by the part he was compelled to play and by the thought of what Mattie must think of him. Confused impulses struggled in him as he strode along to the village. He had made up his mind to do something, but he did not know what it would be.

The early mist had vanished and the fields lay like a silver shield under the sun. It was one of the days when the glitter of winter shines through a pale haze of spring. Every yard of the road was alive with Mattie's presence, and there was hardly a branch against the sky or a tangle of brambles on the bank in which some bright shred of memory was not caught. Once, in the stillness, the call of a bird in a mountain ash was so like her laughter that his heart tightened and then grew large; and all these things made him see that something must be done at once.

Suddenly it occurred to him that Andrew Hale, who was a kind-hearted man, might be induced to reconsider his refusal and advance a small sum on the lumber if he were told that Zeena's ill-health made it necessary to hire a servant. Hale, after all, knew enough of Ethan's situation to make it possible for the latter to renew his appeal without too much loss of pride; and, moreover, how much did pride count in the ebullition of passions in his breast?

The more he considered his plan the more hopeful it seemed. If he could get Mrs. Hale's ear he felt certain of success, and with fifty dollars in his pocket nothing could keep him from Mattie . . .

His first object was to reach Starkfield before Hale had started for his work; he knew the carpenter had a job down the Corbury road and was likely to leave his house early. Ethan's long strides grew more rapid with the accelerated beat of his thoughts, and as he reached the foot of School House Hill he caught sight of Hale's sleigh in the distance. He hurried forward to meet it, but as it drew nearer he saw that it was driven by the carpenter's youngest boy and that the figure at his side, looking like a large upright cocoon in spectacles, was that of Mrs. Hale. Ethan signed to them to stop, and Mrs. Hale leaned forward, her pink wrinkles twinkling with benevolence.

"Mr. Hale? Why, yes, you'll find him down home now. He ain't going to his work this forenoon. He woke up with a touch o' lumbago, and I just made him put on one of old Dr. Kidder's plasters and set right up into the fire."

Beaming maternally on Ethan, she bent over to add: "I on'y just heard from Mr. Hale 'bout Zeena's going over to Bettsbridge to see that new doctor. I'm real sorry she's feeling so bad again! I hope he thinks he can do something for her. I don't know anybody round here's had more sickness than Zeena. I always tell Mr. Hale I don't know what she'd 'a' done if she hadn't 'a' had you to look after her; and I used to say the same thing 'bout your mother. You've had an awful mean time, Ethan Frome."

She gave him a last nod of sympathy while her son chirped to the horse; and Ethan, as she drove off, stood in the middle of the road and stared after the retreating sleigh.

It was a long time since any one had spoken to him as kindly as Mrs. Hale. Most people were either indifferent to his troubles, or disposed to think it natural that a young fellow of his age should have carried without repining the burden of three crippled lives. But Mrs. Hale had said, "You've had an awful mean time, Ethan Frome," and he felt less alone with his misery. If the Hales were sorry for him they would surely respond to his appeal . . .

He started down the road toward their house, but at the end of a few yards he pulled up sharply, the blood in his face. For the first time, in the light of the words he had just heard, he saw what he was about to do. He was planning to take advantage of the Hales' sympathy to obtain money from them on false pretences. That was a plain statement of the cloudy purpose which had driven him in headlong to Starkfield.

With the sudden perception of the point to which his madness had carried him, the madness fell and he saw his life before him as it was. He was a poor man, the husband of a sickly woman, whom his desertion would leave alone and destitute; and even if he had had the heart to desert her he could have done so only by deceiving two kindly people who had pitied him.

He turned and walked slowly back to the farm.

9

At the kitchen door Daniel Byrne sat in his sleigh behind a big-boned grey who pawed the snow and swung his long head restlessly from side to side.

Ethan went into the kitchen and found his wife by the stove. Her head was wrapped in her shawl, and she was reading a book called "Kidney Troubles and Their Cure" on which he had had to pay extra postage only a few days before.

Zeena did not move or look up when he entered, and after a moment he asked: "Where's Mattie?"

Without lifting her eyes from the page she replied: "I presume she's getting down her trunk."

The blood rushed to his face. "Getting down her trunk—alone?"

"Jotham Powell's down in the wood-lot, and Dan'l Byrne says he darsn't leave that horse," she returned.

Her husband, without stopping to hear the end of the phrase, had left the kitchen and sprung up the stairs. The door of Mattie's room was shut, and he wavered a moment on the landing. "Matt," he said in a low voice; but there was no answer, and he put his hand on the door-knob.

He had never been in her room except once, in the early summer, when he had gone there to plaster up a leak in the eaves, but he remembered exactly how everything had looked: the red-and-white quilt on her narrow bed, the pretty pin-cushion on the chest of drawers, and over it the enlarged photograph of her mother, in an oxydized frame, with a bunch of dyed grasses at the back. Now these and all other tokens of her presence had vanished and the room looked as bare and comfortless as when Zeena had shown her into it on the day of her arrival. In the middle of the floor stood her trunk, and on the trunk she sat in her Sunday dress, her back turned to the door and her face in her hands. She had not heard Ethan's call because she was sobbing and she did not hear his step till he stood close behind her and laid his hands on her shoulders.

"Matt—oh, don't—oh, *Matt!*"

She started up, lifting her wet face to his. "Ethan—I thought I wasn't ever going to see you again!"

He took her in his arms, pressing her close, and with a trembling hand smoothed away the hair from her forehead.

"Not see me again? What do you mean?"

She sobbed out: "Jotham said you told him we wasn't to wait dinner for you, and I thought——"

"You thought I meant to cut it?" he finished for her grimly.

She clung to him without answering, and he laid his lips on her hair, which was soft yet springy, like certain mosses on warm slopes, and had the faint woody fragrance of fresh sawdust in the sun.

Through the door they heard Zeena's voice calling out from below: "Dan'l Byrne says you better hurry up if you want him to take that trunk."

They drew apart with stricken faces. Words of resistance rushed to Ethan's lips and died there. Mattie found her handkerchief and dried her eyes; then, bending down, she took hold of a handle of the trunk.

Ethan put her aside. "You let go, Matt," he ordered her.

She answered: "It takes two to coax it round the corner"; and submitting to this argument he grasped the other handle, and together they manœuvred the heavy trunk out to the landing.

"Now let go," he repeated; then he shouldered the trunk and carried it down the stairs and across the passage to the kitchen. Zeena, who had gone back to her seat by the stove, did not lift her head from her book as he passed. Mattie followed him out of the door and helped him to lift the trunk into the back of the sleigh. When it was in place they stood side by side on the door-step, watching Daniel Byrne plunge off behind his fidgety horse.

It seemed to Ethan that his heart was bound with cords which an unseen hand was tightening with every tick of the clock. Twice he opened his lips to speak to Mattie and found no breath. At length, as she turned to re-enter the house, he laid a detaining hand on her.

"I'm going to drive you over, Matt," he whispered.

She murmured back: "I think Zeena wants I should go with Jotham."

"I'm going to drive you over," he repeated; and she went into the kitchen without answering.

At dinner Ethan could not eat. If he lifted his eyes they rested on Zeena's pinched face, and the corners of her straight lips seemed to quiver away into a smile. She ate well, declaring that the mild weather made her feel better, and pressed a second helping of beans on Jotham Powell, whose wants she generally ignored.

Mattie, when the meal was over, went about her usual task of clearing the table and washing up the dishes. Zeena, after feeding the cat, had returned to her rocking-chair by the stove, and Jotham Powell, who always lingered last, reluctantly pushed back his chair and moved toward the door.

On the threshold he turned back to say to Ethan: "What time'll I come round for Mattie?"

Ethan was standing near the window, mechanically filling his pipe while he watched Mattie move to and fro. He answered: "You needn't come round; I'm going to drive her over myself."

He saw the rise of the colour in Mattie's averted cheek, and the quick lifting of Zeena's head.

"I want you should stay here this afternoon, Ethan," his wife said. "Jotham can drive Mattie over."

Mattie flung an imploring glance at him, but he repeated curtly: "I'm going to drive her over myself."

Zeena continued in the same even tone: "I wanted you should stay and fix up that stove in Mattie's room afore the girl gets here. It ain't been drawing right for nigh on a month now."

Ethan's voice rose indignantly. "If it was good enough for Mattie I guess it's good enough for a hired girl."

"That girl that's coming told me she was used to a house where they had a furnace," Zeena persisted with the same monotonous mildness.

"She'd better ha' stayed there then," he flung back at her; and turning to Mattie he added in a hard voice: "You be ready by three, Matt; I've got business at Corbury."

Jotham Powell had started for the barn, and Ethan strode down after him aflame with anger. The pulses in his temples throbbed and a fog was in his eyes. He went about his task without knowing what force directed him, or whose hands and feet were fulfilling its orders.

It was not till he led out the sorrel and backed him between the shafts of the sleigh that he once more became conscious of what he was doing. As he passed the bridle over the horse's head, and wound the traces around the shafts, he remembered the day when he had made the same preparations in order to drive over and meet his wife's cousin at the Flats. It was little more than a year ago, on just such a soft afternoon, with a "feel" of spring in the air. The sorrel, turning the same big ringed eye on him, nuzzled the palm of his hand in the same way; and one by one all the days between rose up and stood before him . . .

He flung the bearskin into the sleigh, climbed to the seat, and drove up to the house. When he entered the kitchen it was empty, but Mattie's bag and shawl lay ready by the door. He went to the foot of the stairs and listened. No sound reached him from above, but presently he thought he heard some one moving about in his deserted study, and pushing open the door he saw Mattie, in her hat and jacket, standing with her back to him near the table.

She started at his approach and turning quickly, said: "Is it time?"

"What are you doing here, Matt?" he asked her.

She looked at him timidly. "I was just taking a look round—that's all," she answered, with a wavering smile.

They went back into the kitchen without speaking, and Ethan picked up her bag and shawl.

"Where's Zeena?" he asked.

"She went upstairs right after dinner. She said she had those shooting pains again, and didn't want to be disturbed."

"Didn't she say good-bye to you?"

"No. That was all she said."

Ethan, looking slowly about the kitchen, said to himself with a shudder than in a few hours he would be returning to it alone. Then the sense of unreality overcame him once more, and he could not bring himself to believe that Mattie stood there for the last time before him.

"Come on," he said almost gaily, opening the door and putting her bag into the sleigh. He sprang to his seat and bent over to tuck the rug about her as she slipped into the place at his side. "Now then, go 'long," he said, with a shake of the reins that sent the sorrel placidly jogging down the hill.

"We got lots of time for a good ride, Matt!" he cried, seeking her hand beneath the fur and pressing it in his. His face tingled and he

felt dizzy, as if he had stopped in at the Starkfield saloon on a zero
day for a drink.

At the gate, instead of making for Starkfield, he turned the sorrel
to the right, up the Bettsbridge road. Mattie sat silent, giving no sign
of surprise; but after a moment she said: "Are you going round by
Shadow Pond?"

He laughed and answered: "I knew you'd know!"

She drew closer under the bearskin, so that, looking sideways
around his coat-sleeve, he could just catch the tip of her nose and a
blown brown wave of hair. They drove slowly up the road between
fields glistening under the pale sun, and then bent to the right down
a lane edged with spruce and larch. Ahead of them, a long way off, a
range of hills stained by mottlings of black forest flowed away in
round white curves against the sky. The lane passed into a pine-wood
with boles reddening in the afternoon sun and delicate blue shadows
on the snow. As they entered it the breeze fell and a warm stillness
seemed to drop from the branches with the dropping needles. Here
the snow was so pure that the tiny tracks of wood-animals had left
on it intricate lace-like patterns, and the bluish cones caught in its
surface stood out like ornaments of bronze.

Ethan drove on in silence till they reached a part of the wood
where the pines were more widely spaced, then he drew up and
helped Mattie to get out of the sleigh. They passed between the aromatic trunks, the snow breaking crisply under their feet, till they
came to a small sheet of water with steep wooded sides. Across its
frozen surface, from the farther bank, a single hill rising against the
western sun threw the long conical shadow which gave the lake its
name. It was a shy secret spot, full of the same dumb melancholy
that Ethan felt in his heart.

He looked up and down the little pebbly beach till his eye lit on a
fallen tree-trunk half submerged in snow.

"There's where we sat at the picnic," he reminded her.

The entertainment of which he spoke was one of the few that they
had taken part in together: a "church picnic" which, on a long afternoon of the preceding summer, had filled the retired place with
merry-making. Mattie had begged him to go with her but he had refused. Then, toward sunset, coming down from the mountain where
he had been felling timber, he had been caught by some strayed
revellers and drawn into the group by the lake, where Mattie, encircled by facetious youths, and bright as a blackberry under her

spreading hat, was brewing coffee over a gipsy fire. He remembered the shyness he had felt at approaching her in his uncouth clothes, and then the lighting up of her face, and the way she had broken through the group to come to him with a cup in her hand. They had sat for a few minutes on the fallen log by the pond, and she had missed her gold locket, and set the young men searching for it; and it was Ethan who had spied it in the moss. . . . That was all; but all their intercourse had been made up of just such inarticulate flashes, when they seemed to come suddenly upon happiness as if they had surprised a butterfly in the winter woods . . .

"It was right there I found your locket," he said, pushing his foot into a dense tuft of blueberry bushes.

"I never saw anybody with such sharp eyes!" she answered.

She sat down on the tree-trunk in the sun and he sat down beside her.

"You were as pretty as a picture in that pink hat," he said.

She laughed with pleasure. "Oh, I guess it was the hat!" she rejoined.

They had never before avowed their inclination so openly, and Ethan, for a moment, had the illusion that he was a free man, wooing the girl he meant to marry. He looked at her hair and longed to touch it again, and to tell her that it smelt of the woods; but he had never learned to say such things.

Suddenly she rose to her feet and said: "We mustn't stay here any longer."

He continued to gaze at her vaguely, only half-roused from his dream. "There's plenty of time," he answered.

They stood looking at each other as if the eyes of each were straining to absorb and hold fast the other's image. There were things he had to say to her before they parted, but he could not say them in that place of summer memories, and he turned and followed her in silence to the sleigh. As they drove away the sun sank behind the hill and the pine-boles turned from red to grey.

By a devious track between the fields they wound back to the Starkfield road. Under the open sky the light was still clear, with a reflection of cold red on the eastern hills. The clumps of trees in the snow seemed to draw together in ruffled lumps, like birds with their heads under their wings; and the sky, as it paled, rose higher, leaving the earth more alone.

As they turned into the Starkfield road Ethan said: "Matt, what do you mean to do?"

She did not answer at once, but at length she said: "I'll try to get a place in a store."

"You know you can't do it. The bad air and the standing all day nearly killed you before."

"I'm a lot stronger than I was before I came to Starkfield."

"And now you're going to throw away all the good it's done you!"

There seemed to be no answer to this, and again they drove on for a while without speaking. With every yard of the way some spot where they had stood, and laughed together or been silent, clutched at Ethan and dragged him back.

"Isn't there any of your father's folks could help you?"

"There isn't any of 'em I'd ask."

He lowered his voice to say: "You know there's nothing I wouldn't do for you if I could."

"I know there isn't."

"But I can't——"

She was silent, but he felt a slight tremor in the shoulder against his.

"Oh, Matt," he broke out, "if I could ha' gone with you now I'd ha' done it——"

She turned to him, pulling a scrap of paper from her breast. "Ethan—I found this," she stammered. Even in the failing light he saw it was the letter to his wife that he had begun the night before and forgotten to destroy. Through his astonishment there ran a fierce thrill of joy. "Matt—" he cried; "if I could ha' done it, would you?"

"Oh, Ethan, Ethan—what's the use?" With a sudden movement she tore the letter in shreds and sent them fluttering off into the snow.

"Tell me, Matt! Tell me!" he adjured her.

She was silent for a moment; then she said, in such a low tone that he had to stoop his head to hear her: "I used to think of it sometimes, summer nights, when the moon was so bright I couldn't sleep."

His heart reeled with the sweetness of it. "As long ago as that?"

She answered, as if the date had long been fixed for her: "The first time was at Shadow Pond."

"Was that why you gave me my coffee before the others?"

"I don't know. Did I? I was dreadfully put out when you wouldn't

go to the picnic with me; and then, when I saw you coming down
the road, I thought maybe you'd gone home that way o' purpose;
and that made me glad."

They were silent again. They had reached the point where the
road dipped to the hollow by Ethan's mill and as they descended the
darkness descended with them, dropping down like a black veil from
the heavy hemlock boughs.

"I'm tied hand and foot, Matt. There isn't a thing I can do," he
began again.

"You must write to me sometimes, Ethan."

"Oh, what good'll writing do? I want to put my hand out and
touch you. I want to do for you and care for you. I want to be there
when you're sick and when you're lonesome."

"You mustn't think but what I'll do all right."

"You won't need me, you mean? I suppose you'll marry!"

"Oh, Ethan!" she cried.

"I don't know how it is you make me feel, Matt. I'd a'most rather
have you dead than that!"

"Oh, I wish I was, I wish I was!" she sobbed.

The sound of her weeping shook him out of his dark anger, and he
felt ashamed.

"Don't let's talk that way," he whispered.

"Why shouldn't we, when it's true? I've been wishing it every
minute of the day."

"Matt! You be quiet! Don't you say it."

"There's never anybody been good to me but you."

"Don't say that either, when I can't lift a hand for you!"

"Yes; but it's true just the same."

They had reached the top of School House Hill and Starkfield lay
below them in the twilight. A cutter, mounting the road from the
village, passed them by in a joyous flutter of bells, and they
straightened themselves and looked ahead with rigid faces. Along the
main street lights had begun to shine from the house-fronts and stray
figures were turning in here and there at the gates. Ethan, with a
touch of his whip, roused the sorrel to a languid trot.

As they drew near the end of the village the cries of children
reached them, and they saw a knot of boys, with sleds behind them,
scattering across the open space before the church.

"I guess this'll be their last coast for a day or two," Ethan said,
looking up at the mild sky.

Mattie was silent, and he added: "We were to have gone down last night."

Still she did not speak and, prompted by an obscure desire to help himself and her through their miserable last hour, he went on discursively: "Ain't it funny we haven't been down together but just that once last winter?"

She answered: "It wasn't often I got down to the village."

"That's so," he said.

They had reached the crest of the Corbury road, and between the indistinct white glimmer of the church and the black curtain of the Varnum spruces the slope stretched away below them without a sled on its length. Some erratic impulse prompted Ethan to say: "How'd you like me to take you down now?"

She forced a laugh. "Why, there isn't time!"

"There's all the time we want. Come along!" His one desire now was to postpone the moment of turning the sorrel toward the Flats.

"But the girl," she faltered. "The girl'll be waiting at the station."

"Well, let her wait. You'd have to if she didn't. Come!"

The note of authority in his voice seemed to subdue her, and when he had jumped from the sleigh she let him help her out, saying only, with a vague feint of reluctance: "But there isn't a sled round anywheres."

"Yes, there is! Right over there under the spruces."

He threw the bearskin over the sorrel, who stood passively by the roadside, hanging a meditative head. Then he caught Mattie's hand and drew her after him toward the sled.

She seated herself obediently and he took his place behind her, so close that her hair brushed his face. "All right, Matt?" he called out, as if the width of the road had been between them.

She turned her head to say: "It's dreadfully dark. Are you sure you can see?"

He laughed contemptuously: "I could go down this coast with my eyes tied!" and she laughed with him, as if she liked his audacity. Nevertheless he sat still a moment, straining his eyes down the long hill, for it was the most confusing hour of the evening, the hour when the last clearness from the upper sky is merged with the rising night in a blur that disguises landmarks and falsifies distances.

"Now!" he cried.

The sled started with a bound, and they flew on through the dusk, gathering smoothness and speed as they went, with the hollow night opening out below them and the air singing by like an organ. Mattie sat perfectly still, but as they reached the bend at the foot of the hill, where the big elm thrust out a deadly elbow, he fancied that she shrank a little closer.

"Don't be scared, Matt!" he cried exultantly, as they spun safely past it and flew down the second slope; and when they reached the level ground beyond, and the speed of the sled began to slacken, he heard her give a little laugh of glee.

They sprang off and started to walk back up the hill. Ethan dragged the sled with one hand and passed the other through Mattie's arm.

"Were you scared I'd run you into the elm?" he asked with a boyish laugh.

"I told you I was never scared with you," she answered.

The strange exaltation of his mood had brought on one of his rare fits of boastfulness. "It *is* a tricky place, though. The least swerve, and we'd never ha' come up again. But I can measure distances to a hair's-breadth—always could."

She murmured: "I always say you've got the surest eye . . ."

Deep silence had fallen with the starless dusk, and they leaned on each other without speaking; but at every step of their climb Ethan said to himself: "It's the last time we'll ever walk together."

They mounted slowly to the top of the hill. When they were abreast of the church he stooped his head to her to ask: "Are you tired?" and she answered, breathing quickly: "It was splendid!"

With a pressure of his arm he guided her toward the Norway spruces. "I guess this sled must be Ned Hale's. Anyhow I'll leave it where I found it." He drew the sled up to the Varnum gate and rested it against the fence. As he raised himself he suddenly felt Mattie close to him among the shadows.

"Is this where Ned and Ruth kissed each other?" she whispered breathlessly, and flung her arms about him. Her lips, groping for his, swept over his face, and he held her fast in a rapture of surprise.

"Good-bye—good-bye," she stammered, and kissed him again.

"Oh, Matt, I can't let you go!" broke from him in the same old cry.

She freed herself from his hold and he heard her sobbing. "Oh, I can't go either!" she wailed.

"Matt! What'll we do? What'll we do?"

They clung to each other's hands like children, and her body shook with desperate sobs.

Through the stillness they heard the church clock striking five.

"Oh, Ethan, it's time!" she cried.

He drew her back to him. "Time for what? You don't suppose I'm going to leave you now?"

"If I missed my train where'd I go?"

"Where are you going if you catch it?"

She stood silent, her hands lying cold and relaxed in his.

"What's the good of either of us going anywheres without the other one now?" he said.

She remained motionless, as if she had not heard him. Then she snatched her hands from his, threw her arms about his neck, and pressed a sudden drenched cheek against his face. "Ethan! Ethan! I want you to take me down again!"

"Down where?"

"The coast. Right off," she panted. "So 't we'll never come up any more."

"Matt! What on earth do you mean?"

She put her lips close against his ear to say: "Right into the big elm. You said you could. So 't we'd never have to leave each other any more."

"Why, what are you talking of? You're crazy!"

"I'm not crazy; but I will be if I leave you."

"Oh, Matt, Matt—" he groaned.

She tightened her fierce hold about his neck. Her face lay close to his face.

"Ethan, where'll I go if I leave you? I don't know how to get along alone. You said so yourself just now. Nobody but you was ever good to me. And there'll be that strange girl in the house . . . and she'll sleep in my bed, where I used to lay nights and listen to hear you come up the stairs . . ."

The words were like fragments torn from his heart. With them came the hated vision of the house he was going back to—of the stairs he would have to go up every night, of the woman who would wait for him there. And the sweetness of Mattie's avowal, the wild wonder of knowing at last that all that had happened to him had happened to her too, made the other vision more abhorrent, the other life more intolerable to return to . . .

Her pleadings still came to him between short sobs, but he no longer heard what she was saying. Her hat had slipped back and he was stroking her hair. He wanted to get the feeling of it into his hand, so that it would sleep there like a seed in winter. Once he found her mouth again, and they seemed to be by the pond together in the burning August sun. But his cheek touched hers, and it was cold and full of weeping, and he saw the road to the Flats under the night and heard the whistle of the train up the line.

The spruces swathed them in blackness and silence. They might have been in their coffins underground. He said to himself: "Perhaps it'll feel like this . . ." and then again: "After this I sha'n't feel anything . . ."

Suddenly he heard the old sorrel whinny across the road, and thought: "He's wondering why he doesn't get his supper. . ."

"Come," Mattie whispered, tugging at his hand.

Her sombre violence constrained him: she seemed the embodied instrument of fate. He pulled the sled out, blinking like a night-bird as he passed from the shade of the spruces into the transparent dusk of the open. The slope below them was deserted. All Starkfield was at supper, and not a figure crossed the open space before the church. The sky, swollen with the clouds that announce a thaw, hung as low as before a summer storm. He strained his eyes through the dimness, and they seemed less keen, less capable than usual.

He took his seat on the sled and Mattie instantly placed herself in front of him. Her hat had fallen into the snow and his lips were in her hair. He stretched out his legs, drove his heels into the road to keep the sled from slipping forward, and bent her head back between his hands. Then suddenly he sprang up again.

"Get up," he ordered her.

It was the tone she always heeded, but she cowered down in her seat, repeating vehemently: "No, no, no!"

"Get up!"

"Why?"

"I want to sit in front."

"No, no! How can you steer in front?"

"I don't have to. We'll follow the track."

They spoke in smothered whispers, as though the night were listening.

"Get up! Get up " he urged her; but she kept on repeating: "Why do you want to sit in front?"

"Because I—because I want to feel you holding me," he stammered, and dragged her to her feet.

The answer seemed to satisfy her, or else she yielded to the power of his voice. He bent down, feeling in the obscurity for the glassy slide worn by preceding coasters, and placed the runners carefully between its edges. She waited while he seated himself with crossed legs in the front of the sled; then she crouched quickly down at his back and clasped her arms about him. Her breath in his neck set him shuddering again, and he almost sprang from his seat. But in a flash he remembered the alternative. She was right: this was better than parting. He leaned back and drew her mouth to his. . .

Just as they started he heard the sorrel's whinny again, and the familiar wistful call, and all the confused images it brought with it, went with him down the first reach of the road. Half-way down there was a sudden drop, then a rise, and after that another long delirious descent. As they took wing for this it seemed to him that they were flying indeed, flying far up into the cloudy night, with Starkfield immeasurably below them, falling away like a speck in space. . . Then the big elm shot up ahead, lying in wait for them at the bend of the road, and he said between his teeth: "We can fetch it; I know we can fetch it——"

As they flew toward the tree Mattie pressed her arms tighter, and her blood seemed to be in his veins. Once or twice the sled swerved a little under them. He slanted his body to keep it headed for the elm, repeating to himself again and again: "I know we can fetch it"; and little phrases she had spoken ran through his head and danced before him on the air. The big tree loomed bigger and closer, and as they bore down on it he thought: "It's waiting for us: it seems to know." But suddenly his wife's face, with twisted monstrous lineaments, thrust itself between him and his goal, and he made an instinctive movement to brush it aside. The sled swerved in response, but he righted it again, kept it straight, and drove down on the black projecting mass. There was a last instant when the air shot past him like millions of fiery wires; and then the elm . . .

The sky was still thick, but looking straight up he saw a single star, and tried vaguely to reckon whether it were Sirius, or—or— The effort tired him too much, and he closed his heavy lids and thought that he would sleep. . . The stillness was so profound that he heard a little animal twittering somewhere near by under the snow. It made a small frightened *cheep* like a field mouse, and he wondered languidly if it were hurt. Then he understood that it must be in pain: pain so excruciating that he seemed, mysteriously, to feel it shooting through his own body. He tried in vain to roll over in the direction of the sound, and stretched his left arm out across the snow. And now it was as though he felt rather than heard the twittering; it seemed to be under his palm, which rested on something soft and springy. The thought of the animal's suffering was intolerable to him and he struggled to raise himself, and could not because a rock, or some huge mass, seemed to be lying on him. But he continued to finger about cautiously with his left hand, thinking he might get hold of the little creature and help it; and all at once he knew that the soft thing he had touched was Mattie's hair and that his hand was on her face.

He dragged himself to his knees, the monstrous load on him moving with him as he moved, and his hand went over and over her face, and he felt that the twittering came from her lips . . .

He got his face down close to hers, with his ear to her mouth, and in the darkness he saw her eyes open and heard her say his name.

"Oh, Matt, I thought we'd fetched it," he moaned; and far off, up the hill, he heard the sorrel whinny, and thought: "I ought to be getting him his feed. . ."

10

THE QUERULOUS DRONE ceased as I entered Frome's kitchen, and of the two women sitting there I could not tell which had been the speaker.

One of them, on my appearing, raised her tall bony figure from her seat, not as if to welcome me—for she threw me no more than a brief glance of surprise—but simply to set about preparing the meal which Frome's absence had delayed. A slatternly calico wrapper hung from her shoulders and the wisps of her thin grey hair were drawn away from a high forehead and fastened at the back by a broken comb. She had pale opaque eyes which revealed nothing and reflected nothing, and her narrow lips were of the same sallow colour as her face.

The other woman was much smaller and slighter. She sat huddled in an arm-chair near the stove, and when I came in she turned her head quickly toward me, without the least corresponding movement of her body. Her hair was as grey as her companion's, her face as bloodless and shrivelled, but amber-tinted, with swarthy shadows sharpening the nose and hollowing the temples. Under her shapeless dress her body kept its limp immobility, and her dark eyes had the bright witch-like stare that disease of the spine sometimes gives.

Even for that part of the country the kitchen was a poor-looking place. With the exception of the dark-eyed woman's chair, which looked like a soiled relic of luxury bought at a country auction, the furniture was of the roughest kind. Three coarse china plates and a broken-nosed milk-jug had been set on a greasy table scored with knife-cuts, and a couple of straw-bottomed chairs and a kitchen dresser of unpainted pine stood meagrely against the plaster walls.

"My, it's cold here! The fire must be 'most out," Frome said, glancing about him apologetically as he followed me in.

The tall woman, who had moved away from us toward the dresser, took no notice; but the other, from her cushioned niche, answered complainingly, in a high thin voice. "It's on'y just been made up this very minute. Zeena fell asleep and slep' ever so long, and I thought I'd be frozen stiff before I could wake her up and get her to 'tend to it."

I knew then that it was she who had been speaking when we entered.

Her companion, who was just coming back to the table with the remains of a cold mince-pie in a battered pie-dish, set down her unappetising burden without appearing to hear the accusation brought against her.

Frome stood hesitatingly before her as she advanced; then he looked at me and said: "This is my wife, Mis' Frome." After another interval he added, turning toward the figure in the arm-chair: "And this is Miss Mattie Silver. . ."

.   .   .   .   .

Mrs. Hale, tender soul, had pictured me as lost in the Flats and buried under a snow-drift; and so lively was her satisfaction on seeing me safely restored to her the next morning that I felt my peril had caused me to advance several degrees in her favour.

Great was her amazement, and that of old Mrs. Varnum, on learning that Ethan Frome's old horse had carried me to and from Corbury Junction through the worst blizzard of the winter; greater still their surprise when they heard that his master had taken me in for the night.

Beneath their wondering exclamations I felt a secret curiosity to know what impressions I had received from my night in the Frome household, and divined that the best way of breaking down their reserve was to let them try to penetrate mine. I therefore confined myself to saying, in a matter-of-fact tone, that I had been received with great kindness, and that Frome had made a bed for me in a room on the ground-floor which seemed in happier days to have been fitted up as a kind of writing-room or study.

"Well," Mrs. Hale mused, "in such a storm I suppose he felt he couldn't do less than take you in—but I guess it went hard with Ethan. I don't believe but what you're the only stranger has set foot in that house for over twenty years. He's that proud he don't even like his oldest friends to go there; and I don't know as any do, any more, except myself and the doctor. . ."

"You still go there, Mrs. Hale?" I ventured.

"I used to go a good deal after the accident, when I was first married; but after awhile I got to think it made 'em feel worse to see us. And then one thing and another came, and my own troubles . . . But I generally make out to drive over there round about New Year's, and once in the summer. Only I always try to pick a day when Ethan's off somewheres. It's bad enough to see the two women sitting there—but *his* face, when he looks round that bare place, just kills me . . . You see, I can look back and call it up in his mother's day, before their troubles."

Old Mrs. Varnum, by this time, had gone up to bed, and her daughter and I were sitting alone, after supper, in the austere seclusion of the horse-hair parlour. Mrs. Hale glanced at me tentatively, as though trying to see how much footing my conjectures gave her; and I guessed that if she had kept silence till now it was because she had been waiting, through all the years, for some one who should see what she alone had seen.

I waited to let her trust in me gather strength before I said: "Yes, it's pretty bad, seeing all three of them there together."

She drew her mild brows into a frown of pain. "It was just awful from the beginning. I was here in the house when they were carried up—they laid Mattie Silver in the room you're in. She and I were great friends, and she was to have been my bridesmaid in the spring . . . When she came to I went up to her and stayed all night. They gave her things to quiet her, and she didn't know much till to'rd morning, and then all of a sudden she woke up just like herself, and looked straight at me out of her big eyes, and said . . . Oh, I don't know why I'm telling you all this," Mrs. Hale broke off, crying.

She took off her spectacles, wiped the moisture from them, and put them on again with an unsteady hand. "It got about the next day," she went on, "that Zeena Frome had sent Mattie off in a hurry because she had a hired girl coming, and the folks here could never rightly tell what she and Ethan were doing that night coasting, when they'd ought to have been on their way to the Flats to ketch the train . . . I never knew myself what Zeena thought—I don't to this day. Nobody knows Zeena's thoughts. Anyhow, when she heard o' the accident she came right in and stayed with Ethan over to the minister's, where they'd carried him. And as soon as the doctors said that Mattie could be moved, Zeena sent for her and took her back to the farm."

"And there she's been ever since?"

Mrs. Hale answered simply: "There was nowhere else for her to go;" and my heart tightened at the thought of the hard compulsions of the poor.

"Yes, there she's been," Mrs. Hale continued, "and Zeena's done for her, and done for Ethan, as good as she could. It was a miracle, considering how sick she was—but she seemed to be raised right up just when the call came to her. Not as she's ever given up doctoring, and she's had sick spells right along; but she's had the strength given her to care for those two for over twenty years, and before the accident came she thought she couldn't even care for herself."

Mrs. Hale paused a moment, and I remained silent, plunged in the vision of what her words evoked. "It's horrible for them all," I murmured.

"Yes: it's pretty bad. And they ain't any of 'em easy people either. Mattie *was*, before the accident; I never knew a sweeter nature. But she's suffered too much—that's what I always say when folks tell me how she's soured. And Zeena, she was always cranky. Not but what she bears with Mattie wonderful—I've seen that myself. But sometimes the two of them get going at each other, and then Ethan's face'd break your heart . . . When I see that, I think it's *him* that suffers most . . . anyhow it ain't Zeena, because she ain't got the time . . . It's a pity, though," Mrs. Hale ended, sighing, "that they're all shut up there'n that one kitchen. In the summertime, on pleasant days, they move Mattie into the parlour, or out in the dooryard, and that makes it easier . . . but winters there's the fires to be thought of; and there ain't a dime to spare up at the Fromes'."

Mrs. Hale drew a deep breath, as though her memory were eased of its long burden, and she had no more to say; but suddenly an impulse of complete avowal seized her.

She took off her spectacles again, leaned toward me across the bead-work table-cover, and went on with lowered voice: "There was one day, about a week after the accident, when they all thought Mattie couldn't live. Well, I say it's a pity she *did*. I said it right out to our minister once, and he was shocked at me. Only he wasn't with me that morning when she first came to . . . And I say, if she'd ha' died, Ethan might ha' lived; and the way they are now, I don't see's there's much difference between the Fromes up at the farm and the Fromes down in the graveyard; 'cept that down there they're all quiet, and the women have got to hold their tongues."

Old New York

FALSE DAWN

(*The 'Forties*)

PART ONE

1

HAY, verbena and mignonette scented the languid July day. Large strawberries, crimsoning through sprigs of mint, floated in a bowl of pale yellow cup on the verandah table: an old Georgian bowl, with complex reflections on polygonal flanks, engraved with the Raycie arms between lion's heads. Now and again the gentlemen, warned by a menacing hum, slapped their cheeks, their brows or their bald crowns; but they did so as furtively as possible, for Mr. Halston Raycie, on whose verandah they sat, would not admit that there were mosquitoes at High Point.

The strawberries came from Mr. Raycie's kitchen garden; the Georgian bowl came from his great-grandfather (father of the Signer); the verandah was that of his country-house, which stood on a height above the Sound, at a convenient driving distance from his town house in Canal Street.

"Another glass, Commodore," said Mr. Raycie, shaking out a cambric handkerchief the size of a table-cloth, and applying a corner of it to his steaming brow.

Mr. Jameson Ledgely smiled and took another glass. He was known as "the Commodore" among his intimates because of having been in the Navy in his youth, and having taken part, as a midshipman under Admiral Porter, in the war of 1812. This jolly sunburnt bachelor, whose face resembled that of one of the bronze idols he might have brought back with him, had kept his naval air, though long retired from the service; and his white duck trousers, his gold-braided cap and shining teeth, still made him look as if he might be in command of a frigate. Instead of that, he had just sailed over a party of friends from his own place on the Long Island shore; and his trim white sloop was now lying in the bay below the point.

The Halston Raycie house overlooked a lawn sloping to the Sound. The lawn was Mr. Raycie's pride: it was mown with a scythe once a fortnight, and rolled in the spring by an old white horse specially shod for the purpose. Below the verandah the turf was broken by three rounds of rose-geranium, heliotrope and Bengal roses, which Mrs. Raycie tended in gauntlet gloves, under a small hinged sunshade that folded back on its carved ivory handle. The house, remodelled and enlarged by Mr. Raycie on his marriage, had played a part in the Revolutionary war as the settler's cottage where Benedict Arnold had had his headquarters. A contemporary print of it hung in Mr. Raycie's study; but no one could have detected the humble outline of the old house in the majestic stone-coloured dwelling built of tongued-and-grooved boards, with an angle tower, tall narrow windows, and a verandah on chamfered posts, that figured so confidently as a "Tuscan Villa" in Downing's "Landscape Gardening in America." There was the same difference between the rude lithograph of the earlier house and the fine steel engraving of its successor (with a "specimen" weeping beech on the lawn) as between the buildings themselves. Mr. Raycie had reason to think well of his architect.

He thought well of most things related to himself by ties of blood or interest. No one had ever been quite sure that he made Mrs. Raycie happy, but he was known to have the highest opinion of her. So it was with his daughters, Sarah Anne and Mary Adeline, fresher replicas of the lymphatic Mrs. Raycie; no one would have sworn that they were quite at ease with their genial parent, yet every one knew how loud he was in their praises. But the most remarkable object within the range of Mr. Raycie's self-approval was his son Lewis. And yet, as Jameson Ledgely, who was given to speaking his mind, had once observed, you wouldn't have supposed young Lewis was exactly the kind of craft Halston would have turned out if he'd had the designing of his son and heir.

Mr. Raycie was a monumental man. His extent in height, width and thickness was so nearly the same that whichever way he was turned one had an almost equally broad view of him; and every inch of that mighty circumference was so exquisitely cared for that to a farmer's eye he might have suggested a great agricultural estate of which not an acre is untilled. Even his baldness, which was in proportion to the rest, looked as if it received a special daily polish; and on a hot day his whole person was like some wonderful example of the costliest irrigation. There was so much of him, and he had so many planes, that it was fascinating to watch each runnel of moisture follow its own particular watershed. Even on his large fresh-looking hands the drops divided, trickling in different ways from the ridges of the fingers; and as for his forehead and temples, and the raised cushion of cheek beneath each of his lower lids, every one of these slopes had its own particular stream, its hollow pools and sudden cataracts; and the sight was never unpleasant, because his whole vast bubbling surface was of such a clean and hearty pink, and the exuding moisture so perceptibly flavoured with expensive eau de Cologne and the best French soap.

Mrs. Raycie, though built on a less heroic scale, had a pale amplitude which, when she put on her best watered silk (the kind that stood alone), and framed her countenance in the innumerable blonde lace ruffles and clustered purple grapes of her newest Paris cap, almost balanced her husband's bulk. Yet from this full-rigged pair, as the Commodore would have put it, had issued the lean little runt of a Lewis, a shrimp of a baby, a shaver of a boy, and now a youth as scant as an ordinary man's midday shadow.

All these things, Lewis himself mused, dangling his legs from the verandah rail, were undoubtedly passing through the minds of the four gentlemen grouped about his father's bowl of cup.

Mr. Robert Huzzard, the banker, a tall broad man, who looked big in any company but Mr. Raycie's, leaned back, lifted his glass, and bowed to Lewis.

"Here's to the Grand Tour!"

"Don't perch on that rail like a sparrow, my boy," Mr. Raycie said reprovingly; and Lewis dropped to his feet, and returned Mr. Huzzard's bow.

"I wasn't thinking," he stammered. It was his too frequent excuse.

Mr. Ambrose Huzzard, the banker's younger brother, Mr. Ledgely and Mr. Donaldson Kent, all raised their glasses and cheerily echoed: "The Grand Tour!"

Lewis bowed again, and put his lips to the glass he had forgotten. In reality, he had eyes only for Mr. Donaldson Kent, his father's cousin, a silent man with a lean hawk-like profile, who looked like a retired Revolutionary hero, and lived in daily fear of the most trifling risk or responsibility.

To this prudent and circumspect citizen had come, some years earlier, the unexpected and altogether inexcusable demand that he should look after the daughter of his only brother, Julius Kent. Julius had died in Italy—well, that was his own business, if he chose to live there. But to let his wife die before him, and to leave a minor daughter, and a will entrusting her to the guardianship of his esteemed elder brother, Donaldson Kent Esquire, of Kent's Point, Long Island, and Great Jones Street, New York—well, as Mr. Kent himself said, and as his wife said for him, there had never been anything, anything whatever, in Mr. Kent's attitude or behaviour, to justify the ungrateful Julius (whose debts he had more than once paid) in laying on him this final burden.

The girl came. She was fourteen, she was considered plain, she was small and black and skinny. Her name was Beatrice, which was bad enough, and made worse by the fact that it had been shortened by ignorant foreigners to Treeshy. But she was eager, serviceable and good-tempered, and as Mr. and Mrs. Kent's friends pointed out, her plainness made everything easy. There were two Kent boys growing up, Bill and Donald; and if this penniless cousin had been compounded of cream and roses—well, she would have taken more watching, and might have rewarded the kindness of her uncle and aunt by some act of wicked ingratitude. But this risk being obviated by her appearance, they could be goodnatured to her without afterthought, and to be goodnatured was natural to them. So, as the years passed, she gradually became the guardian of her guardians; since it was equally natural to Mr. and Mrs. Kent to throw themselves in helpless reliance on every one whom they did not nervously fear or mistrust.

"Yes, he's off on Monday," Mr. Raycie said, nodding sharply at Lewis, who had set down his glass after one sip. "Empty it, you shirk!" the nod commanded; and Lewis, throwing back his head, gulped down the draught, though it almost stuck in his lean throat. He had already had to take two glasses, and even this scant conviviality was too much for him, and likely to result in a mood of excited volubility, followed by a morose evening and a head the next morning. And he wanted to keep his mind clear that day, and to think steadily and lucidly of Treeshy Kent.

Of course he couldn't marry her—yet. He was twenty-one that very day, and still entirely dependent on his father. And he wasn't altogether sorry to be going first on this Grand Tour. It was what he had always dreamed of, pined for, from the moment when his infant eyes had first been drawn to the prints of European cities in the long upper passage that smelt of matting. And all that Treeshy had told him about Italy had confirmed and intensified the longing. Oh, to have been going there with her—with her as his guide, his Beatrice! (For she had given him a little Dante of her father's, with a steel-engraved frontispiece of Beatrice; and his sister Mary Adeline, who had been taught Italian by one of the romantic Milanese exiles, had helped her brother out with the grammar.)

The thought of going to Italy with Treeshy was only a dream; but later, as man and wife, they would return there, and by that time, perhaps, it was Lewis who would be her guide, and reveal to her the historic marvels of her birthplace, of which after all she knew so little, except in minor domestic ways that were quaint but unimportant.

The prospect swelled her suitor's bosom, and reconciled him to the idea of their separation. After all, he secretly felt himself to be still a boy, and it was as a man that he would return: he meant to tell her that when they met the next day. When he came back his character would be formed, his knowledge of life (which he already thought considerable) would be complete; and then no one could keep them apart. He smiled in advance to think how little his father's shouting and booming would impress a man on his return from the Grand Tour. . .

The gentlemen were telling anecdotes about their own early experience in Europe. None of them—not even Mr. Raycie—had travelled as extensively as it was intended that Lewis should; but the two Huzzards had been twice to England on banking matters, and Commodore Ledgely, a bold man, to France and Belgium as well—not to speak of his early experience in the Far East. All three had kept a vivid and amused recollection, slightly tinged with disapprobation, of what they had seen— "Oh, those French wenches," the Commodore chuckled through his white teeth—but poor Mr. Kent, who had gone abroad on his honeymoon, had been caught in Paris by the revolution of 1830, had had the fever in Florence, and had nearly been arrested as a spy in Vienna; and the only satisfactory episode in this disastrous, and never repeated, adventure, had been the fact of his having been mistaken for the Duke of Wellington (as he was trying to slip out of a Viennese hotel in his courier's blue surtout) by a crowd who had been— "Well, very gratifying in their enthusiasm," Mr. Kent admitted.

"How my poor brother Julius could have lived in Europe! Well, look at the consequences—" he used to say, as if poor Treeshy's plainness gave an awful point to his moral.

"There's one thing in Paris, my boy, that you must be warned against: those gambling-hells in the Pally Royle," Mr. Kent insisted. "I never set foot in the places myself; but a glance at the outside was enough."

"I knew a feller that was fleeced of a fortune there," Mr. Henry Huzzard confirmed; while the Commodore, at his tenth glass, chuckled with moist eyes: "The trollops, oh, the trollops—"

"As for Vienna—" said Mr. Kent.

"Even in London," said Mr. Ambrose Huzzard, "a young man must be on his look-out against gamblers. Every form of swindling is practised, and the touts are always on the look-out for greenhorns; a term," he added apologetically, "which they apply to any traveller new to the country."

"In Paris," said Mr. Kent, "I was once within an ace of being challenged to fight a duel." He fetched a sigh of horror and relief, and glanced reassuredly down the Sound in the direction of his own peaceful roof-tree.

"Oh, a duel," laughed the Commodore. "A man can fight duels here. I fought a dozen when I was a young feller in New Erleens." The Commodore's mother had been a southern lady, and after his father's death had spent some years with her parents in Louisiana, so that her son's varied experiences had begun early. "'Bout women," he smiled confidentially, holding out his empty glass to Mr. Raycie.

"The ladies—!" exclaimed Mr. Kent in a voice of warning.

The gentlemen rose to their feet, the Commodore quite as prompt and steadily as the others. The drawing-room window opened, and from it emerged Mrs. Raycie, in a ruffled sarsenet dress and Point de Paris cap, followed by her two daughters in starched organdy with pink spencers. Mr. Raycie looked with proud approval at his women-kind.

"Gentlemen," said Mrs. Raycie, in a perfectly even voice, "supper is on the table, and if you will do Mr. Raycie and myself the favour—"

"The favour, ma'am," said Mr. Ambrose Huzzard, "is on your side, in so amiably inviting us."

Mrs. Raycie curtsied, the gentlemen bowed, and Mr. Raycie said: "Your arm to Mrs. Raycie, Huzzard. This little farewell party is a family affair, and the other gentlemen must content themselves with my two daughters. Sarah Anne, Mary Adeline—"

The Commodore and Mr. John Huzzard advanced ceremoniously toward the two girls, and Mr. Kent, being a cousin, closed the procession between Mr. Raycie and Lewis.

Oh, that supper-table! The vision of it used sometimes to rise before Lewis Raycie's eyes in outlandish foreign places; for though not a large or fastidious eater when he was at home, he was afterward, in lands of chestnut-flour and garlic and queer bearded sea-things, to suffer many pangs of hunger at the thought of that opulent board. In the centre stood the Raycie *épergne* of pierced silver, holding aloft a bunch of June roses surrounded by dangling baskets of sugared almonds and striped peppermints; and grouped about this decorative "motif" were Lowestoft platters heavy with piles of raspberries, strawberries and the first Delaware peaches. An outer flanking of heaped-up cookies, crullers, strawberry short-cake, piping hot corn-bread and deep golden butter in moist blocks still bedewed from the muslin swathings of the dairy, led the eye to the Virginia ham in front of Mr. Raycie, and the twin dishes of scrambled eggs on toast and broiled blue-fish over which his wife presided. Lewis could never afterward fit into this intricate pattern the "side-dishes" of devilled turkeylegs and creamed chicken hash, the sliced cucumbers and tomatoes, the heavy silver jugs of butter-coloured cream, the floating-island, "slips" and lemon jellies that were somehow interwoven with the solider elements of the design; but they were all there, either together or successively, and so were the towering piles of waffles reeling on their foundations, and the slender silver jugs of maple syrup perpetually escorting them about the table as black Dinah replenished the supply.

They ate—oh, how they all ate!—though the ladies were supposed only to nibble; but the good things on Lewis's plate remained untouched until, ever and again, an admonishing glance from Mr. Raycie, or an entreating one from Mary Adeline, made him insert a languid fork into the heap.

And all the while Mr. Raycie continued to hold forth.

"A young man, in my opinion, before setting up for himself, must see the world; form his taste; fortify his judgment. He must study the most famous monuments, examine the organization of foreign societies, and the habits and customs of those older civilizations whose yoke it has been our glory to cast off. Though he may see in them much to deplore and to reprove—" ("Some of the gals, though," Commodore Ledgely was heard to interject)—"much that will make him give thanks for the privilege of having been born and brought up under our own Free Institutions, yet I believe he will also"—Mr. Raycie conceded it with magnanimity—"be able to learn much."

"The Sundays, though," Mr. Kent hazarded warningly; and Mrs. Raycie breathed across to her son: "Ah, that's what *I* say!"

Mr. Raycie did not like interruption; and he met it by growing visibly larger. His huge bulk hung a moment, like an avalanche, above the silence which followed Mr. Kent's interjection and Mrs. Raycie's murmur; then he crashed down on both.

"The Sundays—the Sundays? Well, what of the Sundays? What is there to frighten a good Episcopalian in what we call the Continental Sunday? I presume that we're all Churchmen here, eh? No puling Methodists or atheistical Unitarians at my table tonight, that I'm aware of. Nor will I offend the ladies of my household by assuming that they have secretly lent an ear to the Baptist ranter in the chapel at the foot of our lane. No? I thought not! Well, then, I say, what's all this flutter about the Papists? Far be it from me to approve of their heathenish doctrines—but, damn it, they go to church, don't they? And they have a real service as we do, don't they? And real clergy and not a lot of nondescripts dressed like laymen, and damned badly at that, who chat familiarly with the Almighty in their own vulgar lingo? No, sir"—he swung about on the shrinking Mr. Kent—"it's not the Church I'm afraid of in foreign countries, it's the sewers, sir!"

Mrs. Raycie had grown very pale: Lewis knew that she too was deeply perturbed about the sewers. "And the night-air," she scarce-audibly sighed.

But Mr. Raycie had taken up his main theme again. "In my opinion, if a young man travels at all, he must travel as extensively as his —er—means permit; must see as much of the world as he can. Those are my son's sailing orders, Commodore; and here's to his carrying them out to the best of his powers!"

Black Dinah, removing the Virginia ham, or rather such of its bony structure as alone remained on the dish, had managed to make room for a bowl of punch from which Mr. Raycie poured deep ladlefuls of perfumed fire into the glasses ranged before him on a silver tray. The gentlemen rose, the ladies smiled and wept, and Lewis's health and the success of the Grand Tour were toasted with an eloquence which caused Mrs. Raycie, with a hasty nod to her daughters, and a covering rustle of starched flounces, to shepherd them softly from the room.

"After all," Lewis heard her murmur to them on the threshold, "your father's using such language shows that he's in the best of humour with dear Lewis."

2

In spite of his enforced potations, Lewis Raycie was up the next morning before sunrise.

Unlatching his shutters without noise, he looked forth over the wet lawn merged in a blur of shrubberies, and the waters of the Sound dimly seen beneath a sky full of stars. His head ached but his heart glowed; what was before him was thrilling enough to clear a heavier brain than his.

He dressed quickly and completely (save for his shoes), and then, stripping the flowered quilt from his high mahogany bed, rolled it in a tight bundle under his arm. Thus enigmatically equipped he was feeling his way, shoes in hand, through the darkness of the upper story to the slippery oak stairs, when he was startled by a candle-gleam in the pitch-blackness of the hall below. He held his breath, and leaning over the stair-rail saw with amazement his sister Mary Adeline come forth, cloaked and bonneted, but also in stocking-feet, from the passage leading to the pantry. She too carried a double burden: her shoes and the candle in one hand, in the other a large covered basket that weighed down her bare arm.

Brother and sister stopped and stared at each other in the blue dusk: the upward slant of the candle-light distorted Mary Adeline's mild features, twisting them into a frightened grin as Lewis stole down to join her.

"Oh—" she whispered. "What in the world are you doing here? I was just getting together a few things for that poor young Mrs. Poe down the lane, who's so ill—before mother goes to the storeroom. You won't tell, will you?"

Lewis signalled his complicity, and cautiously slid open the bolt of the front door. They durst not say more till they were out of earshot. On the doorstep they sat down to put on their shoes; then they hastened on without a word through the ghostly shrubberies till they reached the gate into the lane.

"But you, Lewis?" the sister suddenly questioned, with an astonished stare at the rolled-up quilt under her brother's arm.

"Oh, I—. Look here, Addy—" he broke off and began to grope in his pocket—"I haven't much about me . . . the old gentleman keeps me as close as ever . . . but here's a dollar, if you think that poor Mrs. Poe could use it. . . I'd be too happy . . . consider it a privilege. . ."

"Oh, Lewis, Lewis, how noble, how generous of you! Of course I can buy a few extra things with it . . . they never see meat unless I can bring them a bit, you know . . . and I fear she's dying of a decline . . . and she and her mother are so fiery-proud. . ." She wept with gratitude, and Lewis drew a breath of relief. He had diverted her attention from the bed-quilt.

"Ah, there's the breeze," he murmured, sniffing the suddenly chilled air.

"Yes; I must be off; I must be back before the sun is up," said Mary Adeline anxiously, "and it would never do if mother knew—"

"She doesn't know of your visits to Mrs. Poe?"

A look of childish guile sharpened Mary Adeline's undeveloped face. "She *does*, of course; but yet she doesn't . . . we've arranged it so. You see, Mr. Poe's an Atheist; and so father—"

"I see," Lewis nodded. "Well, we part here; I'm off for a swim," he said glibly. But abruptly he turned back and caught his sister's arm. "Sister, tell Mrs. Poe, please, that I heard her husband give a reading from his poems in New York two nights ago—"

("Oh, Lewis—*you?* But father says he's a blasphemer!")

"—And that he's a great poet—a Great Poet. Tell her that from me, will you, please, Mary Adeline?"

"Oh, brother, I couldn't . . . we never speak of him," the startled girl faltered, hurrying away.

In the cove where the Commodore's sloop had ridden a few hours earlier a biggish rowing-boat took the waking ripples. Young Raycie paddled out to her, fastened his skiff to the moorings, and hastily clambered into the boat.

From various recesses of his pockets he produced rope, string, a carpet-layer's needle, and other unexpected and incongruous tackle; then, lashing one of the oars across the top of the other, and jamming the latter upright between the forward thwart and the bow, he rigged the flowered bed-quilt on this mast, knotted a rope to the free end of the quilt, and sat down in the stern, one hand on the rudder, the other on his improvised sheet.

Venus, brooding silverly above a line of pale green sky, made a pool of glory in the sea as the dawn-breeze plumped the lover's sail. . .

On the shelving pebbles of another cove, two or three miles down the Sound, Lewis Raycie lowered his queer sail and beached his boat. A clump of willows on the shingle-edge mysteriously stirred and parted, and Treeshy Kent was in his arms.

The sun was just pushing above a belt of low clouds in the east, spattering them with liquid gold, and Venus blanched as the light spread upward. But under the willows it was still dusk, a watery green dusk in which the secret murmurs of the night were caught.

"Treeshy—Treeshy!" the young man cried, kneeling beside her— and then, a moment later: "My angel, are you sure that no one guesses—?"

The girl gave a faint laugh which screwed up her funny nose. She leaned her head on his shoulder, her round forehead and rough braids pressed against his cheek, her hands in his, breathing quickly and joyfully.

"I thought I should never get here," Lewis grumbled, "with that ridiculous bed-quilt—and it'll be broad day soon! To think that I was of age yesterday, and must come to you in a boat rigged like a child's toy on a duck-pond! If you knew how it humiliates me—"

"What does it matter, dear, since you're of age now, and your own master?"

"But am I, though? He says so—but it's only on his own terms; only while I do what he wants! You'll see. . . I've a credit of ten thousand dollars . . . ten . . . thou . . . sand . . . d'you hear? . . . placed to my name in a London bank; and not a penny here to bless myself with meanwhile. . . Why, Treeshy darling, why, what's the matter?"

She flung her arms about his neck, and through their innocent kisses he could taste her tears. "What is it, Treeshy?" he implored her.

"I . . . oh, I'd forgotten it was to be our last day together till you spoke of London—cruel, cruel!" she reproached him; and through the green twilight of the willows her eyes blazed on him like two stormy stars. No other eyes he knew could express such elemental rage as Treeshy's.

"You little spitfire, you!" he laughed back somewhat chokingly. "Yes, it's our last day—but not for long; at our age two years are not so very long, after all, are they? And when I come back to you I'll come as my own master, independent, free—come to claim you in face of everything and everybody! Think of that, darling, and be brave for my sake . . . brave and patient . . . as I mean to be!" he declared heroically.

"Oh, but you—you'll see other girls; heaps and heaps of them; in those wicked old countries where they're so lovely. My uncle Kent says the European countries are all wicked, even my own poor Italy . . ."

"But *you*, Treeshy; you'll be seeing cousins Bill and Donald meanwhile—seeing them all day long and every day. And you know you've a weakness for that great hulk of a Bill. Ah, if only I stood six-foot-one in my stockings I'd go with an easier heart, you fickle child!" he tried to banter her.

"Fickle? Fickle? *Me*—oh, Lewis!"

He felt the premonitory sweep of sobs, and his untried courage failed him. It was delicious, in theory, to hold weeping beauty to one's breast, but terribly alarming, he found, in practice. There came a responsive twitching in his throat.

"No, no; firm as adamant, true as steel; that's what we both mean to be, isn't it, *cara?*"

"*Caro*, yes," she sighed appeased.

"And you'll write to me regularly, Treeshy—long, long letters? I may count on that, mayn't I, wherever I am? And they must all be numbered, every one of them, so that I shall know at once if I've missed one; remember!"

"And, Lewis, you'll wear them here?" (She touched his breast.) "Oh, not *all*," she added, laughing, "for they'd make such a big bundle that you'd soon have a hump in front like Pulcinella—but always at least the last one, just the last one. Promise!"

"Always, I promise—as long as they're kind," he said, still struggling to take a spirited line.

"Oh, Lewis, they will be, as long as yours are—and long, long afterward. . ."

Venus failed and vanished in the sun's uprising.

3

THE crucial moment, Lewis had always known, would be not that of his farewell to Treeshy, but of his final interview with his father.

On that everything hung: his immediate future as well as his more distant prospects. As he stole home in the early sunlight, over the dew-drenched grass, he glanced up apprehensively at Mr. Raycie's windows, and thanked his stars that they were still tightly shuttered.

There was no doubt, as Mrs. Raycie said, that her husband's "using language" before ladies showed him to be in high good humour, relaxed and slippered, as it were—a state his family so seldom saw him in that Lewis had sometimes impertinently wondered to what awful descent from the clouds he and his two sisters owed their timorous being.

It was all very well to tell himself, as he often did, that the bulk of the money was his mother's, and that he could turn her round his little finger. What difference did that make? Mr. Raycie, the day after his marriage, had quietly taken over the management of his wife's property, and deducted, from the very moderate allowance he accorded her, all her little personal expenses, even to the postage-stamps she used, and the dollar she put in the plate every Sunday. He called the allowance her "pin-money," since, as he often reminded her, he paid all the household bills himself, so that Mrs. Raycie's quarterly pittance could be entirely devoted, if she chose, to frills and feathers.

"And will be, if you respect my wishes, my dear," he always added. "I like to see a handsome figure well set-off, and not to have our friends imagine, when they come to dine, that Mrs. Raycie is sick above-stairs, and I've replaced her by a poor relation in *allapacca*." In compliance with which Mrs. Raycie, at once flattered and terrified, spent her last penny in adorning herself and her daughters, and had to stint their bedroom fires, and the servants' meals, in order to find a penny for any private necessity.

Mr. Raycie had long since convinced his wife that this method of dealing with her, if not lavish, was suitable, and in fact "handsome"; when she spoke of the subject to her relations it was with tears of gratitude for her husband's kindness in assuming the management of her property. As he managed it exceedingly well, her hard-headed brothers (glad to have the responsibility off their hands, and convinced that, if left to herself, she would have muddled her money away in ill-advised charities) were disposed to share her approval of Mr. Raycie; though her old mother sometimes said helplessly: "When I think that Lucy Ann can't as much as have a drop of gruel brought up to her without his weighing the oatmeal. . ." But even that was only whispered, lest Mr. Raycie's mysterious faculty of hearing what was said behind his back should bring sudden reprisals on the venerable lady to whom he always alluded, with a tremor in his genial voice, as "my dear mother-in-law—unless indeed she will allow me to call her, more briefly but more truly, my dear mother."

To Lewis, hitherto, Mr. Raycie had meted the same measure as to the females of the household. He had dressed him well, educated him expensively, lauded him to the skies—and counted every penny of his allowance. Yet there was a difference and Lewis was as well aware of it as any one.

The dream, the ambition, the passion of Mr. Raycie's life, was (as his son knew) to found a Family; and he had only Lewis to found it with. He believed in primogeniture, in heirlooms, in entailed estates, in all the ritual of the English "landed" tradition. No one was louder than he in praise of the democratic institutions under which he lived; but he never thought of them as affecting that more private but more important institution, the Family; and to the Family all his care and all his thoughts were given. The result, as Lewis dimly guessed, was, that upon his own shrinking and inadequate head was centred all the passion contained in the vast expanse of Mr. Raycie's breast. Lewis was his very own, and Lewis represented what was most dear to him; and for both these reasons Mr. Raycie set an inordinate value on the boy (a quite different thing, Lewis thought from loving him).

Mr. Raycie was particularly proud of his son's taste for letters. Himself not a wholly unread man, he admired intensely what he called the "cultivated gentleman"—and that was what Lewis was evidently going to be. Could he have combined with this tendency a manlier frame, and an interest in the few forms of sport then popular among gentlemen, Mr. Raycie's satisfaction would have been complete; but whose is, in this disappointing world? Meanwhile he flattered himself that, Lewis being still young and malleable, and his health certainly mending, two years of travel and adventure might send him back a very different figure, physically as well as mentally. Mr. Raycie had himself travelled in his youth, and was persuaded that the experience was formative; he secretly hoped for the return of a bronzed and broadened Lewis, seasoned by independence and adventure, and having discreetly sown his wild oats in foreign pastures, where they would not contaminate the home crop.

All this Lewis guessed; and he guessed as well that these two wander-years were intended by Mr. Raycie to lead up to a marriage and an establishment after Mr. Raycie's own heart, but in which Lewis's was not to have even a consulting voice.

"He's going to give me all the advantages—for his own purpose," the young man summed it up as he went down to join the family at the breakfast table.

Mr. Raycie was never more resplendent than at that moment of the day and season. His spotless white duck trousers, strapped under kid boots, his thin kerseymere coat, and drab *piqué* waistcoat crossed below a snowy stock, made him look as fresh as the morning and as appetizing as the peaches and cream banked before him.

Opposite sat Mrs. Raycie, immaculate also, but paler than usual, as became a mother about to part from her only son; and between the two was Sarah Anne, unusually pink, and apparently occupied in trying to screen her sister's empty seat. Lewis greeted them, and seated himself at his mother's right.

Mr. Raycie drew out his *guillochée* repeating watch, and detaching it from its heavy gold chain laid it on the table beside him.

"Mary Adeline is late again. It is a somewhat unusual thing for a sister to be late at the last meal she is to take—for two years—with her only brother."

"Oh, Mr. Raycie!" Mrs. Raycie faltered.

"I say, the idea is peculiar. Perhaps," said Mr. Raycie sarcastically, "I am going to be blessed with a *peculiar* daughter."

"I'm afraid Mary Adeline is beginning a sick headache, sir. She tried to get up, but really could not," said Sarah Anne in a rush.

Mr. Raycie's only reply was to arch ironic eyebrows, and Lewis hastily intervened: "I'm sorry, sir; but it may be my fault—"

Mrs. Raycie paled, Sarah Anne purpled, and Mr. Raycie echoed with punctilious incredulity: "Your—fault?"

"In being the occasion, sir, of last night's too-sumptuous festivity—"

"Ha—ha—ha!" Mr. Raycie laughed, his thunders instantly dispelled.

He pushed back his chair and nodded to his son with a smile; and the two, leaving the ladies to wash up the teacups (as was still the habit in genteel families) betook themselves to Mr. Raycie's study.

What Mr. Raycie studied in this apartment—except the accounts, and ways of making himself unpleasant to his family—Lewis had never been able to discover. It was a small bare formidable room; and the young man, who never crossed the threshold but with a sinking of his heart, felt it sink lower than ever. "Now!" he thought.

Mr. Raycie took the only easy-chair, and began.

"My dear fellow, our time is short, but long enough for what I have to say. In a few hours you will be setting out on your great journey: an important event in the life of any young man. Your talents and character—combined with your means of improving the opportunity—make me hope that in your case it will be decisive. I expect you to come home from this trip a man—"

So far, it was all to order, so to speak; Lewis could have recited it beforehand. He bent his head in acquiescence.

"A man," Mr. Raycie repeated, "prepared to play a part, a considerable part, in the social life of the community. I expect you to be a figure in New York; and I shall give you the means to be so." He cleared his throat. "But means are not enough—though you must never forget that they are essential. Education, polish, experience of the world; these are what so many of our men of standing lack. What do they know of Art or Letters? We have had little time here to produce either as yet—you spoke?" Mr. Raycie broke off with a crushing courtesy.

"I—oh, no," his son stammered.

"Ah; I thought you might be about to allude to certain blasphemous penny-a-liners whose poetic ravings are said to have given them a kind of pothouse notoriety."

Lewis reddened at the allusion but was silent, and his father went on:

"Where is our Byron—our Scott—our Shakespeare? And in painting it is the same. Where are our Old Masters? We are not without contemporary talent; but for works of genius we must still look to the past; we must, in most cases, content ourselves with copies. . . Ah, here, I know, my dear boy, I touch a responsive chord! Your love of the arts has not passed unperceived; and I mean, I desire, to do all I can to encourage it. Your future position in the world—your duties and obligations as a gentleman and a man of fortune—will not permit you to become, yourself, an eminent painter or a famous sculptor; but I shall raise no objection to your dabbling in these arts as an amateur—at least while you are travelling abroad. It will form your taste, strengthen your judgment, and give you, I hope, the discernment necessary to select for me a few masterpieces which shall *not* be copies. Copies," Mr. Raycie pursued with a deepening emphasis, "are for the less discriminating, or for those less blessed with this world's goods. Yes, my dear Lewis, I wish to create a gallery: a gallery of Heirlooms. Your mother participates in this ambition—she desires to see on our walls a few original specimens of the Italian genius. Raphael, I fear, we can hardly aspire to; but a Domenichino, an Albano, a Carlo Dolci, a Guercino, a Carlo Maratta—one or two of Salvator Rosa's noble landscapes . . . you see my idea? There shall be a Raycie Gallery; and it shall be your mission to get together its nucleus." Mr. Raycie paused, and mopped his flowing forehead. "I believe I could have given my son no task more to his liking."

"Oh, no, sir, none indeed!" Lewis cried, flushing and paling. He had in fact never suspected this part of his father's plan, and his heart swelled with the honour of so unforeseen a mission. Nothing, in truth, could have made him prouder or happier. For a moment he forgot love, forgot Treeshy, forgot everything but the rapture of moving among the masterpieces of which he had so long dreamed, moving not as a mere hungry spectator, but as one whose privilege it should at least be to single out and carry away some of the lesser treasures. He could hardly take in what had happened, and the shock of the announcement left him, as usual, inarticulate.

He heard his father booming on, developing the plan, explaining with his usual pompous precision that one of the partners of the London bank in which Lewis's funds were deposited was himself a noted collector, and had agreed to provide the young traveller with letters of introduction to other connoisseurs, both in France and Italy, so that Lewis's acquisitions might be made under the most enlightened guidance.

"It is," Mr. Raycie concluded, "in order to put you on a footing of equality with the best collectors that I have placed such a large sum at your disposal. I reckon that for ten thousand dollars you can travel for two years in the very best style; and I mean to place another five thousand to your credit"—he paused, and let the syllables drop slowly into his son's brain: "five thousand dollars for the purchase of works of art, which eventually—remember—will be yours; and will be handed on, I trust, to your sons' sons as long as the name of Raycie survives"—a length of time, Mr. Raycie's tone seemed to imply, hardly to be measured in periods less extensive than those of the Egyptian dynasties.

Lewis heard him with a whirling brain. *Five thousand dollars!* The sum seemed so enormous, even in dollars, and so incalculably larger when translated into any continental currency, that he wondered why his father, in advance, had given up all hope of a Raphael. . . "If I travel economically," he said to himself, "and deny myself unnecessary luxuries, I may yet be able to surprise him by bringing one back. And my mother—how magnanimous, how splendid! Now I see why she has consented to all the little economies that sometimes seemed so paltry and so humiliating. . ."

The young man's eyes filled with tears, but he was still silent, though he longed as never before to express his gratitude and admiration to his father. He had entered the study expecting a parting sermon on the subject of thrift, coupled with the prospective announcement of a "suitable establishment" (he could even guess the particular Huzzard girl his father had in view); and instead he had been told to spend his princely allowance in a princely manner, and to return home with a gallery of masterpieces. "At least," he murmured to himself, "it shall contain a Correggio."

"Well, sir?" Mr. Raycie boomed.

"Oh, sir—" his son cried, and flung himself on the vast slope of the parental waistcoat.

Amid all these accumulated joys there murmured deep down in him the thought that nothing had been said or done to interfere with his secret plans about Treeshy. It seemed almost as if his father had tacitly accepted the idea of their unmentioned engagement; and Lewis felt half guilty at not confessing to it then and there. But the gods are formidable even when they unbend; never more so, perhaps, than at such moments. . .

PART TWO

4

Lewis Raycie stood on a projecting rock and surveyed the sublime spectacle of Mont Blanc.

It was a brilliant August day, and the air, at that height, was already so sharp that he had had to put on his fur-lined pelisse. Behind him, at a respectful distance, was the travelling servant who, at a signal, had brought it up to him; below, in the bend of the mountain road, stood the light and elegant carriage which had carried him thus far on his travels.

Scarcely more than a year had passed since he had waved a farewell to New York from the deck of the packet-ship headed down the bay; yet, to the young man confidently facing Mont Blanc, nothing seemed left in him of that fluid and insubstantial being, the former Lewis Raycie, save a lurking and abeyant fear of Mr. Raycie senior. Even that, however, was so attenuated by distance and time, so far sunk below the horizon, and anchored on the far side of the globe, that it stirred in its sleep only when a handsomely folded and wafered letter in his parent's writing was handed out across the desk of some continental counting-house. Mr. Raycie senior did not write often, and when he did it was in a bland and stilted strain. He felt at a disadvantage on paper, and his natural sarcasm was swamped in the rolling periods which it cost him hours of labour to bring forth; so that the dreaded quality lurked for his son only in the curve of certain letters, and in a positively awful way of writing out, at full length, the word *Esquire*.

It was not that Lewis had broken with all the memories of his past of a year ago. Many still lingered in him, or rather had been transferred to the new man he had become—as for instance his tenderness for Treeshy Kent, which, somewhat to his surprise, had obstinately resisted all the assaults of English keep-sake beauties and almond-eyed houris of the East. It startled him, at times to find Treeshy's short dusky face, with its round forehead, the widely spaced eyes and the high cheek-bones, starting out at him suddenly in the street of some legendary town, or in a landscape of languid beauty, just as he had now and again been arrested in an exotic garden by the very scent of the verbena under the verandah at home. His travels had confirmed rather than weakened the family view of Treeshy's plainness; she could not be made to fit into any of the patterns of female beauty so far submitted to him; yet there she was, ensconced in his new heart and mind as deeply as in the old, though her kisses seemed less vivid, and the peculiar rough notes of her voice hardly reached him. Sometimes, half irritably, he said to himself that with an effort he could disperse her once for all; yet she lived on in him, unseen yet ineffaceable, like the image on a daguerreotype plate, no less there because so often invisible.

To the new Lewis, however, the whole business was less important than he had once thought it. His suddenly acquired maturity made Treeshy seem a petted child rather than the guide, the Beatrice, he had once considered her; and he promised himself, with an elderly smile, that as soon as he got to Italy he would write her the long letter for which he was now considerably in her debt.

His travels had first carried him to England. There he spent some weeks in collecting letters and recommendations for his tour, in purchasing his travelling-carriage and its numerous appurtenances, and in driving in it from cathedral town to storied castle, omitting nothing, from Abbotsford to Kenilworth, which deserved the attention of a cultivated mind. From England he crossed to Calais, moving slowly southward to the Mediterranean; and there, taking ship for the Piræus, he plunged into pure romance, and the tourist became a Giaour.

It was the East which had made him into a new Lewis Raycie; the East, so squalid and splendid, so pestilent and so poetic, so full of knavery and romance and fleas and nightingales, and so different, alike in its glories and its dirt, from what his studious youth had dreamed. After Smyrna and the bazaars, after Damascus and Palmyra, the Acropolis, Mytilene and Sunium, what could be left in his mind of Canal Street and the lawn above the Sound? Even the mosquitoes, which seemed at first the only connecting link, were different, because he fought with them in scenes so different; and a young gentleman who had journeyed across the desert in Arabian dress, slept under goats'-hair tents, been attacked by robbers in the Peloponnesus and despoiled by his own escort at Baalbek, and by customs' officials everywhere, could not but look with a smile on the terrors that walk New York and the Hudson river. Encased in security and monotony, that other Lewis Raycie, when his little figure bobbed up to the surface, seemed like a new-born babe preserved in alcohol. Even Mr. Raycie senior's thunders were now no more than the far-off murmur of summer lightning on a perfect evening. Had Mr. Raycie ever really frightened Lewis? Why, now he was not even frightened by Mont Blanc!

He was still gazing with a sense of easy equality at its awful pinnacles when another travelling-carriage paused near his own, and a young man, eagerly jumping from it, and also followed by a servant with a cloak, began to mount the slope. Lewis at once recognized the carriage, and the light springing figure of the young man, his blue coat and swelling stock, and the scar slightly distorting his handsome and eloquent mouth. It was the Englishman who had arrived at the Montanvert inn the night before with a valet, a guide, and such a cargo of books, maps and sketching-materials as threatened to overshadow even Lewis's outfit.

Lewis, at first, had not been greatly drawn to the newcomer, who, seated aloof in the dining-room, seemed not to see his fellow-traveller. The truth was that Lewis was dying for a little conversation. His astonishing experiences were so tightly packed in him (with no outlet save the meagre trickle of his nightly diary) that he felt they would soon melt into the vague blur of other people's travels unless he could give them fresh reality by talking them over. And the stranger with the deep-blue eyes that matched his coat, the scarred cheek and eloquent lip, seemed to Lewis a worthy listener. The Englishman appeared to think otherwise. He preserved an air of moody abstraction, which Lewis's vanity imagined him to have put on as the gods becloud themselves for their secret errands; and the curtness of his goodnight was (Lewis flattered himself) surpassed only by the young New Yorker's.

But today all was different. The stranger advanced affably, raised his hat from his tossed statue-like hair, and enquired with a smile: "Are you by any chance interested in the forms of cirrous clouds?"

His voice was as sweet as his smile, and the two were reinforced by a glance so winning that it made the odd question seem not only pertinent but natural. Lewis, though surprised, was not disconcerted. He merely coloured with the unwonted sense of his ignorance, and replied ingenuously: "I believe, sir, I am interested in everything."

"A noble answer!" cried the other, and held out his hand.

"But I must add," Lewis continued with courageous honesty, "that I have never as yet had occasion to occupy myself particularly with the forms of cirrous clouds."

His companion looked at him merrily. "That," said he, "is no reason why you shouldn't begin to do so now!" To which Lewis as merrily agreed. "For in order to be interested in things," the other continued more gravely, "it is only necessary to see them; and I believe I am not wrong in saying that you are one of the privileged beings to whom the seeing eye has been given."

Lewis blushed his agreement, and his interlocutor continued: "You are one of those who have been on the road to Damascus."

"On the road? I've been to the place itself!" the wanderer exclaimed, bursting with the particulars of his travels; and then blushed more deeply at the perception that the other's use of the name had of course been figurative.

The young Englishman's face lit up. "You've been to Damascus— literally been there yourself? But that may be almost as interesting, in its quite different way, as the formation of clouds or lichens. For the present," he continued with a gesture toward the mountain, "I must devote myself to the extremely inadequate rendering of some of these delicate *aiguilles*; a bit of drudgery not likely to interest you in the face of so sublime a scene. But perhaps this evening—if, as I think, we are staying in the same inn—you will give me a few minutes of your society, and tell me something of your travels. My father," he added with his engaging smile, "has had packed with my paint-brushes a few bottles of a wholly trustworthy Madeira; and if you will favour me with your company at dinner. . ."

He signed to his servant to undo the sketching materials, spread his cloak on the rock, and was already lost in his task as Lewis descended to the carriage.

The Madeira proved as trustworthy as his host had promised. Perhaps it was its exceptional quality which threw such a golden lustre over the dinner; unless it were rather the conversation of the blue-eyed Englishman which made Lewis Raycie, always a small drinker, feel that in his company every drop was nectar.

When Lewis joined his host it had been with the secret hope of at last being able to talk; but when the evening was over (and they kept it up to the small hours) he perceived that he had chiefly listened. Yet there had been no sense of suppression, of thwarted volubility; he had been given all the openings he wanted. Only, whenever he produced a little fact it was instantly overflowed by the other's imagination till it burned like a dull pebble tossed into a rushing stream. For whatever Lewis said was seen by his companion from a new angle, and suggested a new train of thought; each commonplace item of experience became a many-faceted crystal flashing with unexpected fires. The young Englishman's mind moved in a world of associations and references far more richly peopled than Lewis's; but his eager communicativeness, his directness of speech and manner, instantly opened its gates to the simpler youth. It was certainly not the Madeira which sped the hours and flooded them with magic; but the magic gave the Madeira—excellent, and reputed of its kind, as Lewis afterward learned—a taste no other vintage was to have for him.

"Oh, but we must meet again in Italy—there are many things there that I could perhaps help you to see," the young Englishman declared as they swore eternal friendship on the stairs of the sleeping inn.

5

It was in a tiny Venetian church, no more than a chapel, that Lewis Raycie's eyes had been unsealed—in a dull-looking little church not even mentioned in the guidebooks. But for his chance encounter with the young Englishman in the shadow of Mont Blanc, Lewis would never have heard of the place; but then what else that was worth knowing would he ever have heard of, he wondered?

He had stood a long time looking at the frescoes, put off at first— he could admit it now—by a certain stiffness in the attitudes of the people, by the childish elaboration of their dress (so different from the noble draperies which Sir Joshua's Discourses on Art had taught him to admire in the great painters), and by the innocent inexpressive look in their young faces—for even the gray-beards seemed young. And then suddenly his gaze had lit on one of these faces in particular: that of a girl with round cheeks, high cheek-bones and widely set eyes under an intricate headdress of pearl-woven braids. Why, it was Treeshy—Treeshy Kent to the life! And so far from being thought "plain," the young lady was no other than the peerless princess about whom the tale revolved. And what a fairyland she lived in—full of lithe youths and round-faced pouting maidens, rosy old men and burnished blackamoors, pretty birds and cats and nibbling rabbits—and all involved and enclosed in golden balustrades, in colonnades of pink and blue, laurel-garlands festooned from ivory balconies, and domes and minarets against summer seas! Lewis's imagination lost itself in the scene; he forgot to regret the noble draperies, the exalted sentiments, the fuliginous backgrounds, of the artists he had come to Italy to admire—forgot Sassoferrato, Guido Reni, Carlo Dolce, Lo Spagnoletto, the Carracci, and even the Transfiguration of Raphael, though he knew it to be the greatest picture in the world.

After that he had seen almost everything else that Italian art had to offer; had been to Florence, Naples, Rome; to Bologna to study the Eclectic School, to Parma to examine the Correggios and the Giulio Romanos. But that first vision had laid a magic seed between his lips; the seed that makes you hear what the birds say and the grasses whisper. Even if his English friend had not continued at his side, pointing out, explaining, inspiring, Lewis Raycie flattered himself that the round face of the little Saint Ursula would have led him safely and confidently past all her rivals. She had become his touchstone, his star: how insipid seemed to him all the sheep-faced Virgins draped in red and blue paint after he had looked into her wondering girlish eyes and traced the elaborate pattern of her brocades! He could remember now, quite distinctly, the day when he had given up even Beatrice Cenci . . . and as for that fat naked Magdalen of Carlo Dolce's lolling over the book she was not reading, and ogling the spectator in the good old way . . . faugh! Saint Ursula did not need to rescue him from *her*. . .

His eyes had been opened to a new world of art. And this world it was his mission to reveal to others—he, the insignificant and ignorant Lewis Raycie, as "but for the grace of God," and that chance encounter on Mont Blanc, he might have gone on being to the end! He shuddered to think of the army of Neapolitan beggar-boys, bituminous monks, whirling prophets, languishing Madonnas and pink-rumped *amorini* who might have been travelling home with him in the hold of the fast new steam-packet.

His excitement had something of the apostle's ecstasy. He was not only, in a few hours, to embrace Treeshy, and be reunited to his honoured parents; he was also to go forth and preach the new gospel to them that sat in the darkness of Salvator Rosa and Lo Spagnoletto . . .

The first thing that struck Lewis was the smallness of the house on the Sound, and the largeness of Mr. Raycie.

He had expected to receive the opposite impression. In his recollection the varnished Tuscan villa had retained something of its impressiveness, even when compared to its supposed originals. Perhaps the very contrast between their draughty distances and naked floors, and the expensive carpets and bright fires of High Point, magnified his memory of the latter—there were moments when the thought of

its groaning board certainly added to the effect. But the image of
Mr. Raycie had meanwhile dwindled. Everything about him, as his
son looked back, seemed narrow, juvenile, almost childish. His bluster about Edgar Poe, for instance—true poet still to Lewis, though he
had since heard richer notes; his fussy tyranny of his womenkind; his
unconscious but total ignorance of most of the things, books, people,
ideas, that now filled his son's mind; above all, the arrogance and in-
competence of his artistic judgments. Beyond a narrow range of reading—mostly, Lewis suspected, culled in drowsy after-dinner snatches
from Knight's "Half-hours with the Best Authors"—Mr. Raycie
made no pretence to book-learning; left *that*, as he handsomely
said, "to the professors." But on matters of art he was dogmatic and
explicit, prepared to justify his opinions by the citing of eminent au-
thorities and of market-prices, and quite clear, as his farewell talk
with his son had shown, as to which Old Masters should be privileged to figure in the Raycie collection.

The young man felt no impatience of these judgments. America
was a long way from Europe, and it was many years since Mr. Raycie
had travelled. He could hardly be blamed for not knowing that the
things he admired were no longer admirable, still less for not knowing why. The pictures before which Lewis had knelt in spirit had
been virtually undiscovered, even by art-students and critics, in his
father's youth. How was an American gentleman, filled with his own
self-importance, and paying his courier the highest salary to show
him the accredited "Masterpieces"—how was he to guess that whenever he stood rapt before a Sassoferrato or a Carlo Dolce one of
those unknown treasures lurked near by under dust and cobwebs?

No; Lewis felt only tolerance and understanding. Such a view was
not one to magnify the paternal image; but when the young man entered the study where Mr. Raycie sat immobilized by gout, the
swathed leg stretched along his sofa seemed only another reason for
indulgence . . .

Perhaps, Lewis thought afterward, it was his father's prone position, the way his great bulk billowed over the sofa, and the lame leg
reached out like a mountain-ridge, that made him suddenly seem to
fill the room; or else the sound of his voice booming irritably across
the threshold, and scattering Mrs. Raycie and the girls with a fierce:
"And now, ladies, if the hugging and kissing are over, I should be

glad of a moment with my son." But it was odd that, after mother and daughters had withdrawn with all their hoops and flounces, the study seemed to grow even smaller, and Lewis himself to feel more like a David without the pebble.

"Well, my boy," his father cried, crimson and puffing, "here you are at home again, with many adventures to relate, no doubt; and a few masterpieces to show me, as I gather from the drafts on my exchequer."

"Oh, as to the masterpieces, sir, certainly," Lewis simpered, wondering why his voice sounded so fluty, and his smile was produced with such a conscious muscular effort.

"Good—good," Mr. Raycie approved, waving a violet hand which seemed to be ripening for a bandage. "Reedy carried out my orders, I presume? Saw to it that the paintings were deposited with the bulk of your luggage in Canal Street?"

"Oh, yes, sir; Mr. Reedy was on the dock with precise instructions. You know he always carries out your orders," Lewis ventured with a faint irony.

Mr. Raycie stared. "Mr. Reedy," he said, "does what I tell him, if that's what you mean; otherwise he would hardly have been in my employ for over thirty years."

Lewis was silent, and his father examined him critically. "You appear to have filled out: your health is satisfactory? Well . . . well . . . Mr. Robert Huzzard and his daughters are dining here this evening, by the way, and will no doubt be expecting to see the latest French novelties in stocks and waistcoats. Malvina has become a very elegant figure, your sisters tell me." Mr. Raycie chuckled, and Lewis thought: "I *knew* it was the oldest Huzzard girl!" while a slight chill ran down his spine.

"As to the pictures," Mr. Raycie pursued with growing animation, "I am laid low, as you see, by this cursèd affliction, and till the doctors get me up again, here must I lie and try to imagine how your treasures will look in the new gallery. And meanwhile, my dear boy, I need hardly say that no one is to be admitted to see them till they have been inspected by me and suitably hung. Reedy shall begin unpacking at once; and when we move to town next month Mrs. Raycie, God willing, shall give the handsomest evening party New York has yet seen, to show my son's collection, and perhaps . . . eh, well? . . . to celebrate another interesting event in his history."

Lewis met this with a faint but respectful gurgle, and before his blurred eyes rose the wistful face of Treeshy Kent.

"Ah, well, I shall see her tomorrow," he thought, taking heart again as soon as he was out of his father's presence.

6

Mr. Raycie stood silent for a long time after making the round of the room in the Canal Street house where the unpacked pictures had been set out.

He had driven to town alone with Lewis, sternly rebuffing his daughters' timid hints, and Mrs. Raycie's mute but visible yearning to accompany him. Though the gout was over he was still weak and irritable, and Mrs. Raycie, fluttered at the thought of "crossing him," had swept the girls away at his first frown.

Lewis's hopes rose as he followed his parent's limping progress. The pictures, though standing on chairs and tables, and set clumsily askew to catch the light, bloomed out of the half-dusk of the empty house with a new and persuasive beauty. Ah, how right he had been —how inevitable that his father should own it!

Mr. Raycie halted in the middle of the room. He was still silent, and his face, so quick to frown and glare, wore the calm, almost expressionless look known to Lewis as the mask of inward perplexity. "Oh, of course it will take a little time," the son thought, tingling with the eagerness of youth.

At last, Mr. Raycie woke the echoes by clearing his throat; but the voice which issued from it was as inexpressive as his face. "It is singular," he said, "how little the best copies of the Old Masters resemble the originals. For these *are* Originals?" he questioned, suddenly swinging about on Lewis.

"Oh, absolutely, sir! Besides—" The young man was about to add: "No one would ever have taken the trouble to copy them"—but hastily checked himself.

"Besides—?"

"I meant, I had the most competent advice obtainable."

"So I assume; since it was the express condition on which I authorized your purchases."

Lewis felt himself shrinking and his father expanding; but he sent a glance along the wall, and beauty shed her reviving beam on him.

Mr. Raycie's brows projected ominously; but his face remained smooth and dubious. Once more he cast a slow glance about him.

"Let us," he said pleasantly, "begin with the Raphael." And it was evident that he did not know which way to turn.

"Oh, sir, a Raphael nowadays—I warned you it would be far beyond my budget."

Mr. Raycie's face fell slightly. "I had hoped nevertheless . . . for an inferior specimen. . ." Then, with an effort: "The Sassoferrato, then."

Lewis felt more at his ease; he even ventured a respectful smile. "Sassoferrato is *all* inferior, isn't he? The fact is, he no longer stands . . . quite as he used to. . ."

Mr. Raycie stood motionless: his eyes were vacuously fired on the nearest picture.

"Sassoferrato . . . no longer . . . ?"

"Well, sir, *no*; not for a collection of this quality."

Lewis saw that he had at last struck the right note. Something large and uncomfortable appeared to struggle in Mr. Raycie's throat; then he gave a cough which might almost have been said to cast out Sassoferrato.

There was another pause before he pointed with his stick to a small picture representing a snub-nosed young woman with a high forehead and jewelled coif, against a background of delicately interwoven columbines. "Is *that*," he questioned, "your Carlo Dolce? The style is much the same, I see; but it seems to me lacking in his peculiar sentiment."

"Oh, but it's not a Carlo Dolce: it's a Piero della Francesca, sir!" burst in triumph from the trembling Lewis.

His father sternly faced him. "It's a *copy*, you mean? I thought so!"

"No, no; not a copy; it's by a great painter . . . a much greater . . ."

Mr. Raycie had reddened sharply at his mistake. To conceal his natural annoyance he assumed a still more silken manner. "In that case," he said, "I think I should like to see the inferior painters first. Where *is* the Carlo Dolce?"

"There *is* no Carlo Dolce," said Lewis, white to the lips.

The young man's next distinct recollection was of standing, he knew not how long afterward, before the armchair in which his father had sunk down, almost as white and shaken as himself.

"This," stammered Mr. Raycie, "this is going to bring back my gout. . ." But when Lewis entreated: "Oh, sir, do let us drive back quietly to the country, and give me a chance later to explain . . . to put my case" . . . the old gentleman had struck through the pleading with a furious wave of his stick.

"Explain later? Put your case later? It's just what I insist upon doing here and now!" And Mr. Raycie added hoarsely, and as if in actual physical anguish: "I understand that young John Huzzard returned from Rome last week with a Raphael."

After that, Lewis heard himself—as if with the icy detachment of a spectator—marshalling his arguments, pleading the cause he hoped his pictures would have pleaded for him, dethroning the old Powers and Principalities, and setting up these new names in their place. It was first of all the names that stuck in Mr. Raycie's throat: after spending a life-time in committing to memory the correct pronunciation of words like Lo Spagnoletto and Giulio Romano, it was bad enough, his wrathful eyes seemed to say, to have to begin a new set of verbal gymnastics before you could be sure of saying to a friend with careless accuracy: "And *this* is my Giotto da Bondone."

But that was only the first shock, soon forgotten in the rush of greater tribulation. For one might conceivably learn how to pronounce Giotto da Bondone, and even enjoy doing so, provided the friend in question recognized the name and bowed to its authority. But to have your effort received by a blank stare, and the playful request: "You'll have to say that over again, please"—to know that, in going the round of the gallery (the Raycie Gallery!) the same stare and the same request were likely to be repeated before each picture; the bitterness of this was so great that Mr. Raycie, without exaggeration, might have likened his case to that of Agag.

"God! God! God! Carpatcher, you say this other fellow's called? Kept him back till the last because it's the gem of the collection, did you? Carpatcher—well he'd have done better to stick to his trade. Something to do with those new European steam-cars, I suppose eh?" Mr. Raycie was so incensed that his irony was less subtle than usual. "And Angelico you say did that kind of Noah's Ark soldier in pink armour on gold-leaf? Well *there* I've caught you tripping, my boy. Not Angelico, Angelic*a*; Angelica Kauffman was a lady. And the damned swindler who foisted that barbarous daub on you as a picture of hers deserves to be drawn and quartered—and shall be, sir, by God, if the law can reach him! He shall disgorge every penny he's rooked you out of, or my name's not Halston Raycie! A bargain . . . you say the thing was a *bargain?* Why, the price of a clean postage stamp would be too dear for it! God—my son; do you realize you had a *trust* to carry out?"

"Yes, sir, yes; and it's just because—"

"You might have written; you might at least have placed your views before me . . ."

How could Lewis say: "If I had, I knew you'd have refused to let me buy the pictures?" He could only stammer: "I *did* allude to the revolution in taste . . . new names coming up . . . you may remember . . ."

"Revolution! New names! Who says so? I had a letter last week from the London dealers to whom I especially recommended you, telling me that an undoubted Guido Reni was coming into the market this summer."

"Oh, the dealers—*they* don't know!"

"The dealers . . . don't? . . . Who does . . . except yourself?" Mr. Raycie pronounced in a white sneer.

Lewis, as white, still held his ground. "I wrote you, sir, about my friends; in Italy, and afterward in England."

"Well, God damn it, I never heard of one of *their* names before, either; no more'n of these painters of yours here. I supplied you with the names of all the advisers you needed, and all the painters, too; I all but made the collection for you myself, before you started . . . I was explicit enough, in all conscience, wasn't I?"

Lewis smiled faintly. "That's what I hoped the pictures would be . . ."

"What? Be what? What'd you mean?"

"Be explicit. . . Speak for themselves . . . make you see that their painters are already superseding some of the better-known . . ."

Mr. Raycie gave an awful laugh. "They are, are they? In whose estimation? Your friends', I suppose. What's the name, again, of that fellow you met in Italy who picked 'em out for you?"

"Ruskin—John Ruskin," said Lewis.

Mr. Raycie's laugh, prolonged, gathered up into itself a fresh shower of expletives. "Ruskin—Ruskin—just plain John Ruskin, eh? And who *is* this great John Ruskin, who sets God A'mighty right in his judgments? Who'd you say John Ruskin's father was, now?"

"A respected wine-merchant in London, sir."

Mr. Raycie ceased to laugh: he looked at his son with an expression of unutterable disgust.

"Retail?"

"I . . . believe so . . ."

"Faugh!" said Mr. Raycie.

"It wasn't only Ruskin, father. . . I told you of those other friends in London, whom I met on the way home. They inspected the pictures, and all of them agreed that . . . that the collection would some day be very valuable."

"*Some day*—did they give you a date . . . the month and the year? Ah, those other friends; yes. You said there was a Mr. Brown and a Mr. Hunt and a Mr. Rossiter, was it? Well, I never heard of any of those names, either—except perhaps in a trades' directory."

"It's not Rossiter, father: Dante Rossetti."

"Excuse me: Rossetti. And what does Mr. Dante Rossetti's father do? Sell macaroni, I presume?"

Lewis was silent, and Mr. Raycie went on, speaking now with a deadly steadiness: "The friends I sent you to were judges of art, sir; men who know what a picture's worth; not one of 'em but could pick out a genuine Raphael. Couldn't you find 'em when you got to England? Or hadn't they the time to spare for you? You'd better not," Mr. Raycie added, "tell me *that*, for I know how they'd have received your father's son."

"Oh, most kindly . . . they did indeed, sir . . ."

"Ay; but that didn't suit you. You didn't *want* to be advised. You wanted to show off before a lot of ignoramuses like yourself. You wanted—how'd I know what you wanted? It's as if I'd never given you an instruction or laid a charge on you! And the money—God! Where'd it go to? Buying *this*? Nonsense—." Mr. Raycie raised himself heavily on his stick and fixed his angry eyes on his son. "Own up, Lewis; tell me they got it out of you at cards. Professional gamblers the lot, I make no doubt; your Ruskin and your Morris and your Rossiter. Make a business to pick up young American greenhorns on their travels, I daresay. . . No? Not that, you say? Then—women? . . . God A'mighty, Lewis," gasped Mr. Raycie, tottering toward his son with outstretched stick, "I'm no blue-nosed Puritan, sir, and I'd a damn sight rather you told me you'd spent it on a woman, every penny of it, than let yourself be fleeced like a simpleton, buying these things that look more like cuts out o' Foxe's Book of Martyrs than Originals of the Old Masters for a Gentleman's Gallery. . . Youth's youth. . . Gad, sir, I've been young myself . . . a fellow's got to go through his apprenticeship. . . Own up now: women?"

"Oh, not women—"

"Not even!" Mr. Raycie groaned. "All in pictures, then? Well, say no more to me now. . . I'll get home, I'll get home. . ." He cast a last apoplectic glance about the room. "The Raycie Gallery! That pack of bones and mummers' finery! . . . Why, let alone the rest, there's not a full-bodied female among 'em. . . Do you know what those Madonnas of yours are like, my son? Why, there ain't one of 'em that don't remind me of a bad likeness of poor Treeshy Kent. . . I should say you'd hired half the sign-painters of Europe to do her portrait for you—if I could imagine your wanting it. . . No, sir! I don't need your arm," Mr. Raycie snarled, heaving his great bulk painfully across the hall. He withered Lewis with a last look from the doorstep. "And to buy *that* you overdrew your account?—No, I'll drive home alone."

7

Mr. Raycie did not die till nearly a year later; but New York agreed it was the affair of the pictures that had killed him.

The day after his first and only sight of them he sent for his lawyer, and it became known that he had made a new will. Then he took to his bed with a return of the gout, and grew so rapidly worse that it was thought "only proper" to postpone the party Mrs. Raycie was to have given that autumn to inaugurate the gallery. This enabled the family to pass over in silence the question of the works of art themselves; but outside of the Raycie house, where they were never mentioned, they formed, that winter, a frequent and fruitful topic of discussion.

Only two persons besides Mr. Raycie were known to have seen them. One was Mr. Donaldson Kent, who owed the privilege to the fact of having once been to Italy; the other, Mr. Reedy, the agent, who had unpacked the pictures. Mr. Reedy, beset by Raycie cousins and old family friends, had replied with genuine humility: "Why, the truth is, I never was taught to see any difference between one picture and another, except as regards the size of them; and these struck me as smallish . . . on the small side, I would say. . ."

Mr. Kent was known to have unbosomed himself to Mr. Raycie with considerable frankness—he went so far, it was rumoured, as to declare that he had never seen any pictures in Italy like those brought back by Lewis, and begged to doubt if they really came from there. But in public he maintained that noncommittal attitude which passed for prudence, but proceeded only from timidity; no one ever got anything from him but the guarded statement: "The subjects are wholly inoffensive."

It was believed that Mr. Raycie dared not consult the Huzzards.

Young John Huzzard had just brought home a Raphael; it would
have been hard not to avoid comparisons which would have been too
galling. Neither to them, nor to any one else, did Mr. Raycie ever
again allude to the Raycie Gallery. But when his will was opened it
was found that he had bequeathed the pictures to his son. The rest
of his property was left absolutely to his two daughters. The bulk of
the estate was Mrs. Raycie's; but it was known that Mrs. Raycie had
had her instructions, and among them, perhaps, was the order to
fade away in her turn after six months of widowhood. When she had
been laid beside her husband in Trinity church-yard her will (made
in the same week as Mr. Raycie's, and obviously at his dictation) was
found to allow five thousand dollars a year to Lewis during his lifetime; the residue of the fortune, which Mr. Raycie's thrift and good
management had made into one of the largest in New York, was
divided between the daughters. Of these, the one promptly married a Kent and the other a Huzzard; and the latter, Sarah Anne
(who had never been Lewis's favourite), was wont to say in later
years: "Oh, no, I never grudged my poor brother those funny old
pictures. You see, we have a Raphael."

The house stood on the corner of Third Avenue and Tenth Street.
It had lately come to Lewis Raycie as his share in the property of a
distant cousin, who had made an "old New York will" under which
all his kin benefited in proportion to their consanguinity. The neighbourhood was unfashionable, and the house in bad repair; but Mr.
and Mrs. Lewis Raycie, who, since their marriage, had been living in
retirement at Tarrytown, immediately moved into it.

Their arrival excited small attention. Within a year of his father's
death, Lewis had married Treeshy Kent. The alliance had not been
encouraged by Mr. and Mrs. Kent, who went so far as to say that
their niece might have done better; but as that one of their sons who
was still unmarried had always shown a lively sympathy for Treeshy,
they yielded to the prudent thought that, after all, it was better than
having her entangle Bill.

The Lewis Raycies had been four years married, and during that
time had dropped out of the memory of New York as completely as
if their exile had covered half a century. Neither of them had ever
cut a great figure there. Treeshy had been nothing but the Kents'
Cinderella, and Lewis's ephemeral importance, as heir to the Raycie
millions, had been effaced by the painful episode which resulted in
his being deprived of them.

So secluded was their way of living, and so much had it come to be a habit, that when Lewis announced that he had inherited Cousin Ebenezer's house his wife hardly looked up from the baby-blanket she was embroidering.

"Cousin Ebenezer's house in New York?"

He drew a deep breath. "Now I shall be able to show the pictures."

"Oh, Lewis—" She dropped the blanket. "Are we going to live there?"

"Certainly. But the house is so large that I shall turn the two corner rooms on the ground floor into a gallery. They are very suitably lighted. It was there that Cousin Ebenezer was laid out."

"Oh, Lewis—"

If anything could have made Lewis Raycie believe in his own strength of will it was his wife's attitude. Merely to hear that unquestioning murmur of submission was to feel something of his father's tyrannous strength arise in him; but with the wish to use it more humanely.

"You'll like that, Treeshy? It's been dull for you here, I know."

She flushed up. "Dull? With *you*, darling? Besides, I like the country. But I shall like Tenth Street too. Only—you said there were repairs?"

He nodded sternly. "I shall borrow money to make them. If necessary—" he lowered his voice—"I shall mortgage the pictures."

He saw her eyes fill. "Oh, but it won't be! There are so many ways still in which I can economize."

He laid his hand on hers and turned his profile toward her, because he knew it was so much stronger than his full face. He did not feel sure that she quite grasped his intention about the pictures; was not even certain that he wished her to. He went in to New York every week now, occupying himself mysteriously and importantly with plans, specifications and other business transactions with long names; while Treeshy, through the hot summer months, sat in Tarrytown and waited for the baby.

A little girl was born at the end of the summer and christened Louisa; and when she was a few weeks old the Lewis Raycies left the country for New York.

"*Now!*" thought Lewis, as they bumped over the cobblestones of Tenth Street in the direction of Cousin Ebenezer's house.

The carriage stopped, he handed out his wife, the nurse followed with the baby, and they all stood and looked up at the house-front.

"Oh, Lewis—" Treeshy gasped; and even little Louisa set up a sympathetic wail.

Over the door—over Cousin Ebenezer's respectable, conservative and intensely private front-door—hung a large sign-board bearing, in gold letters on a black ground, the inscription:

GALLERY OF CHRISTIAN ART

OPEN ON WEEK-DAYS FROM 2 TO 4

ADMISSION 25 CENTS.   CHILDREN 10 CENTS

Lewis saw his wife turn pale, and pressed her arm in his. "Believe me, it's the only way to make the pictures known. And they *must* be made known," he said with a thrill of his old ardour.

"Yes, dear, of course. But . . . to every one? Publicly?"

"If we showed them only to our friends, of what use would it be? Their opinion is already formed."

She sighed her acknowledgment. "But the . . . the entrance fee . . ."

"If we can afford it later, the gallery will be free. But meanwhile—"

"Oh, Lewis, I quite understand!" And clinging to him, the still-protesting baby in her wake, she passed with a dauntless step under the awful sign-board.

"At last I shall see the pictures properly lighted!" she exclaimed, and turned in the hall to fling her arms about her husband.

"It's all they need . . . to be appreciated," he answered, aglow with her encouragement.

Since his withdrawal from the world it had been a part of Lewis's system never to read the daily papers. His wife eagerly conformed to his example, and they lived in a little air-tight circle of aloofness, as if the cottage at Tarrytown had been situated in another and happier planet.

Lewis, nevertheless, the day after the opening of the Gallery of Christian Art, deemed it his duty to derogate from this attitude, and sallied forth secretly to buy the principal journals. When he reentered his house he went straight up to the nursery where he knew that, at that hour, Treeshy would be giving the little girl her bath. But it was later than he supposed. The rite was over, the baby lay asleep in its modest cot, and the mother sat crouched by the fire, her face hidden in her hands. Lewis instantly guessed that she too had seen the papers.

"Treeshy—you mustn't . . . consider this of any consequence. . . ," he stammered.

She lifted a tear-stained face. "Oh, my darling! I thought you never read the papers."

"Not usually. But I thought it my duty—"

"Yes; I see. But, as you say, what earthly consequence—?"

"None whatever; we must just be patient and persist."

She hesitated, and then, her arms about him, her head on his breast: "Only, dearest, I've been counting up again, ever so carefully; and even if we give up fires everywhere but in the nursery, I'm afraid the wages of the doorkeeper and the guardian . . . especially if the gallery's open to the public every day . . ."

"I've thought of that already, too; and I myself shall hereafter act as doorkeeper and guardian."

He kept his eyes on hers as he spoke. "This is the test," he thought. Her face paled under its brown glow, and the eyes dilated in her effort to check her tears. Then she said gaily: "That will be . . . very interesting, won't it, Lewis? Hearing what the people say. . . Because, as they begin to know the pictures better, and to understand them, they can't fail to say very interesting things . . . can they?" She turned and caught up the sleeping Louisa. "Can they . . . oh, you darling—darling?"

Lewis turned away too. Not another woman in New York would have been capable of that. He could hear all the town echoing with this new scandal of his showing the pictures himself—and she, so much more sensitive to ridicule, so much less carried away by apostolic ardour, how much louder must that mocking echo ring in her ears! But his pang was only momentary. The one thought that possessed him for any length of time was that of vindicating himself by making the pictures known; he could no longer fix his attention on lesser matters. The derision of illiterate journalists was not a thing to wince at; once let the pictures be seen by educated and intelligent people, and they would speak for themselves—especially if he were at hand to interpret them.

8

FOR a week or two a great many people came to the gallery; but, even with Lewis as interpreter, the pictures failed to make themselves heard. During the first days, indeed, owing to the unprecedented idea of holding a paying exhibition in a private house, and to the mockery of the newspapers, the Gallery of Christian Art was thronged with noisy curiosity-seekers; once the astonished metropolitan police had to be invited in to calm their comments and control their movements. But the name of "Christian Art" soon chilled this class of sightseer, and before long they were replaced by a dumb and respectable throng, who roamed vacantly through the rooms and out again, grumbling that it wasn't worth the money. Then these too diminished; and once the tide had turned, the ebb was rapid. Every day from two to four Lewis still sat shivering among his treasures, or patiently measured the length of the deserted gallery: as long as there was a chance of any one coming he would not admit that he was beaten. For the next visitor might always be the one who understood.

One snowy February day he had thus paced the rooms in unbroken solitude for above an hour when carriage-wheels stopped at the door. He hastened to open it, and in a great noise of silks his sister Sarah Anne Huzzard entered.

Lewis felt for a moment as he used to under his father's glance. Marriage and millions had given the moon-faced Sarah something of the Raycie awfulness; but her brother looked into her empty eyes, and his own kept their level.

"Well, Lewis," said Mrs. Huzzard with a simpering sternness, and caught her breath.

"Well, Sarah Anne—I'm happy that you've come to take a look at my pictures."

"I've come to see you and your wife." She gave another nervous gasp, shook out her flounces, and added in a rush: "And to ask you how much longer this . . . this spectacle is to continue. . ."

"The exhibition?" Lewis smiled. She signed a flushed assent.

"Well, there has been a considerable falling-off lately in the number of visitors—"

"Thank heaven!" she interjected.

"But as long as I feel that any one wishes to come . . . I shall be here . . . to open the door, as you see."

She sent a shuddering glance about her. "Lewis—I wonder if you realize . . . ?"

"Oh, fully."

"Then *why* do you go on? Isn't it enough—aren't you satisfied?"

"With the effect they have produced?"

"With the effect *you* have produced—on your family and on the whole of New York. With the slur on poor Papa's memory."

"Papa left me the pictures, Sarah Anne."

"Yes. But not to make yourself a mountebank about them."

Lewis considered this impartially. "Are you sure? Perhaps, on the contrary, he did it for that very reason."

"Oh, don't heap more insults on our father's memory! Things are bad enough without that. How your wife can allow it I can't see. Do you ever consider the humiliation to *her?*"

Lewis gave another dry smile. "She's used to being humiliated. The Kents accustomed her to that."

Sarah Anne reddened. "I don't know why I should stay to be spoken to in this way. But I came with my husband's approval."

"Do you need that to come and see your brother?"

"I need it to—to make the offer I am about to make; and which he authorizes."

Lewis looked at her in surprise, and she purpled up to the lace ruffles inside her satin bonnet.

"Have you come to make an offer for my collection?" he asked her, humorously.

"You seem to take pleasure in insinuating preposterous things. But anything is better than this public slight on our name." Again she ran a shuddering glance over the pictures. "John and I," she announced, "are prepared to double the allowance mother left you on condition that this . . . this ends . . . for good. That that horrible sign is taken down tonight."

Lewis seemed mildly to weigh the proposal. "Thank you very much, Sarah Anne," he said at length. "I'm touched . . . touched and . . . and surprised . . . that you and John should have made this offer. But perhaps, before I decline it, you will accept *mine*: simply to show you my pictures. When once you've looked at them I think you'll understand—"

Mrs. Huzzard drew back hastily, her air of majesty collapsing. "Look at the pictures? Oh, thank you . . . but I can see them very well from here. And besides, I don't pretend to be a judge . . ."

"Then come up and see Treeshy and the baby," said Lewis quietly.

She stared at him, embarrassed. "Oh, thank you," she stammered again; and as she prepared to follow him: "Then it's *no*, really no, Lewis? Do consider, my dear! You say yourself that hardly any one comes. What harm can there be in closing the place?"

"What—when tomorrow the man may come who understands?"

Mrs. Huzzard tossed her plumes despairingly and followed him in silence.

"What—Mary Adeline?" she exclaimed, pausing abruptly on the threshold of the nursery. Treeshy, as usual, sat holding her baby by the fire; and from a low seat opposite her rose a lady as richly furred and feathered as Mrs. Huzzard, but with far less assurance to carry off her furbelows. Mrs. Kent ran to Lewis and laid her plump cheek against his, while Treeshy greeted Sarah Anne.

"I had no idea you were here, Mary Adeline," Mrs. Huzzard murmured. It was clear that she had not imparted her philanthropic project to her sister, and was disturbed at the idea that Lewis might be about to do so. "I just dropped in for a minute," she continued, "to see that darling little pet of an angel child—" and she enveloped the astonished baby in her ample rustlings and flutterings.

"I'm very glad to see you here, Sarah Anne," Mary Adeline answered with simplicity.

"Ah, it's not for want of wishing that I haven't come before! Treeshy knows that, I hope. But the cares of a household like mine . . ."

"Yes; and it's been so difficult to get about in the bad weather," Treeshy suggested sympathetically.

Mrs. Huzzard lifted the Raycie eyebrows. "Has it really? With two pairs of horses one hardly notices the weather. . . Oh, the pretty, pretty, *pretty* baby! . . . Mary Adeline," Sarah Anne continued, turning severely to her sister, "I shall be happy to offer you a seat in my carriage if you're thinking of leaving."

But Mary Adeline was a married woman too. She raised her mild head and her glance crossed her sister's quietly. "My own carriage is at the door, thank you kindly, Sarah Anne," she said; and the baffled Sarah Anne withdrew on Lewis's arm. But a moment later the old habit of subordination reasserted itself. Mary Adeline's gentle countenance grew as timorous as a child's, and she gathered up her cloak in haste.

"Perhaps I was too quick. . . I'm sure she meant it kindly," she exclaimed, overtaking Lewis as he turned to come up the stairs; and with a smile he stood watching his two sisters drive off together in the Huzzard coach.

He returned to the nursery, where Treeshy was still crooning over her daughter.

"Well, my dear," he said, "what do you suppose Sarah Anne came for?" And, in reply to her wondering gaze: "To buy me off from showing the pictures!"

His wife's indignation took just the form he could have wished. She simply went on with her rich cooing laugh and hugged the baby tighter. But Lewis felt the perverse desire to lay a still greater strain upon her loyalty.

"Offered to double my allowance, she and John, if only I'll take down the sign!"

"No one shall touch the sign!" Treeshy flamed.

"Not till I do," said her husband grimly.

She turned about and scanned him with anxious eyes. "Lewis . . . you?"

"Oh, my dear . . . they're right. . . It can't go on forever . . ." He went up to her, and put his arm about her and the child. "You've been braver than an army of heroes; but it won't do. The expenses have been a good deal heavier than I was led to expect. And I . . . I can't raise a mortgage on the pictures. Nobody will touch them."

She met this quickly. "No; I know. That was what Mary Adeline came about."

The blood rushed angrily to Lewis's temples. "Mary Adeline—how the devil did *she* hear of it?"

"Through Mr. Reedy, I suppose. But you must not be angry. She was kindness itself: she doesn't want you to close the gallery, Lewis . . . that is, not as long as you really continue to believe in it. . . She and Donald Kent will lend us enough to go on with for a year longer. That is what she came to say."

For the first time since the struggle had begun, Lewis Raycie's throat was choked with tears. His faithful Mary Adeline! He had a sudden vision of her, stealing out of the house at High Point before daylight to carry a basket of scraps to the poor Mrs. Edgar Poe who was dying of a decline down the lane. . . He laughed aloud in his joy.

"Dear old Mary Adeline! How magnificent of her! Enough to give me a whole year more . . ." He pressed his wet cheek against his wife's in a long silence. "Well, dear," he said at length, "it's for you to say—do we accept?"

He held her off, questioningly, at arm's length, and her wan little smile met his own and mingled with it.

"Of course we accept!"

9

OF THE Raycie family, which prevailed so powerfully in the New York of the 'forties, only one of the name survived in my boyhood, half a century later. Like so many of the descendants of the proud little Colonial society, the Raycies had totally vanished, forgotten by everyone but a few old ladies, one or two genealogists and the sexton of Trinity Church, who kept the record of their graves.

The Raycie blood was of course still to be traced in various allied families: Kents, Huzzards, Cosbys and many others, proud to claim cousinship with a "Signer," but already indifferent or incurious as to the fate of his progeny. These old New Yorkers, who lived so well and spent their money so liberally, vanished like a pinch of dust when they disappeared from their pews and their dinner-tables.

If I happen to have been familiar with the name since my youth, it is chiefly because its one survivor was a distant cousin of my mother's whom she sometimes took me to see on days when she thought I was likely to be good because I had been promised a treat for the morrow.

Old Miss Alethea Raycie lived in a house I had always heard spoken of as "Cousin Ebenezer's." It had evidently, in its day, been an admired specimen of domestic architecture; but was now regarded as the hideous though venerable relic of a bygone age. Miss Raycie, being crippled by rheumatism, sat above stairs in a large cold room, meagrely furnished with beadwork tables, rosewood étagères and portraits of pale sad-looking people in odd clothes. She herself was large and saturnine, with a battlemented black lace cap, and so deaf that she seemed a survival of forgotten days, a Rosetta Stone to which the clue was lost. Even to my mother, nursed in that vanished tradition, and knowing instinctively to whom Miss Raycie alluded when she spoke of Mary Adeline, Sarah Anne or Uncle Doctor, intercourse with her was difficult and languishing, and my juvenile interruptions were oftener encouraged than reproved.

In the course of one of these visits my eyes, listlessly roaming, singled out among the pallid portraits a three-crayon drawing of a little girl with a large forehead and dark eyes, dressed in a plaid frock and embroidered pantalettes, and sitting on a grass-bank. I pulled my mother's sleeve to ask who she was, and my mother answered: "Ah, that was poor little Louisa Raycie, who died of a decline. How old was little Louisa when she died, Cousin Alethea?"

To batter this simple question into Cousin Alethea's brain was the affair of ten laborious minutes; and when the job was done, and Miss Raycie, with an air of mysterious displeasure, had dropped a deep "Eleven," my mother was too exhausted to continue. So she turned to me to add, with one of the private smiles we kept for each other: "It was the poor child who would have inherited the Raycie Gallery." But to a little boy of my age this item of information lacked interest, nor did I understand my mother's surreptitious amusement.

This far-off scene suddenly came back to me last year, when, on one of my infrequent visits to New York, I went to dine with my old friend, the banker, John Selwyn, and came to an astonished stand before the mantelpiece in his new library.

"Hallo!" I said, looking up at the picture above the chimney.

My host squared his shoulders, thrust his hands into his pockets, and affected the air of modesty which people think it proper to assume when their possessions are admired. "The Macrino d'Alba? Y—yes . . . it was the only thing I managed to capture out of the Raycie collection."

"The only thing? Well—"

"Ah, but you should have seen the Mantegna; *and* the Giotto; *and* the Piero della Francesca—hang it, one of the most beautiful Piero della Francescas in the world. . . A girl in profile, with her hair in a pearl net, against a background of columbines; *that* went back to Europe—the National Gallery, I believe. And the Carpaccio, the most exquisite little St. George . . . that went to California . . . *Lord!*" He sat down with the sigh of a hungry man turned away from a groaning board. "Well, it nearly broke me buying *this!*" he murmured, as if at least that fact were some consolation.

I was turning over my early memories in quest of a clue to what he spoke of as the Raycie collection, in a tone which implied that he was alluding to objects familiar to all art-lovers.

Suddenly: "They weren't poor little Louisa's pictures, by any chance?" I asked, remembering my mother's cryptic smile.

Selwyn looked at me perplexedly. "Who the deuce is poor little Louisa?" And, without waiting for my answer, he went on: "They were that fool Netta Cosby's until a year ago—and she never even knew it."

We looked at each other interrogatively, my friend perplexed at my ignorance, and I now absorbed in trying to run down the genealogy of Netta Cosby. I did so finally. "Netta Cosby—you don't mean Netta Kent, the one who married Jim Cosby?"

"That's it. They were cousins of the Raycies', and she inherited the pictures."

I continued to ponder. "I wanted awfully to marry her, the year I left Harvard," I said presently, more to myself than to my hearer.

"Well, if you had you'd have annexed a prize fool; *and* one of the most beautiful collections of Italian Primitives in the world."

"In the world?"

"Well—you wait till you see them; if you haven't already. And I seem to make out that you haven't—that you can't have. How long have you been in Japan? Four years? I thought so. Well, it was only last winter that Netta found out."

"Found out what?"

"What there was in old Alethea Raycie's attic. You must remember the old Miss Raycie who lived in that hideous house in Tenth Street when we were children. She was a cousin of your mother's, wasn't she? Well, the old fool lived there for nearly half a century, with five millions' worth of pictures shut up in the attic over her head. It seems they'd been there ever since the death of a poor young Raycie who collected them in Italy years and years ago. I don't know much about the story; I never was strong on genealogy, and the Raycies have always been rather dim to me. They were everybody's cousins, of course; but as far as one can make out that seems to have been their principal if not their only function. Oh— and I suppose the Raycie Building was called after them; only *they* didn't build it!

"But there was this one young fellow—I wish I could find out more about him. All that Netta seems to know (or to care, for that matter) is that when he was very young—barely out of college—he was sent to Italy by his father to buy Old Masters—in the 'forties, it must have been—and came back with this extraordinary, this unbelievable collection . . . a boy of that age! . . . and was disinherited by the old gentleman for bringing home such rubbish. The young fellow and his wife died ever so many years ago, both of them. It seems he was so laughed at for buying such pictures that they went away and lived like hermits in the depths of the country. There were some funny spectral portraits of them that old Alethea had up in her bedroom. Netta showed me one of them the last time I went to see her: a pathetic drawing of the only child, an anæmic little girl with a big forehead. Jove, but that must have been your little Louisa!"

I nodded. "In a plaid frock and embroidered pantalettes?"

"Yes, something of the sort. Well, when Louisa and her parents died, I suppose the pictures went to old Miss Raycie. At any rate, at some time or other—and it must have been longer ago than you or I can remember—the old lady inherited them with the Tenth Street house; and when *she* died, three or four years ago, her relations found she'd never even been upstairs to look at them."

"Well—?"

"Well, she died intestate, and Netta Kent—Netta Cosby—turned out to be the next of kin. There wasn't much to be got out of the estate (or so they thought) and, as the Cosbys are always hard up, the house in Tenth Street had to be sold, and the pictures were very nearly sent off to the auction room with all the rest of the stuff. But nobody supposed they would bring anything, and the auctioneer said that if you tried to sell pictures with carpets and bedding and kitchen furniture it always depreciated the whole thing; and so, as the Cosbys had some bare walls to cover, they sent for the lot—there were about thirty—and decided to have them cleaned and hang them up. 'After all,' Netta said, 'as well as I can make out through the cobwebs, some of them look like rather jolly copies of early Italian things.' But as she was short of cash she decided to clean them at home instead of sending them to an expert; and one day, while she was operating on this very one before you, with her sleeves rolled up, the man called who always *does* call on such occasions; the man who knows. In the given case, it was a quiet fellow connected with the Louvre, who'd brought her a letter from Paris, and whom she'd invited to one of her stupid dinners. He was announced, and she thought it would be a joke to let him see what she was doing; she has pretty arms, you may remember. So he was asked into the dining-room, where he found her with a pail of hot water and soap-suds, and *this* laid out on the table; and the first thing he did was to grab her pretty arm so tight that it was black and blue, while he shouted out: 'God in heaven! Not *hot* water!' "

My friend leaned back with a sigh of mingled resentment and satisfaction, and we sat silently looking up at the lovely "Adoration" above the mantelpiece.

"That's how I got it a little cheaper—most of the old varnish was gone for good. But luckily for her it was the first picture she had attacked; and as for the others—you must see them, that's all I can say. . . Wait; I've got the catalogue somewhere about . . ."

He began to rummage for it, and I asked, remembering how nearly I had married Netta Kent: "Do you mean to say she didn't keep a single one of them?"

"Oh, yes—in the shape of pearls and Rolls-Royces. And you've seen their new house in Fifth Avenue?" He ended with a grin of irony: "The best of the joke is that Jim was just thinking of divorcing her when the pictures were discovered."

"Poor little Louisa!" I sighed.

THE OLD MAID

(*The 'Fifties*)

PART ONE

1

In the old New York of the 'fifties a few families ruled, in simplicity and affluence. Of these were the Ralstons.

The sturdy English and the rubicund and heavier Dutch had mingled to produce a prosperous, prudent and yet lavish society. To "do things handsomely" had always been a fundamental principle in this cautious world, built up on the fortunes of bankers, India merchants, ship-builders and ship-chandlers. Those well-fed slow-moving people, who seemed irritable and dyspeptic to European eyes only because the caprices of the climate had stripped them of superfluous flesh, and strung their nerves a little tighter, lived in a genteel monotony of which the surface was never stirred by the dumb dramas now and then enacted underground. Sensitive souls in those days were like muted key-boards, on which Fate played without a sound.

In this compact society, built of solidly welded blocks, one of the largest areas was filled by the Ralstons and their ramifications. The Ralstons were of middle-class English stock. They had not come to the colonies to die for a creed but to live for a bank-account. The result had been beyond their hopes, and their religion was tinged by their success. An edulcorated Church of England which, under the conciliatory name of the "Episcopal Church of the United States of America," left out the coarser allusions in the Marriage Service, slid over the comminatory passages in the Athanasian Creed, and thought it more respectful to say "Our Father *who*" than "*which*" in the Lord's Prayer, was exactly suited to the spirit of compromise whereon the Ralstons had built themselves up. There was in all the tribe the same instinctive recoil from new religions as from unaccounted-for people. Institutional to the core, they represented the conservative element that holds new societies together as seaplants bind the seashore.

Compared with the Ralstons, even such traditionalists as the Lovells, the Halseys or the Vandergraves appeared careless, indifferent to money, almost reckless in their impulses and indecisions. Old John Frederick Ralston, the stout founder of the race, had perceived the difference, and emphasized it to his son, Frederick John, in whom he had scented a faint leaning toward the untried and unprofitable.

"You let the Lannings and the Dagonets and the Spenders take risks and fly kites. It's the county-family blood in 'em: we've nothing to do with that. Look how they're petering out already—the men, I mean. Let your boys marry their girls, if you like (they're wholesome and handsome); though I'd sooner see my grandsons take a Lovell or a Vandergrave, or any of our own kind. But don't let your sons go mooning around after their young fellows, horse-racing, and running down south to those d——d Springs, and gambling at New Orleans, and all the rest of it. That's how you'll build up the family, and keep the weather out. The way we've always done it."

Frederick John listened, obeyed, married a Halsey, and passively followed in his father's steps. He belonged to the cautious generation of New York gentlemen who revered Hamilton and served Jefferson, who longed to lay out New York like Washington, and who laid it out instead like a gridiron, lest they should be thought "undemocratic" by people they secretly looked down upon. Shopkeepers to the marrow, they put in their windows the wares there was most demand for, keeping their private opinions for the back-shop, where through lack of use, they gradually lost substance and colour.

The fourth generation of Ralstons had nothing left in the way of convictions save an acute sense of honour in private and business matters; on the life of the community and the state they took their daily views from the newspapers, and the newspapers they already despised. The Ralstons had done little to shape the destiny of their country, except to finance the Cause when it had become safe to do so. They were related to many of the great men who had built the Republic; but no Ralston had so far committed himself as to be great. As old John Frederick said, it was safer to be satisfied with three per cent: they regarded heroism as a form of gambling. Yet by merely being so numerous and so similar they had come to have a weight in the community. People said: "The Ralstons" when they wished to invoke a precedent. This attribution of authority had gradually convinced the third generation of its collective importance, and the fourth, to which Delia Ralston's husband belonged, had the ease and simplicity of a ruling class.

Within the limits of their universal caution, the Ralstons fulfilled their obligations as rich and respected citizens. They figured on the boards of all the old-established charities, gave handsomely to thriving institutions, had the best cooks in New York, and when they travelled abroad ordered statuary of the American sculptors in Rome whose reputation was already established. The first Ralston who had brought home a statue had been regarded as a wild fellow; but when it became known that the sculptor had executed several orders for the British aristocracy it was felt in the family that this too was a three per cent investment.

Two marriages with the Dutch Vandergraves had consolidated these qualities of thrift and handsome living, and the carefully built-up Ralston character was now so congenital that Delia Ralston sometimes asked herself whether, were she to turn her own little boy loose in a wilderness, he would not create a small New York there, and be on all its boards of directors.

Delia Lovell had married James Ralston at twenty. The marriage, which had taken place in the month of September, 1840, had been solemnized, as was then the custom, in the drawing-room of the bride's country home, at what is now the corner of Avenue A and Ninety-first Street, overlooking the Sound. Thence her husband had driven her (in Grandmamma Lovell's canary-coloured coach with a fringed hammer-cloth) through spreading suburbs and untidy elm-shaded streets to one of the new houses in Gramercy Park, which the pioneers of the younger set were just beginning to affect; and there, at five-and-twenty, she was established, the mother of two children, the possessor of a generous allowance of pin-money, and, by common consent, one of the handsomest and most popular "young matrons" (as they were called) of her day.

She was thinking placidly and gratefully of these things as she sat one afternoon in her handsome bedroom in Gramercy Park. She was too near to the primitive Ralstons to have as clear a view of them as, for instance, the son in question might one day command: she lived under them as unthinkingly as one lives under the laws of one's country. Yet that tremor of the muted key-board, that secret questioning which sometimes beat in her like wings, would now and then so divide her from them that for a fleeting moment she could survey them in their relation to other things. The moment was always fleeting; she dropped back from it quickly, breathless and a little pale, to her children, her house-keeping, her new dresses and her kindly Jim.

She thought of him today with a smile of tenderness, remembering how he had told her to spare no expense on her new bonnet. Though she was twenty-five, and twice a mother, her image was still surprisingly fresh. The plumpness then thought seemly in a young wife stretched the grey silk across her bosom, and caused her heavy gold watch-chain—after it left the anchorage of the brooch of St. Peter's in mosaic that fastened her low-cut Cluny collar—to dangle perilously in the void above a tiny waist buckled into a velvet waistband. But the shoulders above sloped youthfully under her Cashmere scarf, and every movement was as quick as a girl's.

Mrs. Jim Ralston approvingly examined the rosy-cheeked oval set in the blonde ruffles of the bonnet on which, in compliance with her husband's instructions, she had spared no expense. It was a cabriolet of white velvet tied with wide satin ribbons and plumed with a crystal-spangled marabout—a wedding bonnet ordered for the marriage of her cousin, Charlotte Lovell, which was to take place that week at St. Mark's-in-the-Bouwerie. Charlotte was making a match exactly like Delia's own: marrying a Ralston, of the Waverly Place branch, than which nothing could be safer, sounder or more—well, usual. Delia did not know why the word had occurred to her, for it could hardly be postulated, even of the young women of her own narrow clan, that they "usually" married Ralstons; but the soundness, safeness, suitability of the arrangement, did make it typical of the kind of alliance which a nice girl in the nicest set would serenely and blushingly forecast for herself.

Yes—and afterward?

Well—what? And what did this new question mean? Afterward: why, of course, there was the startled puzzled surrender to the incomprehensible exigencies of the young man to whom one had at most yielded a rosy cheek in return for an engagement ring; there was the large double-bed; the terror of seeing him shaving calmly the next morning, in his shirt-sleeves, through the dressing-room door; the evasions, insinuations, resigned smiles and Bible texts of one's Mamma; the reminder of the phrase "to obey" in the glittering blur of the Marriage Service; a week or a month of flushed distress, confusion, embarrassed pleasure; then the growth of habit, the insidious lulling of the matter-of-course, the dreamless double slumbers in the big white bed, the early morning discussions and consultations through that dressing-room door which had once seemed to open into a fiery pit scorching the brow of innocence.

And then, the babies; the babies who were supposed to "make up for everything," and didn't—though they were such darlings, and one had no definite notion as to what it was that one had missed, and that they were to make up for.

Yes: Charlotte's fate would be just like hers. Joe Ralston was so like his second cousin Jim (Delia's James), that Delia could see no reason why life in the squat brick house in Waverly Place should not exactly resemble life in the tall brown-stone house in Gramercy Park. Only Charlotte's bedroom would certainly not be as pretty as hers.

She glanced complacently at the French wall-paper that reproduced a watered silk, with a "valanced" border, and tassels between the loops. The mahogany bedstead, covered with a white embroidered counterpane, was symmetrically reflected in the mirror of a wardrobe which matched it. Coloured lithographs of the "Four Seasons" by Léopold Robert surmounted groups of family daguerreotypes in deeply-recessed gilt frames. The ormolu clock represented a shepherdess sitting on a fallen trunk, a basket of flowers at her feet. A shepherd, stealing up, surprised her with a kiss, while her little dog barked at him from a clump of roses. One knew the profession of the lovers by their crooks and the shape of their hats. This frivolous time-piece had been a wedding-gift from Delia's aunt, Mrs. Manson Mingott, a dashing widow who lived in Paris and was received at the Tuileries. It had been entrusted by Mrs. Mingott to young Clement Spender, who had come back from Italy for a short holiday just after Delia's marriage; the marriage which might never have been, if Clem Spender could have supported a wife, or if he had consented to give up painting and Rome for New York and the law. The young man (who looked, already, so odd and foreign and sarcastic) had laughingly assured the bride that her aunt's gift was "the newest thing in the Palais Royal"; and the family, who admired Mrs. Manson Mingott's taste though they disapproved of her "foreignness," had criticized Delia's putting the clock in her bedroom instead of displaying it on the drawing-room mantel. But she liked, when she woke in the morning to see the bold shepherd stealing his kiss.

Charlotte would certainly not have such a pretty clock in her bedroom; but then she had not been used to pretty things. Her father, who had died at thirty of lung-fever, was one of the "poor Lovells."

His widow, burdened with a young family, and living all the year round "up the River," could not do much for her eldest girl; and Charlotte had entered society in her mother's turned garments, and shod with satin sandals handed down from a defunct aunt who had "opened a ball" with General Washington. The old-fashioned Ralston furniture, which Delia already saw herself banishing, would seem sumptuous to Chatty; very likely she would think Delia's gay French time-piece somewhat frivolous, or even not "quite nice." Poor Charlotte had become so serious, so prudish almost, since she had given up balls and taken to visiting the poor! Delia remembered, with ever-recurring wonder, the abrupt change in her: the precise moment at which it had been privately agreed in the family that, after all, Charlotte Lovell was going to be an old maid.

They had not thought so when she came out. Though her mother could not afford to give her more than one new tarlatan dress, and though nearly everything in her appearance was regrettable, from the too bright red of her hair to the too pale brown of her eyes—not to mention the rounds of brick-rose on her cheek-bones, which almost (preposterous thought!) made her look as if she painted—yet these defects were redeemed by a slim waist, a light foot and a gay laugh; and when her hair was well oiled and brushed for an evening party, so that it looked almost brown, and lay smoothly along her delicate cheeks under a wreath of red and white camellias, several eligible young men (Joe Ralston among them) were known to have called her pretty.

Then came her illness. She caught cold on a moonlight sleighing-party, the brick-rose circles deepened, and she began to cough. There was a report that she was "going like her father," and she was hurried off to a remote village in Georgia, where she lived alone for a year with an old family governess. When she came back everyone felt at once that there was a change in her. She was pale, and thinner than ever, but with an exquisitely transparent cheek, darker eyes and redder hair; and the oddness of her appearance was increased by plain dresses of Quakerish cut. She had left off trinkets and watch-chains, always wore the same grey cloak and small close bonnet, and displayed a sudden zeal for visiting the indigent. The family explained that during her year in the south she had been shocked by the hopeless degradation of the "poor whites" and their children, and that this revelation of misery had made it impossible for her to return to the light-hearted life of her young friends. Everyone agreed,

with significant glances, that this unnatural state of mind would
"pass off in time"; and meanwhile old Mrs. Lovell, Chatty's grandmother, who understood her perhaps better than the others, gave her
a little money for her paupers, and lent her a room in the Lovell stables (at the back of the old lady's Mercer Street house) where she
gathered about her, in what would afterward have been called a
"day-nursery," some of the destitute children of the neighbourhood.
There was even, among them, the baby girl whose origin had excited
such intense curiosity two or three years earlier, when a veiled lady in
a handsome cloak had brought it to the hovel of Cyrus Washington,
the Negro handy-man whose wife Jessamine took in Dr. Lanskell's
washing. Dr. Lanskell, the chief medical practitioner of the day, was
presumably versed in the secret history of every household from the
Battery to Union Square; but, though beset by inquisitive patients,
he had invariably declared himself unable to identify Jessamine's
"veiled lady," or to hazard a guess as to the origin of the hundred
dollar bill pinned to the baby's bib.

The hundred dollars were never renewed, the lady never reappeared, but the baby lived healthily and happily with Jessamine's pic-
caninnies, and as soon as it could toddle was brought to Chatty
Lovell's day-nursery, where it appeared (like its fellow paupers) in
little garments cut down from her old dresses, and socks knitted by
her untiring hands. Delia, absorbed in her own babies, had nevertheless dropped in once or twice at the nursery, and had come away
wishing that Chatty's maternal instinct might find its normal outlet
in marriage. The married cousin confusedly felt that her own affection for her handsome children was a mild and measured sentiment
compared with Chatty's fierce passion for the waifs in Grandmamma
Lovell's stable.

And then, to the general surprise, Charlotte Lovell engaged herself
to Joe Ralston. It was known that Joe had "admired her" the year
she came out. She was a graceful dancer, and Joe, who was tall and
nimble, had footed it with her through many a reel and *Schottische*.
By the end of the winter all the match-makers were predicting that
something would come of it; but when Delia sounded her cousin, the
girl's evasive answer and burning brow seemed to imply that her
suitor had changed his mind, and no further questions could be
asked. Now it was clear that there had, in fact, been an old romance
between them, probably followed by that exciting incident, a "misunderstanding"; but at last all was well, and the bells of St. Mark's

were preparing to ring in happier days for Charlotte. "Ah, when she has her first baby," the Ralston mothers chorused . . .

"Chatty!" Delia exclaimed, pushing back her chair as she saw her cousin's image reflected in the glass over her shoulder.

Charlotte Lovell had paused in the doorway. "They told me you were here—so I ran up."

"Of course, darling. How handsome you do look in your poplin! I always said you needed rich materials. I'm so thankful to see you out of grey cashmere." Delia, lifting her hands, removed the white bonnet from her dark polished head, and shook it gently to make the crystals glitter.

"I hope you like it? It's for your wedding," she laughed.

Charlotte Lovell stood motionless. In her mother's old dove-coloured poplin, freshly banded with narrow rows of crimson velvet ribbon, an ermine tippet crossed on her bosom, and a new beaver bonnet with a falling feather, she had already something of the assurance and majesty of a married woman.

"And you know your hair certainly *is* darker, darling," Delia added, still hopefully surveying her.

"Darker? It's grey," Charlotte suddenly broke out in her deep voice. She pushed back one of the pommaded bands that framed her face, and showed a white lock on her temple. "You needn't save up your bonnet; I'm not going to be married," she added, with a smile that showed her small white teeth in a fleeting glare.

Delia had just enough presence of mind to lay down the bonnet, marabout-up, before she flung herself on her cousin.

"Not going to be married? Charlotte, are you perfectly crazy?"

"Why is it crazy to do what I think right?"

"But people said you were going to marry him the year you came out. And no one understood what happened then. And now—how can it possibly be right? You simply *can't!*" Delia incoherently cried.

"Oh—people!" said Charlotte Lovell wearily.

Her married cousin looked at her with a start. Something thrilled in her voice that Delia had never heard in it, or in any other human voice, before. Its echo seemed to set their familiar world rocking, and the Axminster carpet actually heaved under Delia's shrinking slippers.

Charlotte Lovell stood staring ahead of her with strained lids. In

the pale brown of her eyes Delia noticed the green specks that
floated there when she was angry or excited.

"Charlotte—where on earth have you come from?" she questioned,
drawing the girl down to the sofa.

"Come from?"

"Yes. You look as if you had seen a ghost—an army of ghosts."

The same snarling smile drew up Charlotte's lip. "I've seen Joe,"
she said.

"Well?—Oh, Chatty," Delia exclaimed abruptly illuminated, "you
don't mean to say that you're going to let any little thing in Joe's
past—? Not that I've ever heard the least hint; never. But even if
there were. . ." She drew a deep breath, and bravely proceeded to extremities. "Even if you've heard that he's been . . . that he's had a
child—of course he would have provided for it before. . ."

The girl shook her head. "I know: you needn't go on. 'Men will be
men'; but it's not that."

"Tell me what it is."

Charlotte Lovell looked about the sunny prosperous room as if it
were the image of her world, and that world were a prison she must
break out of. She lowered her head. "I want—to get away," she
panted.

"Get away? From Joe?"

"From his ideas—the Ralston ideas."

Delia bridled—after all, she was a Ralston! "The Ralston ideas? I
haven't found them—so unbearably unpleasant to live with," she
smiled a little tartly.

"No. But it was different with you: they didn't ask you to give up
things."

"What things?" What in the world (Delia wondered) had poor
Charlotte that any one could want her to give up? She had always
been in the position of taking rather than of having to surrender.
"Can't you explain to me, dear?" Delia urged.

"My poor children—he says I'm to give them up," cried the girl in
a stricken whisper.

"Give them up? Give up helping them?"

"Seeing them—looking after them. Give them up altogether. He
got his mother to explain to me. After—after we have children . . .
he's afraid . . . afraid our children might catch things. . .He'll give
me money, of course, to pay some one . . . a hired person, to look
after them. He thought that handsome," Charlotte broke out with a

sob. She flung off her bonnet and smothered her prostrate weeping in the cushions.

Delia sat perplexed. Of all unforeseen complications this was surely the least imaginable. And with all the acquired Ralston that was in her she could not help seeing the force of Joe's objection, could almost find herself agreeing with him. No one in New York had forgotten the death of the poor Henry van der Luydens' only child, who had caught small-pox at the circus to which an unprincipled nurse had surreptitiously taken him. After such a warning as that, parents felt justified in every precaution against contagion. And poor people were so ignorant and careless, and their children, of course, so perpetually exposed to everything catching. No, Joe Ralston was certainly right, and Charlotte almost insanely unreasonable. But it would be useless to tell her so now. Instinctively, Delia temporized.

"After all," she whispered to the prone ear, "if it's only after you have children—you may not have any—for some time."

"Oh, yes, I shall!" came back in anguish from the cushions.

Delia smiled with matronly superiority. "Really, Chatty, I don't quite see how you can know. You don't understand."

Charlotte Lovell lifted herself up. Her collar of Brussels lace had come undone and hung in a wisp on her crumpled bodice, and through the disorder of her hair the white lock glimmered haggardly. In her pale brown eyes the little green specks floated like leaves in a trout-pool.

"Poor girl," Delia thought, "how old and ugly she looks! More than ever like an old maid; and she doesn't seem to realize in the least that she'll never have another chance."

"You must try to be sensible, Chatty dear. After all, one's own babies have the first claim."

"That's just it." The girl seized her fiercely by the wrists. "How can I give up my own baby?"

"Your—your—?" Delia's world again began to waver under her. "Which of the poor little waifs, dearest, do you call your own baby?" she questioned patiently.

Charlotte looked her straight in the eyes. "I call my own baby my own baby."

"Your own—? Take care—you're hurting my wrists, Chatty!" Delia freed herself, forcing a smile. "Your own—?"

"My own little girl. The one that Jessamine and Cyrus—"

"Oh—" Delia Ralston gasped.

The two cousins sat silent, facing each other; but Delia looked away. It came over her with a shudder of repugnance that such things, even if they had to be said, should not have been spoken in her bedroom, so near the spotless nursery across the passage. Mechanically she smoothed the organ-like folds of her silk skirt, which her cousin's embrace had tumbled. Then she looked again at Charlotte's eyes, and her own melted.

"Oh, poor Chatty—my poor Chatty!" She held out her arms to her cousin.

2

THE shepherd continued to steal his kiss from the shepherdess, and the clock in the fallen trunk continued to tick out the minutes.

Delia, petrified, sat unconscious of their passing, her cousin clasped to her. She was dumb with the horror and amazement of learning that her own blood ran in the veins of the anonymous foundling, the "hundred dollar baby" about whom New York had so long furtively jested and conjectured. It was her first contact with the nether side of the smooth social surface, and she sickened at the thought that such things were, and that she, Delia Ralston, should be hearing of them in her own house, and from the lips of the victim! For Chatty of course was a victim—but whose? She had spoken no name, and Delia could put no question: the horror of it sealed her lips. Her mind had instantly raced back over Chatty's past; but she saw no masculine figure in it but Joe Ralston's. And to connect Joe with the episode was obviously unthinkable. Some one in the south, then—? But no: Charlotte had been ill when she left—and in a flash Delia understood the real nature of that illness, and of the girl's disappearance. But from such speculations too her mind recoiled, and instinctively she fastened on something she could still grasp: Joe Ralston's attitude about Chatty's paupers. Of course Joe could not let his wife risk bringing contagion into their home—that was safe ground to dwell on. Her own Jim would have felt in the same way; and she would certainly have agreed with him.

Her eyes travelled back to the clock. She always thought of Clem Spender when she looked at the clock, and suddenly she wondered—if things had been different—what *he* would have said if she had made such an appeal to him as Charlotte had made to Joe. The thing was hard to imagine; yet in a flash of mental readjustment

Delia saw herself as Clem's wife, she saw her children as his, she pictured herself asking him to let her go on caring for the poor waifs in the Mercer Street stable, and she distinctly heard his laugh and his light answer: "Why on earth did you ask, you little goose? Do you take me for such a Pharisee as that?"

Yes, that was Clem Spender all over—tolerant, reckless, indifferent to consequences, always doing the kind thing at the moment, and too often leaving others to pay the score. "There's something cheap about Clem," Jim had once said in his heavy way. Delia Ralston roused herself and pressed her cousin closer. "Chatty, tell me," she whispered.

"There's nothing more."

"I mean, about yourself . . . this thing . . . this. . ." Clem Spender's voice was still in her ears. "You loved some one," she breathed.

"Yes, that's over—. Now it's only the child. . . And I could love Joe—in another way." Chatty Lovell straightened herself, wan and frowning.

"I need the money—I must have it for my baby. Or else they'll send it to an Institution." She paused. "But that's not all. I want to marry—to be a wife, like all of you. I should have loved Joe's children—our children. Life doesn't stop . . ."

"No; I suppose not. But you speak as if . . . as if . . . the person who took advantage of you . . ."

"No one took advantage of me. I was lonely and unhappy. I met some one who was lonely and unhappy. People don't all have your luck. We were both too poor to marry each other . . . and mother would never have consented. And so one day . . . one day before he said goodbye . . ."

"He said goodbye?"

"Yes. He was going to leave the country."

"He left the country—knowing?"

"How was he to know? He doesn't live here. He'd just come back —come back to see his family—for a few weeks . . ." She broke off, her thin lips pressed together upon her secret.

There was a silence. Blindly Delia stared at the bold shepherd.

"Come back from where?" she asked at length in a low tone.

"Oh, what does it matter? You wouldn't understand," Charlotte broke off, in the very words her married cousin had compassionately addressed to her virginity.

A slow blush rose to Delia's cheek: she felt oddly humiliated by the rebuke conveyed in that contemptuous retort. She seemed to herself shy, ineffectual, as incapable as an ignorant girl of dealing with the abominations that Charlotte was thrusting on her. But suddenly some fierce feminine intuition struggled and woke in her. She forced her eyes upon her cousin's.

"You won't tell me who it was?"

"What's the use? I haven't told anybody."

"Then why have you come to me?"

Charlotte's stony face broke up in weeping. "It's for my baby . . . my baby . . ."

Delia did not heed her. "How can I help you if I don't know?" she insisted in a harsh dry voice: her heart-beats were so violent that they seemed to send up throttling hands to her throat.

Charlotte made no answer.

"Come back from where?" Delia doggedly repeated; and at that, with a long wail, the girl flung her hands up, screening her eyes. "He always thought you'd wait for him," she sobbed out, "and then, when he found you hadn't . . . and that you were marrying Jim. . . He heard it just as he was sailing. . . He didn't know it till Mrs. Mingott asked him to bring the clock back for your wedding . . ."

"Stop—stop," Delia cried, springing to her feet. She had provoked the avowal, and now that it had come she felt that it had been gratuitously and indecently thrust upon her. Was this New York, *her* New York, her safe friendly hypocritical New York, was this James Ralston's house, and this his wife listening to such revelations of dishonour?

Charlotte Lovell stood up in her turn. "I knew it—I knew it! You think worse of my baby now, instead of better. . . Oh, why did you make me tell you? I knew you'd never understand. I'd always cared for him, ever since I came out; that was why I wouldn't marry any one else. But I knew there was no hope for me . . . he never looked at anybody but you. And then, when he came back four years ago, and there was no *you* for him any more, he began to notice me, to be kind, to talk to me about his life and his painting. . ." She drew a deep breath, and her voice cleared. "That's over—all over. It's as if I couldn't either hate him or love him. There's only the child now— my child. He doesn't even know of it—why should he? It's none of his business; it's nobody's business but mine. But surely you must see that I can't give up my baby."

Delia Ralston stood speechless, looking away from her cousin in a growing horror. She had lost all sense of reality, all feeling of safety and self-reliance. Her impulse was to close her ears to the other's appeal as a child buries its head from midnight terrors. At last she drew herself up, and spoke with dry lips.

"But what do you mean to do? Why have you come to me? Why have you told me all this?"

"Because he loved you!" Charlotte Lovell stammered out; and the two women stood and faced each other.

Slowly the tears rose to Delia's eyes and rolled down her cheeks, moistening her parched lips. Through the tears she saw her cousin's haggard countenance waver and droop like a drowning face under water. Things half-guessed, obscurely felt, surged up from unsuspected depths in her. It was almost as if, for a moment, this other woman were telling her of her own secret past, putting into crude words all the trembling silences of her own heart.

The worst of it was, as Charlotte said, that they must act now; there was not a day to lose. Chatty was right—it was impossible that she should marry Joe if to do so meant giving up the child. But, in any case, how could she marry him without telling him the truth? And was it conceivable that, after hearing it, he should repudiate her? All these questions spun agonizingly through Delia's brain, and through them glimmered the persistent vision of the child—Clem Spender's child—growing up on charity in a Negro hovel, or herded in one of the plague-houses they called Asylums. No: the child came first—she felt it in every fibre of her body. But what should she do, of whom take counsel, how advise the wretched creature who had come to her in Clement's name? Delia glanced about her desperately, and then turned back to her cousin.

"You must give me time. I must think. You ought not to marry him—and yet all the arrangements are made; and the wedding presents . . . There would be a scandal . . . it would kill Granny Lovell . . ."

Charlotte answered in a low voice: "There *is* no time. I must decide now."

Delia pressed her hands against her breast. "I tell you I must think. I wish you would go home.—Or, no: stay here: your mother mustn't see your eyes. Jim's not coming home till late; you can wait in this room till I come back." She had opened the wardrobe and was reaching up for a plain bonnet and heavy veil.

"Stay here? But where are you going?"

"I don't know. I want to walk—to get the air. I think I want to be alone." Feverishly, Delia unfolded her Paisley shawl, tied on bonnet and veil, thrust her mittened hands into her muff. Charlotte, without moving, stared at her dumbly from the sofa.

"You'll wait," Delia insisted, on the threshold.

"Yes: I'll wait."

Delia shut the door and hurried down the stairs.

3

She had spoken the truth in saying that she did not know where she was going. She simply wanted to get away from Charlotte's unbearable face, and from the immediate atmosphere of her tragedy. Outside, in the open, perhaps it would be easier to think.

As she skirted the park-rails she saw her rosy children playing, under their nurse's eyes, with the pampered progeny of other square-dwellers. The little girl had on her new plaid velvet bonnet and white tippet, and the boy his Highland cap and broad-cloth spencer. How happy and jolly they looked! The nurse spied her, but she shook her head, waved at the group and hurried on.

She walked and walked through the familiar streets decked with bright winter sunshine. It was early afternoon, an hour when the gentlemen had just returned to their offices, and there were few pedestrians in Irving Place and Union Square. Delia crossed the Square to Broadway.

The Lovell house in Mercer Street was a sturdy old-fashioned brick dwelling. A large stable adjoined it, opening on an alley such as Delia, on her honey-moon trip to England, had heard called a "mews." She turned into the alley, entered the stable court, and pushed open a door. In a shabby white-washed room a dozen children, gathered about a stove, were playing with broken toys. The Irishwoman who had charge of them was cutting out small garments on a broken-legged deal table. She raised a friendly face, recognizing Delia as the lady who had once or twice been to see the children with Miss Charlotte.

Delia paused, embarrassed.

"I—I came to ask if you need any new toys," she stammered.

"That we do, ma'am. And many another thing too, though Miss

Charlotte tells me I'm not to beg of the ladies that comes to see our poor darlin's."

"Oh, you may beg of me, Bridget," Mrs. Ralston answered, smiling. "Let me see your babies—it's so long since I've been here."

The children had stopped playing and, huddled against their nurse, gazed up open-mouthed at the rich rustling lady. One little girl with pale brown eyes and scarlet cheeks was dressed in a plaid alpaca frock trimmed with imitation coral buttons that Delia remembered. Those buttons had been on Charlotte's "best dress" the year she came out. Delia stopped and took up the child. Its curly hair was brown, the exact colour of the eyes—thank heaven! But the eyes had the same little green spangles floating in their transparency. Delia sat down, and the little girl, standing on her knee, gravely fingered her watch-chain.

"Oh, ma'am—maybe her shoes'll soil your skirt. The floor here ain't none too clean."

Delia shook her head, and pressed the child against her. She had forgotten the other gazing babies and their wardress. The little creature on her knee was made of different stuff—it had not needed the plaid alpaca and coral buttons to single her out. Her brown curls grew in points on her high forehead, exactly as Clement Spender's did. Delia laid a burning cheek against the forehead.

"Baby want my lovely yellow chain?"

Baby did.

Delia unfastened the gold chain and hung it about the child's neck. The other babies clapped and crowed, but the little girl, gravely dimpling, continued to finger the links in silence.

"Oh, ma'am, you can't leave that fine chain on little Teeny. When she has to go back to those blacks . . ."

"What is her name?"

"Teena they call her, I believe. It don't seem a Christian name, har'ly."

Delia was silent.

"What I say is, her cheeks is too red. And she coughs too easy. Always one cold and another. Here, Teeny, leave the lady go."

Delia stood up, loosening the tender arms.

"She doesn't want to leave go of you, ma'am. Miss Chatty ain't been in today, and the little thing's kinder lonesome without her. She don't play like the other children, somehow. . . Teeny, you look at that lovely chain you've got . . . there, there now . . ."

"Goodbye, Clementina," Delia whispered below her breath. She kissed the pale brown eyes, the curly crown, and dropped her veil on rushing tears. In the stable-yard she dried them on her large embroidered handkerchief, and stood hesitating. Then with a decided step she turned toward home.

The house was as she had left it, except that the children had come in; she heard them romping in the nursery as she went down the passage to her bedroom. Charlotte Lovell was seated on the sofa, upright and rigid, as Delia had left her.

"Chatty—Chatty, I've thought it out. Listen. Whatever happens, the baby shan't stay with those people. I mean to keep her."

Charlotte stood up, tall and white. The eyes in her thin face had grown so dark that they seemed like spectral hollows in a skull. She opened her lips to speak, and then, snatching at her handkerchief, pressed it to her mouth, and sank down again. A red trickle dripped through the handkerchief onto her poplin skirt.

"Charlotte—Charlotte," Delia screamed, on her knees beside her cousin. Charlotte's head slid back against the cushions and the trickle ceased. She closed her eyes, and Delia, seizing a vinaigrette from the dressing-table, held it to her pinched nostrils. The room was filled with an acrid aromatic scent.

Charlotte's lids lifted. "Don't be frightened. I still spit blood sometimes—not often. My lung is nearly healed. But it's the terror—"

"No, no: there's to be no terror. I tell you I've thought it all out. Jim is going to let me take the baby."

The girl raised herself haggardly. "Jim? Have you told him? Is that where you've been?"

"No, darling. I've only been to see the baby."

"Oh," Charlotte moaned, leaning back again. Delia took her own handkerchief, and wiped away the tears that were raining down her cousin's cheeks.

"You mustn't cry, Chatty; you must be brave. Your little girl and his—how could you think? But you must give me time: I must manage it in my own way. . . Only trust me . . ."

Charlotte's lips stirred faintly.

"The tears . . . don't dry them, Delia. . . . I like to feel them . . ."

The two cousins continued to lean against each other without speaking. The ormolu clock ticked out the measure of their mute communion in minutes, quarters, a half-hour, then an hour: the day declined and darkened, the shadows lengthened across the garlands of the Axminster and the broad white bed. There was a knock.

"The children's waiting to say their grace before supper, ma'am."

"Yes, Eliza. Let them say it to you. I'll come later." As the nurse's steps receded Charlotte Lovell disengaged herself from Delia's embrace.

"Now I can go," she said.

"You're not too weak, dear? I can send for a coach to take you home."

"No, no; it would frighten mother. And I shall like walking now, in the darkness. Sometimes the world used to seem all one awful glare to me. There were days when I thought the sun would never set. And then there was the moon at night." She laid her hands on her cousin's shoulders. "Now it's different. Bye and bye I shan't hate the light."

The two women kissed each other, and Delia whispered: "To-morrow."

4

THE Ralstons gave up old customs reluctantly, but once they had adopted a new one they found it impossible to understand why everyone else did not immediately do likewise.

When Delia, who came of the laxer Lovells, and was naturally inclined to novelty, had first proposed to her husband to dine at six o'clock instead of two, his malleable young face had become as relentless as that of the old original Ralston in his grim Colonial portrait. But after a two days' resistance he had come round to his wife's view, and now smiled contemptuously at the obstinacy of those who clung to a heavy midday meal and high tea.

"There's nothing I hate like narrow-mindedness. Let people eat when they like, for all I care; it's their narrow-mindedness that I can't stand."

Delia was thinking of this as she sat in the drawing-room (her mother would have called it the parlour) waiting for her husband's return. She had just had time to smooth her glossy braids, and slip on the black-and-white striped moiré with cherry pipings which was his favourite dress. The drawing-room, with its Nottingham lace curtains looped back under florid gilt cornices, its marble centre-table on a carved rosewood foot, and its old-fashioned mahogany armchairs covered with one of the new French silk damasks in a tart shade of apple-green, was one for any young wife to be proud of. The rosewood what-nots on each side of the folding doors that led into the dining-room were adorned with tropical shells, feldspar vases, an alabaster model of the Leaning Tower of Pisa, a pair of obelisks made of scraps of porphyry and serpentine picked up by the young couple in the Roman Forum, a bust of Clytie in chalk-white biscuit de Sèvres, and four old-fashioned figures of the Seasons in Chelsea

ware, that had to be left among the newer ornaments because they
had belonged to great-grandmamma Ralston. On the walls hung
large dark steel-engravings of Cole's "Voyage of Life," and between
the windows stood the life-size statue of "A Captive Maiden" executed for Jim Ralston's father by the celebrated Harriet Hosmer, im-
mortalized in Hawthorne's novel of the Marble Faun. On the table
lay handsomely tooled copies of Turner's Rivers of France, Drake's
Culprit Fay, Crabbe's Tales, and the Book of Beauty containing portraits of the British peeresses who had participated in the Earl of
Eglinton's tournament.

As Delia sat there, before the hard-coal fire in its arched opening
of black marble, her citron-wood work-table at her side, and one of
the new French lamps shedding a pleasant light on the centre-table
from under a crystal-fringed shade, she asked herself how she could
have passed, in such a short time, so completely out of her usual circle of impressions and convictions—so much farther than ever before
beyond the Ralston horizon. Here it was, closing in on her again, as
if the very plaster ornaments of the ceiling, the forms of the furniture, the cut of her dress, had been built out of Ralston prejudices,
and turned to adamant by the touch of Ralston hands.

She must have been mad, she thought, to have committed herself
so far to Charlotte; yet, turn about as she would in the ever-tighten-
ing circle of the problem, she could still find no other issue. Somehow, it lay with her to save Clem Spender's baby.

She heard the sound of the latch-key (her heart had never beat so
high at it), and the putting down of a tall hat on the hall console—
or of two tall hats, was it? The drawing-room door opened, and two
high-stocked and ample-coated young men came in: two Jim Ralstons, so to speak. Delia had never before noticed how much her husband and his cousin Joe were alike; it made her feel how justified she
was in always thinking of the Ralstons collectively.

She would not have been young and tender, and a happy wife, if
she had not thought Joe but an indifferent copy of her Jim; yet, allowing for defects in the reproduction, there remained a striking likeness between the two tall athletic figures, the short sanguine faces
with straight noses, straight whiskers, straight brows, candid blue
eyes and sweet selfish smiles. Only, at the present moment, Joe
looked like Jim with a tooth-ache.

"Look here, my dear: here's a young man who's asked to take potluck with us," Jim smiled, with the confidence of a well-nourished husband who knows that he can always bring a friend home.

"How nice of you, Joe!—Do you suppose he can put up with oyster soup and a stuffed goose?" Delia beamed upon her husband.

"I knew it! I told you so, my dear chap! He said you wouldn't like it—that you'd be fussed about the dinner. Wait till you're married, Joseph Ralston—." Jim brought down a genial paw on his cousin's bottle-green shoulder, and Joe grimaced as if the tooth had stabbed him.

"It's excessively kind of you, cousin Delia, to take me in this evening. The fact is—"

"Dinner first, my boy, if you don't mind! A bottle of Burgundy will brush away the blue devils. Your arm to your cousin, please; I'll just go and see that the wine is brought up."

Oyster soup, broiled bass, stuffed goose, apple fritters and green peppers, followed by one of Grandmamma Ralston's famous caramel custards: through all her mental anguish, Delia was faintly aware of a secret pride in her achievement. Certainly it would serve to confirm the rumour that Jim Ralston could always bring a friend home to dine without notice. The Ralston and Lovell wines rounded off the effect, and even Joe's drawn face had mellowed by the time the Lovell Madeira started westward. Delia marked the change when the two young men rejoined her in the drawing-room.

"And now, my dear fellow, you'd better tell her the whole story," Jim counselled, pushing an armchair toward his cousin.

The young woman, bent above her wool-work, listened with lowered lids and flushed cheeks. As a married woman—as a mother—Joe hoped she would think him justified in speaking to her frankly: he had her husband's authority to do so.

"Oh, go ahead, go ahead," chafed the exuberant after-dinner Jim from the hearth-rug.

Delia listened, considered, let the bride-groom flounder on through his embarrassed exposition. Her needle hung like a sword of Damocles above the canvas; she saw at once that Joe depended on her trying to win Charlotte over to his way of thinking. But he was very much in love: at a word from Delia, she understood that he would yield, and Charlotte gain her point, save the child, and marry him . . .

How easy it was, after all! A friendly welcome, a good dinner, a

ripe wine, and the memory of Charlotte's eyes—so much the more
expressive for all that they had looked upon. A secret envy stabbed
the wife who had lacked this last enlightenment.

How easy it was—and yet it must not be! Whatever happened, she
could not let Charlotte Lovell marry Joe Ralston. All the traditions
of honour and probity in which she had been brought up forbade her
to connive at such a plan. She could conceive—had already conceived—of high-handed measures, swift and adroit defiances of precedent, subtle revolts against the heartlessness of the social routine.
But a lie she could never connive at. The idea of Charlotte's marrying Joe Ralston—her own Jim's cousin—without revealing her past to
him, seemed to Delia as dishonourable as it would have seemed to
any Ralston. And to tell him the truth would at once put an end to
the marriage; of that even Chatty was aware. Social tolerance was
not dealt in the same measure to men and to women, and neither
Delia nor Charlotte had ever wondered why: like all the young
women of their class they simply bowed to the ineluctable.

No; there was no escape from the dilemma. As clearly as it was
Delia's duty to save Clem Spender's child, so clearly, also, she
seemed destined to sacrifice his mistress. As the thought pressed on
her she remembered Charlotte's wistful cry: "I want to be married,
like all of you," and her heart tightened. But yet it must not be.

"I make every allowance" (Joe was droning on) "for my sweet
girl's ignorance and inexperience—for her lovely purity. How could a
man wish his future wife to be—to be otherwise? You're with me,
Jim? And Delia? I've told her, you understand, that she shall always
have a special sum set apart for her poor children—in addition to her
pin-money; on that she may absolutely count. God! I'm willing to
draw up a deed, a settlement, before a lawyer, if she says so. I admire, I appreciate her generosity. But I ask you, Delia, as a mother—
mind you, now, I want your frank opinion. If you think I can stretch
a point—can let her go on giving her personal care to these children
until . . . until . . ." A flush of pride suffused the potential father's
brow . . . "till nearer duties claim her, why, I'm more than ready
. . . if you'll tell her so. I undertake," Joe proclaimed, suddenly tingling with the memory of his last glass, "to make it right with my
mother, whose prejudices, of course, while I respect them, I can never
allow to—to come between me and my own convictions." He sprang
to his feet, and beamed on his dauntless double in the chimney-mirror.
"My convictions," he flung back at it.

"Hear, hear!" cried Jim emotionally.

Delia's needle gave the canvas a sharp prick, and she pushed her work aside.

"I think I understand you both, Joe. Certainly, in Charlotte's place, I could never give up those children."

"There you are, my dear fellow!" Jim triumphed, as proud of this vicarious courage as of the perfection of the dinner.

"Never," said Delia. "Especially, I mean, the foundlings—there are two, I think. Those children always die if they are sent to asylums. That is what is haunting Chatty."

"Poor innocents! How I love her for loving them! That there should be such scoundrels upon this earth unpunished—. Delia, will you tell her that I'll do whatever—"

"Gently, old man, gently," Jim admonished him, with a flash of Ralston caution.

"Well, that is to say, whatever—in reason—"

Delia lifted an arresting hand. "I'll tell her, Joe: she will be grateful. But it's of no use—"

"No use? What more—?"

"Nothing more: except this. Charlotte has had a return of her old illness. She coughed blood here today. You must not marry her."

There: it was done. She stood up, trembling in every bone, and feeling herself pale to the lips. Had she done right? Had she done wrong? And would she ever know?

Poor Joe turned on her a face as wan as hers: he clutched the back of his armchair, his head drooping forward like an old man's. His lips moved, but made no sound.

"My God!" Jim stammered. "But you know you've got to buck up, old boy."

"I'm—I'm so sorry for you, Joe. She'll tell you herself tomorrow," Delia faltered, while her husband continued to proffer heavy consolations.

"Take it like a man, old chap. Think of yourself—your future. Can't be, you know. Delia's right; she always *is*. Better get it over— better face the music now than later."

"Now than later," Joe echoed with a tortured grin; and it occurred to Delia that never before in the course of his easy good-natured life had he had—any more than her Jim—to give up anything his heart was set on. Even the vocabulary of renunciation, and its conventional gestures, were unfamiliar to him.

"But I don't understand. I can't give her up," he declared, blinking away a boyish tear.

"Think of the children, my dear fellow; it's your duty," Jim insisted, checking a glance of pride at Delia's wholesome comeliness.

In the long conversation that followed between the cousins—argument, counter-argument, sage counsel and hopeless protest—Delia took but an occasional part. She knew well enough what the end would be. The bride-groom who had feared that his bride might bring home contagion from her visits to the poor would not knowingly implant disease in his race. Nor was that all. Too many sad instances of mothers prematurely fading, and leaving their husbands alone with a young flock to rear, must be pressing upon Joe's memory. Ralstons, Lovells, Lannings, Archers, van der Luydens—which one of them had not some grave to care for in a distant cemetery: graves of young relatives "in a decline," sent abroad to be cured by balmy Italy? The Protestant grave-yards of Rome and Pisa were full of New York names; the vision of that familiar pilgrimage with a dying wife was one to turn the most ardent Ralston cold. And all the while, as she listened with bent head, Delia kept repeating to herself: "This is easy; but how am I going to tell Charlotte?"

When poor Joe, late that evening, wrung her hand with a stammered farewell, she called him back abruptly from the threshold.

"You must let me see her first, please; you must wait till she sends for you—" and she winced a little at the alacrity of his acceptance. But no amount of rhetorical bolstering-up could make it easy for a young man to face what lay ahead of Joe; and her final glance at him was one of compassion . . .

The front door closed upon Joe, and she was roused by her husband's touch on her shoulder.

"I never admired you more, darling. My wise Delia!"

Her head bent back, she took his kiss, and then drew apart. The sparkle in his eyes she understood to be as much an invitation to her bloom as a tribute to her sagacity.

She held him at arms' length. "What should you have done, Jim, if I'd had to tell you about myself what I've just told Joe about Chatty?"

A slight frown showed that he thought the question negligible, and hardly in her usual taste. "Come," his strong arm entreated her.

She continued to stand away from him, with grave eyes. "Poor Chatty! Nothing left now—"

His own eyes grew grave, in instant sympathy. At such moments he was still the sentimental boy whom she could manage.

"Ah, poor Chatty, indeed!" He groped for the readiest panacea. "Lucky, now, after all, that she has those paupers, isn't it? I suppose a woman *must* have children to love——somebody else's if not her own." It was evident that the thought of the remedy had already relieved his pain.

"Yes," Delia agreed, "I see no other comfort for her. I'm sure Joe will feel that too. Between us, darling—" and now she let him have her hands—"between us, you and I must see to it that she keeps her babies."

"Her babies?" He smiled at the possessive pronoun. "Of course, poor girl! Unless indeed she's sent to Italy?"

"Oh, she won't be that—where's the money to come from? And, besides, she'd never leave Aunt Lovell. But I thought, dear, if I might tell her tomorrow—you see, I'm not exactly looking forward to my talk with her—if I might tell her that you would let me look after the baby she's most worried about, the poor little foundling girl who has no name and no home—if I might put aside a fixed sum from my pin-money . . ."

Their hands flowed together, she lifted her flushing face to his. Manly tears were in his eyes; ah, how he triumphed in her health, her wisdom, her generosity!

"Not a penny from your pin-money—never!"

She feigned discouragement and wonder. "Think, dear—if I'd had to give you up!"

"Not a penny from your pin-money, I say—but as much more as you need, to help poor Chatty's pauper. There—will that content you?"

"Dearest! When I think of our own, upstairs!" They held each other, awed by that evocation.

5

CHARLOTTE LOVELL, at the sound of her cousin's step, lifted a fevered face from the pillow.

The bedroom, dim and close, smelt of eau de Cologne and fresh linen. Delia, blinking in from the bright winter sun, had to feel her way through a twilight obstructed by dark mahogany.

"I want to see your face, Chatty: unless your head aches too much?"

Charlotte signed "No," and Delia drew back the heavy window curtains and let in a ray of light. In it she saw the girl's head, livid against the bed-linen, the brick-rose circles again visible under darkly shadowed lids. Just so, she remembered, poor cousin So-and-so had looked the week before she sailed for Italy!

"Delia!" Charlotte breathed.

Delia drew near the bed, and stood looking down at her cousin with new eyes. Yes: it had been easy enough, the night before, to dispose of Chatty's future as if it were her own. But now?

"Darling—"

"Oh, begin, please," the girl interrupted, "or I shall know that what's coming is too dreadful!"

"Chatty, dearest, if I promised you too much—"

"Jim won't let you take my child? I knew it! Shall I always go on dreaming things that can never be?"

Delia, her tears running down, knelt by the bed and gave her fresh hand into the other's burning clutch.

"Don't think that, dear: think only of what you'd like best . . ."

"Like best?" The girl sat up sharply against her pillows, alive to the hot fingertips.

"You can't marry Joe, dear—can you—and keep little Tina?" Delia continued.

"Not keep her with me, no: but somewhere where I could slip off to see her—oh, I had hoped such follies!"

"Give up follies, Charlotte. Keep her where? See your own child in secret? Always in dread of disgrace? Of wrong to your other children? Have you ever thought of that?"

"Oh, my poor head won't think! You're trying to tell me that I must give her up?"

"No, dear; but that you must not marry Joe."

Charlotte sank back on the pillow, her eyes half-closed. "I tell you I must make my child a home. Delia, you're too blest to understand!"

"Think yourself blest too, Chatty. You shan't give up your baby. She shall live with you: you shall take care of her—for me."

"For you?"

"I promised you I'd take her, didn't I? But not that you should marry Joe. Only that I would make a home for your baby. Well, that's done; you two shall be always together."

Charlotte clung to her and sobbed. "But Joe—I can't tell him, I can't!" She put back Delia suddenly. "You haven't told him of my— of my baby? I couldn't bear to hurt him as much as that."

"I told him that you coughed blood yesterday. He'll see you presently: he's dreadfully unhappy. He has been given to understand that, in view of your bad health, the engagement is broken by your wish—and he accepts your decision; but if he weakens, or if you weaken, I can do nothing for you or for little Tina. For heaven's sake remember that!"

Delia released her hold, and Charlotte leaned back silent, with closed eyes and narrowed lips. Almost like a corpse she lay there. On a chair near the bed hung the poplin with red velvet ribbons which had been made over in honour of her betrothal. A pair of new slippers of bronze kid peeped from beneath it. Poor Chatty! She had hardly had time to be pretty . . .

Delia sat by the bed motionless, her eyes on her cousin's closed face. They followed the course of a tear that forced a way between Charlotte's tight lids, hung on the lashes, glittered slowly down the cheeks. As the tear reached the narrowed lips they spoke.

"Shall I live with her somewhere, do you mean? Just she and I together?"

"Just you and she."

"In a little house?"

"In a little house . . ."

"You're sure, Delia?"

"Sure, my dearest."

Charlotte once more raised herself on her elbow and sent a hand groping under the pillow. She drew out a narrow ribbon on which hung a diamond ring.

"I had taken it off already," she said simply, and handed it to Delia.

PART TWO

6

You could always have told, every one agreed afterward, that Charlotte Lovell was meant to be an old maid. Even before her illness it had been manifest: there was something prim about her in spite of her fiery hair. Lucky enough for her, poor girl, considering her wretched health in her youth: Mrs. James Ralston's contemporaries, for instance, remembered Charlotte as a mere ghost, coughing her lungs out—that, of course, had been the reason for her breaking her engagement with Joe Ralston.

True, she had recovered very rapidly, in spite of the peculiar treatment she was given. The Lovells, as every one knew, couldn't afford to send her to Italy; the previous experiment in Georgia had been unsuccessful; and so she was packed off to a farm-house on the Hudson—a little place on the James Ralstons' property—where she lived for five or six years with an Irish servant-woman and a foundling baby. The story of the foundling was another queer episode in Charlotte's history. From the time of her first illness, when she was only twenty-two or three, she had developed an almost morbid tenderness for children, especially for the children of the poor. It was said—Dr. Lanskell was understood to have said—that the baffled instinct of motherhood was peculiarly intense in cases where lung-disease prevented marriage. And so, when it was decided that Chatty must break her engagement to Joe Ralston and go to live in the country, the doctor had told her family that the only hope of saving her lay in not separating her entirely from her pauper children, but in letting her choose one of them, the youngest and most pitiable, and devote herself to its care. So the James Ralstons had lent her their little farm-house, and Mrs. Jim, with her extraordinary gift of taking things in at a glance, had at once arranged everything, and even pledged herself to look after the baby if Charlotte died.

Charlotte did not die. She lived to grow robust and middle-aged, energetic and even tyrannical. And as the transformation in her character took place she became more and more like the typical old maid: precise, methodical, absorbed in trifles, and attaching an exaggerated importance to the smallest social and domestic observances. Such was her reputation as a vigilant house-wife that, when poor Jim Ralston was killed by a fall from his horse, and left Delia, still young, with a boy and girl to bring up, it seemed perfectly natural that the heart-broken widow should take her cousin to live with her and share her task. But Delia Ralston never did things quite like other people. When she took Charlotte she took Charlotte's foundling too: a dark-haired child with pale brown eyes, and the odd incisive manner of children who have lived too much with their elders. The little girl was called Tina Lovell: it was vaguely supposed that Charlotte had adopted her. She grew up on terms of affectionate equality with her young Ralston cousins, and almost as much so—it might be said—with the two women who mothered her. But, impelled by an instinct of imitation which no one took the trouble to correct, she always called Delia Ralston "Mamma" and Charlotte Lovell "Aunt Chatty." She was a brilliant and engaging creature, and people marvelled at poor Chatty's luck in having chosen so interesting a specimen among her foundlings (for she was by this time supposed to have had a whole asylum-full to choose from).

The agreeable elderly bachelor, Sillerton Jackson, returning from a prolonged sojourn in Paris (where he was understood to have been made much of by the highest personages) was immensely struck by Tina's charms when he saw her at her coming-out ball, and asked Delia's permission to come some evening and dine alone with her and her young people. He complimented the widow on the rosy beauty of her own young Delia; but the mother's keen eye perceived that all the while he was watching Tina, and after dinner he confided to the older ladies that there was something "very French" in the girl's way of doing her hair, and that in the capital of all the Elegances she would have been pronounced extremely stylish.

"Oh—" Delia deprecated, beamingly, while Charlotte Lovell sat bent over her work with pinched lips; but Tina, who had been laughing with her cousins at the other end of the room, was around upon her elders in a flash.

"I heard what Mr. Sillerton said! Yes, I did, Mamma: he says I do my hair stylishly. Didn't I always tell you so? I *know* it's more

becoming to let it curl as it wants to than to plaster it down with
bandoline like Aunty's—"

"Tina, Tina—you always think people are admiring you!" Miss
Lovell protested.

"Why shouldn't I, when they do?" the girl laughingly challenged;
and, turning her mocking eyes on Sillerton Jackson: "Do tell Aunt
Charlotte not to be so dreadfully old-maidish!"

Delia saw the blood rise to Charlotte Lovell's face. It no longer
painted two brick-rose circles on her thin cheek-bones, but diffused a
harsh flush over her whole countenance, from the collar fastened
with an old-fashioned garnet brooch to the pepper-and-salt hair
(with no trace of red left in it) flattened down over her hollow temples.

That evening, when they went up to bed, Delia called Tina into
her room.

"You ought not to speak to your Aunt Charlotte as you did this
evening, dear. It's disrespectful—you must see that it hurts her."

The girl overflowed with compunction. "Oh, I'm so sorry! Because
I said she was an old maid? But she *is*, isn't she, Mamma? In her inmost soul, I mean. I don't believe she's ever been young—ever
thought of fun or admiration or falling in love—do you? That's why
she never understands me, and you always do, you darling dear
Mamma." With one of her light movements, Tina was in the widow's arms.

"Child, child," Delia softly scolded, kissing the dark curls planted
in five points on the girl's forehead.

There was a soft foot-fall in the passage, and Charlotte Lovell
stood in the door. Delia, without moving, sent her a glance of welcome over Tina's shoulder.

"Come in, Charlotte, I'm scolding Tina for behaving like a spoilt
baby before Sillerton Jackson. What will he think of her?"

"Just what she deserves, probably," Charlotte returned with a cold
smile. Tina went toward her, and her thin lips touched the girl's
proffered forehead just where Delia's warm kiss had rested. "Goodnight, child," she said in her dry tone of dismissal.

The door closed on the two women, and Delia signed to Charlotte
to take the armchair opposite to her own.

"Not so near the fire," Miss Lovell answered. She chose a straight-
backed seat, and sat down with folded hands. Delia's eyes rested ab-

sently on the thin ringless fingers: she wondered why Charlotte never wore her mother's jewels.

"I overheard what you were saying to Tina, Delia. You were scolding her because she called me an old maid."

It was Delia's turn to colour. "I scolded her for being disrespectful, dear; if you heard what I said you can't think that I was too severe."

"Not too severe: no. I've never thought you too severe with Tina; on the contrary."

"You think I spoil her?"

"Sometimes."

Delia felt an unreasoning resentment. "What was it I said that you object to?"

Charlotte returned her glance steadily. "I would rather she thought me an old maid than—"

"Oh—" Delia murmured. With one of her quick leaps of intuition she had entered into the other's soul, and once more measured its shuddering loneliness.

"What else," Charlotte inexorably pursued, "*can* she possibly be allowed to think me—ever?"

"I see . . . I see . . ." the widow faltered.

"A ridiculous narrow-minded old maid—nothing else," Charlotte Lovell insisted, getting to her feet, "or I shall never feel safe with her."

"Goodnight, my dear," Delia said compassionately. There were moments when she almost hated Charlotte for being Tina's mother, and others, such as this, when her heart was wrung by the tragic spectacle of that unavowed bond.

Charlotte seemed to have divined her thought.

"Oh, but don't pity me! She's mine," she murmured, going.

7

DELIA RALSTON sometimes felt that the real events of her life did not begin until both her children had contracted—so safely and suitably—their irreproachable New York alliances. The boy had married first, choosing a Vandergrave in whose father's bank at Albany he was to have an immediate junior partnership; and young Delia (as her mother had foreseen she would) had selected John Junius, the safest and soundest of the many young Halseys, and followed him to his parents' house the year after her brother's marriage.

After young Delia had left the house in Gramercy Park it was inevitable that Tina should take the centre front of its narrow stage. Tina had reached the marriageable age, she was admired and sought after; but what hope was there of her finding a husband? The two watchful women did not propound this question to each other; but Delia Ralston, brooding over it day by day, and taking it up with her when she mounted at night to her bedroom, knew that Charlotte Lovell, at the same hour, carried the same problem with her to the floor above.

The two cousins, during their eight years of life together, had seldom openly disagreed. Indeed, it might almost have been said that there was nothing open in their relation. Delia would have had it otherwise: after they had once looked so deeply into each other's souls it seemed unnatural that a veil should fall between them. But she understood that Tina's ignorance of her origin must at all costs be preserved, and that Charlotte Lovell, abrupt, passionate and inarticulate, knew of no other security than to wall herself up in perpetual silence.

So far had she carried this self-imposed reticence that Mrs. Ralston was surprised at her suddenly asking, soon after young Delia's marriage, to be allowed to move down into the small bedroom next to Tina's that had been left vacant by the bride's departure.

"But you'll be so much less comfortable there, Chatty. Have you thought of that? Or is it on account of the stairs?"

"No; it's not the stairs," Charlotte answered with her usual bluntness. How could she avail herself of the pretext Delia offered her, when Delia knew that she still ran up and down the three flights like a girl? "It's because I should be next to Tina," she said, in a low voice that jarred like an untuned string.

"Oh—very well. As you please." Mrs. Ralston could not tell why she felt suddenly irritated by the request, unless it were that she had already amused herself with the idea of fitting up the vacant room as a sitting-room for Tina. She had meant to do it in pink and pale green, like an opening flower.

"Of course, if there is any reason—" Charlotte suggested, as if reading her thought.

"None whatever; except that—well, I'd meant to surprise Tina by doing the room up as a sort of little boudoir where she could have her books and things, and see her girl friends."

"You're too kind, Delia; but Tina mustn't have boudoirs," Miss Lovell answered ironically, the green specks showing in her eyes.

"Very well: as you please," Delia repeated, in the same irritated tone. "I'll have your things brought down tomorrow."

Charlotte paused in the doorway. "You're sure there's no other reason?"

"Other reason? Why should there be?" The two women looked at each other almost with hostility, and Charlotte turned to go.

The talk once over, Delia was annoyed with herself for having yielded to Charlotte's wish. Why must it always be she who gave in, she who, after all, was the mistress of the house, and to whom both Charlotte and Tina might almost be said to owe their very existence, or at least all that made it worth having? Yet whenever any question arose about the girl it was invariably Charlotte who gained her point, Delia who yielded: it seemed as if Charlotte, in her mute obstinate way, were determined to take every advantage of the dependence that made it impossible for a woman of Delia's nature to oppose her.

In truth, Delia had looked forward more than she knew to the quiet talks with Tina to which the little boudoir would have lent itself. While her own daughter inhabited the room, Mrs. Ralston had been in the habit of spending an hour there every evening, chatting with the two girls while they undressed, and listening to their comments on the incidents of the day. She always knew beforehand exactly what her own girl would say; but Tina's views and opinions were a perpetual delicious shock to her. Not that they were strange or unfamiliar; there were moments when they seemed to well straight up from the dumb depths of Delia's own past. Only they expressed feelings she had never uttered, ideas she had hardly avowed to herself: Tina sometimes said things which Delia Ralston, in faroff self-communions, had imagined herself saying to Clement Spender.

And now there would be an end to these evening talks: if Charlotte had asked to be lodged next to her daughter, might it not conceivably be because she wished them to end? It had never before occurred to Delia that her influence over Tina might be resented; now the discovery flashed a light far down into the abyss which had always divided the two women. But a moment later Delia reproached herself for attributing feelings of jealousy to her cousin. Was it not rather to herself that she should have ascribed them? Charlotte, as Tina's mother, had every right to wish to be near her, near her in all senses of the word; what claim had Delia to oppose to that natural privilege? The next morning she gave the order that Charlotte's things should be taken down to the room next to Tina's.

That evening, when bedtime came, Charlotte and Tina went upstairs together; but Delia lingered in the drawing-room, on the pretext of having letters to write. In truth, she dreaded to pass the threshold where, evening after evening, the fresh laughter of the two girls used to waylay her while Charlotte Lovell already slept her old-maid sleep on the floor above. A pang went through Delia at the thought that henceforth she would be cut off from this means of keeping her hold on Tina.

An hour later, when she mounted the stairs in her turn, she was guiltily conscious of moving as noiselessly as she could along the heavy carpet of the corridor, and of pausing longer than was necessary over the putting out of the gas-jet on the landing. As she lingered she strained her ears for the sound of voices from the adjoining doors behind which Charlotte and Tina slept; she would have been secretly hurt at hearing talk and laughter from within. But none came, nor was there any light beneath the doors. Evidently Charlotte, in her hard methodical way, had said goodnight to her daughter, and gone straight to bed as usual. Perhaps she had never approved of Tina's vigils, of the long undressing punctuated with mirth and confidences; she might have asked for the room next to her daughter's simply because she did not want the girl to miss her "beauty sleep."

Whenever Delia tried to explore the secret of her cousin's actions she returned from the adventure humiliated and abashed by the base motives she found herself attributing to Charlotte. How was it that she, Delia Ralston, whose happiness had been open and avowed to the world, so often found herself envying poor Charlotte the secret of her scanted motherhood? She hated herself for this movement of envy whenever she detected it, and tried to atone for it by a softened manner and a more anxious regard for Charlotte's feelings; but the attempt was not always successful, and Delia sometimes wondered if Charlotte did not resent any show of sympathy as an indirect glance at her misfortune. The worst of suffering such as hers was that it left one sore to the gentlest touch . . .

Delia, slowly undressing before the same lace-draped toilet-glass which had reflected her bridal image, was turning over these thoughts when she heard a light knock. She opened the door, and there stood Tina, in a dressing-gown, her dark curls falling over her shoulders.

With a happy heart-beat Delia held out her arms.

"I had to say goodnight, Mamma," the girl whispered.

"Of course, dear." Delia pressed a long kiss on her lifted forehead. "Run off now, or you might disturb your aunt. You know she sleeps badly, and you must be as quiet as a mouse now she's next to you."

"Yes, I know," Tina acquiesced, with a grave glance that was almost of complicity.

She asked no further question, she did not linger: lifting Delia's hand she held it a moment against her cheek, and then stole out as noiselessly as she had come.

8

"But you must see," Charlotte Lovell insisted, laying aside the *Evening Post*, "that Tina has changed. You do see that?"

The two women were sitting alone by the drawing-room fire in Gramercy Park. Tina had gone to dine with her cousin, young Mrs. John Junius Halsey, and was to be taken afterward to a ball at the Vandergraves', from which the John Juniuses had promised to see her home. Mrs. Ralston and Charlotte, their early dinner finished, had the long evening to themselves. Their custom, on such occasions, was for Charlotte to read the news aloud to her cousin, while the latter embroidered; but tonight, all through Charlotte's conscientious progress from column to column, without a slip or an omission, Delia had felt her, for some special reason, alert to take advantage of her daughter's absence.

To gain time before answering, Mrs. Ralston bent over a stitch in her delicate white embroidery.

"Tina changed? Since when?" she questioned.

The answer flashed out instantly. "Since Lanning Halsey has been coming here so much."

"Lanning? I used to think he came for Delia," Mrs. Ralston mused, speaking at random to gain still more time.

"It's natural you should suppose that every one came for Delia," Charlotte rejoined dryly; "but as Lanning continues to seek every chance of being with Tina—"

Mrs. Ralston raised her head and stole a swift glance at her cousin. She had in truth noticed that Tina had changed, as a flower changes at the mysterious moment when the unopened petals flush from within. The girl had grown handsomer, shyer, more silent, at times more irrelevantly gay. But Delia had not associated these variations of mood with the presence of Lanning Halsey, one of the numerous youths who had haunted the house before young Delia's marriage. There had, indeed, been a moment when Mrs. Ralston's eye had been fixed, with a certain apprehension, on the handsome Lanning. Among all the sturdy and stolid Halsey cousins he was the only one to whom a prudent mother might have hesitated to entrust her daughter; it would have been hard to say why, except that he was handsomer and more conversable than the rest, chronically unpunctual, and totally unperturbed by the fact. Clem Spender had been like that; and what if young Delia—?

But young Delia's mother was speedily reassured. The girl, herself arch and appetizing, took no interest in the corresponding graces except when backed by more solid qualities. A Ralston to the core, she demanded the Ralston virtues, and chose the Halsey most worthy of a Ralston bride.

Mrs. Ralston felt that Charlotte was waiting for her to speak. "It will be hard to get used to the idea of Tina's marrying," she said gently. "I don't know what we two old women shall do, alone in this empty house—for it will be an empty house then. But I suppose we ought to face the idea."

"I *do* face it," said Charlotte Lovell gravely.

"And you dislike Lanning? I mean, as a husband for Tina?"

Miss Lovell folded the evening paper, and stretched out a thin hand for her knitting. She glanced across the citron-wood work-table at her cousin. "Tina must not be too difficult—" she began.

"Oh—" Delia protested, reddening.

"Let us call things by their names," the other evenly pursued. "That's my way, when I speak at all. Usually, as you know, I say nothing."

The widow made a sign of assent, and Charlotte went on: "It's better so. But I've always known a time would come when we should have to talk this thing out."

"Talk this thing out? You and I? What thing?"

"Tina's future."

There was a silence. Delia Ralston, who always responded instantly to the least appeal to her sincerity, breathed a deep sigh of relief. At last the ice in Charlotte's breast was breaking up!

"My dear," Delia murmured, "you know how much Tina's happiness concerns me. If you disapprove of Lanning Halsey as a husband, have you any other candidate in mind?"

Miss Lovell smiled one of her faint hard smiles. "I am not aware that there is a queue at the door. Nor do I disapprove of Lanning Halsey as a husband. Personally, I find him very agreeable; I understand his attraction for Tina."

"Ah—Tina *is* attracted?"

"Yes."

Mrs. Ralston pushed aside her work and thoughtfully considered her cousin's sharp-lined face. Never had Charlotte Lovell more completely presented the typical image of the old maid than as she sat there, upright on her straight-backed chair, with narrowed elbows and clicking needles, and imperturbably discussed her daughter's marriage.

"I don't understand, Chatty. Whatever Lanning's faults are—and I don't believe they're grave—I share your liking for him. After all—" Mrs. Ralston paused—"what is it that people find so reprehensible in him? Chiefly, as far as I can hear, that he can't decide on the choice of a profession. The New York view about that is rather narrow, as we know. Young men may have other tastes . . . artistic . . . literary . . . they may even have difficulty in deciding . . ."

Both women coloured slightly, and Delia guessed that the same reminiscence which shook her own bosom also throbbed under Charlotte's strait bodice.

Charlotte spoke. "Yes: I understand that. But hesitancy about a profession may cause hesitancy about . . . other decisions . . ."

"What do you mean? Surely not that Lanning—?"

"Lanning has not asked Tina to marry him."

Charlotte paused. The steady click of her needles punctuated the silence as once, years before, it had been punctuated by the tick of the Parisian clock on Delia's mantel. As Delia's memory fled back to that scene she felt its mysterious tension in the air.

Charlotte spoke. "Lanning is not hesitating any longer: he has decided *not* to marry Tina. But he has also decided—not to give up seeing her."

Delia flushed abruptly; she was irritated and bewildered by Charlotte's oracular phrases, doled out between parsimonious lips.

"You don't mean that he has offered himself and then drawn back? I can't think him capable of such an insult to Tina."

"He has not insulted Tina. He has simply told her that he can't afford to marry. Until he chooses a profession his father will allow

him only a few hundred dollars a year; and that may be suppressed if
—if he marries against his parents' wishes."

It was Delia's turn to be silent. The past was too overwhelmingly
resuscitated in Charlotte's words. Clement Spender stood before her,
irresolute, impecunious, persuasive. Ah, if only she had let herself be
persuaded!

"I'm very sorry that this should have happened to Tina. But as
Lanning appears to have behaved honourably, and withdrawn with-
out raising false expectations, we must hope . . . we must hope. . ."
Delia paused, not knowing what they must hope.

Charlotte Lovell laid down her knitting. "You know as well as I
do, Delia, that every young man who is inclined to fall in love with
Tina will find as good reasons for not marrying her."

"Then you think Lanning's excuses are a pretext?"

"Naturally. The first of many that will be found by his successors
—for of course he will have successors. Tina—attracts."

"Ah," Delia murmured.

Here they were at last face to face with the problem which,
through all the years of silence and evasiveness, had lain as close to
the surface as a corpse too hastily buried! Delia drew another deep
breath, which again was almost one of relief. She had always known
that it would be difficult, almost impossible, to find a husband for
Tina; and much as she desired Tina's happiness, some inmost
selfishness whispered how much less lonely and purposeless the close
of her own life would be should the girl be forced to share it. But
how say this to Tina's mother?

"I hope you exaggerate, Charlotte. There may be disinterested
characters. . . But, in any case, surely Tina need not be unhappy
here, with us who love her so dearly."

"Tina an old maid? Never!" Charlotte Lovell rose abruptly, her
closed hand crashing down on the slender work-table. "My child
shall have her life . . . her own life . . . whatever it costs me . . ."

Delia's ready sympathy welled up. "I understand your feeling. I
should want also . . . hard as it will be to let her go. But surely there
is no hurry—no reason for looking so far ahead. The child is not
twenty. Wait."

Charlotte stood before her, motionless, perpendicular. At such moments she made Delia think of lava struggling through granite: there
seemed no issue for the fires within.

"Wait? But if *she* doesn't wait?"

"But if he has withdrawn—what do you mean?"

"He has given up marrying her—but not seeing her."

Delia sprang up in her turn, flushed and trembling.

"Charlotte! Do you know what you're insinuating?"

"Yes: I know."

"But it's too outrageous. No decent girl—"

The words died on Delia's lips. Charlotte Lovell held her eyes inexorably. "Girls are not always what you call decent," she declared.

Mrs. Ralston turned slowly back to her seat. Her tambour frame had fallen to the floor; she stooped heavily to pick it up. Charlotte's gaunt figure hung over her, relentless as doom.

"I can't imagine, Charlotte, what is gained by saying such things—even by hinting them. Surely you trust your own child."

Charlotte laughed. "My mother trusted me," she said.

"How dare you—how dare you?" Delia began; but her eyes fell, and she felt a tremor of weakness in her throat.

"Oh, I dare anything for Tina, even to judging her as she is," Tina's mother murmured.

"As she is? She's perfect!"

"Let us say then that she must pay for my imperfections. All I want is that she shouldn't pay too heavily."

Mrs. Ralston sat silent. It seemed to her that Charlotte spoke with the voice of all the dark destinies coiled under the safe surface of life; and that to such a voice there was no answer but an awed acquiescence.

"Poor Tina!" she breathed.

"Oh, I don't intend that she shall suffer! It's not for that I've waited . . . waited. Only I've made mistakes: mistakes that I understand now, and must remedy. You've been too good to us—and we must go."

"Go?" Delia gasped.

"Yes. Don't think me ungrateful. You saved my child once—do you suppose I can forget? But now it's my turn—it's I who must save her. And it's only by taking her away from everything here—from everything she's known till now—that I can do it. She's lived too long among unrealities: and she's like me. They won't content her."

"Unrealities?" Delia echoed vaguely.

"Unrealities for her. Young men who make love to her and can't marry her. Happy households where she's welcomed till she's suspected of designs on a brother or a husband—or else exposed to their insults. How could we ever have imagined, either of us, that the child could escape disaster? I thought only of her present happiness —of all the advantages, for both of us, of being with you. But this affair with young Halsey has opened my eyes. I must take Tina away. We must go and live somewhere where we're not known, where we shall be among plain people, leading plain lives. Somewhere where she can find a husband, and make herself a home."

Charlotte paused. She had spoken in a rapid monotonous tone, as if by rote; but now her voice broke and she repeated painfully: "I'm not ungrateful."

"Oh, don't let's speak of gratitude! What place has it between you and me?"

Delia had risen and begun to move uneasily about the room. She longed to plead with Charlotte, to implore her not to be in haste, to picture to her the cruelty of severing Tina from all her habits and associations, of carrying her inexplicably away to lead "a plain life among plain people." What chance was there, indeed, that a creature so radiant would tamely submit to such a fate, or find an acceptable husband in such conditions? The change might only precipitate a tragedy. Delia's experience was too limited for her to picture exactly what might happen to a girl like Tina, suddenly cut off from all that sweetened life for her; but vague visions of revolt and flight— of a "fall" deeper and more irretrievable than Charlotte's—flashed through her agonized imagination.

"It's too cruel—it's too cruel," she cried, speaking to herself rather than to Charlotte.

Charlotte, instead of answering, glanced abruptly at the clock.

"Do you know what time it is? Past midnight. I mustn't keep you sitting up for my foolish girl."

Delia's heart contracted. She saw that Charlotte wished to cut the conversation short, and to do so by reminding her that only Tina's mother had a right to decide what Tina's future should be. At that moment, though Delia had just protested that there could be no question of gratitude between them, Charlotte Lovell seemed to her a monster of ingratitude, and it was on the tip of her tongue to cry out: "Have all the years then given me no share in Tina?" But at the same instant she had put herself once more in Charlotte's place, and was feeling the mother's fierce terrors for her child. It was natural enough that Charlotte should resent the faintest attempt to usurp in private the authority she could never assert in public. With a pang of compassion Delia realized that she herself was literally the one being on earth before whom Charlotte could act the mother. "Poor thing—ah, let her!" she murmured inwardly.

"But why should you sit up for Tina? She has the key, and Delia is to bring her home."

Charlotte Lovell did not immediately answer. She rolled up her knitting, looked severely at one of the candelabra on the mantelpiece, and crossed over to straighten it. Then she picked up her work-bag.

"Yes, as you say—why should any one sit up for her?" She moved about the room, putting out the lamps, covering the fire, assuring herself that the windows were bolted, while Delia passively watched her. Then the two cousins lit their bedroom candles and walked upstairs through the darkened house. Charlotte seemed determined to make no further allusion to the subject of their talk. On the landing she paused, bending her head toward Delia's nightly kiss.

"I hope they've kept up your fire," she said, with her capable housekeeping air; and on Delia's hasty reassurance the two murmured a simultaneous "Goodnight," and Charlotte turned down the passage to her room.

9

DELIA's fire had been kept up, and her dressing-gown was warming on an armchair near the hearth. But she neither undressed nor yet seated herself. Her conversation with Charlotte had filled her with a deep unrest.

For a few moments she stood in the middle of the floor, looking slowly about her. Nothing had ever been changed in the room which, even as a bride, she had planned to modernize. All her dreams of renovation had faded long ago. Some deep central indifference had gradually made her regard herself as a third person, living the life meant for another woman, a woman totally unrelated to the vivid Delia Lovell who had entered that house so full of plans and visions. The fault, she knew, was not her husband's. With a little managing and a little wheedling she would have gained every point as easily as she had gained the capital one of taking the foundling baby under her wing. The difficulty was that, after that victory, nothing else seemed worth trying for. The first sight of little Tina had somehow decentralized Delia Ralston's whole life, making her indifferent to everything else, except indeed the welfare of her own husband and children. Ahead of her she saw only a future full of duties, and these she had gaily and faithfully accomplished. But her own life was over; she felt as detached as a cloistered nun.

The change in her was too deep not to be visible. The Ralstons openly gloried in dear Delia's conformity. Each acquiescence passed for a concession, and the family doctrine was fortified by such fresh proofs of its durability. Now, as Delia glanced about her at the Léopold Robert lithographs, the family daguerreotypes, the rosewood and mahogany, she understood that she was looking at the walls of her own grave.

The change had come on the day when Charlotte Lovell, cowering on that very lounge, had made her terrible avowal. Then for the first time Delia, with a kind of fearful exaltation, had heard the blind forces of life groping and crying underfoot. But on that day also she had known herself excluded from them, doomed to dwell among shadows. Life had passed her by, and left her with the Ralstons.

Very well, then! She would make the best of herself, and of the Ralstons. The vow was immediate and unflinching; and for nearly twenty years she had gone on observing it. Once only had she been not a Ralston but herself; once only had it seemed worth while. And now perhaps the same challenge had sounded again; again, for a moment, it might be worth while to live. Not for the sake of Clement Spender—poor Clement, married years ago to a plain determined cousin, who had hunted him down in Rome, and enclosing him in an unrelenting domesticity, had obliged all New York on the grand tour to buy his pictures with a resigned grimace. No, not for Clement Spender, hardly for Charlotte or even for Tina; but for her own sake, hers, Delia Ralston's, for the sake of her one missed vision, her forfeited reality, she would once more break down the Ralston barriers and reach out into the world.

A faint sound through the silent house disturbed her meditation. Listening, she heard Charlotte Lovell's door open and her stiff petticoats rustle toward the landing. A light glanced under the door and vanished; Charlotte had passed Delia's threshold on her way downstairs.

Without moving, Delia continued to listen. Perhaps the careful Charlotte had gone down to make sure that the front door was not bolted, or that she had really covered up the fire. If that were her object, her step would presently be heard returning. But no step sounded; and it became gradually evident that Charlotte had gone down to wait for her daughter. Why?

Delia's bedroom was at the front of the house. She stole across the heavy carpet, drew aside the curtains and cautiously folded back the inner shutters. Below her lay the empty square, white with moonlight, its tree-trunks patterned on a fresh sprinkling of snow. The houses opposite slept in darkness; not a footfall broke the white surface, not a wheel-track marred the brilliant street. Overhead a heaven full of stars swam in the moonlight.

Of the households around Gramercy Park Delia knew that only two others had gone to the ball: the Petrus Vandergraves and their

cousins the young Parmly Ralstons. The Lucius Lannings had just
entered on their three years of mourning for Mrs. Lucius's mother
(it was hard on their daughter Kate, just eighteen, who would be unable to "come out" till she was twenty-one); young Mrs. Marcy Mingott was "expecting her third," and consequently secluded from the
public eye for nearly a year; and the other denizens of the square
belonged to the undifferentiated and uninvited.

Delia pressed her forehead against the pane. Before long carriages
would turn the corner, the sleeping square ring with hoof-beats, fresh
laughter and young farewells mount from the door-steps. But why
was Charlotte waiting for her daughter downstairs in the darkness?

The Parisian clock struck one. Delia came back into the room,
raked the fire, picked up a shawl, and wrapped in it, returned to her
vigil. Ah, how old she must have grown that she should feel the cold
at such a moment! It reminded her of what the future held for her:
neuralgia, rheumatism, stiffness, accumulating infirmities. And never
had she kept a moonlight watch with a lover's arms to warm her . . .

The square still lay silent. Yet the ball must surely be ending: the
gayest dances did not last long after one in the morning, and the
drive from University Place to Gramercy Park was a short one. Delia
leaned in the embrasure and listened.

Hoof-beats, muffled by the snow, sounded in Irving Place, and the
Petrus Vandergraves' family coach drew up before the opposite
house. The Vandergrave girls and their brother sprang out and
mounted the steps; then the coach stopped again a few doors farther
on, and the Parmly Ralstons, brought home by their cousins, descended at their own door. The next carriage that rounded the
corner must therefore be the John Juniuses', bringing Tina.

The gilt clock struck half-past one. Delia wondered, knowing that
young Delia, out of regard for John Junius's business hours, never
stayed late at evening parties. Doubtless Tina had delayed her; Mrs.
Ralston felt a little annoyed with Tina's thoughtlessness in keeping
her cousin up. But the feeling was swept away by an immediate wave
of sympathy. "We must go away somewhere, and lead plain lives
among plain people." If Charlotte carried out her threat—and Delia
knew she would hardly have spoken unless her resolve had been
taken—it might be that at that very moment poor Tina was dancing
her last *valse*.

Another quarter of an hour passed; then, just as the cold was
finding a way through Delia's shawl, she saw two people turn into

the deserted square from Irving Place. One was a young man in opera hat and ample cloak. To his arm clung a figure so closely wrapped and muffled that, until the corner light fell on it, Delia hesitated. After that, she wondered that she had not at once recognized Tina's dancing step, and her manner of tilting her head a little sideways to look up at the person she was talking to.

Tina—Tina and Lanning Halsey, walking home alone in the small hours from the Vandergrave ball! Delia's first thought was of an accident: the carriage might have broken down, or else her daughter been taken ill and obliged to return home. But no; in the latter case she would have sent the carriage on with Tina. And if there had been an accident of any sort the young people would have been hastening to apprise Mrs. Ralston; instead of which, through the bitter brilliant night, they sauntered like lovers in a midsummer glade, and Tina's thin slippers might have been falling on daisies instead of snow.

Delia began to tremble like a girl. In a flash she had the answer to a question which had long been the subject of her secret conjectures. How did lovers like Charlotte and Clement Spender contrive to meet? What Latmian solitude hid their clandestine joys? In the exposed compact little society to which they all belonged, how was it possible—literally—for such encounters to take place? Delia would never have dared to put the question to Charlotte; there were moments when she almost preferred not to know, not even to hazard a guess. But now, at a glance, she understood. How often Charlotte Lovell, staying alone in town with her infirm grandmother, must have walked home from evening parties with Clement Spender, how often have let herself and him into the darkened house in Mercer Street, where there was no one to spy upon their coming but a deaf old lady and her aged servants, all securely sleeping overhead! Delia, at the thought, saw the grim drawing-room which had been their moonlit forest, the drawing-room into which old Mrs. Lovell no longer descended, with its swathed chandelier and hard Empire sofas, and the eyeless marble caryatids of the mantel; she pictured the shaft of moonlight falling across the swans and garlands of the faded carpet, and in that icy light two young figures in each other's arms.

Yes: it must have been some such memory that had roused Charlotte's suspicions, excited her fears, sent her down in the darkness to confront the culprits. Delia shivered at the irony of the confrontation. If Tina had but known! But to Tina, of course, Charlotte was still what she had long since resolved to be: the image of prudish spinsterhood. And Delia could imagine how quietly and decently the scene below stairs would presently be enacted: no astonishment, no reproaches, no insinuations, but a smiling and resolute ignoring of excuses.

"What, Tina? You walked home with Lanning? You imprudent child—in this wet snow! Ah, I see: Delia was worried about the baby, and ran off early, promising to send back the carriage—and it never came? Well, my dear, I congratulate you on finding Lanning to see you home. . . Yes—I sat up because I couldn't for the life of me remember whether you'd taken the latch-key—was there ever such a flighty old aunt? But don't tell your Mamma, dear, or she'd scold me for being so forgetful, and for staying downstairs in the cold. . . You're quite sure you have the key? Ah, Lanning has it? Thank you, Lanning; so kind! Goodnight—or one really ought to say, good morning."

As Delia reached this point in her mute representation of Charlotte's monologue the front door slammed below, and young Lanning Halsey walked slowly away across the square. Delia saw him pause on the opposite pavement, look up at the house-front, and then turn lingeringly away. His dismissal had taken exactly as long as Delia had calculated it would. A moment later she saw a passing light under her door, heard the starched rustle of Charlotte's petticoats, and knew that mother and daughter had reached their rooms.

Slowly, with stiff motions, she began to undress, blew out her candles, and knelt by her bedside, her face hidden.

10

Lying awake till morning, Delia lived over every detail of the fateful day when she had assumed the charge of Charlotte's child. At the time she had been hardly more than a child herself, and there had been no one for her to turn to, no one to fortify her resolution, or to advise her how to put it into effect. Since then, the accumulated experiences of twenty years ought to have prepared her for emergencies, and taught her to advise others instead of seeking their guidance. But these years of experience weighed on her like chains binding her down to her narrow plot of life; independent action struck her as more dangerous, less conceivable, than when she had first ventured on it. There seemed to be so many more people to "consider" now ("consider" was the Ralston word): her children, their children, the families into which they had married. What would the Halseys say, and what the Ralstons? Had she then become a Ralston through and through?

A few hours later she sat in old Dr. Lanskell's library, her eyes on his sooty Smyrna rug. For some years now Dr. Lanskell had no longer practised: at most, he continued to go to a few old patients, and to give consultations in "difficult" cases. But he remained a power in his former kingdom, a sort of lay Pope or medical Elder to whom the patients he had once healed of physical ills often returned for moral medicine. People were agreed that Dr. Lanskell's judgments was sound; but what secretly drew them to him was the fact that, in the most totem-ridden of communities, he was known not to be afraid of anything.

Now, as Delia sat and watched his massive silver-headed figure moving ponderously about the room, between rows of medical books in calf bindings and the Dying Gladiators and Young Augustuses of grateful patients, she already felt the reassurance given by his mere bodily presence.

"You see, when I first took Tina I didn't perhaps consider sufficiently—"

The Doctor halted behind his desk and brought his fist down on it with a genial thump. "Thank goodness you didn't! There are considerers enough in this town without you, Delia Lovell."

She looked up quickly. "Why do you call me Delia Lovell?"

"Well, because today I rather suspect you *are*," he rejoined astutely; and she met this with a wistful laugh.

"Perhaps, if I hadn't been, once before—I mean, if I'd always been a prudent deliberate Ralston it would have been kinder to Tina in the end."

Dr. Lanskell sank his gouty bulk into the armchair behind his desk, and beamed at her through ironic spectacles. "I hate in-the-end kindnesses: they're about as nourishing as the third day of cold mutton."

She pondered. "Of course I realize that if I adopt Tina—"

"Yes?"

"Well, people will say. . ." A deep blush rose to her throat, covered her cheeks and brow, and ran like fire under her decently-parted hair.

He nodded: "Yes."

"Or else—" the blush darkened—"that she's Jim's—"

Again Dr. Lanskell nodded. "That's what they're more likely to think; and what's the harm if they do? I know Jim: he asked you no questions when you took the child—but he knew whose she was."

She raised astonished eyes. "He knew—?"

"Yes: he came to me. And—well—in the baby's interest I violated professional secrecy. That's how Tina got a home. You're not going to denounce me, are you?"

"Oh, Dr. Lanskell—" Her eyes filled with painful tears. "Jim knew? And didn't tell me?"

"No. People didn't tell each other things much in those days, did they? But he admired you enormously for what you did. And if you assume—as I suppose you do—that he's now in a world of completer enlightenment, why not take it for granted that he'll admire you still more for what you're going to do? Presumably," the Doctor concluded sardonically, "people realize in heaven that it's a devilish sight harder, on earth, to do a brave thing at forty-five than at twenty-five."

"Ah, that's what I was thinking this morning," she confessed.

"Well, you're going to prove the contrary this afternoon." He looked at his watch, stood up and laid a fatherly hand on her shoulder. "Let people think what they choose; and send young Delia to me if she gives you any trouble. Your boy won't, you know, nor John Junius either; it must have been a woman who invented that third-and-fourth generation idea . . ."

An elderly maid-servant looked in, and Delia rose; but on the threshold she halted.

"I have an idea it's Charlotte I may have to send to you."

"Charlotte?"

"She'll hate what I'm going to do, you know."

Dr. Lanskell lifted his silver eyebrows. "Yes: poor Charlotte? I suppose she's jealous? That's where the truth of the third-and-fourth generation business comes in, after all. Somebody always has to foot the bill."

"Ah—if only Tina doesn't!"

"Well—that's just what Charlotte will come to recognize in time. So your course is clear."

He guided her out through the dining-room, where some poor people and one or two old patients were already waiting.

Delia's course, in truth, seemed clear enough till, that afternoon, she summoned Charlotte alone to her bedroom. Tina was lying down with a headache: it was in those days the accepted state of young ladies in sentimental dilemmas, and greatly simplified the communion of their elders.

Delia and Charlotte had exchanged only conventional phrases over their midday meal; but Delia still had the sense that her cousin's decision was final. The events of the previous evening had no doubt confirmed Charlotte's view that the time had come for such a decision.

Miss Lovell, closing the bedroom door with her dry deliberateness, advanced toward the chintz lounge between the windows.

"You wanted to see me, Delia?"

"Yes.—Oh, don't sit there," Mrs. Ralston exclaimed uncontrollably.

Charlotte stared: was it possible that she did not remember the sobs of anguish she had once smothered in those very cushions?

"Not—?"

"No; come nearer to me. Sometimes I think I'm a little deaf," Delia nervously explained, pushing a chair up to her own.

"Ah." Charlotte seated herself. "I hadn't remarked it. But if you are, it may have saved you from hearing at what hour of the morning Tina came back from the Vandergraves' last night. She would never forgive herself—inconsiderate as she is—if she thought she'd waked you."

"She didn't wake me," Delia answered. Inwardly she thought: "Charlotte's mind is made up; I shan't be able to move her."

"I suppose Tina enjoyed herself very much at the ball?" she continued.

"Well, she's paying for it with a headache. Such excitements are not meant for her, I've already told you—"

"Yes," Mrs. Ralston interrupted. "It's to continue our talk of last night that I've asked you to come up."

"To continue it?" The brick-red circles appeared on Charlotte's dried cheeks. "Is it worth while? I think I ought to tell you at once that my mind's made up. I suppose you'll admit that I know what's best for Tina."

"Yes; of course. But won't you at least allow me a share in your decision?"

"A share?"

Delia leaned forward, laying a warm hand on her cousin's interlocked fingers. "Charlotte, once in this room, years ago, you asked me to help you—you believed I could. Won't you believe it again?"

Charlotte's lips grew rigid. "I believe the time has come for me to help myself."

"At the cost of Tina's happiness?"

"No; but to spare her greater unhappiness."

"But, Charlotte, Tina's happiness is all I want."

"Oh, I know. You've done all you could do for my child."

"No; not all." Delia rose, and stood before her cousin with a kind of solemnity. "But now I'm going to." It was as if she had pronounced a vow.

Charlotte Lovell looked up at her with a glitter of apprehension in her hunted eyes.

"If you mean that you're going to use your influence with the Halseys—I'm very grateful to you; I shall always be grateful. But I don't want a compulsory marriage for my child."

Delia flushed at the other's incomprehension. It seemed to her that her tremendous purpose must be written on her face. "I'm going to adopt Tina—give her my name," she announced.

Charlotte Lovell stared at her stonily. "Adopt her—adopt her?"

"Don't you see dear, the difference it will make? There's my mother's money—the Lovell money; it's not much, to be sure; but Jim always wanted it to go back to the Lovells. And my Delia and her brother are so handsomely provided for. There's no reason why my little fortune shouldn't go to Tina. And why she shouldn't be known as Tina Ralston." Delia paused. "I believe—I think I know—that Jim would have approved of that too."

"Approved?"

"Yes. Can't you see that when he let me take the child he must have foreseen and accepted whatever—whatever might eventually come of it?"

Charlotte stood up also. "Thank you, Delia. But nothing more must come of it, except our leaving you; our leaving you now. I'm sure that's what Jim would have approved."

Mrs. Ralston drew back a step or two. Charlotte's cold resolution benumbed her courage, and she could find no immediate reply.

"Ah, then it's easier for you to sacrifice Tina's happiness than your pride?" she exclaimed.

"My pride? I've no right to any pride, except in my child. And that I'll never sacrifice."

"No one asks you to. You're not reasonable. You're cruel. All I want is to be allowed to help Tina, and you speak as if I were interfering with your rights."

"My rights?" Charlotte echoed the words with a desolate laugh. "What are they? I have no rights, either before the law or in the heart of my own child."

"How can you say such things? You know how Tina loves you."

"Yes; compassionately—as I used to love my old-maid aunts. There were two of them—you remember? Like withered babies! We children used to be warned never to say anything that might shock Aunt Josie or Aunt Nonie; exactly as I heard you telling Tina the other night—"

"Oh—" Delia murmured.

Charlotte Lovell continued to stand before her, haggard, rigid, unrelenting. "No, it's gone on long enough. I mean to tell her everything; and to take her away."

"To tell her about her birth?"

"I was never ashamed of it," Charlotte panted.

"You do sacrifice her, then—sacrifice her to your desire for mastery?"

The two women faced each other, both with weapons spent. Delia, through the tremor of her own indignation, saw her antagonist slowly waver, step backward, sink down with a broken murmur on the lounge. Charlotte hid her face in the cushions, clenching them with violent hands. The same fierce maternal passion that had once flung her down upon those same cushions was now bowing her still lower, in the throes of a bitterer renunciation. Delia seemed to hear the old cry: "But how can I give up my baby?" Her own momentary resentment melted, and she bent over the mother's labouring shoulders.

"Chatty—it won't be like giving her up this time. Can't we just go on loving her together?"

Charlotte did not answer. For a long time she lay silent, immovable, her face hidden: she seemed to fear to turn it to the face bent down to her. But presently Delia was aware of a gradual relaxing of the stretched muscles, and saw that one of her cousin's arms was faintly stirring and grouping. She lowered her hand to the seeking fingers, and it was caught and pressed to Charlotte's lips.

11

Tina Lovell—now Miss Clementina Ralston—was to be married in July to Lanning Halsey. The engagement had been announced only in the previous April; and the female elders of the tribe had begun by crying out against the indelicacy of so brief a betrothal. It was unanimously agreed in the New York of those times that "young people should be given the chance to get to know each other"; though the greater number of the couples constituting New York society had played together as children, and been born of parents as long and as familiarly acquainted, yet some mysterious law of decorum required that the newly affianced should always be regarded as being also newly known to each other. In the southern states things were differently conducted: headlong engagements, even runaway marriages, were not uncommon in their annals; but such rashness was less consonant with the sluggish blood of New York, where the pace of life was still set with a Dutch deliberateness.

In a case as unusual as Tina Ralston's, however, it was no great surprise to any one that tradition should have been disregarded. In the first place, everybody knew that she was no more Tina Ralston than you or I; unless, indeed, one were to credit the rumours about poor Jim's unsuspected "past," and his widow's magnanimity. But the opinion of the majority was against this. People were reluctant to charge a dead man with an offense from which he could not clear himself; and the Ralstons unanimously declared that, thoroughly as they disapproved of Mrs. James Ralston's action, they were convinced that she would not have adopted Tina if her doing so could have been construed as "casting a slur" on her late husband.

No: the girl was perhaps a Lovell—though even that idea was not generally held—but she was certainly not a Ralston. Her brown eyes

and flighty ways too obviously excluded her from the clan for any
formal excommunication to be needful. In fact, most people believed
that—as Dr. Lanskell had always affirmed—her origin was really
undiscoverable, that she represented one of the unsolved mysteries
which occasionally perplex and irritate well-regulated societies, and
that her adoption by Delia Ralston was simply one more proof of
the Lovell clannishness, since the child had been taken in by Mrs.
Ralston only because her cousin Charlotte was so attached to it. To
say that Mrs. Ralston's son and daughter were pleased with the idea
of Tina's adoption would be an exaggeration; but they abstained
from comment, minimizing the effect of their mother's whim by a
dignified silence. It was the old New York way for families thus to
screen the eccentricities of an individual member, and where there
was "money enough to go round" the heirs would have been thought
vulgarly grasping to protest at the alienation of a small sum from the
general inheritance.

Nevertheless, Delia Ralston, from the moment of Tina's adoption,
was perfectly aware of a different attitude on the part of both her
children. They dealt with her patiently, almost parentally, as with a
minor in whom one juvenile lapse has been condoned, but who must
be subjected, in consequence, to a stricter vigilance; and society
treated her in the same indulgent but guarded manner.

She had (it was Sillerton Jackson who first phrased it) an undoubted way of "carrying things off"; since that dauntless woman,
Mrs. Manson Mingott, had broken her husband's will, nothing so
like her attitude had been seen in New York. But Mrs. Ralston's
method was different, and less easy to analyze. What Mrs. Manson
Mingott had accomplished by dint of epigram, invective, insistency
and runnings to and fro, the other achieved without raising her voice
or seeming to take a step from the beaten path. When she had persuaded Jim Ralston to take in the foundling baby, it had been done
in the turn of a hand, one didn't know when or how; and the next
day he and she were as untroubled and beaming as usual. And now,
this adoption—! Well, she had pursued the same method; as Sillerton Jackson said, she behaved as if her adopting Tina had always
been an understood thing, as if she wondered that people should
wonder. And in face of her wonder theirs seemed foolish, and they
gradually desisted.

In reality, behind Delia's assurance there was a tumult of doubts
and uncertainties. But she had once learned that one can do almost

anything (perhaps even murder) if one does not attempt to explain it; and the lesson had never been forgotten. She had never explained the taking over of the foundling baby; nor was she now going to explain its adoption. She was just going about her business as if nothing had happened that needed to be accounted for; and a long inheritance of moral modesty helped her to keep her questionings to herself.

These questionings were in fact less concerned with public opinion than with Charlotte Lovell's private thoughts. Charlotte, after her first moment of tragic resistance, had shown herself pathetically, almost painfully, grateful. That she had reason to be, Tina's attitude abundantly revealed. Tina, during the first days after her return from the Vandergrave ball, had shown a closed and darkened face that terribly reminded Delia of the ghastliness of Charlotte Lovell's sudden reflection, years before, in Delia's own bedroom mirror. The first chapter of the mother's history was already written in the daughter's eyes; and the Spender blood in Tina might well precipitate the sequence. During those few days of silent observation Delia discovered, with terror and compassion, the justification of Charlotte's fears. The girl had nearly been lost to them both: at all costs such a risk must not be renewed.

The Halseys, on the whole, had behaved admirably. Lanning wished to marry dear Delia Ralston's protégée—who was shortly, it was understood, to take her adopted mother's name, and inherit her fortune. To what better could a Halsey aspire than one more alliance with a Ralston? The families had always intermarried. The Halsey parents gave their blessing with a precipitation which showed that they too had their anxieties, and that the relief of seeing Lanning "settled" would more than compensate for the conceivable drawbacks of the marriage; though, once it was decided on, they would not admit even to themselves that such drawbacks existed. Old New York always thought away whatever interfered with the perfect propriety of its arrangements.

Charlotte Lovell of course perceived and recognized all this. She accepted the situation—in her private hours with Delia—as one more in the long list of mercies bestowed on an undeserving sinner. And one phrase of hers perhaps gave the clue to her acceptance: "Now at least she'll never suspect the truth." It had come to be the poor creature's ruling purpose that her child should never guess the tie between them . . .

But Delia's chief support was the sight of Tina. The older woman, whose whole life had been shaped and coloured by the faint reflection of a rejected happiness, hung dazzled in the light of bliss accepted. Sometimes, as she watched Tina's changing face, she felt as though her own blood were beating in it, as though she could read every thought and emotion feeding those tumultuous currents. Tina's love was a stormy affair, with continual ups and downs of rapture and depression, arrogance and self-abasement; Delia saw displayed before her, with an artless frankness, all the visions, cravings and imaginings of her own stifled youth.

What the girl really thought of her adoption it was not easy to discover. She had been given, at fourteen, the current version of her origin, and had accepted it as carelessly as a happy child accepts some remote and inconceivable fact which does not alter the familiar order of things. And she accepted her adoption in the same spirit. She knew that the name of Ralston had been given to her to facilitate her marriage with Lanning Halsey; and Delia had the impression that all irrelevant questionings were submerged in an overwhelming gratitude. "I've always thought of you as my Mamma; and now, you dearest, you really are," Tina had whispered, her cheek against Delia's; and Delia had laughed back: "Well, if the lawyers can make me so!" But there the matter dropped, swept away on the current of Tina's bliss. They were all, in those days, Delia, Charlotte, even the gallant Lanning, rather like straws whirling about on a sunlit torrent.

The golden flood bore them onward, nearer and nearer to the enchanted date; and Delia, deep in bridal preparations, wondered at the comparative indifference with which she had ordered and inspected her own daughter's twelve-dozen-of-everything. There had been nothing to quicken the pulse in young Delia's placid bridal; but as Tina's wedding approached imagination burgeoned like the year. The wedding was to be celebrated at Lovell Place, the old house on the Sound where Delia Lovell had herself been married, and where, since her mother's death, she spent her summers. Although the neighbourhood was already overspread with a net-work of mean streets, the old house, with its thin colonnaded verandah, still looked across an uncurtailed lawn and leafy shrubberies to the narrows of Hell Gate; and the drawing-rooms kept their frail slender settees, their Sheraton consoles and cabinets. It had been thought useless to discard them for more fashionable furniture, since the growth of the city made it certain that the place must eventually be sold.

Tina, like Mrs. Ralston, was to have a "house-wedding," though Episcopalian society was beginning to disapprove of such ceremonies, which were regarded as the despised *pis-aller* of Baptists, Methodists, Unitarians and the other altarless sects. In Tina's case, however, both Delia and Charlotte felt that the greater privacy of a marriage in the house made up for its more secular character; and the Halseys favoured their decision. The ladies accordingly settled themselves at Lovell Place before the end of June, and every morning young Lanning Halsey's cat-boat was seen beating across the bay, and furling its sail at the anchorage below the lawn.

There had never been a fairer June in any one's memory. The damask roses and mignonette below the verandah had never sent such a breath of summer through the tall French windows; the gnarled orange-trees brought out from the old arcaded orange-house had never been so thickly blossomed; the very haycocks on the lawn gave out whiffs of Araby.

The evening before the wedding Delia Ralston sat on the verandah watching the moon rise across the Sound. She was tired with the multitude of last preparations, and sad at the thought of Tina's going. On the following evening the house would be empty: till death came, she and Charlotte would sit alone together beside the evening lamp. Such repinings were foolish—they were, she reminded herself, "not like her." But too many memories stirred and murmured in her: her heart was haunted. As she closed the door on the silent drawing-room—already transformed into a chapel, with its lace-hung altar, the tall alabaster vases awaiting their white roses and June lilies, the strip of red carpet dividing the rows of chairs from door to chancel—she felt that it had perhaps been a mistake to come back to Lovell Place for the wedding. She saw herself again, in her high-waisted "India mull" embroidered with daisies, her flat satin sandals, her Brussels veil—saw again her reflection in the shallow pier-glass as she had left that same room on Jim Ralston's triumphant arm, and the one terrified glance she had exchanged with her own image before she took her stand under the bell of white roses in the hall, and smiled upon the congratulating company. Ah, what a different image the pier-glass would reflect tomorrow!

Charlotte Lovell's brisk step sounded indoors, and she came out and joined Mrs. Ralston.

"I've been to the kitchen to tell Melissa Grimes that she'd better count on at least two hundred plates of ice-cream."

"Two hundred? Yes—I suppose she had, with all the Philadelphia connection coming." Delia pondered. "How about the doylies?" she enquired.

"With your aunt Cecilia Vandergrave's we shall manage beautifully."

"Yes.—Thank you, Charlotte, for taking all this trouble."

"Oh—" Charlotte protested, with her flitting sneer; and Delia perceived the irony of thanking a mother for occupying herself with the details of her own daughter's wedding.

"Do sit down, Chatty," she murmured, feeling herself redden at her blunder.

Charlotte, with a sigh of fatigue, sat down on the nearest chair.

"We shall have a beautiful day tomorrow," she said, pensively surveying the placid heaven.

"Yes. Where is Tina?"

"She was very tired. I've sent her upstairs to lie down."

This seemed so eminently suitable that Delia made no immediate answer. After an interval she said: "We shall miss her."

Charlotte's reply was an inarticulate murmur.

The two cousins remained silent, Charlotte as usual bolt upright, her thin hands clutched on the arms of her old-fashioned rush-bottomed seat, Delia somewhat heavily sunk into the depths of a high-backed armchair. The two had exchanged their last remarks on the preparations for the morrow; nothing more remained to be said as to the number of guests, the brewing of the punch, the arrangements for the robing of the clergy, and the disposal of the presents in the best spare-room.

Only one subject had not yet been touched upon, and Delia, as she watched her cousin's profile grimly cut upon the melting twilight, waited for Charlotte to speak. But Charlotte remained silent.

"I have been thinking," Delia at length began, a slight tremor in her voice, "that I ought presently—"

She fancied she saw Charlotte's hands tighten on the knobs of the chair-arms.

"You ought presently—?"

"Well, before Tina goes to bed, perhaps go up for a few minutes—"

Charlotte remained silent, visibly resolved on making no effort to assist her.

"Tomorrow," Delia continued, "we shall be in such a rush from the earliest moment that I don't see how, in the midst of all the interruptions and excitement, I can possibly—"

"Possibly?" Charlotte monotonously echoed.

Delia felt her blush deepening through the dusk. "Well, I suppose you agree with me, don't you, that a word ought to be said to the child as to the new duties and responsibilities that—well—what is usual, in fact, at such a time?" she falteringly ended.

"Yes, I have thought of that," Charlotte answered. She said no more, but Delia divined in her tone the stirring of that obscure opposition which, at the crucial moments of Tina's life, seemed automatically to declare itself. She could not understand why Charlotte should, at such times, grow so enigmatic and inaccessible, and in the present case she saw no reason why this change of mood should interfere with what she deemed to be her own duty. Tina must long for her guiding hand into the new life as much as she herself yearned for the exchange of half-confidences which would be her real farewell to her adopted daughter. Her heart beating a little more quickly than usual, she rose and walked through the open window into the shadowy drawing-room. The moon, between the columns of the verandah, sent a broad band of light across the rows of chairs, irradiated the lace-decked altar with its empty candlesticks and vases, and outlined with silver Delia's heavy reflection in the pier-glass.

She crossed the room toward the hall.

"Delia!" Charlotte's voice sounded behind her. Delia turned, and the two women scrutinized each other in the revealing light. Charlotte's face looked as it had looked on the dreadful day when Delia had suddenly seen it in the looking-glass above her shoulder.

"You were going up now to speak to Tina?" Charlotte asked.

"I—yes. It's nearly nine. I thought . . ."

"Yes; I understand." Miss Lovell made a visible effort at self-control. "Please understand me too, Delia, if I ask you—not to."

Delia looked at her cousin with a vague sense of apprehension. What new mystery did this strange request conceal? But no—such a doubt as flitted across her mind was inadmissible. She was too sure of her Tina!

"I confess I don't understand, Charlotte. You surely feel that, on the night before her wedding, a girl ought to have a mother's counsel, a mother's . . ."

"Yes; I feel that." Charlotte Lovell took a hurried breath. "But the question is: *which of us is her mother?*"

Delia drew back involuntarily. "Which of us—?" she stammered.

"Yes. Oh, don't imagine it's the first time I've asked myself the question! There—I mean to be calm; quite calm. I don't intend to go back to the past. I've accepted—accepted everything—gratefully. Only tonight—just tonight . . ."

Delia felt the rush of pity which always prevailed over every other sensation in her rare interchanges of truth with Charlotte Lovell. Her throat filled with tears, and she remained silent.

"Just tonight," Charlotte concluded, "*I'm* her mother."

"Charlotte! You're not going to tell her so—not now?" broke involuntarily from Delia.

Charlotte gave a faint laugh. "If I did, should you hate it as much as all that?"

"Hate it? What a word, between us!"

"Between us? But it's the word that's been between us since the beginning—the very beginning! Since the day when you discovered that Clement Spender hadn't quite broken his heart because he wasn't good enough for you; since you found your revenge and your triumph in keeping me at your mercy, and in taking his child from me!" Charlotte's words flamed up as if from the depth of the infernal fires; then the blaze dropped, her head sank forward, and she stood before Delia dumb and stricken.

Delia's first movement was one of an indignant recoil. Where she had felt only tenderness, compassion, the impulse to help and befriend, these darknesses had been smouldering in the other's breast! It was as if a poisonous smoke had swept over some pure summer landscape. . .

Usually such feelings were quickly followed by a reaction of sympathy. But now she felt none. An utter weariness possessed her.

"Yes," she said slowly, "I sometimes believe you really have hated me from the very first; hated me for everything I've tried to do for you."

Charlotte raised her head sharply. "To do for me? But everything you've done has been done for Clement Spender!"

Delia stared at her with a kind of terror. "You are horrible, Charlotte. Upon my honour, I haven't thought of Clement Spender for years."

"Ah, but you have—you have! You've always thought of him in

thinking of Tina—of him and nobody else! A woman never stops thinking of the man she loves. She thinks of him years afterward, in all sorts of unconscious ways, in thinking of all sorts of things—books, pictures, sunsets, a flower or a ribbon—or a clock on the mantelpiece," Charlotte broke off with her sneering laugh. "That was what I gambled on, you see—that's why I came to you that day. I knew I was giving Tina another mother."

Again the poisonous smoke seemed to envelop Delia: that she and Charlotte, two spent old women, should be standing before Tina's bridal altar and talking to each other of hatred, seemed unimaginably hideous and degrading.

"You wicked woman—you *are* wicked!" she exclaimed.

Then the evil mist cleared away, and through it she saw the baffled pitiful figure of the mother who was not a mother, and who, for every benefit accepted, felt herself robbed of a privilege. She moved nearer to Charlotte and laid a hand on her arm.

"Not here! Don't let us talk like this here."

The other drew away from her. "Wherever you please, then. I'm not particular!"

"But tonight, Charlotte—the night before Tina's wedding? Isn't every place in this house full of her? How could we go on saying cruel things to each other anywhere?" Charlotte was silent, and Delia continued in a steadier voice: "Nothing you say can really hurt me—for long; and I don't want to hurt you—I never did."

"You tell me that—and you've left nothing undone to divide me from my daughter! Do you suppose it's been easy, all these years, to hear her call you 'mother'? Oh, I know, I know—it was agreed that she must never guess . . . but if you hadn't perpetually come between us she'd have had no one but me, she'd have felt about me as a child feels about its mother, she'd have *had* to love me better than any one else. With all your forbearances and your generosities you've ended by robbing me of my child. And I've put up with it all for her sake—because I knew I had to. But tonight—tonight she belongs to me. Tonight I can't bear that she should call you 'mother'."

Delia Ralston made no immediate reply. It seemed to her that for the first time she had sounded the deepest depths of maternal passion, and she stood awed of the echoes it gave back.

"How you must love her—to say such things to me," she murmured; then, with a final effort: "Yes, you're right. I won't go up to her. It's you who must go."

Charlotte started toward her impulsively; but with a hand lifted as if in defense, Delia moved across the room and out again to the verandah. As she sank down in her chair she heard the drawing-room door open and close, and the sound of Charlotte's feet on the stairs.

Delia sat alone in the night. The last drop of her magnanimity had been spent, and she tried to avert her shuddering mind from Charlotte. What was happening at this moment upstairs? With what dark revelations were Tina's bridal dreams to be defaced? Well, that was not matter for conjecture either. She, Delia Ralston, had played her part, done her utmost: there remained nothing now but to try to lift her spirit above the embittering sense of failure.

There was a strange element of truth in some of the things that Charlotte had said. With what divination her maternal passion had endowed her! Her jealousy seemed to have a million feelers. Yes; it was true that the sweetness and peace of Tina's bridal eve had been filled, for Delia, with visions of her own unrealized past. Softly, imperceptibly, it had reconciled her to the memory of what she had missed. All these last days she had been living the girl's life, she had been Tina, and Tina had been her own girlish self, the far-off Delia Lovell. Now for the first time, without shame, without self-reproach, without a pang or a scruple, Delia could yield to that vision of requited love from which her imagination had always turned away. She had made her choice in youth, and she had accepted it in maturity; and here in this bridal joy, so mysteriously her own, was the compensation for all she had missed and yet never renounced.

Delia understood now that Charlotte had guessed all this, and that the knowledge had filled her with a fierce resentment. Charlotte had said long ago that Clement Spender had never really belonged to her; now she had perceived that it was the same with Clement Spender's child. As the truth stole upon Delia her heart melted with the old compassion for Charlotte. She saw that it was a terrible, a sacrilegious thing to interfere with another's destiny, to lay the tenderest touch upon any human being's right to love and suffer after his own fashion. Delia had twice intervened in Charlotte Lovell's life: it was natural that Charlotte should be her enemy. If only she did not revenge herself by wounding Tina!

The adopted mother's thoughts reverted painfully to the little white room upstairs. She had meant her half-hour with Tina to leave the girl with thoughts as fragrant as the flowers she was to find beside her when she woke. And now—.

Delia started up from her musing. There was a step on the stair—Charlotte coming down through the silent house. Delia rose with a vague impulse of escape: she felt that she could not face her cousin's eyes. She turned the corner of the verandah, hoping to find the shutters of the dining-room unlatched, and to slip away unnoticed to her room; but in a moment Charlotte was beside her.

"Delia!"

"Ah, it's you? I was going up to bed." For the life of her Delia could not keep an edge of hardness from her voice.

"Yes: it's late. You must be very tired." Charlotte paused; her own voice was strained and painful.

"I *am* tired," Delia acknowledged.

In the moonlit hush the other went up to her, laying a timid touch on her arm.

"Not till you've seen Tina."

Delia stiffened. "Tina? But it's late! Isn't she sleeping? I thought you'd stay with her until—"

"I don't know if she's sleeping," Charlotte paused. "I haven't been in—but there's a light under her door."

"You haven't been in?"

"No: I just stood in the passage, and tried—"

"Tried—?"

"To think of something . . . something to say to her without . . . without her guessing. . ." A sob stopped her, but she pressed on with a final effort. "It's no use. You were right: there's nothing I can say. You're her real mother. Go to her. It's not your fault—or mine."

"Oh—" Delia cried.

Charlotte clung to her in inarticulate abasement. "You said I was wicked—I'm not wicked. After all, she was mine when she was little!"

Delia put an arm about her shoulder.

"Hush, dear! We'll go to her together."

The other yielded automatically to her touch, and side by side the two women mounted the stairs, Charlotte timing her impetuous step to Delia's stiffened movements. They walked down the passage to Tina's door; but there Charlotte Lovell paused and shook her head.

"No—you," she whispered, and turned away.

Tina lay in bed, her arms folded under her head, her happy eyes reflecting the silver space of sky which filled the window. She smiled at Delia through her dream.

"I knew you'd come."

Delia sat down beside her, and their clasped hands lay down upon the coverlet. They did not say much, after all; or else their communion had no need of words. Delia never knew how long she sat by the child's side: she abandoned herself to the spell of the moonlit hour.

But suddenly she thought of Charlotte, alone behind the shut door of her own room, watching, struggling, listening. Delia must not, for her own pleasure, prolong that tragic vigil. She bent down to kiss Tina goodnight; then she paused on the threshold and turned back.

"Darling! Just one thing more."

"Yes?" Tina murmured through her dream.

"I want you to promise me—"

"Everything, everything, you darling mother!"

"Well, then, that when you go away tomorrow—at the very last moment, you understand—"

"Yes?"

"After you've said goodbye to me, and to everybody else—just as Lanning helps you into the carriage—"

"Yes?"

"That you'll give your last kiss to Aunt Charlotte. Don't forget—the very last."

THE SPARK

(*The 'Sixties*)

1

"You idiot!" said his wife, and threw down her cards.

I turned my head away quickly, to avoid seeing Hayley Delane's face; though why I wished to avoid it I could not have told you, much less why I should have imagined (if I did) that a man of his age and importance would notice what was happening to the wholly negligible features of a youth like myself.

I turned away so that he should not see how it hurt me to hear him called an idiot, even in joke—well, at least half in joke; yet I often thought him an idiot myself, and bad as my own poker was, I knew enough of the game to judge that his—when he wasn't attending—fully justified such an outburst from his wife. Why her sally disturbed me I couldn't have said; nor why, when it was greeted by a shrill guffaw from her "latest," young Bolton Byrne, I itched to cuff the little bounder; nor why, when Hayley Delane, on whom banter always dawned slowly but certainly, at length gave forth his low rich gurgle of appreciation—why then, most of all, I wanted to blot the whole scene from my memory. Why?

There they sat, as I had so often seen them, in Jack Alstrop's luxurious bookless library (I'm sure the rich rows behind the glass doors were hollow), while beyond the windows the pale twilight thickened to blue over Long Island lawns and woods and a moonlit streak of sea. No one ever looked out at *that*, except to conjecture what sort of weather there would be the next day for polo, or hunting, or racing, or whatever use the season required the face of nature to be put to; no one was aware of the twilight, the moon or the blue shadows—and Hayley Delane least of all. Day after day, night after night, he sat anchored at somebody's poker-table, and fumbled absently with his cards. . .

Yes; that was the man. He didn't even (as it was once said of a great authority on heraldry) know his own silly business; which was to hang about in his wife's train, play poker with her friends, and giggle at her nonsense and theirs. No wonder Mrs. Delane was sometimes exasperated. As she said, *she* hadn't asked him to marry her! Rather not: all their contemporaries could remember what a thunderbolt it had been on his side. The first time he had seen her—at the theatre, I think: "Who's that? Over there—with the heaps of hair?"— "Oh, Leila Gracy? Why, she's not *really* pretty. . ." "Well, I'm going to marry her—" "Marry her? But her father's that old scoundrel Bill Gracy . . . the one. . ." "I'm going to marry her. . ." "The one who's had to resign from all his clubs. . ." "I'm going to marry her. . ." And he did; and it was she, if you please, who kept him dangling, and who would and who wouldn't, until some whipper-snapper of a youth, who was meanwhile making up his mind about *her*, had finally decided in the negative.

Such had been Hayley Delane's marriage; and such, I imagined, his way of conducting most of the transactions of his futile clumsy life. . . Big bursts of impulse—storms he couldn't control—then long periods of drowsing calm, during which, something made me feel, old regrets and remorses woke and stirred under the indolent surface of his nature. And yet, wasn't I simply romanticizing a commonplace case? I turned back from the window to look at the group. The bringing of candles to the card-tables had scattered pools of illumination throughout the shadowy room; in their radiance Delane's harsh head stood out like a cliff from a flowery plain. Perhaps it was only his bigness, his heaviness and swarthiness—perhaps his greater age, for he must have been at least fifteen years older than his wife and most of her friends; at any rate, I could never look at him without feeling that he belonged elsewhere, not so much in another society as in another age. For there was no doubt that the society he lived in suited him well enough. He shared cheerfully in all the amusements of his little set—rode, played polo, hunted and drove his four-in-hand with the best of them (you will see, by the last allusion, that we were still in the archaic 'nineties). Nor could I guess what other occupations he would have preferred, had he been given his choice. In spite of my admiration for him I could not bring myself to think it was Leila Gracy who had subdued him to what she worked in. What would he have chosen to do if he had not met her that night at the play? Why, I rather thought, to meet and marry some-

body else just like her. No; the difference in him was not in his tastes
—it was in something ever so much deeper. Yet what is deeper in a
man than his tastes?

In another age, then, he would probably have been doing the
equivalent of what he was doing now: idling, taking much violent exercise, eating more than was good for him, laughing at the same kind
of nonsense, and worshipping, with the same kind of dull routine-
worship, the same kind of woman, whether dressed in a crinoline, a
farthingale, a peplum or the skins of beasts—it didn't much matter
under what sumptuary dispensation one placed her. Only in that
other age there might have been outlets for other faculties, now dormant, perhaps even atrophied, but which must—yes, really must—
have had something to do with the building of that big friendly forehead, the monumental nose, and the rich dimple which now and
then furrowed his cheek with light. Did the dimple even mean no
more than Leila Gracy?

Well, perhaps it was *I* who was the idiot, if she'd only known it;
an idiot to believe in her husband, be obsessed by him, oppressed by
him, when, for thirty years now, he'd been only the Hayley Delane
whom everybody took for granted, and was glad to see, and immediately forgot. Turning from my contemplation of that great structural
head, I looked at his wife. Her head was still like something in the
making, something just flowering, a girl's head ringed with haze.
Even the kindly candles betrayed the lines in her face, the paint on
her lips, the peroxide on her hair; but they could not lessen her
fluidity of outline, or the girlishness that lurked in her eyes, floating
up from their depths like a startled Naïad. There was an irreducible
innocence about her, as there so often is about women who have
spent their time in amassing sentimental experiences. As I looked at
the husband and wife, thus confronted above the cards, I marvelled
more and more that it was she who ruled and he who bent the neck.
You will see by this how young I still was.

So young, indeed, that Hayley Delane had dawned on me in my
school-days as an accomplished fact, a finished monument: like Trinity Church, the Reservoir or the Knickerbocker Club. A New Yorker
of my generation could no more imagine him altered or away than
any of those venerable institutions. And so I had continued to take
him for granted till, my Harvard days over, I had come back after an
interval of world-wandering to settle down in New York, and he had

broken on me afresh as something still not wholly accounted for, and more interesting than I had suspected.

I don't say the matter kept me awake. I had my own business (in a down-town office), and the pleasures of my age; I was hard at work discovering New York. But now and then the Hayley Delane riddle would thrust itself between me and my other interests, as it had done tonight just because his wife had sneered at him, and he had laughed and thought her funny. And at such times I found myself moved and excited out of all proportion to anything I knew about him, or had observed in him, to justify such emotions.

The game was over, the dressing-bell had rung. It rang again presently, with a discreet insistence: Alstrop, easy in all else, preferred that his guests should not be more than half an hour late for dinner.

"I say—*Leila!*" he finally remonstrated.

The golden coils drooped above her chips. "Yes—yes. Just a minute. Hayley, you'll have to pay for me.— There, I'm going!" She laughed and pushed back her chair.

Delane, laughing also, got up lazily. Byrne flew to open the door for Mrs. Delane; the other women trooped out with her. Delane, having settled her debts, picked up her gold-mesh bag and cigarette-case, and followed.

I turned toward a window opening on the lawn. There was just time to stretch my legs while curling-tongs and powder were being plied above stairs. Alstrop joined me, and we stood staring up at a soft dishevelled sky in which the first stars came and went.

"Curse it—looks rotten for our match tomorrow!"

"Yes—but what a good smell the coming rain does give to things!"

He laughed. "You're an optimist—like old Hayley."

We strolled across the lawn toward the woodland.

"Why like old Hayley?"

"Oh, he's a regular philosopher. I've never seen him put out, have you?"

"No. That must be what makes him look so sad," I exclaimed.

"Sad? Hayley? Why, I was just saying—"

"Yes, I know. But the only people who are never put out are the people who don't care; and not caring is about the saddest occupation there is. I'd like to see him in a rage just once."

My host gave a faint whistle, and remarked: "By Jove, I believe the wind's hauling round to the north. If it does—" He moistened his finger and held it up.

I knew there was no use in theorizing with Alstrop; but I tried another tack. "What on earth has Delane done with himself all these years?" I asked. Alstrop was forty, or thereabouts, and by a good many years better able than I to cast a backward glance over the problem.

But the effort seemed beyond him. "Why—what years?"

"Well—ever since he left college."

"Lord! How do I know? I wasn't there. Hayley must be well past fifty."

It sounded formidable to my youth; almost like a geological era. And that suited him, in a way—I could imagine him drifting, or silting, or something measurable by aeons, at the rate of about a millimetre a century.

"How long has he been married?" I asked.

"I don't know that either; nearly twenty years, I should say. The kids are growing up. The boys are both at Groton. Leila doesn't look it, I must say—not in some lights."

"Well, then, what's he been doing since he married?"

"Why, what should he have done? He's always had money enough to do what he likes. He's got his partnership in the bank, of course. They say that rascally old father-in-law, whom he refuses to see, gets a good deal of money out of him. You know he's awfully soft-hearted. But he can swing it all, I fancy. Then he sits on lots of boards—Blind Asylum, Children's Aid, S.P.C.A., and all the rest. And there isn't a better sport going."

"But that's not what I mean," I persisted.

Alstrop looked at me through the darkness. "You don't mean women? I never heard—but then one wouldn't, very likely. He's a shut-up fellow."

We turned back to dress for dinner. Yes, that was the word I wanted; he was a shut-up fellow. Even the rudimentary Alstrop felt it. But shut-up consciously, deliberately—or only instinctively, congenitally? There the mystery lay.

2

THE big polo match came off the next day. It was the first of the season, and, taking respectful note of the fact, the barometer, after a night of showers, jumped back to Fair.

All Fifth Avenue had poured down to see New York versus Hempstead. The beautifully rolled lawns and freshly painted club stand were sprinkled with spring dresses and abloom with sunshades, and coaches and other vehicles without number enclosed the farther side of the field.

Hayley Delane still played polo, though he had grown so heavy that the cost of providing himself with mounts must have been considerable. He was, of course, no longer regarded as in the first rank; indeed, in these later days, when the game has become an exact science, I hardly know to what use such a weighty body as his could be put. But in that far-off dawn of the sport his sureness and swiftness of stroke caused him to be still regarded as a useful back, besides being esteemed for the part he had taken in introducing and establishing the game.

I remember little of the beginning of the game, which resembled many others I had seen. I never played myself, and I had no money on: for me the principal interest of the scene lay in the May weather, the ripple of spring dresses over the turf, the sense of youth, fun, gaiety, of young manhood and womanhood weaving their eternal pattern under the conniving sky. Now and then they were interrupted for a moment by a quick "Oh" which turned all those tangled glances the same way, as two glittering streaks of men and horses dashed across the green, locked, swayed, rayed outward into starry figures, and rolled back. But it was for a moment only—then eyes wandered again, chatter began, and youth and sex had it their own way till the next charge shook them from their trance.

I was of the number of these divided watchers. Polo as a spectacle did not amuse me for long, and I saw about as little of it as the pretty girls perched beside their swains on coach-tops and club stand. But by chance my vague wanderings brought me to the white palings enclosing the field, and there, in a cluster of spectators, I caught sight of Leila Delane.

As I approached I was surprised to notice a familiar figure shouldering away from her. One still saw old Bill Gracy often enough in the outer purlieus of the big race-courses; but I wondered how he had got into the enclosure of a fashionable Polo Club. There he was, though, unmistakably; who could forget that swelling chest under the shabby-smart racing-coat, the gray top-hat always pushed back from his thin auburn curls, and the mixture of furtiveness and swagger which made his liquid glance so pitiful? Among the figures that rose here and there like warning ruins from the dead-level of old New York's respectability, none was more typical than Bill Gracy's; my gaze followed him curiously as he shuffled away from his daughter. "Trying to get more money out of her," I concluded; and remembered what Alstrop had said of Delane's generosity.

"Well, if I were Delane," I thought, "I'd pay a good deal to keep that old ruffian out of sight."

Mrs. Delane, turning to watch her father's retreat, saw me and nodded. At the same moment Delane, on a tall deep-chested pony, ambled across the field, stick on shoulder. As he rode thus, heavily yet mightily, in his red-and-black shirt and white breeches, his head standing out like a bronze against the turf, I whimsically recalled the figure of Guidoriccio da Foligno, the famous mercenary, riding at a slow powerful pace across the fortressed fresco of the Town Hall of Siena. Why a New York banker of excessive weight and more than middle age, jogging on a pony across a Long Island polo field, should have reminded me of a martial figure on an armoured war-horse, I find it hard to explain. As far as I knew there were no turreted fortresses in Delane's background; and his too juvenile polo cap and gaudy shirt were a poor substitute for Guidoriccio's coat of mail. But it was the kind of trick the man was always playing: reminding me, in his lazy torpid way, of times and scenes and people greater than he could know. That was why he kept on interesting me.

It was this interest which caused me to pause by Mrs. Delane, whom I generally avoided. After a vague smile she had already turned her gaze on the field.

"You're admiring your husband?" I suggested, as Delane's trot carried him across our line of vision.

She glanced at me dubiously. "You think he's too fat to play, I suppose?" she retorted, a little snappishly.

"I think he's the finest figure in sight. He looks like a great general, a great soldier of fortune—in an old fresco, I mean."

She stared, perhaps suspecting irony, as she always did beneath the unintelligible.

"Ah, *he* can pay anything he likes for his mounts!" she murmured; and added, with a wandering laugh: "Do you mean it as a compliment? Shall I tell him what you say?"

"I wish you would."

But her eyes were off again, this time to the opposite end of the field. Of course—Bolton Byrne was playing on the other side! The fool of a woman was always like that—absorbed in her latest adventure. Yet there had been so many, and she must by this time have been so radiantly sure there would be more! But at every one the girl was born anew in her: she blushed, palpitated, "sat out" dances, plotted for tête-à-têtes, pressed flowers (I'll wager) in her copy of "Omar Khayyám," and was all white muslin and wild roses while it lasted. And the Byrne fever was then at its height.

It did not seem polite to leave her immediately, and I continued to watch the field at her side. "It's their last chance to score," she flung at me, leaving me to apply the ambiguous pronoun; and after that we remained silent.

The game had been a close one; the two sides were five each, and the crowd about the rails hung breathless on the last minutes. The struggle was short and swift, and dramatic enough to hold even the philanderers on the coach-tops. Once I stole a glance at Mrs. Delane, and saw the colour rush to her cheek. Byrne was hurling himself across the field, crouched on the neck of his somewhat weedy mount, his stick swung like a lance—a pretty enough sight, for he was young and supple, and light in the saddle.

"They're going to win!" she gasped with a happy cry.

But just then Byrne's pony, unequal to the pace stumbled, faltered, and came down. His rider dropped from the saddle, hauled the animal to his feet, and stood for a minute half-dazed before he scrambled up again. That minute made the difference. It gave the other side their chance. The knot of men and horses tightened, wavered, grew loose, broke up in arrowing flights; and suddenly a ball

—Delane's—sped through the enemy's goal, victorious. A roar of delight went up; "Good for old Hayley!" voices shouted. Mrs. Delane gave a little sour laugh. "That—that beastly pony; I warned him it was no good—and the ground still so slippery," she broke out.

"The pony? Why, he's a ripper. It's not every mount that will carry Delane's weight," I said. She stared at me unseeingly and turned away with twitching lips. I saw her speeding off toward the enclosure.

I followed hastily, wanting to see Delane in the moment of his triumph. I knew he took all these little sporting successes with an absurd seriousness, as if, mysteriously, they were the shadow of more substantial achievements, dreamed of, or accomplished, in some previous life. And perhaps the elderly man's vanity in holding his own with the youngsters was also an element of his satisfaction; how could one tell, in a mind of such monumental simplicity?

When I reached the saddling enclosure I did not at once discover him; an unpleasant sight met my eyes instead. Bolton Byrne, livid and withered—his face like an old woman's, I thought—rode across the empty field, angrily lashing his pony's flanks. He slipped to the ground, and as he did so, struck the shivering animal a last blow clean across the head. An unpleasant sight—

But retribution fell. It came like a black-and-red thunderbolt descending on the wretch out of the heaven. Delane had him by the collar, had struck him with his whip across the shoulders, and then flung him off like a thing too mean for human handling. It was over in the taking of a breath—then, while the crowd hummed and closed in, leaving Byrne to slink away as if he had become invisible, I saw my big Delane, grown calm and apathetic, turn to the pony and lay a soothing hand on its neck.

I was pushing forward, moved by the impulse to press that hand, when his wife went up to him. Though I was not far off I could not hear what she said; people did not speak loud in those days, or "make scenes," and the two or three words which issued from Mrs. Delane's lips must have been inaudible to everyone but her husband. On his dark face they raised a sudden redness; he made a motion of his free arm (the other hand still on the pony's neck), as if to wave aside an importunate child; then he felt in his pocket, drew out a cigarette, and lit it. Mrs. Delane, white as a ghost, was hurrying back to Alstrop's coach.

I was turning away too when I saw her husband hailed again. This

time it was Bill Gracy, shoving and yet effacing himself, as his manner was, who came up, a facile tear on his lashes, his smile half tremulous, half defiant, a yellow-gloved hand held out.

"God bless you for it, Hayley—God bless you, my dear boy!"

Delane's hand reluctantly left the pony's neck. It wavered for
an instant, just touched the other's palm, and was instantly engulfed
in it. Then Delane, without speaking, turned toward the shed where
his mounts were being rubbed down, while his father-in-law swag-
gered from the scene.

I had promised, on the way home, to stop for tea at a friend's
house half-way between the Polo Club and Alstrop's. Another friend,
who was also going there, offered me a lift, and carried me on to Alstrop's afterward.

During our drive, and about the tea-table, the talk of course dwelt
mainly on the awkward incident of Bolton Byrne's thrashing. The
women were horrified or admiring, as their humour moved them; but
the men all agreed that it was natural enough. In such a case any
pretext was permissible, they said; though it was stupid of Hayley to
air his grievance on a public occasion. But then he *was* stupid—that
was the consensus of opinion. If there was a blundering way of doing
a thing that needed to be done, trust him to hit on it! For the rest,
everyone spoke of him affectionately, and agreed that Leila was a
fool . . . and nobody particularly liked Byrne, an "outsider" who had
pushed himself into society by means of cheek and showy horsemanship. But Leila, it was agreed, had always had a weakness for
"outsiders," perhaps because their admiration flattered her extreme
desire to be thought "in."

"Wonder how many of the party you'll find left—this affair must
have caused a good deal of a shake-up," my friend said, as I got down
at Alstrop's door; and the same thought was in my own mind. Byrne
would be gone, of course; and no doubt, in another direction, Delane
and Leila. I wished I had a chance to shake that blundering hand of
Hayley's. . .

Hall and drawing-room were empty; the dressing-bell must have
sounded its discreet appeal more than once, and I was relieved to
find it had been heeded. I didn't want to stumble on any of my
fellow-guests till I had seen our host. As I was dashing upstairs I
heard him call me from the library, and turned back.

"No hurry—dinner put off till nine," he said cheerfully; and

added, on a note of inexpressible relief: "We've had a tough job of it
—*ouf!*"

The room looked as if they had: the card tables stood untouched,
and the deep armchair, gathered into confidential groups, seemed
still deliberating on the knotty problem. I noticed that a good deal
of whiskey and soda had gone toward its solution.

"What happened? Has Byrne left?"

"Byrne? No—thank goodness!" Alstrop looked at me almost re-
proachfully. "Why should he? That was just what we wanted to
avoid."

"I don't understand. You don't mean that *he's* stayed and the
Delanes have gone?"

"Lord forbid! Why should they, either? Hayley's apologized!"

My jaw fell, and I returned my host's stare.

"Apologized? To that hound? For what?"

Alstrop gave an impatient shrug. "Oh, for God's sake don't reopen
the cursèd question," it seemed to say. Aloud he echoed: "For what?
Why, after all, a man's got a right to thrash his own pony, hasn't he?
It was beastly unsportsmanlike, of course—but it's nobody's business
if Byrne chooses to be that kind of a cad. That's what Hayley saw—
when he cooled down."

"Then I'm sorry he cooled down."

Alstrop looked distinctly annoyed. "I don't follow you. We had a
hard enough job. You said you wanted to see him in a rage just once;
but you don't want him to go on making an ass of himself, do you?"

"I don't call it making an ass of himself to thrash Byrne."

"And to advertise his conjugal difficulties all over Long Island,
with twenty newspaper reporters at his heels?"

I stood silent, baffled but incredulous. "I don't believe he ever
gave that a thought. I wonder who put it to him first in that way?"

Alstrop twisted his unlit cigarette about in his fingers. "We all did
—as delicately as we could. But it was Leila who finally convinced
him. I must say Leila was very game."

I still pondered: the scene in the paddock rose again before me,
the quivering agonized animal, and the way Delane's big hand had
been laid reassuringly on its neck.

"Nonsense! I don't believe a word of it!" I declared.

"A word of what I've been telling you?"

"Well, of the official version of the case."

To my surprise, Alstrop met my glance with an eye neither puzzled nor resentful. A shadow seemed to be lifted from his honest face.

"What *do* you believe?" he asked.

"Why, that Delane thrashed that cur for ill-treating the pony, and not in the least for being too attentive to Mrs. Delane. I was there, I tell you— I saw him."

Alstrop's brow cleared completely. "There's something to be said for that theory," he agreed, smiling over the match he was holding to his cigarette.

"Well, then—what was there to apologize for?"

"Why, for *that*—butting in between Byrne and his horse. Don't you see, you young idiot? If Hayley hadn't apologized, the mud was bound to stick to his wife. Everybody would have said the row was on her account. It's as plain as the knob on the door—there wasn't anything else for him to do. He saw it well enough after she'd said a dozen words to him—"

"I wonder what those words are," I muttered.

"Don't know. He and she came downstairs together. He looked a hundred years old, poor old chap. 'It's the cruelty, it's the cruelty,' he kept saying: 'I hate cruelty.' I rather think he knows we're all on his side. Anyhow, it's all patched up and well patched up; and I've ordered my last 'eighty-four Georges Goulet brought up for dinner. Meant to keep it for my own wedding-breakfast; but since this afternoon I've rather lost interest in that festivity," Alstrop concluded with a celibate grin.

"Well," I repeated, as though it were a relief to say, "I could swear he did it for the pony."

"Oh, so could I," my host acquiesced as we went upstairs together.

On my threshold, he took me by the arm and followed me in. I saw there was still something on his mind.

"Look here, old chap—you say you were in there when it happened?"

"Yes. Close by—"

"Well," he interrupted, "for the Lord's sake don't allude to the subject tonight, will you?"

"Of course not."

"Thanks a lot. Truth is, it was a narrow squeak, and I couldn't help admiring the way Leila played up. She was in a fury with Hayley; but she got herself in hand in no time, and behaved very decently. She told me privately he was often like that—flaring out all of a sudden like a madman. You wouldn't imagine it, would you, with that quiet way of his? She says she thinks it's his old wound."

"What old wound?"

"Didn't you know he was wounded—where was it? Bull Run, I believe. In the head—"

No, I hadn't known; hadn't even heard, or remembered, that Delane had been in the Civil War. I stood and stared in my astonishment.

"Hayley Delane? In the war?"

"Why, of course. All through it."

"But Bull Run—Bull Run was at the very beginning." I broke off to go through a rapid mental calculation. "Look here, Jack, it can't be; he's not over fifty-three. You told me so yourself. If he was in it from the beginning he must have gone into it as a schoolboy."

"Well, that's just what he did: ran away from school to volunteer. His family didn't know what had become of him till he was wounded. I remember hearing my people talk about it. Great old sport, Hayley. I'd have given a lot not to have this thing happen; not at my place anyhow; but it *has*, and there's no help for it. Look here, you swear you won't make a sign, will you? I've got all the others into line, and if you'll back us up we'll have a regular Happy Family Evening. Jump into your clothes—it's nearly nine."

3

THIS is not a story-teller's story; it is not even the kind of episode capable of being shaped into one. Had it been, I should have reached my climax, or at any rate its first stage, in the incident at the Polo Club, and what I have left to tell would be the effect of that incident on the lives of the three persons concerned.

It is not a story, or anything in the semblance of a story, but merely an attempt to depict for you—and in so doing, perhaps make clearer to myself—the aspect and character of a man whom I loved, perplexedly but faithfully, for many years. I make no apology, therefore, for the fact that Bolton Byrne, whose evil shadow ought to fall across all my remaining pages, never again appears in them; and that the last I saw of him (for my purpose) was when, after our exaggeratedly cheerful and even noisy dinner that evening at Jack Alstrop's, I observed him shaking hands with Hayley Delane, and declaring, with pinched lips and a tone of falsetto cordiality: "Bear malice? Well, rather not—why, what rot! All's fair in—in polo, ain't it? I should say so! Yes—off first thing tomorrow. S'pose of course you're staying on with Jack over Sunday? I wish I hadn't promised the Gildermeres—." And therewith he vanishes, having served his purpose as a passing lantern-flash across the twilight of Hayley Delane's character.

All the while, I continued to feel that it was not Bolton Byrne who mattered. While clubs and drawing-rooms twittered with the episode, and friends grew portentous in trying to look unconscious, and said "I don't know what you mean," with eyes beseeching you to speak if you knew more than they did, I had already discarded the whole affair, as I was sure Delane had. "It *was* the pony, and nothing but the pony," I chuckled to myself, as pleased as if I had owed

Mrs. Delane a grudge, and were exulting in her abasement; and still there ran through my mind the phrase which Alstrop said Delane had kept repeating: "It was the cruelty—it was the cruelty. I hate cruelty."

How it fitted in, now, with the other fact my host had let drop— the fact that Delane had fought all through the civil war! It seemed incredible that it should have come to me as a surprise; that I should have forgotten, or perhaps never even known, this phase of his history. Yet in young men like myself, just out of college in the 'nineties, such ignorance was more excusable than now seems possible.

That was the dark time of our national indifference, before the country's awakening; no doubt the war seemed much farther from us, much less a part of us, than it does to the young men of today. Such was the case, at any rate, in old New York, and more particularly, perhaps, in the little clan of well-to-do and indolent old New Yorkers among whom I had grown up. Some of these, indeed, had fought bravely through the four years: New York had borne her part, a memorable part, in the long struggle. But I remember with what perplexity I first wakened to the fact—it was in my school-days—that if certain of my father's kinsmen and contemporaries had been in the war, others—how many!—had stood aside. I recall especially the shock with which, at school, I had heard a boy explain his father's lameness: "He's never got over that shot in the leg he got at Chancellorsville."

I stared; for my friend's father was just my own father's age. At the moment (it was at a school foot-ball match) the two men were standing side by side, in full sight of us—*his* father stooping, halt and old, mine, even to filial eyes, straight and youthful. Only an hour before I had been bragging to my friend about the wonderful shot my father was (he had taken me down to his North Carolina shooting at Christmas); but now I stood abashed.

The next time I went home for the holidays I said to my mother, one day when we were alone: "Mother, why didn't father fight in the war?" My heart was beating so hard that I thought she must have seen my excitement and been shocked. But she raised an untroubled face from her embroidery.

"Your father, dear? Why, because he was a married man." She had a reminiscent smile. "Molly was born already—she was six months old when Fort Sumter fell. I remember I was nursing her when Papa came in with the news. We couldn't believe it." She paused to match a silk placidly. "Married men weren't called upon to fight," she explained.

"But they *did*, though, Mother! Payson Gray's father fought. He was so badly wounded at Chancellorsville that he's had to walk with a stick ever since."

"Well, my dear, I don't suppose you would want your Papa to be like that, would you?" She paused again, and finding I made no answer, probably thought it pained me to be thus convicted of heartlessness, for she added, as if softening the rebuke: "Two of your father's cousins *did* fight: his cousins Harold and James. They were young men, with no family obligations. And poor Jamie was killed, you remember."

I listened in silence, and never again spoke to my mother of the war. Nor indeed to anyone—even myself. I buried the whole business out of sight, out of hearing, as I thought. After all, the war had all happened long ago; it had been over ten years when I was born. And nobody ever talked about it nowadays. Still, one did, of course, as one grew up, meet older men of whom it was said: "Yes, so-and-so was in the war." Many of them even continued to be known by the military titles with which they had left the service: Colonel Ruscott, Major Detrancy, old General Scole. People smiled a little, but admitted that, if it pleased them to keep their army rank, it was a right they had earned. Hayley Delane, it appeared, thought differently. He had never allowed himself to be called "Major" or "Colonel" (I think he had left the service a Colonel). And besides he was years younger than these veterans. To find that he had fought at their side was like discovering that the grandmother one could remember playing with had been lifted up by her nurse to see General Washington. I always thought of Hayley Delane as belonging to my own generation rather than to my father's; though I knew him to be so much older than myself, and occasionally called him "sir," I felt on an equality with him, the equality produced by sharing the same amusements and talking of them in the same slang. And indeed he must have been ten or fifteen years younger than the few men I knew who had been in the war, none of whom, I was sure, had had to run away from school to volunteer; so that my forgetfulness (or perhaps even ignorance) of his past was not inexcusable.

Broad and Delane had been, for two or three generations, one of the safe and conservative private banks of New York. My friend Hayley had been made a partner early in his career; the post was almost hereditary in his family. It happened that, not long after the scene at Alstrop's, I was offered a position in the house. The offer came, not through Delane, but through Mr. Frederick Broad, the senior member, who was an old friend of my father's. The chance was too advantageous to be rejected, and I transferred to a desk at Broad and Delane's my middling capacities and my earnest desire to do my best. It was owing to this accidental change that there gradually grew up between Hayley Delane and myself a sentiment almost filial on my part, elder-brotherly on his—for paternal one could hardly call him, even with his children.

My job need not have thrown me in his way, for his business duties sat lightly on him, and his hours at the bank were neither long nor regular. But he appeared to take a liking to me, and soon began to call on me for the many small services which, in the world of affairs, a young man can render his elders. His great perplexity was the writing of business letters. He knew what he wanted to say; his sense of the proper use of words was clear and prompt; I never knew anyone more impatient of the hazy verbiage with which American primary culture was already corrupting our speech. He would put his finger at once on these laborious inaccuracies, growling: "For God's sake, translate it into English—" but when he had to write, or worse still dictate, a letter his friendly forehead and big hands grew damp, and he would mutter, half to himself and half to me: "How the devil shall I say: 'Your letter of the blankth came yesterday, and after thinking over what you propose I don't like the looks of it'?"— "Why, say just that," I would answer; but he would shake his head and object: "My dear fellow, you're as bad as I am. You don't know how *to write good English.*" In his mind there was a gulf fixed between speaking and writing the language. I could never get his imagination to bridge this gulf, or to see that the phrases which fell from his lips were "better English" than the written version, produced after much toil and pen-biting, which consisted in translating the same statement into some such language as: "I am in receipt of your communication of the 30th ultimo, and regret to be compelled to inform you in reply that, after mature consideration of the proposals therein contained, I find myself unable to pronounce a favourable judgment upon the same"—usually sending a furious dash through "the same" as "counterjumper's lingo," and then groaning over his inability to find a more Johnsonian substitute.

"The trouble with me," he used to say, "is that both my parents

were martinets on grammar, and never let any of us children use a
vulgar expression without correcting us." (By "vulgar" he meant either familiar or inexact.) "We were brought up on the best books—
Scott and Washington Irving, old what's-his-name who wrote the
Spectator, and Gibbon and so forth; and though I'm not a literary
man, and never set up to be, I can't forget my early training, and
when I see the children reading a newspaper-fellow like Kipling I
want to tear the rubbish out of their hands. Cheap journalism—
that's what most modern books are. And you'll excuse my saying,
dear boy, that even you are too young to know how English ought to
be *written*."

It was quite true—though I had at first found it difficult to believe
—that Delane must once have been a reader. He surprised me, one
night, as we were walking home from a dinner where we had met, by
apostrophizing the moon, as she rose, astonished, behind the steeple
of the "Heavenly Rest," with "She walks in beauty like the night";
and he was fond of describing a victorious charge in a polo match by
saying: "Tell you what, we came down on 'em like the Assyrian."
Nor had Byron been his only fare. There had evidently been a time
when he had known the whole of Gray's "Elegy" by heart, and I
once heard him murmuring to himself, as we stood together one autumn evening on the terrace of his country-house:

> Now fades the glimmering landscape on the sight,
> And all the air a solemn stillness holds . . .

Little sympathy as I felt for Mrs. Delane, I could not believe it
was his marriage which had checked Delane's interest in books. To
judge from his very limited stock of allusions and quotations, his
reading seemed to have ceased a good deal earlier than his first meeting with Leila Gracy. Exploring him like a geologist, I found, for several layers under the Leila stratum, no trace of any interest in letters;
and I concluded that, like other men I knew, his mind had been
receptive up to a certain age, and had then snapped shut on what it
possessed, like a replete crustacean never reached by another high
tide. People, I had by this time found, all stopped living at one time
or another, however many years longer they continued to be alive;
and I suspected that Delane had stopped at about nineteen. That
date would roughly coincide with the end of the Civil War, and
with his return to the common-place existence from which he had

never since deviated. Those four years had apparently filled to the brim every crevice of his being. For I could not hold that he had gone through them unawares, as some famous figures, puppets of fate, have been tossed from heights to depths of human experience without once knowing what was happening to them—forfeiting a crown by the insistence on some prescribed ceremonial, or by carrying on their flight a certain monumental dressing-case.

No, Hayley Delane had felt the war, had been made different by it; how different I saw only when I compared him to the other "veterans" who, from being regarded by me as the dullest of my father's dinner-guests, were now become figures of absorbing interest. Time was when, at my mother's announcement that General Scole or Major Detrancy was coming to dine, I had invariably found a pretext for absenting myself; now, when I knew they were expected, my chief object was to persuade her to invite Delane.

"But he's so much younger—he cares only for the sporting set. He won't be flattered at being asked with old gentlemen." And my mother, with a slight smile, would add: "If Hayley has a weakness, it's the wish to be thought younger than he is—on his wife's account, I suppose."

Once, however, she did invite him, and he accepted: and we got over having to ask Mrs. Delane (who undoubtedly *would* have been bored) by leaving out Mrs. Scole and Mrs. Ruscott, and making it a "man's dinner" of the old-fashioned sort, with canvas-backs, a bowl of punch, and my mother the only lady present—the kind of evening my father still liked best.

I remember, at that dinner, how attentively I studied the contrasts, and tried to detect the point of resemblance, between General Scole, old Detrancy and Delane. Allusions to the war—anecdotes of Bull Run and Andersonville, of Lincoln, Seward and MacClellan, were often on Major Detrancy's lips, especially after the punch had gone round. "When a fellow's been through the war," he used to say as a preface to almost everything, from expressing his opinion of last Sunday's sermon to praising the roasting of a canvas-back. Not so General Scole. No one knew exactly why he had been raised to the rank he bore, but he tacitly proclaimed his right to it by never alluding to the subject. He was a tall and silent old gentleman with a handsome shock of white hair, half-shut blue eyes, glinting between veined lids, and an impressively upright carriage. His manners were perfect—so perfect that they stood him in lieu of language, and people would say afterward how agreeable he had been when he had only bowed and smiled, and got up and sat down again, with an absolute mastery of those difficult arts. He was said to be a judge of horses and Madeira, but he never rode, and was reported to give very indifferent wines to the rare guests he received in his grim old house in Irving Place.

He and Major Detrancy had one trait in common—the extreme caution of the old New Yorker. They viewed with instinctive distrust anything likely to derange their habits, diminish their comfort, or lay on them any unwonted responsibilities, civic or social; and slow as their other mental processes were, they showed a supernatural quickness in divining when a seemingly harmless conversation might draw them into "signing a paper," backing up even the mildest attempt at municipal reform, or pledging them to support, on however small a scale, any new and unfamiliar cause.

According to their creed, gentlemen subscribed as handsomely as their means allowed to the Charity Organization Society, the Patriarchs' Balls, the Children's Aid, and their own parochial charities. Everything beyond savoured of "politics," revivalist meetings, or the attempts of vulgar persons to buy their way into the circle of the elect; even the Society for the Prevention of Cruelty to Animals, being of more recent creation, seemed open to doubt, and they thought it rash of certain members of the clergy to lend it their names. "But then," as Major Detrancy said, "in this noisy age some people will do anything to attract notice." And they breathed a joint sigh over the vanished "Old New York" of their youth, the exclusive and impenetrable New York to which Rubini and Jenny Lind had sung and Mr. Thackeray lectured, the New York which had declined to receive Charles Dickens, and which, out of revenge, he had so scandalously ridiculed.

Yet Major Detrancy and General Scole had fought all through the war, had participated in horrors and agonies untold, endured all manner of hardships and privations, suffered the extremes of heat and cold, hunger, sickness and wounds; and it had all faded like an indigestion comfortably slept off, leaving them perfectly commonplace and happy.

The same was true, with a difference, of Colonel Ruscott, who, though not by birth of the same group, had long since been received into it, partly because he was a companion in arms, partly because of having married a Hayley connection. I can see Colonel Ruscott still:

a dapper handsome little fellow, rather too much of both, with a lustrous wave to his hair (or was it a wig?), and a dash too much of Cologne on too-fine cambric. He had been in the New York militia in his youth, had "gone out" with the great Seventh; and the Seventh, ever since, had been the source and centre of his being, as still, to some octogenarians, their University dinner is.

Colonel Ruscott specialized in chivalry. For him the war was "the blue and the grey," the rescue of lovely Southern girls, anecdotes about Old Glory, and the carrying of vital despatches through the enemy lines. Enchantments seemed to have abounded in his path during the four years which had been so drab and desolate to many; and the punch (to the amusement of us youngsters, who were not above drawing him) always evoked from his memory countless situations in which by prompt, respectful yet insinuating action, he had stamped his image indelibly on some proud Southern heart, while at the same time discovering where Jackson's guerillas lay, or at what point the river was fordable.

And there sat Hayley Delane, so much younger than the others, yet seeming at such times so much their elder that I thought to myself: "But if *he* stopped growing up at nineteen, they're still in long-clothes!" But it was only morally that he had gone on growing. Intellectually they were all on a par. When the last new play at Wallack's was discussed, or my mother tentatively alluded to the last new novel by the author of *Robert Elsmere* (it was her theory that, as long as the hostess was present at a man's dinner, she should keep the talk at the highest level), Delane's remarks were no more penetrating than his neighbours'—and he was almost sure not to have read the novel.

It was when any social question was raised: any of the problems concerning club administration, charity, or the relation between "gentlemen" and the community, that he suddenly stood out from them, not so much opposed as aloof.

He would sit listening, stroking my sister's long skye-terrier (who, defying all rules, had jumped up to his knees at dessert), with a grave half-absent look on his heavy face; and just as my mother (I knew) was thinking how bored he was, that big smile of his would reach out and light up his dimple, and he would say, with enough diffidence to mark his respect for his elders, yet a complete independence of their views: "After all, what does it matter who makes the first move? The thing is to get the business done."

That was always the gist of it. To everyone else, my father included, what mattered in everything, from Diocesan Meetings to Patriarchs' Balls, was just what Delane seemed so heedless of: the standing of the people who make up the committee or headed the movement. To Delane, only the movement itself counted; if the thing was worth doing, he pronounced in his slow lazy way, get it done somehow, even if its backers *were* Methodists or Congregationalists, or people who dined in the middle of the day.

"If they were convicts from Sing Sing I shouldn't care," he affirmed, his hand lazily flattering the dog's neck as I had seen it caress Byrne's terrified pony.

"Or lunatics out of Bloomingdale—as these 'reformers' usually are," my father added, softening the remark with his indulgent smile.

"Oh, well," Delane murmured, his attention flagging, "I daresay we're well enough off as we are."

"Especially," added Major Detrancy with a playful sniff, "with the punch in the offing, as I perceive it to be."

The punch struck the note for my mother's withdrawal. She rose with her shy circular smile, while the gentlemen, all on their feet, protested gallantly at her desertion.

"Abandoning us to go back to Mr. Elsmere—we shall be jealous of the gentleman!" Colonel Ruscott declared, chivalrously reaching the door first; and as he opened it my father said, again with his indulgent smile: "Ah, my wife—she's a great reader."

Then the punch was brought.

4

"You'll admit," Mrs. Delane challenged me, "that Hayley's perfect."

Don't imagine you have yet done with Mrs. Delane, any more than Delane had, or I. Hitherto I have shown you only one side, or rather one phase, of her; that during which, for obvious reasons, Hayley became an obstacle or a burden. In the intervals between her great passions, when somebody had to occupy the vacant throne in her bosom, her husband was always reinstated there; and during these interlunar periods he and the children were her staple subjects of conversation. If you had met her then for the first time you would have taken her for the perfect wife and mother, and wondered if Hayley ever got a day off; and you would have not been far wrong in conjecturing that he seldom did.

Only these intervals were rather widely spaced, and usually of short duration; and at other times, his wife being elsewhere engaged, it was Delane who elder-brothered his big boys and their little sister. Sometimes, on these occasions—when Mrs. Delane was abroad or at Newport—Delane used to carry me off for a week to the quiet old house in the New Jersey hills, full of Hayley and Delane portraits, of heavy mahogany furniture and the mingled smell of lavender bags and leather—leather boots, leather gloves, leather luggage, all the aromas that emanate from the cupboards and passages of a house inhabited by hard riders.

When his wife was at home he never seemed to notice the family portraits or the old furniture. Leila carried off her own regrettable origin by professing a democratic scorn of ancestors in general. "I know enough bores in the flesh without bothering to remember all the dead ones," she said one day, when I had asked her the name of

a stern-visaged old forebear in breast-plate and buff jerkin who hung
on the library wall: and Delane, so practised in sentimental duplici-
ties, winked jovially at the children, as who should say: "There's the
proper American spirit for you, my dears! That's the way we all
ought to feel."

Perhaps, however, he detected a tinge of irritation in my own look,
for that evening, as we sat over the fire after Leila had yawned her-
self off to bed, he glanced up at the armoured image, and said,
"That's old Durward Hayley—the friend of Sir Harry Vane the
Younger and all that lot. I have some curious letters somewhere. . .
But Leila's right, you know," he added loyally.

"In not being interested?"

"In regarding all that old past as dead. It *is* dead. We've got no
use for it over here. That's what that queer fellow in Washington always used to say to me. . ."

"What queer fellow in Washington?"

"Oh, a sort of big backwoodsman who was awfully good to me
when I was in hospital . . . after Bull Run. . ."

I sat up abruptly. It was the first time that Delane had mentioned
his life during the war. I thought my hand was on the clue; but it
wasn't.

"You were in hospital in Washington?"

"Yes; for a longish time. They didn't know much about disinfect-
ing wounds in those days. . . But Leila," he resumed with his smiling obstinacy, "Leila's dead right, you know. It's a better world now.
Think of what has been done to relieve suffering since then!" When
he pronounced the word "suffering" the vertical furrows in his forehead deepened as though he felt the actual pang of his old wound.
"Oh, I believe in progress every bit as much as *she* does—I believe
we're working out toward something better. If we weren't. . ." He
shrugged his mighty shoulders, reached lazily for the adjoining tray,
and mixed my glass of whiskey-and-soda.

"But the war—you were wounded at Bull Run?"

"Yes." He looked at his watch. "But I'm off to bed now. I promised the children to take them for an early canter tomorrow, before
lessons, and I have to have my seven or eight hours of sleep to feel
fit. I'm getting on, you see. Put out the lights when you come up."

No; he wouldn't talk about the war.

It was not long afterward that Mrs. Delane appealed to me to tes-

tify to Hayley's perfection. She had come back from her last absence
—a six weeks' flutter at Newport—rather painfully subdued and
pinched-looking. For the first time I saw in the corners of her mouth
that middle-aged droop which has nothing to do with the loss of
teeth. "How common-looking she'll be in a few years!" I thought un-
charitably.

"Perfect—perfect," she insisted; and then, plaintively: "And yet—"
I echoed coldly: "And yet?"

"With the children, for instance. He's everything to them. He's
cut me out with my own children." She was half joking, half whim-
pering.

Presently she stole an eye-lashed look at me, and added: "And at
times he's so *hard*."

"Delane?"

"Oh, I know you won't believe it. But in business matters——have
you never noticed? You wouldn't admit it, I suppose. But there are
times when one simply can't move him." We were in the library, and
she glanced up at the breast-plated forebear. "He's as hard to the
touch as *that*." She pointed to the steel convexity.

"Not the Delane I know," I murmured, embarrassed by these
confidences.

"Ah, you think you know him?" she half-sneered; then, with a du-
tiful accent: "I've always said he was a perfect father—and he's made
the children think so. And yet—"

He came in, and dropping a pale smile on him she drifted away,
calling to her children.

I thought to myself: "She's getting on, and something has told her
so at Newport. Poor thing!"

Delane looked as preoccupied as she did; but he said nothing till
after she had left us that evening. Then he suddenly turned to me.

"Look here. You're a good friend of ours. Will you help me to
think out a rather bothersome question?"

"Me, sir?" I said, surprised by the "ours," and overcome by so solemn an appeal from my elder.

He made a wan grimace. "Oh, don't call me 'sir'; not during this
talk." He paused, and then added: "You're remembering the difference in our ages. Well, that's just why I'm asking you. I want
the opinion of somebody who hasn't had time to freeze into his rut
—as most of my contemporaries have. The fact is, I'm trying to make
my wife see that we've got to let her father come and live with us."

My open-mouthed amazement must have been marked enough to pierce his gloom, for he gave a slight laugh. "Well, yes—"

I sat dumbfounded. All New York knew what Delane thought of his suave father-in-law. He had married Leila in spite of her antecedents; but Bill Gracy, at the outset, had been given to understand that he would not be received under the Delane roof. Mollified by the regular payment of a handsome allowance, the old gentleman, with tears in his eyes, was wont to tell his familiars that personally he didn't blame his son-in-law. "Our tastes differ: that's all. Hayley's not a bad chap at heart; give you my word he isn't." And the familiars, touched by such magnanimity, would pledge Hayley in the champagne provided by his last remittance.

Delane, as I still remained silent, began to explain. "You see, somebody's got to look after him—who else is there?"

"But—" I stammered.

"You'll say he's always needed looking after? Well, I've done my best; short of having him here. For a long time that seemed impossible; I quite agreed with Leila—" (So it was Leila who had banished her father!) "But now," Delane continued, "it's different. The poor old chap's getting on: he's been breaking up very fast this last year. And some bloodsucker of a woman has got hold of him, and threatened to rake up old race-course rows, and I don't know what. If we don't take him in he's bound to go under. It's his last chance—he feels it is. He's scared; he wants to come."

I was still silent, and Delane went on: "You think, I suppose, what's the use? Why not let him stew in his own juice? With a decent allowance, of course. Well, I can't say . . . I can't tell you . . . only I feel it mustn't be. . ."

"And Mrs. Delane?"

"Oh, I see her point. The children are growing up; they've hardly known their grandfather. And having him in the house isn't going to be like having a nice old lady in a cap knitting by the fire. He takes up room, Gracy does; it's not going to be pleasant. She thinks we ought to consider the children first. But I don't agree. The world's too ugly a place; why should anyone grow up thinking it's a flower-garden? Let 'em take their chance. . . . And then"—he hesitated, as if embarrassed—"well, you know her; she's fond of society. Why shouldn't she be? She's made for it. And of course it'll cut us off, prevent our inviting people. She won't like that, though she doesn't admit that it has anything to do with her objecting."

So, after all, he judged the wife he still worshipped! I was beginning to see why he had that great structural head, those large quiet
movements. There *was* something—

"What alternative does Mrs. Delane propose?"

He coloured. "Oh, more money. I sometimes fancy," he brought
out, hardly above a whisper, "that she thinks I've suggested having
him here because I don't want to give more money. She won't understand, you see, that more money would just precipitate things."

I coloured too, ashamed of my own thought. Had she not, perhaps, understood; was it not her perspicacity which made her hold
out? If her father was doomed to go under, why prolong the process?
I could not be sure, now, that Delane did not suspect this also, and
allow for it. There was apparently no limit to what he allowed for.

"*You'll* never be frozen into a rut," I ventured, smiling.

"Perhaps not frozen; but sunk down deep. I'm that already. Give
me a hand up, do!" He answered my smile.

I was still in the season of cocksureness, and at a distance could no
doubt have dealt glibly with the problem. But at such short range,
and under those melancholy eyes, I had a chastening sense of inexperience.

"You don't care to tell me what you think?" He spoke almost re-
proachfully.

"Oh, it's not that . . . I'm trying to. But it's so—so awfully evangel-
ical," I brought out—for some of us were already beginning to read
the Russians.

"Is it? Funny, that, too. For I have an idea I got it, with other
things, from an old heathen; that chap I told you about, who used to
come and talk to me by the hour in Washington."

My interest revived. "That chap in Washington—was he a heathen?"

"Well, he didn't go to church." Delane did, regularly taking the
children, while Leila slept off the previous night's poker, and joining
in the hymns in a robust baritone, always half a tone flat.

He seemed to guess that I found his reply inadequate, and added
helplessly: "You know I'm no scholar: I don't know what you'd call
him." He lowered his voice to add: "I don't think he believed in our
Lord. Yet he taught me Christian charity."

"He must have been an unusual sort of man, to have made such
an impression on you. What was his name?"

"There's the pity! I must have heard it, but I was all foggy with fever most of the time, and can't remember. Nor what became of him either. One day he didn't turn up—that's all I recall. And soon afterward I was off again, and didn't think of him for years. Then, one day, I had to settle something with myself, and, by George, there he was, telling me the right and wrong of it! Queer—he comes like that, at long intervals; turning-points, I suppose." He frowned, his heavy head sunk forward, his eyes distant, pursuing the vision.

"Well—hasn't he come this time?"

"Rather! That's my trouble—I can't see things in any way but his. And I want another eye to help me."

My heart was beating rather excitedly. I felt small, trivial and inadequate, like an intruder on some grave exchange of confidences.

I tried to postpone my reply, and at the same time to satisfy another curiosity. "Have you ever told Mrs. Delane about—about him?"

Delane roused himself and turned to look at me. He lifted his shaggy eyebrows slightly, protruded his lower lip, and sank once more into abstraction.

"Well, sir," I said, answering the look, "I believe in him."

The blood rose in his dark cheek. He turned to me again, and for a second the dimple twinkled through his gloom. "That's your answer?"

I nodded breathlessly.

He got up, walked the length of the room, and came back, pausing in front of me. "He just vanished. I never even knew his name. . ."

5

DELANE was right; having Bill Gracy under one's roof was not like harbouring a nice old lady. I looked on at the sequence of our talk and marvelled.

New York—the Delanes' New York—sided unhesitatingly with Leila. Society's attitude toward drink and dishonesty was still inflexible: a man who had had to resign from his clubs went down into a pit presumably bottomless. The two or three people who thought Delane's action "rather fine" made haste to add: "But he ought to have taken a house for the old man in some quiet place in the country." Bill Gracy cabined in a quiet place in the country! Within a week he would have set the neighbourhood on fire. He was simply not to be managed by proxy; Delane had understood that, and faced it.

Nothing in the whole unprecedented situation was more odd, more unexpected and interesting, than Mr. Gracy's own perception of it. He too had become aware that his case was without alternative.

"They *had* to have me here, by gad; I see that myself. Old firebrand like me . . . couldn't be trusted! Hayley saw it from the first— fine fellow, my son-in-law. He made no bones about telling me so. Said: 'I can't trust you, father' . . . said it right out to me. By gad, if he'd talked to me like that a few years sooner I don't answer for the consequences! But I ain't my own man any longer. . . I've got to put up with being treated like a baby. . . I forgave him on the spot, sir— on the spot." His fine eye filled, and he stretched a soft old hand, netted with veins and freckles, across the table to me.

In the virtual seclusion imposed by his presence I was one of the few friends the Delanes still saw. I knew Leila was grateful to me for coming; but I did not need that incentive. It was enough that I could give even a negative support to Delane. The first months were horrible; but he was evidently saying to himself: "Things will settle down gradually," and just squaring his great shoulders to the storm.

Things didn't settle down; as embodied in Bill Gracy they continued in a state of effervescence. Filial care, good food and early hours restored the culprit to comparative health; he became exuberant, arrogant and sly. Happily his first imprudence caused a relapse alarming even to himself. He saw that his powers of resistance were gone, and, tremulously tender over his own plight, he relapsed into a plaintive burden. But he was never a passive one. Some part or other he had to play, usually to somebody's detriment.

One day a strikingly dressed lady forced her way in to see him, and the house echoed with her recriminations. Leila objected to the children's assisting at such scenes, and when Christmas brought the boys home she sent them to Canada with a tutor, and herself went with the little girl to Florida. Delane, Gracy and I sat down alone to our Christmas turkey, and I wondered what Delane's queer friend of the Washington hospital would have thought of that festivity. Mr. Gracy was in a melting mood, and reviewed his past with an edifying prolixity. "After all, women and children have always loved me," he summed up, a tear on his lashes. "But I've been a curse to you and Leila, and I know it, Hayley. That's my only merit, I suppose—that I *do* know it! Well, here's to turning over a new leaf . . ." and so forth.

One day, a few months later, Mr. Broad, the head of the firm, sent for me, I was surprised, and somewhat agitated at the summons, for I was not often called into his august presence.

"Mr. Delane has a high regard for your ability," he began affably.

I bowed, thrilled at what I supposed to be a hint of promotion; but Mr. Broad went on: "I know you are at his house a great deal. In spite of the difference in age he always speaks of you as an old friend." Hopes of promotion faded, yet left me unregretful. Somehow, this was even better. I bowed again.

Mr. Broad was becoming embarrassed. "You see Mr. William Gracy rather frequently at his son-in-law's?"

"He's living there," I answered bluntly.

Mr. Broad heaved a sigh. "Yes. It's a fine thing of Mr. Delane . . . but does he quite realize the consequences? His own family side with his wife. You'll wonder at my speaking with such frankness . . . but I've been asked . . . it has been suggested . . ."

"If he weren't there he'd be in the gutter."

Mr. Broad sighed more deeply. "Ah, it's a problem. . . You may ask why I don't speak directly to Mr. Delane . . . but it's so delicate, and he's so uncommunicative. Still, there are Institutions. . . You don't feel there's anything to be done?"

I was silent, and he shook hands, murmured: "This is confidential," and made a motion of dismissal. I withdrew to my desk, feeling that the situation must indeed be grave if Mr. Broad could so emphasize it by consulting me.

New York, to ease its mind of the matter, had finally decided that Hayley Delane was "queer." There were the two of them, madmen both, hobnobbing together under his roof; no wonder poor Leila found the place untenable! That view, bruited about, as things are, with a mysterious underground rapidity, prepared me for what was to follow.

One day during the Easter holidays I went to dine with the Delanes, and finding my host alone with old Gracy I concluded that Leila had again gone off with the children. She had: she had been gone a week, and had just sent a letter to her husband saying that she was sailing from Montreal with the little girl. The boys would be sent back to Groton with a trusted servant. She would add nothing more, as she did not wish to reflect unkindly on what his own family agreed with her in thinking an act of ill-advised generosity. He knew that she was worn out by the strain he had imposed on her, and would understand her wishing to get away for a while. . .

She had left him.

Such events were not, in those days, the matters of course they have since become; and I doubt if, on a man like Delane, the blow would ever have fallen lightly. Certainly that evening was the grimmest I ever passed in his company. I had the same impression as on the day of Bolton Byrne's chastisement: the sense that Delane did not care a fig for public opinion. His knowing that it sided with his wife did not, I believe, affect him in the least; nor did her own view of his conduct—and for that I was unprepared. What really ailed him, I discovered, was his loneliness. He missed her, he wanted her back—her trivial irritating presence was the thing in the world he could least dispense with. But when he told me what she had done he simply added: "I see no help for it; we've both of us got a right to our own opinion."

Again I looked at him with astonishment. Another voice seemed to be speaking through his lips, and I had it on mine to say: "Was that what your old friend in Washington would have told you?" But at the door of the dining-room, where we had lingered, Mr. Gracy's flushed countenance and unreverend auburn locks appeared between us.

"Look here, Hayley; what about our little game? If I'm to be packed off to bed at ten like a naughty boy you might at least give me my hand of poker first." He winked faintly at me as we passed into the library, and added, in a hoarse aside: "If he thinks he's going to boss me like Leila he's mistaken. Flesh and blood's one thing; now she's gone I'll be damned if I take any bullying."

That threat was the last flare of Mr. Gracy's indomitable spirit. The act of defiance which confirmed it brought on a severe attack of pleurisy. Delane nursed the old man with dogged patience, and he emerged from the illness diminished, wizened, the last trace of auburn gone from his scant curls, and nothing left of his old self but a harmless dribble of talk.

Delane taught him to play patience, and he used to sit for hours by the library fire, puzzling over the cards, or talking to the children's parrot, which he fed and tended with a touching regularity. He also devoted a good deal of time to collecting stamps for his youngest grandson, and his increasing gentleness and playful humour so endeared him to the servants that a trusted housemaid had to be dismissed for smuggling cocktails into his room. On fine days Delane, coming home earlier from the bank, would take him for a short stroll; and one day, happening to walk up Fifth Avenue behind them, I noticed that the younger man's broad shoulders were beginning to stoop like the other's, and that there was less lightness in his gait than in Bill Gracy's jaunty shamble. They looked like two old men doing their daily mile on the sunny side of the street. Bill Gracy was no longer a danger to the community, and Leila might have come home. But I understood from Delane that she was still abroad with her daughter.

Society soon grows used to any state of things which is imposed upon it without explanation. I had noticed that Delane never explained; his chief strength lay in that negative quality. He was probably hardly aware that people were beginning to say: "Poor old Gracy —after all, he's making a decent end. It was the proper thing for

Hayley to do—but his wife ought to come back and share the burden
with him." In important matters he was so careless of public opinion
that he was not likely to notice its veering. He wanted Leila to come
home; he missed her and the little girl more and more; but for him
there was no "ought" about the matter.

And one day she came. Absence had rejuvenated her, she had
some dazzling new clothes, she had made the acquaintance of a
charming Italian nobleman who was coming to New York on the
next steamer . . . she was ready to forgive her husband, to be tolerant, resigned and even fond. Delane, with his amazing simplicity,
took all this for granted; the effect of her return was to make him
feel he had somehow been in the wrong, and he was ready to bask in
her forgiveness. Luckily for her own popularity she arrived in time to
soothe her parent's declining moments. Mr. Gracy was now a mere
mild old pensioner and Leila used to drive out with him regularly,
and refuse dull invitations "because she had to be with Papa." After
all, people said, she had a heart. Her husband thought so too, and
triumphed in the conviction. At that time life under the Delane
roof, though melancholy, was idyllic; it was a pity old Gracy could
not have been kept alive longer, so miraculously did his presence
unite the household it had once divided. But he was beyond being
aware of this, and from a cheerful senility sank into coma and death.
The funeral was attended by the whole of New York, and Leila's
crape veil was of exactly the right length—a matter of great importance in those days.

Life has a way of overgrowing its achievements as well as its ruins.
In less time than seemed possible in so slow-moving a society, the
Delanes' family crisis had been smothered and forgotten. Nothing
seemed changed in the mutual attitude of husband and wife, or in
that of their little group toward the couple. If anything, Leila had
gained in popular esteem by her assiduity at her father's bedside;
though as a truthful chronicler I am bound to add that she partly
forfeited this advantage by plunging into a flirtation with the Italian
nobleman before her crape trimmings had been replaced by *pas-
sementerie*. On such fundamental observances old New York still
took its stand.

As for Hayley Delane, he emerged older, heavier, more stooping,
but otherwise unchanged, from the ordeal. I am not sure that anyone
except myself was aware that there had been an ordeal. But my con-

viction remained. His wife's return had changed him back into a card-playing, ball-going, race-frequenting elderly gentleman; but I had seen the waters part, and a granite rock thrust up from them. Twice the upheaval had taken place; and each time in obedience to motives unintelligible to the people he lived among. Almost any man can take a stand on a principle his fellow-citizens are already occupying; but Hayley Delane held out for things his friends could not comprehend, and did it for reasons he could not explain. The central puzzle subsisted.

Does it subsist for me to this day? Sometimes, walking up town from the bank where in my turn I have become an institution, I glance through the rails of Trinity churchyard and wonder. He has lain there ten years or more now; his wife has married the President of a rising Western University, and grown intellectual and censorious; his children are scattered and established. Does the old Delane vault hold his secret, or did I surprise it one day; did he and I surprise it together?

It was one Sunday afternoon, I remember, not long after Bill Gracy's edifying end. I had not gone out of town that week-end, and after a long walk in the frosty blue twilight of Central Park I let myself into my little flat. To my surprise I saw Hayley Delane's big overcoat and tall hat in the hall. He used to drop in on me now and then, but mostly on the way home from a dinner where we happened to have met; and I was rather startled at his appearance at that hour and on a Sunday. But he lifted an untroubled face from the morning paper.

"You didn't expect a call on a Sunday? Fact is, I'm out of a job. I wanted to go down to the country, as usual, but there's some grand concert or other that Leila was booked for this afternoon; and a dinner tonight at Alstrop's. So I dropped in to pass the time of day. What *is* there to do on a Sunday afternoon, anyhow?"

There he was, the same old usual Hayley, as much put to it as the merest fribble of his set to employ an hour unfilled by poker! I was glad he viewed me as a possible alternative, and laughingly told him so. He laughed too—we were on terms of brotherly equality—and told me to go ahead and read two or three notes which had arrived in my absence. "Gad—how they shower down on a fellow at your age!" he chuckled.

I broke the seals and was glancing through the letters when I heard an exclamation at my back.

"By Jove—there he is!" Hayley Delane shouted. I turned to see what he meant.

He had taken up a book—an unusual gesture, but it lay at his elbow, and I suppose he had squeezed the newspapers dry. He held the volume out to me without speaking, his forefinger resting on the open page; his swarthy face was in a glow, his hand shook a little. The page to which his finger pointed bore the steel engraving of a man's portrait.

"It's him to the life—I'd know those old clothes of his again anywhere," Delane exulted, jumping up from his seat.

I took the book and stared first at the portrait and then at my friend.

"Your pal in Washington?"

He nodded excitedly. "That chap I've often told you about—yes!" I shall never forget the way his smile flew out and reached the dimple. There seemed a network of them spangling his happy face. His eyes had grown absent, as if gazing down invisible vistas. At length they travelled back to me.

"How on earth did the old boy get his portrait in a book? Has somebody been writing something about him?" His sluggish curiosity awakened, he stretched his hand for the volume. But I held it back.

"Lots of people have written about him; but this book is his own."

"You mean he wrote it?" He smiled incredulously. "Why, the poor chap hadn't any education!"

"Perhaps he had more than you think. Let me keep the book a moment longer, and read you something from it."

He signed an assent, though I could see the apprehension of the printed page already clouding his interest.

"What sort of things did he write?"

"Things for *you*. Now listen."

He settled back into his armchair, composing a painfully attentive countenance, and I sat down and began:

A sight in camp in the day-break grey and dim.
As from my tent I emerge so early, sleepless,
As slow I walk in the cool fresh air, the path near by the hospital
*   tent,*
Three forms I see on stretchers lying, brought out there, untended
*   lying,*

Over each the blanket spread, ample brownish woollen blanket,
Grey and heavy blanket, folding, covering all.

Curious, I halt, and silent stand:
Then with light fingers I from the face of the nearest, the first, just
    lift the blanket:
Who are you, elderly man so gaunt and grim, with well-grey'd hair,
    and flesh all sunken about the eyes?
Who are you, my dear comrade?
Then to the second I step—And who are you, my child and darling?
Who are you, sweet boy, with cheeks yet blooming?

Then to the third—a face nor child, nor old, very calm, as of beauti-
    ful yellow-white ivory;
Young man, I think I know you—I think this face of yours is the
    face of the Christ himself;
Dead and divine, and brother of all, and here again he lies.

I laid the open book on my knee, and stole a glance at Delane. His
face was a blank, still composed in the heavy folds of enforced attention. No spark had been struck from him. Evidently the distance was
too great between the far-off point at which he and English poetry
had parted company, and this new strange form it had put on. I
must find something which would bring the matter closely enough
home to surmount the unfamiliar medium.

> *Vigil strange I kept on the field one night,*
> *When you, my son and my comrade, dropt at my side. . .*

The starlit murmur of the verse flowed on, muffled, insistent; my
throat filled with it, my eyes grew dim. I said to myself, as my voice
sank on the last line: "He's reliving it all now, seeing it again—knowing for the first time that someone else saw it as he did."

Delane stirred uneasily in his seat, and shifted his crossed legs one
over the other. One hand absently stroked the fold of his carefully
ironed trousers. His face was still a blank. The distance had not yet
been bridged between Gray's "Elegy" and this unintelligible harmony. But I was not discouraged. I ought not to have expected any

of it to reach him—not just at first—except by way of the closest personal appeal. I turned from the "Lovely and Soothing Death," at which I had reopened the book, and looked for another page. My listener leaned back resignedly.

> *Bearing the bandages, water and sponge,*
> *Straight and swift to my wounded I go. . .*

I read on to the end. Then I shut the book and looked up again. Delane sat silent, his great hands clasping the arms of his chair, his head slightly sunk on his breast. His lids were dropped, as I imagined reverentially. My own heart was beating with a religious emotion; I had never felt the oft-read lines as I felt them then.

A little timidly, he spoke at length, "Did *he* write that?"

"Yes; just about the time you were seeing him, probably."

Delane still brooded; his expression grew more and more timid. "What do you . . . er . . . call it . . . exactly?" he ventured.

I was puzzled for a moment; then: "Why, poetry . . . rather a free form, of course. . . You see, he was an originator of new verse-forms . . ."

"New verse-forms?" Delane echoed forlornly. He stood up in his heavy way, but did not offer to take the book from me again. I saw in his face the symptoms of approaching departure.

"Well, I'm glad to have seen his picture after all these years," he said; and on the threshold he paused to ask: "What was his name, by the way?"

When I told him he repeated it with a smile of slow relish. "Yes; that's it. Old Walt—that was what all the fellows used to call him. He was a great chap: I'll never forget him.—I rather wish, though," he added, in his mildest tone of reproach, "you hadn't told me that he wrote all that rubbish."

NEW YEAR'S DAY

(The 'Seventies)

1

"She was *bad* . . . always. They used to meet at the Fifth Avenue Hotel," said my mother, as if the scene of the offence added to the guilt of the couple whose past she was revealing. Her spectacles slanted on her knitting, she dropped the words in a hiss that might have singed the snowy baby-blanket which engaged her indefatigable fingers. (It was typical of my mother to be always employed in benevolent actions while she uttered uncharitable words.)

"They used to meet at the Fifth Avenue Hotel"; how the precision of the phrase characterized my old New York! A generation later, people would have said, in reporting an affair such as Lizzie Hazeldean's with Henry Prest: "They met in hotels"—and today who but a few superannuated spinsters, still feeding on the venom secreted in their youth, would take any interest in the tracing of such topographies?

Life has become too telegraphic for curiosity to linger on any given point in a sentimental relation; as old Sillerton Jackson, in response to my mother, grumbled through his perfect "china set": "Fifth Avenue Hotel? They might meet in the middle of Fifth Avenue nowadays, for all that anybody cares."

But what a flood of light my mother's tart phrase had suddenly focussed on an unremarked incident of my boyhood!

The Fifth Avenue Hotel . . . Mrs. Hazeldean and Henry Prest . . . the conjunction of these names had arrested her darting talk on a single point of my memory, as a search-light, suddenly checked in its gyrations, is held motionless while one notes each of the unnaturally sharp and lustrous images it picks out.

At the time I was a boy of twelve, at home from school for the holidays. My mother's mother, Grandmamma Parrett, still lived in the house in West Twenty-third Street which Grandpapa had built in his pioneering youth, in days when people shuddered at the perils of living north of Union Square—days that Grandmamma and my parents looked back to with a joking incredulity as the years passed and the new houses advanced steadily Park-ward, outstripping the Thirtieth Streets, taking the Reservoir at a bound, and leaving us in what, in my school-days, was already a dullish back-water between Aristocracy to the south and Money to the north.

Even then fashion moved quickly in New York, and my infantile memory barely reached back to the time when Grandmamma, in lace lappets and creaking "*moiré*," used to receive on New Year's Day, supported by her handsome married daughters. As for old Sillerton Jackson, who, once a social custom had dropped into disuse, always affected never to have observed it, he stoutly maintained that the New Year's Day ceremonial had never been taken seriously except among families of Dutch descent, and that that was why Mrs. Henry van der Luyden had clung to it, in a reluctant half-apologetic way, long after her friends had closed their doors on the first of January, and the date had been chosen for those out-of-town parties which are so often used as a pretext for absence when the unfashionable are celebrating their rites.

Grandmamma of course, no longer received. But it would have seemed to her an exceedingly odd thing to go out of town in winter, especially now that the New York houses were luxuriously warmed by the new hot-air furnaces, and searchingly illuminated by gas chandeliers. No, thank you—no country winters for the chilblained generation of prunella sandals and low-necked sarcenet, the generation brought up in unwarmed and unlit houses, and shipped off to die in Italy when they proved unequal to the struggle of living in New York! Therefore Grandmamma, like most of her contemporaries, remained in town on the first of January, and marked the day by a family reunion, a kind of supplementary Christmas—though to us juniors the absence of presents and plum-pudding made it but a pale and moonlike reflection of the Feast.

Still, the day was welcome as a lawful pretext for over-eating, dawdling, and looking out of the window: a Dutch habit still extensively practised in the best New York circles. On the day in question, however, we had not yet placed ourselves behind the plate-glass whence it would presently be so amusing to observe the funny gentlemen who trotted about, their evening ties hardly concealed behind their overcoat collars, darting in and out of chocolate-coloured house-fronts on their sacramental round of calls. We were still engaged in placidly digesting around the ravaged luncheon table when a servant dashed in to say that the Fifth Avenue Hotel was on fire.

Oh, then the fun began—and what fun it was! For Grand-mamma's house was just opposite the noble edifice of white marble which I associated with such deep-piled carpets, and such a rich sultry smell of anthracite and coffee, whenever I was bidden to "step across" for a messenger-boy, or to buy the evening paper for my elders.

The hotel, for all its sober state, was no longer fashionable. No one, in my memory, had ever known any one who went there; it was frequented by "politicians" and "Westerners," two classes of citizens whom my mother's intonation always seemed to deprive of their vote by ranking them with illiterates and criminals.

But for that very reason there was all the more fun to be expected from the calamity in question; for had we not, with infinite amuse-ment, watched the arrival, that morning, of monumental "floral pieces" and towering frosted cakes for the New Year's Day reception across the way? The event was a communal one. All the ladies who were the hotel's "guests" were to receive together in the densely lace-curtained and heavily chandeliered public parlours, and gentlemen with long hair, imperials and white gloves had been hastening since two o'clock to the scene of revelry. And now, thanks to the oppor-tune conflagration, we were going to have the excitement not only of seeing the Fire Brigade in action (supreme joy of the New York youngster), but of witnessing the flight of the ladies and their visi-tors, staggering out through the smoke in gala array. The idea that the fire might be dangerous did not mar these pleasing expectations. The house was solidly built; New York's invincible Brigade was al-ready at the door, in a glare of polished brass, coruscating helmets and horses shining like table-silver; and my tall cousin Hubert Wes-son, dashing across at the first alarm, had promptly returned to say that all risk was over, though the two lower floors were so full of smoke and water that the lodgers, in some confusion, were being transported to other hotels. How then could a small boy see in the event anything but an unlimited lark?

Our elders, once reassured, were of the same mind. As they stood behind us in the windows, looking over our heads, we heard chuckles of amusement mingled with ironic comment.

"Oh, my dear, look—here they all come! The New Year ladies! Low neck and short sleeves in broad daylight, every one of them! Oh, and the fat one with the paper roses in her hair . . . they *are* paper, my dear . . . off the frosted cake, probably! Oh! Oh! Oh! *Oh!*"

Aunt Sabina Wesson was obliged to stuff her lace handkerchief between her lips, while her firm poplin-cased figure rocked with delight.

"Well, my dear," Grandmamma gently reminded her, "in my youth we wore low-necked dresses all day long and all the year around."

No one listened. My cousin Kate, who always imitated Aunt Sabina, was pinching my arm in an agony of mirth. "Look at them scuttling! The parlours must be full of smoke. Oh, but this one is still funnier; the one with the tall feather in her hair! Granny, did you wear feathers in your hair in the daytime? Oh, don't ask me to believe it! And the one with the diamond necklace! And all the gentlemen in white ties! Did Grandpapa wear a white tie at two o'clock in the afternoon?" Nothing was sacred to Kate, and she feigned not to notice Grandmamma's mild frown of reproval.

"Well, they do in Paris, to this day, at weddings—wear evening clothes and white ties," said Sillerton Jackson with authority. "When Minnie Transome of Charleston was married at the Madeleine to the Duc de . . ."

But no one listened even to Sillerton Jackson. One of the party had abruptly exclaimed: "Oh, there's a lady running out of the hotel who's not in evening dress!"

The exclamation caused all our eyes to turn toward the person indicated, who had just reached the threshold; and someone added, in an odd voice: "Why, her figure looks like Lizzie Hazeldean's—"

A dead silence followed. The lady who was not in evening dress paused. Standing on the door-step with lifted veil, she faced our window. Her dress was dark and plain—almost conspicuously plain—and in less time than it takes to tell she had put her hand to her closely-patterned veil and pulled it down over her face. But my young eyes were keen and far-sighted; and in that hardly perceptible interval I had seen a vision. Was she beautiful—or was she only someone apart? I felt the shock of a small pale oval, dark eyebrows curved with one sure stroke, lips made for warmth, and now drawn up in a grimace of terror; and it seemed as if the mysterious something, rich, secret and insistent, that broods and murmurs behind a boy's conscious thoughts, had suddenly peered out at me. . . As the dart reached me her veil dropped.

"But it *is* Lizzie Hazeldean!" Aunt Sabina gasped. She had stopped laughing, and her crumpled handkerchief fell to the carpet.

"Lizzie—*Lizzie?*" The name was echoed over my head with varying intonations of reprobation, dismay and half-veiled malice.

Lizzie Hazeldean? Running out of the Fifth Avenue Hotel on New Year's Day with all those dressed-up women? But what on earth could she have been doing there? No; nonsense! It was impossible. . .

"There's Henry Prest with her," continued Aunt Sabina in a precipitate whisper.

"With her?" someone gasped; and "*Oh—*" my mother cried with a shudder.

The men of the family said nothing, but I saw Hubert Wesson's face crimson with surprise. Henry Prest! Hubert was forever boring us youngsters with his Henry Prest! That was the kind of chap Hubert meant to be at thirty: in his eyes Henry Prest embodied all the manly graces. Married? No, thank you! That kind of man wasn't made for the domestic yoke. Too fond of ladies' society, Hubert hinted with his undergraduate smirk; and handsome, rich, independent—an all-round sportsman, good horseman, good shot, crack yachtsman (had his pilot's certificate, and always sailed his own sloop, whose cabin was full of racing trophies); gave the most delightful little dinners, never more than six, with cigars that beat old Beaufort's; was awfully decent to the younger men, chaps of Hubert's age included—all combined, in short, all the qualities, mental and physical, which make up, in such eyes as Hubert's, that oracular and irresistible figure, the man of the world. "Just the fellow," Hubert always solemnly concluded, "that I should go straight to if ever I got into any kind of row that I didn't want the family to know about"; and our blood ran pleasantly cold at the idea of our old Hubert's ever being in such an unthinkable predicament.

I felt sorry to have missed a glimpse of this legendary figure; but my gaze had been enthralled by the lady, and now the couple had vanished in the crowd.

The group in our window continued to keep an embarrassed silence. They looked almost frightened; but what struck me even more deeply was that not one of them looked surprised. Even to my boyish sense it was clear that what they had just seen was only the confirmation of something they had long been prepared for. At length one of my uncles emitted a whistle, was checked by a severe glance from his wife, and muttered: "I'll be damned"; another uncle began an unheeded narrative of a fire at which he had been present in his youth, and my mother said to me severely: "You ought to be at home preparing your lessons—a big boy like you!" a remark so obviously unfair that it served only to give the measure of her agitation.

"I don't believe it," said Grandmamma, in a low voice of warning, protest and appeal. I saw Hubert steal a grateful look at her.

But nobody else listened: every eye still strained through the window. Livery-stable "hacks," of the old blue-curtained variety, were driving up to carry off the fair fugitives; for the day was bitterly cold, and lit by one of those harsh New York suns of which every ray seems an icicle. Into these ancient vehicles the ladies, now regaining their composure, were being piled with their removable possessions, while their kid-gloved callers ("So like the White Rabbit!" Kate exulted) appeared and reappeared in the doorway, gallantly staggering after them under bags, reticules, bird-cages, pet dogs and heaped-up finery. But to all this—as even I, a little boy, was aware—nobody in Grandmamma's window paid the slightest attention. The thoughts of one and all, with a mute and guarded eagerness, were still following the movements of those two who were so obviously unrelated to the rest. The whole business—discovery, comment, silent visual pursuit—could hardly, all told, have filled a minute, perhaps not as much; before the sixty seconds were over, Mrs. Hazeldean and Henry Prest had been lost in the crowd, and, while the hotel continued to empty itself into the street, had gone their joint or separate ways. But in my grandmother's window the silence continued unbroken.

"Well, it's over: here are the firemen coming out again," someone said at length.

We youngsters were all alert at that; yet I felt that the grown-ups lent but a half-hearted attention to the splendid sight which was New York's only pageant: the piling of scarlet ladders on scarlet carts, the leaping up on the engine of the helmeted flame-fighters, and the disciplined plunge forward of each pair of broad-chested black steeds, as one after another the chariots of fire rattled off.

Silently, almost morosely, we withdrew to the drawing-room hearth; where, after an interval of languid monosyllables, my mother, rising first, slipped her knitting into its bag, and turning on me with renewed severity, said: "This racing after fire-engines is what makes you too sleepy to prepare your lessons"—a comment so wide of the mark that once again I perceived, without understanding, the extent of the havoc wrought in her mind by the sight of Mrs. Hazeldean and Henry Prest coming out of the Fifth Avenue Hotel together.

It was not until many years later that chance enabled me to relate this fugitive impression to what had preceded and what came after it.

2

Mrs. Hazeldean paused at the corner of Fifth Avenue and Madison Square. The crowd attracted by the fire still enveloped her; it was safe to halt and take breath.

Her companion, she knew, had gone in the opposite direction. Their movements, on such occasions, were as well-ordered and as promptly executed as those of the New York Fire Brigade; and after their precipitate descent to the hall, the discovery that the police had barred their usual exit, and the quick: "You're all right?" to which her imperceptible nod had responded, she was sure he had turned down Twenty-third Street toward Sixth Avenue.

"The Parretts' windows were full of people," was her first thought.

She dwelt on it a moment, and then reflected: "Yes, but in all that crowd and excitement nobody would have been thinking of *me!*"

Instinctively she put her hand to her veil, as though recalling that her features had been exposed when she ran out, and unable to remember whether she had covered them in time or not.

"What a fool I am! It can't have been off my face for more than a second—" but immediately afterward another disquieting possibility assailed her. "I'm almost sure I saw Sillerton Jackson's head in one of the windows, just behind Sabina Wesson's. No one else has that particularly silvery gray hair." She shivered, for everyone in New York knew that Sillerton Jackson saw everything, and could piece together seemingly unrelated fragments of fact with the art of a skilled china-mender.

Meanwhile, after sending through her veil the circular glance which she always shot about her at that particular corner, she had begun to walk up Broadway. She walked well—fast, but not too fast;

easily, assuredly, with the air of a woman who knows that she has a good figure, and expects rather than fears to be identified by it. But under this external appearance of ease she was covered with cold beads of sweat.

Broadway, as usual at that hour, and on a holiday, was nearly deserted; the promenading public still slowly poured up and down Fifth Avenue.

"Luckily there was such a crowd when we came out of the hotel that no one could possibly have noticed me," she murmured over again, reassured by the sense of having the long thoroughfare to herself. Composure and presence of mind were so necessary to a woman in her situation that they had become almost a second nature to her, and in a few minutes her thick uneven heart-beats began to subside and to grow steadier. As if to test their regularity, she paused before a florist's window, and looked appreciatively at the jars of roses and forced lilac, the compact bunches of lilies-of-the-valley and violets, the first pots of close-budded azaleas. Finally she opened the shop-door, and after examining the Jacqueminots and Marshal Niels, selected with care two perfect specimens of a new silvery-pink rose, waited for the florist to wrap them in cotton-wool, and slipped their long stems into her muff for more complete protection.

"It's so simple, after all," she said to herself as she walked on. "I'll tell him that as I was coming up Fifth Avenue from Cousin Cecilia's I heard the fire-engines turning into Twenty-third Street, and ran after them. Just what *he* would have done . . . once . . ." she ended on a sigh.

At Thirty-first Street she turned the corner with a quicker step. The house she was approaching was low and narrow; but the Christmas holly glistening between frilled curtains, the well-scrubbed steps, the shining bell and door-knob, gave it a welcoming look. From garret to basement it beamed like the abode of a happy couple.

As Lizzie Hazeldean reached the door a curious change came over her. She was conscious of it at once—she had so often said to herself, when her little house rose before her: "It makes me feel younger as soon as I turn the corner." And it was true even today. In spite of her agitation she was aware that the lines between her eyebrows were smoothing themselves out, and that a kind of inner lightness was replacing the heavy tumult of her breast. The lightness revealed itself in her movements, which grew as quick as a girl's as she ran up the steps. She rang twice—it was her signal—and turned an unclouded smile on her elderly parlourmaid.

"Is Mr. Hazeldean in the library, Susan? I hope you've kept up the fire for him."

"Oh, yes, ma'am. But Mr. Hazeldean's not in," said Susan returning the smile respectfully.

"*Not in?* With his cold—and in this weather?"

"That's what I told him, ma'am. But he just laughed—"

"Just laughed? What do you mean, Susan?" Lizzie Hazeldean felt herself turning pale. She rested her hand quickly on the hall table.

"Well, ma'am, the minute he heard the fire-engine, off he rushed like a boy. It seems the Fifth Avenue Hotel's on fire: there's where he's gone."

The blood left Mrs. Hazeldean's lips; she felt it shuddering back to her heart. But a second later she spoke in a tone of natural and good-humoured impatience.

"What madness! How long ago—can you remember?" Instantly, she felt the possible imprudence of the question, and added: "The doctor said he ought not to be out more than a quarter of an hour, and only at the sunniest time of the day."

"I know that, ma'am, and so I reminded him. But he's been gone nearly an hour, I should say."

A sense of deep fatigue overwhelmed Mrs. Hazeldean. She felt as if she had walked for miles against an icy gale: her breath came laboriously.

"How could you let him go?" she wailed; then, as the parlourmaid again smiled respectfully, she added: "Oh, I know—sometimes one can't stop him. He gets so restless, being shut up with these long colds."

"That's what I *do* feel, ma'am."

Mistress and maid exchanged a glance of sympathy, and Susan felt herself emboldened to suggest: "Perhaps the outing will do him good," with the tendency of her class to encourage favoured invalids in disobedience.

Mrs. Hazeldean's look grew severe. "Susan! I've often warned you against talking to him in that way—"

Susan reddened, and assumed a pained expression. "How can you think it, ma'am?—me that never say anything to anybody, as all in the house will bear witness."

Her mistress made an impatient movement. "Oh, well, I daresay he won't be long. The fire's over."

"Ah—you knew of it too, then, ma'am?"

"Of the fire? Why, of course, I *saw* it, even—" Mrs. Hazeldean smiled. "I was walking home from Washington Square—from Miss Cecilia Winter's—and at the corner of Twenty-third Street there was a huge crowd, and clouds of smoke. . . It's very odd that I shouldn't have run across Mr. Hazeldean." She looked limpidly at the parlour-maid. "But, then, of course, in all that crowd and confusion . . ."

Half-way up the stairs she turned to call back: "Make up a good fire in the library, please, and bring the tea up. It's too cold in the drawing-room."

The library was on the upper landing. She went in, drew the two roses from her muff, tenderly unswathed them, and put them in a slim glass on her husband's writing-table. In the doorway she paused to smile at this touch of summer in the firelit wintry room; but a moment later her frown of anxiety reappeared. She stood listening intently for the sound of a latch-key; then, hearing nothing, passed on to her bedroom.

It was a rosy room, hung with one of the new English chintzes, which also covered the deep sofa, and the bed with its rose-lined pillow-covers. The carpet was cherry red, the toilet-table ruffled and looped like a ball-dress. Ah, how she and Susan had ripped and sewn and hammered, and pieced together old scraps of lace and ribbon and muslin, in the making of that airy monument! For weeks after she had done over the room her husband never came into it without saying: "I can't think how you managed to squeeze all this loveliness out of that last cheque of your stepmother's."

On the dressing-table Lizzie Hazeldean noticed a long florist's box, one end of which had been cut open to give space to the still longer stems of a bunch of roses. She snipped the string, and extracted from the box an envelope which she flung into the fire without so much as a glance at its contents. Then she pushed the flowers aside, and after rearranging her dark hair before the mirror, carefully dressed herself in a loose garment of velvet and lace which lay awaiting her on the sofa, beside her high-heeled slippers and stockings of open-work silk.

She had been one of the first women in New York to have tea every afternoon at five, and to put off her walking-dress for a tea-gown.

3

Sʜᴇ returned to the library, where the fire was beginning to send a bright blaze through the twilight. It flashed on the bindings of Hazeldean's many books, and she smiled absently at the welcome it held out. A latch-key rattled, and she heard her husband's step, and the sound of his cough below in the hall.

"What madness—what madness!" she murmured.

Slowly—how slowly for a young man!—he mounted the stairs, and still coughing came into the library. She ran to him and took him in her arms.

"Charlie! How could you! In this weather? It's nearly dark!"

His long thin face lit up with a deprecating smile. "I suppose Susan's betrayed me, eh? Don't be cross. You've missed such a show! The Fifth Avenue Hotel's been on fire."

"Yes; I know." She paused, just perceptibly. "I *didn't* miss it, though—I rushed across Madison Square for a look at it myself."

"You did? You were there too? What fun!" The idea appeared to him with boyish amusement.

"Naturally I was! On my way home from Cousin Cecilia's . . ."

"Ah, of course. I'd forgotten you were going there. But how odd, then, that we didn't meet!"

"If we *had* I should have dragged you home long ago. I've been in at least half an hour, and the fire was already over when I got there. What a baby you are to have stayed out so long, staring at smoke and a fire-engine!"

He smiled, still holding her, and passing his gaunt hand softly and wistfully over her head. "Oh, don't worry, I've been indoors, safely sheltered, and drinking old Mrs. Parrett's punch. The old lady saw me from her window, and sent one of the Wesson boys across the street to fetch me in. They had just finished a family luncheon. And Sillerton Jackson, who was there, drove me home. So you see,—"

He released her, and moved toward the fire, and she stood motionless, staring blindly ahead, while the thoughts spun through her mind like a mill-race.

"Sillerton Jackson—" she echoed, without in the least knowing what she said.

"Yes; he has the gout again—luckily for me!—and his sister's brougham came to the Parretts' to fetch him."

She collected herself. "You're coughing more than you did yesterday," she accused him.

"Oh, well—the air's sharpish. But I shall be all right presently. . . Oh, those roses!" He paused in admiration before his writing-table.

Her face glowed with a reflected pleasure, though all the while the names he had pronounced—"The Parretts, the Wessons, Sillerton Jackson"—were clanging through her brain like a death-knell.

"They *are* lovely, aren't they?" she beamed.

"Much too lovely for me. You must take them down to the drawing-room."

"No; we're going to have tea up here."

"That's jolly—it means there'll be no visitors, I hope?"

She nodded, smiling.

"Good! But the roses—no, they mustn't be wasted on this desert air. You'll wear them in your dress this evening?"

She started perceptibly, and moved slowly back toward the hearth.

"This evening? . . . Oh, I'm going to Mrs. Struthers's," she said, remembering.

"Yes, you are. Dearest—I want you to!"

"But what shall you do alone all the evening? With that cough, you won't go to sleep till late."

"Well, if I don't, I've a lot of new books to keep me busy."

"Oh, your books—!" She made a little gesture, half teasing, half impatient, in the direction of the freshly cut volumes stacked up beside his student lamp. It was an old joke between them that she had never been able to believe anyone could really "care for reading." Long as she and her husband had lived together, this passion of his remained for her as much of a mystery as on the day when she had first surprised him, mute and absorbed, over what the people she had always lived with would have called "a deep book." It was her first encounter with a born reader; or at least, the few she had known had been, like her stepmother, the retired opera-singer, feverish devourers of circulating library fiction: she had never before lived in a house with books in it. Gradually she had learned to take a pride in Hazeldean's reading, as if it had been some rare accomplishment; she had perceived that it reflected credit on him, and was even conscious of its adding to the charm of his talk, a charm she had always felt without being able to define it. But still, in her heart of hearts she regarded books as a mere expedient, and felt sure that they were only an aid to patience, like jackstraws or a game of patience, with the disadvantage of requiring a greater mental effort.

"Shan't you be too tired to read tonight?" she questioned wistfully.

"Too tired? Why, you goose, reading is the greatest rest in the world!—I want you to go to Mrs. Struthers's, dear; I want to see you again in the black velvet dress," he added with his coaxing smile.

The parlourmaid brought in the tray, and Mrs. Hazeldean busied herself with the tea-caddy. Her husband had stretched himself out in the deep armchair which was his habitual seat. He crossed his arms behind his neck, leaning his head back wearily against them, so that, as she glanced at him across the hearth, she saw the salient muscles in his long neck, and the premature wrinkles about his ears and chin. The lower part of his face was singularly ravaged; only the eyes, those quiet ironic grey eyes, and the white forehead above them, reminded her of what he had been seven years before. Only seven years!

She felt a rush of tears: no, there were times when fate was too cruel, the future too horrible to contemplate, and the past—the past, oh, how much worse! And there he sat, coughing, coughing—and thinking God knows what, behind those quiet half-closed lids. At such times he grew so mysteriously remote that she felt lonelier than when he was not in the room.

"Charlie!"

He roused himself. "Yes?"

"Here's your tea."

He took it from her in silence, and she began, nervously, to wonder why he was not talking. Was it because he was afraid it might make him cough again, afraid she would be worried, and scold him? Or was it because he was thinking—thinking of things he had heard at old Mrs. Parrett's, or on the drive home with Sillerton Jackson . . . hints they might have dropped . . . insinuations . . . she didn't know what . . . or of something he had *seen*, perhaps, from old Mrs. Parrett's window? She looked across at his white forehead, so smooth and impenetrable in the lamplight, and thought: "Oh, God, it's like a locked door. I shall dash my brains out against it some day!"

For, after all, it was not impossible that he had actually seen her, seen her from Mrs. Parrett's window, or even from the crowd around the door of the hotel. For all she knew, he might have been near enough, in that crowd, to put out his hand and touch her. And he might have held back, benumbed, aghast, not believing his own eyes. . . She couldn't tell. She had never yet made up her mind how he would look, how he would behave, what he would say, if ever he *did* see or hear anything. . .

No! That was the worst of it. They had lived together for nearly nine years—and how closely!—and nothing that she knew of him, or had observed in him, enabled her to forecast exactly what, in that particular case, his state of mind and his attitude would be. In his profession, she knew, he was celebrated for his shrewdness and insight; in personal matters he often seemed, to her alert mind, oddly absent-minded and indifferent. Yet that might be merely his instinctive way of saving his strength for things he considered more important. There were times when she was sure he was quite deliberate and self-controlled enough to feel in one way and behave in another: perhaps even to have thought out a course in advance—just as, at the first bad symptoms of illness, he had calmly made his will, and planned everything about her future, the house and the servants. . . No, she couldn't tell; there always hung over her the thin glittering menace of a danger she could neither define nor localize—like that avenging lightning which groped for the lovers in the horrible poem he had once read aloud to her (what a choice!) on a lazy afternoon of their wedding journey, as they lay stretched under Italian stone-pines.

The maid came in to draw the curtains and light the lamps. The fire glowed, the scent of the roses drifted on the warm air, and the clock ticked out the minutes, and softly struck a half hour, while Mrs. Hazeldean continued to ask herself, as she so often had before: "Now, what would be the *natural* thing for me to say?"

And suddenly the words escaped from her, she didn't know how: "I wonder you didn't see me coming out of the hotel—for I actually squeezed my way in."

Her husband made no answer. Her heart jumped convulsively; then she lifted her eyes and saw that he was asleep. How placid his face looked—years younger than when he was awake! The immensity of her relief rushed over her in a warm glow, the counterpart of the icy sweat which had sent her chattering homeward from the fire. After all, if he could fall asleep, fall into such a peaceful sleep as that —tired, no doubt, by his imprudent walk, and the exposure to the cold—it meant, beyond all doubt, beyond all conceivable dread, that he knew nothing, had seen nothing, suspected nothing: that she was safe, safe, safe!

The violence of the reaction made her long to spring to her feet and move about the room. She saw a crooked picture that she wanted to straighten, she would have liked to give the roses another tilt in their glass. But there he sat, quietly sleeping, and the long habit of vigilance made her respect his rest, watching over it as patiently as if it had been a sick child's.

She drew a contented breath. Now she could afford to think of his outing only as it might affect his health; and she knew that this sudden drowsiness, even if it were a sign of extreme fatigue, was also the natural restorative for that fatigue. She continued to sit behind the tea-tray, her hands folded, her eyes on his face, while the peace of the scene entered into her, and held her under brooding wings.

4

At Mrs. Struthers's, at eleven o'clock that evening, the long over-lit drawing-rooms were already thronged with people.

Lizzie Hazeldean paused on the threshold and looked about her. The habit of pausing to get her bearings, of sending a circular glance around any assemblage of people, any drawing-room, concert-hall or theatre that she entered, had become so instinctive that she would have been surprised had anyone pointed out to her the unobservant expression and careless movements of the young women of her acquaintance, who also looked about them, it is true, but with the vague unseeing stare of youth, and of beauty conscious only of itself.

Lizzie Hazeldean had long since come to regard most women of her age as children in the art of life. Some savage instinct of self-defence, fostered by experience, had always made her more alert and perceiving than the charming creatures who passed from the nursery to marriage as if lifted from one rose-lined cradle into another. "Rocked to sleep—that's what they've always been," she used to think sometimes, listening to their innocuous talk during the long after-dinners in hot drawing-rooms, while their husbands, in the smoking-rooms below, exchanged ideas which, if no more striking, were at least based on more direct experiences.

But then, as all the old ladies said, Lizzie Hazeldean had always preferred the society of men.

The man she now sought was not visible, and she gave a little sigh of ease. "If only he has had the sense to stay away!" she thought.

She would have preferred to stay away herself; but it had been her husband's whim that she should come. "You know you always enjoy yourself at Mrs. Struthers's—everybody does. The old girl somehow manages to have the most amusing house in New York. Who is it who's going to sing tonight? . . . If you don't go, I shall know it's because I've coughed two or three times oftener than usual, and you're worrying about me. My dear girl, it will take more than the Fifth Avenue Hotel fire to kill *me*. . . My heart's feeling unusually steady. . . Put on your black velvet, will you?—with these two roses. . ."

So she had gone. And here she was, in her black velvet, under the glitter of Mrs. Struthers's chandeliers, amid all the youth and good looks and gaiety of New York; for, as Hazeldean said, Mrs. Struthers's house was more amusing than anybody else's, and whenever she opened her doors the world flocked through them.

As Mrs. Hazeldean reached the inner drawing-room the last notes of a rich tenor were falling on the attentive silence. She saw Campanini's low-necked throat subside into silence above the piano, and the clapping of many tightly-fitting gloves was succeeded by a general movement, and the usual irrepressible outburst of talk.

In the breaking-up of groups she caught a glimpse of Sillerton Jackson's silvery crown. Their eyes met across bare shoulders, he bowed profoundly, and she fancied that a dry smile lifted his moustache. "He doesn't usually bow to me as low as that," she thought apprehensively.

But as she advanced into the room her self-possession returned. Among all these stupid pretty women she had such a sense of power, of knowing almost everything better than they did, from the way of doing her hair to the art of keeping a secret! She felt a thrill of pride in the slope of her white shoulders above the black velvet, in the one curl escaping from her thick chignon, and the slant of the gold arrow tipped with diamonds which she had thrust in to retain it. And she had done it all without a maid, with no one cleverer than Susan to help her! Ah, as a woman she knew her business. . .

Mrs. Struthers, plumed and ponderous, with diamond stars studding her black wig like a pin-cushion, had worked her resolute way back to the outer room. More people were coming in; and with her customary rough skill she was receiving, distributing, introducing them. Suddenly her smile deepened; she was evidently greeting an old friend. The group about her scattered, and Mrs. Hazeldean saw that, in her cordial absent-minded way, and while her wandering hostess-eye swept the rooms, she was saying a confidential word to a tall man whose hand she detained. They smiled at each other; then

Mrs. Struthers's glance turned toward the inner room, and her smile seemed to say: "You'll find her there."

The tall man nodded. He looked about him composedly, and began to move toward the centre of the throng, speaking to everyone, appearing to have no object beyond that of greeting the next person in his path, yet quietly, steadily pursuing that path, which led straight to the inner room.

Mrs. Hazeldean had found a seat near the piano. A good-looking youth, seated beside her, was telling her at considerable length what he was going to wear at the Beauforts' fancy-ball. She listened, approved, suggested; but her glance never left the advancing figure of the tall man.

Handsome? Yes, she said to herself; she had to admit that he was handsome. A trifle too broad and florid, perhaps; though his air and his attitude so plainly denied it that, on second thoughts, one agreed that a man of his height had, after all, to carry some ballast. Yes; his assurance made him, as a rule, appear to people exactly as he chose to appear; that is, as a man over forty, but carrying his years carelessly, an active muscular man, whose blue eyes were still clear, whose fair hair waved ever so little less thickly than it used to on a low sunburnt forehead, over eyebrows almost silvery in their blondness, and blue eyes the bluer for their thatch. Stupid-looking? By no means. His smile denied that. Just self-sufficient enough to escape fatuity, yet so cool that one felt the fundamental coldness, he steered his way through life as easily and resolutely as he was now working his way through Mrs. Struthers's drawing-rooms.

Half-way, he was detained by a tap of Mrs. Wesson's red fan. Mrs. Wesson—surely, Mrs. Hazeldean reflected, Charles had spoken of Mrs. Sabina Wesson's being with her mother, old Mrs. Parrett, while they watched the fire? Sabina Wesson was a redoubtable woman, one of the few of her generation and her clan who had broken with tradition, and gone to Mrs. Struthers's almost as soon as the Shoe-Polish Queen had bought her house in Fifth Avenue, and issued her first challenge to society. Lizzie Hazeldean shut her eyes for an instant; then, rising from her seat, she joined the group about the singer. From there she wandered on to another knot of acquaintances.

"Look here: the fellow's going to sing again. Let's get into that corner over there."

She felt ever so slight a touch on her arm, and met Henry Prest's composed glance.

A red-lit and palm-shaded recess divided the drawing-rooms from the dining-room, which ran across the width of the house at the back. Mrs. Hazeldean hesitated; then she caught Mrs. Wesson's watchful glance, lifted her head with a smile and followed her companion.

They sat down on a small sofa under the palms, and a couple, who had been in search of the same retreat, paused on the threshold, and with an interchange of glances passed on. Mrs. Hazeldean smiled more vividly.

"Where are my roses? Didn't you get them?" Prest asked. He had a way of looking her over from beneath lowered lids, while he affected to be examining a glove-button or contemplating the tip of his shining boot.

"Yes, I got them," she answered.

"You're not wearing them. I didn't order those."

"No."

"Whose are they, then?"

She unfolded her mother-of-pearl fan, and bent above its complicated traceries.

"Mine," she pronounced.

"Yours? Well, obviously. But I suppose someone sent them to you?"

"I did." She hesitated a second. "I sent them to myself."

He raised his eyebrows a little. "Well, they don't suit you—that washy pink! May I ask why you didn't wear mine?"

"I've already told you. . . I've often asked you never to send flowers . . . on the day. . ."

"Nonsense. That's the very day. . . What's the matter? Are you still nervous?"

She was silent for a moment; then she lowered her voice to say: "You ought not to have come here tonight."

"My dear girl, how unlike you! You *are* nervous."

"Didn't you see all those people in the Parretts' window?"

"What, opposite? Lord, no; I just took to my heels! It was the deuce, the back way being barred. But what of it? In all that crowd, do you suppose for a moment—"

"My husband was in the window with them," she said, still lower.

His confident face fell for a moment, and then almost at once regained its look of easy arrogance.

"Well—?"

"Oh, nothing—as yet. Only I ask you . . . to go away now."

"Just as you asked me not to come! Yet *you* came, because you
had the sense to see that if you didn't . . . and I came for the same
reason. Look here, my dear, for God's sake don't lose your head!"

The challenge seemed to rouse her. She lifted her chin, glanced
about the thronged room which they commanded from their corner,
and nodded and smiled invitingly at several acquaintances, with the
hope that some one of them might come up to her. But though they
all returned her greetings with a somewhat elaborate cordiality, not
one advanced toward her secluded seat.

She turned her head slightly toward her companion. "I ask you
again to go," she repeated.

"Well, I will then, after the fellow's sung. But I'm bound to say
you're a good deal pleasanter—"

The first bars of "*Salve, Dimora*" silenced him, and they sat side
by side in the meditative rigidity of fashionable persons listening to
expensive music. She had thrown herself into a corner of the sofa,
and Henry Prest, about whom everything was discreet but his eyes,
sat apart from her, one leg crossed over the other, one hand holding
his folded opera-hat on his knee, while the other hand rested beside
him on the sofa. But an end of her tulle scarf lay in the space between them; and without looking in his direction, without turning
her glance from the singer, she was conscious that Prest's hand had
reached and drawn the scarf toward him. She shivered a little, made
an involuntary motion as though to gather it about her—and then
desisted. As the song ended, he bent toward her slightly, said: "Darling" so low that it seemed no more than a breath on her cheek, and
then, rising, bowed, and strolled into the other room.

She sighed faintly, and, settling herself once more in her corner,
lifted her brilliant eyes to Sillerton Jackson, who was approaching.
"It *was* good of you to bring Charlie home from the Parretts' this afternoon." She held out her hand, making way for him at her side.

"Good of me?" he laughed. "Why, I was glad of the chance of
getting him safely home; it was rather naughty of *him* to be where
he was, I suspect." She fancied a slight pause, as if he waited to see
the effect of this, and her lashes beat her cheeks. But already he was
going on: "Do you encourage him, with that cough, to run about
town after fire-engines?"

She gave back the laugh.

"I don't discourage him—ever—if I can help it. But it *was* foolish of him to go out today," she agreed; and all the while she kept on asking herself, as she had that afternoon, in her talk with her husband: "Now, what would be the *natural* thing for me to say?"

Should she speak of having been at the fire herself—or should she not? The question dinned in her brain so loudly that she could hardly hear what her companion was saying; yet she had, at the same time, a queer feeling of his never having been so close to her, or rather so closely intent on her, as now. In her strange state of nervous lucidity, her eyes seemed to absorb with a new precision every facial detail of whoever approached her; and old Sillerton Jackson's narrow mask, his withered pink cheeks, the veins in the hollow of his temples, under the carefully-tended silvery hair, and the tiny bloodspecks in the white of his eyes as he turned their cautious blue gaze on her, appeared as if presented under some powerful lens. With his eye-glasses dangling over one white-gloved hand, the other supporting his opera-hat on his knee, he suggested, behind that assumed carelessness of pose, the patient fixity of a naturalist holding his breath near the crack from which some tiny animal might suddenly issue—if one watched long enough, or gave it, completely enough, the impression of not looking for it, or dreaming it was anywhere near. The sense of that tireless attention made Mrs. Hazeldean's temples ache as if she sat under a glare of light even brighter than that of the Struthers' chandeliers—a glare in which each quiver of a half-formed thought might be as visible behind her forehead as the faint lines wrinkling its surface into an uncontrollable frown of anxiety. Yes, Prest was right; she was losing her head—losing it for the first time in the dangerous year during which she had had such continual need to keep it steady.

"What is it? What has happened to me?" she wondered.

There had been alarms before—how could it be otherwise? But they had only stimulated her, made her more alert and prompt; whereas tonight she felt herself quivering away into she knew not what abyss of weakness. What was different, then? Oh, she knew well enough! It was Charles . . . that haggard look in his eyes, and the lines of his throat as he had leaned back sleeping. She had never before admitted to herself how ill she thought him; and now, to have to admit it, and at the same time not to have the complete certainty that the look in his eyes was caused by illness only, made the strain unbearable.

She glanced about her with a sudden sense of despair. Of all the people in those brilliant animated groups—of all the women who called her Lizzie, and the men who were familiars at her house—she knew that not one, at that moment, guessed, or could have understood, what she was feeling. . . Her eyes fell on Henry Prest, who had come to the surface a little way off, bending over the chair of the handsome Mrs. Lyman. "And *you* least of all!" she thought. "Yet God knows," she added with a shiver, "they all have their theories about me!"

"My dear Mrs. Hazeldean, you look a little pale. Are you cold? Shall I get you some champagne?" Sillerton Jackson was officiously suggesting.

"If you think the other women look blooming! My dear man, it's this hideous vulgar overhead lighting. . ." She rose impatiently. It had occurred to her that the thing to do—the "natural" thing— would be to stroll up to Jinny Lyman, over whom Prest was still attentively bending. *Then* people would see if she was nervous, or ill— or afraid!

But half-way she stopped and thought: "Suppose the Parretts and Wessons *did* see me? Then my joining Jinny while he's talking to her will look—how will it look?" She began to regret not having had it out on the spot with Sillerton Jackson, who could be trusted to hold his tongue on occasion, especially if a pretty woman threw herself on his mercy. She glanced over her shoulder as if to call him back; but he had turned away, been absorbed into another group, and she found herself, instead, abruptly face to face with Sabina Wesson. Well, perhaps that was better still. After all, it all depended on how much Mrs. Wesson had seen, and what line she meant to take, supposing she *had* seen anything. She was not likely to be as inscrutable as old Sillerton. Lizzie wished now that she had not forgotten to go to Mrs. Wesson's last party.

"Dear Mrs. Wesson, it was so kind of you—"

But Mrs. Wesson was not there. By the exercise of that mysterious protective power which enables a woman desirous of not being waylaid to make herself invisible, or to transport herself, by means imperceptible, to another part of the earth's surface, Mrs. Wesson, who, two seconds earlier, appeared in all her hard handsomeness to be bearing straight down on Mrs. Hazeldean, with a scant yard of clear *parquet* between them—Mrs. Wesson, as her animated back and her active red fan now called on all the company to notice, had never been there at all, had never seen Mrs. Hazeldean (*Was* she at

Mrs. Struthers's last Sunday? How odd! I must have left before she got there—"), but was busily engaged, on the farther side of the piano, in examining a picture to which her attention appeared to have been called by the persons nearest her.

"Ah, how *life-like!* That's what I always feel when I see a Meissonier," she was heard to exclaim, with her well-known instinct for the fitting epithet.

Lizzie Hazeldean stood motionless. Her eyes dazzled as if she had received a blow on the forehead. "So *that's* what it feels like!" she thought. She lifted her head very high, looked about her again, tried to signal to Henry Prest, but saw him still engaged with the lovely Mrs. Lyman, and at the same moment caught the glance of young Hubert Wesson, Sabina's eldest, who was standing in disengaged expectancy near the supper-room door.

Hubert Wesson, as his eyes met Mrs. Hazeldean's, crimsoned to the forehead, hung back a moment, and then came forward, bowing low—again that too low bow! "So *he* saw me too," she thought. She put her hand on his arm with a laugh. "Dear me, how ceremonious you are! Really, I'm not as old as that bow of yours implies. My dear boy, I hope you want to take me in to supper at once. I was out in the cold all the afternoon, gazing at the Fifth Avenue Hotel fire, and I'm simply dying of hunger and fatigue."

There, the die was cast—she had said it loud enough for all the people nearest her to hear! And she was sure now that it was the right, the "natural" thing to do.

Her spirits rose, and she sailed into the supper-room like a goddess, steering Hubert to an unoccupied table in a flowery corner.

"No—I think we're very well by ourselves, don't you? Do you want that fat old bore of a Lucy Vanderlow to join us? If you *do*, of course . . . I can see she's dying to . . . but then, I warn you, I shall ask a young man! Let me see—shall I ask Henry Prest? You see he's hovering! No, it *is* jollier with just you and me, isn't it?" She leaned forward a little, resting her chin on her clasped hands, her elbows on the table, in an attitude which the older women thought shockingly free, but the younger ones were beginning to imitate.

"And now, some champagne, please—and *hot* terrapin! . . . But I suppose you were at the fire yourself, weren't you?" she leaned still a little nearer to say.

The blush again swept over young Wesson's face, rose to his forehead, and turned the lobes of his large ears to balls of fire ("It looks," she thought, "as if he had on huge coral earrings."). But she forced him to look at her, laughed straight into his eyes, and went on: "Did you ever see a funnier sight than all those dressed-up absurdities rushing out into the cold? It looked like the end of an Inauguration Ball! I was so fascinated that I actually pushed my way into the hall. The firemen were furious, but they couldn't stop me—nobody can stop me at a fire! You should have seen the ladies scuttling downstairs—the fat ones! Oh, but I beg your pardon; I'd forgotten that you admire . . . avoirdupois. No? But . . . Mrs. Van . . . so stupid of me! Why, you're actually blushing! I assure you, you're as red as your mother's fan—and visible from as great a distance! Yes, please; a little more champagne. . ."

And then the inevitable began. She forgot the fire, forgot her anxieties, forgot Mrs. Wesson's affront, forgot everything but the amusement, the passing childish amusement, of twirling around her little finger this shy clumsy boy, as she had twirled so many others, old and young, not caring afterward if she ever saw them again, but so absorbed in the sport, and in her sense of knowing how to do it better than the other women—more quietly, more insidiously, without ogling, bridling or grimacing—that sometimes she used to ask herself with a shiver: "What was the gift given to me for?" Yes; it always amused her at first: the gradual dawn of attraction in eyes that had regarded her with indifference, the blood rising to the face, the way she could turn and twist the talk as though she had her victim on a leash, spinning him after her down winding paths of sentimentality, irony, caprice . . . and leaving him, with beating heart and dazzled eyes, to visions of an all-promising morrow. . . "My only accomplishment!" she murmured to herself as she rose from the table followed by young Wesson's fascinated gaze, while already, on her own lips, she felt the taste of cinders.

"But at any rate," she thought, "he'll hold his tongue about having seen me at the fire."

5

S<small>HE</small> let herself in with her latch-key, glanced at the notes and letters on the hall-table (the old habit of allowing nothing to escape her), and stole up through the darkness to her room.

A fire still glowed in the chimney, and its light fell on two vases of crimson roses. The room was full of their scent.

Mrs. Hazeldean frowned, and then shrugged her shoulders. It had been a mistake, after all, to let it appear that she was indifferent to the flowers; she must remember to thank Susan for rescuing them. She began to undress, hastily yet clumsily, as if her deft fingers were all thumbs; but first, detaching the two faded pink roses from her bosom, she put them with a reverent touch into a glass on the toilet-table. Then, slipping on her dressing-gown, she stole to her husband's door. It was shut, and she leaned her ear to the keyhole. After a moment she caught his breathing, heavy, as it always was when he had a cold, but regular, untroubled. . . With a sigh of relief she tiptoed back. Her uncovered bed, with its fresh pillows and satin coverlet, sent her a rosy invitation; but she cowered down by the fire, hugging her knees and staring into the coals.

"So *that's* what it feels like!" she repeated.

It was the first time in her life that she had ever been deliberately "cut"; and the cut was a deadly injury in old New York. For Sabina Wesson to have used it, consciously, deliberately—for there was no doubt that she had purposely advanced toward her victim—she must have done so with intent to kill. And to risk that, she must have been sure of her facts, sure of corroborating witnesses, sure of being backed up by all her clan.

Lizzie Hazeldean had her clan too—but it was a small and weak one, and she hung on its outer fringe by a thread of little-regarded cousinship. As for the Hazeldean tribe, which was large and stronger (though nothing like the great organized Wesson-Parrett *gens*, with half New York and all Albany at its back)—well, the Hazeldeans were not much to be counted on, and would even, perhaps, in a furtive negative way, be not too sorry ("if it were not for poor Charlie") that poor Charlie's wife should at last be made to pay for her good looks, her popularity, above all for being, in spite of her origin, treated by poor Charlie as if she were one of them!

Her origin was, of course, respectable enough. Everybody knew all about the Winters—she had been Lizzie Winter. But the Winters were very small people, and her father, the Reverend Arcadius Winter, the sentimental over-popular Rector of a fashionable New York church, after a few seasons of too great success as preacher and director of female consciences, had suddenly had to resign and go to Bermuda for his health—or was it France?—to some obscure watering-place, it was rumoured. At any rate, Lizzie, who went with him (with a crushed bed-ridden mother), was ultimately, after the mother's death, fished out of a girls' school in Brussels—they seemed to have been in so many countries at once!—and brought back to New York by a former parishioner of poor Arcadius's, who had always "believed in him," in spite of the Bishop and who took pity on his lonely daughter.

The parishioner, Mrs. Mant, was "one of the Hazeldeans." She was a rich widow, given to generous gestures which she was often at a loss how to complete; and when she had brought Lizzie Winter home, and sufficiently celebrated her own courage in doing so, she did not quite know what step to take next. She had fancied it would be pleasant to have a clever handsome girl about the house; but her housekeeper was not of the same mind. The spare-room sheets had not been out of lavender for twenty years—and Miss Winter always left the blinds up in her room, and the carpet and curtains, unused to such exposure, suffered accordingly. Then young men began to call—they called in numbers. Mrs. Mant had not supposed that the daughter of a clergyman—and a clergyman "under a cloud"—would expect visitors. She had imagined herself taking Lizzie Winter to Church Fairs, and having the stitches of her knitting picked up by the young girl, whose "eyes were better" than her benefactress's. But Lizzie did not know how to knit—she possessed no useful accomplishments—and she was visibly bored by Church Fairs, where her presence was of little use, since she had no money to spend. Mrs.

Mant began to see her mistake; and the discovery made her dislike her protégée, whom she secretly regarded as having intentionally misled her.

In Mrs. Mant's life, the transition from one enthusiasm to another was always marked by an interval of disillusionment, during which, Providence having failed to fulfill her requirements, its existence was openly called into question. But in this flux of moods there was one fixed point: Mrs. Mant was a woman whose life revolved about a bunch of keys. What treasures they gave access to, what disasters would have ensued had they been forever lost, was not quite clear; but whenever they were missed the household was in an uproar, and as Mrs. Mant would trust them to no one but herself, these occasions were frequent. One of them arose at the very moment when Mrs. Mant was recovering from her enthusiasm for Miss Winter. A minute before, the keys had been there, in a pocket of her work-table; she had actually touched them in hunting for her buttonhole-scissors. She had been called away to speak to the plumber about the bath-room leak, and when she left the room there was no one in it but Miss Winter. When she returned, the keys were gone. The house had been turned inside out; everyone had been, if not accused, at least suspected; and in a rash moment Mrs. Mant had spoken of the police. The housemaid had thereupon given warning, and her own maid threatened to follow; when suddenly the Bishop's hints recurred to Mrs. Mant. The Bishop had always implied that there had been something irregular in Dr. Winter's accounts, besides the other unfortunate business.

Very mildly, she had asked Miss Winter if she might not have seen the keys, and "picked them up without thinking." Miss Winter permitted herself to smile in denying the suggestion; the smile irritated Mrs. Mant; and in a moment the floodgates were opened. She saw nothing to smile at in her question—unless it was of a kind that Miss Winter was already used to, prepared for . . . with that sort of background . . . her unfortunate father. . .

"Stop!" Lizzie Winter cried. She remembered now, as if it had happened yesterday, the abyss suddenly opening at her feet. It was her first direct contact with human cruelty. Suffering, weakness, frailties other than Mrs. Mant's restricted fancy could have pictured, the girl had known, or at least suspected; but she had found as much kindness as folly in her path, and no one had ever before attempted to visit upon her the dimly-guessed shortcomings of her poor old fa-

ther. She shook with horror as much as with indignation, and her
"Stop!" blazed out so violently that Mrs. Mant, turning white, feebly
groped for the bell.

And it was then, at that very moment, that Charles Hazeldean
came in—Charles Hazeldean, the favourite nephew, the pride of the
tribe. Lizzie had seen him only once or twice, for he had been absent
since her return to New York. She had thought him distinguished-
looking, but rather serious and sarcastic; and he had apparently
taken little notice of her—which perhaps accounted for her opinion.

"Oh, Charles, dearest Charles—that you should be here to hear
such things said to me!" his aunt gasped, her hand on her outraged
heart.

"What things? Said by whom? I see no one here to say them but
Miss Winter," Charles had laughed, taking the girl's icy hand.

"Don't shake hands with her! She has insulted me! She has ordered me to keep silence—in my own house. 'Stop!' she said, when I
was trying, in the kindness of my heart, to get her to admit privately
. . . Well, if she prefers to have the police. . ."

"I do! I ask you to send for them!" Lizzie cried.

How vividly she remembered all that followed: the finding of the
keys, Mrs. Mant's reluctant apologies, her own cold acceptance of
them, and the sense on both sides of the impossibility of continuing
their life together! She had been wounded to the soul, and her own
plight first revealed to her in all its destitution. Before that, despite
the ups and downs of a wandering life, her youth, her good looks,
the sense of a certain bright power over people and events, had hurried her along on a spring tide of confidence; she had never thought
of herself as the dependent, the beneficiary, of the persons who were
kind to her. Now she saw herself, at twenty, a penniless girl, with a
feeble discredited father carrying his snowy head, his unctuous voice,
his edifying manner from one cheap watering-place to another,
through an endless succession of sentimental and pecuniary en-
tanglements. To him she could be of no more help than he to her;
and save for him she was alone. The Winter cousins, as much humiliated by his disgrace as they had been puffed-up by his triumphs, let
it be understood, when the breach with Mrs. Mant became known,
that they were not in a position to interfere; and among Dr. Winter's former parishioners none was left to champion him. Almost at
the same time, Lizzie heard that he was about to marry a Portuguese

opera-singer and be received into the Church of Rome; and this crowning scandal too promptly justified his family.

The situation was a grave one, and called for energetic measures. Lizzie understood it—and a week later she was engaged to Charles Hazeldean.

She always said afterward that but for the keys he would never have thought of marrying her; while he laughingly affirmed that, on the contrary, but for the keys she would never have looked at *him*.

But what did it all matter, in the complete and blessed understanding which was to follow on their hasty union? If all the advantages on both sides had been weighed and found equal by judicious advisers, harmony more complete could hardly have been predicted. As a matter of fact, the advisers, had they been judicious, would probably have found only elements of discord in the characters concerned. Charles Hazeldean was by nature an observer and a student, brooding and curious of mind: Lizzie Winter (as she looked back at herself)—what was she, what would she ever be, but a quick, ephemeral creature, in whom a perpetual and adaptable activity simulated mind, as her grace, her swiftness, her expressiveness simulated beauty? So others would have judged her; so, now, she judged herself. And she knew that in fundamental things she was still the same. And yet she had satisfied him: satisfied him, to all appearances, as completely in the quiet later years as in the first flushed hours. As completely, or perhaps even more so. In the early months, dazzled gratitude made her the humbler, fonder worshipper; but as her powers expanded in the warm air of comprehension, as she felt herself grow handsomer, cleverer, more competent and more companionable than he had hoped, or she had dreamed herself capable of becoming, the balance was imperceptibly reversed, and the triumph in his eyes when they rested on her.

The Hazeldeans were conquered; they had to admit it. Such a brilliant recruit to the clan was not to be disowned. Mrs. Mant was left to nurse her grievance in solitude, till she too fell into line, carelessly but handsomely forgiven.

Ah, those first years of triumph! They frightened Lizzie now as she looked back. One day, the friendless defenceless daughter of a discredited man; the next, almost, the wife of Charlie Hazeldean, the popular successful young lawyer, with a good practice already assured, and the best of professional and private prospects. His own parents were dead, and had died poor; but two or three childless relatives were understood to be letting their capital accumulate for his benefit, and meanwhile in Lizzie's thrifty hands his earnings were largely sufficient.

Ah, those first years! There had been barely six; but even now there were moments when their sweetness drenched her to the soul. . . Barely six; and then the sharp re-awakening of an inherited weakness of the heart that Hazeldean and his doctors had imagined to be completely cured. Once before, for the same cause, he had been sent off, suddenly, for a year of travel in mild climate and distant scenes; and his first return had coincided with the close of Lizzie's sojourn at Mrs. Mant's. The young man felt sure enough of the future to marry and take up his professional duties again, and for the following six years he had led, without interruption, the busy life of a successful lawyer; then had come a second breakdown, more unexpectedly, and with more alarming symptoms. The "Hazeldean heart" was a proverbial boast in the family; the Hazeldeans privately considered it more distinguished than the Sillerton gout, and far more refined than the Wesson liver; and it had permitted most of them to survive, in valetudinarian ease, to a ripe old age, when they died of some quite other disorder. But Charles Hazeldean had defied it, and it took its revenge, and took it savagely.

One by one, hopes and plans faded. The Hazeldeans went south for a winter; he lay on a deck-chair in a Florida garden, and read and dreamed, and was happy with Lizzie beside him. So the months passed; and by the following autumn he was better, returned to New York, and took up his profession. Intermittently but obstinately, he had continued the struggle for two more years; but before they were over husband and wife understood that the good days were done.

He could be at his office only at lengthening intervals; he sank gradually into invalidism without submitting to it. His income dwindled; and, indifferent for himself, he fretted ceaselessly at the thought of depriving Lizzie of the least of her luxuries.

At heart she was indifferent to them too; but she could not convince him of it. He had been brought up in the old New York tradition, which decreed that a man, at whatever cost, must provide his wife with what she had always "been accustomed to"; and he had gloried too much in her prettiness, her elegance, her easy way of wearing her expensive dresses, and his friends' enjoyment of the good dinners she knew how to order, not to accustom her to everything which could enhance such graces. Mrs. Mant's secret satisfaction rankled in him. She sent him Baltimore terrapin, and her famous clam broth, and a dozen of the old Hazeldean port, and said "I told you so" to her confidants when Lizzie was mentioned; and Charles Hazeldean knew it, and swore at it.

"I won't be pauperized by her!" he declared; but Lizzie smiled away his anger, and persuaded him to taste the terrapin and sip the port.

She was smiling faintly at the memory of the last passage between him and Mrs. Mant when the turning of the bedroom door-handle startled her. She jumped up, and he stood there. The blood rushed to her forehead; his expression frightened her; for an instant she stared at him as if he had been an enemy. Then she saw that the look in his face was only the remote lost look of excessive physical pain.

She was at his side at once, supporting him, guiding him to the nearest armchair. He sank into it, and she flung a shawl over him, and knelt at his side while his inscrutable eyes continued to repel her.

"Charles . . . Charles," she pleaded.

For a while he could not speak; and she said to herself that she would perhaps never know whether he had sought her because he was ill, or whether illness had seized him as he entered her room to question, accuse, or reveal what he had seen or heard that afternoon.

Suddenly he lifted his hand and pressed back her forehead, so that her face lay bare under his eyes.

"Love, love, you've been happy?"

"*Happy?*" The word choked her. She clung to him, burying her anguish against his knees. His hand stirred weakly in her hair, and gathering her whole strength into the gesture, she raised her head again, looked into his eyes, and breathed back: "And you?"

He gave her one full look; all their life together was in it, from the first day to the last. His hand brushed her once more, like a blessing, and then dropped. The moment of their communion was over; the next she was preparing remedies, ringing for the servants, ordering the doctor to be called. Her husband was once more the harmless helpless captive that sickness makes of the most dreaded and the most loved.

6

It was in Mrs. Mant's drawing-room that, some half-year later, Mrs. Charles Hazeldean, after a moment's hesitation, said to the servant that, yes, he might show in Mr. Prest.

Mrs. Mant was away. She had been leaving for Washington to visit a new protégée when Mrs. Hazeldean arrived from Europe, and after a rapid consultation with the clan had decided that it would not be "decent" to let poor Charles's widow go to an hotel. Lizzie had therefore the strange sensation of returning, after nearly nine years, to the house from which her husband had triumphantly rescued her; of returning there, to be sure, in comparative independence, and without danger of falling into her former bondage, yet with every nerve shrinking from all that the scene revived.

Mrs. Mant, the next day, had left for Washington; but before starting she had tossed a note across the breakfast-table to her visitor.

"Very proper—he was one of Charlie's oldest friends, I believe?" she said, with her mild frosty smile. Mrs. Hazeldean glanced at the note, turned it over as if to examine the signature, and restored it to her hostess.

"Yes. But I don't think I care to see anyone just yet."

There was a pause, during which the butler brought in fresh griddle-cakes, replenished the hot milk, and withdrew. As the door closed on him, Mrs. Mant said, with a dangerous cordiality: "No one would misunderstand your receiving an old friend of your husband's . . . like Mr. Prest."

Lizzie Hazeldean cast a sharp glance at the large empty mysterious face across the table. They *wanted* her to receive Henry Prest, then? Ah, well . . . perhaps she understood. . .

"Shall I answer this for you, my dear? Or will you?" Mrs. Mant pursued.

"Oh, as you like. But don't fix a day, please. Later—"

Mrs. Mant's face again became vacuous. She murmured: "You must not shut yourself up too much. It will not do to be morbid. I'm sorry to have to leave you here alone—"

Lizzie's eyes filled: Mrs. Mant's sympathy seemed more cruel than her cruelty. Every word that she used had a veiled taunt for its counterpart.

"Oh, you mustn't think of giving up your visit—"

"My dear, how can I? It's a *duty*. I'll send a line to Henry Prest, then. . . If you would sip a little port at luncheon and dinner we should have you looking less like a ghost. . ."

Mrs. Mant departed; and two days later—the interval was "decent"—Mr. Henry Prest was announced. Mrs. Hazeldean had not seen him since the previous New Year's Day. Their last words had been exchanged in Mrs. Struthers's crimson boudoir, and since then half a year had elapsed. Charles Hazeldean had lingered for a fortnight; but though there had been ups and downs, and intervals of hope when none could have criticised his wife for seeing her friends, her door had been barred against everyone. She had not excluded Henry Prest more rigorously than the others; he had simply been one of the many who received, day by day, the same answer: "Mrs. Hazeldean sees no one but the family."

Almost immediately after her husband's death she had sailed for Europe on a long-deferred visit to her father, who was now settled at Nice; but from this expedition she had presumably brought back little comfort, when she arrived in New York her relations were struck by her air of ill-health and depression. It spoke in her favour, however; they were agreed that she was behaving with propriety.

She looked at Henry Prest as if he were a stranger: so difficult was it, at the first moment, to fit his robust and splendid person into the region of twilight shades which, for the last months, she had inhabited. She was beginning to find that everyone had an air of remoteness; she seemed to see people and life through the confusing blur of the long crape veil in which it was a widow's duty to shroud her affliction. But she gave him her hand without perceptible reluctance.

He lifted it toward his lips, in an obvious attempt to combine gallantry with condolence, and then, half-way up, seemed to feel that the occasion required him to release it.

"Well—you'll admit that I've been patient!" he exclaimed.

"Patient? Yes. What else was there to be?" she rejoined with a faint smile, as he seated himself beside her, a little too near.

"Oh, well . . . of course! I understood all that, I hope you'll believe. But mightn't you at least have answered my letters—one or two of them?"

She shook her head. "I couldn't write."

"Not to anyone? Or not to me?" he queried, with ironic emphasis.

"I wrote only the letters I had to—no others."

"Ah, I see." He laughed slightly. "And you didn't consider that letters to *me* were among them?"

She was silent, and he stood up and took a turn across the room. His face was redder than usual, and now and then a twitch passed over it. She saw that he felt the barrier of her crape, and that it left him baffled and resentful. A struggle was still perceptibly going on in him between his traditional standard of behaviour at such a meeting, and primitive impulses renewed by the memory of their last hours together. When he turned back and paused before her his ruddy flush had paled, and he stood there, frowning, uncertain, and visibly resenting the fact that she made him so.

"You sit there like a stone!" he said.

"I feel like a stone."

"Oh, come—!"

She knew well enough what he was thinking: that the only way to bridge over such a bad beginning was to get the woman into your arms—and talk afterward. It was the classic move. He had done it dozens of times, no doubt, and was evidently asking himself why the deuce he couldn't do it now. . . But something in her look must have benumbed him. He sat down again beside her.

"What you must have been through, dearest!" He waited and coughed. "I can understand your being—all broken up. But I know nothing; remember, I know nothing as to what actually happened. . ."

"Nothing happened."

"As to—what we feared? No hint—?"

She shook her head.

He cleared his throat before the next question. "And you don't think that in your absence he may have spoken—to anyone?"

"Never!"

"Then, my dear, we seem to have had the most unbelievable good luck; and I can't see—"

He had edged slowly nearer, and now laid a large ringed hand on her sleeve. How well she knew those rings—the two dull gold snakes with malevolent jewelled eyes! She sat as motionless as if their coils were about her, till slowly his tentative grasp relaxed.

"Lizzie, you know"—his tone was discouraged—"this is morbid. . ."

"Morbid?"

"When you're safe out of the worst scrape . . . and free, my darling, *free!* Don't you realize it? I suppose the strain's been too much for you; but I want you to feel that now—"

She stood up suddenly, and put half the length of the room between them.

"Stop! Stop! Stop!" she almost screamed, as she had screamed long ago at Mrs. Mant.

He stood up also, darkly red under his rich sunburn, and forced a smile.

"Really," he protested, "all things considered—and after a separation of six months!" She was silent. "My dear," he continued mildly, "will you tell me what you expect me to think?"

"Oh, don't take that tone," she murmured.

"What tone?"

"As if—as if—you still imagined we could go back—"

She saw his face fall. Had he ever before, she wondered, stumbled upon an obstacle in that smooth walk of his? It flashed over her that this was the danger besetting men who had a "way with women" —the day came when they might follow it too blindly.

The reflection evidently occurred to him almost as soon as it did to her. He summoned another propitiatory smile, and drawing near, took her hand gently. "But I don't want to go back. . . I want to go forward, dearest. . . Now that at last you're free."

She seized on the word as if she had been waiting for her cue. "Free! Oh, that's it—*free!* Can't you see, can't you understand, that I mean to stay free?"

Again a shadow of distrust crossed his face, and the smile he had begun for her reassurance seemed to remain on his lips for his own.

"But of course! Can you imagine that I want to put you in chains? I want you to be as free as you please—free to love me as much as you choose!" He was visibly pleased with the last phrase.

She drew away her hand, but not unkindly. "I'm sorry—I *am* sorry, Henry. But you don't understand."

"What don't I understand?"

"That what you ask is quite impossible—ever. I can't go on . . . in the old way. . ."

She saw his face working nervously. "In the old way? You mean—?" Before she could explain he hurried on with an increasing majesty of manner: "Don't answer! I see—I understand. When you spoke of freedom just now I was misled for a moment—I frankly own I was— into thinking that, after your wretched marriage, you might prefer discreeter ties . . . an apparent independence which would leave us both. . . I say *apparent*, for on my side there has never been the least wish to conceal. . . But if I was mistaken, if on the contrary what you wish is . . . is to take advantage of your freedom to regularize our . . . our attachment. . ."

She said nothing, not because she had any desire to have him complete the phrase, but because she found nothing to say. To all that concerned their common past she was aware of offering a numbed soul. But her silence evidently perplexed him, and in his perplexity he began to lose his footing, and to flounder in a sea of words.

"Lizzie! Do you hear me? If I was mistaken, I say—and I hope I'm not above owning that at times I *may* be mistaken; if I was—why, by God, my dear, no woman ever heard me speak the words before; but here I am to have and to hold, as the Book says! Why, hadn't you realized it? Lizzie, look up—! *I'm asking you to marry me.*"

Still, for a moment, she made no reply, but stood gazing about her as if she had the sudden sense of unseen presences between them. At length she gave a faint laugh. It visibly ruffled her visitor.

"I'm not conscious," he began again, "of having said anything particularly laughable—" He stopped and scrutinized her narrowly, as though checked by the thought that there might be some thing not quite normal. . . Then, apparently reassured, he half-murmured his only French phrase: "*La joie fait peur* . . . eh?"

She did not seem to hear. "I wasn't laughing at you," she said, "but only at the coincidences of life. It was in this room that my husband asked me to marry him."

"Ah?" Her suitor appeared politely doubtful of the good taste, or the opportunity, of producing this reminiscence. But he made another call on his magnanimity. "Really? But, I say, my dear, I couldn't be expected to know it, could I? If I'd guessed that such a painful association—"

"Painful?" She turned upon him. "A painful association? Do you think that was what I meant?" Her voice sank. "This room is sacred to me."

She had her eyes on his face, which, perhaps because of its architectural completeness, seemed to lack the mobility necessary to follow such a leap of thought. It was so ostensibly a solid building, and not a nomad's tent. He struggled with a ruffled pride, rose again to playful magnanimity, and murmured: "Compassionate angel!"

"Oh, compassionate? To whom? Do you imagine—did I ever say anything to make you doubt the truth of what I'm telling you?"

His brows fretted: his temper was up. "*Say* anything? No," he insinuated ironically; then, in a hasty plunge after his lost forbearance, added with exquisite mildness: "Your tact was perfect . . . always. I've invariably done you that justice. No one could have been more thoroughly the . . . the lady. I never failed to admire your goodbreeding in avoiding any reference to your . . . your other life."

She faced him steadily: "Well, that other life *was* my life—my only life! Now you know."

There was a silence. Henry Prest drew out a monogrammed handkerchief and passed it over his dry lips. As he did so, a whiff of his eau de Cologne reached her, and she winced a little. It was evident that he was seeking what to say next; wondering, rather helplessly, how to get back his lost command of the situation. He finally induced his features to break again into a persuasive smile.

"Not your *only* life, dearest," he reproached her.

She met it instantly. "Yes; so you thought—because I chose you should."

"You chose—?" The smile became incredulous.

"Oh, deliberately. But I suppose I've no excuse that you would not dislike to hear. . . Why shouldn't we break off now?"

"Break off . . . this conversation?" His tone was aggrieved. "Of course I've no wish to force myself—"

She interrupted him with a raised hand. "Break off for good, Henry."

"For good?" He stared, and gave a quick swallow, as though the dose were choking him. "For good? Are you really—? You and I? Is this serious, Lizzie?"

"Perfectly. But if you prefer to hear . . . what can only be painful. . ."

He straightened himself, threw back his shoulders, and said in an uncertain voice: "I hope you don't take me for a coward."

She made no direct reply, but continued: "Well, then, you thought I loved you, I suppose—"

He smiled again, revived his moustache with a slight twist, and gave a hardly perceptible shrug. "You . . . ah . . . managed to produce the illusion. . ."

"Oh, well, yes: a woman *can*—so easily! That's what men often forget. You thought I was a lovelorn mistress; and I was only an expensive prostitute."

"Elizabeth!" he gasped, pale now to the ruddy eyelids. She saw that the word had wounded more than his pride, and that, before realizing the insult to his love, he was shuddering at the offence to his taste. Mistress! Prostitute! Such words were banned. No one reproved coarseness of language in women more than Henry Prest; one of Mrs. Hazeldean's greatest charms (as he had just told her) had been her way of remaining, "through it all," so ineffably "the lady." He looked at her as if a fresh doubt of her sanity had assailed him.

"Shall I go on?" she smiled.

He bent his head stiffly. "I am still at a loss to imagine for what purpose you made a fool of me."

"Well, then, it was as I say. I wanted money—money for my husband."

He moistened his lips. "For your husband?"

"Yes; when he began to be so ill; when he needed comforts, luxury, the opportunity to get away. He saved me, when I was a girl, from untold humiliation and wretchedness. No one else lifted a finger to help me—not one of my own family. I hadn't a penny or a friend. Mrs. Mant had grown sick of me, and was trying to find an excuse to throw me over. Oh, you don't know what a girl has to put up with—a girl alone in the world—who depends for her clothes, and her food, and the roof over her head, on the whims of a vain capricious old woman! It was because *he* knew, because he understood, that he married me. . . He took me out of misery into blessedness. He put me up above them all . . . he put me beside himself. I didn't care for anything but that; I didn't care for the money or the freedom; I cared only for him. I would have followed him into the desert —I would have gone barefoot to be with him. I would have starved, begged, done anything for him—*anything*." She broke off, her voice lost in a sob. She was no longer aware of Prest's presence—all her consciousness was absorbed in the vision she had evoked. "It was *he* who cared—who wanted me to be rich and independent and admired! He wanted to heap everything on me—during the first years I could hardly persuade him to keep enough money for himself. . . And then he was taken ill; and as he got worse, and gradually dropped out of affairs, his income grew smaller, and then stopped altogether; and all the while there were new expenses piling up—nurses, doctors, travel; and he grew frightened; frightened not for himself but for me. . . And what was I to do? I had to pay for things somehow. For the first year I managed to put off paying—then I borrowed small sums here and there. But that couldn't last. And all the while I had to keep on looking pretty and prosperous, or else he began to worry, and think we were ruined, and wonder what would become of me if he didn't get well. By the time you came I was desperate—I would have done anything, anything! He thought the money came from my Portuguese stepmother. She really was rich, as it happens. Unluckily my poor father tried to invest her money, and lost it all; but when they were first married she sent a thousand dollars—and all the rest, all you gave me, I built on that."

She paused pantingly, as if her tale were at an end. Gradually her consciousness of present things returned, and she saw Henry Prest, as if far off, a small indistinct figure looming through the mist of her blurred eyes. She thought to herself: "He doesn't believe me," and the thought exasperated her.

"You wonder, I suppose," she began again, "that a woman should dare confess such things about herself—"

He cleared his throat. "About herself? No; perhaps not. But about her husband."

The blood rushed to her forehead. "About her husband? But you don't dare to imagine—?"

"You leave me," he rejoined icily, "no other inference that I can see." She stood dumbfounded, and he added: "At any rate, it certainly explains your extraordinary coolness—pluck, I used to think it. I perceived that I needn't have taken such precautions."

She considered this. "You think, then, that he knew? You think, perhaps, that I knew he did?" She pondered again painfully, and then her face lit up. "He never knew—never! That's enough for me—and for you it doesn't matter. Think what you please. He was happy to the end—that's all I care for."

"There can be no doubt about your frankness," he said with pinched lips.

"There's no longer any reason for not being frank."

He picked up his hat, and studiously considered its lining; then he took the gloves he had laid in it, and drew them thoughtfully through his hands. She thought: "Thank God, he's going!"

But he set the hat and gloves down on a table, and moved a little nearer to her. His face looked as ravaged as a reveller's at daybreak.

"You—leave positively nothing to the imagination!" he murmured.

"I told you it was useless—" she began; but he interrupted her: "Nothing, that is—if I believed you." He moistened his lips again, and tapped them with his handkerchief. Again she had a whiff of the eau de Cologne. "But I don't!" he proclaimed. "Too many memories . . . too many . . . proofs, my dearest. . ." He stopped, smiling somewhat convulsively. She saw that he imagined the smile would soothe her.

She remained silent, and he began once more, as if appealing to her against her own verdict: "I know better, Lizzie. In spite of everything, *I know you're not that kind of woman.*"

"I took your money—"

"As a favour. I knew the difficulties of your position. . . I understood completely. I beg of you never again to allude to—all that." It dawned on her that anything would be more endurable to him than to think he had been a dupe—and one of two dupes! The part was not one that he could conceive of having played. His pride was up in arms to defend her, not so much for her sake as for his own. The discovery gave her a baffling sense of helplessness; against that impenetrable self-sufficiency all her affirmations might spend themselves in vain.

"No man who has had the privilege of being loved by you could ever for a moment. . ."

She raised her head and looked at him. "You have never had that privilege," she interrupted.

His jaw fell. She saw his eyes from uneasy supplication to a cold anger. He gave a little inarticulate grunt before his voice came back to him.

"You spare no pains in degrading yourself in my eyes."

"I am not degrading myself. I am telling you the truth. I needed money. I knew no way of earning it. You were willing to give it . . . for what you call the privilege. . ."

"Lizzie," he interrupted solemnly, "don't go on! I believe I enter into all your feelings—I believe I always have. In so sensitive, so hypersensitive a nature, there are moments when every other feeling

is swept away by scruples. . . For those scruples I only honour you
the more. But I won't hear another word now. If I allowed you to go
on in your present state of . . . nervous exaltation . . . you might be
the first to deplore. . . I wish to forget everything you have said. . .
I wish to look forward, not back. . ." He squared his shoulders, took
a deep breath, and fixed her with a glance of recovered confidence.
"How little you know me if you believe that I could fail you *now!*"

She returned his look with a weary steadiness. "You are kind—you
mean to be generous, I'm sure. But don't you see that I *can't* marry
you?"

"I only see that, in the natural rush of your remorse—"

"Remorse? Remorse?" She broke in with a laugh. "Do you imagine I feel any remorse? I'd do it all over again tomorrow—for the
same object! I got what I wanted—I gave him that last year, that last
good year. It was the relief from anxiety that kept him alive, that
kept him happy. Oh, he *was* happy—I know that!" She turned to
Prest with a strange smile. "I do thank you for that—I'm not ungrateful."

"You . . . you . . . *ungrateful?* This . . . is really . . . indecent. . ." He took up his hat again, and stood in the middle of the
room as if waiting to be waked from a bad dream.

"You are—rejecting an opportunity—" he began.

She made a faint motion of assent.

"You do realize it? I'm still prepared to—to help you, if you
should. . ." She made no answer, and he continued: "How do you
expect to live—since you have chosen to drag in such considerations?"

"I don't care how I live. I never wanted the money for myself."

He raised a deprecating hand. "Oh, don't—*again!* The woman I
had meant to. . ." Suddenly, to her surprise, she saw a glitter of
moisture on his lower lids. He applied his handkerchief to them, and
the waft of scent checked her momentary impulse of compunction.
That Cologne water! It called up picture after picture with a hideous
precision. "Well, it was worth it," she murmured doggedly.

Henry Prest restored his handkerchief to his pocket. He waited,
glanced about the room, turned back to her.

"If your decision is final—"

"Oh, final!"

He bowed. "There is one thing more—which I should have mentioned if you had ever given me the opportunity of seeing you after—

after last New Year's Day. Something I preferred not to commit to writing—"

"Yes?" she questioned indifferently.

"Your husband, you are positively convinced, had no idea . . . that day . . . ?"

"None."

"Well, others, it appears, had." He paused. "Mrs. Wesson saw us."

"So I suppose. I remember now that she went out of her way to cut me that evening at Mrs. Struthers's."

"Exactly. And she was not the only person who saw us. If people had not been disarmed by your husband's falling ill that very day you would have found yourself—ostracized."

She made no comment, and he pursued, with a last effort: "In your grief, your solitude, you haven't yet realized what your future will be—how difficult. It is what I wished to guard you against—it was my purpose in asking you to marry me." He drew himself up and smiled as if he were looking at his own reflection in a mirror, and thought favourably of it. "A man who has had the misfortune to compromise a woman is bound in honour—Even if my own inclination were not what it is, I should consider. . ."

She turned to him with a softened smile. Yes, he had really brought himself to think that he was proposing to marry her to save her reputation. At this glimpse of the old hackneyed axioms on which he actually believed that his conduct was based, she felt anew her remoteness from the life he would have drawn her back to.

"My poor Henry, don't you see how far I've got beyond the Mrs. Wessons? If all New York wants to ostracize me, let it! I've had my day . . . no woman has more than one. Why shouldn't I have to pay for it? I'm ready."

"Good heavens!" he murmured.

She was aware that he had put forth his last effort. The wound she had inflicted had gone to the most vital spot; she had prevented his being magnanimous, and the injury was unforgivable. He was glad, yes, actually glad now, to have her know that New York meant to cut her; but, strive as she might, she could not bring herself to care either for the fact, or for his secret pleasure in it. Her own secret pleasures were beyond New York's reach and his.

"I'm sorry," she reiterated gently. He bowed, without trying to take her hand, and left the room.

As the door closed she looked after him with a dazed stare. "He's right, I suppose; I don't realize yet—" She heard the shutting of the outer door, and dropped to the sofa, pressing her hands against her aching eyes. At that moment, for the first time, she asked herself what the next day, and the next, would be like. . .

"If only I cared more about reading," she moaned, remembering how vainly she had tried to acquire her husband's tastes, and how gently and humorously he had smiled at her efforts. "Well—there are always cards; and when I get older, knitting and patience, I suppose. And if everybody cuts me I shan't need any evening dresses. That will be an economy, at any rate," she concluded with a little shiver.

7

. . . . . .

"SHE was *bad* . . . always. They used to meet at the Fifth Avenue Hotel."

I must go back now to this phrase of my mother's—the phrase from which, at the opening of my narrative, I broke away for a time in order to project more vividly on the scene that anxious moving vision of Lizzie Hazeldean: a vision in which memories of my one boyish glimpse of her were pieced together with hints collected afterward.

When my mother uttered her condemnatory judgment I was a young man of twenty-one, newly graduated from Harvard, and at home again under the family roof in New York. It was long since I had heard Mrs. Hazeldean spoken of. I had been away, at school and at Harvard, for the greater part of the interval, and in the holidays she was probably not considered a fitting subject of conversation, especially now that my sisters came to the table.

At any rate, I had forgotten everything I might ever have picked up about her when, on the evening after my return, my cousin Hubert Wesson—now towering above me as a pillar of the Knickerbocker Club, and a final authority on the ways of the world—suggested our joining her at the opera.

"Mrs. Hazeldean? But I don't know her. What will she think?"

"That it's all right. Come along. She's the jolliest woman I know. We'll go back afterward and have supper with her—jolliest house I know." Hubert twirled a self-conscious moustache.

We were dining at the Knickerbocker, to which I had just been elected, and the bottle of Pommery we were finishing disposed me to think that nothing could be more fitting for two men of the world

than to end their evening in the box of the jolliest woman Hubert
knew. I groped for my own moustache, gave a twirl in the void, and
followed him, after meticulously sliding my overcoat sleeve around
my silk hat as I had seen him do.

But once in Mrs. Hazeldean's box I was only an overgrown boy
again, bathed in such blushes as used, at the same age, to visit
Hubert, forgetting that I had a moustache to twirl, and knocking my
hat from the peg on which I had just hung it, in my zeal to pick up a
programme she had not dropped.

For she was really too lovely—too formidably lovely. I was used by
now to mere unadjectived loveliness, the kind that youth and spirits
hang like a rosy veil over commonplace features, an average outline
and a pointless merriment. But this was something calculated, accomplished, finished—and just a little worn. It frightened me with
my first glimpse of the infinity of beauty and the multiplicity of her
pit-falls. What! There were women who need not fear crow's-feet,
were more beautiful for being pale, could let a silver hair or two
show among the dark, and their eyes brood inwardly while they
smiled and chatted? But then no young man was safe for a moment!
But then the world I had hitherto known had been only a warm
pink nursery, while this new one was a place of darkness, perils and
enchantments. . .

It was the next day that one of my sisters asked me where I had
been the evening before, and that I puffed out my chest to answer:
"With Mrs. Hazeldean—at the opera." My mother looked up, but
did not speak till the governess had swept the girls off; then she said
with pinched lips: "Hubert Wesson took you to Mrs. Hazeldean's
box?"

"Yes."

"Well, a young man may go where he pleases. I hear Hubert is
still infatuated; it serves Sabina right for not letting him marry the
youngest Lyman girl. But don't mention Mrs. Hazeldean again before your sisters. . . They say her husband never knew—I suppose if
he *had* she would never have got old Miss Cecilia Winter's money."
And it was then that my mother pronounced the name of Henry
Prest, and added that phrase about the Fifth Avenue Hotel which
suddenly woke my boyish memories. . .

In a flash I saw again, under its quickly-lowered veil, the face with
the exposed eyes and the frozen smile, and felt through my grown-up
waistcoat the stab to my boy's heart and the loosened murmur of my

soul; felt all this, and at the same moment tried to relate that former face, so fresh and clear despite its anguish, to the smiling guarded countenance of Hubert's "jolliest woman I know."

I was familiar with Hubert's indiscriminate use of his one adjective, and had not expected to find Mrs. Hazeldean "jolly" in the literal sense: in the case of the lady he happened to be in love with the epithet simply meant that she justified his choice. Nevertheless, as I compared Mrs. Hazeldean's earlier face to this one, I had my first sense of what may befall in the long years between youth and maturity, and of how short a distance I had travelled on that mysterious journey. If only she would take me by the hand!

I was not wholly unprepared for my mother's comment. There was no other lady in Mrs. Hazeldean's box when we entered; none joined her during the evening, and our hostess offered no apology for her isolation. In the New York of my youth every one knew what to think of a woman who was seen "alone at the opera"; if Mrs. Hazeldean was not openly classed with Fanny Ring, our one conspicuous "professional," it was because, out of respect for her social origin, New York preferred to avoid such juxtapositions. Young as I was, I knew this social law, and had guessed, before the evening was over, that Mrs. Hazeldean was not a lady on whom other ladies called, though she was not, on the other hand, a lady whom it was forbidden to mention to other ladies. So I did mention her, with bravado.

No ladies showed themselves at the opera with Mrs. Hazeldean; but one or two dropped in to the jolly supper announced by Hubert, an entertainment whose jollity consisted in a good deal of harmless banter over broiled canvas-backs and celery, with the best of champagne. These same ladies I sometimes met at her house afterward. They were mostly younger than their hostess, and still, though precariously, within the social pale: pretty trivial creatures, bored with a monotonous prosperity, and yearning for such unlawful joys as cigarettes, plain speaking, and a drive home in the small hours with the young man of the moment. But such daring spirits were few in old New York, their appearances infrequent and somewhat furtive. Mrs. Hazeldean's society consisted mainly of men, men of all ages, from her bald or grey-headed contemporaries to youths of Hubert's accomplished years and raw novices of mine.

A great dignity and decency prevailed in her little circle. It was not the oppressive respectability which weighs on the reformed *déclassée*, but the air of ease imparted by a woman of distinction who has wearied of society and closed her doors to all save her intimates. One always felt, at Lizzie Hazeldean's, that the next moment one's grandmother and aunts might be announced; and yet so pleasantly certain that they wouldn't be.

What is there in the atmosphere of such houses that makes them so enchanting to a fastidious and imaginative youth? Why is it that "those women" (as the others call them) alone know how to put the awkward at ease, check the familiar, smile a little at the over-knowing, and yet encourage naturalness in all? The difference of atmosphere is felt on the very threshold. The flowers grow differently in their vases, the lamps and easy-chairs have found a cleverer way of coming together, the books on the table are the very ones that one is longing to get hold of. The most perilous coquetry may not be in a woman's way of arranging her dress but in her way of arranging her drawing-room; and in this art Mrs. Hazeldean excelled.

I have spoken of books; even then they were usually the first objects to attract me in a room, whatever else of beauty it contained; and I remember, on the evening of that first "jolly supper," coming to an astonished pause before the crowded shelves that took up one wall of the drawing-room. What! The goddess read, then? She could accompany one on those flights too? Lead one, no doubt? My heart beat high. . .

But I soon learned that Lizzie Hazeldean did not read. She turned but languidly even the pages of the last Ouida novel; and I remember seeing Mallock's *New Republic* uncut on her table for weeks. It took me no long time to make the discovery: at my very next visit she caught my glance of surprise in the direction of the rich shelves, smiled, coloured a little, and met it with the confession: "No, I can't read them. I've tried—I *have* tried—but print makes me sleepy. Even novels do. . ." "They" were the accumulated treasures of English poetry, and a rich and varied selection of history, criticism, letters, in English, French and Italian—she spoke these languages, I knew—books evidently assembled by a sensitive and widely-ranging reader. We were alone at the time, and Mrs. Hazeldean went on in a lower tone: "I kept just the few he liked best—my husband, you know." It was the first time that Charles Hazeldean's name had been spoken between us, and my surprise was so great that my candid cheek must have reflected the blush on hers. I had fancied that women in her situation avoided alluding to their husbands. But she continued to look at me, wistfully, humbly almost, as if there were something more that she wanted to say, and was inwardly entreating me to understand.

"He was a great reader: a student. And he tried so hard to make me read too—he wanted to share everything with me. And I *did* like poetry—some poetry—when he read it aloud to me. After his death I thought: 'There'll be his books. I can go back to them—I shall find him there.' And I tried—oh, so hard—but it's no use. They've lost their meaning . . . as most things have." She stood up, lit a cigarette, pushed back a log on the hearth. I felt that she was waiting for me to speak. If life had but taught me how to answer her, what was there of her story I might not have learned? But I was too inexperienced; I could not shake off my bewilderment. What! This woman whom I had been pitying for matrimonial miseries which seemed to justify her seeking solace elsewhere—this woman could speak of her husband in such a tone! I had instantly perceived that the tone was not feigned; and a confused sense of the complexity—or the chaos—of human relations held me as tongue-tied as a schoolboy to whom a problem beyond his grasp is suddenly propounded.

Before the thought took shape she had read it, and with the smile which drew such sad lines about her mouth, had continued gaily: "What are you up to this evening, by the way? What do you say to going to the "Black Crook" with your cousin Hubert and one or two others? I have a box."

It was inevitable that, not long after this candid confession, I should have persuaded myself that a taste for reading was boring in a woman, and that one of Mrs. Hazeldean's chief charms lay in her freedom from literary pretensions. The truth was, of course, that it lay in her sincerity; in her humble yet fearless estimate of her own qualities and short-comings. I had never met its like in a woman of any age, and coming to me in such early days, and clothed in such looks and intonations, it saved me, in after years, from all peril of meaner beauties.

But before I had come to understand that, or to guess what falling in love with Lizzie Hazeldean was to do for me, I had quite unwittingly and fatuously done the falling. The affair turned out, in the perspective of the years, to be but an incident of our long friendship; and if I touch on it here it is only to illustrate another of my poor friend's gifts. If she could not read books she could read hearts; and she bent a playful yet compassionate gaze on mine while it still floundered in unawareness.

I remember it all as if it were yesterday. We were sitting alone in her drawing-room, in the winter twilight, over the fire. We had reached—in her company it was not difficult—the degree of fellowship when friendly talk lapses naturally into a friendlier silence, and she had taken up the evening paper while I glowered dumbly at the embers. One little foot, just emerging below her dress, swung, I remember, between me and the fire, and seemed to hold her all in the spring of its instep. . .

"Oh," she exclaimed, "poor Henry Prest—." She dropped the paper. "His wife is dead—poor fellow," she said simply.

The blood rushed to my forehead: my heart was in my throat. She had named him—named him at last, the recreant lover, the man who had "dishonoured" her! My hands were clenched: if he had entered the room they would have been at his throat. . .

And then, after a quick interval, I had again the humiliating disheartening sense of not understanding: of being too young, too inexperienced, to know. This woman, who spoke of her deceived husband with tenderness, spoke compassionately of her faithless lover! And she did the one as naturally as the other, not as if this impartial charity were an attitude she had determined to assume, but as if it were part of the lesson life had taught her.

"I didn't know he was married," I growled between my teeth.

She meditated absently. "Married? Oh, yes, when was it? The year after . . ." her voice dropped again . . . "after my husband died. He married a quiet cousin, who had always been in love with him, I believe. They had two boys.—You knew him?" she abruptly questioned.

I nodded grimly.

"People always thought he would never marry—he used to say so himself," she went on, still absently.

I burst out: "The—hound!"

"Oh!" she exclaimed. I started up, our eyes met, and hers filled with tears of reproach and understanding. We sat looking at each other in silence. Two of the tears overflowed, hung on her lashes, melted down her cheeks. I continued to stare at her shamefacedly; then I got to my feet, drew out my handkerchief, and tremblingly, reverently, as if I had touched a sacred image, I wiped them away.

My love-making went no farther. In another moment she had contrived to put a safe distance between us. She did not want to turn a boy's head; long since (she told me afterward) such amusements had ceased to excite her. But she did want my sympathy, wanted it overwhelmingly: amid the various feelings she was aware of arousing, she let me see that sympathy, in the sense of a moved understanding, had always been lacking. "But then," she added ingenuously, "I've never really been sure, because I've never told anyone my story. Only I take it for granted that, if I haven't, it's *their* fault rather than mine. . ." She smiled half-deprecatingly, and my bosom swelled, acknowledging the distinction. "And now I want to tell *you—*" she began.

I have said that my love for Mrs. Hazeldean was a brief episode in our long relation. At my age, it was inevitable that it should be so. The "fresher face" soon came, and in its light I saw my old friend as a middle-aged woman, turning grey, with a mechanical smile and haunted eyes. But it was in the first glow of my feeling that she had told me her story; and when the glow subsided, and in the afternoon light of a long intimacy I judged and tested her statements, I found that each detail fitted into the earlier picture.

My opportunities were many; for once she had told the tale she always wanted to be retelling it. A perpetual longing to relive the past, a perpetual need to explain and justify herself—the satisfaction of these two cravings, once she had permitted herself to indulge them, became the luxury of her empty life. She had kept it empty—emotionally, sentimentally empty—from the day of her husband's death, as the guardian of an abandoned temple might go on forever sweeping and tending what had once been the god's abode. But this duty performed, she had no other. She had done one great—or abominable—thing; rank it as you please, it had been done heroically. But there was nothing in her to keep her at that height. Her tastes, her interests, her conceivable occupations, were all on the level of a middling domesticity; she did not know how to create for herself any inner life in keeping with that one unprecedented impulse.

Soon after her husband's death, one of her cousins, the Miss Cecilia Winter of Washington Square to whom my mother had referred, had died also, and left Mrs. Hazeldean a handsome legacy. And a year or two later Charles Hazeldean's small estate had undergone the favourable change that befell New York realty in the 'eighties. The property he had bequeathed to his wife had doubled, then tripled, in value; and she found herself, after a few years of widowhood, in possession of an income large enough to supply her with all the luxuries which her husband had struggled so hard to provide. It was the peculiar irony of her lot to be secured from temptation when all danger

of temptation was over; for she would never, I am certain, have held
out the tip of her finger to any man to obtain such luxuries for her
own enjoyment. But if she did not value her money for itself, she
owed to it—and the service was perhaps greater than she was aware—
the power of mitigating her solitude, and filling it with the trivial dis-
tractions without which she was less and less able to live.

She had been put into the world, apparently, to amuse men and
enchant them; yet, her husband dead, her sacrifice accomplished, she
would have preferred, I am sure, to shut herself up in a lonely monumental attitude, with thoughts and pursuits on a scale with her one
great hour. But what was she to do? She had known of no way of
earning money except by her graces; and now she knew no way of
filling her days except with cards and chatter and theatre-going. Not
one of the men who approached her passed beyond the friendly barrier she had opposed to me. Of that I was sure. She had not shut out
Henry Prest in order to replace him—her face grew white at the suggestion. But what else was there to do, she asked me; what? The days
had to be spent somehow; and she was incurably, disconsolately sociable.

So she lived, in a cold celibacy that passed for I don't know what
licence; so she lived, withdrawn from us all, yet needing us so desperately, inwardly faithful to her one high impulse, yet so incapable of
attuning her daily behaviour to it! And so, at the very moment when
she ceased to deserve the blame of society, she found herself cut off
from it, and reduced to the status of the "fast" widow noted for her
jolly suppers.

I bent bewildered over the depths of her plight. What else, at any
stage of her career, could she have done, I often wondered? Among
the young women now growing up about me I find none with
enough imagination to picture the helpless incapacity of the pretty
girl of the 'seventies, the girl without money or vocation, seemingly
put into the world only to please, and unlearned in any way of main-
taining herself there by her own efforts. Marriage alone could save
such a girl from starvation, unless she happened to run across an old
lady who wanted her dogs exercised and her *Churchman* read aloud
to her. Even the day of painting wild-roses on fans, of colouring photographs to "look like" miniatures, of manufacturing lamp-shades
and trimming hats for more fortunate friends—even this precarious
beginning of feminine independence had not dawned. It was inconceivable to my mother's generation that a portionless girl should not

be provided for by her relations until she found a husband; and that, having found him, she should have to help him to earn a living, was more inconceivable still. The self-sufficing little society of that vanished New York attached no great importance to wealth, but regarded poverty as so distasteful that it simply took no account of it.

These things pleaded in favour of poor Lizzie Hazeldean, though to superficial observers her daily life seemed to belie the plea. She had known no way of smoothing her husband's last years but by being false to him; but once he was dead, she expiated her betrayal by a rigidity of conduct for which she asked no reward but her own inner satisfaction. As she grew older, and her friends scattered, married, or were kept away from one cause or another, she filled her depleted circle with a less fastidious hand. One met in her drawing-room dull men, common men, men who too obviously came there because they were not invited elsewhere, and hoped to use her as a social stepping-stone. She was aware of the difference—her eyes said so whenever I found one of these newcomers installed in my arm-chair—but never, by word or sign, did she admit it. She said to me once: "You find it duller here than it used to be. It's my fault, perhaps; I think I knew better how to draw out my old friends." And another day: "Remember, the people you meet here now come out of kindness. I'm an old woman, and I consider nothing else." That was all.

She went more assiduously than ever to the theatre and the opera; she performed for her friends a hundred trivial services; in her eagerness to be always busy she invented superfluous attentions, oppressed people by offering assistance they did not need, verged at times—for all her tact—on the officiousness of the desperately lonely. At her little suppers she surprised us with exquisite flowers and novel delicacies. The champagne and cigars grew better and better as the quality of the guests declined; and sometimes, as the last of her dull company dispersed, I used to see her, among the scattered ash-trays and liqueur decanters, turn a stealthy glance at her reflection in the mirror, with haggard eyes which seemed to ask: "Will even *these* come back tomorrow?"

I should be loth to leave the picture at this point; my last vision of her is more satisfying. I had been away, travelling for a year at the other end of the world; the day I came back I ran across Hubert Wesson at my club. Hubert had grown pompous and heavy. He drew me into a corner, and said, turning red, and glancing cautiously over his shoulder: "Have you seen our old friend Mrs. Hazeldean? She's very ill, I hear."

I was about to take up the "I hear"; then I remembered that in my absence Hubert had married, and that his caution was probably a tribute to his new state. I hurried at once to Mrs. Hazeldean's; and on her door-step, to my surprise, I ran against a Catholic priest, who looked gravely at me, bowed and passed out.

I was unprepared for such an encounter, for my old friend had never spoken to me of religious matters. The spectacle of her father's career had presumably shaken whatever incipient faith was in her; though in her little-girlhood, as she often told me, she had been as deeply impressed by Dr. Winter's eloquence as any grown-up member of his flock. But now, as soon as I laid eyes on her, I understood. She was very ill, she was visibly dying; and in her extremity, fate, not always kind, had sent her the solace which she needed. Had some obscure inheritance of religious feeling awaked in her? Had she remembered that her poor father, after his long life of mental and moral vagabondage, had finally found rest in the ancient fold? I never knew the explanation—she probably never knew it herself.

But she knew that she had found what she wanted. At last she could talk of Charles, she could confess her sin, she could be absolved of it. Since cards and suppers and chatter were over, what more blessed barrier could she find against solitude? All her life, henceforth, was a long preparation for that daily hour of expansion and consolation. And then this merciful visitor, who understood her so well, could also tell her things about Charles: knew where he was, how he felt, what exquisite daily attentions could still be paid to him, and how, with all unworthiness washed away, she might at last hope to reach him. Heaven could never seem strange, so interpreted; each time that I saw her, during the weeks of her slow fading, she was more and more like a traveller with her face turned homeward, yet smilingly resigned to await her summons. The house no longer seemed lonely, nor the hours tedious; there had even been found for her, among the books she had so often tried to read, those books which had long looked at her with such hostile faces, two or three (they were always on her bed) containing messages from the world where Charles was waiting.

Thus provided and led, one day she went to him.